"Is it really you? Can it indeed be that you are alive?"
(from "The Adventure of the Empty House," page 8)

It was indeed like old times when, at that hour, I found myself seated beside him in a hansom, my revolver in my pocket, and the thrill of adventure in my heart. Holmes was cold and stern and silent. As the gleam of the street-lamps flashed upon his austere features, I saw that his brows were drawn down in thought and his thin lips compressed. I knew not what wild beast we were about to hunt down in the dark jungle of criminal London, but I was well assured, from the bearing of this master huntsman, that the adventure was a most grave one.
(from "The Adventure of the Empty House," pages 11–12)

"What one man can invent another can discover."
(from "The Adventure of the Dancing Men," page 56)

"When a man embarks upon a crime, he is morally guilty of any other crime which may spring from it."
(from "The Adventure of the Priory School," page 92)

"I've seen you handle a good many cases, Mr. Holmes, but I don't know that I ever knew a more workmanlike one than that. We're not jealous of you at Scotland Yard. No, sir, we are very proud of you, and if you come down to-morrow, there's not a man, from the oldest inspector to the youngest constable, who wouldn't be glad to shake you by the hand."
(from "The Adventure of the Six Napoleons," page 141)

"Come, Watson, come!" he cried. "The game is afoot. Not a word! Into your clothes and come!"
(from "The Adventure of the Abbey Grange," page 191)

"The motives of women are so inscrutable."
(from "The Adventure of the Second Stain," page 216)

Sherlock Holmes had pushed away his untasted breakfast and lit the unsavoury pipe which was the companion of his deepest meditations.
(from *The Valley of Fear*, page 236)

Mediocrity knows nothing higher than itself; but talent instantly recognizes genius.
(from *The Valley of Fear*, page 238)

"The blunt accusation, the brutal tap upon the shoulder—what can one make of such a *dénouement*? But the quick inference, the subtle trap, the clever forecast of coming events, the triumphant vindication of bold theories—are these not the pride and the justification of our life's work?"
(from *The Valley of Fear*, page 283)

"My mind is like a racing engine, tearing itself to pieces because it is not connected up with the work for which it was built. Life is commonplace; the papers are sterile; audacity and romance seem to have passed forever from the criminal world."

(from "The Adventure of Wisteria Lodge," pages 359–360)

"It may be very much deeper than appears on the surface. The first thing that strikes one is the obvious possibility that the person now in the rooms may be entirely different from the one who engaged them."

(from "The Adventure of the Red Circle," page 400)

"It shows, my dear Watson, that we are dealing with an exceptionally astute and dangerous man."

(from "The Disappearance of Lady Frances Carfax," page 452)

"When you follow two separate chains of thought, Watson, you will find some point of intersection which should approximate to the truth."

(from "The Disappearance of Lady Frances Carfax," page 455)

"To revenge crime is important, but to prevent it is more so."

(from "The Adventure of the Illustrious Client," page 498)

"The faculty of deduction is certainly contagious, Watson."

(from "The Problem of Thor Bridge," page 582)

"By Jove, Mr. Holmes, I think you have hit it."

(from "The Adventure of the Lion's Mane," page 625)

"My dear fellow, I fear your deductions have not been so happy as I should have wished." (from "How Watson Learned the Trick," page 675)

THE COMPLETE SHERLOCK HOLMES, VOLUME II

Sir Arthur Conan Doyle

With an Introduction and Notes
by Kyle Freeman

George Stade
Consulting Editorial Director

JB

BARNES & NOBLE CLASSICS

NEW YORK

ฦ
BARNES & NOBLE CLASSICS
NEW YORK

Published by Barnes & Noble Books
122 Fifth Avenue
New York, NY 10011

www.barnesandnoble.com/classics

The Valley of Fear was first published in 1914. The stories in *The Return of Sherlock Holmes* were first collected and published in 1903, those in *His Last Bow* in 1917, and those in *The Case Book of Sherlock Holmes* in 1927.

"The Creeping Man," "The Sussex Vampire," "The Veiled Lodger," "The Retired Colourman," "Shoscombe Old Place," "How Watson Learned the Trick," "The Truth about Sherlock Holmes," and "Some Personalia about Mr. Sherlock Holmes" are protected by copyright in the United States of America and are reprinted here courtesy of the Estate of Dame Jean Conan Doyle.

Published in 2003 by Barnes & Noble Classics with new Introduction, Notes, Biography, Chronology, A Note on Conveyances, Inspired By, Comments & Questions, and For Further Reading.

General Introduction, Introduction to Volume II, A Note on Conveyances, Notes, and For Further Reading Copyright © 2003 by Kyle Freeman.

Note on Sir Arthur Conan Doyle, The World of Sir Arthur Conan Doyle and *Sherlock Holmes*, Inspired by *Sherlock Holmes*, and Comments & Questions Copyright © 2003 by Barnes & Noble, Inc.

The Complete Sherlock Holmes, Volume II
ISBN-13: 978-1-59308-040-2
ISBN-10: 1-59308-040-9
LC Control Number 2003102759

Produced and published in conjunction with:
Fine Creative Media, Inc.
322 Eighth Avenue
New York, NY 10001

Michael J. Fine, President and Publisher

Printed in the United States of America

QM

11 13 15 17 19 20 18 16 14 12

SIR ARTHUR CONAN DOYLE

Arthur Conan Doyle had many careers—physician, writer of popular fiction and nonfiction, war correspondent, historian, and spiritualist—but it was the creation of the cultural icon Sherlock Holmes that was to be his enduring legacy. The author was born in Edinburgh, Scotland, on May 22, 1859. His mother raised ten children on her husband's small income; his father's poor health and heavy drinking made that a daunting task. Despite this adversity, his mother's willfulness and her exhaustive genealogical research instilled in Arthur a decided sense of purpose.

After early education in Jesuit schools, Conan Doyle enrolled in Edinburgh University, where he earned a medical degree while working part-time to support his family. At the university one of his instructors was Dr. Joseph Bell, who had an uncanny ability to deduce the histories of his patients and who later became a template for Sherlock Holmes. Another teacher, an eccentric Professor Rutherford, inspired the character of Professor George Edward Challenger in *The Lost World* and two other novels.

Having had a taste of adventure on a trip to Greenland while still a student, Conan Doyle longed to travel after graduation and so took a position as doctor on a ship en route to West Africa. Returning to England, he set up as a physician in 1882. His practice was small at first, so he had time to do some writing. In 1887 the first Sherlock Holmes story appeared, titled *A Study in Scarlet*. Over the next few years, Conan Doyle would write a historical novel, open a new ocular practice, explore spiritualism, and send Holmes on further thrilling exploits. A second novel, *The Sign of Four*, came out in 1890, and starting in 1891 the Holmes stories regularly appeared in the *Strand Magazine*. Two collections, *The Adventures of Sherlock Holmes* in 1892 and *The Memoirs of Sherlock Holmes* in 1893, collected a total of twenty-four of the mysteries. However, Conan Doyle felt that work on the Holmes stories was keeping him from writing on more serious historical topics. To the shock of his readers, in the 1893 story called "The Final Problem" he described the death of his famous sleuth.

In 1894 Conan Doyle published *Round the Red Lamp*, a collection of short stories with a medical theme; in 1895 *The Stark Munro Letters*, an autobiographical novel; and in 1896 *The Exploits of Brigadier Gerard*, set in the Napoleonic Wars. In 1900 he traveled to South Africa in the capacity of war-time physician in Cape Town; his treatise on the Boer War, a defense of Britain's tactics, earned him a knighthood in 1902. That same year Conan Doyle published *The Hound of the Baskervilles*, set before the story that had finished Holmes off in 1893. In 1903 new Holmes stories started to appear in the *Strand*.

In the coming years, Conan Doyle produced more popular books on a variety of subjects, including three new collections of stories—*The Return of Sherlock Holmes* (1905), *His Last Bow* (1917), and *The Case Book of Sherlock Holmes* (1927)—plus a final Holmes novel, *The Valley of Fear* (1915). Among many other non-Holmes projects were the three Challenger novels, historical fiction and nonfiction, and several books on spiritualism. He also championed the rights of the wrongly accused, in two separate cases exonerating innocent men.

With the onset of World War I, Conan Doyle served as a war correspondent on several major European battlefields. Following the war, he became a passionate advocate of spiritualism, which he embraced in part to communicate with his eldest son, Kingsley, who had died from influenza aggravated by war wounds. From 1920 until his death, the author wrote, traveled, and lectured to promote his belief in a spiritual life after the death of the body. After a long, demanding journey through Scandinavia, Arthur Conan Doyle suffered a heart attack; he died a few months later, on July 7, 1930, in Sussex.

TABLE OF CONTENTS

THE WORLD OF SIR ARTHUR CONAN DOYLE AND *SHERLOCK HOLMES*

1859 Arthur Conan Doyle is born on May 22 in Edinburgh, Scotland, the second child and eldest son of ten children that will be born to Charles and Mary Foley Doyle. Darwin's *On the Origin of Species by Natural Selection* and Charles Dickens's *A Tale of Two Cities* are published.

1868 Arthur attends school with the Jesuits in England; later he will reject Catholicism.

1871 Lewis Carroll's *Through the Looking Glass* is published. The first book of George Eliot's *Middlemarch* is published. Royal Albert Hall, one of Britain's most important concert venues, opens in London.

1876 Conan Doyle enrolls in the University of Edinburgh Medical School. As a student, he takes various jobs to help his family, including serving as a ship's doctor on an Arctic voyage. While at Edinburgh, he meets Dr. Joseph Bell, whose analytical capabilities amaze his patients and students; Bell later becomes a model for Sherlock Holmes.

1879 "The Mystery of Sasassa Valley," Conan Doyle's first story, is published in *Chambers's Journal*, an Edinburgh weekly.

1881 Conan Doyle receives his Bachelor of Medicine and Master of Surgery qualifications, and takes a position as ship's doctor on a steamer en route to West Africa.

1882 He returns to Great Britain and establishes his medical practice.

1885 Conan Doyle receives his M.D. degree. He marries Louise Hawkins; her poor health makes the marriage a difficult one.

1887 *A Study in Scarlet*, the debut Sherlock Holmes story, is published in *Beeton's Christmas Annual*.

1889 Conan Doyle's short novel *The Mystery of Cloomber*, which is concerned with the paranormal, is published, as is *Micah Clarke*, a popular novel about the Monmouth Rebellion of 1685.

1890 The second Holmes novel, *The Sign of Four* is published, in February in *Lippincott's Monthly Magazine* and in October as a book. The story had been commissioned at the same dinner party at which Oscar Wilde was offered a contract for *The Picture of Dorian Gray*, also published in *Lippincott's* this year.

1891 *The White Company*, a tale of fourteenth-century chivalry, is published. Conan Doyle closes his medical practice to devote more time to his writing career. Stories featuring Sherlock Holmes begin to appear regularly in the *Strand Magazine*.

1892   The story collection *The Adventures of Sherlock Holmes* is published.

1893   The year proves stressful, as the author's father dies and his wife is diagnosed with tuberculosis. Hoping to help Louise's condition, the family travels to Switzerland, where Conan Doyle visits Reichenbach Falls, the site he chooses for the murder of Sherlock Holmes in "The Final Problem"; he intends for this to be the last Holmes story so that he can turn to literary work he considers more important. He joins the British Society for Psychical Research, which will provide the basis for his belief in spiritualism. The story collection *The Memoirs of Sherlock Holmes* is published.

1894   *Round the Red Lamp*, a collection of medical short stories, is published.

1895   *The Stark Munro Letters*, a fictionalized autobiography, is published.

1896   *The Exploits of Brigadier Gerard*, about a hero in the Napoleonic Wars, is published.

1897   Conan Doyle meets Jean Leckie and falls in love with her; the two maintain a platonic relationship until their marriage in 1907. Bram Stoker's *Dracula* is published.

1900   Conan Doyle travels to South Africa to serve as a hospital doctor in the Boer War; he publishes *The Great Boer War*, an account of that conflict. Oscar Wilde dies.

1901   Queen Victoria dies.

1902   *The Hound of the Baskervilles*, a Holmes novel set before "The Final Problem" (1893), is published. Conan Doyle's work in a field hospital and his treatise on the Boer War, *The War in South Africa: Its Cause and Conduct*, earn him a knighthood.

1903   New Holmes stories begin to appear in the *Strand Magazine*.

1905   The story collection *The Return of Sherlock Holmes* is published.

1906   Louise dies of tuberculosis at age forty-nine. Conan Doyle begins investigations that will exonerate George Edalji, a man who had been wrongfully accused and sent to jail. *Sir Nigel*, a companion piece to *The White Company* (1891), is published.

1907   Conan Doyle marries Jean Leckie. *Through the Magic Door*, about the importance of books in his life, is published.

1909   *The Crime of the Congo*, about Belgian atrocities in the Congo, is published.

1910   Conan Doyle investigates the case of Oscar Slater, another wrongfully accused man. E. M. Forster's *Howards End* is published.

1912   *The Lost World* is published; the first of a series of science fiction novels featuring the skeptical Professor George Edward Challenger, it is the best known of the author's non-Holmes stories.

1913   The second Challenger novel, *The Poison Belt*, is published.

1914   Conan Doyle visits New York City and Canada. World War I begins. James Joyce's *Dubliners* is published.

1915   The final Holmes novel, *The Valley of Fear*, is published.

1916   Conan Doyle announces his belief in spiritualism, which holds that the spirit has a life after the death of the body; he will become one of its best-known advocates. James Joyce's *Portrait of the Artist as a Young Man* is published.

1917   The Holmes story collection *His Last Bow* is published.

1918   The author's eldest son, Kingsley, dies from war wounds and influenza. World War I ends. Conan Doyle publishes *The New Revelation*, his first book on spiritualism. Gerard Manley Hopkins's *Poems* is published.

1919   Conan Doyle's brother, Innes, dies from pneumonia. Another book on spiritualism, *The Vital Message*, is published.

1920   From this year until his death, the author acts as an advocate for spiritualism.

1921   Conan Doyle's mother, Mary, dies. Jean experiments with automatic writing.

1922   Conan Doyle tours America in support of spiritualism. T. S. Eliot's *The Wasteland* and James Joyce's *Ulysses* are published.

1924   Conan Doyle's autobiography, *Memories and Adventures*, is published.

1926   The last Challenger novel, *The Land of Mist*, is published, as is Conan Doyle's two-volume *History of Spiritualism*.

1927   The final Holmes story collection, *The Case Book of Sherlock Holmes*, is published. Virginia Woolf's *To the Lighthouse* is published.

1930   Sir Arthur Conan Doyle dies on July 7 at his home in Sussex from an illness resulting from a heart attack.

GENERAL INTRODUCTION

Sir Arthur Conan Doyle lived an interesting life by any standard. As a young ship's surgeon he sailed the Arctic in a whaling ship, and later he steamed down the west coast of Africa on a cargo vessel. In midlife his fame as a writer opened doors all over the world. He taught Rudyard Kipling to play golf in a Connecticut field, and argued in the newspapers with his neighbor, Bernard Shaw, about the *Titanic*. He climbed the top of the Great Pyramid in Giza, and lectured the deacons in the Great Mormon Tabernacle in Utah. As a champion of spiritualism he proclaimed that a pharaoh's curse could indeed have caused the death of Lord Carnarvon, the patron of the Tutankhamun expedition, and assured the public that Agatha Christie, who had mysteriously disappeared, would show up safe and sound because a psychic to whom he had taken one of her gloves predicted it. He was knighted by King Edward VII for writing a pamphlet justifying the British cause in the Boer War. He wrote what he thought were important historical novels in the manner of Sir Walter Scott and through them hoped to establish his legacy. Ironically enough, all these events have a chance to be remembered only because he also created what he regarded as "a lower stratum of literary achievement," his peerless detective, Sherlock Holmes.

Holmes has become as famous as any character in literature. His name is synonymous with brilliant deduction. Call someone "Sherlock" and everyone knows what you mean. The stories have been in print continuously since the time the first one, *A Study in Scarlet*, was published in 1887. In addition Holmes has been the leading character in hundreds of plays, films, and television shows. He made his debut in films even before Conan Doyle had finished writing the stories. Long before Basil Rathbone and Nigel Bruce created their memorable roles of Holmes and Watson in films of the late 1930s and the 1940s, the celebrated sleuth had already been played by a host of actors on stage and screen. The stories continue to be filmed today. You have probably seen one of the excellent Granada Television episodes with Jeremy Brett, which may well be the reason you are reading this book.

Sherlock Holmes has such a strong hold on the popular imagination that he is no longer moored to the books in which he first appeared. Not satisfied by the fifty-six short stories and four novellas of the Holmes canon, writers first adopted the character by completing cases Dr. Watson had mentioned only in passing. Soon they constructed new episodes for the master detective. Film directors followed suit. Though many films have been scrupulously true to the plots of the stories, some have created their own plots. Such films include *Young Sherlock Holmes* (1985), which invented a childhood for the detective. In it Holmes and Watson meet as teenagers at a boarding school where Professor Moriarty, Holmes's great nemesis in the books, is an encouraging teacher. It also introduces a love interest for Holmes, a young girl whose death at the hands of Moriarty, who turns into a deadly foe, explains why Holmes was never the marrying kind. *The Seven-Per-Cent Solution* (1976) sends Holmes to Vienna to meet Sigmund Freud, who traces Holmes's obsession with Moriarty to a repressed memory of his mother in the arms of the professor. In perhaps the boldest reimagining of the stories, and certainly the most amusing, *Without a Clue* (1988) reveals that Watson was the real detective genius and that Holmes was his fictional creation; when the public clamored to meet Holmes, Watson hired a dim-witted actor to play the role.

So powerful is the Holmes persona that even tangential connections attract viewers. In 2000 and 2002 the Public Broadcasting System aired a joint British-American series of mysteries that featured Conan Doyle and his teacher, Dr. Joseph Bell, on whom Holmes was partly modeled, as characters solving crimes in the manner of Holmes and Watson. Called *Murder Rooms: The Dark Beginnings of Sherlock Holmes*, the episodes weave incidents from Conan Doyle's life into fictional plots that foreshadow the great stories to come. But clearly the draw for the series is the name of the immortal detective.

So how did this all begin? While the springs of creation are always ultimately mysterious, they are never entirely hidden. As with every mystery, there are clues. The most promising sources, as with most writers, are biographical.

Arthur Conan Doyle was born in Edinburgh, Scotland, in 1859. He was a healthy, athletic lad, who appeared to have a happy childhood. He grew up in a middle-class family with a keen sense of its place in society and history. His family was originally from Ireland. His grandfather, John Doyle, like many gifted Irishmen, had moved to London, where he made his name as a political cartoonist. His four sons all became artists of one sort or another. Conan Doyle's Uncle Richard knew Dickens; a warm letter from the great novelist survives in the family archives. Richard was also a friend of William Thackeray, whose works he had illustrated. The author of *Vanity Fair* once bounced young Arthur on his knee while paying a visit to Conan Doyle's father, Charles. Charles worked as a young architect in the Government Office of Works, though he carried on the family's artistic tradition by painting in his spare time. Arthur's mother, Mary, also of Irish parentage, traced her descent back to the Plantagenets on one side and Sir Walter Scott on the other, both sources of considerable pride. Arthur Conan Doyle grew up in a stable society well worth valuing. Nothing in his early life gave him any reason to be a reformer. His great detective would one day uphold the values of this social order, acting as a mainstay of the status quo.

Arthur had a very good education. His thorough knowledge of both ancient and modern classics is clear from reading the Holmes stories. His parents sent him to Jesuit boarding schools, where he initially rebelled against their harsh discipline, as well as the dullness of his studies. His outlook changed when he discovered the essays of English historian and poet Thomas Macaulay, who died the year Conan Doyle was born. Though hardly anyone reads Macaulay today, he was immensely influential in the nineteenth century. Conan Doyle was entranced by his language and his sharp, colorful pronouncements. Macaulay made history a source of wonder and romance. He was also an unapologetic believer in the superiority of British life. It is not as if there weren't a thousand springs from which any young British boy could drink in this notion, but Macaulay supplied a river of it to Conan Doyle. He carried a volume of the essays around with him the rest of his life, claiming Macaulay had influenced him more than anyone else.

After graduation from boarding school, it was time to choose a career. Since it appeared that Conan Doyle did not inherit the family's artistic genes, he decided on a career in medicine. It was at the medical school in Edinburgh that he met the two men who would have the most influence on his conception of Holmes. The first was the surgeon Dr. Joseph Bell; Conan Doyle later claimed he was the model for Sherlock Holmes. Bell regularly amazed his students by deducing facts about his patients from minute observations of their appearance and behavior. Conan Doyle's autobiography, *Memories and Adventures* (see "For Further Reading"), lists only one example of the doctor's deductive powers.

> In one of his best cases he said to a civilian patient: 'Well, my man, you've served in the army.' 'Aye, Sir.' 'Not long discharged?' 'No, Sir.' 'A Highland regiment?' 'Aye, Sir.' 'A non-com officer?' 'Aye, Sir.' 'Stationed at Barbados?' 'Aye, Sir.' 'You see, gentlemen,' he would explain, 'the man was a respectful man but did not remove his hat. They do not in the army, but he would have learned civilian ways had he been long discharged. He has an air of authority and he is obviously Scottish. As to Barbados, his complaint is Elephantiasis, which is West Indian, and not British' (p. 330).

That could well be Sherlock Holmes interrogating a visitor to 221B Baker Street. Bell's reasoning powers made so strong an impression on Conan Doyle that he turned to those memories when he decided to write a detective novel. When the first twelve stories were published in book form as *The Adventures of Sherlock Holmes*, Conan Doyle asked Bell if he might dedicate them to him. Robert Louis Stevenson, who also knew Bell, wrote to congratulate Conan Doyle on "your very ingenious and very interesting adventures of Sherlock Holmes." At the end of the letter Stevenson asks, "Only one thing troubles me: can this be my old friend Joe Bell?"

Dr. Bell wasn't the only model, though. Some aspects of Holmes were derived from George Budd, a fellow medical student Conan Doyle met on the school's rugby team. Brilliant but mercurial, Budd could talk expansively on subject after subject, then lapse into moody silence. The life of the party at one moment, he could turn murderously violent the next. The two were friends at medical school, but they lost track of one another when Budd moved away after graduation in 1881. In 1882, after Conan Doyle had spent some postgraduate time at sea, Budd summoned him to Plymouth, England, to start a practice there.

Budd had made a tremendous success of his practice by flouting every rule of medical etiquette. He yelled at his patients, pushed some against walls, cursed others, told many they ate too much, drank too much, and slept too much. Sometimes Budd refused even to see them, proclaiming to an anxious clutch in the waiting room that he was going to spend the day in the country. Despite this bizarre behavior, or perhaps because of it, his consulting services were enormously popular. No doubt a contributing reason was that he charged no fee for his diagnoses. It was no coincidence, however, that Budd prescribed medicine for every patient. Their pills could be conveniently purchased down the hall, where Mrs. Budd typed up the labels for the bottles and took the patients' money. Budd earned a fortune from this dubious practice. He made a point each day on his way to the bank to carry his earnings in a big bag through the doctors' quarter of the city, jingling it as he went, just to rankle his fellow practitioners. He was convinced that the rules of medical ethics were a con game to keep young, energetic doctors subservient to their elders.

Conan Doyle was both appalled and amused by this display. When Budd offered to help him start a practice of his own, however, he accepted. Budd furnished Conan Doyle with a consulting room in his clinic, then flooded him with advice on how to run his life. One suggestion was to start a novel that very day. Although he had already published one short story, Conan Doyle hadn't considered writing anything as ambitious as a novel. But because he had no patients as yet and thus plenty of time on his hands, he gave it a try.

There is no evidence that Sherlock Holmes was born out of this circumstance, or that Budd contributed anything more to the character than his energy, range of interests, and black moods. But he contributed something else essential that runs throughout Doyle's work. Through Budd, Conan Doyle experienced deception and betrayal for the first time. Of course Conan Doyle knew, as we all do, that people can lie and turn against former friends, but it makes a different and certainly deeper impression when it happens to you personally. It came about in the following way.

During his time in Budd's clinic, Conan Doyle's mother wrote him letters expressing her displeasure at his involvement with Budd, whom she considered an unscrupulous character. Budd apparently sneaked the letters out of Conan Doyle's room, read them without Conan Doyle's knowledge, and developed a bitter resentment against his friend. At some point he complained that his own practice was dwindling because of Conan Doyle. As Conan Doyle, unlike Budd, really was a man of honor, he immediately went to his office door with a hammer and pulled off his nameplate.

   This display of character softened Budd's resentment, at least for a while. He proposed to lend Conan Doyle a pound a week to help him set up a practice in Portsmouth. Once Conan Doyle moved to that city to restart his medical career, Budd reneged on the payment. He wrote to Conan Doyle, quoting what he considered slanderous passages from a letter of Conan Doyle's mother, which he claimed the maid had found torn in pieces under the grate. This kind of back-stabbing carried on under his roof was a betrayal he couldn't forgive, said Budd. He would have nothing more to do with Conan Doyle.

   Conan Doyle was stunned. Upon thinking it over, he couldn't remember ever tearing up any of his letters. Searching through his pockets he found the very one from which Budd had quoted. He realized Budd's lie about finding the letter meant Budd was lying and must have been reading his mail surreptitiously. He wrote back to say he had seen through the clumsy plot, thanking Budd for removing the only disagreement between himself and his mother by confirming her low opinion of Budd. He assured Budd that any attempt to harm him had backfired.

   The incident left a haunting memory. Conan Doyle wrote later, "It was as though in the guise and dress of a man I had caught a sudden glimpse of something subhuman—of something so outside my own range of thought that I was powerless against it" (*The Stark Munro Letters*, p. 271). He was also powerless to explain it. Whenever he depicts some descent into the abyss of vice, it is inevitably without any insight into how a soul makes such a journey: It is always taken as merely a fact of existence.

   It was a few years later, in 1886, after he had set up a mildly profitable medical practice of his own, that Conan Doyle first turned to the idea of a detective novel. In addition to his Edinburgh models, Sherlock Holmes had literary sources, too. Conan Doyle had read and admired the detective stories of Edgar Allan Poe, the creator of the genre, as well as the detective novels of Émile Gaboriau, whose Monsieur Lecoq solved some baffling crimes. Holmes's methods are similar to those of Poe's C. Auguste Dupin, and the stories have a structure reminiscent of Gaboriau's work, but his personality owes nothing to either of those Parisian detectives. And ultimately it is his personality that makes Holmes so compelling.

   Just what is it about Sherlock Holmes that has captivated people for so long? It's easy to see some of the reasons for his popularity. His intelligence, his self-assurance, his mastery of every situation, and his unerring judgment are all enormously appealing. We are also attracted by Holmes's sense of humor. From the very first Holmes not only sprinkles the stories with his dry retorts and ironic asides, he also laughs, chuckles, smiles, and jokes throughout. This quality goes a long way toward humanizing him, making it easier to feel affection for a character whose abilities could well make him seem more machine than human.

   His eccentricities add to his appeal. An unwritten rule says that every commentator must mention the tobacco he keeps in the toe end of his Persian slipper, the cigars he keeps in a coal-shuttle, and the unanswered correspondence he transfixes by a jack-knife into the very center of his wooden mantelpiece. But his odd qualities extend further than these surface details. They are really only shallow tricks that add some local color, perhaps, to his characterization, but reveal little about his character. More revealing of just how truly eccentric he is are the passions central to his mind and the lengths he is willing to go in their service.

Devoting his life to fighting crime, for instance, is surely unusual. With his skills and connections, one would think he could have had his choice of careers. What sort of person dedicates himself to catching people who commit crimes? We don't need a psychiatrist's shingle to conclude that someone who feels this need must have suffered some sort of injustice as a child. As we can never know what this sad event was, we can only speculate, and many have. Whatever it was, it has made Holmes a moralist. It is not the law that he upholds, but his own conception of justice. Several times he substitutes this conception for the letter of British law by letting someone go who is guilty of a crime. Several other times he violates the law himself in order to bring about some higher justice. Those are some of the things we admire about him. Because we always agree with his judgment in those instances, his willingness to become the final arbiter of justice makes him heroic.

Holmes is of course a gentleman, with all the notions of class in nineteenth-century England that the word implies. Yet he does things no gentleman would dream of doing. On one occasion he disguises himself as a beggar, on another as an opium addict, and, most improbably of all, on another as an old woman. Since these disguises help him get to the truth, we think of them, if we think of them at all, as merely techniques, albeit clever and entertaining ones, for solving crimes. But respectable men in London in the 1890s would be aghast at seeing a fellow they knew sauntering forth in a frock and a wig, or holed up in an opium den. Neither would such men pay any but the most begrudging and uncomfortable notice to street urchins beseeching them for alms. Yet Holmes not only befriends such boys, he enlists them as extra eyes and ears. Dubbing them "the Baker Street Irregulars," he also seems to feel affection and sympathy for them. But then "respectability" is achieved by conforming to an external set of shared beliefs. Holmes couldn't care less what any one else might think of his actions, so long as those actions help him bring criminals to their just deserts. His self-worth comes from measuring up to his own moral code.

Holmes's attitude toward class distinctions is also unusual for his time, and may be an added reason he is popular in America. His judgments about people arise from the content of their characters, not from the color of their coats of arms. He shows the most respect for characters who display loyalty to someone they love, particularly when they also exhibit courage. Irene Adler in "A Scandal in Bohemia," Grant Munro in "The Yellow Face," and Captain Jack Crocker in "The Adventure of the Abbey Grange" all gain his respect because they show these qualities. It's surely significant that none of those characters are upper class. Aristocrats and even royalty usually fare rather less well in his estimation. His acidic assessment of the King of Bohemia seems to go right over the royal head. Holmes sternly rebukes Lord Holdernesse in "The Adventure of the Priory School" as if he were a judge scolding a prisoner in the dock. He can scarcely conceal his distaste for Lord Robert St. Simon in "The Adventure of the Noble Bachelor," and we read in "The Adventure of the Three Garridebs" that he refused an offer of knighthood from Edward VII. It isn't that he dislikes these people because of their class. He accepts an emerald pin from Queen Victoria in "The Adventure of the Bruce-Partington Plans," and he's perfectly gracious to the title family in "The Musgrave Ritual." It's that he expects everyone, irrespective of their class, to live up to a common set of human values.

Lest he seem impossibly superior, Holmes is given some counterbalancing weaknesses. He is wrong from time to time, though usually about something trifling. He is inclined to be critical of the people around him, including Watson, when they haven't met what seems like some impossibly high standard. Some could see this trait as one of his strengths, though, since he holds himself to the same standard. More important, he is what we would call today a manic-depressive. He comes alive only when on the trail of crime, but not just any crime. It must have some special feature that baffles ordinary mortals. When no crime worthy of his skills is currently afoot, he lapses into listlessness, requiring cocaine for stimulation. Cocaine was not illegal at the time; these were the 1880s and 1890s, the time of bohemians in the European capitals, the absinthe drinkers of Degas, and the drug-induced estheticism of the fin-de-siècle. Though not illicit this dependency is clearly a character flaw.

The sum of all his qualities makes Sherlock Holmes seem like a real person. This sense of his reality sets these stories apart from other literature, and from the very beginning the illusion of his existence was powerful. On October 29, 1892, an article called "The Real Sherlock Holmes" by "Our Special Correspondent" appeared in the *National Observer*. It quoted Sherlock Holmes complaining about the way Conan Doyle had plagiarized Dr. Watson. Holmes also expressed indignation at Conan Doyle's misrepresentations of some of his cases. He didn't make any of those little mistakes Conan Doyle ascribes to him. The *Strand Magazine*, which published all the short stories, received letters wanting to know if Holmes were a real person. The magazine cagily replied that it had not made his personal acquaintance but would certainly call upon him if ever it needed a mystery investigated.

Even after it was well known that Holmes was a fictional creation, a curious phenomenon developed that has no other parallel in literature. It has become a good-humored convention for Holmes scholars to treat the stories as historical events and the protagonists as real figures. Conan Doyle is often referred to as the literary agent for Dr. John H. Watson. Several biographies have been written about Holmes, and the current residents of Baker Street still get mail addressed to him. In October 2002 the Royal Society of Chemistry in Britain awarded an Honorary Fellowship to Sherlock Holmes, its first fictional inductee, on the hundredth anniversary of his coming out of retirement to solve the case of *The Hound of the Baskervilles*.

In addition to his own characteristics, Holmes is popular for other reasons. The plots and the atmospheres of the stories deserve no small credit for creating the Holmes appeal. Conan Doyle's skill in vividly describing London has made countless readers feel they know the city. The inclusion of so many accurate details from daily life in the city—from train stations and schedules, concert series, real-life performers, streets and buildings they passed every day—gave contemporaneous readers a sense they might be reading an account from the newspapers. The inclusion of many real historical characters strengthens the sense that we are reading a personal memoir. The stories were also initially popular because of the novelty of the scientific method used by Holmes in solving his mysteries, something we can't help but take for granted now.

Holmes profits enormously by having his exploits narrated by an admirer. Nearly as well known but much less appreciated, the good Dr. Watson provides not only a contrast as the Everyman to Holmes's Superman, he also perfectly embodies the British man in the street. Conan Doyle himself has often been thought the model for Holmes's friend and chronicler. Like Watson, Conan Doyle was a doctor. Also like Watson, who we learn was a rugby player in his youth, Conan Doyle was an avid footballer. He was also a boxer, cricket player, and golfer. He was an all-round sportsman, and like other sportsmen, then and now, he had an uncomplicated attitude toward the world. Conan Doyle was like Watson in another way that's scarcely believable except for the testimony of people who knew him. He was apparently as little likely to deduce something about you as Watson was. Hesketh Pearson reports a conversation Conan Doyle had with Hugh Kingsmill: " 'Arnold Lunn is a son of Sir Henry Lunn, is he not?' asked Conan Doyle. 'Yes.' 'And you are a brother of Arnold Lunn?' 'Yes.' (After a minute's pause for reflection) 'Then you also are a son of Sir Henry Lunn?' 'Yes' " (*Conan Doyle: His Life and Art*, pp. 183–184). The obvious difference between Conan Doyle and Watson is that Watson did not have the capacity to invent a character like Sherlock Holmes. Generations of readers have been grateful that Arthur Conan Doyle did, and that he used that capacity to enrich our imaginations by creating a hero who reassures us that even the most baffling mysteries can be solved by reason, and who challenges us to use our powers of observation.

If you are reading these stories for the first time or renewing your acquaintance with them after decades of fond but faded memories, I urge you, as other editors of these stories have urged their readers before me, to proceed directly to the sitting room at 221B Baker Street, where you may test your detective powers against the Master's. Come back to the following essay after you've finished. We'll have much to talk about.

                                                                    —Kyle Freeman

INTRODUCTION TO VOLUME II

When in 1893 Sherlock Holmes tumbled to his apparent death over the falls at Reichenbach in Switzerland, locked in the embrace of the sinister Professor Moriarty, readers all over the world were stunned and saddened. Letters poured in to Arthur Conan Doyle and to his publisher, the *Strand Magazine*, urging the revival of the beloved detective. Conan Doyle was adamant that he wouldn't do it. "I couldn't revive him if I would, at least not for years," he wrote to a friend, "for I have had such an overdose of him that I feel towards him as I do towards *pâté-de-foie-gras*, of which I once ate too much, so that the name of it gives me a sickly feeling to this day" (Baring-Gould, *The Annotated Sherlock Holmes*, vol. 1, p. 16; see "For Further Reading"). Then seven years later, after a young friend told him a legend from Dartmoor about a supernatural hound, Conan Doyle relented by writing *The Hound of the Baskervilles*. He was careful, however, to make it a reminiscence, not a resurrection, of his famous consulting detective. The story was set in 1889, two years before the Swiss misadventure. The resumption of writing about his most famous creation must have set into motion something in Conan Doyle's soul, for in an interview quoted in the *Harper's Weekly* issue of August 31, 1901, the month *The Hound* was first serialized, one can see his resolve starting to weaken. "I know that my friend Dr. Watson is a most trustworthy man, and I gave the utmost credit to his story of the dreadful affair in Switzerland. He may have been mistaken, of course. It may not have been Mr. Holmes who fell from the ledge at all, or the whole affair might be the result of hallucination." It wasn't long before Conan Doyle decided—perhaps after a wistful look at his bank balance—that the enforced absence of his sleuth had gone on for too long. In 1903 he called on his friend Dr. Watson once more for another series of stories about his colleague, and in October 1903 the *Strand* published "The Adventure of the Empty House." There it was revealed, almost plausibly, that only Moriarty had gone over the falls at Reichenbach. Thus readers learned to their delight that they would be treated to many more adventures of the world's greatest detective, Sherlock Holmes.

A series of twelve more stories followed, ending with "The Adventure of the Second Stain," the last published in the December 1904 issue of the *Strand Magazine*. In quick order the series was published as a book by George Newnes of London in 1905, under the title *The Return of Sherlock Holmes*, with sixteen illustrations by Sidney Paget, the great illustrator whose drawings for the first *Strand* stories had done so much to establish the popular image of Holmes. The new stories appeared to take up just where the old ones left off. Holmes and Watson resumed their cozy relationship; Holmes continued to solve mysteries that baffled Watson, Scotland Yard, and the reader; and the world of 221B Baker Street seemed as solid and unchanging as ever.

It seems that way only until one examines the stories more carefully. A closer reading reveals subtle but significant changes in Holmes. The first one we might notice is Holmes's willingness to take the law into his own hands. In one of the early Sherlock Holmes stories, "The Boscombe Valley Mystery," we recall that Holmes did not divulge the name of John Turner as the man responsible for the death of his neighbor, Mr. McCarthy, when Holmes learned that McCarthy was a blackmailer and that Turner didn't have long to live. Technically it's a crime to conceal such evidence, but in view of the circumstances few would quarrel with Holmes's decision. But before his resurrection, such behavior by Holmes was unique to that story, and we might note that he merely withheld information he had deduced himself—passive misbehavior at worst. In his defense we might also recall that in the case of "The Greek Interpreter" in the second series of stories, Holmes insisted on getting a warrant to search the premises of kidnappers.

In *The Return* such niceties are almost scornfully dismissed. Holmes aggressively pursues his own justice, actively breaking the law on several occasions and coming close to morally censurable conduct on several others. We first see this change in "The Adventure of the Priory School," where we learn that the murder of a German teacher named Heidegger and the kidnapping of the son of the Duke of Holdernesse were part of a plot by the duke's illegitimate son. It's clear that the son, acting as the duke's secretary, and the duke himself were complicit in aiding the killer's escape. Holmes, claiming he is a poor man, agrees to keep silent about the whole nasty business in exchange for a huge check from his lordship. This is rather shocking. Unlike the previous case in Boscombe Valley, where we feel some sympathy for the wronged man, who will die soon anyway, we have no extenuating circumstances here. In fact, we have a prime example of the high-handedness of aristocracy in covering up its dirty family business at the cost of other people's lives. Holmes's acceptance of an enormous check could be seen as a bribe. When we compare this with his acid-toned retort in "The Problem of Thor Bridge,"—" 'My professional charges are upon a fixed scale,' said Holmes coldly. 'I do not vary them, save when I remit them altogether' "—it looks as if Holmes has sold out here.

Those are likely to be fighting words to many Holmes fans. If you're one of them, consider some further evidence before reaching for your brass knuckles. After he solves the mystery in "The Adventure of the Six Napoleons," which, by the by, reprises the jewel-hidden-inside-another-object trick found in "The Adventure of the Blue Carbuncle," Holmes tells Watson to put the stolen jewel they have just recovered, "the famous black pearl of the Borgias," in his own safe rather than return it to the authorities. Since Inspector Lestrade from Scotland Yard is standing right there, one would think there could be no better time to settle accounts. Holmes appears to think he has the right to stolen property just because he found it. This finders-keepers attitude would be, of course, antithetical to the law. What can Holmes be thinking?

Then there is the troubling case of "The Adventure of Charles Augustus Milverton." In that story Holmes abandons the moral code he followed in previous stories. First, while spying on Milverton, Holmes pledges to marry Milverton's housemaid in order to get information out of her about her boss. When Watson reacts with shock to this admission, Holmes nonchalantly replies, "You can't help it, my dear Watson." Then before he and Watson break into Milverton's house (no talk of a search warrant here!), Holmes tells Watson that they will "take no articles save those which are used for an illegal purpose." Later, however, when he empties the contents of Milverton's safe into the fire, he doesn't stop to examine which papers are for such purposes and which are not. Most serious of all, he stays Watson's hand when a wronged woman pulls a pistol on the blackmailer and shoots him; then Holmes refuses to cooperate with the police in finding her. Milverton may have been what Holmes calls him, "the worst man in London," but blackmail is not a hanging crime. Holmes admits that Milverton got "the best of the first exchanges" between them, then vows, "but my self-respect and my reputation are concerned to fight it to a finish." Holmes seems to act out of revenge for his wounded pride, the law be damned.

Finally, in "The Adventure of the Abbey Grange" Holmes takes it upon himself to be judge and jury for Captain Croker. ("Hold on!" you may object: "Holmes quite explicitly makes Watson the jury." True enough, but Holmes knew with certainty what Watson's judgment would be, and thus only pretends to let him decide Croker's fate.) Here we again sympathize with his judgment, as Croker is an admirable fellow in every way. The man he kills, Sir Eustace Brackenstall, is not only a drunken brute, but his implied sexual mistreatment of his refined wife is more than enough to convince us that the world is a better place without him. (We might note here another case of corrupt aristocracy, a common element of the entire Saga.) The speed and assurance with which Holmes takes upon himself this authority, even enlisting Watson's conscious intercession, is the noteworthy point of this story. He is coming more and more to feel and act like an embodiment of Justice itself.

What can be the cause of this change in Holmes? It stems in part from Conan Doyle's exasperation with the English legal system. Because people assumed that the author of the Sherlock Holmes stories was every bit as clever as his fictional creation, Conan Doyle often received requests to solve mysteries or to set straight the course of justice gone awry. A prominent example, although it occurred in 1906, after the publication of *The Return*, illustrates the kind of thing that frustrated him. George Edalji, the son of an Indian minister, was convicted of killing farm animals on evidence that was obviously trumped up. His main crime seemed to be that he was Indian at a time when there was much anti-Indian sentiment in

England. Conan Doyle took up his case, collected evidence overlooked by the investigators, interviewed witnesses not called at trial, and for years made speeches, wrote articles, and badgered officials to set the poor bloke free. He did the same a few years later for another man framed for murder, Oscar Slater. In each case it took nearly twenty years before either man got any justice from the legal system. Holmes reflects his creator's impatience with letting an obviously flawed human institution decide crucial questions when it's clear to any intelligent person what the outcome should be.

This change in Holmes makes him more human. He has weaknesses; he makes mistakes; he succumbs to emotions from time to time, even ugly ones. His character becomes more interesting to his readers and his creator alike when it evolves and deepens. The vehicle for this change can only be his relationship with Watson. The development of that relationship will be one of the themes that most interested Conan Doyle in these late stories. We'll see further examples of it later.

In addition to the changes in Holmes, one also notices about *The Return* that many of the plots are remakes of older ones. As noted earlier, "The Adventure of the Six Napoleons" reprises "The Blue Carbuncle." "The Adventure of the Norwood Builder" uses the same trick of feigning fire found in "A Scandal in Bohemia." "The Second Stain" recaps several earlier themes. The important letter of state that goes missing recalls the same kind of letter in the "The Naval Treaty"; it is also returned to its owner as if it had never been gone, again like the one in "The Naval Treaty"; the theme of blackmail over an indiscreet love letter recalls "A Scandal in Bohemia." "The Adventure of the Solitary Cyclist" repeats elements of "The Greek Interpreter." The pressure to come up with new plots had always been the source of Conan Doyle's irritation with the Holmes stories. Without such new plots, and under a time limit to come up with them, he simply recycled some golden oldies.

He also returned to the oldest theme in detective fiction, revenge. It's a prominent theme in both the first two series and again in this one. "The Empty House" revolves around Colonel Sebastian Moran getting revenge on Holmes for Moriarty's death. Jonas Oldacre of "The Norwood Builder" wants revenge on the woman who rejected his romantic attentions thirty years previously, so he stages his own death and frames her son for it. Abe Slaney kills Hilton Cubitt in "The Adventure of the Dancing Men" because Cubitt fired at him first while Slaney was talking to Mrs. Cubitt, a woman he had once wooed in the United States. Although he didn't set out to revenge his lost love, the end result proved to be exactly that. The title character of "Charles Augustus Milverton" is murdered by a woman he had ruined because she wouldn't pay him blackmail. And perhaps worst of all, by allowing Milverton's murder and shielding his killer, Holmes himself resorts to revenge on Milverton for upsetting Holmes's calculations to catch him.

One last note about *The Return* before we turn to the next series of stories, *His Last Bow*. While everyone has his or her favorites among the stories, a number are always bridesmaids, never brides. No one ever champions "The Adventure of the Three Students" or "The Adventure of the Missing Three-Quarter," as the problems Holmes solves in those stories seem so trivial. The latter story, while dull as a detective yarn, becomes more interesting when one learns that Conan Doyle's first wife, Louise, was an invalid for the last years of her life. During this time, Conan Doyle formed a strong attachment to another woman, Jean Leckie, who moved to a house near the Conan Doyles. Conan Doyle saw her whenever he could, but from all we know about them, their love was strictly platonic. A year after the death of Louise, Conan Doyle and Jean married. The story of the rugby player who keeps his sick wife in a secret hideaway merges the two women in Conan Doyle's life into one. While this story may not appeal greatly to us, we can be sure it had a special resonance for its conflicted creator.

After *The Return*, Conan Doyle thought again that he was through with Mr. Sherlock Holmes. The last story in the volume, "The Adventure of the Second Stain," begins by claiming that Holmes "has definitely retired from London and betaken himself to study and bee-farming on the Sussex Downs." Conan Doyle never committed himself to another series of stories. He wrote his publisher in March 1908, however, that he would contribute a number of occasional new Holmes tales, to be called "Reminiscences of Sherlock Holmes," but at his own pace, subject to no time pressure. These stories, as that initial title suggests, would reflect particular concerns of Conan Doyle going beyond exciting whodunit plots. Holmes would be made the vehicle for exploring changes in the modern world and other themes especially interesting to Conan Doyle.

Conan Doyle began the first such story, "The Adventure of Wisteria Lodge," just days after King Leopold II had given up personal control of large areas of the Congo to Belgium in March 1908. A year later Conan Doyle wrote a blistering indictment of the Belgian treatment of the people of the Congo, but his first go at the cruelties of the African empire came in this thinly disguised fictional form. The plot concerns a dictator who has ruined a small country, fleeing with much of its wealth. Six months after the events in the beginning of the story he is found dead in a Madrid hotel in what is assumed to be a revenge murder by the widow of a diplomat he had killed. Watson tells us, "We could not doubt that justice, if belated, had come at last." To Conan Doyle the story takes a stand against the immoralities of nation-plundering; to most readers, the story induces heavy sleep. *The World Bibliography of Sherlock Holmes and Dr. Watson*, a complete list of articles published about the Holmes cycle, had yet to show a single article about this story as late as 1974 (though several have been written since). When Conan Doyle set his Holmes stories the task of reflecting world concerns, rather than providing exciting mysteries, his readers weren't so eager to follow.

In this story Conan Doyle continues to humanize Holmes. He gives him little work to do. In fact, because Holmes is so competitive with the local Inspector Baynes, they nearly cancel each other out, leaving it to the dictator's gardener to save the day. Though still capable of remarkable insight and brilliant deductions, Holmes isn't the superman he appeared to be in the early tales. His list of mistakes will grow in this series, setting up a new pattern that in its turn will be broken to surprise us.

The second story in the cycle to be published, "The Adventure of the Bruce-Partington Plans," appeared in December 1908.* Conan Doyle was very much concerned about the laxity of the government's defense of Britain against the growing power of other European nations, particularly Germany. This story functions as a cautionary tale for ministers oblivious to mounting danger. It also continues the theme of Holmes as ordinary mortal. He has to ask Mycroft for the names of the spies most likely to be involved in the matter; we recall that in "The Adventure of the Second Stain" he knew them without having to ask. Although he makes some clever deductions about the reason for the odd placement of the body of Cadogan West and the absence of blood at the presumed murder scene, he's completely off-track about West's involvement. He has been steered away by Mycroft from the true source of treason, the brother of Sir James Walter, because the elder Holmes can't imagine that a long-time government minister could be involved in any kind of intrigue against his government. Sir James is protected by the same kind of "he's one of us" feeling that later sheltered Kim Philby, Guy Burgess, and Donald Maclean when they were Soviet moles working inside British Intelligence. Holmes suspects everyone but the real villain. When he discovers the truth, Holmes says to Watson, " 'You can write me down an ass this time, Watson,' said he. 'This is not the bird that I was looking for.' "

This story adds to the growing list of crimes Holmes is ready to commit in order to get at the source of worse crimes. Although there's talk of getting a warrant to search the premises of Hugo Oberstein, Holmes concludes that the evidence he has wouldn't persuade a magistrate. When Watson agrees to be the lookout while Holmes once again turns to breaking and entering, a moment of personal affection follows that in some ways is more rewarding to readers than another demonstration of Holmes as supersleuth. "He sprang up and shook me by the hand. 'I knew you would not shrink at the last,' said he, and for a moment I saw something in his eyes which was nearer to tenderness than I had ever seen."

In February 1909, two months after this story was published Conan Doyle was recuperating from an illness when a Cornish boatman said something to him that must have stung him, for he repeated the incident many times in later years. " 'I think, sir,' the boatman said, expressing the popular reaction to the resumption of Holmes's career, 'when Holmes fell over the cliff, he may not have killed himself, but all the same he was never quite the same man afterwards.' " (*Memories and Adventures*, p. 116). This implied criticism spurred Conan Doyle to set his next story

---

*The order of the stories in book form and in this collection are not the same as the original publication order.

in Cornwall. "The Adventure of the Devil's Foot," published in December 1910, combines a number of themes. First, Holmes returns to his old form by solving a string of baffling murders. The adventure also deepens the relationship between Holmes and Watson, as Holmes would have either been killed or driven insane had not Watson pulled him out of the deadly vapors to which Holmes had subjected them both as an experiment. We have never seen Holmes so vulnerable. Holmes's face, "white, rigid and drawn with horror," his "clammy forehead" and "unsteady voice" testify to his mortality. The terrors of the hallucinatory visions produced by the spell of the drug show us that even his admirably balanced mind might sink into madness. Watson's response to Holmes's apology is one of the more touching rewards of the entire series. " 'You know,' I answered with some emotion, for I had never seen so much of Holmes's heart before, 'that it is my greatest joy and privilege to help you.' " Only one other passage, to come a few years later, equals this intensity of feeling between the two men.

Further, "The Adventure of the Devil's Foot" revisits another personal theme mentioned earlier: Conan Doyle's long platonic love for Jean Leckie. One of the murderers in this story, Leon Sterndale, has had a long platonic love for Brenda Treginnis. "For years I have loved her. For years she has loved me. . . . For years Brenda waited. For years I waited." She is killed, however, by her brother, Mortimer, who was hoping just to drive her insane so that he could inherit the family estate. Sterndale then avenges her death by forcing Mortimer Treginnis to breathe the same deadly fumes that Mortimer had used to kill his sister. Sterndale's grief at the death of his beloved is so profound that once again Holmes becomes justice itself, letting the broken man go in peace, with the full assent of Watson and every reader with an ounce of pity.

Not long after this story, Conan Doyle had another occasion to change his writing in reaction to outside commentary, this time from a highly learned source. In 1912 Ronald Knox, who later became well known as a monsignor in the Catholic Church, published a talk he had given the year before to a student union about the eleven points common to the Sherlock Holmes stories. Conan Doyle read it, then sent Knox a polite, appreciative letter in response. But in his very next story, "The Adventure of the Dying Detective," he intentionally set out to break the patterns so astutely adduced by Knox. No one likes to think his or her mind is an open book to other people. In the previous stories, the plots had mysteries for the reader to try to solve, but the framework for those plots was predictable. In "The Dying Detective" Conan Doyle varied some of those predictable elements. First, the story doesn't begin as usual in Baker Street, but in Watson's rooms during his marriage. Then the first words spoken are from the heretofore silent Mrs. Hudson, Holmes's landlady. Holmes doesn't have a visitor bring him a case, nor does he go out to survey the scene of any mystery: The action comes to him. But then Conan Doyle plays a really crafty trick on us. After reading of his rheumatism and seeing the series of mistakes Holmes had made in the last few stories, we have been conditioned to the physical weaknesses age has visited on him. When he seems to be dying from a rare tropical disease, his infirmity is believable. Then Conan Doyle turns the tables on our expectations when Holmes, once again his invincible old self, pops up, calmly lights a cigarette, and informs a killer that the jig is up.

Conan Doyle continued until 1917 to publish the stories that ultimately formed *His Last Bow*. He took a break after publishing "The Dying Detective" in December 1913 to start a more substantial project. Out of the blue, and to the delight of his publisher, Conan Doyle wrote to the *Strand* in January 1914 that he had already written half of a new Sherlock Holmes novel. The last time he sent the *Strand* a Holmes novel, *The Hound of the Baskervilles*, sales of the magazine shot up by 30,000 copies. Conan Doyle finished his first and only draft by mid-April, but the novel didn't appear in serialization in the *Strand* until September, after the Great War had begun. The last chapter concluded in May 1915. It was also serialized in the United States by the Associated Sunday Newspapers, which published a Sunday magazine as a supplement to the regular newspaper, much like *Parade Magazine* in the United States today. The U.S. version was printed once a week, while in England the *Strand* published chapters once a month, so the novel actually first appeared in full in the United States.

Conan Doyle expressed his apologies to his English editors for contributing only this trifling distraction instead of something more important to the war effort. He was doubly wrong: On the one hand, he could scarcely have provided anything more conducive to public morale than a new adventure by the always reassuring Sherlock Holmes, which gave citizens something to take their minds off the grisly business across the Channel. On the other hand, this particular novel ends with the implication that the forces of darkness are unconquerable, a disquieting thought in the face of the implacable Hun facing the Allies across the trenches.

Conan Doyle writes in the preface to *Sherlock Holmes: The Complete Long Stories* (1929) that "*The Valley of Fear* had its origin through my reading a graphic account of the Molly McQuire [sic] outrages in the coalfields of Pennsylvania." That account was Allan Pinkerton's *The Molly Maguires and the Detectives*, published in 1877, which details the experiences of James McParlan, a Pinkerton employee who masqueraded as James McKenna to build a case against a group of lawless Irish labor terrorists in Pennsylvania. Conan Doyle became a friend of Pinkerton's son William, who apparently confided some information about his father's career that Conan Doyle used in his new novel. When *The Valley of Fear* was published, Pinkerton considered suing Conan Doyle for using this confidential information without asking permission. Exactly what Conan Doyle learned from Pinkerton we don't know, but it's one of those nice ironies that the son of the most famous American detective should have unwittingly provided information that formed an adventure of the world's most famous fictional detective.

The Pinkerton liaison came several years after Conan Doyle learned of a similar infiltration of lawless gangs. In 1892 Thomas Beach had published *Twenty-five Years in the Secret Service*, which detailed his penetration of a group of Irish revolutionaries in America, much like the Molly Maguires. Using the name Major Henri Le Caron, he gave evidence against them and then had to be guarded by the British government for years afterward for fear of reprisals. His death on April 1, 1894 had attracted Conan Doyle's attention, for its announcement was much publicized and Le Caron was buried in Norwood, near where Conan Doyle was living at the time. The fact that the announcement came on April Fool's Day gave rise to a rumor that the master spy's demise was a ruse to throw killers off his trail, a feature Conan Doyle used in *The Valley of Fear* by having Douglas fake his own death for the same reason.

So there was historical precedence for the novel's story. The new novel was originally written with a third-person narrator telling the entire story. By the time it was finally published in September 1915, Conan Doyle either had had second thoughts about the wisdom of that decision, or he was urged by someone to revise the work so that once again we have Watson as our trusty guide. As in *A Study in Scarlet*, the long flashback to experiences in America is written from a third-person point of view. We are told that Douglas presents Holmes and Watson with a manuscript explaining the provenance of the current situation. That manuscript is clearly the basis for the long flashback, but it isn't clear whose words we are reading.

On first glance this would seem to be a step backward. After the awkward third-person flashback of *A Study in Scarlet*, Conan Doyle had gotten better and better about introducing the distant past into his novels. *The Sign of Four* lets two of the characters, Sholto and Small, each tell part of the previous story, so that no omniscient narrator obtrudes with testimony Watson couldn't have heard. *The Hound of the Baskervilles* needs only a two-page letter about the history of the curse of the Baskervilles, read by Doctor Mortimer, to explain how the past is prologue to the present. Most readers don't think of it as a flashback at all. At this point in his career, after reaching the peak of his ability to construct plots, why would Conan Doyle revert to a clumsy tactic of his youth?

A second glance—indeed, a long, hard stare, perhaps—reveals that Conan Doyle was trying something here that he couldn't have begun to bring off in his younger days. We're being asked to judge Douglas in a way that would be impossible if Watson were our guide. Watson is an admirable example of the dependable narrator. We believe what he says. The success of this story depends on our doubts about McMurdo/Edwards/Douglas. That doubt is first sown when Douglas reveals that an intruder, armed with a shotgun, was "accidentally" shot square in the face during a struggle. In view of the plan to use this accident to his advantage, one can't help but wonder if in fact Douglas managed to capture Ted Baldwin, the intruder, and then cold-bloodedly execute him as the realization sank in that he would never be free from the retributive arm of the

Scowrers. It seems a little too convenient for Baldwin's face to be oblit-erated; and how exactly would an intruder get into a castle like Birlstone Manor, with a moat and a drawbridge, and then be surprised so quickly that he couldn't get off a shot with a shotgun? It seems more likely that someone else with a gun got the drop on him. Part II convinces us that Baldwin was a killer who got just what was coming to him. But his pre-meditated killing, even if it saves Douglas's life, would put Douglas in a morally ambiguous state. Our doubts about Douglas only grow when we note that Holmes doesn't congratulate him for his escape. Holmes is strangely quiet, perhaps pondering this very ambiguity.

When we then read the story of Douglas's career as secret agent, we have to wonder just how he managed to rise so high in an organization of killers, thieves, and scoundrels of all stripes without committing any crimes himself. The unknown narrator gives him plenty of attractive fea-tures, despite the reprehensible circumstances in which he finds himself, so that we like him, and we see that the best people in the town also like him. His ascendancy in the Scowrers occurs without any serious moral compromise on his part. It's hard to believe that this group of hard-edged men would cede authority to someone from the outside without more of a test than we hear McMurdo has undergone. Because the seed of doubt about him was sown in the first part, we can't read this account without wondering what it omits. We begin to mistrust the narrator. Although Mc-Murdo's ultimate goal was to put an end to the criminal enterprise that locks the valley in a grip of fear, to do so he must surely have been forced to commit some crimes to gain the trust of a show-me cadre of leaders. The entire flashback seems to avoid the question at its center: Just how much evil can one commit in the name of good and not become evil one-self? McMurdo/Edwards is surrounded by moral ambiguity. Some of this ambiguity is transferred to the narration itself, something new in the Holmes Canon.

Then there is the question of Moriarty. Right away we hear of the archvillain whom readers of the series would instantly remember as the man they thought had plunged their detective hero to his watery death twenty years before. But in that story, "The Final Problem," Watson re-sponds to Holmes's question about the Professor by saying he had never heard of him. Here, in "the early days at the end of the 'eighties,'" well before the unpleasant incident at Reichenbach Falls, Watson knows all about him. This contradiction could be the result of negligence, but that seems unlikely. If we assume that Conan Doyle hadn't forgotten what he had written earlier, he must have thought he had more to gain from the inclusion of Moriarty's name than he would lose by the glaring inconsis-tency of Watson's knowledge of him. What *The Valley of Fear* gained was a sense of menace supplied by the mere mention of the Napoleon of crime. If Holmes had never managed to connect Moriarty with a crime several years after the date of this story, the implication that Holmes won't connect him this time must hang over this scene like a dark cloud. If Moriarty is out to get Douglas, we must fear that he will succeed, as in fact he does. Moriarty's name is a guarantee of ultimate doom. It's the beginning of fear, and a guarantee that its span stretches far past the valley in Pennsylvania.

After *The Valley of Fear* was published, Conan Doyle contributed one more story, "His Last Bow," in 1917 before collecting the series of tales written since *The Return* into a new volume entitled *His Last Bow*. When it was published in late 1917, its title implied once again that readers had seen the last of the remarkable consulting detective. But again, Conan Doyle, for whatever reason, had a change of heart. Over the next ten years he wrote a series of stories at odd intervals that was published in 1927 as *The Case Book of Sherlock Holmes*. This group presents a unique problem in Conan Doyle scholarship: The poor quality of many of them, the details that differ significantly from the earlier stories, and the erratic characterization of Holmes himself, all lead us to ask if all of these stories were actually written by Conan Doyle himself? A number of devoted Holmes critics have concluded that several stories are spurious. The evidence for such conclusions rests primarily on an examination of the texts themselves. What biographical support there is for this contention is very slender. What we know is that Conan Doyle was so hard up for plots for his detective stories that he suggested a public contest for ideas to turn into Holmes adventures. He wrote in his autobiography that "the difficulty of the Holmes work was that every story really needed as clear-cut and original a plot as a longish book would do. One cannot without effort spin plots at such a rate. They are apt to become thin and break" (*Memories and Adventures*, pp. 91–92). The editor of the Oxford editions of all the stories, Owen Dudley Edwards, states that he hardly ever questioned changes editors suggested to him (*A Study in Scarlet*, p. viii), but that is disputed by Cameron Hollyer's study of the letters between Conan Doyle and his publisher in "Author to Editor: Arthur Conan Doyle's Correspondence with H. Greenhough Smith." But on the other hand, when William Gillette, an American actor, first went on stage in New York with a play titled *Sherlock Holmes*, he asked Conan Doyle's permission to allow Holmes to be married. Conan Doyle replied, "You may marry or murder or do what you like with him" (Howlett, "The Impersonators: Sherlock Holmes on Stage and Screen," *Beyond Baker Street*, p. 188). Also he was careful in crafting the details of all his writing. The slapdash skid marks all over some of these stories are at great variance with the rest of his writing. All of these facts warrant at least the strong suspicion that many of these last stories were written by Conan Doyle but then changed, perhaps by someone much younger who may have thought the old-style Holmes stories weren't sophisticated enough.

This supposition, however, is complicated by a couple of things we know about Conan Doyle. First, despite his reputation for hating Sherlock Holmes, Conan Doyle knew he would be best remembered for his remarkable sleuth; we can't doubt that he was quietly proud of his creation. We wouldn't think, therefore, that he would consent to letting a patently inferior work bear his name unless he produced it himself. And some very inferior stories have been in the canon now for nearly seventy-five years. Second, Conan Doyle has claimed he wrote the stories; he was an honorable man when honor meant something. We have the stories in his handwriting. For someone else to have written them, or even materially changed them, would mean that Conan Doyle conspired with someone whose identity has yet to be discovered to defraud the world about his involvement in what, for better or for worse, would be his chief legacy. In the absence of any hard facts to the contrary, it's hard to believe that such a man would do this.

But it's also hard to believe that such a conscientious writer produced the stylistic turn-around some of these stories represent. Take, for example, the story most at odds with all the facts about Holmes and Watson that Conan Doyle had established over nearly forty years, "The Adventure of the Mazarin Stone." It was an adaptation of his earlier unproduced play about Holmes, *The Crown Diamond*. When polls of various Holmes Societies are taken about the relative merit of the stories, it regularly places last. The reasons aren't hard to fathom. First, it's one of only three stories in which neither Holmes nor Watson is the narrator. A third-person narrator works for many kinds of fiction, but not for these stories, which depend so much on their realism that many people thought Sherlock Holmes was alive, and societies now devoted to him self-consciously maintain that whimsical illusion. A narrator like the one in "The Mazarin Stone" accentuates the fictional quality of the story, most unwelcome to many Holmes admirers.

In addition, the story is a rehash of several plot elements that had previously appeared in the Saga. Watson reminds us that the decoy bust of Holmes, in case we've forgotten, appeared earlier in "The Empty House": "We used something of the sort once before," he says. There, it was used to fool Colonel Sebastian Moran, "the best heavy game shot that our Eastern Empire has ever produced," who carried a new weapon, the air-gun. In "The Mazarin Stone" the bust fools Sam Merton, about whom Holmes says, "Possibly you have heard of his reputation as a shooter of big game." Sam, as Holmes refers to him several times (another un-Holmesian trait), has just bought an air-gun. Then at the story's conclusion, Holmes slips the jewel into the pocket of Lord Cantlemere. This plot element of putting a stolen item under a client's very nose for him to find was used in "The Adventure of the Naval Treaty" and again in "The Adventure of the Second Stain."

This repetition of plot elements wouldn't be so suspicious in itself. After all, in many of the stories since *The Return*, Conan Doyle had recycled plots. "The Mazarin Stone," however, is also full of details inconsistent with all the other tales. Early in the story we hear of a waiting room and a second exit in the apartment at 221B Baker Street, things Conan Doyle had neglected to mention before. The choice of the name "Negretto Sylvius"—the Italian word for "black" and Latin for "woods"—happens to be the name of a rival magazine (*Blackwood's*) that once accepted a submission by Conan Doyle but then never published it. This was not the sort of witty wordplay that Conan Doyle engaged in. The way Holmes talks in this story doesn't sound at all like the dignified figure we've come to know over the previous fifty stories. He's become a kind of jokester right out of the music halls. And when Holmes sends Watson to contact someone at Scotland Yard, he tells him to see Youghal, as if we're supposed to know who he is, yet it's a name we've never heard before.

In addition to all this, the plot is perhaps the weakest of all the Holmes stories. It depends on a number of accidents, rather than ingenious deductions or a carefully laid trap into which the criminal inevitably falls. Why, for instance, would any crooks who had stolen a world-famous gem worth a hundred thousand pounds bring it with them to the apartment of Sherlock Holmes, whose address was surely well known among members of the underworld? How could any but the dimmest of bulbs have mistaken one of those early gramophones for a real violin in the next room? Or have failed to notice Holmes exchanging places with the wax bust of himself in the same room? Or attempt to exchange the jewel in Holmes's apartment, even if he were playing the violin in the next room? The whole thing is preposterous. We might say about this story what Samuel Johnson once said to a man who asked his opinion about a book the man had written: "Your manuscript is both good and original; but the part that is good is not original, and the part that is original is not good."

To give one more example, consider "The Adventure of the Three Gables." There Holmes taunts a servant, whom he calls by her first name ("Oh, Susan! Language!" and "Good-bye, Susan. Paregoric is the stuff"), two things a gentleman never does, and Holmes is every inch a gentleman. To make matters worse, he sarcastically refers to her as "the fair Susan." He also twice insults a black man, whom he also calls by his first name, by claiming he has a peculiar smell. Most repugnant of all, a character in this story refers to the black man as "the big nigger"; it's true that the term is spoken by a pompous and dim-witted policeman, but it seems inconceivable for the man who wrote the appeal for racial harmony in "The Yellow Face" and the indictment of the Ku Klux Klan in "The Five Orange Pips" to have penned this. In addition to obvious affronts like these, the prose style itself furnishes more subtle clues that an unseen hand may have been at work. After you've read hundreds and hundreds of pages of Conan Doyle's prose, you become so accustomed to its rhythms, its diction, its tone, that sudden departures from his style jump out at you. Almost nothing about either of "The Mazarin Stone" or "The Three Gables" has the true ring of Conan Doyle's style about them.

One could suggest that, after all, these stories were written at the end of Conan Doyle's life, by which time his creative powers had begun to flag. He was also in ill health during these years. This might be a reasonable explanation, were it not that some of these last stories still show remarkable power. "The Adventure of the Illustrious Client" and "The Problem of Thor Bridge," for example, are superior to some of the stories in the first two volumes of Holmes's exploits. Some of the other less successful stories also have passages of considerable power, making a judgment that parts were written by someone other than Conan Doyle extremely difficult to sustain.

Not everything in *The Case Book* is cartoon fiction, however. In "The Adventure of the Veiled Lodger," Holmes solves no crime, nor does he even clear up any sort of mystery. The lodger, a woman who had been horribly disfigured by a lion while trying to kill her husband, simply wants to confess her crime of years ago before taking her own life. Holmes, after listening to the confession, dissuades the lady from ending it all by telling her "your life is not your own." Days later she sends him the bottle of poison she was planning to swallow to show him he has saved her from despair. We see in this story that Conan Doyle chose to make Holmes fulfill functions other than just avenging crimes. Here he takes on the role of priest, hearing a last confession before giving a secular absolution. By the time of this story, Conan Doyle was nearly seventy. Like most people, he grew sadder as he grew older. In addition to the usual woes that afflict us all, he suffered a few not everyone experiences. He lost his first wife in 1906 after a long illness, his son and his brother to World War I, and he saw the devastation that war wrought on a whole generation of young English men. He may well have come to think that gallivanting around the countryside peering at footprints and carriage tracks was ultimately a trivial pursuit for his fictional creature. If he were to continue to write stories about Holmes, Conan Doyle wanted him to serve some higher purpose than just putting away the odd criminal or two. Unfortunately, paragons of virtue rarely make good reading. While Holmes is out saving souls, he is not performing the feats most readers have come to expect of him, and many are left cold by this change of mission.

The Case Book brings to an end the development of a forty-year relationship between two of the most oddly paired characters in fiction. Most of that time the personal relationship between Holmes and Watson was unstated. Victorian men weren't accustomed to express emotion, especially about their male friends. Before his resurrection, Holmes scarcely noticed Watson, save to chide him for placing the wrong emphasis on his accounts, or for bungling a reconnaissance on which Holmes has sent him, or for completely misdeducing some obvious string of inferences. We've seen a couple of scenes where that pattern was broken by a show of feeling by Holmes, but the ultimate epiphany of Holmes's emotion for Watson occurs in "The Adventure of the Three Garridebs," after Watson has been shot by Killer Evans. The passage bears repeating in full.

Then my friend's wiry arms were round me, and he was leading me to a chair.

"You're not hurt, Watson? For God's sake, say that you are not hurt!"

It was worth a wound—it was worth many wounds—to know the depth of loyalty and love which lay behind that cold mask. The clear, hard eyes were dimmed for a moment, and the firm lips were shaking. For the one and only time I caught a glimpse of a great heart as well as of a great brain. All my years of humble but single-minded service culminated in that moment of revelation (p. 580).

This is the closest Holmes ever comes to expressing love for another human being. It's all the more touching because he has been so aloof from ordinary human passions for most of his life. When we imagine him in his retirement, in proud isolation on Sussex Downs, tending his bees, creatures who are the very emblem of passionless, mechanical activity, do we not feel, mixed with our admiration, a hint of sorrow that his life has been largely untouched by love, that his remarkable personality never found its soul mate? Of course looking at the imagined life of a fictional character this way is clearly out of bounds for ordinary literary criticism. There's always been something special about Sherlock Holmes, however, that has inspired this sort of speculation into his unwritten life. Early on, admiring readers and critics adopted the convention that Holmes was a real person, who never died. Naturally this is tongue in cheek, as we know that Holmes never really lived, and if he had, he'd be 150 years old now, a bit long for even his iron constitution to hold out. But in another sense, those admirers are right: Sherlock Holmes is still alive, and always will be as long as human affairs have mysteries at their center, and readers feel the impulse to identify with heroes who are braver, bolder, and more clever than they are.

Kyle Freeman, a Sherlock Holmes enthusiast for many years, earned two graduate degrees in English literature from Columbia University, where his major was twentieth-century British literature. He has seen almost all the Holmes movies of the last sixty years, as well as the television series with Jeremy Brett. Now working as a computer consultant, he constantly puts into practice Sherlock Holmes's famous statement "Eliminate all other factors, and the one which remains, however improbable, must be the truth."

A NOTE ON CONVEYANCES

During the course of their adventures, Holmes and Watson travel in a number of different vehicles. During the period of the stories, London had more than 8,000 horse-drawn carriages of many types. These are the ones that appear most often:

Landau: This heavy, four-wheeled carriage accommodated four people, who sat on facing seats; the coachman drove four horses from a raised front seat. The top of the carriage was in two sections that could be folded down or removed, and the bottom was cut away at the ends so that the door was the lowest point on the body. The landau was popular in England starting in the eighteenth century.

Hansom: The driver sat above and behind the closed carriage of this light, two-wheeled vehicle and spoke through a trapdoor to passengers, who entered from the front through a folding door and perched on a seat for two positioned above the axle. The hansom was in wide use as a public cab.

Brougham: This light four-wheeled carriage was usually drawn by one horse. The low, closed body appeared cut away in front, though there were many variations in the basic design. Inside was a two-passenger seat; a third passenger could ride up front with the driver.

Trap: This two-wheeled carriage on springs was drawn by one horse.

Dog-cart: Called a dog-cart because its back seat could be converted into a compartment for carrying a dog, this two-wheeled horse cart had two seats placed back to back.

The generic term *cab* can refer to any of the above, but it mainly describes two-wheelers. A four-wheeled, two-horse vehicle is more likely to be called a *coach.* Generally, four-wheeled carriages offered a smoother ride, with more privacy, while a dog-cart or trap offered the greatest speed. When the game was afoot, though, the first vehicle that presented itself often had to do.

To travel to places outside London, Holmes and Watson take the train. Waterloo, Charing Cross, Paddington, Victoria, London Bridge, Woolwich, Aldersgate, Gloucester Road, Blackheath, High Street, King's Cross, Euston, and Metropolitan are all railway stations in London.

Sometimes speakers drop the word "station"; when a character says she arrived at Waterloo or Victoria, she means the railway station. The names of railway stations outside London are generally the name of the town where the train stops.

THE COMPLETE
SHERLOCK HOLMES,
VOLUME II

THE RETURN OF
SHERLOCK HOLMES

THE ADVENTURE OF THE
EMPTY HOUSE

It was in the spring of the year 1894 that all London was interested, and the fashionable world dismayed, by the murder of the Honourable Ronald Adair under most unusual and inexplicable circumstances. The public has already learned those particulars of the crime which came out in the police investigation, but a good deal was suppressed upon that occasion, since the case for the prosecution was so overwhelmingly strong that it was not necessary to bring forward all the facts. Only now, at the end of nearly ten years, am I allowed to supply those missing links which make up the whole of that remarkable chain. The crime was of interest in itself, but that interest was as nothing to me compared to the inconceivable sequel, which afforded me the greatest shock and surprise of any event in my adventurous life. Even now, after this long interval, I find myself thrilling as I think of it, and feeling once more that sudden flood of joy, amazement, and incredulity which utterly submerged my mind. Let me say to that public, which has shown some interest in those glimpses which I have occasionally given them of the thoughts and actions of a very remarkable man, that they are not to blame me if I have not shared my knowledge with them, for I should have considered it my first duty to do so, had I not been barred by a positive prohibition from his own lips, which was only withdrawn upon the third of last month.

It can be imagined that my close intimacy with Sherlock Holmes had interested me deeply in crime, and that after his disappearance I never failed to read with care the various problems which came before the public. And I even attempted, more than once, for my own private satisfaction, to employ his methods in their solution, though with indifferent success. There was none, however, which appealed to me like this tragedy of Ronald Adair. As I read the evidence at the inquest, which led up to a verdict of wilful murder against some person or persons unknown, I realized more clearly than I had ever done the loss which the community had sustained by the death of Sherlock Holmes. There were points about this strange business which would, I was sure, have specially appealed to him, and the efforts of the police would have been supplemented, or more probably anticipated, by the trained observation and the alert mind of the first criminal agent in Europe. All day, as I drove upon my round, I turned over the case in my mind and found no explanation which appeared to me to be adequate. At the risk of telling a twice-told tale, I will recapitulate the facts as they were known to the public at the conclusion of the inquest.

The Honourable Ronald Adair was the second son of the Earl of Maynooth, at that time governor of one of the Australian colonies. Adair's mother had returned from Australia to undergo the operation for cataract, and she, her son Ronald, and her daughter Hilda were living together at 427 Park Lane. The youth moved in the best society—had, so far as was known, no enemies and no particular vices. He had been engaged to Miss Edith Woodley, of Carstairs, but the engagement had been broken off by mutual consent some months before, and there was no sign that it had left any very profound feeling behind it. For the rest of the man's life moved in a narrow and conventional circle, for his habits were quiet and his nature unemotional. Yet it was upon this easy-going young aristocrat that death came, in most strange and unexpected form, between the hours of ten and eleven-twenty on the night of March 30, 1894.

Ronald Adair was fond of cards—playing continually, but never for such stakes as would hurt him. He was a member of the Baldwin, the Cavendish, and the Bagatelle card clubs. It was shown that, after dinner on the day of his death, he had played a rubber of whist at the latter club. He had also played there in the afternoon. The evidence of those who had played with him—Mr. Murray, Sir John Hardy, and Colonel Moran—showed that the game was whist, and that there was a fairly equal fall of the cards. Adair might have lost five pounds, but not more. His fortune was a considerable one, and such a loss could not in any way affect him. He had played nearly every day at one club or other, but he was a cautious player, and usually rose a winner. It came out in evidence that, in partnership with Colonel Moran, he had actually won as much as four hundred and twenty pounds in a sitting, some weeks before, from Godfrey Milner and Lord Balmoral. So much for his recent history as it came out at the inquest.

On the evening of the crime, he returned from the club exactly at ten. His mother and sister were out spending the evening with a relation. The servant deposed that she heard him enter the front room on the second floor, generally used as his sitting-room. She had lit a fire there, and as it smoked she had opened the window. No sound was heard from the room until eleven-twenty, the hour of the return of Lady Maynooth and her daughter. Desiring to say good-night, she attempted to enter her son's room. The door was locked on the inside, and no answer could be got to their cries and knocking. Help was obtained, and the door forced. The unfortunate young man was found lying near the table. His head had been horribly mutilated by an expanding revolver bullet, but no weapon of any sort was to be found in the room. On the table lay two banknotes for ten pounds each and seventeen pounds ten in silver and gold, the money arranged in little piles of varying amount. There were some figures also upon a sheet of paper, with the names of some club friends opposite to them, from which it was conjectured that before his death he was endeavouring to make out his losses or winnings at cards.

A minute examination of the circumstances served only to make the case more complex. In the first place, no reason could be given why the young man should have fastened the door upon the inside. There was the possibility that the murderer had done this, and had afterwards escaped by the window. The drop was at least twenty feet, however, and a bed of crocuses in full bloom lay beneath. Neither the flowers nor the earth showed any sign of having been disturbed, nor were there any marks upon the narrow strip of grass which separated the house from the road. Apparently, therefore, it was the young man himself who had fastened the door. But how did he come by his death? No one could have climbed up to the window without leaving traces. Suppose a man had fired through the window, he would indeed be a remarkable shot who could with a revolver inflict so deadly a wound. Again, Park Lane is a frequented thoroughfare; there is a cab stand within a hundred yards of the house. No one had heard a shot. And yet there was the dead man, and there the revolver bullet, which had mushroomed out, as soft-nosed bullets will, and so inflicted a wound which must have caused instantaneous death. Such were the circumstances of the Park Lane Mystery, which were further complicated by entire absence of motive, since, as I have said, young Adair was not known to have any enemy, and no attempt had been made to remove the money or valuables in the room.

All day I turned these facts over in my mind, endeavouring to hit some theory which could reconcile them all, and to find that line of least resistance which my poor friend had declared to be the starting-point of every investigation. I confess that I made little progress. In the evening I strolled across the Park, and found myself about six o'clock at the Oxford Street end of Park Lane. A group of loafers upon the pavements, all staring up at a particular window, directed me to the house which I had come to see. A tall, thin man with coloured glasses, whom I strongly suspected of being a plain-clothes detective, was pointing out some theory of his own, while the others crowded round to listen to what he said. I got as near him as I could, but his observations seemed to me to be absurd, so I withdrew again in some disgust. As I did so I struck against an elderly, deformed man, who had been behind me, and I knocked down several books which he was carrying. I remember that as I picked them up, I observed the title of one of them, *The Origin of Tree Worship*, and it struck me that the fellow must be some poor bibliophile, who, either as a trade or as a hobby, was a collector of obscure volumes. I endeavoured to apologize for the accident, but it was evident that these books which I had so unfortunately maltreated were very precious objects in the eyes of their owner. With a snarl of contempt he turned upon his heel, and I saw his curved back and white side-whiskers disappear among the throng.

My observations of No. 427 Park Lane did little to clear up the problem in which I was interested. The house was separated from the street by a low wall and railing, the whole not more than five feet high. It was perfectly easy, therefore, for anyone to get into the garden, but the window was entirely inaccessible, since there was no waterpipe or anything which could help the most active man to climb it. More puzzled than ever, I retraced my steps to Kensington. I had not been in my study five minutes when the maid entered to say that a person desired to see me. To my astonishment it was none other than my strange old book collector, his sharp, wizened face peering out from a frame of white hair, and his precious volumes, a dozen of them at least, wedged under his right arm.

"You're surprised to see me, sir," said he, in a strange, croaking voice. I acknowledged that I was.

"Well, I've a conscience, sir, and when I chanced to see you go into this house, as I came hobbling after you, I thought to myself, I'll just step in and see that kind gentleman, and tell him that if I was a bit gruff in my manner there was not any harm meant, and that I am much obliged to him for picking up my books."

"You make too much of a trifle," said I. "May I ask how you knew who I was?"

"Well, sir, if it isn't too great a liberty, I am a neighbour of yours, for you'll find my little bookshop at the corner of Church Street, and very happy to see you, I am sure. Maybe you collect yourself, sir. Here's *British Birds*, and *Catullus*, and *The Holy War*—a bargain, every one of them. With five volumes you could just fill that gap on that second shelf. It looks untidy, does it not, sir?"

I moved my head to look at the cabinet behind me. When I turned again, Sherlock Holmes was standing smiling at me across my study table. I rose to my feet, stared at him for some seconds in utter amazement, and then it appears that I must have fainted for the first and the last time in my life. Certainly a gray mist swirled before my eyes, and when it cleared I found my collar-ends undone and the tingling after-taste of brandy upon my lips. Holmes was bending over my chair, his flask in his hand.

"My dear Watson," said the well-remembered voice, "I owe you a thousand apologies. I had no idea that you would be so affected."

I gripped him by the arms.

"Holmes!" I cried. "Is it really you? Can it indeed be that you are alive? Is it possible that you succeeded in climbing out of that awful abyss?"

"Wait a moment," said he. "Are you sure that you are really fit to discuss things? I have given you a serious shock by my unnecessarily dramatic reappearance."

"I am all right, but indeed, Holmes, I can hardly believe my eyes. Good heavens! to think that you—you of all men—should be standing in my study." Again I gripped him by the sleeve, and felt the thin, sinewy arm beneath it. "Well, you're not a spirit, anyhow," said I. "My dear chap, I'm overjoyed to see you. Sit down, and tell me how you came alive out of that dreadful chasm."

He sat opposite to me, and lit a cigarette in his old, nonchalant manner. He was dressed in the seedy frockcoat of the book merchant, but the rest of that individual lay in a pile of white hair and old books upon the table. Holmes looked even thinner and keener than of old, but there was a dead-white tinge in his aquiline face which told me that his life recently had not been a healthy one.

"I am glad to stretch myself, Watson," said he. "It is no joke when a tall man has to take a foot off his stature for several hours on end. Now, my dear fellow, in the matter of these explanations, we have, if I may ask for your cooperation, a hard and dangerous night's work in front of us.

Perhaps it would be better if I gave you an account of the whole situation when that work is finished."

"I am full of curiosity. I should much prefer to hear now."

"You'll come with me to-night?"

"When you like and where you like."

"This is, indeed, like the old days. We shall have time for a mouthful of dinner before we need go. Well, then, about that chasm. I had no serious difficulty in getting out of it, for the very simple reason that I never was in it."

"You never were in it?"

"No, Watson, I never was in it. My note to you was absolutely genuine. I had little doubt that I had come to the end of my career when I perceived the somewhat sinister figure of the late Professor Moriarty standing upon the narrow pathway which led to safety. I read an inexorable purpose in his gray eyes. I exchanged some remarks with him, therefore, and obtained his courteous permission to write the short note which you afterwards received. I left it with my cigarette-box and my stick, and I walked along the pathway, Moriarty still at my heels. When I reached the end I stood at bay. He drew no weapon, but he rushed at me and threw his long arms around me. He knew that his own game was up, and was only anxious to revenge himself upon me. We tottered together upon the brink of the fall. I have some knowledge, however, of baritsu, or the Japanese system of wrestling, which has more than once been very useful to me. I slipped through his grip, and he with a horrible scream kicked madly for a few seconds, and clawed the air with both his hands. But for all his efforts he could not get his balance, and over he went. With my face over the brink, I saw him fall for a long way. Then he struck a rock, bounded off, and splashed into the water."

I listened with amazement to this explanation, which Holmes delivered between the puffs of his cigarette.

"But the tracks!" I cried. "I saw, with my own eyes, that two went down the path and none returned."

"It came about in this way. The instant that the Professor had disappeared, it struck me what a really extraordinarily lucky chance Fate had placed in my way. I knew that Moriarty was not the only man who had sworn my death. There were at least three others whose desire for vengeance upon me would only be increased by the death of their leader. They were all most dangerous men. One or other would certainly get me. On the other hand, if all the world was convinced that I was dead they would take liberties, these men, they would soon lay themselves open, and sooner or later I could destroy them. Then it would be time for me to announce that I was still in the land of the living. So rapidly does the brain act that I believe I had thought this all out before Professor Moriarty had reached the bottom of the Reichenbach Fall.

"I stood up and examined the rocky wall behind me. In your picturesque account of the matter, which I read with great interest some months later, you assert that the wall was sheer. That was not literally true. A few small footholds presented themselves, and there was some indication of a ledge. The cliff is so high that to climb it all was an obvious impossibility, and it was equally impossible to make my way along the wet path without leaving some tracks. I might, it is true, have reversed my boots, as I have done on similar occasions, but the sight of three sets of tracks in one direction would certainly have suggested a deception. On the whole, then, it was best that I should risk the climb. It was not a pleasant business, Watson. The fall roared beneath me. I am not a fanciful person, but I give you my word that I seemed to hear Moriarty's voice screaming at me out of the abyss. A mistake would have been fatal. More than once, as tufts of grass came out in my hand or my foot slipped in the wet notches of the rock, I thought that I was gone. But I struggled upward, and at last I reached a ledge several feet deep and covered with soft green moss, where I could lie unseen, in the most perfect comfort. There I was stretched, when you, my dear Watson, and all your following were investigating in the most sympathetic and inefficient manner the circumstances of my death.

"At last, when you had all formed your inevitable and totally erroneous conclusions, you departed for the hotel, and I was left alone. I had imagined that I had reached the end of my adventures, but a very unexpected occurrence showed me that there were surprises still in store for me. A huge rock, falling from above, boomed past me, struck the path, and bounded over into the chasm. For an instant I thought that it was an accident, but a moment later, looking up, I saw a man's head against the darkening sky, and another stone struck the very ledge upon which I was stretched, within a foot of my head. Of course, the meaning of this was obvious. Moriarty had not been alone. A confederate—and even that one glance had told me how dangerous a man that confederate was—had kept guard while the Professor had attacked me. From a distance, unseen by me, he had been a witness of his friend's death and of my escape. He had waited, and then making his way round to the top of the cliff, he had endeavoured to succeed where his comrade had failed.

"I did not take long to think about it, Watson. Again I saw that grim face look over the cliff, and I knew that it was the precursor of another stone. I scrambled down on to the path. I don't think I could have done it in cold blood. It was a hundred times more difficult than getting up. But I had no time to think of the danger, for another stone sang past me as I hung by my hands from the edge of the ledge. Halfway down I slipped, but, by the blessing of God, I landed, torn and bleeding, upon the path. I took to my heels, did ten miles over the mountains in the darkness, and a week later I found myself in Florence, with the certainty that no one in the world knew what had become of me.

"I had only one confidant—my brother Mycroft. I owe you many apologies, my dear Watson, but it was all-important that it should be thought I was dead, and it is quite certain that you would not have written so convincing an account of my unhappy end had you not yourself thought that it was true. Several times during the last three years I have taken up my pen to write to you, but always I feared lest your affectionate regard for me should tempt you to some indiscretion which would betray my secret. For that reason I turned away from you this evening when you upset my books, for I was in danger at the time, and any show of surprise and emotion upon your part might have drawn attention to my identity and led to the most deplorable and irreparable results. As to Mycroft, I had to confide in him in order to obtain the money which I needed. The course of events in London did not run so well as I had hoped, for the trial of the Moriarty gang left two of its most dangerous members, my own most vindictive enemies, at liberty. I travelled for two years in Tibet, therefore, and amused myself by visiting Lhassa, and spending some days with the head lama. You may have read of the remarkable explorations of a Norwegian named Sigerson, but I am sure that it never occurred to you that you were receiving news of your friend. I then passed through Persia, looked in at Mecca, and paid a short but interesting visit to the Khalifa at Khartoum, the results of which I have communicated to the Foreign Office. Returning to France, I spent some months in a research into the coal-tar derivatives, which I conducted in a laboratory at Montpellier, in the south of France. Having concluded this to my satisfaction and learning that only one of my enemies was now left in London, I was about to return when my movements were hastened by the news of this very remarkable Park Lane Mystery, which not only appealed to me by its own merits, but which seemed to offer some most peculiar personal opportunities. I came over at once to London, called in my own person at Baker Street, threw Mrs. Hudson into violent hysterics, and found that Mycroft had preserved my rooms and my papers exactly as they had always been. So it was, my dear Watson, that at two o'clock to-day I found myself in my old armchair in my own old room, and only wishing that I could have seen my old friend Watson in the other chair which he has so often adorned."

Such was the remarkable narrative to which I listened on that April evening—a narrative which would have been utterly incredible to me had it not been confirmed by the actual sight of the tall, spare figure and the keen, eager face, which I had never thought to see again. In some manner he had learned of my own sad bereavement,* and his sympathy was shown in his manner rather than in his words. "Work is the best antidote to sorrow, my dear Watson," said he; "and I have a piece of work for us both to-night which, if we can bring it to a successful conclusion, will in itself justify a man's life on this planet." In vain I begged him to tell me more. "You will hear and see enough before morning," he answered. "We have three years of the past to discuss. Let that suffice until half-past nine, when we start upon the notable adventure of the empty house."

It was indeed like old times when, at that hour, I found myself seated beside him in a hansom, my revolver in my pocket, and the thrill of ad-

---

*The death of Mary Marston Watson, his wife.

venture in my heart. Holmes was cold and stern and silent. As the gleam of the street-lamps flashed upon his austere features, I saw that his brows were drawn down in thought and his thin lips compressed. I knew not what wild beast we were about to hunt down in the dark jungle of criminal London, but I was well assured, from the bearing of this master huntsman, that the adventure was a most grave one—while the sardonic smile which occasionally broke through his ascetic gloom boded little good for the object of our quest.

I had imagined that we were bound for Baker Street, but Holmes stopped the cab at the corner of Cavendish Square. I observed that as he stepped out he gave a most searching glance to right and left, and at every subsequent street corner he took the utmost pains to assure that he was not followed. Our route was certainly a singular one. Holmes's knowledge of the byways of London was extraordinary, and on this occasion he passed rapidly and with an assured step through a network of mews and stables, the very existence of which I had never known. We emerged at last into a small road, lined with old, gloomy houses, which led us into Manchester Street, and so to Blandford Street. Here he turned swiftly down a narrow passage, passed through a wooden gate into a deserted yard, and then opened with a key the back door of a house. We entered together, and he closed it behind us.

The place was pitch dark, but it was evident to me that it was an empty house. Our feet creaked and crackled over the bare planking, and my outstretched hand touched a wall from which the paper was hanging in ribbons. Holmes's cold, thin fingers closed round my wrist and led me forward down a long hall, until I dimly saw the murky fanlight over the door. Here Holmes turned suddenly to the right, and we found ourselves in a large, square, empty room, heavily shadowed in the corners, but faintly lit in the centre from the lights of the street beyond. There was no lamp near, and the window was thick with dust, so that we could only just discern each other's figures within. My companion put his hand upon my shoulder and his lips close to my ear.

"Do you know where we are?" he whispered.

"Surely that is Baker Street," I answered, staring through the dim window.

"Exactly. We are in Camden House, which stands opposite to our own old quarters."

"But why are we here?"

"Because it commands so excellent a view of that picturesque pile. Might I trouble you, my dear Watson, to draw a little nearer to the window, taking every precaution not to show yourself, and then to look up at our old rooms—the starting-point of so many of your little fairy-tales? We will see if my three years of absence have entirely taken away my power to surprise you."

I crept forward and looked across at the familiar window. As my eyes fell upon it, I gave a gasp and a cry of amazement. The blind was down, and a strong light was burning in the room. The shadow of a man who was seated in a chair within was thrown in hard, black outline upon the luminous screen of the window. There was no mistaking the poise of the head, the squareness of the shoulders, the sharpness of the features. The face was turned half-round, and the effect was that of one of those black silhouettes which our grandparents loved to frame. It was a perfect reproduction of Holmes. So amazed was I that I threw out my hand to make sure that the man himself was standing beside me. He was quivering with silent laughter.

"Well?" said he.

"Good heavens!" I cried. "It is marvellous."

"I trust that age doth not wither nor custom stale my infinite variety,"* said he, and I recognized in his voice the joy and pride which the artist takes in his own creation. "It really is rather like me, is it not?"

"I should be prepared to swear that it was you."

"The credit of the execution is due to Monsieur Oscar Meunier, of Grenoble, who spent some days in doing the moulding. It is a bust in wax. The rest I arranged myself during my visit to Baker Street this afternoon."

"But why?"

"Because, my dear Watson, I had the strongest possible reason for wishing certain people to think that I was there when I was really elsewhere."

"And you thought the rooms were watched?"

"I *knew* that they were watched."

"By whom?"

"By my old enemies, Watson. By the charming society whose leader lies in the Reichenbach Fall. You must remember that they knew, and only they knew, that I was still alive. Sooner or later they believed that I should come back to my rooms. They watched them continuously, and this morning they saw me arrive."

"How do you know?"

"Because I recognized their sentinel when I glanced out of my window. He is a harmless enough fellow, Parker by name, a garroter by trade, and a remarkable performer upon the jew's-harp. I cared nothing for him. But I cared a great deal for the much more formidable person who was behind him, the bosom friend of Moriarty, the man who dropped the rocks over the cliff, the most cunning and dangerous criminal in London. That is the man who is after me to-night, Watson, and that is the man who is quite unaware that we are after *him*."

My friend's plans were gradually revealing themselves. From this convenient retreat, the watchers were being watched and the trackers tracked. That angular shadow up yonder was the bait, and we were the hunters. In silence we stood together in the darkness and watched the

---

*Holmes refers to Shakespeare's *Antony and Cleopatra* (act 2, scene 2): "Age cannot wither her, nor custom stale / Her infinite variety."

hurrying figures who passed and repassed in front of us. Holmes was silent and motionless; but I could tell that he was keenly alert, and that his eyes were fixed intently upon the stream of passers-by. It was a bleak and boisterous night, and the wind whistled shrilly down the long street. Many people were moving to and fro, most of them muffled in their coats and cravats. Once or twice it seemed to me that I had seen the same figure before, and I especially noticed two men who appeared to be sheltering themselves from the wind in the doorway of a house some distance up the street. I tried to draw my companion's attention to them; but he gave a little ejaculation of impatience, and continued to stare into the street. More than once he fidgeted with his feet and tapped rapidly with his fingers upon the wall. It was evident to me that he was becoming uneasy, and that his plans were not working out altogether as he had hoped. At last, as midnight approached and the street gradually cleared, he paced up and down the room in uncontrollable agitation. I was about to make some remark to him, when I raised my eyes to the lighted window, and again experienced almost as great a surprise as before. I clutched Holmes's arm, and pointed upward.

"The shadow has moved!" I cried.

It was indeed no longer the profile, but the back, which was turned towards us.

Three years had certainly not smoothed the asperities of his temper or his impatience with a less active intelligence than his own.

"Of course it has moved," said he. "Am I such a farcical bungler, Watson, that I should erect an obvious dummy, and expect that some of the sharpest men in Europe would be deceived by it? We have been in this room two hours, and Mrs. Hudson has made some change in that figure eight times, or once in every quarter of an hour. She works it from the front, so that her shadow may never be seen. Ah!" He drew in his breath with a shrill, excited intake. In the dim light I saw his head thrown forward, his whole attitude rigid with attention. Outside the street was absolutely deserted. Those two men might still be crouching in the doorway, but I could no longer see them. All was still and dark, save only that brilliant yellow screen in front of us with the black figure outlined upon its centre. Again in the utter silence I heard that thin, sibilant note which spoke of intense suppressed excitement. An instant later he pulled me back into the blackest corner of the room, and I felt his warning hand upon my lips. The fingers which clutched me were quivering. Never had I known my friend more moved, and yet the dark street still stretched lonely and motionless before us.

But suddenly I was aware of that which his keener senses had already distinguished. A low, stealthy sound came to my ears, not from the direction of Baker Street, but from the back of the very house in which we lay concealed. A door opened and shut. An instant later steps crept down the passage—steps which were meant to be silent, but which reverberated harshly through the empty house. Holmes crouched back against the wall, and I did the same, my hand closing upon the handle of my revolver.

Peering through the gloom, I saw the vague outline of a man, a shade blacker than the blackness of the open door. He stood for an instant, and then he crept forward, crouching, menacing, into the room. He was within three yards of us, this sinister figure, and I had braced myself to meet his spring, before I realized that he had no idea of our presence. He passed close beside us, stole over to the window, and very softly and noiselessly raised it for half a foot. As he sank to the level of this opening, the light of the street, no longer dimmed by the dusty glass, fell full upon his face. The man seemed to be beside himself with excitement. His two eyes shone like stars, and his features were working convulsively. He was an elderly man, with a thin, projecting nose, a high, bald forehead, and a huge grizzled moustache. An opera hat was pushed to the back of his head, and an evening dress shirt-front gleamed out through his open overcoat. His face was gaunt and swarthy, scored with deep, savage lines. In his hand he carried what appeared to be a stick, but as he laid it down upon the floor it gave a metallic clang. Then from the pocket of his overcoat he drew a bulky object, and he busied himself in some task which ended with a loud, sharp click, as if a spring or bolt had fallen into its place. Still kneeling upon the floor he bent forward and threw all his weight and strength upon some lever, with the result that there came a long, whirling, grinding noise, ending once more in a powerful click. He straightened himself then, and I saw that what he held in his hand was a sort of gun, with a curiously misshapen butt. He opened it at the breech, put something in, and snapped the breech-lock. Then, crouching down, he rested the end of the barrel upon the ledge of the open window, and I saw his long moustache droop over the stock and his eye gleam as it peered along the sights. I heard a little sigh of satisfaction as he cuddled the butt into his shoulder, and saw that amazing target, the black man on the yellow ground, standing clear at the end of his foresight. For an instant he was rigid and motionless. Then his finger tightened on the trigger. There was a strange, loud whiz and a long, silvery tinkle of broken glass. At that instant Holmes sprang like a tiger on to the marksman's back, and hurled him flat upon his face. He was up again in a moment, and with convulsive strength he seized Holmes by the throat, but I struck him on the head with the butt of my revolver, and he dropped again upon the floor. I fell upon him, and as I held him my comrade blew a shrill call upon a whistle. There was the clatter of running feet upon the pavement, and two policemen in uniform, with one plain-clothes detective, rushed through the front entrance and into the room.

"That you, Lestrade?" said Holmes.

"Yes, Mr. Holmes. I took the job myself. It's good to see you back in London, sir."

"I think you want a little unofficial help. Three undetected murders in one year won't do, Lestrade. But you handled the Molesey Mystery with less than your usual—that's to say, you handled it fairly well."

We had all risen to our feet, our prisoner breathing hard, with a stalwart constable on each side of him. Already a few loiterers had begun to collect in the street. Holmes stepped up to the window, closed it, and dropped the blinds. Lestrade had produced two candles, and the policemen had uncovered their lanterns. I was able at last to have a good look at our prisoner.

It was a tremendously virile and yet sinister face which was turned towards us: With the brow of a philosopher above and the jaw of a sensualist below, the man must have started with great capacities for good or for evil. But one could not look upon his cruel blue eyes, with their drooping, cynical lids, or upon the fierce, aggressive nose and the threatening, deep-lined brow, without reading Nature's plainest danger-signals. He took no heed of any of us, but his eyes were fixed upon Holmes's face with an expression in which hatred and amazement were equally blended. "You fiend!" he kept on muttering. "You clever, clever fiend!"

"Ah, Colonel!" said Holmes, arranging his rumpled collar. " 'Journeys end in lovers' meetings,' as the old play says.* I don't think I have had the pleasure of seeing you since you favoured me with those attentions as I lay on the ledge above the Reichenbach Fall."

The colonel still stared at my friend like a man in a trance. "You cunning, cunning fiend!" was all that he could say.

"I have not introduced you yet," said Holmes. "This, gentlemen, is Colonel Sebastian Moran, once of Her Majesty's Indian Army, and the best heavy-game shot that our Eastern Empire has ever produced. I believe I am correct, Colonel, in saying that your bag of tigers still remains unrivalled?"

The fierce old man said nothing, but still glared at my companion. With his savage eyes and bristling moustache he was wonderfully like a tiger himself.

"I wonder that my very simple stratagem could deceive so old a *shikari*,"† said Holmes. "It must be very familiar to you. Have you not tethered a young kid under a tree, lain above it with your rifle, and waited for the bait to bring up your tiger? This empty house is my tree, and you are my tiger. You have possibly had other guns in reserve in case there should be several tigers, or in the unlikely supposition of your own aim failing you. These," he pointed around, "are my other guns. The parallel is exact."

Colonel Moran sprang forward with a snarl of rage, but the constables dragged him back. The fury upon his face was terrible to look at.

"I confess that you had one small surprise for me," said Holmes. "I did not anticipate that you would yourself make use of this empty house and this convenient front window. I had imagined you as operating from the street, where my friend Lestrade and his merry men were awaiting you. With that exception, all has gone as I expected."

---

*Misquote from Shakespeare's *Twelfth Night* (act 2, scene 3): "Journeys end in lovers meeting."

†Hindu term for a hunter.

Colonel Moran turned to the official detective.

"You may or may not have just cause for arresting me," said he, "but at least there can be no reason why I should submit to the gibes of this person. If I am in the hands of the law, let things be done in a legal way."

"Well, that's reasonable enough," said Lestrade. "Nothing further you have to say, Mr. Holmes, before we go?"

Holmes had picked up the powerful air-gun from the floor, and was examining its mechanism.

"An admirable and unique weapon," said he, "noiseless and of tremendous power: I knew Von Herder, the blind German mechanic, who constructed it to the order of the late Professor Moriarty. For years I have been aware of its existence, though I have never before had the opportunity of handling it. I commend it very specially to your attention, Lestrade, and also the bullets which fit it."

"You can trust us to look after that, Mr. Holmes," said Lestrade, as the whole party moved towards the door. "Anything further to say?"

"Only to ask what charge you intend to prefer?"

"What charge, sir? Why, of course, the attempted murder of Mr. Sherlock Holmes."

"Not so, Lestrade. I do not propose to appear in the matter at all. To you, and to you only, belongs the credit of the remarkable arrest which you have effected. Yes, Lestrade, I congratulate you! With your usual happy mixture of cunning and audacity, you have got him."

"Got him! Got whom, Mr. Holmes?"

"The man that the whole force has been seeking in vain—Colonel Sebastian Moran, who shot the Honourable Ronald Adair with an expanding bullet from an air-gun through the open window of the second-floor front of No. 427 Park Lane, upon the thirtieth of last month. That's the charge, Lestrade. And now, Watson, if you can endure the draught from a broken window, I think that half an hour in my study over a cigar may afford you some profitable amusement."

Our old chambers had been left unchanged through the supervision of Mycroft Holmes and the immediate care of Mrs. Hudson. As I entered I saw, it is true, an unwonted tidiness, but the old landmarks were all in their place. There were the chemical corner and the acid-stained, deal-topped table. There upon a shelf was the row of formidable scrap-books and books of reference which many of our fellow-citizens would have been so glad to burn. The diagrams, the violin-case, and the pipe-rack—even the Persian slipper which contained the tobacco—all met my eyes as I glanced round me. There were two occupants of the room—one, Mrs. Hudson, who beamed upon us both as we entered—the other, the strange dummy which had played so important a part in the evening's adventures. It was a wax-coloured model of my friend, so admirably done that it was a perfect facsimile. It stood on a small pedestal table with an old dressing-gown of Holmes's so draped round it that the illusion from the street was absolutely perfect.

"I hope you observed all precautions, Mrs. Hudson?" said Holmes.

"I went to it on my knees, sir, just as you told me."

"Excellent. You carried the thing out very well. Did you observe where the bullet went?"

"Yes, sir. I'm afraid it has spoilt your beautiful bust, for it passed right through the head and flattened itself on the wall. I picked it up from the carpet. Here it is!"

Holmes held it out to me. "A soft revolver bullet, as you perceive, Watson. There's genius in that, for who would expect to find such a thing fired from an air-gun? All right, Mrs. Hudson. I am much obliged for your assistance. And now, Watson, let me see you in your old seat once more, for there are several points which I should like to discuss with you."

He had thrown off the seedy frockcoat, and now he was the Holmes of old in the mouse-coloured dressing-gown which he took from his effigy.

"The old *shikari's* nerves have not lost their steadiness, nor his eyes their keenness," said he, with a laugh, as he inspected the shattered forehead of his bust.

"Plumb in the middle of the back of the head and smack through the brain. He was the best shot in India, and I expect that there are few better in London. Have you heard the name?"

"No, I have not."

"Well, well, such is fame! But, then, if I remember right, you had not heard the name of Professor James Moriarty, who had one of the great brains of the century. Just give me down my index of biographies from the shelf."

He turned over the pages lazily, leaning back in his chair and blowing great clouds from his cigar.

"My collection of M's is a fine one," said he. "Moriarty himself is enough to make any letter illustrious, and here is Morgan the poisoner, and Merridew of abominable memory, and Mathews; who knocked out my left canine in the waiting-room at Charing Cross, and, finally, here is our friend of to-night."

He handed over the book, and I read:

Moran, Sebastian, Colonel. Unemployed. Formerly 1st Bangalore Pioneers. Born London, 1840. Son of Sir Augustus Moran, C.B., once British Minister to Persia. Educated Eton and Oxford. Served in Jowaki Campaign, Afghan Campaign, Charasiab (despatches), Sherpur, and Cabul. Author of *Heavy Game of the Western Himalayas* (1881); *Three Months in the Jungle* (1884). Address: Conduit Street. Clubs: The Anglo-Indian, the Tankerville, the Bagatelle Card Club.

On the margin was written, in Holmes's precise hand:

The second most dangerous man in London.

"This is astonishing," said I, as I handed back the volume. "The man's career is that of an honourable soldier."

"It is true," Holmes answered. "Up to a certain point he did well. He was always a man of iron nerve, and the story is still told in India how he crawled down a drain after a wounded man-eating tiger. There are some trees, Watson, which grow to a certain height, and then suddenly develop some unsightly eccentricity. You will see it often in humans. I have a theory that the individual represents in his development the whole procession of his ancestors, and that such a sudden turn to good or evil stands for some strong influence which came into the line of his pedigree. The person becomes, as it were, the epitome of the history of his own family."

"It is surely rather fanciful."

"Well, I don't insist upon it. Whatever the cause, Colonel Moran began to go wrong. Without any open scandal, he still made India too hot to hold him. He retired, came to London, and again acquired an evil name. It was at this time that he was sought out by Professor Moriarty, to whom for a time he was chief of the staff. Moriarty supplied him liberally with money, and used him only in one or two very high-class jobs, which no ordinary criminal could have undertaken. You may have some recollection of the death of Mrs. Stewart, of Lauder, in 1887. Not? Well, I am sure Moran was at the bottom of it, but nothing could be proved. So cleverly was the colonel concealed that, even when the Moriarty gang was broken up, we could not incriminate him. You remember at that date, when I called upon you in your rooms, how I put up the shutters for fear of air-guns? No doubt you thought me fanciful. I knew exactly what I was doing, for I knew of the existence of this remarkable gun, and I knew also that one of the best shots in the world would be behind it. When we were in Switzerland he followed us with Moriarty, and it was undoubtedly he who gave me that evil five minutes on the Reichenbach ledge.

"You may think that I read the papers with some attention during my sojourn in France, on the look-out for any chance of laying him by the heels. So long as he was free in London, my life would really not have been worth living. Night and day the shadow would have been over me, and sooner or later his chance must have come. What could I do? I could not shoot him at sight, or I should myself be in the dock. There was no use appealing to a magistrate. They cannot interfere on the strength of what would appear to them to be a wild suspicion. So I could do nothing. But I watched the criminal news, knowing that sooner or later I should get him. Then came the death of this Ronald Adair. My chance had come at last. Knowing what I did, was it not certain that Colonel Moran had done it? He had played cards with the lad, he had followed him home from the club, he had shot him through the open window. There was not a doubt of it. The bullets alone are enough to put his head in a noose. I came over at once. I was seen by the sentinel, who would, I knew, direct the colonel's attention to my presence. He could not fail to connect my sudden return with his crime, and to be terribly alarmed. I was sure that he would make an attempt to get me out of the way *at once*, and would bring round his murderous weapon for that purpose. I left him an excellent mark in the window, and, having warned the police that they might be needed—by the way, Watson, you spotted their presence in that doorway with unerring accuracy—I took up what seemed to me to be a judicious post for observation, never dreaming that he would choose the same spot for his attack. Now, my dear Watson, does anything remain for me to explain?"

"Yes," said I. "You have not made it clear what was Colonel Moran's motive in murdering the Honourable Ronald Adair?"

"Ah! my dear Watson, there we come into those realms of conjecture, where the most logical mind may be at fault. Each may form his own hypothesis upon the present evidence, and yours is as likely to be correct as mine."

"You have formed one, then?"

"I think that it is not difficult to explain the facts. It came out in evidence that Colonel Moran and young Adair had, between them, won a considerable amount of money. Now, Moran undoubtedly played foul—of that I have long been aware. I believe that on the day of the murder Adair had discovered that Moran was cheating. Very likely he had spoken to him privately, and had threatened to expose him unless he voluntarily resigned his membership of the club, and promised not to play cards again. It is unlikely that a youngster like Adair would at once make a hideous scandal by exposing a well known man so much older than himself. Probably he acted as I suggest. The exclusion from his clubs would mean ruin to Moran, who lived by his ill-gotten card-gains. He therefore murdered Adair, who at the time was endeavouring to work out how much money he should himself return, since he could not profit by his partner's foul play. He locked the door lest the ladies should surprise him and insist upon knowing what he was doing with these names and coins. Will it pass?"

"I have no doubt that you have hit upon the truth."

"It will be verified or disproved at the trial. Meanwhile, come what may, Colonel Moran will trouble us no more. The famous air-gun of Von Herder will embellish the Scotland Yard Museum, and once again Mr. Sherlock Holmes is free to devote his life to examine those interesting little problems which the complex life of London so plentifully presents."

THE ADVENTURE OF THE
NORWOOD BUILDER

From the point of view of the criminal expert," said Mr. Sherlock Holmes, "London has become a singularly uninteresting city since the death of the late lamented Professor Moriarty."

"I can hardly think that you would find many decent citizens to agree with you," I answered.

"Well, well, I must not be selfish," said he, with a smile, as he pushed back his chair from the breakfast-table. "The community is certainly the gainer, and no one the loser, save the poor out-of-work specialist, whose occupation has gone. With that man in the field, one's morning paper presented infinite possibilities. Often it was only the smallest trace, Watson, the faintest indication, and yet it was enough to tell me that the great malignant brain was there, as the gentlest tremors of the edges of the web remind one of the foul spider which lurks in the centre. Petty thefts, wanton assaults, purposeless outrage—to the man who held the clue all could be worked into one connected whole. To the scientific student of the higher criminal world, no capital in Europe offered the advantages which London then possessed. But now—" He shrugged his shoulders in humorous deprecation of the state of things which he had himself done so much to produce.

At the time of which I speak, Holmes had been back for some months, and I at his request had sold my practice and returned to share the old quarters in Baker Street. A young doctor, named Verner, had purchased my small Kensington practice, and given with astonishingly little demur the highest price that I ventured to ask—an incident which only explained itself some years later, when I found that Verner was a distant relation of Holmes, and that it was my friend who had really found the money.

Our months of partnership had not been so uneventful as he had stated, for I find, on looking over my notes, that this period includes the case of the papers of ex-President Murillo, and also the shocking affair of the Dutch steamship *Friesland*, which so nearly cost us both our lives. His cold and proud nature was always averse, however, from anything in the shape of public applause, and he bound me in the most stringent terms to say no further word of himself, his methods, or his successes—a prohibition which, as I have explained, has only now been removed.

Mr. Sherlock Holmes was leaning back in his chair after his whimsical protest, and was unfolding his morning paper in a leisurely fashion, when our attention was arrested by a tremendous ring at the bell, followed immediately by a hollow drumming sound, as if someone were beating on the outer door with his fist. As it opened there came a tumultuous rush into the hall, rapid feet clattered up the stair, and an instant later a wild-eyed and frantic young man, pale, dishevelled, and palpitating, burst into the room. He looked from one to the other of us, and under our gaze of inquiry he became conscious that some apology was needed for this un-ceremonious entry.

"I'm sorry, Mr. Holmes," he cried. "You mustn't blame me. I am nearly mad. Mr. Holmes, I am the unhappy John Hector McFarlane."

He made the announcement as if the name alone would explain both his visit and its manner, but I could see, by my companion's unresponsive face, that it meant no more to him than to me.

"Have a cigarette, Mr. McFarlane," said he, pushing his case across. "I am sure that, with your symptoms, my friend Dr. Watson here would pre-scribe a sedative. The weather has been so very warm these last few days. Now, if you feel a little more composed, I should be glad if you would sit down in that chair, and tell us very slowly and quietly who you are, and what it is that you want. You mentioned your name, as if I should recog-nize it, but I assure you that, beyond the obvious facts that you are a bach-elor, a solicitor, a Freemason, and an asthmatic, I know nothing whatever about you."

Familiar as I was with my friend's methods, it was not difficult for me to follow his deductions, and to observe the untidiness of attire, the sheaf of legal papers, the watch-charm, and the breathing which had prompted them. Our client, however, stared in amazement.

"Yes, I am all that, Mr. Holmes; and, in addition, I am the most unfor-tunate man at this moment in London. For heaven's sake, don't abandon me, Mr. Holmes! If they come to arrest me before I have finished my story, make them give me time, so that I may tell you the whole truth. I could go to jail happy if I knew that you were working for me outside."

"Arrest you!" said Holmes. "This is really most grati—most interest-ing. On what charge do you expect to be arrested?"

"Upon the charge of murdering Mr. Jonas Oldacre, of Lower Nor-wood."

My companion's expressive face showed a sympathy which was not, I am afraid, entirely unmixed with satisfaction.

"Dear me," said he, "it was only this moment at breakfast that I was saying to my friend, Dr. Watson, that sensational cases had disappeared out of our papers."

Our visitor stretched forward a quivering hand and picked up the *Daily Telegraph*, which still lay upon Holmes's knee.

"If you had looked at it, sir, you would have seen at a glance what the errand is on which I have come to you this morning. I feel as if my name and my misfortune must be in every man's mouth." He turned it over to expose the central page. "Here it is, and with your permission I will read it to you. Listen to this, Mr. Holmes. The headlines are: 'Mysterious Af-fair at Lower Norwood. Disappearance of a Well Known Builder. Suspi-cion of Murder and Arson. A Clue to the Criminal.' That is the clue which they are already following, Mr. Holmes, and I know that it leads infallibly to me. I have been followed from London Bridge Station, and I am sure that they are only waiting for the warrant to arrest me. It will break my mother's heart—it will break her heart!" He wrung his hands in an agony of apprehension, and swayed backward and forward in his chair.

I looked with interest upon this man, who was accused of being the perpetrator of a crime of violence. He was flaxen-haired and handsome, in a washed-out negative fashion, with frightened blue eyes, and a clean-shaven face, with a weak, sensitive mouth. His age may have been about twenty-seven, his dress and bearing that of a gentleman. From the pocket of his light summer overcoat protruded the bundle of endorsed papers which proclaimed his profession.

"We must use what time we have," said Holmes. "Watson, would you have the kindness to take the paper and to read the paragraph in question?"

Underneath the vigorous headlines which our client had quoted, I read the following suggestive narrative:

"Late last night, or early this morning, an incident occurred at Lower Norwood which points, it is feared, to a serious crime. Mr. Jonas Oldacre is a well known resident of that suburb, where he has carried on his business as a builder for many years. Mr. Oldacre is a bachelor, fifty-two years of age, and lives in Deep Dene House, at the Sydenham end of the road of that name. He has had the reputation of being a man of eccentric habits, secretive and retiring. For some years he has practically withdrawn from the business, in which he is said to have massed considerable wealth. A small timber-yard still exists, however, at the back of the house, and last night, about twelve o'-clock, an alarm was given that one of the stacks was on fire. The engines were soon upon the spot, but the dry wood burned with great fury, and it was impossible to arrest the conflagration until the stack had been entirely consumed. Up to this point the incident bore the appearance of an ordinary accident, but fresh indications seem to point to serious crime. Surprise was expressed at the absence of the master of the establishment from the scene of the fire, and an inquiry followed, which showed that he had disappeared from the house. An examination of his room revealed that the bed had not been slept in, that a safe which stood in it was open, that a number of important papers were scattered about the room, and finally, that there were signs of a murderous struggle, slight traces of blood being found within the room, and an oaken walking-stick, which also showed stains of blood upon the handle. It is known that Mr. Jonas Oldacre had received a late visitor in his bedroom upon that night, and the stick found has been identified as the property of this person, who is a young London solicitor named John Hector McFarlane, junior partner of Graham and McFarlane, of 426 Gresham Buildings, E. C. The police believe that they have evidence in their possession which supplies a very convincing motive for the crime, and altogether it cannot be doubted that sensational developments will follow.

"LATER.—It is rumoured as we go to press that Mr. John Hector McFarlane has actually been arrested on the charge of the murder of Mr. Jonas Oldacre. It is at least certain that a warrant has been issued. There have been further and sinister developments in the investigation at Norwood. Besides the signs of a struggle in the room of the unfortunate builder it is now known that the French windows of his bedroom (which is on the ground floor) were found to be open, that there were marks as if some bulky object had been dragged across to the wood-pile, and, finally, it is asserted that charred remains have been found among the charcoal ashes of the fire. The police theory is that a most sensational crime has been committed, that the victim was clubbed to death in his own bedroom, his papers rifled, and his dead body dragged across to the wood-stack, which was then ignited so as to hide all traces of the crime. The conduct of the criminal investigation has been left in the experienced hands of Inspector Lestrade, of Scotland Yard, who is following up the clues with his accustomed energy and sagacity."

Sherlock Holmes listened with closed eyes and fingertips together to this remarkable account.

"The case has certainly some points of interest," said he, in his languid fashion. "May I ask, in the first place, Mr. McFarlane, how it is that you are still at liberty, since there appears to be enough evidence to justify your arrest?"

"I live at Torrington Lodge, Blackheath, with my parents, Mr. Holmes, but last night, having to do business very late with Mr. Jonas Oldacre, I stayed at an hotel in Norwood, and came to my business from there. I knew nothing of this affair until I was in the train, when I read what you have just heard. I at once saw the horrible danger of my position, and I hurried to put the case into your hands. I have no doubt that I should have been arrested either at my city office or at my home. A man followed me from London Bridge Station, and I have no doubt——Great heaven! what is that?"

It was a clang of the bell, followed instantly by heavy steps upon the stair. A moment later, our old friend Lestrade appeared in the doorway. Over his shoulder I caught a glimpse of one or two uniformed policemen outside.

"Mr. John Hector McFarlane?" said Lestrade.

Our unfortunate client rose with a ghastly face.

"I arrest you for the wilful murder of Mr. Jonas Oldacre, of Lower Norwood."

McFarlane turned to us with a gesture of despair, and sank into his chair once more like one who is crushed.

"One moment, Lestrade," said Holmes. "Half an hour more or less can make no difference to you, and the gentleman was about to give us an account of this very interesting affair, which might aid us in clearing it up."

"I think there will be no difficulty in clearing it up," said Lestrade, grimly.

"None the less, with your permission, I should be much interested to hear his account."

"Well, Mr. Holmes, it is difficult for me to refuse you anything, for you have been of use to the force once or twice in the past, and we owe you a good turn at Scotland Yard," said Lestrade. "At the same time I must remain with my prisoner, and I am bound to warn him that anything he may say will appear in evidence against him."

"I wish nothing better," said our client. "All I ask is that you should hear and recognize the absolute truth."

Lestrade looked at his watch. "I'll give you half an hour," said he.

"I must explain first," said McFarlane. "that I knew nothing of Mr. Jonas Oldacre. His name was familiar to me, for many years ago my parents were acquainted with him, but they drifted apart. I was very much surprised, therefore, when yesterday, about three o'clock in the afternoon, he walked into my office in the city. But I was still more astonished when he told me the object of his visit. He had in his hand several sheets of a notebook, covered with scribbled writing—here they are—and he laid them on my table.

" 'Here is my will,' said he. 'I want you, Mr. McFarlane, to cast it into proper legal shape. I will sit here while you do so.'

"I set myself to copy it, and you can imagine my astonishment when I found that, with some reservations, he had left all his property to me. He was a strange little ferret-like man, with white eyelashes, and when I looked up at him I found his keen gray eyes fixed upon me with an amused expression. I could hardly believe my own senses as I read the terms of the will; but he explained that he was a bachelor with hardly any living relation, that he had known my parents in his youth, and that he had always heard of me as a very deserving young man, and was assured that his money would be in worthy hands. Of course, I could only stammer out my thanks. The will was duly finished, signed, and witnessed by my clerk. This is it on the blue paper, and these slips, as I have explained, are the rough draft. Mr. Jonas Oldacre then informed me that there were a number of documents—building leases, title-deeds, mortgages, scrip, and so forth—which it was necessary that I should see and understand. He said that his mind would not be easy until the whole thing was settled, and he begged me to come out to his house at Norwood that night, bringing the will with me, and to arrange matters. 'Remember, my boy, not one word to your parents about the affair until everything is settled. We will keep it as a little surprise for them.' He was very insistent upon this point, and made me promise it faithfully.

"You can imagine, Mr. Holmes, that I was not in a humour to refuse him anything that he might ask. He was my benefactor, and all my desire was to carry out his wishes in every particular. I sent a telegram home, therefore, to say that I had important business on hand, and that it was impossible for me to say how late I might be. Mr. Oldacre had told me that he would like me to have supper with him at nine, as he might not be home before that hour. I had some difficulty in finding his house, however, and it was nearly half-past before I reached it. I found him——"

"One moment!" said Holmes. "Who opened the door?"

"A middle-aged woman, who was, I suppose, his housekeeper."

"And it was she, I presume, who mentioned your name?"

"Exactly," said McFarlane.

"Pray proceed."

McFarlane wiped his damp brow, and then continued his narrative:

"I was shown by this woman into a sitting-room, where a frugal supper was laid out. Afterwards, Mr. Jonas Oldacre led me into his bedroom, in which there stood a heavy safe. This he opened and took out a mass of documents, which we went over together. It was between eleven and twelve when we finished. He remarked that we must not disturb the housekeeper. He showed me out through his own French window, which had been open all this time."

"Was the blind down?" asked Holmes.

"I will not be sure, but I believe that it was only half down. Yes, I remember how he pulled it up in order to swing open the window. I could not find my stick, and he said, 'Never mind, my boy, I shall see a good deal of you now, I hope, and I will keep your stick until you come back to claim it.' I left him there, the safe open, and the papers made up in packets upon the table. It was so late that I could not get back to Blackheath, so I spent the night at the Anerley Arms, and I knew nothing more until I read of this horrible affair in the morning."

"Anything more that you would like to ask, Mr. Holmes?" said Lestrade, whose eyebrows had gone up once or twice during this remarkable explanation.

"Not until I have been to Blackheath."

"You mean to Norwood," said Lestrade.

"Oh, yes, no doubt that is what I must have meant," said Holmes, with his enigmatical smile. Lestrade had learned by more experiences than he would care to acknowledge that that razor-like brain could cut through that which was impenetrable to him. I saw him look curiously at my companion.

"I think I should like to have a word with you presently, Mr. Sherlock Holmes," said he. "Now, Mr. McFarlane, two of my constables are at the door, and there is a four-wheeler waiting." The wretched young man arose, and with a last beseeching glance at us walked from the room. The officers conducted him to the cab, but Lestrade remained.

Holmes had picked up the pages which formed the rough draft of the will, and was looking at them with the keenest interest upon his face.

"There are some points about that document, Lestrade, are there not?" said he, pushing them over.

The official looked at them with a puzzled expression.

"I can read the first few lines, and these in the middle of the second page, and one or two at the end. Those are as clear as print," said he, "but the writing in between is very bad, and there are three places where I cannot read it at all."

"What do you make of that?" said Holmes.

"Well, what do *you* make of it?"

"That it was written in a train. The good writing represents stations, the bad writing movement, and the very bad writing passing over points. A scientific expert would pronounce at once that this was drawn up on a suburban line, since nowhere save in the immediate vicinity of a great city could there be so quick a succession of points. Granting that his whole journey was occupied in drawing up the will, then the train was an express, only stopping once between Norwood and London Bridge."

Lestrade began to laugh.

"You are too much for me when you begin to get on your theories, Mr. Holmes," said he. "How does this bear on the case?"

"Well, it corroborates the young man's story to the extent that the will was drawn up by Jonas Oldacre in his journey yesterday. It is curious—is it not?—that a man should draw up so important a document in so haphazard a fashion. It suggests that he did not think it was going to be of much practical importance. If a man drew up a will which he did not intend ever to be effective, he might do it so."

"Well, he drew up his own death warrant at the same time," said Lestrade.

"Oh, you think so?"

"Don't you?"

"Well, it is quite possible, but the case is not clear to me yet."

"Not clear? Well, if that isn't clear, what *could* be clear? Here is a young man who learns suddenly that, if a certain older man dies, he will succeed to a fortune. What does he do? He says nothing to anyone, but he arranges that he shall go out on some pretext to see his client that night. He waits until the only other person in the house is in bed, and then in the solitude of a man's room he murders him, burns his body in the wood-pile, and departs to a neighbouring hotel. The blood-stains in the room and also on the stick are very slight. It is probable that he imagined his crime to be a bloodless one, and hoped that if the body were consumed it would hide all traces of the method of his death—traces which, for some reason, must have pointed to him. Is not all this obvious?"

"It strikes me, my good Lestrade, as being just a trifle too obvious," said Holmes. "You do not add imagination to your other great qualities, but if you could for one moment put yourself in the place of this young man, would you choose the very night after the will had been made to commit your crime? Would it not seem dangerous to you to make so very close a relation between the two incidents? Again, would you choose an occasion when you are known to be in the house, when a servant has let you in? And, finally, would you take the great pains to conceal the body, and yet leave your own stick as a sign that you were the criminal? Confess, Lestrade, that all this is very unlikely."

"As to the stick, Mr. Holmes, you know as well as I do that a criminal is often flurried, and does such things, which a cool man would avoid. He was very likely afraid to go back to the room. Give me another theory that would fit the facts."

"I could very easily give you half a dozen," said Holmes. "Here, for example, is a very possible and even probable one. I make you a free present of it. The older man is showing documents which are of evident value. A passing tramp sees them through the window, the blind of which is only half down. Exit the solicitor. Enter the tramp! He seizes a stick, which he observes there, kills Oldacre, and departs after burning the body."

"Why should the tramp burn the body?"

"For the matter of that, why should McFarlane?"

"To hide some evidence."

"Possibly the tramp wanted to hide that any murder at all had been committed."

"And why did the tramp take nothing?"

"Because they were papers that he could not negotiate."

Lestrade shook his head, though it seemed to me that his manner was less absolutely assured than before.

"Well, Mr. Sherlock Holmes, you may look for your tramp, and while you are finding him we will hold on to our man. The future will show which is right. Just notice this point, Mr. Holmes: that so far as we know, none of the papers were removed, and that the prisoner is the one man in the world who had no reason for removing them, since he was heir-at-law, and would come into them in any case."

My friend seemed struck by this remark.

"I don't mean to deny that the evidence is in some ways very strongly in favour of your theory," said he. "I only wish to point out that there are other theories possible. As you say, the future will decide. Good-morning! I dare say that in the course of the day I shall drop in at Norwood and see how you are getting on."

When the detective departed, my friend rose and made his preparations for the day's work with the alert air of a man who has a congenial task before him.

"My first movement, Watson," said he, as he bustled into his frock-coat, "must, as I said, be in the direction of Blackheath."

"And why not Norwood?"

"Because we have in this case one singular incident coming close to the heels of another singular incident. The police are making the mistake of concentrating their attention upon the second, because it happens to be the one which is actually criminal. But it is evident to me that the logical way to approach the case is to begin by trying to throw some light upon the first incident—the curious will, so suddenly made, and to so unexpected an heir. It may do something to simplify what followed. No, my dear fellow, I don't think you can help me. There is no prospect of danger, or I should not dream of stirring out without you. I trust that when I see you in the evening, I will be able to report that I have been able to do something for this unfortunate youngster, who has thrown himself upon my protection."

It was late when my friend returned, and I could see, by a glance at his haggard and anxious face, that the high hopes with which he had started had not been fulfilled. For an hour he droned away upon his violin, endeavouring to soothe his own ruffled spirits. At last he flung down the instrument, and plunged into a detailed account of his misadventures.

"It's all going wrong, Watson—all as wrong as it can go. I kept a bold face before Lestrade, but, upon my soul, I believe that for once the fellow is on the right track and we are on the wrong. All my instincts are one way, and all the facts are the other, and I much fear that British juries have not yet attained that pitch of intelligence when they will give the preference to my theories over Lestrade's facts."

"Did you go to Blackheath?"

"Yes, Watson, I went there, and I found very quickly that the late lamented Oldacre was a pretty considerable blackguard. The father was away in search of his son. The mother was at home—a little, fluffy, blue-eyed person, in a tremor of fear and indignation. Of course, she would not admit even the possibility of his guilt. But she would not express either surprise or regret over the fate of Oldacre. On the contrary, she spoke of him with such bitterness that she was unconsciously considerably strengthening the case of the police for, of course, if her son had heard her speak of the man in this fashion, it would predispose him towards hatred and violence. 'He was more like a malignant and cunning ape than a human being,' said she, 'and he always was, ever since he was a young man.'

"'You knew him at that time?' said I.

"'Yes, I knew him well, in fact, he was an old suitor of mine. Thank heaven that I had the sense to turn away from him and to marry a better, if poorer, man. I was engaged to him, Mr. Holmes, when I heard a shocking story of how he had turned a cat loose in an aviary, and I was so horrified at his brutal cruelty that I would have nothing more to do with him.' She rummaged in a bureau, and presently she produced a photograph of a woman, shamefully defaced and mutilated with a knife. 'That is my own photograph,' she said. 'He sent it to me in that state, with his curse, upon my wedding morning.'

"'Well,' said I, 'at least he has forgiven you now, since he has left all his property to your son.'

"'Neither my son nor I want anything from Jonas Oldacre, dead or alive!' she cried, with a proper spirit. 'There is a God in heaven, Mr. Holmes, and that same God who has punished that wicked man will show, in His own good time, that my son's hands are guiltless of his blood.'

"Well, I tried one or two leads, but could get at nothing which would help our hypothesis, and several points which would make against it. I gave it up at last, and off I went to Norwood.

"This place, Deep Dene House, is a big modern villa of staring brick, standing back in its own grounds, with a laurel-clumped lawn in front of it. To the right and some distance back from the road was the timber-yard which had been the scene of the fire. Here's a rough plan on a leaf of my notebook. This window on the left is the one which opens into Oldacre's room. You can look into it from the road, you see. That is about the only bit of consolation I have had to-day. Lestrade was not there, but his head constable did the honours. They had just found a great treasure-trove. They had spent the morning raking among the ashes of the burned wood-pile, and besides the charred organic remains they had secured several discoloured metal discs. I examined them with care, and there was no doubt that they were trouser buttons. I even distinguished that one of them was marked with the name of 'Hyams,' who was Oldacre's tailor. I then worked the lawn very carefully for signs and traces, but this drought has made everything as hard as iron. Nothing was to be seen save that some body or bundle had been dragged through a low privet hedge which is in a line with the wood-pile. All that, of course, fits in with the official theory. I crawled about the lawn with an August sun on my back, but I got up at the end of an hour no wiser than before.

"Well, after this fiasco I went into the bedroom and examined that also. The blood-stains were very slight, mere smears and discolourations, but undoubtedly fresh. The stick had been removed, but there also the marks were slight. There is no doubt about the stick belonging to our client. He admits it. Footmarks of both men could be made out on the carpet, but none of any third person, which again is a trick for the other side. They were piling up their score all the time and we were at a stand-still.

"Only one little gleam of hope did I get—and yet it amounted to nothing. I examined the contents of the safe, most of which had been taken out and left on the table. The papers had been made up into sealed envelopes, one or two of which had been opened by the police. They were not, so far as I could judge, of any great value, nor did the bank-book show that Mr. Oldacre was in such very affluent circumstances. But it seemed to me that all the papers were not there. There were allusions to some deeds—possibly the more valuable—which I could not find. This, of course, if we could definitely prove it, would turn Lestrade's argument against himself; for who would steal a thing if he knew that he would shortly inherit it?

"Finally, having drawn every other cover and picked up no scent, I tried my luck with the housekeeper. Mrs. Lexington is her name—a little, dark, silent person, with suspicious and sidelong eyes. She could tell us something if she would—I am convinced of it. But she was as close as wax.* Yes, she had let Mr. McFarlane in at half-past nine. She wished her hand had withered before she had done so. She had gone to bed at half-past ten. Her room was at the other end of the house, and she could hear nothing of what passed. Mr. McFarlane had left his hat, and to the best of

---

*As silent as if made out of wax.

her belief his stick, in the hall. She had been awakened by the alarm of fire. Her poor, dear master had certainly been murdered. Had he any enemies? Well, every man had enemies, but Mr. Oldacre kept himself very much to himself, and only met people in the way of business. She had seen the buttons, and was sure that they belonged to the clothes which he had worn last night. The wood-pile was very dry, for it had not rained for a month. It burned like tinder, and by the time she reached the spot, nothing could be seen but flames. She and all the firemen smelled the burned flesh from inside it. She knew nothing of the papers, nor of Mr. Oldacre's private affairs.

"So, my dear Watson, there's my report of a failure. And yet—and yet—" he clenched his thin hands in a paroxysm of conviction—"I *know* it's all wrong. I feel it in my bones. There is something that has not come out, and that housekeeper knows it. There was a sort of sulky defiance in her eyes, which only goes with guilty knowledge. However, there's no good talking any more about it, Watson; but unless some lucky chance comes our way I fear that the Norwood Disappearance Case will not figure in that chronicle of our successes which I foresee that a patient public will sooner or later have to endure."

"Surely," said I, "the man's appearance would go far with any jury?"

"That is a dangerous argument, my dear Watson. You remember that terrible murderer, Bert Stevens, who wanted us to get him off in '87? Was there ever a more mild-mannered, Sunday-school young man?"

"It is true."

"Unless we succeed in establishing an alternative theory, this man is lost. You can hardly find a flaw in the case which can now be presented against him, and all further investigation has served to strengthen it. By the way, there is one curious little point about those papers which may serve us as the starting-point for an inquiry. On looking over the bank-book I found that the low state of the balance was principally due to large checks which have been made out during the last year to Mr. Cornelius. I confess that I should be interested to know who this Mr. Cornelius may be with whom a retired builder has had such very large transactions. Is it possible that he has had a hand in the affair? Cornelius might be a broker, but we have found no scrip to correspond with these large payments. Failing any other indication, my researches must now take the direction of an inquiry at the bank for the gentleman who has cashed these checks. But I fear, my dear fellow, that our case will end ingloriously by Lestrade hanging our client, which will certainly be a triumph for Scotland Yard."

I do not know how far Sherlock Holmes took any sleep that night, but when I came down to breakfast I found him pale and harassed, his bright eyes the brighter for the dark shadows round them. The carpet round his chair was littered with cigarette-ends and with the early editions of the morning papers. An open telegram lay upon the table.

"What do you think of this, Watson?" he asked, tossing it across.

It was from Norwood, and ran as follows:

Important fresh evidence to hand. McFarlane's guilt definitely established. Advise you to abandon case.

LESTRADE.

"This sounds serious," said I.

"It is Lestrade's little cock-a-doodle of victory," Holmes answered; with a bitter smile. "And yet it may be premature to abandon the case. After all, important fresh evidence is a two-edged thing, and may possibly cut in a very different direction to that which Lestrade imagines. Take your breakfast, Watson, and we will go out together and see what we can do. I feel as if I shall need your company and your moral support to-day."

My friend had no breakfast himself, for it was one of his peculiarities that in his more intense moments he would permit himself no food, and I have known him presume upon his iron strength until he has fainted from pure inanition. "At present I cannot spare energy and nerve force for digestion," he would say in answer to my medical remonstrances. I was not surprised, therefore, when this morning he left his untouched meal behind him, and started with me for Norwood. A crowd of morbid sightseers were still gathered round Deep Dene House, which was just such a suburban villa as I had pictured. Within the gates Lestrade met us, his face flushed with victory, his manner grossly triumphant.

"Well, Mr. Holmes, have you proved us to be wrong yet? Have you found your tramp?" he cried.

"I have formed no conclusion whatever," my companion answered.

"But we formed ours yesterday, and now it proves to be correct, so you must acknowledge that we have been a little in front of you this time, Mr. Holmes."

"You certainly have the air of something unusual having occurred," said Holmes.

Lestrade laughed loudly.

"You don't like being beaten any more than the rest of us do," said he. "A man can't expect always to have it his own way, can he, Dr. Watson? Step this way, if you please, gentlemen, and I think I can convince you once for all that it was John McFarlane who did this crime."

He led us through the passage and out into a dark hall beyond.

"This is where young McFarlane must have come out to get his hat after the crime was done," said he. "Now look at this." With dramatic suddenness he struck a match, and by its light exposed a stain of blood upon the whitewashed wall. As he held the match nearer, I saw that it was more than a stain. It was the well-marked print of a thumb.

"Look at that with your magnifying glass, Mr. Holmes."

"Yes, I am doing so."

"You are aware that no two thumb-marks are alike?"

"I have heard something of the kind."

"Well, then, will you please compare that print with this wax impression of young McFarlane's right thumb, taken by my orders this morning?"

As he held the waxen print close to the blood-stain, it did not take a magnifying glass to see that the two were undoubtedly from the same thumb. It was evident to me that our unfortunate client was lost.

"That is final," said Lestrade.

"Yes, that is final," I involuntarily echoed.

"It is final," said Holmes.

Something in his tone caught my ear, and I turned to look at him. An extraordinary change had come over his face. It was writhing with inward merriment. His two eyes were shining like stars. It seemed to me that he was making desperate efforts to restrain a convulsive attack of laughter.

"Dear me! Dear me!" he said at last. "Well, now, who would have thought it? And how deceptive appearances may be, to be sure! Such a nice young man to look at! It is a lesson to us not to trust our own judgment, is it not, Lestrade?"

"Yes, some of us are a little too much inclined to be cock-sure, Mr. Holmes," said Lestrade. The man's insolence was maddening, but we could not resent it.

"What a providential thing that this young man should press his right thumb against the wall in taking his hat from the peg! Such a very natural action, too, if you come to think if it." Holmes was outwardly calm, but his whole body gave a wriggle of suppressed excitement as he spoke.

"By the way, Lestrade, who made this remarkable discovery?"

"It was the housekeeper, Mrs. Lexington, who drew the night constable's attention to it."

"Where was the night constable?"

"He remained on guard in the bedroom where the crime was committed, so as to see that nothing was touched."

"But why didn't the police see this mark yesterday?"

"Well, we had no particular reason to make a careful examination of the hall. Besides, it's not in a very prominent place, as you see."

"No, no—of course not. I suppose there is no doubt that the mark was there yesterday?"

Lestrade looked at Holmes as if he thought he was going out of his mind. I confess that I was myself surprised both at his hilarious manner and at his rather wild observation.

"I don't know whether you think that McFarlane came out of jail in the dead of the night in order to strengthen the evidence against himself," said Lestrade. "I leave it to any expert in the world whether that is not the mark of his thumb."

"It is unquestionably the mark of his thumb."

"There, that's enough." said Lestrade. "I am a practical man, Mr. Holmes, and when I have got my evidence I come to my conclusions. If you have anything to say, you will find me writing my report in the sitting-room."

Holmes had recovered his equanimity, though I still seemed to detect gleams of amusement in his expression.

"Dear me, this is a very sad development, Watson, is it not?" said he.

"And yet there are singular points about it which hold out some hopes for our client."

"I am delighted to hear it," said I, heartily. "I was afraid it was all up with him."

"I would hardly go so far as to say that, my dear Watson. The fact is that there is one really serious flaw in this evidence to which our friend attaches so much importance."

"Indeed, Holmes! What is it?"

"Only this: that I *know* that that mark was not there when I examined the hall yesterday. And now, Watson, let us have a little stroll round in the sunshine."

With a confused brain, but with a heart into which some warmth of hope was returning, I accompanied my friend in a walk round the garden. Holmes took each face of the house in turn, and examined it with great interest. He then led the way inside, and went over the whole building from basement to attic. Most of the rooms were unfurnished, but none the less Holmes inspected them all minutely. Finally, on the top corridor, which ran outside three untenanted bedrooms, he again was seized with a spasm of merriment.

"There are really some very unique features about this case, Watson," said he. "I think it is time now that we took our friend Lestrade into our confidence. He has had his little smile at our expense, and perhaps we may do as much by him, if my reading of this problem proves to be correct. Yes, yes, I think I see how we should approach it."

The Scotland Yard inspector was still writing in the parlour when Holmes interrupted him.

"I understood that you were writing a report of this case" said he.

"So I am."

"Don't you think it may be a little premature? I can't help thinking that your evidence is not complete."

Lestrade knew my friend too well to disregard his words. He laid down his pen and looked curiously at him.

"What do you mean, Mr. Holmes?"

"Only that there is an important witness whom you have not seen."

"Can you produce him?"

"I think I can."

"Then do so."

"I will do my best. How many constables have you?"

"There are three within call."

"Excellent!" said Holmes. "May I ask if they are all large, able-bodied men with powerful voices?"

"I have no doubt they are, though I fail to see what their voices have to do with it."

"Perhaps I can help you to see that and one or two other things as well," said Holmes. "Kindly summon your men, and I will try."

Five minutes later, three policemen had assembled in the hall.

"In the outhouse you will find a considerable quantity of straw," said

Holmes. "I will ask you to carry in two bundles of it. I think it will be of the greatest assistance in producing the witness whom I require. Thank you very much. I believe you have some matches in your pocket, Watson. Now, Mr. Lestrade, I will ask you all to accompany me to the top landing."

As I have said, there was a broad corridor there, which ran outside three empty bedrooms. At one end of the corridor we were all marshalled by Sherlock Holmes, the constables grinning and Lestrade staring at my friend with amazement, expectation, and derision chasing each other across his features. Holmes stood before us with the air of a conjurer who is performing a trick.

"Would you kindly send one of your constables for two buckets of water? Put the straw on the floor here, free from the wall on either side. Now I think that we are all ready."

Lestrade's face had begun to grow red and angry.

"I don't know whether you are playing a game with us, Mr. Sherlock Holmes," said he. "If you know anything, you can surely say it without all this tomfoolery."

"I assure you, my good Lestrade, that I have an excellent reason for everything that I do. You may possibly remember that you chaffed me a little, some hours ago, when the sun seemed on your side of the hedge, so you must not grudge me a little pomp and ceremony now. Might I ask you, Watson, to open that window, and then to put a match to the edge of the straw?"

I did so, and driven by the draught, a coil of gray smoke swirled down the corridor, while the dry straw crackled and flamed.

"Now we must see if we can find this witness for you, Lestrade. Might I ask you all to join in the cry of 'Fire!'? Now then; one, two, three——"

"Fire!" we all yelled.

"Thank you. I will trouble you once again."

"Fire!"

"Just once more, gentlemen, and all together."

"Fire!" The shout must have rung over Norwood.

It had hardly died away when an amazing thing happened. A door suddenly flew open out of what appeared to be solid wall at the end of the corridor, and a little, wizened man darted out of it, like a rabbit out of its burrow.

"Capital!" said Holmes, calmly. "Watson, a bucket of water over the straw. That will do! Lestrade, allow me to present you with your principal missing witness, Mr. Jonas Oldacre."

The detective stared at the newcomer with blank amazement. The latter was blinking in the bright light of the corridor, and peering at us and at the smouldering fire. It was an odious face—crafty, vicious, malignant, with shifty, light-gray eyes and white lashes.

"What's this, then?" said Lestrade, at last. "What have you been doing all this time, eh?"

Oldacre gave an uneasy laugh; shrinking back from the furious red face of the angry detective.

"I have done no harm."

"No harm? You have done your best to get an innocent man hanged. If it wasn't for this gentleman here, I am not sure that you would not have succeeded."

The wretched creature began to whimper.

"I am sure, sir, it was only my practical joke."

"Oh! a joke, was it? You won't find the laugh on your side. I promise you. Take him down, and keep him in the sitting-room until I come. Mr. Holmes," he continued, when they had gone, "I could not speak before the constables, but I don't mind saying, in the presence of Dr. Watson, that this is the brightest thing that you have done yet, though it is a mystery to me how you did it. You have saved an innocent man's life, and you have prevented a very grave scandal, which would have ruined my reputation in the Force."

Holmes smiled, and clapped Lestrade upon the shoulder.

"Instead of being ruined, my good sir, you will find that your reputation has been enormously enhanced. Just make a few alterations in that report which you were writing, and they will understand how hard it is to throw dust in the eyes of Inspector Lestrade."

"And you don't want your name to appear?"

"Not at all. The work is its own reward. Perhaps I shall get the credit also at some distant day, when I permit my zealous historian to lay out his foolscap once more—eh, Watson? Well, now, let us see where this rat has been lurking."

A lath-and-plaster partition had been run across the passage six feet from the end, with a door cunningly concealed in it. It was lit within by slits under the eaves. A few articles of furniture and a supply of food and water were within, together with a number of books and papers.

"There's the advantage of being a builder," said Holmes, as we came out. "He was able to fix up his own little hiding-place without any confederate—save, of course, that precious housekeeper of his, whom I should lose no time in adding to your bag, Lestrade."

"I'll take your advice. But how did you know of this place, Mr. Holmes?"

"I made up my mind that the fellow was in hiding in the house. When I paced one corridor and found it six feet shorter than the corresponding one below, it was pretty clear where he was. I thought he had not the nerve to lie quiet before an alarm of fire. We could, of course, have gone in and taken him, but it amused me to make him reveal himself. Besides, I owed you a little mystification, Lestrade, for your chaff in the morning."

"Well, sir, you certainly got equal with me on that. But how in the world did you know that he was in the house at all?"

"The thumb-mark, Lestrade. You said it was final; and so it was, in a very different sense. I knew it had not been there the day before. I pay a good deal of attention to matters of detail, as you may have observed, and

I had examined the hall, and was sure that the wall was clear. Therefore, it had been put on during the night."

"But how?"

"Very simply. When those packets were sealed up, Jonas Oldacre got McFarlane to secure one of the seals by putting his thumb upon the soft wax. It would be done so quickly and so naturally, that I daresay the young man himself has no recollection of it. Very likely it just so happened, and Oldacre had himself no notion of the use he would put it to. Brooding over the case in that den of his, it suddenly struck him what absolutely damning evidence he could make against McFarlane by using that thumb-mark. It was the simplest thing in the world for him to take a wax impression from the seal, to moisten it in as much blood as he could get from a pin-prick, and to put the mark upon the wall during the night, either with his own hand or with that of his housekeeper. If you examine among those documents which he took with him into his retreat, I will lay you a wager that you find the seal with the thumbmark upon it."

"Wonderful!" said Lestrade. "Wonderful! It's all as clear as crystal, as you put it. But what is the object of this deep deception, Mr. Holmes?"

It was amusing to me to see how the detective's overbearing manner had changed suddenly to that of a child asking questions of its teacher.

"Well, I don't think that is very hard to explain. A very deep, malicious, vindictive person is the gentleman who is now waiting for us downstairs. You know that he was once refused by McFarlane's mother? You don't! I told you that you should go to Blackheath first and Norwood afterwards. Well, this injury, as he would consider it, has rankled in his wicked, scheming brain, and all his life he has longed for vengeance, but never seen his chance. During the last year or two, things have gone against him—secret speculation, I think—and he finds himself in a bad way. He determines to swindle his creditors, and for this purpose he pays large checks to a certain Mr. Cornelius, who is, I imagine, himself under another name. I have not traced these checks yet, but I have no doubt that they were banked under that name at some provincial town where Oldacre from time to time led a double existence. He intended to change his name altogether, draw this money, and vanish, starting life again elsewhere.

"Well, that's likely enough."

"It would strike him that in disappearing he might throw all pursuit off his track, and at the same time have an ample and crushing revenge upon his old sweetheart, if he could give the impression that he had been murdered by her only child. It was a masterpiece of villainy, and he carried it out like a master. The idea of the will, which would give an obvious motive for the crime, the secret visit unknown to his own parents, the retention of the stick, the blood, and the animal remains and buttons in the wood-pile, all were admirable. It was a net from which it seemed to me, a few hours ago, that there was no possible escape. But he had not that supreme gift of the artist, the knowledge of when to stop. He wished to improve that which was already perfect—to draw the rope tighter yet round the neck of his unfortunate victim—and so he ruined all. Let us descend, Lestrade. There are just one or two questions that I would ask him."

The malignant creature was seated in his own parlour, with a policeman upon each side of him.

"It was a joke, my good sir—a practical joke, nothing more," he whined incessantly. "I assure you, sir, that I simply concealed myself in order to see the effect of my disappearance, and I am sure that you would not be so unjust as to imagine that I would have allowed any harm to befall poor young Mr. McFarlane."

"That's for a jury to decide," said Lestrade. "Anyhow, we shall have you on a charge of conspiracy, if not for attempted murder."

"And you'll probably find that your creditors will impound the banking account of Mr. Cornelius," said Holmes.

The little man started, and turned his malignant eyes upon my friend.

"I have to thank you for a good deal," said he. "Perhaps I'll pay my debt some day."

Holmes smiled indulgently.

"I fancy that, for some few years, you will find your time very fully occupied," said he. "By the way, what was it you put into the wood-pile besides your old trousers? A dead dog, or rabbits, or what? You won't tell? Dear me, how very unkind of you! Well, well, I daresay that a couple of rabbits would account both for the blood and for the charred ashes. If ever you write an account, Watson, you can make rabbits serve your turn."

THE ADVENTURE OF THE DANCING MEN

Holmes had been seated for some hours in silence with his long, thin back curved over a chemical vessel in which he was brewing a particularly malodorous product. His head was sunk upon his breast, and he looked from my point of view like a strange, lank bird, with dull gray plumage and a black top-knot.

"So, Watson," said he, suddenly, "you do not propose to invest in South African securities?"

I gave a start of astonishment. Accustomed as I was to Holmes's curious faculties, this sudden intrusion into my most intimate thoughts was utterly inexplicable.

"How on earth do you know that?" I asked.

He wheeled round upon his stool, with a steaming test-tube in his hand, and a gleam of amusement in his deep-set eyes.

"Now, Watson, confess yourself utterly taken aback," said he.

"I am."

"I ought to make you sign a paper to that effect."

"Why?"

"Because in five minutes you will say that it is all so absurdly simple."

"I am sure that I shall say nothing of the kind."

"You see, my dear Watson"—he propped his test-tube in the rack, and began to lecture with the air of a professor addressing his class—"it is not really difficult to construct a series of inferences, each dependent upon its predecessor and each simple in itself. If, after doing so, one simply knocks out all the central inferences and presents one's audience with the starting-point and the conclusion, one may produce a startling, though possibly a meretricious, effect. Now, it was not really difficult, by an inspection of the groove between your left forefinger and thumb, to feel sure that you did *not* propose to invest your small capital in the gold fields."

"I see no connection."

"Very likely not; but I can quickly show you a close connection. Here are the missing links of the very simple chain: 1. You had chalk between your left finger and thumb when you returned from the club last night. 2. You put chalk there when you play billiards, to steady the cue. 3. You never play billiards except with Thurston. 4. You told me, four weeks ago, that Thurston had an option on some South African property which would expire in a month, and which he desired you to share with him. 5. Your check book is locked in my drawer, and you have not asked for the key. 6. You do not propose to invest your money in this manner."

"How absurdly simple!" I cried.

"Quite so!" said he, a little nettled. "Every problem becomes very childish when once it is explained to you. Here is an unexplained one. See what you can make of that, friend Watson." He tossed a sheet of paper upon the table, and turned once more to his chemical analysis.

I looked with amazement at the absurd hieroglyphics upon the paper.

"Why, Holmes, it is a child's drawing," I cried.

"Oh, that's your idea!"

"What else should it be?"

"That is what Mr. Hilton Cubitt, of Riding Thorpe Manor, Norfolk, is very anxious to know. This little conundrum came by the first post, and he was to follow by the next train. There's a ring at the bell, Watson. I should not be very much surprised if this were he."

A heavy step was heard upon the stairs, and an instant later there entered a tall, ruddy, clean-shaven gentleman, whose clear eyes and florid cheeks told of a life led far from the fogs of Baker Street. He seemed to bring a whiff of his strong, fresh, bracing, east-coast air with him as he entered. Having shaken hands with each of us, he was about to sit down, when his eye rested upon the paper with the curious markings, which I had just examined and left upon the table.

"Well, Mr. Holmes, what do you make of these?" he cried. "They told me that you were fond of queer mysteries, and I don't think you can find a queerer one than that. I sent the paper on ahead, so that you might have time to study it before I came."

"It is certainly rather a curious production," said Holmes. "At first sight it would appear to be some childish prank. It consists of a number of absurd little figures dancing across the paper upon which they are drawn. Why should you attribute any importance to so grotesque an object?"

"I never should, Mr. Holmes. But my wife does. It is frightening her to death. She says nothing, but I can see terror in her eyes. That's why I want to sift the matter to the bottom."

Holmes held up the paper so that the sunlight shone full upon it. It was a page torn from a notebook. The markings were done in pencil, and ran in this way:

Holmes examined it for some time, and then, folding it carefully up, he placed it in his pocketbook.

"This promises to be a most interesting and unusual case," said he. "You gave me a few particulars in your letter, Mr. Hilton Cubitt, but I should be very much obliged if you would kindly go over it all again for the benefit of my friend, Dr. Watson."

"I'm not much of a story-teller," said our visitor, nervously clasping and unclasping his great, strong hands. "You'll just ask me anything that I don't make clear. I'll begin at the time of my marriage last year, but I want to say first of all that, though I'm not a rich man, my people have been at Riding Thorpe for a matter of five centuries, and there is no better known family in the County of Norfolk. Last year I came up to London for the Jubilee, and I stopped at a boardinghouse in Russell Square, because Parker, the vicar of our parish, was staying in it. There was an American young lady there—Patrick was the name—Elsie Patrick. In some way we became friends, until before my month was up I was as much in love as man could be. We were quietly married at a registry office, and we returned to Norfolk a wedded couple. You'll think it very mad, Mr. Holmes, that a man of a good old family should marry a wife in this fashion, knowing nothing of her past or of her people, but if you saw her and knew her, it would help you to understand.

"She was very straight about it, was Elsie. I can't say that she did not give me every chance of getting out of it if I wished to do so. 'I have had some very disagreeable associations in my life,' said she, 'I wish to forget all about them. I would rather never allude to the past, for it is very painful to me. If you take me, Hilton, you will take a woman who has nothing that she need be personally ashamed of; but you will have to be content with my word for it, and to allow me to be silent as to all that passed up to the time when I became yours. If these conditions are too hard, then go back to Norfolk, and leave me to the lonely life in which you found me.' It was only the day before our wedding that she said those very words to me. I told her that I was content to take her on her own terms, and I have been as good as my word.

"Well, we have been married now for a year, and very happy we have been. But about a month ago, at the end of June, I saw for the first time signs of trouble. One day my wife received a letter from America. I saw the American stamp. She turned deadly white, read the letter, and threw it into the fire. She made no allusion to it afterwards, and I made none, for a promise is a promise, but she has never known an easy hour from that moment. There is always a look of fear upon her face—a look as if she were waiting and expecting. She would do better to trust me. She would find that I was her best friend. But until she speaks, I can say nothing. Mind you, she is a truthful woman, Mr. Holmes, and whatever trouble there may have been in her past life it has been no fault of hers. I am only a simple Norfolk squire, but there is not a man in England who ranks his family honour more highly than I do. She knows it well, and she knew it well before she married me. She would never bring any stain upon it— of that I am sure.

"Well, now I come to the queer part of my story. About a week ago— it was the Tuesday of last week—I found on one of the window-sills a number of absurd little dancing figures like these upon the paper. They were scrawled with chalk. I thought that it was the stable-boy who had drawn them, but the lad swore he knew nothing about it. Anyhow, they had come there during the night. I had them washed out, and I only mentioned the matter to my wife afterwards. To my surprise, she took it very seriously, and begged me if any more came to let her see them. None did come for a week, and then yesterday morning I found this paper lying on the sundial in the garden. I showed it to Elsie, and down she dropped in a dead faint. Since then she has looked like a woman in a dream, half dazed, and with terror always lurking in her eyes. It was then that I wrote and sent the paper to you, Mr. Holmes. It was not a thing that I could take to the police, for they would have laughed at me, but you will tell me what to do. I am not a rich man, but if there is any danger threatening my little woman, I would spend my last copper to shield her."

He was a fine creature, this man of the old English soil—simple, straight, and gentle, with his great, earnest blue eyes and broad, comely face. His love for his wife and his trust in her shone in his features. Holmes had listened to his story with the utmost attention, and now he sat for some time in silent thought.

"Don't you think, Mr. Cubitt," said he, at last, "that your best plan would be to make a direct appeal to your wife, and to ask her to share her secret with you?"

Hilton Cubitt shook his massive head.

"A promise is a promise, Mr. Holmes. If Elsie wished to tell me she would. If not, it is not for me to force her confidence. But I am justified in taking my own line—and I will."

"Then I will help you with all my heart. In the first place, have you heard of any strangers being seen in your neighbourhood?"

"No."

"I presume that it is a very quiet place. Any fresh face would cause comment?"

"In the immediate neighbourhood, yes. But we have several small watering-places not very far away. And the farmers take in lodgers."

"These hieroglyphics have evidently a meaning. If it is a purely arbitrary one, it may be impossible for us to solve it. If, on the other hand, it is systematic, I have no doubt that we shall get to the bottom of it. But this particular sample is so short that I can do nothing, and the facts which you have brought me are so indefinite that we have no basis for an investigation. I would suggest that you return to Norfolk, that you keep a keen lookout, and that you take an exact copy of any fresh dancing men which may appear. It is a thousand pities that we have not a reproduction of those which were done in chalk upon the window-sill. Make a discreet inquiry also as to any strangers in the neighbourhood. When you have collected some fresh evidence, come to me again. That is the best advice which I can give you, Mr. Hilton Cubitt. If there are any pressing fresh developments, I shall be always ready to run down and see you in your Norfolk home."

The interview left Sherlock Holmes very thoughtful, and several times in the next few days I saw him take his slip of paper from his notebook and look long and earnestly at the curious figures inscribed upon it. He made no allusion to the affair, however, until one afternoon a fortnight or so later. I was going out when he called me back.

"You had better stay here, Watson."

"Why?"

"Because I had a wire from Hilton Cubitt this morning. You remember Hilton Cubitt, of the dancing men? He was to reach Liverpool Street at one-twenty. He may be here at any moment. I gather from his wire that there have been some new incidents of importance."

We had not long to wait, for our Norfolk squire came straight from the station as fast as a hansom could bring him. He was looking worried and depressed, with tired eyes and a lined forehead.

"It's getting on my nerves, this business, Mr. Holmes," said he, as he sank, like a wearied man, into an armchair. "It's bad enough to feel that you are surrounded by unseen, unknown folk, who have some kind of design upon you, but when, in addition to that, you know that it is just killing your wife by inches, then it becomes as much as flesh and blood can endure. She's wearing away under it—just wearing away before my eyes."

"Has she said anything yet?"

"No, Mr. Holmes, she has not. And yet there have been times when the poor girl has wanted to speak, and yet could not quite bring herself to take the plunge. I have tried to help her, but I daresay I did it clumsily, and scared her from it. She has spoken about my old family, and our reputation in the county, and our pride in our unsullied honour, and I always felt it was leading to the point, but somehow it turned off before we got there."

"But you have found out something for yourself?"

"A good deal, Mr. Holmes. I have several fresh dancing-men pictures for you to examine, and, what is more important, I have seen the fellow."

"What, the man who draws them?"

"Yes, I saw him at his work. But I will tell you everything in order. When I got back after my visit to you, the very first thing I saw next morning was a fresh crop of dancing men. They had been drawn in chalk upon the black wooden door of the tool-house, which stands beside the lawn in full view of the front windows. I took an exact copy, and here it is." He unfolded a paper and laid it upon the table. Here is a copy of the hieroglyphics:

"Excellent!" said Holmes. "Excellent! Pray continue."

"When I had taken the copy, I rubbed out the marks, but, two mornings later, a fresh inscription had appeared. I have a copy of it here":

Holmes rubbed his hands and chuckled with delight.

"Our material is rapidly accumulating," said he.

"Three days later a message was left scrawled upon paper, and placed under a pebble upon the sundial. Here it is. The characters are, as you see, exactly the same as the last one. After that I determined to lie in wait, so I got out my revolver and I sat up in my study, which overlooks the lawn and garden. About two in the morning I was seated by the window, all being dark save for the moonlight outside, when I heard steps behind me, and there was my wife in her dressing-gown. She implored me to come to bed. I told her frankly that I wished to see who it was who played such absurd tricks upon us. She answered that it was some senseless practical joke, and that I should not take any notice of it.

" 'If it really annoys you, Hilton, we might go and travel, you and I, and so avoid this nuisance.'

" 'What, be driven out of our own house by a practical joker?' said I. 'Why, we should have the whole county laughing at us.'

" 'Well, come to bed,' said she, 'and we can discuss it in the morning.'

"Suddenly, as she spoke, I saw her white face grow whiter yet in the moonlight, and her hand tightened upon my shoulder. Something was moving in the shadow of the tool-house. I saw a dark, creeping figure which crawled round the corner and squatted in front of the door. Seizing my pistol, I was rushing out, when my wife threw her arms round me and held me with convulsive strength. I tried to throw her off, but she clung to me most desperately. At last I got clear, but by the time I had opened the door and reached the house the creature was gone. He had left a trace of his presence, however, for there on the door was the very same arrangement of dancing men which had already twice appeared, and which I have copied on that paper. There was no other sign of the fellow anywhere, though I ran all over the grounds. And yet the amazing thing is that he must have been there all the time, for when I examined the door again in the morning, he had scrawled some more of his pictures under the line which I had already seen."

"Have you that fresh drawing?"

"Yes, it is very short, but I made a copy of it, and here it is." Again he produced a paper. The new dance was in this form:

"Tell me," said Holmes—and could see by his eyes that he was much excited—"was this a mere addition to the first or did it appear to be entirely separate?"

"It was on a different panel of the door."

"Excellent! This is by far the most important of all for our purpose. It fills me with hopes. Now, Mr. Hilton Cubitt, please continue your most interesting statement."

"I have nothing more to say, Mr. Holmes, except that I was angry with my wife that night for having held me back when I might have caught the skulking rascal. She said that she feared that I might come to harm. For an instant it had crossed my mind that perhaps what she really feared was that *he* might come to harm, for I could not doubt that she knew who this man was, and what he meant by these strange signals. But there is a tone in my wife's voice, Mr. Holmes, and a look in her eyes which forbid doubt, and I am sure that it was indeed my own safety that was in her mind. There's the whole case, and now I want your advice as to what I ought to do. My own inclination is to put half a dozen of my farm lads in the shrubbery, and when this fellow comes again to give him such a hiding that he will leave us in peace for the future."

"I fear it is too deep a case for such simple remedies," said Holmes. "How long can you stay in London?"

"I must go back today. I would not leave my wife alone all night for anything. She is very nervous, and begged me to come back."

"I daresay you are right. But if you could have stopped, I might possibly have been able to return with you in a day or two. Meanwhile you will leave me these papers, and I think that it is very likely that I shall be able to pay you a visit shortly and to throw some light upon your case."

Sherlock Holmes preserved his calm professional manner until our visitor had left us, although it was easy for me, who knew him so well, to see that he was profoundly excited. The moment that Hilton Cubitt's broad back had disappeared through the door my comrade rushed to the table, laid out all the slips of paper containing dancing men in front of him, and threw himself into an intricate and elaborate calculation. For two hours I watched him as he covered sheet after sheet of paper with figures and letters, so completely absorbed in his task that he had evidently forgotten my presence. Sometimes he was making progress and whistled and sang at his work; sometimes he was puzzled, and would sit for long spells with a furrowed brow and a vacant eye. Finally he sprang from his chair with a cry of satisfaction, and walked up and down the room rubbing his hands together. Then he wrote a long telegram upon a cable form. "If my answer to this is as I hope, you will have a very pretty case to add to your collection, Watson," said he. "I expect that we shall be able to go down to Norfolk tomorrow, and to take our friend some very definite news as to the secret of his annoyance."

I confess that I was filled with curiosity, but I was aware that Holmes liked to make his disclosures at his own time and in his own way, so I waited until it should suit him to take me into his confidence.

But there was a delay in that answering telegram, and two days of impatience followed, during which Holmes pricked up his ears at every ring of the bell. On the evening of the second there came a letter from Hilton

Cubitt. All was quiet with him, save that a long inscription had appeared that morning upon the pedestal of the sundial. He inclosed a copy of it, which is here reproduced:

Holmes bent over this grotesque frieze for some minutes, and then suddenly sprang to his feet with an exclamation of surprise and dismay. His face was haggard with anxiety.

"We have let this affair go far enough," said he. "Is there a train to North Walsham to-night?"

I turned up the time-table. The last had just gone. "Then we shall breakfast early and take the very first in the morning," said Holmes. "Our presence is most urgently needed. Ah! here is our expected cablegram. One moment, Mrs. Hudson, there may be an answer. No, that is quite as I expected. This message makes it even more essential that we should not lose an hour in letting Hilton Cubitt know how matters stand, for it is a singular and a dangerous web in which our simple Norfolk squire is entangled."

So, indeed, it proved, and as I come to the dark conclusion of a story which had seemed to me to be only childish and bizarre, I experience once again the dismay and horror with which I was filled. Would that I had some brighter ending to communicate to my readers, but these are the chronicles of fact, and I must follow to their dark crisis the strange chain of events which for some days made Riding Thorpe Manor a household word through the length and breadth of England.

We had hardly alighted at North Walsham, and mentioned the name of our destination, when the stationmaster hurried towards us. "I suppose that you are the detectives from London?" said he.

A look of annoyance passed over Holmes's face.

"What makes you think such a thing?"

"Because Inspector Martin from Norwich has just passed through. But maybe you are the surgeons. She's not dead—or wasn't by last accounts. You may be in time to save her yet—though it be for the gallows."

Holmes's brow was dark with anxiety.

"We are going to Riding Thorpe Manor," said he, "but we have heard nothing of what has passed there."

"It's a terrible business," said the stationmaster. "They are shot, both Mr. Hilton Cubitt and his wife. She shot him and then herself—so the servants say. He's dead and her life is despaired of. Dear, dear, one of the oldest families in the county of Norfolk, and one of the most honoured."

Without a word Holmes hurried to a carriage, and during the long seven miles' drive he never opened his mouth. Seldom have I seen him so utterly despondent. He had been uneasy during all our journey from town, and I had observed that he had turned over the morning papers with anxious attention, but now this sudden realization of his worst fears left him in a blank melancholy. He leaned back in his seat, lost in gloomy speculation. Yet there was much around to interest us, for we were passing through as singular a countryside as any in England, where a few scattered cottages represented the population of to-day, while on every hand enormous square-towered churches bristled up from the flat green landscape and told of the glory and prosperity of old East Anglia. At last the violet rim of the German Ocean* appeared over the green edge of the Norfolk coast, and the driver pointed with his whip to two old brick and timber gables which projected from a grove of trees. "That's Riding Thorpe Manor," said he.

As we drove up to the porticoed front door, I observed in front of it, beside the tennis lawn, the black tool-house and the pedestalled sundial with which we had such strange associations. A dapper little man, with a quick, alert manner and a waxed moustache, had just descended from a high dog-cart. He introduced himself as Inspector Martin, of the Norfolk Constabulary, and he was considerably astonished when he heard the name of my companion.

"Why, Mr. Holmes, the crime was only committed at three this morning. How could you hear of it in London and get to the spot as soon as I?"

"I anticipated it. I came in the hope of preventing it."

"Then you must have important evidence, of which we are ignorant, for they were said to be a most united couple."

"I have only the evidence of the dancing men," said Holmes. "I will explain the matter to you later. Meanwhile, since it is too late to prevent this tragedy, I am very anxious that I should use the knowledge which I possess in order to insure that justice be done. Will you associate me in your investigation, or will you prefer that I should act independently?"

"I should be proud to feel that we were acting together, Mr. Holmes," said the inspector, earnestly.

"In that case I should be glad to hear the evidence and to examine the premises without an instant of unnecessary delay."

Inspector Martin had the good sense to allow my friend to do things in his own fashion, and contented himself with carefully noting the results. The local surgeon, an old, white-haired man, had just come down from Mrs. Hilton Cubitt's room, and he reported that her injuries were serious, but not necessarily fatal. The bullet had passed through the front of her brain, and it would probably be some time before she could regain consciousness. On the question of whether she had been shot or had shot herself, he would not venture to express any decided opinion. Certainly the bullet had been discharged at very close quarters. There was only the one

---

*Another name for the North Sea.

pistol found in the room, two barrels of which had been emptied. Mr. Hilton Cubitt had been shot through the heart. It was equally conceivable that he had shot her and then himself, or that she had been the criminal, for the revolver lay upon the floor midway between them.

"Has he been moved?" asked Holmes.

"We have moved nothing except the lady. We could not leave her lying wounded upon the floor."

"How long have you been here, Doctor?"

"Since four o'clock."

"Anyone else?"

"Yes, the constable here."

"And you have touched nothing?"

"Nothing."

"You have acted with great discretion. Who sent for you?"

"The housemaid, Saunders."

"Was it she who gave the alarm?"

"She and Mrs. King, the cook."

"Where are they now?"

"In the kitchen, I believe."

"Then I think we had better hear their story at once."

The old hall, oak-panelled and high-windowed, had been turned into a court of investigation. Holmes sat in a great, old-fashioned chair, his inexorable eyes gleaming out of his haggard face. I could read in them a set purpose to devote his life to this quest until the client whom he had failed to save should at last be avenged. The trim Inspector Martin, the old, gray-headed country doctor, myself, and a stolid village policeman made up the rest of that strange company.

The two women told their story clearly enough. They had been aroused from their sleep by the sound of an explosion, which had been followed a minute later by a second one. They slept in adjoining rooms, and Mrs. King had rushed in to Saunders. Together they had descended the stairs. The door of the study was open, and a candle was burning upon the table. Their master lay upon his face in the centre of the room. He was quite dead. Near the window his wife was crouching, her head leaning against the wall. She was horribly wounded, and the side of her face was red with blood. She breathed heavily, but was incapable of saying anything. The passage, as well as the room, was full of smoke and the smell of powder. The window was certainly shut and fastened upon the inside. Both women were positive upon the point. They had at once sent for the doctor and for the constable. Then, with the aid of the groom and the stable-boy, they had conveyed their injured mistress to her room. Both she and her husband had occupied the bed. She was clad in her dress—he in his dressing-gown, over his night clothes. Nothing had been moved in the study. So far as they knew, there had never been any quarrel between husband and wife. They had always looked upon them as a very united couple.

These were the main points of the servants' evidence. In answer to Inspector Martin, they were clear that every door was fastened upon the inside, and that no one could have escaped from the house. In answer to Holmes, they both remembered that they were conscious of the smell of powder from the moment that they ran out of their rooms upon the top floor. "I commend that fact very carefully to your attention," said Holmes to his professional colleague. "And now I think that we are in a position to undertake a thorough examination of the room."

The study proved to be a small chamber, lined on three sides with books, and with a writing-table facing an ordinary window, which looked out upon the garden. Our first attention was given to the body of the unfortunate squire, whose huge frame lay stretched across the room. His disordered dress showed that he had been hastily aroused from sleep. The bullet had been fired at him from the front, and had remained in his body, after penetrating the heart. His death had certainly been instantaneous and painless. There was no powder-marking either upon his dressing-gown or on his hands. According to the country surgeon, the lady had stains upon her face, but none upon her hand.

"The absence of the latter means nothing, though its presence may mean everything," said Holmes. "Unless the powder from a badly fitting cartridge happens to spurt backward, one may fire many shots without leaving a sign. I would suggest that Mr. Cubitt's body may now be removed. I suppose, Doctor, you have not recovered the bullet which wounded the lady?"

"A serious operation will be necessary before that can be done. But there are still four cartridges in the revolver. Two have been fired and two wounds inflicted, so that each bullet can be accounted for."

"So it would seem," said Holmes. "Perhaps you can account also for the bullet which has so obviously struck the edge of the window?"

He had turned suddenly, and his long, thin finger was pointing to a hole which had been drilled right through the lower windowsash, about an inch above the bottom.

"By George!" cried the inspector. "How ever did you see that?"

"Because I looked for it."

"Wonderful!" said the country doctor. "You are certainly right, sir. Then a third shot has been fired, and therefore a third person must have been present. But who could that have been, and how could he have got away?"

"That is the problem which we are now about to solve," said Sherlock Holmes. "You remember, Inspector Martin, when the servants said that on leaving their room they were at once conscious of a smell of powder, I remarked that the point was an extremely important one?"

"Yes, sir; but I confess I did not quite follow you."

"It suggested that at the time of the firing, the window as well as the door of the room had been open. Otherwise the fumes of powder could not have been blown so rapidly through the house. A draught in the room was necessary for that. Both door and window were only open for a very short time, however."

"How do you prove that?"

"Because the candle was not guttered."

"Capital!" cried the inspector. "Capital!"

"Feeling sure that the window had been open at the time of the tragedy, I conceived that there might have been a third person in the affair, who stood outside this opening and fired through it. Any shot directed at this person might hit the sash. I looked, and there, sure enough, was the bullet mark!"

"But how came the window to be shut and fastened?"

"The woman's first instinct would be to shut and fasten the window. But, halloa! what is this?"

It was a lady's hand-bag which stood upon the study table—a trim little handbag of crocodile-skin and silver. Holmes opened it and turned the contents out. There were twenty fifty-pound notes of the Bank of England, held together by an india-rubber band—nothing else.

"This must be preserved, for it will figure in the trial," said Holmes, as he handed the bag with its contents to the inspector. "It is now necessary that we should try to throw some light upon this third bullet, which has clearly, from the splintering of the wood, been fired from inside the room. I should like to see Mrs. King, the cook, again. You said, Mrs. King, that you were awakened by a *loud* explosion. When you said that, did you mean that it seemed to you to be louder than the second one?"

"Well, sir, it wakened me from my sleep, so it is hard to judge. But it did seem very loud."

"You don't think that it might have been two shots fired almost at the same instant?"

"I am sure I couldn't say, sir."

"I believe that it was undoubtedly so. I rather think, Inspector Martin, that we have now exhausted all that this room can teach us. If you will kindly step round with me, we shall see what fresh evidence the garden has to offer."

A flower-bed extended up to the study window, and we all broke into an exclamation as we approached it. The flowers were trampled down, and the soft soil was imprinted all over with footmarks. Large, masculine feet they were, with peculiarly long, sharp toes. Holmes hunted about among the grass and leaves like a retriever after a wounded bird. Then, with a cry of satisfaction, he bent forward and picked up a little brazen cylinder.

"I thought so," said he; "the revolver had an ejector, and here is the third cartridge. I really think, Inspector Martin, that our case is almost complete."

The country inspector's face had shown his intense amazement at the rapid and masterful progress of Holmes's investigation. At first he had shown some disposition to assert his own position, but now he was overcome with admiration, and ready to follow without question wherever Holmes led.

"Whom do you suspect?" he asked.

"I'll go into that later. There are several points in this problem which I have not been able to explain to you yet. Now that I have got so far, I had best proceed on my own lines, and then clear the whole matter up once and for all."

"Just as you wish, Mr. Holmes, so long as we get our man."

"I have no desire to make mysteries, but it is impossible at the moment of action to enter into long and complex explanations. I have the threads of this affair all in my hand. Even if this lady should never recover consciousness, we can still reconstruct the events of last night, and insure that justice be done. First of all, I wish to know whether there is any inn in this neighbourhood known as 'Elrige's'?"

The servants were cross-questioned, but none of them had heard of such a place. The stable-boy threw a light upon the matter by remembering that a farmer of that name lived some miles off, in the direction of East Ruston.

"Is it a lonely farm?"

"Very lonely, sir."

"Perhaps they have not heard yet of all that happened here during the night?"

"Maybe not, sir."

Holmes thought for a little, and then a curious smile played over his face.

"Saddle a horse, my lad," said he. "I shall wish you to take a note to Elrige's Farm."

He took from his pocket the various slips of the dancing men. With these in front of him he worked for some time at the study-table. Finally he handed a note to the boy, with directions to put it into the hands of the person to whom it was addressed, and especially to answer no questions of any sort which might be put to him. I saw the outside of the note, addressed in straggling, irregular characters, very unlike Holmes's usual precise hand. It was consigned to Mr. Abe Slaney, Elrige's Farm, East Ruston, Norfolk.

"I think, Inspector," Holmes remarked, "that you would do well to telegraph for an escort, as, if my calculations prove to be correct, you may have a particularly dangerous prisoner to convey to the county jail. The boy who takes this note could no doubt forward your telegram. If there is an afternoon train to town, Watson, I think we should do well to take it, as I have a chemical analysis of some interest to finish, and this investigation draws rapidly to a close."

When the youth had been dispatched with the note, Sherlock Holmes gave his instructions to the servants. If any visitor were to call asking for Mrs. Hilton Cubitt, no information should be given as to her condition, but he was to be shown at once into the drawing-room. He impressed these points upon them with the utmost earnestness. Finally he led the way into the drawing-room, with the remark that the business was now out of our hands, and that we must while away the time as best we might until we could see what was in store for us. The doctor had departed to his patients and only the inspector and myself remained.

"I think that I can help you to pass an hour in an interesting and profitable manner," said Holmes, drawing his chair up to the table, and spreading out in front of him the various papers upon which were recorded the antics of the dancing men. "As to you, friend Watson, I owe you every atonement for having allowed your natural curiosity to remain so long unsatisfied. To you, Inspector, the whole incident may appeal as a remarkable professional study. I must tell you, first of all, the interesting circumstances connected with the previous consultations which Mr. Hilton Cubitt has had with me in Baker Street." He then shortly recapitulated the facts which have already been recorded. "I have here in front of me these singular productions, at which one might smile, had they not proved themselves to be the forerunners of so terrible a tragedy. I am fairly familiar with all forms of secret writings, and am myself the author of a trifling monograph upon the subject, in which I analyze one hundred and sixty separate ciphers, but I confess that this is entirely new to me. The object of those who invented the system has apparently been to conceal that these characters convey a message, and to give the idea that they are the mere random sketches of children.

"Having once recognized, however, that the symbols stood for letters, and having applied the rules which guide us in all forms of secret writings, the solution was easy enough. The first message submitted to me was so short that it was impossible for me to do more than to say, with some confidence, that the symbol stood for E. As you are aware, E is the most common letter in the English alphabet, and it predominates to so marked an extent that even in a short sentence one would expect to find it most often. Out of fifteen symbols in the first message, four were the same, so it was reasonable to set this down as E. It is true that in some cases the figure was bearing a flag, and in some cases not, but it was probable, from the way in which the flags were distributed, that they were used to break the sentence up into words. I accepted this as a hypothesis, and noted that E was represented by .

"But now came the real difficulty of the inquiry. The order of the English letters after E is by no means well marked, and any preponderance which may be shown in an average of a printed sheet may be reversed in a single short sentence. Speaking roughly, T, A, O, I, N, S, H, R, D, and L are the numerical order in which letters occur; but T, A, O, and I are very nearly abreast of each other, and it would be an endless task to try each combination until a meaning was arrived at. I therefore waited for fresh material. In my second interview with Mr. Hilton Cubitt he was able to give me two other short sentences and one message, which appeared—since there was no flag—to be a single word. Here are the symbols. Now, in the single word I have already got the two E's coming second and fourth in a word of five letters. It might be 'sever,' or 'lever,' or 'never.' There can be no question that the latter as a reply to an appeal is far the most probable, and the circumstances pointed to its being a reply written by the lady. Accepting it as correct, we are now able to say that the

symbols ⚇⚇⚇ stand respectively for N, V, and R.

"Even now I was in considerable difficulty, but a happy thought put me in possession of several other letters. It occurred to me that if these appeals came, as I expected, from someone who had been intimate with the lady in her early life, a combination which contained two E's with three letters between might very well stand for the name 'ELSIE.' On examination I found that such a combination formed the termination of the message which was three times repeated. It was certainly some appeal to 'Elsie.' In this way I had got my L, S, and I. But what appeal could it be? There were only four letters in the word which preceded 'Elsie,' and it ended in E. Surely the word must be 'COME.' I tried all other four letters ending in E, but could find none to fit the case. So now I was in possession of C, O, and M, and I was in a position to attack the first message once more, dividing it into words and putting dots for each symbol which was still unknown. So treated, it worked out in this fashion:

. M . ERE . . E SL . NE.

"Now the first letter *can* only be A, which is a most useful discovery, since it occurs no fewer than three times in this short sentence, and the H is also apparent in the second word. Now it becomes:

AM HERE A. E SLANE.

Or, filling in the obvious vacancies in the name:

AM HERE ABE SLANEY.

I had so many letters now that I could proceed with considerable confidence to the second message, which worked out in this fashion:

A . ELRI . ES.

Here I could only make sense by putting T and G for the missing letters, and supposing that the name was that of some house or inn at which the writer was staying."

Inspector Martin and I had listened with the utmost interest to the full and clear account of how my friend had produced results which had led to so complete a command over our difficulties.

"What did you do then, sir?" asked the inspector.

"I had every reason to suppose that this Abe Slaney was an American, since Abe is an American contraction, and since a letter from America had been the starting-point of all the trouble. I had also every cause to think that there was some criminal secret in the matter. The lady's allusions to her past, and her refusal to take her husband into her confidence, both pointed in that direction. I therefore cabled to my friend, Wilson Hargreave, of the New York Police Bureau, who has more than once made use of my knowledge of London crime. I asked him whether the name of Abe Slaney was known to him. Here is his reply: 'The most dangerous crook in Chicago.' On the very evening upon which I had his answer, Hilton Cubitt sent me the last message from Slaney. Working with known letters, it took this form:

ELSIE . RE . ARE TO MEET THY GO.

The addition of a P and a D completed a message which showed me that the rascal was proceeding from persuasion to threats, and my knowledge of the crooks of Chicago prepared me to find that he might very rapidly put his words into action. I at once came to Norfolk with my friend and colleague, Dr. Watson, but, unhappily, only in time to find that the worst had already occurred."

"It is a privilege to be associated with you in the handling of a case," said the inspector, warmly. "You will excuse me, however, if I speak frankly to you. You are only answerable to yourself, but I have to answer to my superiors. If this Abe Slaney, living at Elrige's, is indeed the murderer, and if he has made his escape while I am seated here, I should certainly get into serious trouble."

"You need not be uneasy. He will not try to escape."

"How do you know?"

"To fly would be a confession of guilt."

"Then let us go to arrest him."

"I expect him here every instant."

"But why should he come?"

"Because I have written, and asked him."

"But this is incredible, Mr. Holmes! Why should he come because you have asked him? Would not such a request rather rouse his suspicions and cause him to fly?"

"I think I have known how to frame the letter," said Sherlock Holmes. "In fact, if I am not very much mistaken, here is the gentleman himself coming up the drive."

A man was striding up the path which led to the door. He was a tall, handsome, swarthy fellow, clad in a suit of gray flannel, with a Panama hat, a bristling black beard, and a great, aggressive hooked nose, and flourishing a cane as he walked. He swaggered up the path as if the place belonged to him, and we heard his loud, confident peal at the bell.

"I think, gentlemen," said Holmes, quietly, "that we had best take up our position behind the door. Every precaution is necessary when dealing with such a fellow. You will need your handcuffs, Inspector. You can leave the talking to me."

We waited in silence for a minute—one of those minutes which one can never forget. Then the door opened and the man stepped in. In an instant Holmes clapped a pistol to his head, and Martin slipped the handcuffs over his wrists. It was all done so swiftly and deftly that the fellow was helpless before he knew that he was attacked. He glared from one to the other of us with a pair of blazing black eyes. Then he burst into a bitter laugh.

"Well, gentlemen, you have the drop on me this time. I seem to have knocked up against something hard. But I came here in answer to a letter from Mrs. Hilton Cubitt. Don't tell me that she is in this? Don't tell me that she helped to set a trap for me?"

"Mrs. Hilton Cubitt was seriously injured, and is at death's door."

The man gave a hoarse cry of grief, which rang through the house.

"You're crazy!" he cried, fiercely. "It was he that was hurt, not she. Who would have hurt little Elsie? I may have threatened her—God forgive me!—but I would not have touched a hair of her pretty head. Take it back—you! Say that she is not hurt!"

"She was found, badly wounded, by the side of her dead husband."

He sank with a deep groan on to the settee, and buried his face in his manacled hands. For five minutes he was silent. Then he raised his face once more, and spoke with the cold composure of despair.

"I have nothing to hide from you, gentlemen," said he. "If I shot the man he had his shot at me, and there's no murder in that. But if you think I could have hurt that woman, then you don't know either me or her. I tell you, there was never a man in this world loved a woman more than I loved her. I had a right to her. She was pledged to me years ago. Who was this Englishman that he should come between us? I tell you that I had the first right to her, and that I was only claiming my own."

"She broke away from your influence when she found the man that you are," said Holmes, sternly. "She fled from America to avoid you, and she married an honourable gentleman in England. You dogged her and followed her and made her life a misery to her, in order to induce her to abandon the husband whom she loved and respected in order to fly with you, whom she feared and hated. You have ended by bringing about the death of a noble man and driving his wife to suicide. That is your record in this business, Mr. Abe Slaney, and you will answer for it to the law."

"If Elsie dies, I care nothing what becomes of me," said the American. He opened one of his hands, and looked at a note crumpled up in his palm. "See here, mister," he cried, with a gleam of suspicion in his eyes, "you're not trying to scare me over this, are you? If the lady is hurt as bad as you say, who was it that wrote this note?" He tossed it forward on to the table.

"I wrote it, to bring you here."

"You wrote it? There was no one on earth outside the Joint who knew the secret of the dancing men. How came you to write it?"

"What one man can invent another can discover," said Holmes. "There is a cab coming to convey you to Norwich, Mr. Slaney. But, meanwhile, you have time to make some small reparation for the injury you have wrought. Are you aware that Mrs. Hilton Cubitt has herself lain under grave suspicion of the murder of her husband, and that it was only my presence here, and the knowledge which I happened to possess, which has saved her from the accusation? The least that you owe her is to make it clear to the whole world that she was in no way, directly or indirectly, responsible for his tragic end."

"I ask nothing better," said the American. "I guess the very best case I can make for myself is the absolute naked truth."

"It is my duty to warn you that it will be used against you," cried the inspector, with the magnificent fair play of the British criminal law.

Slaney shrugged his shoulders.

"I'll chance that," said he. "First of all, I want you gentlemen to understand that I have known this lady since she was a child. There were seven of us in a gang in Chicago, and Elsie's father was the boss of the Joint. He was a clever man, was old Patrick. It was he who invented that writing, which would pass as a child's scrawl unless you just happened to have the key to it. Well, Elsie learned some of our ways, but she couldn't stand the business, and she had a bit of honest money of her own, so she gave us all the slip and got away to London. She had been engaged to me, and she would have married me, I believe, if I had taken over another profession, but she would have nothing to do with anything on the cross.* It was only after her marriage to this Englishman that I was able to find out where she was. I wrote to her, but got no answer. After that I came over, and, as letters were no use, I put my messages where she could read them.

"Well, I have been here a month now. I lived in that farm, where I had a room down below, and could get in and out every night, and no one the wiser. I tried all I could to coax Elsie away. I knew that she read the messages, for once she wrote an answer under one of them. Then my temper got the better of me, and I began to threaten her. She sent me a letter then, imploring me to go away, and saying that it would break her heart if any scandal should come upon her husband. She said that she would come down when her husband was asleep at three in the morning, and speak with me through the end window, if I would go away afterwards and leave her in peace. She came down and brought money with her, trying to bribe me to go. This made me mad and I caught her arm and tried to pull her through the window. At that moment in rushed the husband with his revolver in his hand. Elsie had sunk down upon the floor, and we were face to face. I was heeled also, and I held up my gun to scare him off and let me get away. He fired and missed me. I pulled off almost at the same instant, and down he dropped. I made away across the garden, and

---

*Counter to honesty; crossing the bounds of legality.

as I went I heard the window shut behind me. That's God's truth, gentlemen, every word of it; and I heard no more about it until that lad came riding up with a note which made me walk in here, like a jay, and give myself into your hands."

A cab had driven up whilst the American had been talking. Two uniformed policemen sat inside. Inspector Martin rose and touched his prisoner on the shoulder.

"It is time for us to go."

"Can I see her first?"

"No, she is not conscious. Mr. Sherlock Holmes, I only hope that, if ever again I have an important case, I shall have the good fortune to have you by my side."

We stood at the window and watched the cab drive away. As I turned back, my eye caught the pellet of paper which the prisoner had tossed upon the table. It was the note with which Holmes had decoyed him.

"See if you can read it, Watson," said he, with a smile.

It contained no word, but this little line of dancing men:

"If you use the code which I have explained," said Holmes, "you will find that it simply means 'Come here at once.' I was convinced that it was an invitation which he would not refuse, since he could never imagine that it could come from anyone but the lady. And so, my dear Watson, we have ended by turning the dancing men to good when they have so often been the agents of evil, and I think that I have fulfilled my promise of giving you something unusual for your notebook. Three-forty is our train, and I fancy we should be back in Baker Street for dinner."

Only one word of epilogue. The American, Abe Slaney, was condemned to death at the winter assizes at Norwich, but his penalty was changed to penal servitude in consideration of mitigating circumstances, and the certainty that Hilton Cubitt had fired the first shot. Of Mrs. Hilton Cubitt I only know that I have heard she recovered entirely, and that she still remains a widow, devoting her whole life to the care of the poor and to the administration of her husband's estate.

THE ADVENTURE OF THE
SOLITARY CYCLIST

From the years 1894 to 1901 inclusive, Mr. Sherlock Holmes was a very busy man. It is safe to say that there was no public case of any difficulty in which he was not consulted during those eight years, and there were hundreds of private cases, some of them of the most intricate and extraordinary character, in which he played a prominent part. Many startling successes and a few unavoidable failures were the outcome of this long period of continuous work. As I have preserved very full notes of all these cases, and was myself personally engaged in many of them, it may be imagined that it is no easy task to know which I should select to lay before the public. I shall, however, preserve my former rule, and give the preference to those cases which derive their interest not so much from the brutality of the crime as from the ingenuity and dramatic quality of the solution. For this reason I will now lay before the reader the facts connected with Miss Violet Smith, the solitary cyclist of Charlington, and the curious sequel of our investigation, which culminated in unexpected tragedy. It is true that the circumstance did not admit of any striking illustration of those powers for which my friend was famous, but there were some points about the case which made it stand out in those long records of crime from which I gather the material for these little narratives.

On referring to my notebook for the year 1895, I find that it was upon Saturday, the 23d of April, that we first heard of Miss Violet Smith. Her visit was, I remember, extremely unwelcome to Holmes, for he was immersed at the moment in a very abstruse and complicated problem concerning the peculiar persecution to which John Vincent Harden, the well known tobacco millionaire, had been subjected. My friend, who loved above all things precision and concentration of thought, resented anything which distracted his attention from the matter in hand. And yet, without a harshness which was foreign to his nature, it was impossible to refuse to listen to the story of the young and beautiful woman, tall, graceful, and queenly, who presented herself at Baker Street late in the evening, and implored his assistance and advice. It was vain to urge that his time was already fully occupied, for the young lady had come with the determination to tell her story, and it was evident that nothing short of force could get her out of the room until she had done so. With a resigned air and a somewhat weary smile, Holmes begged the beautiful intruder to take a seat, and to inform us what it was that was troubling her.

"At least it cannot be your health," said he, as his keen eyes darted over her; "so ardent a bicyclist must be full of energy."

She glanced down in surprise at her own feet, and I observed the slight roughening of the side of the sole caused by the friction of the edge of the pedal.

"Yes, I bicycle a good deal, Mr. Holmes, and that has something to do with my visit to you to-day."

My friend took the lady's ungloved hand, and examined it with as close an attention and as little sentiment as a scientist would show to a specimen.

"You will excuse me, I am sure. It is my business," said he, as he dropped it. "I nearly fell into the error of supposing that you were typewriting. Of course, it is obvious that it is music. You observe the spatulate finger-ends, Watson, which is common to both professions? There is a spirituality about the face, however"—she gently turned it towards the light—"which the typewriter does not generate. This lady is a musician."

"Yes, Mr. Holmes, I teach music."

"In the country, I presume, from your complexion."

"Yes, sir, near Farnham, on the borders of Surrey."

"A beautiful neighbourhood, and full of the most interesting associations. You remember, Watson, that it was near there that we took Archie Stamford, the forger. Now, Miss Violet, what has happened to you, near Farnham, on the borders of Surrey?"

The young lady, with great clearness and composure, made the following curious statement:

"My father is dead, Mr. Holmes. He was James Smith, who conducted the orchestra at the old Imperial Theatre. My mother and I were left without a relation in the world except one uncle, Ralph Smith, who went to Africa twenty-five years ago, and we have never had a word from him since. When father died, we were left very poor, but one day we were told that there was an advertisement in the *Times*, inquiring for our whereabouts. You can imagine how excited we were, for we thought that someone had left us a fortune. We went at once to the lawyer whose name was given in the paper. There we met two gentlemen, Mr. Carruthers and Mr. Woodley, who were home on a visit from South Africa. They said that my uncle was a friend of theirs, that he had died some months before in great poverty in Johannesburg, and that he had asked them with his last breath to hunt up his relations, and see that they were in no want. It seemed strange to us that Uncle Ralph, who took no notice of us when he was alive, should be so careful to look after us when he was dead, but Mr. Carruthers explained that the reason was that my uncle had just heard of the death of his brother, and so felt responsible for our fate."

"Excuse me," said Holmes. "When was this interview?"

"Last December—four months ago."

"Pray proceed."

"Mr. Woodley seemed to me to be a most odious person. He was for ever making eyes at me—a coarse, puffy-faced, red-moustached young man, with his hair plastered down on each side of his forehead. I thought that he was perfectly hateful—and I was sure that Cyril would not wish me to know such a person."

"Oh, Cyril is his name!" said Holmes, smiling.

The young lady blushed and laughed.

"Yes, Mr. Holmes, Cyril Morton, an electrical engineer, and we hope to be married at the end of the summer. Dear me, how did I get talking about him? What I wished to say was that Mr. Woodley was perfectly odious, but that Mr. Carruthers, who was a much older man, was more agreeable. He was a dark, sallow, clean-shaven, silent person, but he had polite manners and a pleasant smile. He inquired how we were left, and on finding that we were very poor, he suggested that I should come and teach music to his only daughter, aged ten. I said that I did not like to leave my mother, on which he suggested that I should go home to her every week-end, and he offered me a hundred a year, which was certainly splendid pay. So it ended by my accepting, and I went down to Chiltern Grange, about six miles from Farnham. Mr. Carruthers was a widower, but he had engaged a lady housekeeper, a very respectable, elderly person, called Mrs. Dixon, to look after his establishment. The child was a dear, and everything promised well. Mr. Carruthers was very kind and very musical, and we had most pleasant evenings together. Every week-end I went home to my mother in town.

"The first flaw in my happiness was the arrival of the red-moustached Mr. Woodley. He came for a visit of a week, and oh! it seemed three months to me. He was a dreadful person—a bully to everyone else, but to me something infinitely worse. He made odious love to me, boasted of his wealth, said that if I married him I could have the finest diamonds in London, and finally, when I would have nothing to do with him, he seized me in his arms one day after dinner—he was hideously strong—and swore that he would not let me go until I had kissed him. Mr. Carruthers came in and tore him from me, on which he turned upon his own host, knocking him down and cutting his face open. That was the end of his visit, as you can imagine. Mr. Carruthers apologized to me next day, and assured me that I should never be exposed to such an insult again. I have not seen Mr. Woodley since.

"And now, Mr. Holmes, I come at last to the special thing which has caused me to ask your advice to-day. You must know that every Saturday forenoon I ride on my bicycle to Farnham Station, in order to get the 12:22 to town. The road from Chiltern Grange is a lonely one, and at one spot it is particularly so, for it lies for over a mile between Charlington Heath upon one side and the woods which lie round Charlington Hall upon the other. You could not find a more lonely tract of road anywhere, and it is quite rare to meet so much as a cart, or a peasant, until you reach the high road near Crooksbury Hill. Two weeks ago I was passing this place, when I chanced to look back over my shoulder, and about two hundred yards behind me I saw a man, also on a bicycle. He seemed to be a middle-aged man, with a short, dark beard. I looked back before I reached Farnham, but the man was gone, so I thought no more about it. But you can imagine how surprised I was, Mr. Holmes, when, on my return on the Monday, I saw the same man on the same stretch of road. My astonishment was increased when the incident occurred again, exactly as before, on the following Saturday and Monday. He always kept his dis-

tance and did not molest me in any way, but still it certainly was very odd.
I mentioned it to Mr. Carruthers, who seemed interested in what I said,
and told me that he had ordered a horse and trap, so that in future I
should not pass over these lonely roads without some companion.

"The horse and trap were to have come this week, but for some reason they were not delivered, and again I had to cycle to the station. That
was this morning. You can think that I looked out when I came to Charlington Heath, and there, sure enough, was the man, exactly as he had
been the two weeks before. He always kept so far from me that I could
not clearly see his face, but it was certainly someone whom I did not
know. He was dressed in a dark suit with a cloth cap. The only thing about
his face that I could clearly see was his dark beard. To-day I was not
alarmed, but I was filled with curiosity, and I determined to find out who
he was and what he wanted. I slowed down my machine, but he slowed
down his. Then I stopped altogether, but he stopped also. Then I laid a
trap for him. There is a sharp turning of the road, and I pedalled very
quickly round this, and then I stopped and waited. I expected him to
shoot round and pass me before he could stop. But he never appeared.
Then I went back and looked round the corner. I could see a mile of road,
but he was not on it. To make it the more extraordinary, there was no side
road at this point down which he could have gone."

Holmes chuckled and rubbed his hands. "This case certainly presents
some features of its own," said he. "How much time elapsed between
your turning the corner and your discovery that the road was clear?"

"Two or three minutes."

"Then he could not have retreated down the road, and you say that
there are no side roads?"

"None."

"Then he certainly took a footpath on one side or the other."

"It could not have been on the side of the heath, or I should have seen
him."

"So, by the process of exclusion, we arrive at the fact that he made his
way toward Charlington Hall, which, as I understand, is situated in its
own grounds on one side of the road. Anything else?"

"Nothing, Mr. Holmes, save that I was so perplexed that I felt I should
not be happy until I had seen you and had your advice."

Holmes sat in silence for some little time.

"Where is the gentleman to whom you are engaged?" he asked at last.

"He is in the Midland Electrical Company, at Coventry."

"He would not pay you a surprise visit?"

"Oh, Mr. Holmes! As if I should not know him!"

"Have you had any other admirers?"

"Several before I knew Cyril."

"And since?"

"There was this dreadful man, Woodley, if you can call him an admirer."

"No one else?"

Our fair client seemed a little confused.

"Who was he?" asked Holmes.

"Oh, it may be a mere fancy of mine; but it had seemed to me sometimes that my employer, Mr. Carruthers, takes a great deal of interest in me. We are thrown rather together. I play his accompaniments in the evening. He has never said anything. He is a perfect gentleman. But a girl always knows."

"Ha!" Holmes looked grave. "What does he do for a living?"

"He is a rich man."

"No carriages or horses?"

"Well, at least he is fairly well-to-do. But he goes into the city two or three times a week. He is deeply interested in South African gold shares."

"You will let me know any fresh development, Miss Smith. I am very busy just now, but I will find time to make some inquiries into your case. In the meantime, take no step without letting me know. Good-bye, and I trust that we shall have nothing but good news from you."

"It is part of the settled order of Nature that such a girl should have followers," said Holmes, as he pulled at his meditative pipe, "but for choice not on bicycles in lonely country roads. Some secretive lover, beyond all doubt. But there are curious and suggestive details about the case, Watson."

"That he should appear only at that point?"

"Exactly. Our first effort must be to find who are the tenants of Charlington Hall. Then, again, how about the connection between Carruthers and Woodley, since they appear to be men of such a different type? How came they *both* to be so keen upon looking up Ralph Smith's relations? One more point. What sort of a ménage is it which pays double the market price for a governess but does not keep a horse, although six miles from the station? Odd, Watson—very odd!"

"You will go down?"

"No, my dear fellow, you will go down. This may be some trifling intrigue, and I cannot break my other important research for the sake of it. On Monday you will arrive early at Farnham; you will conceal yourself near Charlington Heath; you will observe these facts for yourself, and act as your own judgment advises. Then, having inquired as to the occupants of the Hall, you will come back to me and report. And now, Watson, not another word of the matter until we have a few solid stepping-stones on which we may hope to get across to our solution."

We had ascertained from the lady that she went down upon the Monday by the train which leaves Waterloo at 9:50, so I started early and caught the 9:13. At Farnham Station I had no difficulty in being directed to Charlington Heath. It was impossible to mistake the scene of the young lady's adventure, for the road runs between the open heath on one side and an old yew hedge upon the other, surrounding a park which is studded with magnificent trees. There was a main gateway of lichen-studded stone, each side pillar surmounted by mouldering heraldic emblems, but besides this central carriage drive I observed several points where there were gaps in the hedge and paths leading through them. The house was invisible from the road, but the surroundings all spoke of gloom and decay.

The heath was covered with golden patches of flowering gorse, gleaming magnificently in the light of the bright spring sunshine. Behind one of these clumps I took up my position, so as to command both the gateway of the Hall and a long stretch of the road upon either side. It had been deserted when I left it, but now I saw a cyclist riding down it from the opposite direction to that in which I had come. He was clad in a dark suit, and I saw that he had a black beard. On reaching the end of the Charlington grounds, he sprang from his machine and led it through a gap in the hedge, disappearing from my view.

A quarter of an hour passed, and then a second cyclist appeared. This time it was the young lady coming from the station. I saw her look about her as she came to the Charlington hedge. An instant later the man emerged from his hiding-place, sprang upon his cycle, and followed her. In all the broad landscape those were the only moving figures, the graceful girl sitting very straight upon her machine, and the man behind her bending low over his handle-bar with a curiously furtive suggestion in every movement. She looked back at him and slowed her pace. He slowed also. She stopped. He at once stopped, too, keeping two hundred yards behind her. Her next movement was as unexpected as it was spirited. She suddenly whisked her wheels round and dashed straight at him. He was as quick as she, however, and darted off in desperate flight. Presently she came back up the road again, her head haughtily in the air, not deigning to take any further notice of her silent attendant. He had turned also, and still kept his distance until the curve of the road hid them from my sight.

I remained in my hiding-place, and it was well that I did so, for presently the man reappeared, cycling slowly back. He turned in at the Hall gates, and dismounted from his machine. For some minutes I could see him standing among the trees. His hands were raised, and he seemed to be settling his necktie. Then he mounted his cycle, and rode away from me down the drive towards the Hall. I ran across the heath and peered through the trees. Far away I could catch glimpses of the old gray building with its bristling Tudor chimneys, but the drive ran through a dense shrubbery, and I saw no more of my man.

However, it seemed to me that I had done a fairly good morning's work, and I walked back in high spirits to Farnham. The local house agent could tell me nothing about Charlington Hall, and referred me to a well known firm in Pall Mall. There I halted on my way home, and met with courtesy from the representative. No, I could not have Charlington Hall for the summer. I was just too late. It had been let about a month ago. Mr. Williamson was the name of the tenant. He was a respectable, elderly gentleman. The polite agent was afraid he could say no more, as the affairs of his clients were not matters which he could discuss.

Mr. Sherlock Holmes listened with attention to the long report which I was able to present to him that evening, but it did not elicit that word of curt praise which I had hoped for and should have valued. On the contrary, his austere face was even more severe than usual as he commented upon the things that I had done and the things that I had not.

"Your hiding-place, my dear Watson, was very faulty. You should have been behind the hedge, then you would have had a close view of this interesting person. As it is, you were some hundreds of yards away and can tell me even less than Miss Smith. She thinks she does not know the man; I am convinced she does. Why, otherwise, should he be so desperately anxious that she should not get so near him as to see his features? You describe him as bending over the handle-bar. Concealment again, you see. You really have done remarkably badly. He returns to the house, and you want to find out who he is. You come to a London house agent!"

"What should I have done?" I cried, with some heat.

"Gone to the nearest public-house. That is the centre of country gossip. They would have told you every name, from the master to the scullery-maid. Williamson? It conveys nothing to my mind. If he is an elderly man he is not this active cyclist who sprints away from that young lady's athletic pursuit. What have we gained by your expedition? The knowledge that the girl's story is true. I never doubted it. That there is a connection between the cyclist and the Hall. I never doubted that either. That the Hall is tenanted by Williamson. Who's the better for that? Well, well, my dear sir, don't look so depressed. We can do little more until next Saturday, and in the meantime I may make one or two inquiries myself."

Next morning, we had a note from Miss Smith, recounting shortly and accurately the very incidents which I had seen, but the pith of the letter lay in the postscript:

> I am sure that you will respect my confidence, Mr. Holmes, when I tell you that my place here has become difficult, owing to the fact that my employer has proposed marriage to me. I am convinced that his feelings are most deep and most honourable. At the same time, my promise is of course given. He took my refusal very seriously, but also very gently. You can understand, however, that the situation is a little strained.

"Our young friend seems to be getting into deep waters," said Holmes, thoughtfully, as he finished the letter. "The case certainly presents more features of interest and more possibility of development than I had originally thought. I should be none the worse for a quiet, peaceful day in the country, and I am inclined to run down this afternoon and test one or two theories which I have formed."

Holmes's quiet day in the country had a singular termination, for he arrived at Baker Street late in the evening, with a cut lip and a discoloured lump upon his forehead, besides a general air of dissipation which would have made his own person the fitting object of a Scotland Yard investigation. He was immensely tickled by his own adventures and laughed heartily as he recounted them.

"I get so little active exercise that it is always a treat," said he. "You are aware that I have some proficiency in the good old British sport of boxing. Occasionally, it is of service; today, for example, I should have come to very ignominious grief without it."

I begged him to tell me what had occurred.

"I found that country pub which I had already recommended to your notice, and there I made my discreet inquiries. I was in the bar, and a garrulous landlord was giving me all that I wanted. Williamson is a white-bearded man, and he lives alone with a small staff of servants at the Hall. There is some rumor that he is or has been a clergyman, but one or two incidents of his short residence at the Hall struck me as peculiarly unecclesiastical. I have already made some inquiries at a clerical agency, and they tell me that there *was* a man of that name in orders, whose career has been a singularly dark one. The landlord further informed me that there are usually weekend visitors—'a warm lot, sir'—at the Hall, and especially one gentleman with a red moustache, Mr. Woodley by name, who was always there. We had got as far as this, when who should walk in but the gentleman himself, who had been drinking his beer in the tap-room and had heard the whole conversation. Who was I? What did I want? What did I mean by asking questions? He had a fine flow of language, and his adjectives were very vigorous. He ended a string of abuse by a vicious backhander, which I failed to entirely avoid. The next few minutes were delicious. It was a straight left against a slogging ruffian. I emerged as you see me. Mr. Woodley went home in a cart. So ended my country trip, and it must be confessed that, however enjoyable, my day on the Surrey border has not been much more profitable than your own."

The Thursday brought us another letter from our client.

You will not be surprised, Mr. Holmes [said she] to hear that I am leaving Mr. Carruthers's employment. Even the high pay cannot reconcile me to the discomforts of my situation. On Saturday I come up to town, and I do not intend to return. Mr. Carruthers has got a trap, and so the dangers of the lonely road, if there ever were any dangers, are now over.

As to the special cause of my leaving, it is not merely the strained situation with Mr. Carruthers, but it is the reappearance of that odious man, Mr. Woodley. He was always hideous, but he looks more awful than ever now, for he appears to have had an accident, and he is much disfigured. I saw him out of the window, but I am glad to say I did not meet him. He had a long talk with Mr. Carruthers, who seemed much excited afterwards. Woodley must be staying in the neighbourhood, for he did not sleep here, and yet I caught a glimpse of him again this morning, slinking about in the shrubbery. I would sooner have a savage wild animal loose about the place. I loathe and fear him more than I can say. How *can* Mr. Carruthers endure such a creature for a moment? However, all my troubles will be over on Saturday.

"So I trust, Watson, so I trust," said Holmes, gravely. "There is some deep intrigue going on round that little woman, and it is our duty to see that no one molests her upon that last journey. I think, Watson, that we must spare time to run down together on Saturday morning and make sure that this curious and inclusive investigation has no untoward ending."

I confess that I had not up to now taken a very serious view of the case, which had seemed to me rather grotesque and bizarre than dangerous. That a man should lie in wait for and follow a very handsome woman is no unheard-of thing, and if he has so little audacity that he not only dared not address her, but even fled from her approach, he was not a very formidable assailant. The ruffian Woodley was a very different person, but, except on one occasion, he had not molested our client, and now he visited the house of Carruthers without intruding upon her presence. The man on the bicycle was doubtless a member of those week-end parties at the Hall of which the publican* had spoken, but who he was, or what he wanted, was as obscure as ever. It was the severity of Holmes's manner and the fact that he slipped a revolver into his pocket before leaving our rooms which impressed me with the feeling that tragedy might prove to lurk behind this curious train of events.

A rainy night had been followed by a glorious morning, and the heath-covered countryside, with the glowing clumps of flowering gorse, seemed all the more beautiful to eyes which were weary of the duns and drabs and slate grays of London. Holmes and I walked along the broad, sandy road inhaling the fresh morning air and rejoicing in the music of the birds and the fresh breath of the spring. From a rise of the road on the shoulder of Crooksbury Hill, we could see the grim Hall bristling out from amidst the ancient oaks, which, old as they were, were still younger than the building which they surrounded. Holmes pointed down the long tract of road which wound, a reddish yellow band, between the brown of the heath and the budding green of the woods. Far away, a black dot, we could see a vehicle moving in our direction. Holmes gave an exclamation of impatience.

"I have given a margin of half an hour," said he. "If that is her trap, she must be making for the earlier train. I fear, Watson, that she will be past Charlington before we can possibly meet her."

From the instant that we passed the rise, we could no longer see the vehicle, but we hastened onward at such a pace that my sedentary life began to tell upon me, and I was compelled to fall behind. Holmes, however, was always in training, for he had inexhaustible stores of nervous energy upon which to draw. His springy step never slowed until suddenly, when he was a hundred yards in front of me, he halted, and I saw him throw up his hand with a gesture of grief and despair. At the same instant an empty dog-cart, the horse cantering, the reins trailing, appeared round the curve of the road and rattled swiftly towards us.

---

*Tavernkeeper.

"Too late, Watson, too late!" cried Holmes, as I ran panting to his side. "Fool that I was not to allow for that earlier train! It's abduction, Watson—abduction! Murder! Heaven knows what! Block the road! Stop the horse! That's right. Now, jump in, and let us see if I can repair the consequences of my own blunder."

We had sprung into the dog-cart, and Holmes, after turning the horse, gave it a sharp cut with the whip, and we flew back along the road. As we turned the curve, the whole stretch of road between the Hall and the heath was opened up. I grasped Holmes's arm.

"That's the man!" I gasped.

A solitary cyclist was coming towards us. His head was down and his shoulders rounded, as he put every ounce of energy that he possessed on to the pedals. He was flying like a racer. Suddenly he raised his bearded face, saw us close to him, and pulled up, springing from his machine. That coal-black beard was in singular contrast to the pallor of his face, and his eyes were as bright as if he had a fever. He stared at us and at the dog-cart. Then a look of amazement came over his face.

"Halloa! Stop there!" he shouted, holding his bicycle to block our road. "Where did you get that dog-cart? Pull up, man!" he yelled, drawing a pistol from his side pocket. "Pull up, I say, or, by George, I'll put a bullet into your horse."

Holmes threw the reins into my lap and sprang down from the cart.

"You're the man we want to see. Where is Miss Violet Smith?" he said, in his quick, clear way.

"That's what I'm asking you. You're in her dog-cart. You ought to know where she is."

"We met the dog-cart on the road. There was no one in it. We drove back to help the young lady."

"Good Lord! Good Lord! What shall I do?" cried the stranger, in an ecstasy of despair. "They've got her, that hell-hound Woodley and the blackguard parson. Come, man, come, if you really are her friend. Stand by me and we'll save her, if I have to leave my carcass in Charlington Wood."

He ran distractedly, his pistol in his hand, towards a gap in the hedge. Holmes followed him, and I, leaving the horse grazing beside the road, followed Holmes.

"This is where they came through," said he, pointing to the marks of several feet upon the muddy path. "Halloa! Stop a minute! Who's this in the bush?"

It was a young fellow about seventeen, dressed like an ostler, with leather cords and gaiters. He lay upon his back, his knees drawn up, a terrible cut upon his head. He was insensible, but alive. A glance at his wound told me that it had not penetrated the bone.

"That's Peter, the groom," cried the stranger. "He drove her. The beasts have pulled him off and clubbed him. Let him lie; we can't do him any good, but we may save her from the worst fate that can befall a woman."

We ran frantically down the path, which wound among the trees. We had reached the shrubbery which surrounded the house when Holmes pulled up.

"They didn't go to the house. Here are their marks on the left—here, beside the laurel bushes. Ah! I said so."

As he spoke, a woman's shrill scream—a scream which vibrated with a frenzy of horror—burst from the thick, green clump of bushes in front of us. It ended suddenly on its highest note with a choke and a gurgle.

"This way! This way! They are in the bowling-alley," cried the stranger, darting through the bushes. "Ah, the cowardly dogs! Follow me, gentlemen! Too late! too late! by the living Jingo!"

We had broken suddenly into a lovely glade of greensward surrounded by ancient trees. On the farther side of it, under the shadow of a mighty oak, there stood a singular group of three people. One was a woman, our client, drooping and faint, a handkerchief round her mouth. Opposite her stood a brutal, heavy-faced, red-moustached young man, his gaitered legs parted wide, one arm akimbo, the other waving a riding crop, his whole attitude suggestive of triumphant bravado. Between them an elderly, gray-bearded man, wearing a short surplice over a light tweed suit, had evidently just completed the wedding service, for he pocketed his prayer-book as we appeared, and slapped the sinister bridegroom upon the back in jovial congratulation.

"They're married?" I gasped.

"Come on!" cried our guide; "come on!" He rushed across the glade, Holmes and I at his heels. As we approached, the lady staggered against the trunk of the tree for support. Williamson, the ex-clergyman, bowed to us with mock politeness, and the bully, Woodley, advanced with a shout of brutal and exultant laughter.

"You can take your beard off, Bob," said he. "I know you, right enough. Well, you and your pals have just come in time for me to be able to introduce you to Mrs. Woodley."

Our guide's answer was a singular one. He snatched off the dark beard which had disguised him and threw it on the ground, disclosing a long, sallow, clean-shaven face below it. Then he raised his revolver and covered the young ruffian, who was advancing upon him with his dangerous riding crop swinging in his hand.

"Yes," said our ally, "I *am* Bob Carruthers. and I'll see this woman righted, if I have to swing for it. I told you what I'd do if you molested her, and, by the Lord! I'll be as good as my word."

"You're too late. She's my wife."

"No, she's your widow."

His revolver cracked, and I saw the blood spurt from the front of Woodley's waistcoat. He spun round with a scream and fell upon his back, his hideous red face turning suddenly to a dreadful mottled pallor. The old man, still clad in his surplice, burst into such a string of foul oaths as I have never heard, and pulled out a revolver of his own, but, before he could raise it, he was looking down the barrel of Holmes's weapon.

"Enough of this," said my friend, coldly. "Drop that pistol! Watson, pick it up! Hold it to his head! Thank you. You, Carruthers, give me that revolver. We'll have no more violence. Come, hand it over!"

"Who are you, then?"

"My name is Sherlock Holmes."

"Good Lord!"

"You have heard of me, I see. I will represent the official police until their arrival. Here, you!" he shouted to a frightened groom, who had appeared at the edge of the glade. "Come here. Take this note as hard as you can ride to Farnham." He scribbled a few words upon a leaf from his notebook. "Give it to the superintendent at the police-station. Until he comes, I must detain you all under my personal custody."

The strong, masterful personality of Holmes dominated the tragic scene, and all were equally puppets in his hands. Williamson and Carruthers found themselves carrying the wounded Woodley into the house, and I gave my arm to the frightened girl. The injured man was laid on his bed, and at Holmes's request I examined him. I carried my report to where he sat in the old tapestry-hung dining-room with his two prisoners before him.

"He will live," said I.

"What!" cried Carruthers, springing out of his chair. "I'll go upstairs and finish him first. Do you tell me that that girl, that angel, is to be tied to Roaring Jack Woodley for life?"

"You need not concern yourself about that," said Holmes. "There are two very good reasons why she should, under no circumstances, be his wife. In the first place, we are very safe in questioning Mr. Williamson's right to solemnize a marriage."

"I have been ordained," cried the old rascal.

"And also unfrocked."

"Once a clergyman, always a clergyman."

"I think not. How about the licence?"

"We had a licence for the marriage. I have it here in my pocket."

"Then you got it by a trick. But, in any case, a forced marriage is no marriage, but it is a very serious felony, as you will discover before you have finished. You'll have time to think the point out during the next ten years or so, unless I am mistaken. As to you, Carruthers, you would have done better to keep your pistol in your pocket."

"I begin to think so, Mr. Holmes, but when I thought of all the precaution I had taken to shield this girl—for I loved her, Mr. Holmes, and it is the only time that ever I knew what love was—it fairly drove me mad to think that she was in the power of the greatest brute and bully in South Africa—a man whose name is a holy terror from Kimberley to Johannesburg. Why, Mr. Holmes, you'll hardly believe it, but ever since that girl has been in my employment I never once let her go past this house, where I knew the rascals were lurking, without following her on my bicycle, just to see that she came to no harm. I kept my distance from her, and I wore a beard, so that she should not recognize me, for she is a good and high-spirited girl, and she wouldn't have stayed in my employment long if she had thought that I was following her about the country roads."

"Why didn't you tell her of her danger?"

"Because then, again, she would have left me, and I couldn't bear to face that. Even if she couldn't love me, it was a great deal to me just to see her dainty form about the house, and to hear the sound of her voice."

"Well," said I, "you call that love, Mr. Carruthers, but I should call it selfishness."

"Maybe the two things go together. Anyhow, I couldn't let her go. Besides, with this crowd about, it was well that she should have someone near to look after her. Then, when the cable came, I knew they were bound to make a move."

"What cable?"

Carruthers took a telegram from his pocket.

"That's it," said he.

It was short and concise:

THE OLD MAN IS DEAD.

"Hum!" said Holmes. "I think I see how things worked, and I can understand how this message would, as you say, bring them to a head. But while you wait, you might tell me what you can."

The old reprobate with the surplice burst into a volley of bad language.

"By heaven!" said he, "if you squeal on us, Bob Carruthers, I'll serve you as you served Jack Woodley. You can bleat about the girl to your heart's content, for that's your own affair, but if you round on your pals to this plain-clothes copper, it will be the worst day's work that ever you did."

"Your reverence need not be excited," said Holmes, lighting a cigarette. "The case is clear enough against you, and all I ask is a few details for my private curiosity. However, if there's any difficulty in your telling me, I'll do the talking, and then you will see how far you have a chance of holding back your secrets. In the first place, three of you came from South Africa on this game—you Williamson, you Carruthers, and Woodley."

"Lie number one," said the old man; "I never saw either of them until two months ago, and I have never been in Africa in my life, so you can put that in your pipe and smoke it, Mr. Busybody Holmes!"

"What he says is true," said Carruthers.

"Well, well, two of you came over. His reverence is our own home-made article. You had known Ralph Smith in South Africa. You had reason to believe he would not live long. You found out that his niece would inherit his fortune. How's that—eh?"

Carruthers nodded and Williamson swore.

"She was next of kin, no doubt, and you were aware that the old fellow would make no will."

"Couldn't read or write," said Carruthers.

"So you came over, the two of you, and hunted up the girl. The idea was that one of you was to marry her, and the other have a share of the plunder. For some reason, Woodley was chosen as the husband. Why was that?"

"We played cards for her on the voyage. He won."

"I see. You got the young lady into your service, and there Woodley was to do the courting. She recognized the drunken brute that he was, and would have nothing to do with him. Meanwhile, your arrangement was rather upset by the fact that you had yourself fallen in love with the lady. You could no longer bear the idea of this ruffian owning her?"

"No, by George, I couldn't!"

"There was a quarrel between you. He left you in a rage, and began to make his own plans independently of you."

"It strikes me, Williamson, there isn't very much that we can tell this gentleman," cried Carruthers, with a bitter laugh. "Yes, we quarreled, and he knocked me down. I am level with him on that, anyhow. Then I lost sight of him. That was when he picked up with this outcast padre here. I found that they had set up housekeeping together at this place on the line that she had to pass for the station. I kept my eye on her after that, for I knew there was some devilry in the wind. I saw them from time to time, for I was anxious to know what they were after. Two days ago Woodley came up to my house with this cable, which showed that Ralph Smith was dead. He asked me if I would stand by the bargain. I said I would not. He asked me if I would marry the girl myself and give him a share. I said I would willingly do so, but that she would not have me. He said, 'Let us get her married first, and after a week or two she may see things a bit different.' I said I would have nothing to do with violence. So he went off cursing, like the foul-mouthed blackguard that he was, and swearing that he would have her yet. She was leaving me this week-end, and I had got a trap to take her to the station, but I was so uneasy in my mind that I followed her on my bicycle. She had got a start, however, and before I could catch her, the mischief was done. The first thing I knew about it was when I saw you two gentlemen driving back in her dog-cart."

Holmes rose and tossed the end of his cigarette into the grate. "I have been very obtuse, Watson," said he. "When in your report you said that you had seen the cyclist as you thought arrange his necktie in the shrubbery, that alone should have told me all. However, we may congratulate ourselves upon a curious and, in some respects, a unique case. I perceive three of the county constabulary in the drive, and I am glad to see that the little ostler is able to keep pace with them, so it is likely that neither he nor the interesting bridegroom will be permanently damaged by their morning's adventures. I think, Watson, that in your medical capacity, you might wait upon Miss Smith and tell her that if she is sufficiently recovered, we shall be happy to escort her to her mother's home. If she is not quite convalescent, you will find that a hint that we were about to telegraph to a young electrician in the Midlands would probably complete the cure. As to you, Mr. Carruthers, I think that you have done what you could to make amends for your share in an evil plot. There is my card, sir, and if my evidence can be of help in your trial, it shall be at your disposal."

In the whirl of our incessant activity, it has often been difficult for me, as the reader has probably observed, to round off my narratives, and to give those final details which the curious might expect. Each case has been the prelude to another, and the crisis once over, the actors have passed for ever out of our busy lives. I find, however, a short note at the end of my manuscript dealing with this case, in which I have put it upon record that Miss Violet Smith did indeed inherit a large fortune, and that she is now the wife of Cyril Morton, the senior partner of Morton & Kennedy, the famous Westminster electricians. Williamson and Woodley were both tried for abduction and assault, the former getting seven years and the latter ten. Of the fate of Carruthers, I have no record, but I am sure that his assault was not viewed very gravely by the court, since Woodley had the reputation of being a most dangerous ruffian, and I think that a few months were sufficient to satisfy the demands of justice.

THE ADVENTURE OF THE
PRIORY SCHOOL

We have had some dramatic entrances and exits upon our small stage at Baker Street, but I cannot recollect anything more sudden and startling than the first appearance of Thorneycroft Huxtable, M.A., Ph.D., etc. His card, which seemed too small to carry the weight of his academic distinctions, preceded him by a few seconds, and then he entered himself—so large, so pompous, and so dignified that he was the very embodiment of self-possession and solidity. And yet his first action, when the door had closed behind him, was to stagger against the table, whence he slipped down upon the floor, and there was that majestic figure prostrate and insensible upon our bearskin hearthrug.

We had sprung to our feet, and for a few moments we stared in silent amazement at this ponderous piece of wreckage, which told of some sudden and fatal storm far out on the ocean of life. Then Holmes hurried with a cushion for his head, and I with brandy for his lips. The heavy, white face was seamed with lines of trouble, the hanging pouches under the closed eyes were leaden in colour, the loose mouth drooped dolorously at the corners, the rolling chins were unshaven. Collar and shirt bore the grime of a long journey, and the hair bristled unkempt from the well-shaped head. It was a sorely stricken man who lay before us.

"What is it, Watson?" asked Holmes.

"Absolute exhaustion—possibly mere hunger and fatigue," said I, with my finger on the thready pulse, where the stream of life trickled thin and small.

"Return ticket from Mackleton, in the north of England," said Holmes, drawing it from the watch-pocket. "It is not twelve o'clock yet. He has certainly been an early starter."

The puckered eyelids had begun to quiver, and now a pair of vacant gray eyes looked up at us. An instant later the man had scrambled on to his feet, his face crimson with shame.

"Forgive this weakness, Mr. Holmes, I have been a little overwrought. Thank you, if I might have a glass of milk and a biscuit, I have no doubt that I should be better. I came personally, Mr. Holmes, in order to insure that you would return with me. I feared that no telegram would convince you of the absolute urgency of the case."

"When you are quite restored——"

"I am quite well again. I cannot imagine how I came to be so weak. I wish you, Mr. Holmes, to come to Mackleton with me by the next train."

My friend shook his head.

"My colleague, Dr. Watson, could tell you that we are very busy at present. I am retained in this case of the Ferrers Documents, and the Abergavenny murder is coming up for trial. Only a very important issue could call me from London at present."

"Important!" Our visitor threw up his hands. "Have you heard nothing of the abduction of the only son of the Duke of Holdernesse?"

"What! the late Cabinet Minister?"

"Exactly. We had tried to keep it out of the papers, but there was some rumor in the *Globe* last night. I thought it might have reached your ears."

Holmes shot out his long, thin arm and picked out Volume "H" in his encyclopædia of reference.

"'Holdernesse, 6th Duke, K.G.,* P.C.†—half the alphabet! 'Baron Beverley, Earl of Carston'—dear me, what a list! 'Lord Lieutenant of Hallamshire since 1900. Married Edith, daughter of Sir Charles Appledore, 1888. Heir and only child, Lord Saltire. Owns about two hundred and fifty thousand acres. Minerals in Lancashire and Wales. Address: Canton House Terrace; Holdernesse Hall, Hallamshire; Carston Castle, Bangor, Wales. Lord of the Admiralty, 1872; Chief Secretary of State for—' Well, well, this man is certainly one of the greatest subjects of the Crown!"

"The greatest and perhaps the wealthiest. I am aware, Mr. Holmes, that you take a very high line in professional matters, and that you are prepared to work for the work's sake. I may tell you, however, that his Grace has already intimated that a check for five thousand pounds will be handed over to the person who can tell him where his son is, and another thousand to him who can name the man or men who have taken him."

"It is a princely offer," said Holmes. "Watson, I think that we shall accompany Dr. Huxtable back to the north of England. And now, Dr. Huxtable, when you have consumed that milk, you will kindly tell me what has happened, when it happened, how it happened, and, finally, what Dr. Thorneycroft Huxtable, of the Priory School, near Mackleton, has to do with the matter, and why he comes three days after an event— the state of your chin gives the date—to ask for my humble services."

Our visitor had consumed his milk and biscuits. The light had come back to his eyes and the colour to his cheeks, as he set himself with great vigour and lucidity to explain the situation.

"I must inform you, gentlemen, that the Priory is a preparatory school, of which I am the founder and principal. *Huxtable's Sidelights on Horace* may possibly recall my name to your memories. The Priory is, without exception, the best and most select preparatory school in England. Lord Leverstoke, the Earl of Blackwater, Sir Cathcart Soames—they all have intrusted their sons to me. But I felt that my school had reached its zenith when, three weeks ago, the Duke of Holdernesse sent Mr. James Wilder, his secretary, with the intimation that young Lord Saltire, ten years old, his only son and heir, was about to be committed to my charge. Little did

---

*Knight of the Garter; member of the most exclusive Order in Britain.

†Privy Councillor; an appointed member to a mostly ceremonial council that advises the sovereign.

I think that this would be the prelude to the most crushing misfortune of my life.

"On May 1st the boy arrived, that being the beginning of the summer term. He was a charming youth, and he soon fell into our ways. I may tell you—I trust that I am not indiscreet, but half-confidences are absurd in such a case—that he was not entirely happy at home. It is an open secret that the Duke's married life had not been a peaceful one, and the matter had ended in a separation by mutual consent, the Duchess taking up her residence in the south of France. This had occurred very shortly before, and the boy's sympathies are known to have been strongly with his mother. He moped after her departure from Holdernesse Hall, and it was for this reason that the Duke desired to send him to my establishment. In a fortnight the boy was quite at home with us and was apparently absolutely happy.

"He was last seen on the night of May 13th—that is, the night of last Monday. His room was on the second floor and was approached through another larger room, in which two boys were sleeping. These boys saw and heard nothing, so that it is certain that young Saltire did not pass out that way. His window was open, and there is a stout ivy plant leading to the ground. We could trace no footmarks below, but it is sure that this is the only possible exit.

"His absence was discovered at seven o'clock on Tuesday morning. His bed had been slept in. He had dressed himself fully, before going off, in his usual school suit of black Eton jacket and dark gray trousers. There were no signs that anyone had entered the room, and it is quite certain that anything in the nature of cries or a struggle would have been heard, since Caunter, the elder boy in the inner room, is a very light sleeper.

"When Lord Saltire's disappearance was discovered, I at once called a roll of the whole establishment—boys, masters, and servants. It was then that we ascertained that Lord Saltire had not been alone in his flight. Heidegger, the German master, was missing. His room was on the second floor, at the farther end of the building, facing the same way as Lord Saltire's. His bed had also been slept in, but he had apparently gone away partly dressed, since his shirt and socks were lying on the floor. He had undoubtedly let himself down by the ivy, for we could see the marks of his feet where he had landed on the lawn. His bicycle was kept in a small shed beside this lawn, and it also was gone.

"He had been with me for two years, and came with the best references, but he was a silent, morose man, not very popular either with masters or boys. No trace could be found of the fugitives, and now, on Thursday morning, we are as ignorant as we were on Tuesday. Inquiry was, of course, made at once at Holdernesse Hall. It is only a few miles away, and we imagined that, in some sudden attack of homesickness, he had gone back to his father, but nothing had been heard of him. The Duke is greatly agitated, and, as to me, you have seen yourselves the state of nervous prostration to which the suspense and the responsibility have reduced me. Mr. Holmes, if ever you put forward your full powers, I implore you to do so now, for never in your life could you have a case which is more worthy of them."

Sherlock Holmes had listened with the utmost intentness to the statement of the unhappy schoolmaster. His drawn brows and the deep furrow between them showed that he needed no exhortation to concentrate all his attention upon a problem which, apart from the tremendous interests involved, must appeal so directly to his love of the complex and the unusual. He now drew out his notebook and jotted down one or two memoranda.

"You have been very remiss in not coming to me sooner," said he, severely. "You start me on my investigation with a very serious handicap. It is inconceivable, for example, that this ivy and this lawn would have yielded nothing to an expert observer."

"I am not to blame, Mr. Holmes. His Grace was extremely desirous to avoid all public scandal. He was afraid of his family unhappiness being dragged before the world. He has a deep horror of anything of the kind."

"But there has been some official investigation?"

"Yes, sir, and it has proved most disappointing. An apparent clue was at once obtained, since a boy and a young man were reported to have been seen leaving a neighbouring station by an early train. Only last night we had news that the couple had been hunted down in Liverpool, and they prove to have no connection whatever with the matter in hand. Then it was that in my despair and disappointment, after a sleepless night, I came straight to you by the early train."

"I suppose the local investigation was relaxed while this false clue was being followed up?"

"It was entirely dropped."

"So that three days have been wasted: The affair has been most deplorably handled."

"I feel it and admit it."

"And yet the problem should be capable of ultimate solution. I shall be very happy to look into it. Have you been able to trace any connection between the missing boy and this German master?"

"None at all."

"Was he in the master's class?"

"No, he never exchanged a word with him, so far as I know."

"That is certainly very singular. Had the boy a bicycle?"

"No."

"Was any other bicycle missing?"

"No."

"Is that certain?"

"Quite."

"Well, now, you do not mean to seriously suggest that this German rode off upon a bicycle in the dead of the night, bearing the boy in his arms?"

"Certainly not."

"Then what is the theory in your mind?"

"The bicycle may have been a blind. It may have been hidden somewhere, and the pair gone off on foot."

"Quite so, but it seems rather an absurd blind, does it not? Were there other bicycles in this shed?"

"Several."

"Would he not have hidden *a couple*, had he desired to give the idea that they had gone off upon them?"

"I suppose he would."

"Of course he would. The blind theory won't do. But the incident is an admirable starting-point for an investigation. After all, a bicycle is not an easy thing to conceal or to destroy. One other question. Did anyone call to see the boy on the day before he disappeared?"

"No."

"Did he get any letters?"

"Yes, one letter."

"From whom?"

"From his father."

"Do you open the boys' letters?"

"No."

"How do you know it was from the father?"

"The coat of arms was on the envelope, and it was addressed in the Duke's peculiar stiff hand. Besides, the Duke remembers having written."

"When had he a letter before that?"

"Not for several days."

"Had he ever one from France?"

"No, never."

"You see the point of my questions, of course. Either the boy was carried off by force or he went of his own free will. In the latter case, you would expect that some prompting from outside would be needed to make so young a lad do such a thing. If he has had no visitors, that prompting must have come in letters; hence I try to find out who were his correspondents."

"I fear I cannot help you much. His only correspondent, so far as I know, was his own father."

"Who wrote to him on the very day of his disappearance. Were the relations between father and son very friendly?"

"His Grace is never very friendly with anyone. He is completely immersed in large public questions, and is rather inaccessible to all ordinary emotions. But he was always kind to the boy in his own way."

"But the sympathies of the latter were with the mother?"

"Yes."

"Did he say so?"

"No."

"The Duke, then?"

"Good heaven, no!"

"Then how could you know?"

"I have had some confidential talks with Mr. James Wilder, his Grace's secretary. It was he who gave me the information about Lord Saltire's feelings."

"I see. By the way, that last letter of the Duke's—was it found in the boy's room after he was gone?"

"No, he had taken it with him. I think, Mr. Holmes, it is time that we were leaving for Euston."

"I will order a four-wheeler. In a quarter of an hour, we shall be at your service. If you are telegraphing home, Dr. Huxtable, it would be well to allow the people in your neighbourhood to imagine that the inquiry is still going on in Liverpool, or wherever else that red herring led your pack. In the meantime I will do a little quiet work at your own doors, and perhaps the scent is not so cold but that two old hounds like Watson and myself may get a sniff of it."

That evening found us in the cold, bracing atmosphere of the Peak country, in which Dr. Huxtable's famous school is situated. It was already dark when we reached it. A card was lying on the hall table, and the butler whispered something to his master, who turned to us with agitation in every heavy feature.

"The Duke is here," said he. "The Duke and Mr. Wilder are in the study. Come, gentlemen, and I will introduce you."

I was, of course, familiar with the pictures of the famous statesman, but the man himself was very different from his representation. He was a tall and stately person, scrupulously dressed, with a drawn, thin face, and a nose which was grotesquely curved and long. His complexion was of a dead pallor, which was more startling by contrast with a long, dwindling beard of vivid red, which flowed down over his white waistcoat, with his watch-chain gleaming through its fringe. Such was the stately presence who looked stonily at us from the centre of Dr. Huxtable's hearthrug. Beside him stood a very young man, whom I understood to be Wilder, the private secretary. He was small, nervous, alert, with intelligent light-blue eyes and mobile features. It was he who at once, in an incisive and positive tone, opened the conversation.

"I called this morning, Dr. Huxtable, too late to prevent you from starting for London. I learned that your object was to invite Mr. Sherlock Holmes to undertake the conduct of this case. His Grace is surprised, Dr. Huxtable, that you should have taken such a step without consulting him."

"When I learned that the police had failed——"

"His Grace is by no means convinced that the police have failed."

"But surely, Mr. Wilder——"

"You are well aware, Dr. Huxtable, that his Grace is particularly anxious to avoid all public scandal. He prefers to take as few people as possible into his confidence."

"The matter can be easily remedied," said the browbeaten doctor; "Mr. Sherlock Holmes can return to London by the morning train."

"Hardly that, Doctor, hardly that," said Holmes, in his blandest voice. "This northern air is invigorating and pleasant, so I propose to spend a few days upon your moors, and to occupy my mind as best I may.

Whether I have the shelter of your roof or of the village inn is, of course, for you to decide."

I could see that the unfortunate doctor was in the last stage of indecision, from which he was rescued by the deep, sonorous voice of the red-bearded Duke, which boomed out like a dinner-gong.

"I agree with Mr. Wilder, Dr. Huxtable, that you would have done wisely to consult me. But since Mr. Holmes has already been taken into your confidence, it would indeed be absurd that we should not avail ourselves of his services. Far from going to the inn, Mr. Holmes, I should be pleased if you would come and stay with me at Holdernesse Hall."

"I thank your Grace. For the purposes of my investigation, I think that it would be wiser for me to remain at the scene of the mystery."

"Just as you like, Mr. Holmes. Any information which Mr. Wilder or I can give you is, of course, at your disposal."

"It will probably be necessary for me to see you at the Hall," said Holmes. "I would only ask you now, sir, whether you have formed any explanation in your own mind as to the mysterious disappearance of your son?"

"No, sir, I have not."

"Excuse me if I allude to that which is painful to you, but I have no alternative. Do you think that the Duchess had anything to do with the matter?"

The great minister showed perceptible hesitation.

"I do not think so," he said, at last.

"The other most obvious explanation is that the child has been kidnapped for the purpose of levying ransom. You have not had any demand of the sort?"

"No, sir."

"One more question, your Grace. I understand that you wrote to your son upon the day when this incident occurred."

"No, I wrote upon the day before."

"Exactly. But he received it on that day?"

"Yes."

"Was there anything in your letter which might have unbalanced him or induced him to take such a step?"

"No, sir, certainly not."

"Did you post that letter yourself?"

The nobleman's reply was interrupted by his secretary, who broke in with some heat.

"His Grace is not in the habit of posting letters himself," said he. "This letter was laid with others upon the study table, and I myself put them in the post-bag."

"You are sure this one was among them?"

"Yes, I observed it."

"How many letters did your Grace write that day?"

"Twenty or thirty. I have a large correspondence. But surely this is somewhat irrelevant?"

"Not entirely," said Holmes.

"For my own part," the Duke continued, "I have advised the police to turn their attention to the south of France. I have already said that I do not believe that the Duchess would encourage so monstrous an action, but the lad had the most wrong-headed opinions, and it is possible that he may have fled to her, aided and abetted by this German. I think, Dr. Huxtable, that we will now return to the Hall."

I could see that there were other questions which Holmes would have wished to put, but the nobleman's abrupt manner showed that the interview was at an end. It was evident that to his intensely aristocratic nature this discussion of his intimate family affairs with a stranger was most abhorrent, and that he feared lest every fresh question would throw a fiercer light into the discreetly shadowed corners of his ducal history.

When the nobleman and his secretary had left, my friend flung himself at once with characteristic eagerness into the investigation.

The boy's chamber was carefully examined, and yielded nothing save the absolute conviction that it was only through the window that he could have escaped. The German master's room and effects gave no further clue. In his case a trailer of ivy had given way under his weight, and we saw by the light of a lantern the mark on the lawn where his heels had come down. That one dint in the short, green grass was the only material witness left of this inexplicable nocturnal flight.

Sherlock Holmes left the house alone, and only returned after eleven. He had obtained a large ordnance map of the neighbourhood, and this he brought into my room, where he laid it out on the bed, and, having balanced the lamp in the middle of it, he began to smoke over it, and occasionally to point out objects of interest with the reeking amber of his pipe.

"This case grows upon me, Watson," said he. "There are decidedly some points of interest in connection with it. In this early stage, I want you to realize those geographical features which may have a good deal to do with our investigation.

"Look at this map. This dark square is the Priory School. I'll put a pin in it. Now, this line is the main road. You see that it runs east and west past the school, and you see also that there is no side road for a mile either way. If these two folk passed away by road, it was *this* road."

"Exactly."

"By a singular and happy chance, we are able to some extent to check what passed along this road during the night in question. At this point, where my pipe is now resting, a county constable was on duty from twelve to six. It is, as you perceive, the first cross-road on the east side. This man declares that he was not absent from his post for an instant, and he is positive that neither boy nor man could have gone that way unseen. I have spoken with this policeman to-night, and he appears to me to be a perfectly reliable person. That blocks this end. We have now to deal with the other. There is an inn here, the Red Bull, the landlady of which was ill. She had sent to Mackleton for a doctor, but he did not arrive until morning, being absent at another case. The people at the inn were alert all

HOLMES'S MAP OF THE NEIGHBOURHOOD OF THE SCHOOL

night, awaiting his coming, and one or other of them seems to have continually had an eye upon the road. They declare that no one passed. If their evidence is good, then we are fortunate enough to be able to block the west, and also to be able to say that the fugitives did *not* use the road at all."

"But the bicycle?" I objected.

"Quite so. We will come to the bicycle presently. To continue our reasoning: if these people did not go by the road, they must have traversed the country to the north of the house or to the south of the house. That is certain. Let us weigh the one against the other. On the south of the house is, as you perceive, a large district of arable land, cut up into small fields, with stone walls between them. There, I admit that a bicycle is impossible. We can dismiss the idea. We turn to the country on the north. Here there lies a grove of trees, marked as the 'Ragged Shaw,' and on the farther side stretches a great rolling moor, Lower Gill Moor, extending for ten miles and sloping gradually upward. Here, at one side of this wilderness, is Holdernesse Hall, ten miles by road, but only six across the moor. It is a peculiarly desolate plain. A few moor farmers have small holdings, where they rear sheep and cattle. Except these, the plover and the curlew are the only inhabitants until you come to the Chesterfield high road. There is a church there, you see, a few cottages, and an inn. Beyond that the hills become precipitous. Surely it is here to the north that our quest must lie."

"But the bicycle?" I persisted.

"Well, well!" said Holmes, impatiently. "A good cyclist does not need a high road. The moor is intersected with paths, and the moon was at the full. Halloa! what is this?"

There was an agitated knock at the door, and an instant afterwards Dr. Huxtable was in the room. In his hand he held a blue cricket-cap with a white chevron on the peak.

"At last we have a clue!" he cried. "Thank heaven! at last we are on the dear boy's track! It is his cap."

"Where was it found?"

"In the van of the gipsies who camped on the moor. They left on Tuesday. To-day the police traced them down and examined their caravan. This was found."

"How do they account for it?"

"They shuffled and lied—said that they found it on the moor on Tuesday morning. They know where he is, the rascals! Thank goodness, they are all safe under lock and key. Either the fear of the law or the Duke's purse will certainly get out of them all that they know."

"So far, so good," said Holmes, when the doctor had at last left the room. "It at least bears out the theory that it is on the side of the Lower Gill Moor that we must hope for results. The police have really done nothing locally, save the arrest of these gipsies. Look here, Watson! There is a watercourse across the moor. You see it marked here in the map. In some parts it widens into a morass. This is particularly so in the region between Holdernesse Hall and the school. It is vain to look elsewhere for tracks in this dry weather, but at *that* point there is certainly a chance of some record being left. I will call you early to-morrow morning, and you and I will try if we can throw some little light upon the mystery."

The day was just breaking when I woke to find the long, thin form of Holmes by my bedside. He was fully dressed, and had apparently already been out.

"I have done the lawn and the bicycle shed," said he. "I have also had a ramble through the Ragged Shaw. Now, Watson, there is cocoa ready in the next room. I must beg you to hurry, for we have a great day before us."

His eyes shone, and his cheek was flushed with the exhilaration of the master workman who sees his work lie ready before him. A very different Holmes, this active, alert man, from the introspective and pallid dreamer of Baker Street. I felt, as I looked upon that supple figure, alive with nervous energy, that it was indeed a strenuous day that awaited us.

And yet it opened in the blackest disappointment. With high hopes we struck across the peaty, russet moor, intersected with a thousand sheep paths, until we came to the broad, light-green belt which marked the morass between us and Holdernesse. Certainly, if the lad had gone homeward, he must have passed this, and he could not pass it without leaving his traces. But no sign of him or the German could be seen. With a darkening face my friend strode along the margin, eagerly observant of every muddy stain upon the mossy surface. Sheep-marks there were in profusion, and at one place, some miles down, cows had left their tracks. Nothing more.

"Check number one," said Holmes, looking gloomily over the rolling expanse of the moor. "There is another morass down yonder, and a narrow neck between. Halloa! halloa! halloa! what have we here?"

We had come on a small black ribbon of pathway. In the middle of it, clearly marked on the sodden soil, was the track of a bicycle.

"Hurrah!" I cried. "We have it."

But Holmes was shaking his head, and his face was puzzled and expectant rather than joyous.

"A bicycle, certainly, but not *the* bicycle," said he. "I am familiar with forty-two different impressions left by tyres. This, as you perceive, is a Dunlop, with a patch upon the outer cover. Heidegger's tyres were Palmer's, leaving longitudinal stripes. Aveling, the mathematical master, was sure upon the point. Therefore, it is not Heidegger's track."

"The boy's, then?"

"Possibly, if we could prove a bicycle to have been in his possession. But this we have utterly failed to do. This track, as you perceive, was made by a rider who was going from the direction of the school."

"Or towards it?"

"No, no, my dear Watson. The more deeply sunk impression is of course, the hind wheel, upon which the weight rests. You perceive several places where it has passed across and obliterated the more shallow mark of the front one. It was undoubtedly heading away from the school. It may or may not be connected with our inquiry, but we will follow it backwards before we go any farther."

We did so, and at the end of a few hundred yards lost the tracks as we emerged from the boggy portion of the moor. Following the path backwards, we picked out another spot, where a spring trickled across it. Here, once again, was the mark of the bicycle, though nearly obliterated by the hoofs of cows. After that there was no sign, but the path ran right on into Ragged Shaw, the wood which backed on to the school. From this wood the cycle must have emerged. Holmes sat down on a boulder and rested his chin in his hands. I had smoked two cigarettes before he moved.

"Well, well," said he, at last. "It is, of course, possible that a cunning man might change the tyres of his bicycle in order to leave unfamiliar tracks. A criminal who was capable of such a thought is a man whom I should be proud to do business with. We will leave this question undecided and hark back to our morass again, for we have left a good deal unexplored."

We continued our systematic survey of the edge of the sodden portion of the moor, and soon our perseverance was gloriously rewarded. Right across the lower part of the bog lay a miry path. Holmes gave a cry of delight as he approached it. An impression like a fine bundle of telegraph wires ran down the centre of it. It was the Palmer tyres.

"Here is Herr Heidegger, sure enough!" cried Holmes, exultantly. "My reasoning seems to have been pretty sound, Watson."

"I congratulate you."

"But we have a long way still to go. Kindly walk clear of the path. Now let us follow the trail. I fear that it will not lead very far."

We found, however, as we advanced that this portion of the moor is intersected with soft patches, and, though we frequently lost sight of the track, we always succeeded in picking it up once more.

"Do you observe," said Holmes. "that the rider is now undoubtedly forcing the pace? There can be no doubt of it. Look at this impression, where you get both tyres clear. The one is as deep as the other. That can only mean that the rider is throwing his weight on to the handle-bar, as a man does when he is sprinting. By Jove! he has had a fall."

There was a broad, irregular smudge covering some yards of the track. Then there were a few footmarks, and the tyres reappeared once more.

"A side-slip," I suggested.

Holmes held up a crumpled branch of flowering gorse. To my horror I perceived that the yellow blossoms were all dabbled with crimson. On the path, too, and among the heather were dark stains of clotted blood.

"Bad!" said Holmes. "Bad! Stand clear, Watson! Not an unnecessary footstep! What do I read here? He fell wounded—he stood up—he remounted—he proceeded. But there is no other track. Cattle on this side path. He was surely not gored by a bull? Impossible! But I see no traces of anyone else. We must push on, Watson. Surely, with stains as well as the track to guide us, he cannot escape us now."

Our search was not a very long one. The tracks of the tyre began to curve fantastically upon the wet and shining path. Suddenly, as I looked ahead, the gleam of metal caught my eye from amid the thick gorse-bushes. Out of them we dragged a bicycle, Palmer-tyred, one pedal bent, and the whole front of it horribly smeared and slobbered with blood. On the other side of the bushes, a shoe was projecting. We ran round, and there lay the unfortunate rider. He was a tall man, full-bearded, with spectacles, one glass of which had been knocked out. The cause of his death was a frightful blow upon the head, which had crushed in part of his skull. That he could have gone on after receiving such an injury said much for the vitality and courage of the man. He wore shoes, but no socks, and his open coat disclosed a nightshirt beneath it. It was undoubtedly the German master.

Holmes turned the body over reverently, and examined it with great attention. He then sat in deep thought for a time, and I could see by his ruffled brow that this grim discovery had not, in his opinion, advanced us much in our inquiry.

"It is a little difficult to know what to do, Watson," said he, at last. "My own inclinations are to push this inquiry on, for we have already lost so much time that we cannot afford to waste another hour. On the other hand, we are bound to inform the police of the discovery, and to see that this poor fellow's body is looked after."

"I could take a note back."

"But I need your company and assistance. Wait a bit! There is a fellow cutting peat up yonder. Bring him over here, and he will guide the police."

I brought the peasant across, and Holmes dispatched the frightened man with a note to Dr. Huxtable.

"Now, Watson," said he, "we have picked up two clues this morning. One is the bicycle with the Palmer tyre, and we see what that has led to. The other is the bicycle with the patched Dunlop. Before we start to investigate that, let us try to realize what we *do* know, so as to make the most of it, and to separate the essential from the accidental."

"First of all, I wish to impress upon you that the boy certainly left of his own free-will. He got down from his window and he went off, either alone or with someone. That is sure."

I assented.

"Well, now, let us turn to this unfortunate German master. The boy was fully dressed when he fled. Therefore, he foresaw what he would do. But the German went without his socks. He certainly acted on very short notice."

"Undoubtedly."

"Why did he go? Because, from his bedroom window, he saw the flight of the boy; because he wished to overtake him and bring him back. He seized his bicycle, pursued the lad, and in pursuing him met his death."

"So it would seem."

"Now I come to the critical part of my argument. The natural action of a man in pursuing a little boy would be to run after him. He would know that he could overtake him. But the German does not do so. He turns to his bicycle. I am told that he was an excellent cyclist. He would not do this, if he did not see that the boy had some swift means of escape."

"The other bicycle."

"Let us continue our reconstruction. He meets his death five miles from the school—not by a bullet, mark you, which even a lad might conceivably discharge, but by a savage blow dealt by a vigorous arm. The lad, then, *had* a companion in his flight. And the flight was a swift one, since it took five miles before an expert cyclist could overtake them. Yet we survey the ground round the scene of the tragedy. What do we find? A few cattletracks, nothing more. I took a wide sweep round, and there is no path within fifty yards. Another cyclist could have had nothing to do with the actual murder, nor were there any human footmarks."

"Holmes," I cried, "this is impossible."

"Admirable!" he said. "A most illuminating remark. It *is* impossible as I state it, and therefore I must in some respect have stated it wrong. Yet you saw for yourself. Can you suggest any fallacy?"

"He could not have fractured his skull in a fall?"

"In a morass, Watson?"

"I am at my wit's end."

"Tut, tut, we have solved some worse problems. At least we have plenty of material, if we can only use it. Come, then, and, having exhausted the Palmer, let us see what the Dunlop with the patched cover has to offer us."

We picked up the track and followed it onward for some distance, but soon the moor rose into a long, heather-tufted curve, and we left the watercourse behind us. No further help from tracks could be hoped for. At the spot where we saw the last of the Dunlop tyre it might equally have led to Holdernesse Hall, the stately towers of which rose some miles to our left, or to a low, gray village which lay in front of us and marked the position of the Chesterfield high road.

As we approached the forbidding and squalid inn, with the sign of a game-cock above the door, Holmes gave a sudden groan, and clutched me by the shoulder to save himself from falling. He had had one of those violent strains of the ankle which leave a man helpless. With difficulty he limped up to the door, where a squat, dark, elderly man was smoking a black clay pipe.

"How are you, Mr. Reuben Hayes?" said Holmes.

"Who are you, and how do you get my name so pat?" the countryman answered, with a suspicious flash of a pair of cunning eyes.

"Well, it's printed on the board above your head. It's easy to see a man who is master of his own house. I suppose you haven't such a thing as a carriage in your stables?"

"No, I have not."

"I can hardly put my foot to the ground."

"Don't put it to the ground."

"But I can't walk."

"Well, then, hop."

Mr. Reuben Hayes's manner was far from gracious, but Holmes took it with admirable good-humour.

"Look here, my man," said he. "This is really rather an awkward fix for me. I don't mind how I get on."

"Neither do I," said the morose landlord.

"The matter is very important. I would offer you a sovereign for the use of a bicycle."

The landlord pricked up his ears.

"Where do you want to go?"

"To Holdernesse Hall."

"Pals of the Dook, I suppose?" said the landlord, surveying our mud-stained garments with ironical eyes.

Holmes laughed good-naturedly.

"He'll be glad to see us, anyhow."

"Why?"

"Because we bring him news of his lost son."

The landlord gave a very visible start.

"What, you're on his track?"

"He has been heard of in Liverpool. They expect to get him every hour."

Again a swift change passed over the heavy, unshaven face. His manner was suddenly genial.

"I've less reason to wish the Dook well than most men," said he, "for I was his head coachman once, and cruel bad he treated me. It was him that sacked me without a character on the word of a lying corn-chandler.* But I'm glad to hear that the young lord was heard of in Liverpool, and I'll help you to take the news to the Hall."

"Thank you," said Holmes. "We'll have some food first. Then you can bring round the bicycle."

"I haven't got a bicycle."

Holmes held up a sovereign.

"I tell you, man, that I haven't got one. I'll let you have two horses as far as the Hall."

"Well, well," said Holmes, "we'll talk about it when we've had something to eat."

When we were left alone in the stone-flagged kitchen, it was astonishing how rapidly that sprained ankle recovered. It was nearly nightfall, and we had eaten nothing since early morning, so that we spent some time over our meal. Holmes was lost in thought, and once or twice he walked over to the window and stared earnestly out. It opened on to a squalid courtyard. In the far corner was a smithy, where a grimy lad was at work. On the other side were the stables. Holmes had sat down again after one of these excursions, when he suddenly sprang out of his chair with a loud exclamation.

"By heaven, Watson, I believe that I've got it!" he cried. "Yes, yes, it must be so. Watson, do you remember seeing any cow-tracks to-day?"

"Yes, several."

"Where?"

"Well; everywhere. They were at the morass, and again on the path, and again near where poor Heidegger met his death."

"Exactly. Well, now, Watson, how many cows did you see on the moor?"

"I don't remember seeing any."

"Strange, Watson, that we should see tracks all along our line, but never a cow on the whole moor. Very strange, Watson, eh?"

"Yes, it is strange."

"Now, Watson, make an effort, throw your mind back. Can you see those tracks upon the path?"

"Yes, I can."

"Can you recall that the tracks were sometimes like that, Watson"—

---

*A chandler is a dealer in a specified merchandise.

he arranged a number of bread-crumbs in this fashion—: : : : :—"and sometimes like this"—: . : . : . : . —"and occasionally like this"—. ˙. ˙. ˙. "Can you remember that?"

"No, I cannot."

"But I can. I could swear to it. However, we will go back at our leisure and verify it. What a blind beetle I have been, not to draw my conclusion."

"And what is your conclusion?"

"Only that it is a remarkable cow which walks, canters, and gallops. By George! Watson, it was no brain of a country publican that thought out such a blind as that. The coast seems to be clear, save for that lad in the smithy. Let us slip out and see what we can see."

There were two rough-haired, unkempt horses in the tumble-down stable. Holmes raised the hind leg of one of them and laughed aloud.

"Old shoes, but newly shod—old shoes, but new nails. This case deserves to be a classic. Let us go across to the smithy."

The lad continued his work without regarding us. I saw Holmes's eye darting to right and left among the litter of iron and wood which was scattered about the floor. Suddenly, however, we heard a step behind us, and there was the landlord, his heavy eyebrows drawn over his savage eyes, his swarthy features convulsed with passion. He held a short, metal-headed stick in his hand, and he advanced in so menacing a fashion that I was right glad to feel the revolver in my pocket.

"You infernal spies!" the man cried. "What are you doing there?"

"Why, Mr. Reuben Hayes," said Holmes, coolly, "one might think that you were afraid of our finding something out."

The man mastered himself with a violent effort, and his grim mouth loosened into a false laugh, which was more menacing than his frown.

"You're welcome to all you can find out in my smithy," said he. "But look here, mister, I don't care for folk poking about my place without my leave, so the sooner you pay your score and get out of this the better I shall be pleased."

"All right, Mr. Hayes, no harm meant," said Holmes. "We have been having a look at your horses, but I think I'll walk, after all. It's not far, I believe."

"Not more than two miles to the Hall gates. That's the road to the left." He watched us with sullen eyes until we had left his premises.

We did not go very far along the road, for Holmes stopped the instant that the curve hid us from the landlord's view.

"We were warm, as the children say, at that inn," said he. "I seem to grow colder every step that I take away from it. No, no, I can't possibly leave it."

"I am convinced," said I, "that this Reuben Hayes knows all about it. A more self-evident villain I never saw."

"Oh! he impressed you in that way, did he? There are the horses, there is the smithy. Yes, it is an interesting place, this Fighting Cock. I think we shall have another look at it in an unobtrusive way."

A long, sloping hillside, dotted with gray limestone boulders, stretched behind us. We had turned off the road, and were making our way up the hill, when, looking in the direction of Holdernesse Hall, I saw a cyclist coming swiftly along.

"Get down, Watson!" cried Holmes, with a heavy hand upon my shoulder. We had hardly sunk from view when the man flew past us on the road. Amid a rolling cloud of dust, I caught a glimpse of a pale, agitated face—a face with horror in every lineament, the mouth open, the eyes staring wildly in front. It was like some strange caricature of the dapper James Wilder whom we had seen the night before.

"The Duke's secretary!" cried Holmes. "Come, Watson, let us see what he does."

We scrambled from rock to rock, until in a few moments we had made our way to a point from which we could see the front door of the inn. Wilder's bicycle was leaning against the wall beside it. No one was moving about the house, nor could we catch a glimpse of any faces at the windows. Slowly the twilight crept down as the sun sank behind the high towers of Holdernesse Hall. Then, in the gloom, we saw the two side-lamps of a trap light up in the stable-yard of the inn, and shortly afterwards heard the rattle of hoofs, as it wheeled out into the road and tore off at a furious pace in the direction of Chesterfield.

"What do you make of that, Watson?" Holmes whispered.

"It looks like a flight."

"A single man in a dog-cart, so far as I could see. Well, it certainly was not Mr. James Wilder, for there he is at the door."

A red square of light had sprung out of the darkness. In the middle of it was the black figure of the secretary, his head advanced, peering out into the night. It was evident that he was expecting someone. Then at last there were steps in the road, a second figure was visible for an instant against the light, the door shut, and all was black once more. Five minutes later a lamp was lit in a room upon the first floor.

"It seems to be a curious class of custom that is done by the Fighting Cock," said Holmes.

"The bar is on the other side."

"Quite so. These are what one may call the private guests. Now, what in the world is Mr. James Wilder doing in that den at this hour of night, and who is the companion who comes to meet him there? Come, Watson, we must really take a risk and try to investigate this a little more closely."

Together we stole down to the road and crept across to the door of the inn. The bicycle still leaned against the wall. Holmes struck a match and held it to the back wheel, and I heard him chuckle as the light fell upon a patched Dunlop tyre. Up above us was the lighted window.

"I must have a peep through that, Watson. If you bend your back and support yourself upon the wall, I think that I can manage."

An instant later, his feet were on my shoulders, but he was hardly up before he was down again.

"Come, my friend," said he, "our day's work has been quite long enough. I think that we have gathered all that we can. It's a long walk to the school, and the sooner we get started the better."

He hardly opened his lips during that weary trudge across the moor, nor would he enter the school when he reached it, but went on to Mackleton Station, whence he could send some telegrams. Late at night I heard him consoling Dr. Huxtable, prostrated by the tragedy of his master's death, and later still he entered my room as alert and vigorous as he had been when he started in the morning. "All goes well, my friend," said he. "I promise that before to-morrow evening we shall have reached the solution of the mystery."

At eleven o'clock next morning my friend and I were walking up the famous yew avenue of Holdernesse Hall. We were ushered through the magnificent Elizabethan doorway and into his Grace's study. There we found Mr. James Wilder, demure and courtly, but with some trace of that wild terror of the night before still lurking in his furtive eyes and in his twitching features.

"You have come to see his Grace? I am sorry, but the fact is that the Duke is far from well. He has been very much upset by the tragic news. We received a telegram from Dr. Huxtable yesterday afternoon, which told us of your discovery."

"I must see the Duke, Mr. Wilder."

"But he is in his room."

"Then I must go to his room."

"I believe he is in his bed."

"I will see him there."

Holmes's cold and inexorable manner showed the secretary that it was useless to argue with him.

"Very good, Mr. Holmes, I will tell him that you are here."

After an hour's delay, the great nobleman appeared. His face was more cadaverous than ever, his shoulders had rounded, and he seemed to me to be an altogether older man than he had been the morning before. He greeted us with a stately courtesy and seated himself at his desk, his red beard streaming down on the table.

"Well, Mr. Holmes?" said he.

But my friend's eyes were fixed upon the secretary, who stood by his master's chair.

"I think, your Grace, that I could speak more freely in Mr. Wilder's absence."

The man turned a shade paler and cast a malignant glance at Holmes.

"If your Grace wishes——"

"Yes, yes, you had better go. Now, Mr. Holmes, what have you to say?"

My friend waited until the door had closed behind the retreating secretary.

"The fact is, your Grace," said he, "that my colleague, Dr. Watson, and myself had an assurance from Dr. Huxtable that a reward had been offered in this case. I should like to have this confirmed from your own lips."

"Certainly, Mr. Holmes."

"It amounted, if I am correctly informed, to five thousand pounds to anyone who will tell you where your son is?"

"Exactly."

"And another thousand to the man who will name the person or persons who keep him in custody?"

"Exactly."

"Under the latter heading is included, no doubt, not only those who may have taken him away, but also those who conspire to keep him in his present position?"

"Yes, yes," cried the Duke, impatiently. "If you do your work well, Mr. Sherlock Holmes, you will have no reason to complain of niggardly treatment."

My friend rubbed his thin hands together with an appearance of avidity which was a surprise to me, who knew his frugal tastes.

"I fancy that I see your Grace's check-book upon the table," said he. "I should be glad if you would make me out a check for six thousand pounds. It would be as well, perhaps, for you to cross it.* The Capital and Counties Bank, Oxford Street branch are my agents."

His Grace sat very stern and upright in his chair and looked stonily at my friend.

"Is this a joke, Mr. Holmes? It is hardly a subject for pleasantry."

"Not at all, your Grace. I was never more earnest in my life."

"What do you mean, then?"

"I mean that I have earned the reward. I know where your son is, and I know some, at least, of those who are holding him."

The Duke's beard had turned more aggressively red than ever against his ghastly white face.

"Where is he?" he gasped.

"He is, or was last night, at the Fighting Cock Inn, about two miles from your park gate."

The Duke fell back in his chair.

"And whom do you accuse?"

Sherlock Holmes's answer was an astounding one. He stepped swiftly forward and touched the Duke upon the shoulder.

"I accuse *you*," said he. "And now, your Grace, I'll trouble you for that check."

Never shall I forget the Duke's appearance as he sprang up and clawed with his hands, like one who is sinking into an abyss. Then, with an extraordinary effort of aristocratic self-command, he sat down and sank his face in his hands. It was some minutes before he spoke.

"How much do you know?" he asked at last, without raising his head.

---

*Write the name of a bank across the check so Holmes could deposit it.

"I saw you together last night."

"Does anyone else beside your friend know?"

"I have spoken to no one."

The Duke took a pen in his quivering fingers and opened his checkbook.

"I shall be as good as my word, Mr. Holmes. I am about to write your check, however unwelcome the information which you have gained may be to me. When the offer was first made, I little thought the turn which events might take. But you and your friend are men of discretion, Mr. Holmes?"

"I hardly understand your Grace."

"I must put it plainly, Mr. Holmes. If only you two know of this incident, there is no reason why it should go any farther. I think twelve thousand pounds is the sum that I owe you, is it not?"

But Holmes smiled and shook his head.

"I fear, your Grace, that matters can hardly be arranged so easily. There is the death of this schoolmaster to be accounted for."

"But James knew nothing of that. You cannot hold him responsible for that. It was the work of this brutal ruffian whom he had the misfortune to employ."

"I must take the view, your Grace, that when a man embarks upon a crime, he is morally guilty of any other crime which may spring from it."

"Morally, Mr. Holmes. No doubt you are right. But surely not in the eyes of the law. A man cannot be condemned for a murder at which he was not present, and which he loathes and abhors as much as you do. The instant that he heard of it he made a complete confession to me, so filled was he with horror and remorse. He lost not an hour in breaking entirely with the murderer. Oh, Mr. Holmes, you must save him—you must save him! I tell you that you must save him!" The Duke had dropped the last attempt at self-command, and was pacing the room with a convulsed face and with his clenched hands raving in the air. At last he mastered himself and sat down once more at his desk. "I appreciate your conduct in coming here before you spoke to anyone else," said he. "At least, we may take counsel how far we can minimize this hideous scandal."

"Exactly," said Holmes. "I think, your Grace, that this can only be done by absolute frankness between us. I am disposed to help your Grace to the best of my ability, but, in order to do so, I must understand to the last detail how the matter stands. I realize that your words applied to Mr. James Wilder, and that he is not the murderer."

"No, the murderer has escaped."

Sherlock Holmes smiled demurely.

"Your Grace can hardly have heard of any small reputation which I possess, or you would not imagine that it is so easy to escape me. Mr. Reuben Hayes was arrested at Chesterfield, on my information, at eleven o'clock last night. I had a telegram from the head of the local police before I left the school this morning."

The Duke leaned back in his chair and stared with amazement at my friend.

"You seem to have powers that are hardly human," said he. "So Reuben Hayes is taken? I am right glad to hear it, if it will not react upon the fate of James."

"Your secretary?"

"No, sir, my son."

It was Holmes's turn to look astonished.

"I confess that this is entirely new to me, your Grace. I must beg you to be more explicit."

"I will conceal nothing from you. I agree with you that complete frankness, however painful it may be to me, is the best policy in this desperate situation to which James's folly and jealousy have reduced us. When I was a very young man, Mr. Holmes, I loved with such a love as comes only once in a lifetime. I offered the lady marriage, but she refused it on the grounds that such a match might mar my career. Had she lived, I would certainly never have married anyone else. She died, and left this one child, whom for her sake I have cherished and cared for. I could not acknowledge the paternity to the world, but I gave him the best of educations, and since he came to manhood I have kept him near my person. He surprised my secret, and has presumed ever since upon the claim which he has upon me, and upon his power of provoking a scandal which would be abhorrent to me. His presence had something to do with the unhappy issue of my marriage. Above all, he hated my young legitimate heir from the first with a persistent hatred. You may well ask me why, under these circumstances, I still kept James under my roof. I answer that it was because I could see his mother's face in his, and that for her dear sake there was no end to my long-suffering. All her pretty ways too—there was not one of them which he could not suggest and bring back to my memory. I *could* not send him away. But I feared so much lest he should do Arthur— that is, Lord Saltire—a mischief, that I dispatched him for safety to Dr. Huxtable's school.

"James came into contact with this fellow Hayes, because the man was a tenant of mine, and James acted as agent. The fellow was a rascal from the beginning, but, in some extraordinary way, James became intimate with him. He had always a taste for low company. When James determined to kidnap Lord Saltire, it was of this man's service that he availed himself. You remember that I wrote to Arthur upon that last day. Well, James opened the letter and inserted a note asking Arthur to meet him in a little wood called the Ragged Shaw, which is near to the school. He used the Duchess's name, and in that way got the boy to come. That evening James bicycled over—I am telling you what he has himself confessed to me—and he told Arthur, whom he met in the wood, that his mother longed to see him, that she was awaiting him on the moor, and that if he would come back into the wood at midnight he would find a man with a horse, who would take him to her. Poor Arthur fell into the trap. He came to the appointment, and found this fellow Hayes with a led pony. Arthur mounted, and they set off together. It appears—though this James only heard yesterday—that they were pursued, that Hayes struck the pursuer with his stick, and that the man died of his injuries. Hayes brought Arthur to his public-house, the Fighting Cock, where he was confined in an upper room, under the care of Mrs. Hayes, who is a kindly woman, but entirely under the control of her brutal husband.

"Well, Mr. Holmes, that was the state of affairs when I first saw you two days ago. I had no more idea of the truth than you. You will ask me what was James's motive in doing such a deed. I answer that there was a great deal which was unreasoning and fanatical in the hatred which he bore my heir. In his view he should himself have been heir of all my estates, and he deeply resented those social laws which made it impossible. At the same time, he had a definite motive also. He was eager that I should break the entail,* and he was of opinion that it lay in my power to do so. He intended to make a bargain with me—to restore Arthur if I would break the entail, and so make it possible for the estate to be left to him by will. He knew well that I should never willingly invoke the aid of the police against him. I say that he would have proposed such a bargain to me; but he did not actually do so, for events moved too quickly for him, and he had not time to put his plans into practice.

"What brought all his wicked scheme to wreck was your discovery of this man Heidegger's dead body. James was seized with horror at the news. It came to us yesterday, as we sat together in this study. Dr. Huxtable had sent a telegram. James was so overwhelmed with grief and agitation that my suspicions, which had never been entirely absent, rose instantly to a certainty, and I taxed him with the deed. He made a complete voluntary confession. Then he implored me to keep his secret for three days longer, so as to give his wretched accomplice a chance of saving his guilty life. I yielded—as I have always yielded—to his prayers, and instantly James hurried off to the Fighting Cock to warn Hayes and give him the means of flight. I could not go there by daylight without provoking comment, but as soon as night fell I hurried off to see my dear Arthur. I found him safe and well, but horrified beyond expression by the dreadful deed he had witnessed. In deference to my promise, and much against my will, I consented to leave him there for three days, under the charge of Mrs. Hayes, since it was evident that it was impossible to inform the police where he was without telling them also who was the murderer, and I could not see how that murderer could be punished without ruin to my unfortunate James. You asked for frankness, Mr. Holmes, and I have taken you at your word, for I have now told you everything without an attempt at circumlocution or concealment. Do you in turn be as frank with me."

"I will," said Holmes. "In the first place, your Grace, I am bound to tell you that you have placed yourself in a most serious position in the

---

*Predetermined order of succession to the estate.

eyes of the law. You have condoned a felony, and you have aided the escape of a murderer, for I cannot doubt that any money which was taken by James Wilder to aid his accomplice in his flight came from your Grace's purse."

The Duke bowed his assent.

"This is, indeed, a most serious matter. Even more culpable in my opinion, your Grace, is your attitude towards your younger son. You leave him in this den for three days."

"Under solemn promises——"

"What are promises to such people as these? You have no guarantee that he will not be spirited away again. To humour your guilty older son, you have exposed your innocent younger son to imminent and unnecessary danger. It was a most unjustifiable action."

The proud lord of Holdernesse was not accustomed to be so rated in his own ducal hall. The blood flushed into his high forehead, but his conscience held him dumb.

"I will help you, but on one condition only. It is that you ring for the footman and let me give such orders as I like."

Without a word, the Duke pressed the electric bell. A servant entered.

"You will be glad to hear," said Holmes, "that your young master is found. It is the Duke's desire that the carriage shall go at once to the Fighting Cock Inn to bring Lord Saltire home.

"Now," said Holmes, when the rejoicing lackey had disappeared, "having secured the future, we can afford to be more lenient with the past. I am not in an official position, and there is no reason, so long as the ends of justice are served, why I should disclose all that I know. As to Hayes, I say nothing. The gallows awaits him, and I would do nothing to save him from it. What he will divulge I cannot tell, but I have no doubt that your Grace could make him understand that it is to his interest to be silent. From the police point of view he will have kidnapped the boy for the purpose of ransom. If they do not themselves find it out, I see no reason why I should prompt them to take a broader point of view. I would warn your Grace, however, that the continued presence of Mr. James Wilder in your household can only lead to misfortune."

"I understand that, Mr. Holmes, and it is already settled that he shall leave me forever, and go to seek his fortune in Australia."

"In that case, your Grace, since you have yourself stated that any unhappiness in your married life was caused by his presence, I would suggest that you make such amends as you can to the Duchess, and that you try to resume those relations which have been so unhappily interrupted."

"That also I have arranged, Mr. Holmes. I wrote to the Duchess this morning."

"In that case," said Holmes, rising, "I think that my friend and I can congratulate ourselves upon several most happy results from our little visit to the North. There is one other small point upon which I desire some light. This fellow Hayes had shod his horses with shoes which counterfeited the tracks of cows. Was it from Mr. Wilder that he learned so extraordinary a device?"

The Duke stood in thought for a moment, with a look of intense surprise on his face. Then he opened a door and showed us into a large room furnished as a museum. He led the way to a glass case in a corner, and pointed to the inscription.

"These shoes," it ran, "were dug up in the moat of Holdernesse Hall. They are for the use of horses, but they are shaped below with a cloven foot of iron, so as to throw pursuers off the track. They are supposed to have belonged to some of the marauding Barons of Holdernesse in the Middle Ages."

Holmes opened the case, and moistening his finger he passed it along the shoe. A thin film of recent mud was left upon his skin.

"Thank you," said he, as he replaced the glass. "It is the second most interesting object that I have seen in the North."

"And the first?"

Holmes folded up his check and placed it carefully in his notebook. "I am a poor man," said he, as he patted it affectionately, and thrust it into the depths of his inner pocket.

THE ADVENTURE OF BLACK PETER

I have never known my friend to be in better form, both mental and physical, than in the year '95. His increasing fame had brought with it an immense practice, and I should be guilty of an indiscretion if I were even to hint at the identity of some of the illustrious clients who crossed our humble threshold in Baker Street. Holmes, however, like all great artists, lived for his art's sake, and, save in the case of the Duke of Holdernesse, I have seldom known him claim any large reward for his inestimable services. So unworldly was he—or so capricious—that he frequently refused his help to the powerful and wealthy where the problem made no appeal to his sympathies, while he would devote weeks of most intense application to the affairs of some humble client whose case presented those strange and dramatic qualities which appealed to his imagination and challenged his ingenuity.

In this memorable year '95, a curious and incongruous succession of cases had engaged his attention, ranging from his famous investigation of the sudden death of Cardinal Tosca—an inquiry which was carried out by him at the express desire of His Holiness the Pope—down to his arrest of Wilson, the notorious canary-trainer, which removed a plague-spot from the East End of London. Close on the heels of these two famous cases came the tragedy of Woodman's Lee, and the very obscure circumstances which surrounded the death of Captain Peter Carey. No record of the doings of Mr. Sherlock Holmes would be complete which did not include some account of this very unusual affair.

During the first week of July, my friend had been absent so often and so long from our lodgings that I knew he had something on hand. The fact that several rough-looking men called during that time and inquired for Captain Basil made me understand that Holmes was working somewhere under one of the numerous disguises and names with which he concealed his own formidable identity. He had at least five small refuges in different parts of London, in which he was able to change his personality. He said nothing of his business to me, and it was not my habit to force a confidence. The first positive sign which he gave me of the direction which his investigation was taking was an extraordinary one. He had gone out before breakfast, and I had sat down to mine when he strode into the room, his hat upon his head and a huge barbed-headed spear tucked like an umbrella under his arm.

"Good gracious, Holmes!" I cried. "You don't mean to say that you have been walking about London with that thing?"

"I drove to the butcher's and back."

"The butcher's?"

"And I return with an excellent appetite. There can be no question, my dear Watson, of the value of exercise before breakfast. But I am prepared to bet that you will not guess the form that my exercise has taken."

"I will not attempt it."

He chuckled as he poured out the coffee.

"If you could have looked into Allardyce's back shop, you would have seen a dead pig swung from a hook in the ceiling, and a gentleman in his shirt sleeves furiously stabbing at it with this weapon. I was that energetic person, and I have satisfied myself that by no exertion of my strength can I transfix the pig with a single blow. Perhaps you would care to try?"

"Not for worlds. But why were you doing this?"

"Because it seemed to me to have an indirect bearing upon the mystery of Woodman's Lee. Ah, Hopkins, I got your wire last night, and I have been expecting you. Come and join us."

Our visitor was an exceedingly alert man, thirty years of age, dressed in a quiet tweed suit, but retaining the erect bearing of one who was accustomed to official uniform. I recognized him at once as Stanley Hopkins, a young police inspector, for whose future Holmes had high hopes,* while he in turn professed the admiration and respect of a pupil for the scientific methods of the famous amateur. Hopkins's brow was clouded, and he sat down with an air of deep dejection.

"No, thank you, sir. I breakfasted before I came round. I spent the night in town, for I came up yesterday to report."

"And what had you to report?"

"Failure, sir, absolute failure."

"You have made no progress?"

"None."

"Dear me! I must have a look at the matter."

"I wish to heavens that you would, Mr. Holmes. It's my first big chance, and I am at my wit's end. For goodness' sake, come down and lend me a hand."

"Well, well, it just happens that I have already read all the available evidence, including the report of the inquest, with some care. By the way, what do you make of that tobacco pouch, found on the scene of the crime? Is there no clue there?"

Hopkins looked surprised.

"It was the man's own pouch, sir. His initials were inside it. And it was of sealskin—and he was an old sealer."

"But he had no pipe."

"No, sir, we could find no pipe. Indeed, he smoked very little, and yet he might have kept some tobacco for his friends."

"No doubt. I only mention it because, if I had been handling the case, I should have been inclined to make that the starting-point of my investigation. However, my friend, Dr. Watson, knows nothing of this matter,

---

*Perhaps, then, his initials are not a coincidence.

and I should be none the worse for hearing the sequence of events once more. Just give us some short sketches of the essentials."

Stanley Hopkins drew a slip of paper from his pocket.

"I have a few dates here which will give you the career of the dead man, Captain Peter Carey. He was born in '45—fifty years of age. He was a most daring and successful seal and whale fisher. In 1883 he commanded the steam sealer *Sea Unicorn*, of Dundee. He had then had several successful voyages in succession, and in the following year, 1884, he retired. After that he travelled for some years, and finally he bought a small place called Woodman's Lee, near Forest Row, in Sussex. There he has lived for six years, and there he died just a week ago to-day.

"There were some most singular points about the man. In ordinary life, he was a strict Puritan—a silent, gloomy fellow. His household consisted of his wife, his daughter, aged twenty, and two female servants. These last were continually changing, for it was never a very cheery situation, and sometimes it became past all bearing. The man was an intermittent drunkard, and when he had the fit on him he was a perfect fiend. He has been known to drive his wife and daughter out of doors in the middle of the night and flog them through the park until the whole village outside the gates was aroused by their screams.

"He was summoned once for a savage assault upon the old vicar, who had called upon him to remonstrate with him upon his conduct. In short, Mr. Holmes, you would go far before you found a more dangerous man than Peter Carey, and I have heard that he bore the same character when he commanded his ship. He was known in the trade as Black Peter, and the name was given him, not only on account of his swarthy features and the colour of his huge beard, but for the humours which were the terror of all around him. I need not say that he was loathed and avoided by every one of his neighbours, and that I have not heard one single word of sorrow about his terrible end.

"You must have read in the account of the inquest about the man's cabin, Mr. Holmes, but perhaps your friend here has not heard of it. He had built himself a wooden outhouse—he always called it the 'cabin'—a few hundred yards from his house, and it was here that he slept every night. It was a little, single-roomed hut, sixteen feet by ten. He kept the key in his pocket, made his own bed, cleaned it himself, and allowed no other foot to cross the threshold. There are small windows on each side, which were covered by curtains and never opened. One of these windows was turned towards the high road, and when the light burned in it at night the folk used to point it out to each other and wonder what Black Peter was doing in there. That's the window, Mr. Holmes, which gave us one of the few bits of positive evidence that came out at the inquest.

"You remember that a stonemason, named Slater, walking from Forest Row about one o'clock in the morning—two days before the murder— stopped as he passed the grounds and looked at the square of light still shining among the trees. He swears that the shadow of a man's head turned sideways was clearly visible on the blind, and that this shadow was certainly not that of Peter Carey, whom he knew well. It was that of a bearded man, but the beard was short and bristled forward in a way very different from that of the captain. So he says, but he had been two hours in the public-house, and it is some distance from the road to the window. Besides, this refers to the Monday, and the crime was done upon the Wednesday.

"On the Tuesday, Peter Carey was in one of his blackest moods, flushed with drink and as savage as a dangerous wild beast. He roamed about the house, and the women ran for it when they heard him coming. Late in the evening, he went down to his own hut. About two o'clock the following morning, his daughter, who slept with her window open, heard a most fearful yell from that direction, but it was no unusual thing for him to bawl and shout when he was in drink, so no notice was taken. On rising at seven, one of the maids noticed that the door of the hut was open, but so great was the terror which the man caused that it was midday before anyone would venture down to see what had become of him. Peeping into the open door, they saw a sight which sent them flying, with white faces, into the village. Within an hour, I was on the spot and had taken over the case.

"Well, I have fairly steady nerves, as you know, Mr. Holmes, but I give you my word, that I got a shake when I put my head into that little house. It was droning like a harmonium with the flies and bluebottles, and the floor and walls were like a slaughter-house. He had called it a cabin, and a cabin it was, sure enough, for you would have thought that you were in a ship. There was a bunk at one end, a sea-chest, maps and charts, a picture of the *Sea Unicorn*, a line of logbooks on a shelf, all exactly as one would expect to find it in a captain's room. And there, in the middle of it, was the man himself—his face twisted like a lost soul in torment, and his great brindled beard stuck upward in his agony. Right through his broad breast a steel harpoon had been driven, and it had sunk deep into the wood of the wall behind him. He was pinned like a beetle on a card. Of course, he was quite dead, and had been so from the instant that he had uttered that last yell of agony.

"I know your methods, sir, and I applied them. Before I permitted anything to be moved, I examined most carefully the ground outside, and also the floor of the room. There were no footmarks."

"Meaning that you saw none?"

"I assure you, sir, that there were none."

"My good Hopkins, I have investigated many crimes, but I have never yet seen one which was committed by a flying creature. As long as the criminal remains upon two legs so long must there be some indentation, some abrasion, some trifling displacement which can be detected by the scientific searcher. It is incredible that this blood-bespattered room contained no trace which could have aided us. I understand, however, from the inquest that there were some objects which you failed to overlook?"

---

*Reference to Shakespeare's *Henry IV, Part I* (act 2, scene 4): "Nay, that's past praying for."

The young inspector winced at my companion's ironical comments.

"I was a fool not to call you in at the time, Mr. Holmes. However, that's past praying for* now. Yes, there were several objects in the room which called for special attention. One was the harpoon with which the deed was committed. It had been snatched down from a rack on the wall. Two others remained there, and there was a vacant place for the third. On the stock was engraved 'SS. *Sea Unicorn*, Dundee.' This seemed to establish that the crime had been done in a moment of fury, and that the murderer had seized the first weapon which came in his way. The fact that the crime was committed at two in the morning, and yet Peter Carey was fully dressed, suggested that he had an appointment with the murderer, which is borne out by the fact that a bottle of rum and two dirty glasses stood upon the table."

"Yes," said Holmes; "I think that both inferences are permissible. Was there any other spirit but rum in the room?"

"Yes, there was a tantalus containing brandy and whisky on the sea-chest. It is of no importance to us, however, since the decanters were full, and it had therefore not been used."

"For all that, its presence has some significance," said Holmes. "However, let us hear some more about the objects which do seem to you to bear upon the case."

"There was this tobacco-pouch upon the table."

"What part of the table?"

"It lay in the middle. It was of coarse sealskin—the straight-haired skin, with a leather thong to bind it. Inside was 'P. C.' on the flap. There was half an ounce of strong ship's tobacco in it."

"Excellent! What more?"

Stanley Hopkins drew from his pocket a drab-covered notebook. The outside was rough and worn, the leaves discoloured. On the first page were written the initials "J. H. N." and the date "1883." Holmes laid it on the table and examined it in his minute way, while Hopkins and I gazed over each shoulder. On the second page were the printed letters "C. P. R.," and then came several sheets of numbers. Another heading was "Argentine," another "Costa Rica," and another "San Paulo," each with pages of signs and figures after it.

"What do you make of these?" asked Holmes.

"They appear to be lists of Stock Exchange securities. I thought that 'J. H. N.' were the initials of a broker, and that 'C. P. R.' may have been his client."

"Try Canadian Pacific Railway," said Holmes.

Stanley Hopkins swore between his teeth, and struck his thigh with his clenched hand.

"What a fool I have been!" he cried. "Of course, it is as you say. Then 'J. H. N.' are the only initials we have to solve. I have already examined the old Stock Exchange lists, and I can find no one in 1883, either in the house or among the outside brokers, whose initials correspond with these. Yet I feel that the clue is the most important one that I hold. You will admit, Mr. Holmes, that there is a possibility that these initials are those of the second person who was present—in other words, of the murderer. I would also urge that the introduction into the case of a document relating to large masses of valuable securities gives us for the first time some indication of a motive for the crime."

Sherlock Holmes's face showed that he was thoroughly taken aback by this new development.

"I must admit both your points," said he. "I confess that this notebook, which did not appear at the inquest, modifies any views which I may have formed. I had come to a theory of the crime in which I can find no place for this. Have you endeavoured to trace any of the securities here mentioned?"

"Inquiries are now being made at the offices, but I fear that the complete register of the stockholders of these South American concerns is in South America, and that some weeks must elapse before we can trace the shares."

Holmes had been examining the cover of the notebook with his magnifying lens.

"Surely there is some discolouration here," said he.

"Yes, sir, it is a blood-stain. I told you that I picked the book off the floor."

"Was the blood-stain above or below?"

"On the side next to the boards."

"Which proves, of course, that the book was dropped after the crime was committed."

"Exactly, Mr. Holmes. I appreciated that point, and I conjectured that it was dropped by the murderer in his hurried flight. It lay near the door."

"I suppose that none of these securities have been found among the property of the dead man?"

"No, sir."

"Have you any reason to suspect robbery?"

"No, sir. Nothing seemed to have been touched."

"Dear me, it is certainly a very interesting case. Then there was a knife, was there not?"

"A sheath-knife, still in its sheath. It lay at the feet of the dead man. Mrs. Carey has identified it as being her husband's property."

Holmes was lost in thought for some time.

"Well," said he, at last, "I suppose I shall have to come out and have a look at it."

Stanley Hopkins gave a cry of joy.

"Thank you, sir. That will, indeed, be a weight off my mind."

Holmes shook his finger at the inspector.

"It would have been an easier task a week ago," said he. "But even now my visit may not be entirely fruitless. Watson, if you can spare the time, I should be very glad of your company. If you will call a four-wheeler, Hopkins, we shall be ready to start for Forest Row in a quarter of an hour."

Alighting at the small wayside station, we drove for some miles through the remains of widespread woods, which were once part of that great forest which for so long held the Saxon invaders at bay—the impenetrable "weald," for sixty years the bulwark of Britain. Vast sections of it have been cleared, for this is the seat of the first iron-works of the country, and the trees have been felled to smelt the ore. Now the richer fields of the North have absorbed the trade, and nothing save these ravaged groves and great scars in the earth show the work of the past. Here, in a clearing upon the green slope of a hill, stood a long, low, stone house, approached by a curving drive running through the fields. Nearer the road, and surrounded on three sides by bushes, was a small outhouse, one window and the door facing in our direction. It was the scene of the murder.

Stanley Hopkins led us first to the house, where he introduced us to a haggard, gray-haired woman, the widow of the murdered man, whose gaunt and deep-lined face, with the furtive look of terror in the depths of her red-rimmed eyes, told of the years of hardship and ill-usage which she had endured. With her was her daughter, a pale, fair-haired girl, whose eyes blazed defiantly at us as she told us that she was glad that her father was dead, and that she blessed the hand which had struck him down. It was a terrible household that Black Peter Carey had made for himself, and it was with a sense of relief that we found ourselves in the sunlight again and making our way along a path which had been worn across the fields by the feet of the dead man.

The outhouse was the simplest of dwellings, wooden-walled, shingle-roofed, one window beside the door and one on the farther side. Stanley Hopkins drew the key from his pocket and had stooped to the lock, when he paused with a look of attention and surprise upon his face.

"Someone has been tampering with it," he said.

There could be no doubt of the fact. The woodwork was cut, and the scratches showed white through the paint, as if they had been that instant done. Holmes had been examining the window.

"Someone has tried to force this also. Whoever it was has failed to make his way in. He must have been a very poor burglar."

"This is a most extraordinary thing," said the inspector. "I could swear that these marks were not here yesterday evening."

"Some curious person from the village, perhaps," I suggested.

"Very unlikely. Few of them would dare to set foot in the grounds, far less try to force their way into the cabin. What do you think of it, Mr. Holmes?"

"I think that fortune is very kind to us."

"You mean that the person will come again?"

"It is very probable. He came expecting to find the door open. He tried to get in with the blade of a very small penknife. He could not manage it. What would he do?"

"Come again next night with a more useful tool."

"So I should say. It will be our fault if we are not there to receive him. Meanwhile, let me see the inside of the cabin."

The traces of the tragedy had been removed, but the furniture within the little room still stood as it had been on the night of the crime. For two hours, with most intense concentration, Holmes examined every object in turn, but his face showed that his quest was not a successful one. Once only he paused in his patient investigation.

"Have you taken anything off this shelf, Hopkins?"

"No, I have moved nothing."

"Something has been taken. There is less dust in this corner of the shelf than elsewhere. It may have been a book lying on its side. It may have been a box. Well, well, I can do nothing more. Let us walk in these beautiful woods, Watson, and give a few hours to the birds and the flowers. We shall meet you here later, Hopkins, and see if we can come to closer quarters with the gentleman who has paid this visit in the night."

It was past eleven o'clock when we formed our little ambuscade. Hopkins was for leaving the door of the hut open, but Holmes was of the opinion that this would rouse the suspicions of the stranger. The lock was a perfectly simple one, and only a strong blade was needed to push it back. Holmes also suggested that we should wait, not inside the hut, but outside it, among the bushes which grew round the farther window. In this way we should be able to watch our man if he struck a light, and see what his object was in this stealthy nocturnal visit.

It was a long and melancholy vigil, and yet brought with it something of the thrill which the hunter feels when he lies beside the water-pool, and waits for the coming of the thirsty beast of prey. What savage creature was it which might steal upon us out of the darkness? Was it a fierce tiger of crime, which could only be taken fighting hard with flashing fang and claw, or would it prove to be some skulking jackal, dangerous only to the weak and unguarded?

In absolute silence we crouched amongst the bushes, waiting for whatever might come. At first the steps of a few belated villagers, or the sound of voices from the village, lightened our vigil, but one by one these interruptions died away, and an absolute stillness fell upon us, save for the chimes of the distant church, which told us of the progress of the night, and for the rustle and whisper of a fine rain falling amid the foliage which roofed us in.

Half-past two had chimed, and it was the darkest hour which precedes the dawn, when we all started as a low but sharp click came from the direction of the gate. Someone had entered the drive. Again there was a long silence, and I had begun to fear that it was a false alarm, when a stealthy step was heard upon the other side of the hut, and a moment later a metallic scraping and clinking. The man was trying to force the lock. This time his skill was greater or his tool was better, for there was a sudden snap and the creak of the hinges. Then a match was struck, and next instant the steady light from a candle filled the interior of the hut. Through the gauze curtain our eyes were all riveted upon the scene within.

The nocturnal visitor was a young man, frail and thin, with a black moustache, which intensified the deadly pallor of his face. He could not have been much above twenty years of age. I have never seen any human being who appeared to be in such a pitiable fright, for his teeth were visibly chattering, and he was shaking in every limb. He was dressed like a gentleman, in Norfolk jacket and knickerbockers, with a cloth cap upon his head. We watched him staring round with frightened eyes. Then he laid the candle-end upon the table and disappeared from our view into one of the corners. He returned with a large book, one of the logbooks which formed a line upon the shelves. Leaning on the table, he rapidly turned over the leaves of this volume until he came to the entry which he sought. Then, with an angry gesture of his clenched hand, he closed the book, replaced it in the corner, and put out the light. He had hardly turned to leave the hut when Hopkins's hand was on the fellow's collar, and I heard his loud gasp of terror as he understood that he was taken. The candle was relit, and there was our wretched captive, shivering and cowering in the grasp of the detective. He sank down upon the sea-chest, and looked helplessly from one of us to the other.

"Now, my fine fellow," said Stanley Hopkins, "who are you, and what do you want here?"

The man pulled himself together, and faced us with an effort at self-composure.

"You are detectives, I suppose?" said he. "You imagine I am connected with the death of Captain Peter Carey. I assure you that I am innocent."

"We'll see about that," said Hopkins. "First of all, what is your name?"

"It is John Hopley Neligan."

I saw Holmes and Hopkins exchange a quick glance.

"What are you doing here?"

"Can I speak confidentially?"

"No, certainly not."

"Why should I tell you?"

"If you have no answer, it may go badly with you at the trial."

The young man winced.

"Well, I will tell you," he said. "Why should I not? And yet I hate to think of this old scandal gaining a new lease of life. Did you ever hear of Dawson and Neligan?"

I could see, from Hopkins's face, that he never had, but Holmes was keenly interested.

"You mean the West Country bankers," said he. "They failed for a million, ruined half the county families of Cornwall, and Neligan disappeared."

"Exactly. Neligan was my father."

At last we were getting something positive, and yet it seemed a long gap between an absconding banker and Captain Peter Carey pinned against the wall with one of his own harpoons. We all listened intently to the young man's words.

"It was my father who was really concerned. Dawson had retired. I was only ten years of age at the time, but I was old enough to feel the shame and horror of it all. It has always been said that my father stole all the securities and fled. It is not true. It was his belief that if he were given time in which to realize them, all would be well and every creditor paid in full. He started in his little yacht for Norway just before the warrant was issued for his arrest. I can remember that last night, when he bade farewell to my mother. He left us a list of the securities he was taking, and he swore that he would come back with his honour cleared, and that none who had trusted him would suffer. Well, no word was ever heard from him again. Both the yacht and he vanished utterly. We believed, my mother and I, that he and it, with the securities that he had taken with him, were at the bottom of the sea. We had a faithful friend, however, who is a business man, and it was he who discovered some time ago that some of the securities which my father had with him had reappeared on the London market. You can imagine our amazement. I spent months in trying to trace them, and at last, after many doubtings and difficulties, I discovered that the original seller had been Captain Peter Carey, the owner of this hut.

"Naturally, I made some inquiries about the man. I found that he had been in command of a whaler which was due to return from the Arctic seas at the very time when my father was crossing to Norway. The autumn of that year was a stormy one. and there was a long succession of southerly gales. My father's yacht may well have been blown to the north, and there met by Captain Peter Carey's ship. If that were so, what had become of my father? In any case, if I could prove from Peter Carey's evidence how these securities came on the market it would be a proof that my father had not sold them, and that he had no view to personal profit when he took them.

"I came down to Sussex with the intention of seeing the captain, but it was at this moment that his terrible death occurred. I read at the inquest a description of his cabin, in which it stated that the old logbooks of his vessel were preserved in it. It struck me that if I could see what occurred in the month of August, 1883, on board the *Sea Unicorn*, I might settle the mystery of my father's fate. I tried last night to get at these logbooks, but was unable to open the door. To-night I tried again and succeeded, but I find that the pages which deal with that month have been torn from the book. It was at that moment I found myself a prisoner in your hands."

"Is that all?" asked Hopkins.

"Yes, that is all." His eyes shifted as he said it.

"You have nothing else to tell us?"

He hesitated.

"No, there is nothing."

"You have not been here before last night?"

"No."

"Then how do you account for *that?*" cried Hopkins, as he held up the damning notebook, with the initials of our prisoner on the first leaf and the blood-stain on the cover.

The wretched man collapsed. He sank his face in his hands, and trembled all over.

"Where did you get it?" he groaned. "I did not know. I thought I had lost it at the hotel."

"That is enough," said Hopkins, sternly. "Whatever else you have to say, you must say in court. You will walk down with me now to the police-station. Well, Mr. Holmes, I am very much obliged to you and to your friend for coming down to help me. As it turns out your presence was unnecessary, and I would have brought the case to this successful issue without you, but, none the less, I am grateful. Rooms have been reserved for you at the Brambletye Hotel, so we can all walk down to the village together."

"Well, Watson, what do you think of it?" asked Holmes, as we travelled back next morning.

"I can see that you are not satisfied."

"Oh, yes, my dear Watson, I am perfectly satisfied. At the same time, Stanley Hopkins's methods do not commend themselves to me. I am disappointed in Stanley Hopkins. I had hoped for better things from him. One should always look for a possible alternative, and provide against it. It is the first rule of criminal investigation."

"What, then, is the alternative?"

"The line of investigation which I have myself been pursuing. It may give us nothing. I cannot tell. But at least I shall follow it to the end."

Several letters were waiting for Holmes at Baker Street. He snatched one of them up, opened it, and burst out into a triumphant chuckle of laughter.

"Excellent, Watson! The alternative develops. Have you telegraph forms? Just write a couple of messages for me: 'Sumner, Shipping Agent, Ratcliff Highway. Send three men on, to arrive ten to-morrow morning.—Basil.' That's my name in those parts. The other is: 'Inspector Stanley Hopkins, 46 Lord Street, Brixton. Come breakfast to-morrow at nine-thirty. Important. Wire if unable to come.—Sherlock Holmes.' There, Watson, this infernal case has haunted me for ten days. I hereby banish it completely from my presence. To-morrow, I trust that we shall hear the last of it forever."

Sharp at the hour named Inspector Stanley Hopkins appeared, and we sat down together to the excellent breakfast which Mrs. Hudson had prepared. The young detective was in high spirits at his success.

"You really think that your solution must be correct?" asked Holmes.

"I could not imagine a more complete case."

"It did not seem to me conclusive."

"You astonish me, Mr. Holmes. What more could one ask for?"

"Does your explanation cover every point?"

"Undoubtedly. I find that young Neligan arrived at the Brambletye Hotel on the very day of the crime. He came on the pretence of playing golf. His room was on the ground-floor, and he could get out when he liked. That very night he went down to Woodman's Lee, saw Peter Carey at the hut, quarrelled with him, and killed him with the harpoon. Then, horrified by what he had done, he fled out of the hut, dropping the notebook which he had brought with him in order to question Peter Carey about these different securities. You may have observed that some of them were marked with ticks, and the others—the great majority—were not. Those which are ticked have been traced on the London market, but the others, presumably, were still in the possession of Carey, and young Neligan, according to his own account, was anxious to recover them in order to do the right thing by his father's creditors. After his flight he did not dare to approach the hut again for some time, but at last he forced himself to do so in order to obtain the information which he needed. Surely that is all simple and obvious?"

Holmes smiled and shook his head.

"It seems to me to have only one drawback, Hopkins, and that is that it is intrinsically impossible. Have you tried to drive a harpoon through a body? No? Tut, tut, my dear sir, you must really pay attention to these details. My friend Watson could tell you that I spent a whole morning in that exercise. It is no easy matter, and requires a strong and practised arm. But this blow was delivered with such violence that the head of the weapon sank deep into the wall. Do you imagine that this anemic youth was capable of so frightful an assault? Is he the man who hobnobbed in rum and water with Black Peter in the dead of the night? Was it his profile that was seen on the blind two nights before? No, no, Hopkins, it is another and more formidable person for whom we must seek."

The detective's face had grown longer and longer during Holmes's speech. His hopes and his ambitions were all crumbling about him. But he would not abandon his position without a struggle.

"You can't deny that Neligan was present that night, Mr. Holmes. The book will prove that. I fancy that I have evidence enough to satisfy a jury, even if you are able to pick a hole in it. Besides, Mr. Holmes, I have laid my hand upon my man. As to this terrible person of yours, where is he?"

"I rather fancy that he is on the stair," said Holmes, serenely. "I think, Watson, that you would do well to put that revolver where you can reach it." He rose and laid a written paper upon a side-table. "Now we are ready," said he.

There had been some talking in gruff voices outside, and now Mrs. Hudson opened the door to say that there were three men inquiring for Captain Basil.

"Show them in one by one," said Holmes.

The first who entered was a little Ribston pippin* of a man, with ruddy cheeks and fluffy white side-whiskers. Holmes had drawn a letter from his pocket.

"What name?" he asked.

"James Lancaster."

---

*Type of apple.

"I am sorry, Lancaster, but the berth is full. Here is half a sovereign for your trouble. Just step into this room and wait there for a few minutes."

The second man was a long, dried-up creature, with lank hair and sallow cheeks. His name was Hugh Pattins. He also received his dismissal, his half-sovereign, and the order to wait.

The third applicant was a man of remarkable appearance. A fierce bull-dog face was framed in a tangle of hair and beard, and two bold, dark eyes gleamed behind the cover of thick, tufted, overhung eyebrows. He saluted and stood sailor-fashion, turning his cap round in his hands.

"Your name?" asked Holmes.

"Patrick Cairns."

"Harpooner?"

"Yes, sir. Twenty-six voyages."

"Dundee, I suppose?"

"Yes, sir."

"And ready to start with an exploring ship?"

"Yes, sir."

"What wages?"

"Eight pounds a month."

"Could you start at once?"

"As soon as I get my kit."

"Have you your papers?"

"Yes, sir." He took a sheaf of worn and greasy forms from his pocket. Holmes glanced over them and returned them.

"You are just the man I want," said he. "Here's the agreement on the side-table. If you sign it the whole matter will be settled."

The seaman lurched across the room and took up the pen.

"Shall I sign here?" he asked, stooping over the table.

Holmes leaned over his shoulder and passed both hands over his neck.

"This will do," said he.

I heard a click of steel and a bellow like an enraged bull. The next instant Holmes and the seaman were rolling on the ground together. He was a man of such gigantic strength that, even with the handcuffs which Holmes had so deftly fastened upon his wrists, he would have very quickly overpowered my friend had Hopkins and I not rushed to his rescue. Only when I pressed the cold muzzle of the revolver to his temple did he at last understand that resistance was vain. We lashed his ankles with cord, and rose breathless from the struggle.

"I must really apologize, Hopkins," said Sherlock Holmes. "I fear that the scrambled eggs are cold. However, you will enjoy the rest of your breakfast all the better, will you not, for the thought that you have brought your case to a triumphant conclusion,"

Stanley Hopkins was speechless with amazement.

"I don't know what to say, Mr. Holmes," he blurted out at last, with a very red face. "It seems to me that I have been making a fool of myself from the beginning. I understand now, what I should never have forgot-

ten, that I am the pupil and you are the master. Even now I see what you
have done, but I don't know how you did it or what it signifies."

"Well, well," said Holmes, good-humouredly. "We all learn by experience, and your lesson this time is that you should never lose sight of the
alternative. You were so absorbed in young Neligan that you could not
spare a thought to Patrick Cairns, the true murderer of Peter Carey."

The hoarse voice of the seaman broke in on our conversation.

"See here, mister," said he, "I make no complaint of being man-
handled in this fashion, but I would have you call things by their right
names. You say I murdered Peter Carey, I say I *killed* Peter Carey, and
there's all the difference. Maybe you don't believe what I say. Maybe you
think I am just slinging you a yarn."

"Not at all," said Holmes. "Let us hear what you have to say."

"It's soon told, and, by the Lord, every word of it is truth. I knew Black
Peter, and when he pulled out his knife I whipped a harpoon through him
sharp, for I knew that it was him or me. That's how he died. You can call
it murder. Anyhow, I'd as soon die with a rope round my neck as with
Black Peter's knife in my heart."

"How came you there?" asked Holmes.

"I'll tell it you from the beginning. Just sit me up a little, so as I can
speak easy. It was in '83 that it happened—August of that year. Peter
Carey was master of the *Sea Unicorn*, and I was spare harpooner. We
were coming out of the ice-pack on our way home, with head winds and
a week's southerly gale, when we picked up a little craft that had been
blown north. There was one man on her—a landsman. The crew had
thought she would founder and had made for the Norwegian coast in the
dinghy. I guess they were all drowned. Well, we took him on board, this
man, and he and the skipper had some long talks in the cabin. All the
baggage we took off with him was one tin box. So far as I know, the man's
name was never mentioned, and on the second night he disappeared as if
he had never been. It was given out that he had either thrown himself
overboard or fallen overboard in the heavy weather that we were having.
Only one man knew what had happened to him, and that was me, for,
with my own eyes, I saw the skipper tip up his heels and put him over the
rail in the middle watch of a dark night, two days before we sighted the
Shetland Lights.

"Well, I kept my knowledge to myself, and waited to see what would
come of it. When we got back to Scotland it was easily hushed up, and nobody asked any questions. A stranger died by accident, and it was nobody's business to inquire. Shortly after Peter Carey gave up the sea, and
it was long years before I could find where he was. I guessed that he had
done the deed for the sake of what was in that tin box, and that he could
afford now to pay me well for keeping my mouth shut.

"I found out where he was through a sailor man that had met him in
London, and down I went to squeeze him. The first night he was reasonable enough, and was ready to give me what would make me free of the
sea for life. We were to fix it all two nights later. When I came, I found

him three parts drunk and in a vile temper. We sat down and we drank and we yarned about old times, but the more he drank the less I liked the look on his face. I spotted that harpoon upon the wall, and I thought I might need it before I was through. Then at last he broke out at me, spitting and cursing, with murder in his eyes and a great clasp-knife in his hand. He had not time to get it from the sheath before I had the harpoon through him. Heavens! what a yell he gave! and his face gets between me and my sleep. I stood there, with his blood splashing round me, and I waited for a bit, but all was quiet, so I took heart once more. I looked round, and there was the tin box on the shelf. I had as much right to it as Peter Carey, anyhow, so I took it with me and left the hut. Like a fool I left my baccy-pouch upon the table.

"Now I'll tell you the queerest part of the whole story. I had hardly got outside the hut when I heard someone coming, and I hid among the bushes. A man came slinking along, went into the hut, gave a cry as if he had seen a ghost, and legged it as hard as he could run until he was out of sight. Who he was or what he wanted is more than I can tell. For my part I walked ten miles, got a train at Tunbridge Wells, and so reached London, and no one the wiser.

"Well, when I came to examine the box I found there was no money in it, and nothing but papers that I would not dare to sell. I had lost my hold on Black Peter and was stranded in London without a shilling. There was only my trade left. I saw these advertisements about harpooners, and high wages, so I went to the shipping agents, and they sent me here. That's all I know, and I say again that if I killed Black Peter, the law should give me thanks, for I saved them the price of a hempen rope."

"A very clear statement," said Holmes, rising and lighting his pipe. "I think, Hopkins, that you should lose no time in conveying your prisoner to a place of safety. This room is not well adapted for a cell, and Mr. Patrick Cairns occupies too large a proportion of our carpet."

"Mr. Holmes," said Hopkins, "I do not know how to express my gratitude. Even now I do not understand how you attained this result."

"Simply by having the good fortune to get the right clue from the beginning. It is very possible if I had known about this notebook it might have led away my thoughts, as it did yours. But all I heard pointed in the one direction. The amazing strength, the skill in the use of the harpoon, the rum and water, the sealskin tobacco-pouch with the coarse tobacco—all these pointed to a seaman, and one who had been a whaler. I was convinced that the initials 'P. C.' upon the pouch were a coincidence, and not those of Peter Carey, since he seldom smoked, and no pipe was found in his cabin. You remember that I asked whether whisky and brandy were in the cabin. You said they were. How many landsmen are there who would drink rum when they could get these other spirits? Yes, I was certain it was a seaman."

"And how did you find him?"

"My dear sir, the problem had become a very simple one. If it were a seaman, it could only be a seaman who had been with him on the *Sea Uni-*

corn. So far as I could learn he had sailed in no other ship. I spent three days in wiring to Dundee, and at the end of that time I had ascertained the names of the crew of the *Sea Unicorn* in 1883. When I found Patrick Cairns among the harpooners, my research was nearing its end. I argued that the man was probably in London, and that he would desire to leave the country for a time. I therefore spent some days in the East End, devised an Arctic expedition, put forth tempting terms for harpooners who would serve under Captain Basil—and behold the result!"

"Wonderful!" cried Hopkins. "Wonderful!"

"You must obtain the release of young Neligan as soon as possible," said Holmes. "I confess that I think you owe him some apology. The tin box must be returned to him, but, of course, the securities which Peter Carey has sold are lost forever. There's the cab, Hopkins, and you can remove your man. If you want me for the trial, my address and that of Watson will be somewhere in Norway—I'll send particulars later."

THE ADVENTURE OF
CHARLES AUGUSTUS MILVERTON

It is years since the incidents of which I speak took place, and yet it is with diffidence that I allude to them. For a long time, even with the utmost discretion and reticence, it would have been impossible to make the facts public, but now the principal person concerned is beyond the reach of human law, and with due suppression the story may be told in such fashion as to injure no one. It records an absolutely unique experience in the career both of Mr. Sherlock Holmes and of myself. The reader will excuse me if I conceal the date or any other fact by which he might trace the actual occurrence.

We had been out for one of our evening rambles, Holmes and I, and had returned about six o'clock on a cold, frosty winter's evening. As Holmes turned up the lamp the light fell upon a card on the table. He glanced at it, and then, with an ejaculation of disgust, threw it on the floor. I picked it up and read:

CHARLES AUGUSTUS MILVERTON,
Appledore Towers,
Hampstead.

Agent.

"Who is he?" I asked.

"The worst man in London," Holmes answered, as he sat down and stretched his legs before the fire. "Is anything on the back of the card?"

I turned it over.

"Will call at 6:30—C. A. M.," I read.

"Hum! He's about due. Do you feel a creeping, shrinking sensation, Watson, when you stand before the serpents in the Zoo, and see the slithery, gliding, venomous creatures, with their deadly eyes and wicked, flattened faces? Well, that's how Milverton impresses me. I've had to do with fifty murderers in my career, but the worst of them never gave me the repulsion which I have for this fellow. And yet I can't get out of doing business with him—indeed, he is here at my invitation."

"But who is he?"

"I'll tell you, Watson. He is the king of all the blackmailers. Heaven help the man, and still more the woman, whose secret and reputation come into the power of Milverton! With a smiling face and a heart of marble, he will squeeze and squeeze until he has drained them dry. The fellow is a genius in his way, and would have made his mark in some more savoury trade. His method is as follows: He allows it to be known that he is prepared to pay very high sums for letters which compromise people of wealth and position. He receives these wares not only from treacherous valets or maids, but frequently from genteel ruffians, who have gained the confidence and affection of trusting women. He deals with no niggard hand. I happen to know that he paid seven hundred pounds to a footman for a note two lines in length, and that the ruin of a noble family was the result. Everything which is in the market goes to Milverton, and there are hundreds in this great city who turn white at his name. No one knows where his grip may fall, for he is far too rich and far too cunning to work from hand to mouth. He will hold a card back for years in order to play it at the moment when the stake is best worth winning. I have said that he is the worst man in London, and I would ask you how could one compare the ruffian, who in hot blood bludgeons his mate, with this man, who methodically and at his leisure tortures the soul and wrings the nerves in order to add to his already swollen money-bags?"

I had seldom heard my friend speak with such intensity of feeling.

"But surely," said I, "the fellow must be within the grasp of the law?"

"Technically, no doubt, but practically not. What would it profit a woman, for example, to get him a few months' imprisonment if her own ruin must immediately follow? His victims dare not hit back. If ever he blackmailed an innocent person, then indeed we should have him, but he is as cunning as the Evil One. No, no, we must find other ways to fight him."

"And why is he here?"

"Because an illustrious client has placed her piteous case in my hands. It is the Lady Eva Blackwell, the most beautiful debutante of last season. She is to be married in a fortnight to the Earl of Dovercourt. This fiend has several imprudent letters—imprudent, Watson, nothing worse—which were written to an impecunious young squire in the country. They would suffice to break off the match. Milverton will send the letters to the Earl unless a large sum of money is paid him. I have been commissioned to meet him, and—to make the best terms I can."

At that instant there was a clatter and a rattle in the street below. Looking down I saw a stately carriage and pair,* the brilliant lamps gleaming on the glossy haunches of the noble chestnuts. A footman opened the door, and a small, stout man in a shaggy astrakhan overcoat descended. A minute later he was in the room.

Charles Augustus Milverton was a man of fifty, with a large, intellectual head, a round, plump, hairless face, a perpetual frozen smile, and two keen gray eyes, which gleamed brightly from behind broad, gold-rimmed glasses. There was something of Mr. Pickwick's benevolence in his appearance, marred only by the insincerity of the fixed smile and by the hard glitter of those restless and penetrating eyes. His voice was as smooth and suave as his countenance, as he advanced with a plump little hand extended, murmuring his regret for having missed us at his first visit. Holmes disregarded the outstretched hand and looked at him with a face of granite. Milverton's smile broadened, he shrugged his shoulders, re-

---

*Carriage drawn by two horses, here the chestnuts of the next line.

moved his overcoat, folded it with great deliberation over the back of a chair, and then took a seat.

"This gentleman?" said he, with a wave in my direction. "Is it discreet? Is it right?"

"Dr. Watson is my friend and partner."

"Very good, Mr. Holmes. It is only in your client's interests that I protested. The matter is so very delicate——"

"Dr. Watson has already heard of it."

"Then we can proceed to business. You say that you are acting for Lady Eva. Has she empowered you to accept my terms?"

"What are your terms?"

"Seven thousand pounds."

"And the alternative?"

"My dear sir, it is painful for me to discuss it, but if the money is not paid on the 14th, there certainly will be no marriage on the 18th." His insufferable smile was more complacent than ever.

Holmes thought for a little.

"You appear to me," he said, at last, "to be taking matters too much for granted. I am, of course, familiar with the contents of these letters. My client will certainly do what I may advise. I shall counsel her to tell her future husband the whole story and to trust to his generosity."

Milverton chuckled.

"You evidently do not know the Earl," said he.

From the baffled look upon Holmes's face, I could see clearly that he did.

"What harm is there in the letters?" he asked.

"They are sprightly—very sprightly," Milverton answered. "The lady was a charming correspondent. But I can assure you that the Earl of Dovercourt would fail to appreciate them. However, since you think otherwise, we will let it rest at that. It is purely a matter of business. If you think that it is in the best interests of your client that these letters should be placed in the hands of the Earl, then you would indeed be foolish to pay so large a sum of money to regain them." He rose and seized his astrakhan coat.

Holmes was gray with anger and mortification.

"Wait a little," he said. "You go too fast. We should certainly make every effort to avoid scandal in so delicate a matter."

Milverton relapsed into his chair.

"I was sure that you would see it in that light," he purred.

"At the same time," Holmes continued, "Lady Eva is not a wealthy woman. I assure you that two thousand pounds would be a drain upon her resources, and that the sum you name is utterly beyond her power. I beg, therefore, that you will moderate your demands, and that you will return the letters at the price I indicate, which is, I assure you, the highest that you can get."

Milverton's smile broadened and his eyes twinkled humorously.

"I am aware that what you say is true about the lady's resources," said he. "At the same time you must admit that the occasion of a lady's marriage is a very suitable time for her friends and relatives to make some little effort upon her behalf. They may hesitate as to an acceptable wedding present. Let me assure them that this little bundle of letters would give more joy than all the candelabra and butter-dishes in London."

"It is impossible," said Holmes.

"Dear me, dear me, how unfortunate!" cried Milverton, taking out a bulky pocketbook. "I cannot help thinking that ladies are ill-advised in not making an effort. Look at this!" He held up a little note with a coat-of-arms upon the envelope. "That belongs to—well, perhaps it is hardly fair to tell the name until to-morrow morning. But at that time it will be in the hands of the lady's husband. And all because she will not find a beggarly sum which she could get by turning her diamonds into paste. It *is* such a pity! Now, you remember the sudden end of the engagement between the Honourable Miss Miles and Colonel Dorking? Only two days before the wedding, there was a paragraph in the *Morning Post* to say that it was all off. And why? It is almost incredible, but the absurd sum of twelve hundred pounds would have settled the whole question. Is it not pitiful? And here I find you, a man of sense, boggling about terms, when your client's future and honour are at stake. You surprise me, Mr. Holmes."

"What I say is true," Holmes answered. "The money cannot be found. Surely it is better for you to take the substantial sum which I offer than to ruin this woman's career, which can profit you in no way?"

"There you make a mistake, Mr. Holmes. An exposure would profit me indirectly to a considerable extent. I have eight or ten similar cases maturing. If it was circulated among them that I had made a severe example of the Lady Eva, I should find all of them much more open to reason. You see my point?"

Holmes sprang from his chair.

"Get behind him, Watson! Don't let him out! Now, sir, let us see the contents of that notebook."

Milverton had glided as quick as a rat to the side of the room and stood with his back against the wall.

"Mr. Holmes, Mr. Holmes," he said, turning the front of his coat and exhibiting the butt of a large revolver, which projected from the inside pocket. "I have been expecting you to do something original. This has been done so often, and what good has ever come from it? I assure you that I am armed to the teeth, and I am perfectly prepared to use my weapons, knowing that the law will support me. Besides, your supposition that I would bring the letters here in a notebook is entirely mistaken. I would do nothing so foolish. And now, gentlemen, I have one or two little interviews this evening, and it is a long drive to Hampstead." He stepped forward, took up his coat, laid his hand on his revolver, and turned to the door. I picked up a chair, but Holmes shook his head, and I laid it down again. With a bow, a smile, and a twinkle, Milverton was out of the room, and a few moments after we heard the slam of the carriage door and the rattle of the wheels as he drove away.

Holmes sat motionless by the fire, his hands buried deep in his trouser pockets, his chin sunk upon his breast, his eyes fixed upon the glowing embers. For half an hour he was silent and still. Then, with the gesture of a man who has taken his decision, he sprang to his feet and passed into his bedroom. A little later a rakish young workman, with a goatee beard and a swagger, lit his clay pipe at the lamp before descending into the street. "I'll be back some time, Watson," said he, and vanished into the night. I understood that he had opened his campaign against Charles Augustus Milverton, but I little dreamed the strange shape which that campaign was destined to take.

For some days Holmes came and went at all hours in this attire, but beyond a remark that his time was spent at Hampstead, and that it was not wasted, I knew nothing of what he was doing. At last, however, on a wild, tempestuous evening, when the wind screamed and rattled against the windows, he returned from his last expedition, and having removed his disguise he sat before the fire and laughed heartily in his silent inward fashion.

"You would not call me a marrying man, Watson?"

"No, indeed!"

"You'll be interested to hear that I'm engaged."

"My dear fellow! I congrat——"

"To Milverton's housemaid."

"Good heavens, Holmes!"

"I wanted information, Watson."

"Surely you have gone too far?"

"It was a most necessary step. I am a plumber with a rising business, Escott, by name. I have walked out with her each evening, and I have talked with her. Good heavens, those talks! However, I have got all I wanted. I know Milverton's house as I know the palm of my hand."

"But the girl, Holmes?"

He shrugged his shoulders.

"You can't help it, my dear Watson. You must play your cards as best you can when such a stake is on the table. However, I rejoice to say that I have a hated rival, who will certainly cut me out the instant that my back is turned. What a splendid night it is!"

"You like this weather?"

"It suits my purpose. Watson, I mean to burgle Milverton's house tonight."

I had a catching of the breath, and my skin went cold at the words, which were slowly uttered in a tone of concentrated resolution. As a flash of lightning in the night shows up in an instant every detail of a wild landscape, so at one glance I seemed to see every possible result of such an action—the detection, the capture, the honoured career ending in irreparable failure and disgrace, my friend himself lying at the mercy of the odious Milverton.

"For heaven's sake, Holmes, think what you are doing," I cried.

"My dear fellow, I have given it every consideration. I am never precipitate in my actions, nor would I adopt so energetic and, indeed, so dangerous a course, if any other were possible. Let us look at the matter clearly and fairly. I suppose that you will admit that the action is morally justifiable, though technically criminal. To burgle his house is no more than to forcibly take his pocketbook—an action in which you were prepared to aid me."

I turned it over in my mind.

"Yes," I said, "it is morally justifiable so long as our object is to take no articles save those which are used for an illegal purpose."

"Exactly. Since it is morally justifiable, I have only to consider the question of personal risk. Surely a gentleman should not lay much stress upon this, when a lady is in most desperate need of his help?"

"You will be in such a false position."

"Well, that is part of the risk. There is no other possible way of regaining these letters. The unfortunate lady has not the money, and there are none of her people in whom she could confide. To-morrow is the last day of grace, and unless we can get the letters to-night, this villain will be as good as his word and will bring about her ruin. I must, therefore, abandon my client to her fate or I must play this last card. Between ourselves, Watson, it's a sporting duel between this fellow Milverton and me. He had, as you saw, the best of the first exchanges, but my self-respect and my reputation are concerned to fight it to a finish."

"Well, I don't like it, but I suppose it must be," said I. "When do we start?"

"You are not coming."

"Then you are not going," said I. "I give you my word of honour—and I never broke it in my life—that I will take a cab straight to the police-station and give you away, unless you let me share this adventure with you."

"You can't help me."

"How do you know that? You can't tell what may happen. Anyway, my resolution is taken. Other people besides you have self-respect, and even reputations."

Holmes had looked annoyed, but his brow cleared, and he clapped me on the shoulder.

"Well, well, my dear fellow, be it so. We have shared this same room for some years, and it would be amusing if we ended by sharing the same cell. You know, Watson, I don't mind confessing to you that I have always had an idea that I would have made a highly efficient criminal. This is the chance of my lifetime in that direction. See here!" He took a neat little leather case out of a drawer, and opening it he exhibited a number of shining instruments. "This is a first-class, up-to-date burgling kit, with nickel-plated jemmy, diamond-tipped glass-cutter, adaptable keys, and every modern improvement which the march of civilization demands.

Here, too, is my dark lantern. Everything is in order. Have you a pair of silent shoes?"

"I have rubber-soled tennis shoes."

"Excellent! And a mask?"

"I can make a couple out of black silk."

"I can see that you have a strong, natural turn for this sort of thing. Very good, do make the masks. We shall have some cold supper before we start. It is now nine-thirty. At eleven we shall drive as far as Church Row. It is a quarter of an hour's walk from there to Appledore Towers. We shall be at work before midnight. Milverton is a heavy sleeper, and retires punctually at ten-thirty. With any luck we should be back here by two, with the Lady Eva's letters in my pocket."

Holmes and I put on our dress-clothes, so that we might appear to be two theatre-goers homeward bound. In Oxford Street we picked up a hansom and drove to an address in Hampstead. Here we paid off our cab, and with our great coats buttoned up, for it was bitterly cold, and the wind seemed to blow through us, we walked along the edge of the heath.

"It's a business that needs delicate treatment," said Holmes. "These documents are contained in a safe in the fellow's study, and the study is the ante-room of his bed-chamber. On the other hand, like all these stout, little men who do themselves well, he is a plethoric sleeper,* Agatha— that's my fiancée—says it is a joke in the servants' hall that it's impossible to wake the master. He has a secretary who is devoted to his interests, and never budges from the study all day. That's why we are going at night. Then he has a beast of a dog which roams the garden. I met Agatha late the last two evenings, and she locks the brute up so as to give me a clear run. This is the house, this big one in its own grounds. Through the gate— now to the right among the laurels. We might put on our masks here, I think. You see, there is not a glimmer of light in any of the windows, and everything is working splendidly."

With our black silk face-coverings, which turned us into two of the most truculent figures in London, we stole up to the silent, gloomy house. A sort of tiled veranda extended along one side of it, lined by several windows and two doors.

"That's his bedroom," Holmes whispered. "This door opens straight into the study. It would suit us best, but it is bolted as well as locked, and we should make too much noise getting in. Come round here. There's a greenhouse which opens into the drawing-room."

The place was locked, but Holmes removed a circle of glass and turned the key from the inside. An instant afterwards he had closed the door behind us, and we had become felons in the eyes of the law. The thick, warm air of the conservatory and the rich, choking fragrance of exotic plants took us by the throat. He seized my hand in the darkness and led me swiftly past banks of shrubs which brushed against our faces. Holmes had

---

*He sleeps so excessively he can't be awakened.

remarkable powers, carefully cultivated, of seeing in the dark. Still holding my hand in one of his, he opened a door, and I was vaguely conscious that we had entered a large room in which a cigar had been smoked not long before. He felt his way among the furniture, opened another door, and closed it behind us. Putting out my hand I felt several coats hanging from the wall, and I understood that I was in a passage. We passed along it, and Holmes very gently opened a door upon the right-hand side. Something rushed out at us and my heart sprang into my mouth. but I could have laughed when I realized that it was the cat. A fire was burning in this new room, and again the air was heavy with tobacco smoke. Holmes entered on tiptoe, waited for me to follow, and then very gently closed the door. We were in Milverton's study, and a portière* at the farther side showed the entrance to his bedroom.

It was a good fire, and the room was illuminated by it. Near the door I saw the gleam of an electric switch, but it was unnecessary, even if it had been safe, to turn it on. At one side of the fireplace was a heavy curtain which covered the bay window we had seen from outside. On the other side was the door which communicated with the veranda. A desk stood in the centre, with a turning-chair of shining red leather. Opposite was a large bookcase, with a marble bust of Athene† on the top. In the corner, between the bookcase and the wall, there stood a tall green safe, the firelight flashing back from the polished brass knobs upon its face. Holmes stole across and looked at it. Then he crept to the door of the bedroom, and stood with slanting head listening intently. No sound came from within. Meanwhile it had struck me that it would be wise to secure our retreat through the outer door, so I examined it. To my amazement, it was neither locked nor bolted. I touched Holmes on the arm, and he turned his masked face in that direction. I saw him start, and he was evidently as surprised as I.

"I don't like it," he whispered, putting his lips to my very ear. "I can't quite make it out. Anyhow, we have no time to lose."

"Can I do anything?"

"Yes, stand by the door. If you hear anyone come, bolt it on the inside, and we can get away as we came. If they come the other way, we can get through the door if our job is done, or hide behind these window curtains if it is not. Do you understand?"

I nodded, and stood by the door. My first feeling of fear had passed away, and I thrilled now with a keener zest than I had ever enjoyed when we were the defenders of the law instead of its defiers. The high object of our mission, the consciousness that it was unselfish and chivalrous, the villainous character of our opponent, all added to the sporting interest of the adventure. Far from feeling guilty, I rejoiced and exulted in our dangers. With a glow of admiration I watched Holmes unrolling his case of instruments and choosing his tool with the calm, scientific accuracy of a

---

*Heavy curtain hung across a doorway.

†Greek goddess of wisdom, usually spelled Athena.

surgeon who performs a delicate operation. I knew that the opening of safes was a particular hobby with him, and I understood the joy which it gave him to be confronted with this green and gold monster, the dragon which held in its maw the reputations of many fair ladies. Turning up the cuffs of his dress-coat—he had placed his overcoat on a chair—Holmes laid out two drills, a jemmy, and several skeleton keys. I stood at the centre door with my eyes glancing at each of the others, ready for any emergency, though, indeed, my plans were somewhat vague as to what I should do if we were interrupted. For half an hour, Holmes worked with concentrated energy, laying down one tool, picking up another, handling each with the strength and delicacy of the trained mechanic. Finally I heard a click, the broad green door swung open, and inside I had a glimpse of a number of paper packets, each tied, sealed, and inscribed. Holmes picked one out, but it was hard to read by the flickering fire, and he drew out his little dark lantern, for it was too dangerous, with Milverton in the next room, to switch on the electric light. Suddenly I saw him halt, listen intently, and then in an instant he had swung the door of the safe to, picked up his coat, stuffed his tools into the pockets, and darted behind the window curtain, motioning me to do the same.

It was only when I had joined him there that I heard what had alarmed his quicker senses. There was a noise somewhere within the house. A door slammed in the distance. Then a confused, dull murmur broke itself into the measured thud of heavy footsteps rapidly approaching. They were in the passage outside the room. They paused at the door. The door opened. There was a sharp snick as the electric light was turned on. The door closed once more, and the pungent reek of a strong cigar was borne to our nostrils. Then the footsteps continued backward and forward, backward and forward, within a few yards of us. Finally there was a creak from a chair, and the footsteps ceased. Then a key clicked in a lock, and I heard the rustle of papers.

So far I had not dared to look out, but now I gently parted the division of the curtains in front of me and peeped through. From the pressure of Holmes's shoulder against mine, I knew that he was sharing my observations. Right in front of us, and almost within our reach, was the broad, rounded back of Milverton. It was evident that we had entirely miscalculated his movements, that he had never been to his bedroom, but that he had been sitting up in some smoking or billiard room in the farther wing of the house, the windows of which we had not seen. His broad, grizzled head, with its shining patch of baldness, was in the immediate foreground of our vision. He was leaning far back in the red leather chair, his legs outstretched, a long, black cigar projecting at an angle from his mouth. He wore a semi-military smoking jacket, claret-coloured, with a black velvet collar. In his hand he held a long, legal document which he was reading in an indolent fashion, blowing rings of tobacco smoke from his lips as he did so. There was no promise of a speedy departure in his composed bearing and his comfortable attitude.

I felt Holmes's hand steal into mine and give me a reassuring shake, as if to say that the situation was within his powers, and that he was easy in his mind. I was not sure whether he had seen what was only too obvious from my position, that the door of the safe was imperfectly closed, and that Milverton might at any moment observe it. In my own mind I had determined that if I were sure, from the rigidity of his gaze, that it had caught his eye, I would at once spring out, throw my great coat over his head, pinion him, and leave the rest to Holmes. But Milverton never looked up. He was languidly interested by the papers in his hand, and page after page was turned as he followed the argument of the lawyer. At least, I thought, when he has finished the document and the cigar he will go to his room, but before he had reached the end of either, there came a remarkable development, which turned our thoughts into quite another channel.

Several times I had observed that Milverton looked at his watch, and once he had risen and sat down again, with a gesture of impatience. The idea, however, that he might have an appointment at so strange an hour never occurred to me until a faint sound reached my ears from the veranda outside. Milverton dropped his papers and sat rigid in his chair. The sound was repeated, and then there came a gentle tap at the door. Milverton rose and opened it.

"Well," said he, curtly, "you are nearly half an hour late."

So this was the explanation of the unlocked door and of the nocturnal vigil of Milverton. There was the gentle rustle of a woman's dress. I had closed the slit between the curtains as Milverton's face had turned in our direction, but now I ventured very carefully to open it once more. He had resumed his seat, the cigar still projecting at an insolent angle from the corner of his mouth. In front of him, in the full glare of the electric light, there stood a tall, slim, dark woman, a veil over her face, a mantle drawn round her chin. Her breath came quick and fast, and every inch of the lithe figure was quivering with strong emotion.

"Well," said Milverton, "you made me lose a good night's rest, my dear. I hope you'll prove worth it. You couldn't come any other time—eh?"

The woman shook her head.

"Well, if you couldn't you couldn't. If the Countess is a hard mistress, you have your chance to get level with her now. Bless the girl, what are you shivering about? That's right. Pull yourself together. Now, let us get down to business." He took a notebook from the drawer of his desk. "You say that you have five letters which compromise the Countess d'Albert. You want to sell them. I want to buy them. So far so good. It only remains to fix a price. I should want to inspect the letters, of course. If they are really good specimens—Great heavens, is it you?"

The woman, without a word, had raised her veil and dropped the mantle from her chin. It was a dark, handsome, clear-cut face which confronted Milverton—a face with a curved nose, strong, dark eyebrows shading hard, glittering eyes, and a straight, thin-lipped mouth set in a dangerous smile.

"It is I," she said, "the woman whose life you have ruined."

Milverton laughed, but fear vibrated in his voice. "You were so very obstinate," said he. "Why did you drive me to such extremities? I assure you I wouldn't hurt a fly of my own accord, but every man has his business, and what was I to do? I put the price well within your means. You would not pay."

"So you sent the letters to my husband, and he—the noblest gentleman that ever lived, a man whose boots I was never worthy to lace—he broke his gallant heart and died. You remember that last night, when I came through that door, I begged and prayed you for mercy, and you laughed in my face as you are trying to laugh now, only your coward heart cannot keep your lips from twitching. Yes, you never thought to see me here again, but it was that night which taught me how I could meet you face to face, and alone. Well, Charles Milverton, what have you to say?"

"Don't imagine that you can bully me," said he, rising to his feet. "I have only to raise my voice, and I could call my servants and have you arrested. But I will make allowance for your natural anger. Leave the room at once as you came, and I will say no more."

The woman stood with her hand buried in her bosom, and the same deadly smile on her thin lips.

"You will ruin no more lives as you have ruined mine. You will wring no more hearts as you wrung mine. I will free the world of a poisonous thing. Take that, you hound—and that!—and that!—and that!—and that!"

She had drawn a little gleaming revolver, and emptied barrel after barrel into Milverton's body, the muzzle within two feet of his shirt front. He shrank away and then fell forward upon the table, coughing furiously and clawing among the papers. Then he staggered to his feet, received another shot, and rolled upon the floor. "You've done me," he cried, and lay still. The woman looked at him intently, and ground her heel into his upturned face. She looked again, but there was no sound or movement. I heard a sharp rustle, the night air blew into the heated room, and the avenger was gone.

No interference upon our part could have saved the man from his fate, but, as the woman poured bullet after bullet into Milverton's shrinking body I was about to spring out, when I felt Holmes's cold, strong grasp upon my wrist. I understood the whole argument of that firm, restraining grip—that it was no affair of ours, that justice had overtaken a villain, that we had our own duties and our own objects, which were not to be lost sight of. But hardly had the woman rushed from the room when Holmes, with swift, silent steps, was over at the other door. He turned the key in the lock. At the same instant we heard voices in the house and the sound of hurrying feet. The revolver shots had roused the household. With perfect coolness Holmes slipped across to the safe, filled his two arms with bundles of letters, and poured them all into the fire. Again and again he did it, until the safe was empty. Someone turned the handle and beat upon the outside of the door. Holmes looked swiftly round. The letter which had been the messenger of death for Milverton lay, all mottled with his blood, upon the table. Holmes tossed it in among the blazing papers. Then he drew the key from the outer door, passed through after me, and locked it on the outside. "This way, Watson," said he, "we can scale the garden wall in this direction."

I could not have believed that an alarm could have spread so swiftly. Looking back, the huge house was one blaze of light. The front door was open, and figures were rushing down the drive. The whole garden was alive with people, and one fellow raised a view-halloa as we emerged from the veranda and followed hard at our heels. Holmes seemed to know the grounds perfectly, and he threaded his way swiftly among a plantation of small trees, I close at his heels, and our foremost pursuer panting behind us. It was a six-foot wall which barred our path, but he sprang to the top and over. As I did the same I felt the hand of the man behind me grab at my ankle, but I kicked myself free and scrambled over a grass-strewn coping.* I fell upon my face among some bushes, but Holmes had me on my feet in an instant, and together we dashed away across the huge expanse of Hampstead Heath. We had run two miles, I suppose, before Holmes at last halted and listened intently. All was absolute silence behind us. We had shaken off our pursuers and were safe.

We had breakfasted and were smoking our morning pipe on the day after the remarkable experience which I have recorded, when Mr. Lestrade, of Scotland Yard, very solemn and impressive, was ushered into our modest sitting-room.

"Good-morning, Mr. Holmes," said he; "good-morning. May I ask if you are very busy just now?"

"Not too busy to listen to you."

"I thought that, perhaps, if you had nothing particular on hand, you might care to assist us in a most remarkable case, which occurred only last night at Hampstead."

"Dear me!" said Holmes. "What was that?"

"A murder—a most dramatic and remarkable murder. I know how keen you are upon these things, and I would take it as a great favour if you would step down to Appledore Towers, and give us the benefit of your advice. It is no ordinary crime. We have had our eyes upon this Mr. Milverton for some time, and, between ourselves, he was a bit of a villain. He is known to have held papers which he used for blackmailing purposes. These papers have all been burned by the murderers. No article of value was taken, as it is probable that the criminals were men of good position, whose sole object was to prevent social exposure."

"Criminals?" said Holmes. "Plural?"

"Yes, there were two of them. They were as nearly as possible captured red-handed. We have their footmarks, we have their description, it's ten to one that we trace them. The first fellow was a bit too active, but the

---

*Top part of a wall.

second was caught by the undergardener, and only got away after a struggle. He was a middle-sized, strongly built man—square jaw, thick neck, moustache, a mask over his eyes."

"That's rather vague," said Sherlock Holmes. "Why, it might be a description of Watson!"

"It's true," said the inspector, with amusement. "It might be a description of Watson."

"Well, I'm afraid I can't help you, Lestrade," said Holmes. "The fact is that I knew this fellow Milverton, that I considered him one of the most dangerous men in London, and that I think there are certain crimes which the law cannot touch, and which therefore, to some extent, justify private revenge. No, it's no use arguing. I have made up my mind. My sympathies are with the criminals rather than with the victim, and I will not handle this case."

Holmes had not said one word to me about the tragedy which we had witnessed, but I observed all the morning that he was in his most thoughtful mood, and he gave me the impression, from his vacant eyes and his abstracted manner, of a man who is striving to recall something to his memory. We were in the middle of our lunch, when he suddenly sprang to his feet. "By Jove, Watson, I've got it!" he cried. "Take your hat! Come with me!" He hurried at his top speed down Baker Street and along Oxford Street, until we had almost reached Regent Circus. Here, on the left hand, there stands a shop window filled with photographs of the celebrities and beauties of the day. Holmes's eyes fixed themselves upon one of them, and following his gaze I saw the picture of a regal and stately lady in Court dress, with a high diamond tiara upon her noble head. I looked at that delicately curved nose, at the marked eyebrows, at the straight mouth, and the strong little chin beneath it. Then I caught my breath as I read the time-honoured title of the great nobleman and statesman whose wife she had been. My eyes met those of Holmes, and he put his finger to his lips as we turned away from the window.

THE ADVENTURE OF THE
SIX NAPOLEONS

It was no very unusual thing for Mr. Lestrade, of Scotland Yard, to look in upon us of an evening, and his visits were welcome to Sherlock Holmes, for they enabled him to keep in touch with all that was going on at the police headquarters. In return for the news which Lestrade would bring, Holmes was always ready to listen with attention to the details of any case upon which the detective was engaged, and was able occasionally, without any active interference, to give some hint or suggestion drawn from his own vast knowledge and experience.

On this particular evening, Lestrade had spoken of the weather and the newspapers. Then he had fallen silent, puffing thoughtfully at his cigar. Holmes looked keenly at him.

"Anything remarkable on hand?" he asked.

"Oh, no, Mr. Holmes—nothing very particular."

"Then tell me about it."

Lestrade laughed.

"Well, Mr. Holmes, there is no use denying that there *is* something on my mind. And yet it is such an absurd business, that I hesitated to bother you about it. On the other hand, although it is trivial, it is undoubtedly queer, and I know that you have a taste for all that is out of the common. But, in my opinion, it comes more in Dr. Watson's line than ours."

"Disease?" said I.

"Madness, anyhow. And a queer madness, too. You wouldn't think there was anyone living at this time of day who had such a hatred of Napoleon the First that he would break any image of him that he could see."

Holmes sank back in his chair.

"That's no business of mine," said he.

"Exactly. That's what I said. But then, when the man commits burglary in order to break images which are not his own, that brings it away from the doctor and on to the policeman."

Holmes sat up again.

"Burglary! This is more interesting. Let me hear the details."

Lestrade took out his official notebook and refreshed his memory from its pages.

"The first case reported was four days ago," said he. "It was at the shop of Morse Hudson, who has a place for the sale of pictures and statues in the Kennington Road. The assistant had left the front shop for an instant, when he heard a crash, and hurrying in he found a plaster bust of Napoleon, which stood with several other works of art upon the counter, lying shivered into fragments. He rushed out into the road, but, although several passers-by declared that they had noticed a man run out of the shop, he could neither see anyone nor could he find any means of identi-

fying the rascal. It seemed to be one of those senseless acts of Hooligan-
ism which occur from time to time, and it was reported to the constable
on the beat as such. The plaster cast was not worth more than a few
shillings, and the whole affair appeared to be too childish for any particular investigation.

"The second case, however, was more serious, and also more singular.
It occurred only last night.

"In Kennington Road, and within a few hundred yards of Morse Hud-
son's shop, there lives a well-known medical practitioner, named Dr. Bar-
nicot, who has one of the largest practices upon the south side of the
Thames. His residence and principal consulting-room is at Kennington
Road, but he has a branch surgery and dispensary at Lower Brixton
Road, two miles away. This Dr. Barnicot is an enthusiastic admirer of
Napoleon, and his house is full of books, pictures, and relics of the French
Emperor. Some little time ago he purchased from Morse Hudson two duplicate plaster casts of the famous head of Napoleon by the French sculptor, Devine. One of these he placed in his hall in the house at Kennington
Road, and the other on the mantelpiece of the surgery at Lower Brixton.
Well, when Dr. Barnicot came down this morning he was astonished to
find that his house had been burgled during the night, but that nothing
had been taken save the plaster head from the hall. It had been carried
out and had been dashed savagely against the garden wall, under which
its splintered fragments were discovered."

Holmes rubbed his hands.

"This is certainly very novel," said he.

"I thought it would please you. But I have not got to the end yet. Dr.
Barnicot was due at his surgery at twelve o'clock, and you can imagine his
amazement when, on arriving there, he found that the window had been
opened in the night, and that the broken pieces of his second bust were
strewn all over the room. It had been smashed to atoms where it stood.
In neither case were there any signs which could give us a clue as to the
criminal or lunatic who had done the mischief. Now, Mr. Holmes, you
have got the facts."

"They are singular, not to say grotesque," said Holmes. "May I ask
whether the two busts smashed in Dr. Barnicot's rooms were the exact
duplicates of the one which was destroyed in Morse Hudson's shop?"

"They were taken from the same mould."

"Such a fact must tell against the theory that the man who breaks them
is influenced by any general hatred of Napoleon. Considering how many
hundreds of statues of the great Emperor must exist in London, it is too
much to suppose such a coincidence as that a promiscuous iconoclast
should chance to begin upon three specimens of the same bust."

"Well, I thought as you do," said Lestrade. "On the other hand, this
Morse Hudson is the purveyor of busts in that part of London, and these
three were the only ones which had been in his shop for years. So, although, as you say, there are many hundreds of statues in London, it is
very probable that these three were the only ones in that district. There-

fore, a local fanatic would begin with them. What do you think, Dr. Watson?"

"There are no limits to the possibilities of monomania," I answered. "There is the condition which the modern French psychologists have called the *'idée fixe,'* which may be trifling in character, and accompanied by complete sanity in every other way. A man who had read deeply about Napoleon, or who had possibly received some hereditary family injury through the great war, might conceivably form such an *idée fixe* and under its influence be capable of any fantastic outrage."

"That won't do, my dear Watson," said Holmes, shaking his head, "for no amount of *idée fixe* would enable your interesting monomaniac to find out where these busts were situated."

"Well, how do *you* explain it?"

"I don't attempt to do so. I would only observe that there is a certain method in the gentleman's eccentric proceedings. For example, in Dr. Barnicot's hall, where a sound might arouse the family, the bust was taken outside before being broken, whereas in the surgery, where there was less danger of an alarm, it was smashed where it stood. The affair seems absurdly trifling, and yet I dare call nothing trivial when I reflect that some of my most classic cases have had the least promising commencement. You will remember, Watson, how the dreadful business of the Abernetty family was first brought to my notice by the depth which the parsley had sunk into the butter upon a hot day. I can't afford, therefore, to smile at your three broken busts, Lestrade, and I shall be very much obliged to you if you will let me hear of any fresh development of so singular a chain of events."

The development for which my friend had asked came in a quicker and an infinitely more tragic form than he could have imagined. I was still dressing in my bedroom next morning, when there was a tap at the door and Holmes entered, a telegram in his hand. He read it aloud:

"Come instantly, 131 Pitt Street, Kensington.

"LESTRADE."

"What is it, then?" I asked.

"Don't know—may be anything. But I suspect it is the sequel of the story of the statues. In that case our friend the image-breaker has begun operations in another quarter of London. There's coffee on the table, Watson, and I have a cab at the door."

In half an hour we had reached Pitt Street, a quiet little backwater just beside one of the briskest currents of London life. No. 131 was one of a row, all flat-chested, respectable, and most unromantic dwellings. As we drove up, we found the railings in front of the house lined by a curious crowd. Holmes whistled.

"By George! it's attempted murder at the least. Nothing less will hold the London message-boy. There's a deed of violence indicated in that fellow's round shoulders and outstretched neck. What's this, Watson? The top steps swilled down and the other ones dry. Footsteps enough, anyhow! Well, well, there's Lestrade at the front window, and we shall soon know all about it."

The official received us with a very grave face and showed us into a sitting-room, where an exceedingly unkempt and agitated elderly man, clad in a flannel dressing-gown, was pacing up and down. He was introduced to us as the owner of the house—Mr. Horace Harker, of the Central Press Syndicate.

"It's the Napoleon bust business again," said Lestrade. "You seemed interested last night, Mr. Holmes, so I thought perhaps you would be glad to be present now that the affair has taken a very much graver turn."

"What has it turned to, then?"

"To murder. Mr. Harker, will you tell these gentlemen exactly what has occurred?"

The man in the dressing-gown turned upon us with a most melancholy face.

"It's an extraordinary thing," said he, "that all my life I have been collecting other people's news, and now that a real piece of news has come my own way I am so confused and bothered that I can't put two words together. If I had come in here as a journalist, I should have interviewed myself and had two columns in every evening paper. As it is, I am giving away valuable copy by telling my story over and over to a string of different people, and I can make no use of it myself. However, I've heard your name, Mr. Sherlock Holmes, and if you'll only explain this queer business, I shall be paid for my trouble in telling you the story."

Holmes sat down and listened.

"It all seems to centre round that bust of Napoleon which I bought for this very room about four months ago. I picked it up cheap from Harding Brothers, two doors from the High Street Station. A great deal of my journalistic work is done at night, and I often write until the early morning. So it was to-day. I was sitting in my den, which is at the back of the top of the house, about three o'clock, when I was convinced that I heard some sounds downstairs. I listened, but they were not repeated, and I concluded that they came from outside. Then suddenly, about five minutes later, there came a most horrible yell—the most dreadful sound, Mr. Holmes, that ever I heard. It will ring in my ears as long as I live. I sat frozen with horror for a minute or two. Then I seized the poker and went downstairs. When I entered this room I found the window wide open, and I at once observed that the bust was gone from the mantelpiece. Why any burglar should take such a thing passes my understanding, for it was only a plaster cast and of no real value whatever.

"You can see for yourself that anyone going out through that open window could reach the front doorstep by taking a long stride. This was clearly what the burglar had done, so I went round and opened the door. Stepping out into the dark, I nearly fell over a dead man, who was lying there. I ran back for a light, and there was the poor fellow, a great gash in his throat and the whole place swimming in blood. He lay on his back, his knees drawn up, and his mouth horribly open. I shall see him in my dreams. I had just time to blow on my police-whistle, and then I must have fainted, for I knew nothing more until I found the policeman standing over me in the hall."

"Well, who was the murdered man?" asked Holmes.

"There's nothing to show who he was," said Lestrade. "You shall see the body at the mortuary, but we have made nothing of it up to now. He is a tall man, sunburned, very powerful, not more than thirty. He is poorly dressed, and yet does not appear to be a labourer. A horn-handled clasp knife was lying in a pool of blood beside him. Whether it was the weapon which did the deed, or whether it belonged to the dead man, I do not know. There was no name on his clothing, and nothing in his pockets save an apple, some string, a shilling map of London, and a photograph. Here it is."

It was evidently taken by a snapshot from a small camera. It represented an alert, sharp-featured simian man, with thick eyebrows and a very peculiar projection of the lower part of the face, like the muzzle of a baboon.

"And what became of the bust?" asked Holmes, after a careful study of this picture.

"We had news of it just before you came. It has been found in the front garden of an empty house in Campden House Road. It was broken into fragments. I am going round now to see it. Will you come?"

"Certainly. I must just take one look round." He examined the carpet and the window. "The fellow had either very long legs or was a most active man," said he. "With an area beneath, it was no mean feat to reach that window-ledge and open that window. Getting back was comparatively simple. Are you coming with us to see the remains of your bust, Mr. Harker?"

The disconsolate journalist had seated himself at a writing-table.

"I must try and make something of it," said he, "though I have no doubt that the first editions of ther evening papers are out already with full details. It's like my luck! You remember when the stand fell at Doncaster? Well, I was the only journalist in the stand, and my journal the only one that had no account of it, for I was too shaken to write it. And now I'll be too late with a murder done on my own doorstep."

As we left the room, we heard his pen travelling shrilly over the foolscap.

The spot where the fragments of the bust had been found was only a few hundred yards away. For the first time our eyes rested upon this presentment of the great emperor, which seemed to raise such frantic and destructive hatred in the mind of the unknown. It lay scattered, in splintered shards, upon the grass. Holmes picked up several of them and examined them carefully. I was convinced, from his intent face and his purposeful manner, that at last he was upon a clue.

"Well?" asked Lestrade.

Holmes shrugged his shoulders.

"We have a long way to go yet," said he. "And yet—and yet—well, we have some suggestive facts to act upon. The possession of this trifling bust was worth more, in the eyes of this strange criminal, than a human life. That is one point. Then there is the singular fact that he did not break it in the house, or immediately outside the house, if to break it was his sole object."

"He was rattled and bustled by meeting this other fellow. He hardly knew what he was doing."

"Well, that's likely enough. But I wish to call your attention very particularly to the position of this house, in the garden of which the bust was destroyed."

Lestrade looked about him.

"It was an empty house, and so he knew that he would not be disturbed in the garden."

"Yes, but there is another empty house farther up the street which he must have passed before he came to this one. Why did he not break it there, since it is evident that every yard that he carried it increased the risk of someone meeting him?"

"I give it up," said Lestrade.

Holmes pointed to the street lamp above our heads.

"He could see what he was doing here, and he could not there. That was his reason."

"By Jove! that's true," said the detective. "Now that I come to think of it, Dr. Barnicot's bust was broken not far from his red lamp. Well, Mr. Holmes, what are we to do with that fact?"

"To remember it—to docket it. We may come on something later which will bear upon it. What steps do you propose to take now, Lestrade?"

"The most practical way of getting at it, in my opinion, is to identify the dead man. There should be no difficulty about that. When we have found who he is and who his associates are, we should have a good start in learning what he was doing in Pitt Street last night, and who it was who met him and killed him on the doorstep of Mr. Horace Harker. Don't you think so?"

"No doubt; and yet it is not quite the way in which I should approach the case."

"What would you do then?"

"Oh, you must not let me influence you in any way. I suggest that you go on your line and I on mine. We can compare notes afterwards, and each will supplement the other."

"Very good," said Lestrade.

"If you are going back to Pitt Street, you might see Mr. Horace Harker. Tell him for me that I have quite made up my mind, and that it is certain that a dangerous homicidal lunatic, with Napoleonic delusions, was in his house last night. It will be useful for his article."

Lestrade stared.

"You don't seriously believe that?"

Holmes smiled.

"Don't I? Well, perhaps I don't. But I am sure that it will interest Mr. Horace Harker and the subscribers of the Central Press Syndicate. Now, Watson, I think that we shall find that we have a long and rather complex day's work before us. I should be glad, Lestrade, if you could make it convenient to meet us at Baker Street at six o'clock this evening. Until then I should like to keep this photograph, found in the dead man's pocket. It is possible that I may have to ask your company and assistance upon a small expedition which will have to be undertaken tonight, if my chain of reasoning should prove to be correct. Until then good-bye and good luck!"

Sherlock Holmes and I walked together to the High Street, where we stopped at the shop of Harding Brothers, whence the bust had been purchased. A young assistant informed us that Mr. Harding would be absent until afternoon, and that he was himself a newcomer, who could give us no information. Holmes's face showed his disappointment and annoyance.

"Well, well, we can't expect to have it all our own way, Watson," he said, at last. "We must come back in the afternoon, if Mr. Harding will not be here until then. I am, as you have no doubt surmised, endeavouring to trace these busts to their source, in order to find if there is not something peculiar which may account for their remarkable fate. Let us make for Mr. Morse Hudson, of the Kennington Road, and see if he can throw any light upon the problem."

A drive of an hour brought us to the picture-dealer's establishment. He was a small, stout man with a red face and a peppery manner.

"Yes, sir. On my very counter, sir," said he. "What we pay rates and taxes for I don't know, when any ruffian can come in and break one's goods. Yes, sir, it was I who sold Dr. Barnicot his two statues. Disgraceful, sir! A Nihilist plot—that's what I make it. No one but an anarchist would go about breaking statues. Red republicans—that's what I call 'em. Who did I get the statues from? I don't see what that has to do with it. Well, if you really want to know, I got them from Gelder & Co., in Church Street, Stepney. They are a well-known house in the trade, and have been this twenty years. How many had I? Three—two and one are three—two of Dr. Barnicot's, and one smashed in broad daylight on my own counter. Do I know that photograph? No, I don't. Yes, I do, though. Why, it's Beppo. He was a kind of Italian piece-work man, who made himself useful in the shop. He could carve a bit, and gild and frame, and do odd jobs. The fellow left me last week, and I've heard nothing of him since. No, I don't know where he came from nor where he went to. I had nothing against him while he was here. He was gone two days before the bust was smashed."

"Well, that's all we could reasonably expect from Morse Hudson," said Holmes, as we emerged from the shop. "We have this Beppo as a common factor, both in Kennington and in Kensington, so that is worth a ten-mile drive. Now, Watson, let us make for Gelder & Co., of Stepney, the source and origin of the busts. I shall be surprised if we don't get some help down there."

In rapid succession we passed through the fringe of fashionable London, hotel London, theatrical London, literary London, commercial London, and, finally, maritime London, till we came to a riverside city of a hundred thousand souls, where the tenement houses swelter and reek with the outcasts of Europe. Here, in a broad thoroughfare, once the abode of wealthy city merchants, we found the sculpture works for which we searched. Outside was a considerable yard full of monumental masonry. Inside was a large room in which fifty workers were carving or moulding. The manager, a big blond German, received us civilly and gave a clear answer to all Holmes's questions. A reference to his books showed that hundreds of casts had been taken from a marble copy of Devine's head of Napoleon, but that the three which had been sent to Morse Hudson a year or so before had been half of a batch of six, the other three being sent to Harding Brothers, of Kensington. There was no reason why those six should be different from any of the other casts. He could suggest no possible cause why anyone should wish to destroy them—in fact, he laughed at the idea. Their wholesale price was six shillings, but the retailer would get twelve or more. The cast was taken in two moulds from each side of the face, and then these two profiles of plaster of Paris were joined together to make the complete bust. The work was usually done by Italians, in the room we were in. When finished, the busts were put on a table in the passage to dry, and afterwards stored. That was all he could tell us.

But the production of the photograph had a remarkable effect upon the manager. His face flushed with anger, and his brows knotted over his blue Teutonic eyes.

"Ah, the rascal!" he cried. "Yes, indeed, I know him very well. This has always been a respectable establishment, and the only time that we have ever had the police in it was over this very fellow. It was more than a year ago now. He knifed another Italian in the street, and then he came to the works with the police on his heels, and he was taken here. Beppo was his name—his second name I never knew. Serve me right for engaging a man with such a face. But he was a good workman—one of the best."

"What did he get?"

"The man lived and he got off with a year. I have no doubt he is out now, but he has not dared to show his nose here. We have a cousin of his here, and I daresay he could tell you where he is."

"No, no," cried Holmes, "not a word to the cousin—not a word, I beg of you. The matter is very important, and the farther I go with it, the more important it seems to grow. When you referred in your ledger to the sale of those casts I observed that the date was June 3rd of last year. Could you give me the date when Beppo was arrested?"

"I could tell you roughly by the pay-list," the manager answered.

"Yes," he continued, after some turning over of pages, "he was paid last on May 20th."

"Thank you," said Holmes. "I don't think that I need intrude upon your time and patience any more." With a last word of caution that he should say nothing as to our researches, we turned our faces westward once more.

The afternoon was far advanced before we were able to snatch a hasty luncheon at a restaurant. A news-bill at the entrance announced "Kensington Outrage. Murder by a Madman," and the contents of the paper showed that Mr. Horace Harker had got his account into print after all. Two columns were occupied with a highly sensational and flowery rendering of the whole incident. Holmes propped it against the cruet-stand and read it while he ate. Once or twice he chuckled.

"This is all right, Watson," said he. "Listen to this:

"It is satisfactory to know that there can be no difference of opinion upon this case, since Mr. Lestrade, one of the most experienced members of the official force, and Mr. Sherlock Holmes, the well-known consulting expert, have each come to the conclusion that the grotesque series of incidents, which have ended in so tragic a fashion, arise from lunacy rather than from deliberate crime. No explanation save mental aberration can cover the facts.

The Press, Watson, is a most valuable institution, if you only know how to use it. And now, if you have quite finished, we will hark back to Kensington and see what the manager of Harding Brothers has to say on the matter."

The founder of that great emporium proved to be a brisk, crisp little person, very dapper and quick, with a clear head and a ready tongue.

"Yes, sir, I have already read the account in the evening papers. Mr. Horace Harker is a customer of ours. We supplied him with the bust some months ago. We ordered three busts of that sort from Gelder & Co., of Stepney. They are all sold now. To whom? Oh, I daresay by consulting our sales book we could very easily tell you. Yes, we have the entries here. One to Mr. Harker you see, and one to Mr. Josiah Brown, of Laburnum Lodge, Laburnum Vale, Chiswick, and one to Mr. Sandeford, of Lower Grove Road, Reading. No, I have never seen this face which you show me in the photograph. You would hardly forget it, would you, sir, for I've seldom seen an uglier. Have we any Italians on the staff? Yes, sir, we have several among our workpeople and cleaners. I daresay they might get a peep at that sales book if they wanted to. There is no particular reason for keeping a watch upon that book. Well, well, it's a very strange business, and I hope that you will let me know if anything comes of your inquiries."

Holmes had taken several notes during Mr. Harding's evidence, and I could see that he was thoroughly satisfied by the turn which affairs were taking. He made no remark, however, save that, unless we hurried, we should be late for our appointment with Lestrade. Sure enough, when we reached Baker Street the detective was already there, and we found him pacing up and down in a fever of impatience. His look of importance showed that his day's work had not been in vain.

"Well?" he asked. "What luck, Mr. Holmes?"

"We have had a very busy day, and not entirely a wasted one," my friend explained. "We have seen both the retailers and also the wholesale manufacturers. I can trace each of the busts now from the beginning."

"The busts!" cried Lestrade. "Well, well, you have your own methods, Mr. Sherlock Holmes, and it is not for me to say a word against them, but I think I have done a better day's work than you. I have identified the dead man."

"You don't say so?"

"And found a cause for the crime."

"Splendid!"

"We have an inspector who makes a specialty of Saffron Hill and the Italian Quarter. Well, this dead man had some Catholic emblem round his neck, and that, along with his colour, made me think he was from the South. Inspector Hill knew him the moment he caught sight of him. His name is Pietro Venucci, from Naples, and he is one of the greatest cut-throats in London. He is connected with the Mafia, which, as you know, is a secret political society, enforcing its decrees by murder. Now, you see how the affair begins to clear up. The other fellow is probably an Italian also, and a member of the Mafia. He has broken the rules in some fashion. Pietro is set upon his track. Probably the photograph we found in his pocket is the man himself, so that he may not knife the wrong person. He dogs the fellow, he sees him enter a house, he waits outside for him, and in the scuffle he receives his own death-wound. How is that, Mr. Sherlock Holmes?"

Holmes clapped his hands approvingly.

"Excellent, Lestrade, excellent!" he cried. "But I didn't quite follow your explanation of the destruction of the busts."

"The busts! You never can get those busts out of your head. After all, that is nothing; petty larceny, six months at the most. It is the murder that we are really investigating, and I tell you that I am gathering all the threads into my hands."

"And the next stage?"

"Is a very simple one. I shall go down with Hill to the Italian Quarter, find the man whose photograph we have got, and arrest him on the charge of murder. Will you come with us?"

"I think not. I fancy we can attain our end in a simpler way. I can't say for certain, because it all depends—well, it all depends upon a factor which is completely outside our control. But I have great hopes—in fact, the betting is exactly two to one—that if you will come with us to-night I shall be able to help you to lay him by the heels."

"In the Italian Quarter?"

"No, I fancy Chiswick is an address which is more likely to find him. If you will come with me to Chiswick to-night, Lestrade, I'll promise to go to the Italian Quarter with you to-morrow, and no harm will be done by the delay. And now I think that a few hours' sleep would do us all good, for I do not propose to leave before eleven o'clock, and it is unlikely that we shall be back before morning. You'll dine with us, Lestrade, and then you are welcome to the sofa until it is time for us to start. In the meantime, Watson, I should be glad if you would ring for an express messenger, for I have a letter to send and it is important that it should go at once."

Holmes spent the evening in rummaging among the files of the old daily papers with which one of our lumber-rooms was packed. When at last he descended, it was with triumph in his eyes, but he said nothing to either of us as to the result of his researches. For my own part, I had followed step by step the methods by which he had traced the various windings of this complex case, and, though I could not yet perceive the goal which we would reach, I understood clearly that Holmes expected this grotesque criminal to make an attempt upon the two remaining busts, one of which, I remembered, was at Chiswick. No doubt the object of our journey was to catch him in the very act, and I could not but admire the cunning with which my friend had inserted a wrong clue in the evening paper, so as to give the fellow the idea that he could continue his scheme with impunity. I was not surprised when Holmes suggested that I should take my revolver with me. He had himself picked up the loaded hunting-crop,* which was his favourite weapon.

A four-wheeler was at the door at eleven, and in it we drove to a spot at the other side of Hammersmith Bridge. Here the cabman was directed to wait. A short walk brought us to a secluded road fringed with pleasant houses, each standing in its own grounds. In the light of a street lamp we read "Laburnum Villa" upon the gatepost of one of them. The occupants had evidently retired to rest, for all was dark save for a fanlight over the hall door, which shed a single blurred circle on to the garden path. The wooden fence which separated the grounds from the road threw a dense black shadow upon the inner side, and here it was that we crouched.

"I fear that you'll have a long wait," Holmes whispered. "We may thank our stars that it is not raining. I don't think we can even venture to smoke to pass the time. However, it's a two to one chance that we get something to pay us for our trouble."

It proved, however, that our vigil was not to be so long as Holmes had led us to fear, and it ended in a very sudden and singular fashion. In an instant, without the least sound to warn us of his coming, the garden gate swung open, and a lithe, dark figure, as swift and active as an ape, rushed up the garden path. We saw it whisk past the light thrown from over the door and disappear against the black shadow of the house. There was a long pause, during which we held our breath, and then a very gentle creaking sound came to our ears. The window was being opened. The

---

*Short riding whip.

noise ceased, and again there was a long silence. The fellow was making his way into the house. We saw the sudden flash of a dark lantern inside the room. What he sought was evidently not there, for again we saw the flash through another blind, and then through another.

"Let us get to the open window. We will nab him as he climbs out," Lestrade whispered.

But before we could move, the man had emerged again. As he came out into the glimmering patch of light, we saw that he carried something white under his arm. He looked stealthily all round him. The silence of the deserted street reassured him. Turning his back upon us he laid down his burden, and the next instant there was the sound of a sharp tap, followed by a clatter and rattle. The man was so intent upon what he was doing that he never heard our steps as we stole across the grass plot. With the bound of a tiger Holmes was on his back, and an instant later Lestrade and I had him by either wrist, and the handcuffs had been fastened. As we turned him over I saw a hideous, sallow face, with writhing, furious features, glaring up at us, and I knew that it was indeed the man of the photograph whom we had secured.

But it was not our prisoner to whom Holmes was giving his attention. Squatted on the doorstep, he was engaged in most carefully examining that which the man had brought from the house. It was a bust of Napoleon, like the one which we had seen that morning, and it had been broken into similar fragments. Carefully Holmes held each separate shard to the light, but in no way did it differ from any other shattered piece of plaster. He had just completed his examination when the hall lights flew up, the door opened, and the owner of the house, a jovial, rotund figure in shirt and trousers, presented himself.

"Mr. Josiah Brown, I suppose?" said Holmes.

"Yes, sir; and you, no doubt, are Mr. Sherlock Holmes? I had the note which you sent by the express messenger, and I did exactly what you told me. We locked every door on the inside and awaited developments. Well, I'm very glad to see that you have got the rascal. I hope, gentlemen, that you will come in and have some refreshment."

However, Lestrade was anxious to get his man into safe quarters, so within a few minutes our cab had been summoned and we were all four upon our way to London. Not a word would our captive say, but he glared at us from the shadow of his matted hair, and once, when my hand seemed within his reach, he snapped at it like a hungry wolf. We stayed long enough at the police-station to learn that a search of his clothing revealed nothing save a few shillings and a long sheath knife, the handle of which bore copious traces of recent blood.

"That's all right," said Lestrade, as we parted. "Hill knows all these gentry, and he will give a name to him. You'll find that my theory of the Mafia will work out all right. But I'm sure I am exceedingly obliged to you, Mr. Holmes, for the workmanlike way in which you laid hands upon him. I don't quite understand it all yet."

"I fear it is rather too late an hour for explanations," said Holmes.

"Besides, there are one or two details which are not finished off, and it is one of those cases which are worth working out to the very end. If you will come round once more to my rooms at six o'clock to-morrow, I think I shall be able to show you that even now you have not grasped the entire meaning of this business, which presents some features which make it absolutely original in the history of crime. If ever I permit you to chronicle any more of my little problems, Watson, I foresee that you will enliven your pages by an account of the singular adventure of the Napoleonic busts."

When we met again next evening, Lestrade was furnished with much information concerning our prisoner. His name, it appeared, was Beppo, second name unknown. He was a well-known ne'er-do-well among the Italian colony. He had once been a skilful sculptor and had earned an honest living, but he had taken to evil courses and had twice already been in jail—once for a petty theft, and once, as we had already heard, for stabbing a fellow-countryman. He could talk English perfectly well. His reasons for destroying the busts were still unknown, and he refused to answer any questions upon the subject, but the police had discovered that these same busts might very well have been made by his own hands, since he was engaged in this class of work at the establishment of Gelder & Co. To all this information, much of which we already knew, Holmes listened with polite attention, but I, who knew him so well, could clearly see that his thoughts were elsewhere, and I detected a mixture of mingled uneasiness and expectation beneath that mask which he was wont to assume. At last he started in his chair, and his eyes brightened. There had been a ring at the bell. A minute later we heard steps upon the stairs, and an elderly red-faced man with grizzled side-whiskers was ushered in. In his right hand he carried an old-fashioned carpet-bag, which he placed upon the table.

"Is Mr. Sherlock Holmes here?"

My friend bowed and smiled. "Mr. Sandeford, of Reading, I suppose?" said he.

"Yes, sir, I fear that I am a little late, but the trains were awkward. You wrote to me about a bust that is in my possession."

"Exactly."

"I have your letter here. You said, 'I desire to possess a copy of Devine's Napoleon, and am prepared to pay you ten pounds for the one which is in your possession.' Is that right?"

"Certainly."

"I was very much surprised at your letter, for I could not imagine how you knew that I owned such a thing."

"Of course you must have been surprised, but the explanation is very simple. Mr. Harding, of Harding Brothers, said that they had sold you their last copy, and he gave me your address."

"Oh, that was it, was it? Did he tell you what I paid for it?"

"No, he did not."

"Well, I am an honest man, though not a very rich one. I only gave fifteen shillings for the bust, and I think you ought to know that before I take ten pounds from you."

"I am sure the scruple does you honour, Mr. Sandeford. But I have named that price, so I intend to stick to it."

"Well, it is very handsome of you, Mr. Holmes. I brought the bust up with me, as you asked me to do. Here it is!" He opened his bag, and at last we saw placed upon our table a complete specimen of that bust which we had already seen more than once in fragments.

Holmes took a paper from his pocket and laid a ten-pound note upon the table.

"You will kindly sign that paper, Mr. Sandeford, in the presence of these witnesses. It is simply to say that you transfer every possible right that you ever had in the bust to me. I am a methodical man, you see, and you never know what turn events might take afterwards. Thank you, Mr. Sandeford; here is your money, and I wish you a very good evening."

When our visitor had disappeared, Sherlock Holmes's movements were such as to rivet our attention. He began by taking a clean white cloth from a drawer and laying it over the table. Then he placed his newly acquired bust in the centre of the cloth. Finally, he picked up his hunting-crop and struck Napoleon a sharp blow on the top of the head. The figure broke into fragments, and Holmes bent eagerly over the shattered remains. Next instant, with a loud shout of triumph he held up one splinter, in which a round, dark object was fixed like a plum in a pudding.

"Gentlemen," he cried, "let me introduce you to the famous black pearl of the Borgias."*

Lestrade and I sat silent for a moment, and then, with a spontaneous impulse, we both broke out clapping, as at the well-wrought crisis of a play. A flush of colour sprang to Holmes's pale cheeks, and he bowed to us like the master dramatist who receives the homage of his audience. It was at such moments that for an instant he ceased to be a reasoning machine, and betrayed his human love for admiration and applause. The same singularly proud and reserved nature which turned away with disdain from popular notoriety was capable of being moved to its depths by spontaneous wonder and praise from a friend.

"Yes, gentlemen," said he, "it is the most famous pearl now existing in the world, and it has been my good fortune, by a connected chain of inductive reasoning, to trace it from the Prince of Colonna's bedroom at the Dacre Hotel, where it was lost, to the interior of this, the last of the six busts of Napoleon which were manufactured by Gelder & Co., of Stepney. You will remember, Lestrade, the sensation caused by the disappearance of this valuable jewel, and the vain efforts of the London police to recover it. I was myself consulted upon the case, but I was unable to throw any light upon it. Suspicion fell upon the maid of the Princess, who

*Illustrious Italian Renaissance family whose members included popes and poisoners.

was an Italian, and it was proved that she had a brother in London, but we failed to trace any connection between them. The maid's name was Lucretia Venucci, and there is no doubt in my mind that this Pietro who was murdered two nights ago was the brother. I have been looking up the dates in the old files of the paper, and I find that the disappearance of the pearl was exactly two days before the arrest of Beppo, for some crime of violence—an event which took place in the factory of Gelder & Co., at the very moment when these busts were being made. Now you clearly see the sequence of events, though you see them, of course, in the inverse order to the way in which they presented themselves to me. Beppo had the pearl in his possession. He may have stolen it from Pietro, he may have been Pietro's confederate, he may have been the go-between of Pietro and his sister. It is of no consequence to us which is the correct solution.

"The main fact is that he *had* the pearl, and at that moment, when it was on his person, he was pursued by the police. He made for the factory in which he worked, and he knew that he had only a few minutes in which to conceal this enormously valuable prize, which would otherwise be found on him when he was searched. Six plaster casts of Napoleon were drying in the passage. One of them was still soft. In an instant Beppo, a skilful workman, made a small hole in the wet plaster, dropped in the pearl, and with a few touches covered over the aperture once more. It was an admirable hiding-place. No one could possibly find it. But Beppo was condemned to a year's imprisonment, and in the meanwhile his six busts were scattered over London. He could not tell which contained his treasure. Only by breaking them could he see. Even shaking would tell him nothing, for as the plaster was wet it was probable that the pearl would adhere to it—as, in fact, it has done. Beppo did not despair, and he conducted his search with considerable ingenuity and perseverance. Through a cousin who works with Gelder, he found out the retail firms who had bought the busts. He managed to find employment with Morse Hudson, and in that way tracked down three of them. The pearl was not there. Then, with the help of some Italian employé, he succeeded in finding out where the other three busts had gone. The first was at Harker's. There he was dogged by his confederate, who held Beppo responsible for the loss of the pearl, and he stabbed him in the scuffle which followed."

"If he was his confederate, why should he carry his photograph?" I asked.

"As a means of tracing him, if he wished to inquire about him from any third person. That was the obvious reason. Well, after the murder I calculated that Beppo would probably hurry rather than delay his movements. He would fear that the police would read his secret, and so he hastened on before they should get ahead of him. Of course, I could not say that he had not found the pearl in Harker's bust. I had not even concluded for certain that it was the pearl, but it was evident to me that he was looking for something, since he carried the bust past the other houses in order to break it in the garden which had a lamp overlooking it. Since

Harker's bust was one in three, the chances were exactly as I told you— two to one against the pearl being inside it. There remained two busts, and it was obvious that he would go for the London one first. I warned the inmates of the house, so as to avoid a second tragedy, and we went down, with the happiest results. By that time, of course, I knew for certain that it was the Borgia pearl that we were after. The name of the murdered man linked the one event with the other. There only remained a single bust—the Reading one—and the pearl must be there. I bought it in your presence from the owner—and there it lies."

We sat in silence for a moment.

"Well," said Lestrade, "I've seen you handle a good many cases, Mr. Holmes, but I don't know that I ever knew a more workmanlike one than that. We're not jealous of you at Scotland Yard. No, sir, we are very proud of you, and if you come down to-morrow, there's not a man, from the oldest inspector to the youngest constable, who wouldn't be glad to shake you by the hand."

"Thank you!" said Holmes. "Thank you!" and as he turned away, it seemed to me that he was more nearly moved by the softer human emotions than I had ever seen him. A moment later he was the cold and practical thinker once more. "Put the pearl in the safe, Watson," said he, "and get out the papers of the Conk-Singleton forgery case. Good-bye, Lestrade. If any little problem comes your way, I shall be happy, if I can, to give you a hint or two as to its solution."

THE ADVENTURE OF THE
THREE STUDENTS

It was in the year '95 that a combination of events, into which I need not enter, caused Mr. Sherlock Holmes and myself to spend some weeks in one of our great university towns, and it was during this time that the small but instructive adventure which I am about to relate befell us. It will be obvious that any details which would help the reader exactly to identify the college or the criminal would be injudicious and offensive. So painful a scandal may well be allowed to die out. With due discretion the incident itself may, however, be described, since it serves to illustrate some of those qualities for which my friend was remarkable. I will endeavour, in my statement, to avoid such terms as would serve to limit the events to any particular place, or give a clue as to the people concerned.

We were residing at the time in furnished lodgings close to a library where Sherlock Holmes was pursuing some laborious researches in early English charters—researches which led to results so striking that they may be the subject of one of my future narratives. Here it was that one evening we received a visit from an acquaintance, Mr. Hilton Soames, tutor and lecturer at the College of St. Luke's. Mr. Soames was a tall, spare man, of a nervous and excitable temperament. I had always known him to be restless in his manner, but on this particular occasion he was in such a state of uncontrollable agitation that it was clear something very unusual had occurred.

"I trust, Mr. Holmes, that you can spare me a few hours of your valuable time. We have had a very painful incident at St. Luke's, and really, but for the happy chance of your being in town, I should have been at a loss what to do."

"I am very busy just now, and I desire no distractions," my friend answered. "I should much prefer that you called in the aid of the police."

"No, no, my dear sir; such a course is utterly impossible. When once the law is evoked it cannot be stayed again, and this is just one of those cases where, for the credit of the college, it is most essential to avoid scandal. Your discretion is as well known as your powers, and you are the one man in the world who can help me. I beg you, Mr. Holmes, to do what you can."

My friend's temper had not improved since he had been deprived of the congenial surroundings of Baker Street. Without his scrapbooks, his chemicals, and his homely untidiness, he was an uncomfortable man. He shrugged his shoulders in ungracious acquiescence, while our visitor in hurried words and with much excitable gesticulation poured forth his story.

"I must explain to you, Mr. Holmes, that to-morrow is the first day of the examination for the Fortescue Scholarship. I am one of the examiners. My subject is Greek, and the first of the papers consists of a large passage of Greek translation which the candidate has not seen. This passage is printed on the examination paper, and it would naturally be an immense advantage if the candidate could prepare it in advance. For this reason, great care is taken to keep the paper secret.

"To-day, about three o'clock, the proofs of this paper arrived from the printers. The exercise consists of half a chapter of Thucydides. I had to read it over carefully, as the text must be absolutely correct. At four-thirty my task was not yet completed. I had, however, promised to take tea in a friend's rooms, so I left the proof upon my desk. I was absent rather more than an hour.

"You are aware, Mr. Holmes, that our college doors are double—a green baize one within and a heavy oak one without. As I approached my outer door, I was amazed to see a key in it. For an instant I imagined that I had left my own there, but on feeling in my pocket I found that it was all right. The only duplicate which existed, so far as I knew, was that which belonged to my servant, Bannister—a man who has looked after my room for ten years, and whose honesty is absolutely above suspicion. I found that the key was indeed his, that he had entered my room to know if I wanted tea, and that he had very carelessly left the key in the door when he came out. His visit to my room must have been within a very few minutes of my leaving it. His forgetfulness about the key would have mattered little upon any other occasion, but on this one day it has produced the most deplorable consequences.

"The moment I looked at my table, I was aware that someone had rummaged among my papers. The proof was in three long slips. I had left them all together. Now, I found that one of them was lying on the floor, one was on the side table near the window, and the third was where I had left it."

Holmes stirred for the first time.

"The first page on the floor, the second in the window, the third where you left it," said he.

"Exactly, Mr. Holmes. You amaze me. How could you possibly know that?"

"Pray continue your very interesting statement."

"For an instant I imagined that Bannister had taken the unpardonable liberty of examining my papers. He denied it, however, with the utmost earnestness, and I am convinced that he was speaking the truth. The alternative was that someone passing had observed the key in the door, had known that I was out, and had entered to look at the papers. A large sum of money is at stake, for the scholarship is a very valuable one, and an unscrupulous man might very well run a risk in order to gain an advantage over his fellows.

"Bannister was very much upset by the incident. He had nearly fainted when we found that the papers had undoubtedly been tampered with. I gave him a little brandy and left him collapsed in a chair, while I made a most careful examination of the room. I soon saw that the intruder had left other traces of his presence besides the rumpled papers. On the table in the window were several shreds from a pencil which had been sharp-ened. A broken tip of lead was lying there also. Evidently the rascal had copied the paper in a great hurry, had broken his pencil, and had been compelled to put a fresh point to it."

"Excellent!" said Holmes, who was recovering his good-humour as his attention became more engrossed by the case. "Fortune has been your friend."

"This was not all. I have a new writing-table with a fine surface of red leather. I am prepared to swear, and so is Bannister, that it was smooth and unstained. Now I found a clean cut in it about three inches long—not a mere scratch, but a positive cut. Not only this, but on the table I found a small ball of black dough or clay, with specks of something which looks like sawdust in it. I am convinced that these marks were left by the man who rifled the papers. There were no footmarks and no other evidence as to his identity. I was at my wit's end, when suddenly the happy thought oc-curred to me that you were in the town, and I came straight round to put the matter into your hands. Do help me, Mr. Holmes. You see my dilemma. Either I must find the man or else the examination must be postponed until fresh papers are prepared, and since this cannot be done without explanation, there will ensue a hideous scandal, which will throw a cloud not only on the college, but on the university. Above all things, I desire to settle the matter quietly and discreetly."

"I shall be happy to look into it and to give you such advice as I can," said Holmes, rising and putting on his overcoat. "The case is not entirely devoid of interest. Had anyone visited you in your room after the papers came to you?"

"Yes, young Daulat Ras, an Indian student, who lives on the same stair, came in to ask me some particulars about the examination."

"For which he was entered?"

"Yes."

"And the papers were on your table?"

"To the best of my belief, they were rolled up."

"But might be recognized as proofs?"

"Possibly."

"No one else in your room?"

"No."

"Did anyone know that these proofs would be there?"

"No one save the printer."

"Did this man Bannister know?"

"No, certainly not. No one knew."

"Where is Bannister now?"

"He was very ill, poor fellow. I left him collapsed in the chair. I was in such a hurry to come to you."

"You left your door open?"

"I locked up the papers first."

"Then it amounts to this, Mr. Soames: that, unless the Indian student recognized the roll as being proofs, the man who tampered with them came upon them accidentally without knowing that they were there."

"So it seems to me."

Holmes gave an enigmatic smile.

"Well," said he, "let us go round. Not one of your cases, Watson— mental, not physical. All right; come if you want to. Now, Mr. Soames— at your disposal!"

The sitting-room of our client opened by a long, low, latticed window on to the ancient lichen-tinted court of the old college. A Gothic arched door led to a worn stone staircase. On the ground floor was the tutor's room. Above were three students, one on each story. It was already twilight when we reached the scene of our problem. Holmes halted and looked earnestly at the window. Then he approached it, and, standing on tiptoe with his neck craned, he looked into the room.

"He must have entered through the door. There is no opening except the one pane," said our learned guide.

"Dear me!" said Holmes, and he smiled in a singular way as he glanced at our companion. "Well, if there is nothing to be learned here, we had best go inside."

The lecturer unlocked the outer door and ushered us into his room. We stood at the entrance while Holmes made an examination of the carpet.

"I am afraid there are no signs here," said he. "One could hardly hope for any upon so dry a day. Your servant seems to have quite recovered. You left him in a chair, you say. Which chair?"

"By the window there."

"I see. Near this little table. You can come in now. I have finished with the carpet. Let us take the little table first. Of course, what has happened is very clear. The man entered and took the papers, sheet by sheet, from the central table. He carried them over to the window table, because from there he could see if you came across the courtyard, and so could effect an escape."

"As a matter of fact, he could not," said Soames, "for I entered by the side door."

"Ah, that's good! Well, anyhow, that was in his mind. Let me see the three strips. No finger impressions—no! Well, he carried over this one first, and he copied it. How long would it take him to do that, using every possible contraction? A quarter of an hour, not less. Then he tossed it down and seized the next. He was in the midst of that when your return caused him to make a very hurried retreat—*very* hurried, since he had not time to replace the papers which would tell you that he had been there. You were not aware of any hurrying feet on the stair as you entered the outer door?"

"No, I can't say I was."

"Well, he wrote so furiously that he broke his pencil, and had, as you observe, to sharpen it again. This is of interest, Watson. The pencil was not an ordinary one. It was above the usual size, with a soft lead, the outer colour was dark blue, the maker's name was printed in silver lettering, and the piece remaining is only about an inch and a half long. Look for such a pencil, Mr. Soames, and you have got your man. When I add that he possesses a large and very blunt knife, you have an additional aid."

Mr. Soames was somewhat overwhelmed by this flood of information. "I can follow the other points," said he, "but really, in this matter of the length——"

Holmes held out a small chip with the letters NN and a space of clear wood after them.

"You see?"

"No, I fear that even now——"

"Watson, I have always done you an injustice. There are others. What could this NN be? It is at the end of a word. You are aware that Johann Faber is the most common maker's name. Is it not clear that there is just as much of the pencil left as usually follows the Johann?" He held the small table sideways to the electric light. "I was hoping that if the paper on which he wrote was thin, some trace of it might come through upon this polished surface. No, I see nothing. I don't think there is anything more to be learned here. Now for the central table. This small pellet is, I presume, the black, doughy mass you spoke of. Roughly pyramidal in shape and hollowed out, I perceive. As you say, there appear to be grains of sawdust in it. Dear me, this is very interesting. And the cut—a positive tear, I see. It began with a thin scratch and ended in a jagged hole. I am much indebted to you for directing my attention to this case, Mr. Soames. Where does that door lead to?"

"To my bedroom."

"Have you been in it since your adventure?"

"No, I came straight away for you."

"I should like to have a glance round. What a charming, old-fashioned room! Perhaps you will kindly wait a minute, until I have examined the floor. No, I see nothing. What about this curtain? You hang your clothes behind it. If anyone were forced to conceal himself in this room he must do it there, since the bed is too low and the wardrobe too shallow. No one there, I suppose?"

As Holmes drew the curtain I was aware, from some little rigidity and alertness of his attitude, that he was prepared for an emergency. As a matter of fact, the drawn curtain disclosed nothing but three or four suits of clothes hanging from a line of pegs. Holmes turned away, and stooped suddenly to the floor.

"Halloa! What's this?" said he.

It was a small pyramid of black, putty-like stuff, exactly like the one upon the table of the study. Holmes held it out on his open palm in the glare of the electric light.

"Your visitor seems to have left traces in your bedroom as well as in your sitting-room, Mr. Soames."

"What could he have wanted there?"

"I think it is clear enough. You came back by an unexpected way, and so he had no warning until you were at the very door. What could he do? He caught up everything which would betray him, and he rushed into your bedroom to conceal himself."

"Good gracious, Mr. Holmes, do you mean to tell me that, all the time I was talking to Bannister in this room, we had the man prisoner if we had only known it?"

"So I read it."

"Surely there is another alternative, Mr. Holmes. I don't know whether you observed my bedroom window?"

"Lattice-paned, lead framework, three separate windows, one swinging on hinge, and large enough to admit a man."

"Exactly. And it looks out on an angle of the courtyard so as to be partly invisible. The man might have effected his entrance there, left traces as he passed through the bedroom, and finally, finding the door open, have escaped that way."

Holmes shook his head impatiently.

"Let us be practical," said he. "I understand you to say that there are three students who use this stair, and are in the habit of passing your door?"

"Yes, there are."

"And they are all in for this examination?"

"Yes."

"Have you any reason to suspect any one of them more than the others?"

Soames hesitated.

"It is a very delicate question," said he. "One hardly likes to throw suspicion where there are no proofs."

"Let us hear the suspicions. I will look after the proofs."

"I will tell you, then, in a few words the character of the three men who inhabit these rooms. The lower of the three is Gilchrist, a fine scholar and athlete, plays in the Rugby team and the cricket team for the college, and got his Blue* for the hurdles and the long jump. He is a fine, manly fellow. His father was the notorious Sir Jabez Gilchrist, who ruined himself on the turf.† My scholar has been left very poor, but he is hard-working and industrious. He will do well.

"The second floor is inhabited by Daulat Ras, the Indian. He is a quiet, inscrutable fellow; as most of those Indians are. He is well up in his work, though his Greek is his weak subject. He is steady and methodical.

"The top floor belongs to Miles McLaren. He is a brilliant fellow when he chooses to work—one of the brightest intellects of the university; but he is wayward, dissipated, and unprincipled. He was nearly expelled over

---

*Was officially a representative for the school for a sports event.
†Suffered gambling losses at the racetrack.

a card scandal in his first year. He has been idling all this term, and he must look forward with dread to the examination."

"Then it is he whom you suspect?"

"I dare not go so far as that. But, of the three, he is perhaps the least unlikely."

"Exactly. Now, Mr. Soames, let us have a look at your servant, Bannister."

He was a little, white-faced, clean-shaven, grizzly-haired fellow of fifty. He was still suffering from this sudden disturbance of the quiet routine of his life. His plump face was twitching with his nervousness, and his fingers could not keep still.

"We are investigating this unhappy business, Bannister," said his master.

"Yes, sir."

"I understand," said Holmes, "that you left your key in the door?"

"Yes, sir."

"Was it not very extraordinary that you should do this on the very day when there were these papers inside?"

"It was most unfortunate, sir. But I have occasionally done the same thing at other times."

"When did you enter the room?"

"It was about half-past four. That is Mr. Soames's tea time."

"How long did you stay?"

"When I saw that he was absent, I withdrew at once."

"Did you look at these papers on the table?"

"No, sir—certainly not."

"How came you to leave the key in the door?"

"I had the tea-tray in my hand. I thought I would come back for the key. Then I forgot."

"Has the outer door a spring lock?"

"No, sir."

"Then it was open all the time?"

"Yes, sir."

"Anyone in the room could get out?"

"Yes, sir."

"When Mr. Soames returned and called for you, you were very much disturbed?"

"Yes, sir. Such a thing has never happened during the many years that I have been here. I nearly fainted, sir."

"So I understand. Where were you when you began to feel bad?"

"Where was I, sir? Why, here, near the door."

"That is singular, because you sat down in that chair over yonder near the corner. Why did you pass these other chairs?"

"I don't know, sir, it didn't matter to me where I sat."

"I really don't think he knew much about it, Mr. Holmes. He was looking very bad—quite ghastly."

"You stayed here when your master left?"

"Only for a minute or so. Then I locked the door and went to my room."

"Whom do you suspect?"

"Oh, I would not venture to say, sir. I don't believe there is any gentleman in this university who is capable of profiting by such an action. No, sir, I'll not believe it."

"Thank you, that will do," said Holmes. "Oh, one more word. You have not mentioned to any of the three gentlemen whom you attend that anything is amiss?"

"No, sir—not a word."

"You haven't seen any of them?"

"No, sir."

"Very good. Now, Mr. Soames, we will take a walk in the quadrangle, if you please."

Three yellow squares of light shone above us in the gathering gloom.

"Your three birds are all in their nests," said Holmes, looking up. "Halloa! What's that? One of them seems restless enough."

It was the Indian, whose dark silhouette appeared suddenly upon his blind. He was pacing swiftly up and down his room.

"I should like to have a peep at each of them," said Holmes. "Is it possible?"

"No difficulty in the world," Soames answered. "This set of rooms is quite the oldest in the college, and it is not unusual for visitors to go over them. Come along, and I will personally conduct you."

"No names, please!" said Holmes, as we knocked at Gilchrist's door. A tall, flaxen-haired, slim young fellow opened it, and made us welcome when he understood our errand. There were some really curious pieces of mediæval domestic architecture within. Holmes was so charmed with one of them that he insisted on drawing it in his notebook, broke his pencil, had to borrow one from our host, and finally borrowed a knife to sharpen his own. The same curious accident happened to him in the rooms of the Indian—a silent, little, hook-nosed fellow, who eyed us askance, and was obviously glad when Holmes's architectural studies had come to an end. I could not see that in either case Holmes had come upon the clue for which he was searching. Only at the third did our visit prove abortive. The outer door would not open to our knock, and nothing more substantial than a torrent of bad language came from behind it. "I don't care who you are. You can go to blazes!" roared the angry voice. "To-morrow's the exam, and I won't be drawn by anyone."

"A rude fellow," said our guide, flushing with anger as we withdrew down the stair. "Of course, he did not realize that it was I who was knocking, but none the less his conduct was very uncourteous, and, indeed, under the circumstances rather suspicious."

Holmes's response was a curious one.

"Can you tell me his exact height?" he asked.

"Really, Mr. Holmes, I cannot undertake to say. He is taller than the Indian, not so tall as Gilchrist. I suppose five foot six would be about it."

"That is very important," said Holmes. "And now, Mr. Soames, I wish you good-night."

Our guide cried aloud in his astonishment and dismay. "Good gracious, Mr. Holmes, you are surely not going to leave me in this abrupt fashion! You don't seem to realize the position. To-morrow is the examination. I must take some definite action to-night. I cannot allow the examination to be held if one of the papers has been tampered with. The situation must be faced."

"You must leave it as it is. I shall drop round early to-morrow morning and chat the matter over. It is possible that I may be in a position then to indicate some course of action. Meanwhile, you change nothing—nothing at all."

"Very good, Mr. Holmes."

"You can be perfectly easy in your mind. We shall certainly find some way out of your difficulties. I will take the black clay with me, also the pencil cuttings. Good-bye."

When we were out in the darkness of the quadrangle, we again looked up at the windows. The Indian still paced his room. The others were invisible.

"Well, Watson, what do you think of it?" Holmes asked, as we came out into the main Street. "Quite a little parlour game—sort of three-card trick, is it not? There are your three men. It must be one of them. You take your choice. Which is yours?"

"The foul-mouthed fellow at the top. He is the one with the worst record. And yet that Indian was a sly fellow also. Why should he be pacing his room all the time?"

"There is nothing in that. Many men do it when they are trying to learn anything by heart."

"He looked at us in a queer way."

"So would you, if a flock of strangers came in on you when you were preparing for an examination next day, and every moment was of value. No, I see nothing in that. Pencils, too, and knives—all was satisfactory. But that fellow *does* puzzle me."

"Who?"

"Why, Bannister, the servant. What's his game in the matter?"

"He impressed me as being a perfectly honest man."

"So he did me. That's the puzzling part. Why should a perfectly honest man—Well, well, here's a large stationer's. We shall begin our researches here."

There were only four stationers of any consequences in the town, and at each Holmes produced his pencil chips, and bid high for a duplicate. All were agreed that one could be ordered, but that it was not a usual size of pencil, and that it was seldom kept in stock. My friend did not appear to be depressed by his failure, but shrugged his shoulders in half-humorous resignation.

"No good, my dear Watson. This, the best and only final clue, has run to nothing. But, indeed, I have little doubt that we can build up a sufficient case without it. By Jove! my dear fellow, it is nearly nine, and the landlady babbled of green peas at seven-thirty. What with your eternal tobacco, Watson, and your irregularity at meals, I expect that you will get notice to quit, and that I shall share your downfall—not, however, before we have solved the problem of the nervous tutor, the careless servant, and the three enterprising students."

Holmes made no further allusion to the matter that day, though he sat lost in thought for a long time after our belated dinner. At eight in the morning, he came into my room just as I finished my toilet.

"Well, Watson," said he, "it is time we went down to St. Luke's. Can you do without breakfast?"

"Certainly."

"Soames will be in a dreadful fidget until we are able to tell him something positive."

"Have you anything positive to tell him?"

"I think so."

"You have formed a conclusion?"

"Yes, my dear Watson, I have solved the mystery."

"But what fresh evidence could you have got?"

"Aha! It is not for nothing that I have turned myself out of bed at the untimely hour of six. I have put in two hours' hard work and covered at least five miles, with something to show for it. Look at that!"

He held out his hand. On the palm were three little pyramids of black, doughy clay.

"Why, Holmes, you had only two yesterday."

"And one more this morning. It is a fair argument that wherever No. 3 came from is also the source of Nos. 1 and 2. Eh, Watson? Well, come along and put friend Soames out of his pain."

The unfortunate tutor was certainly in a state of pitiable agitation when we found him in his chambers. In a few hours the examination would commence, and he was still in the dilemma between making the facts public and allowing the culprit to compete for the valuable scholarship. He could hardly stand still, so great was his mental agitation, and he ran towards Holmes with two eager hands outstretched.

"Thank heaven that you have come! I feared that you had given it up in despair. What am I to do? Shall the examination proceed?"

"Yes, let it proceed, by all means."

"But this rascal?"

"He shall not compete."

"You know him?"

"I think so. If this matter is not to become public, we must give ourselves certain powers and resolve ourselves into a small private court-martial. You there, if you please, Soames! Watson, you here! I'll take the armchair in the middle. I think that we are now sufficiently imposing to strike terror into a guilty breast. Kindly ring the bell!"

Bannister entered, and shrank back in evident surprise and fear at our judicial appearance.

"You will kindly close the door," said Holmes. "Now, Bannister, will you please tell us the truth about yesterday's incident?"

The man turned white to the roots of his hair.

"I have told you everything, sir."

"Nothing to add?"

"Nothing at all, sir."

"Well, then, I must make some suggestions to you. When you sat down on that chair yesterday, did you do so in order to conceal some object which would have shown who had been in the room?"

Bannister's face was ghastly.

"No, sir, certainly not."

"It is only a suggestion," said Holmes, suavely. "I frankly admit that I am unable to prove it. But it seems probable enough, since the moment that Mr. Soames's back was turned, you released the man who was hiding in that bedroom."

Bannister licked his dry lips.

"There was no man, sir.

"Ah, that's a pity, Bannister. Up to now you may have spoken the truth, but now I know that you have lied."

The man's face set in sullen defiance.

"There was no man, sir."

"Come, come, Bannister!"

"No, sir, there was no one."

"In that case, you can give us no further information. Would you please remain in the room? Stand over there near the bedroom door. Now, Soames, I am going to ask you to have the great kindness to go up to the room of young Gilchrist, and to ask him to step down into yours."

An instant later the tutor returned, bringing with him the student. He was a fine figure of a man, tall, lithe, and agile, with a springy step and a pleasant, open face. His troubled blue eyes glanced at each of us, and finally rested with an expression of blank dismay upon Bannister in the farther corner.

"Just close the door," said Holmes. "Now, Mr. Gilchrist, we are all quite alone here, and no one need ever know one word of what passes between us. We can be perfectly frank with each other. We want to know, Mr. Gilchrist, how you, an honourable man, ever came to commit such an action as that of yesterday?"

The unfortunate young man staggered back, and cast a look full of horror and reproach at Bannister.

"No, no, Mr. Gilchrist, sir, I never said a word—never one word!" cried the servant.

"No, but you have now," said Holmes. "Now, sir, you must see that after Bannister's words your position is hopeless, and that your only chance lies in a frank confession."

For a moment Gilchrist, with upraised hand, tried to control his writhing features. The next he had thrown himself on his knees beside the table, and burying his face in his hands, he had burst into a storm of passionate sobbing.

"Come, come, said Holmes, kindly, "it is human to err, and at least no one can accuse you of being a callous criminal. Perhaps it would be easier for you if I were to tell Mr. Soames what occurred, and you can check me where I am wrong. Shall I do so? Well, well, don't trouble to answer. Listen, and see that I do you no injustice.

"From the moment, Mr. Soames, that you said to me that no one, not even Bannister, could have told that the papers were in your room, the case began to take a definite shape in my mind. The printer one could, of course, dismiss. He could examine the papers in his own office. The Indian I also thought nothing of. If the proofs were in a roll, he could not possibly know what they were. On the other hand, it seemed an unthinkable coincidence that a man should dare to enter the room, and that by chance on that very day the papers were on the table. I dismissed that. The man who entered knew that the papers were there. How did he know?

"When I approached your room, I examined the window. You amused me by supposing that I was contemplating the possibility of someone having in broad daylight, under the eyes of all these opposite rooms, forced himself through it. Such an idea was absurd. I was measuring how tall a man would need to be in order to see, as he passed, what papers were on the central table. I am six feet high, and I could do it with an effort. No one less than that would have a chance. Already you see I had reason to think that, if one of your three students was a man of unusual height, he was the most worth watching of the three.

"I entered, and I took you into my confidence as to the suggestions of the side table. Of the centre table I could make nothing, until in your description of Gilchrist you mentioned that he was a long-distance jumper. Then the whole thing came to me in an instant, and I only needed certain corroborative proofs, which I speedily obtained.

"What happened was this: This young fellow had employed his afternoon at the athletic grounds, where he had been practising the jump. He returned carrying his jumping-shoes, which are provided, as you are aware, with several sharp spikes. As he passed your window he saw, by means of his great height, these proofs upon your table, and conjectured what they were. No harm would have been done had it not been that, as he passed your door, he perceived the key which had been left by the carelessness of your servant. A sudden impulse came over him to enter, and see if they were indeed the proofs. It was not a dangerous exploit, for he could always pretend that he had simply looked in to ask a question.

"Well, when he saw that they were indeed the proofs, it was then that he yielded to temptation. He put his shoes on the table. What was it you put on that chair near the window?"

"Gloves," said the young man.

Holmes looked triumphantly at Bannister. "He put his gloves on the chair, and he took the proofs, sheet by sheet, to copy them. He thought the tutor must return by the main gate, and that he would see him. As we know, he came back by the side gate. Suddenly he heard him at the very door. There was no possible escape. He forgot his gloves, but he caught up his shoes and darted into the bedroom. You observe that the scratch on that table is slight at one side, but deepens in the direction of the bedroom door. That in itself is enough to show us that the shoe had been drawn in that direction, and that the culprit had taken refuge there. The earth round the spike had been left on the table, and a second sample was loosened and fell in the bedroom. I may add that I walked out to the athletic grounds this morning, saw that tenacious black clay is used in the jumping-pit, and carried away a specimen of it, together with some of the fine tan or sawdust which is strewn over it to prevent the athlete from slipping. Have I told the truth, Mr. Gilchrist?"

The student had drawn himself erect.

"Yes, sir, it is true," said he.

"Good heavens! have you nothing to add?" cried Soames.

"Yes, sir, I have, but the shock of this disgraceful exposure has bewildered me. I have a letter here, Mr. Soames, which I wrote to you early this morning in the middle of a restless night. It was before I knew that my sin had found me out. Here it is, sir. You will see that I have said, 'I have determined not to go in for the examination. I have been offered a commission in the Rhodesian Police, and I am going out to South Africa at once.' "

"I am indeed pleased to hear that you did not intend to profit by your unfair advantage," said Soames. "But why did you change your purpose?"

Gilchrist pointed to Bannister.

"There is the man who set me in the right path," said he.

"Come now, Bannister," said Holmes. "It will be clear to you, from what I have said, that only you could have let this young man out, since you were left in the room, and must have locked the door when you went out. As to his escaping by that window, it was incredible. Can you not clear up the last point in this mystery, and tell us the reasons for your action?"

"It was simple enough, sir, if you only had known, but, with all your cleverness, it was impossible that you could know. Time was, sir, when I was butler to old Sir Jabez Gilchrist, this young gentleman's father. When he was ruined I came to the college as servant, but I never forgot my old employer because he was down in the world. I watched his son all I could for the sake of the old days. Well, sir, when I came into this room yesterday, when the alarm was given, the very first thing I saw was Mr. Gilchrist's tan gloves a-lying in that chair. I knew those gloves well, and I understood their message. If Mr. Soames saw them, the game was up. I flopped down into that chair, and nothing would budge me until Mr. Soames went for you. Then out came my poor young master, whom I had dandled on my knee, and confessed it all to me. Wasn't it natural, sir, that I should save him, and wasn't it natural also that I should try to speak to him as his dead father would have done, and make him understand that he could not profit by such a deed? Could you blame me, sir?"

"No, indeed," said Holmes, heartily, springing to his feet. "Well, Soames, I think we have cleared your little problem up, and our breakfast awaits us at home. Come, Watson! As to you, sir, I trust that a bright future awaits you in Rhodesia. For once you have fallen low. Let us see, in the future, how high you can rise."

THE ADVENTURE OF THE
GOLDEN PINCE-NEZ*

When I look at the three massive manuscript volumes which contain our work for the year 1894, I confess that it is very difficult for me, out of such a wealth of material, to select the cases which are most interesting in themselves, and at the same time most conducive to a display of those peculiar powers for which my friend was famous. As I turn over the pages, I see my notes upon the repulsive story of the red leech and the terrible death of Crosby, the banker. Here also I find an account of the Addleton tragedy, and the singular contents of the ancient British barrow. The famous Smith-Mortimer succession case comes also within this period, and so does the tracking and arrest of Huret, the Boulevard assassin—an exploit which won for Holmes an autograph letter of thanks from The French President and the Order of the Legion of Honour. Each of these would furnish a narrative, but on the whole I am of the opinion that none of them unites so many singular points of interest as the episode of Yoxley Old Place, which includes not only the lamentable death of young Willoughby Smith, but also those subsequent developments which threw so curious a light upon the causes of the crime.

It was a wild, tempestuous night, towards the close of November. Holmes and I sat together in silence all the evening, he engaged with a powerful lens deciepering the remains of the original inscription upon a palimpsest,† I deep in a recent treatise upon surgery. Outside the wind howled down Baker Street, while the rain beat fiercely against the windows. It was strange there, in the very depths of the town, with ten miles of man's handiwork on every side of us, to feel the iron grip of Nature, and to be conscious that to the huge elemental forces all London was no more than the molehills that dot the fields. I walked to the window, and looked out on the deserted street. The occasional lamps gleamed on the expanse of muddy road and shining pavement. A single cab was splashing its way from the Oxford Street end.

"Well, Watson, it's as well we have not to turn out to-night," said Holmes, laying aside his lens and rolling up the palimpsest. "I've done enough for one sitting. It is trying work for the eyes. So far as I can make out, it is nothing more exciting than an Abbey's accounts dating from the second half of the fifteenth century. Halloa! halloa! halloa! What's this?"

Amid the droning of the wind there had come the stamping of a horse's hoofs, and the long grind of a wheel as it rasped against the curb. The cab which I had seen had pulled up at our door.

---

*Eyeglasses that fit on the bridge of the nose.
†Parchment or vellum that has been written upon more than once.

"What can he want?" I ejaculated, as a man stepped out of it.

"Want? He wants us. And we, my poor Watson, want overcoats and cravats and goloshes, and every aid that man ever invented to fight the weather. Wait a bit, though! There's the cab off again! There's hope yet. He'd have kept it if he had wanted us to come. Run down, my dear fellow, and open the door, for all virtuous folk have been long in bed."

When the light of the hall lamp fell upon our midnight visitor, I had no difficulty in recognizing him. It was young Stanley Hopkins, a promising detective, in whose career Holmes had several times shown a very practical interest.

"Is he in?" he asked, eagerly.

"Come up, my dear sir," said Holmes's voice from above. "I hope you have no designs upon us on such a night as this."

The detective mounted the stairs, and our lamp gleamed upon his shining waterproof. I helped him out of it, while Holmes knocked a blaze out of the logs in the grate.

"Now, my dear Hopkins, draw up and warm your toes," said he. "Here's a cigar, and the doctor has a prescription containing hot water and a lemon, which is good medicine on a night like this. It must be something important which has brought you out in such a gale."

"It is indeed, Mr. Holmes. I've had a bustling afternoon, I promise you. Did you see anything of the Yoxley case in the latest editions?"

"I've seen nothing later than the fifteenth century to-day."

"Well, it was only a paragraph, and all wrong at that, so you have not missed anything. I haven't let the grass grow under my feet. It's down in Kent, seven miles from Chatham and three from the railway line. I was wired for at 3:15, reached Yoxley Old Place at 5, conducted my investigation, was back at Charing Cross by the last train, and straight to you by cab."

"Which means, I suppose, that you are not quite clear about your case?"

"It means that I can make neither head nor tail of it. So far as I can see, it is just as tangled a business as ever I handled, and yet at first it seemed so simple that one couldn't go wrong. There's no motive, Mr. Holmes. That's what bothers me—I can't put my hand on a motive. Here's a man dead—there's no denying that—but, so far as I can see, no reason on earth why anyone should wish him harm."

Holmes lit his cigar and leaned back in his chair.

"Let us hear about it," said he.

"I've got my facts pretty clear," said Stanley Hopkins. "All I want now is to know what they all mean. The story, so far as I can make it out, is like this. Some years ago this country house, Yoxley Old Place, was taken by an elderly man, who gave the name of Professor Coram. He was an invalid, keeping his bed half the time, and the other half hobbling round the house with a stick or being pushed about the grounds by the gardener in

---

*Chair mounted on wheels for invalids; first used at Bath, noted for its medicinal springs.

a Bath chair.* He was well liked by the few neighbours who called upon him, and he has the reputation down there of being a very learned man. His household used to consist of an elderly housekeeper, Mrs. Marker, and of a maid, Susan Tarlton. These have both been with him since his arrival, and they seem to be women of excellent character. The professor is writing a learned book, and he found it necessary, about a year ago, to engage a secretary. The first two that he tried were not successes, but the third, Mr. Willoughby Smith, a very young man straight from the university, seems to have been just what his employer wanted. His work consisted in writing all the morning to the professor's dictation, and he usually spent the evening in hunting up references and passages which bore upon the next day's work. This Willoughby Smith has nothing against him, either as a boy at Uppingham or as a young man at Cambridge. I have seen his testimonials, and from the first he was a decent, quiet, hard-working fellow, with no weak spot in him at all. And yet this is the lad who has met his death this morning in the professor's study under circumstances which can point only to murder."

The wind howled and screamed at the windows. Holmes and I drew closer to the fire, while the young inspector slowly and point by point developed his singular narrative.

"If you were to search all England," said he, "I don't suppose you could find a household more self-contained or freer from outside influences. Whole weeks would pass, and not one of them go past the garden gate. The professor was buried in his work and existed for nothing else. Young Smith knew nobody in the neighbourhood, and lived very much as his employer did. The two women had nothing to take them from the house. Mortimer, the gardener, who wheels the Bath chair, is an army pensioner—an old Crimean man of excellent character. He does not live in the house, but in a three-roomed cottage at the other end of the garden. Those are the only people that you would find within the grounds of Yoxley Old Place. At the same time, the gate of the garden is a hundred yards from the main London to Chatham road. It opens with a latch, and there is nothing to prevent anyone from walking in.

"Now I will give you the evidence of Susan Tarlton, who is the only person who can say anything positive about the matter. It was in the forenoon, between eleven and twelve. She was engaged at the moment in hanging some curtains in the upstairs front bedroom. Professor Coram was still in bed, for when the weather is bad he seldom rises before midday. The housekeeper was busied with some work in the back of the house. Willoughby Smith had been in his bedroom, which he uses as a sitting-room, but the maid heard him at that moment pass along the passage and descend to the study immediately below her. She did not see him, but she says that she could not be mistaken in his quick, firm tread. She did not hear the study door close, but a minute or so later there was a dreadful cry in the room below. It was a wild, hoarse scream, so strange and unnatural that it might have come either from a man or a woman. At the same instant there was a heavy thud, which shook the old house, and then all was silence. The maid stood petrified for a moment, and then, recovering her courage, she ran downstairs. The study door was shut and she opened it. Inside, young Mr. Willoughby Smith was stretched upon the floor. At first she could see no injury, but as she tried to raise him she saw that blood was pouring from the underside of his neck. It was pierced by a very small but very deep wound, which had divided the carotid artery. The instrument with which the injury had been inflicted lay upon the carpet beside him. It was one of those small sealing-wax knives to be found on old-fashioned writing-tables, with an ivory handle and a stiff blade. It was part of the fittings of the professor's own desk.

"At first the maid thought that young Smith was already dead, but on pouring some water from the carafe over his forehead he opened his eyes for an instant. 'The professor,' he murmured—'it was she.' The maid is prepared to swear that those were the exact words. He tried desperately to say something else, and he held his right hand up in the air. Then he fell back dead.

"In the meantime the housekeeper had also arrived upon the scene; but she was just too late to catch the young man's dying words. Leaving Susan with the body, she hurried to the professor's room. He was sitting up in bed horribly agitated, for he had heard enough to convince him that something terrible had occurred. Mrs. Marker is prepared to swear that the professor was still in his night-clothes, and indeed it was impossible for him to dress without the help of Mortimer, whose orders were to come at twelve o'clock. The professor declares that he heard the distant cry, but that he knows nothing more. He can give no explanation of the young man's last words, 'The professor—it was she,' but imagines that they were the outcome of delirium. He believes that Willoughby Smith had not an enemy in the world, and can give no reason for the crime. His first action was to send Mortimer, the gardener, for the local police. A little later the chief constable sent for me. Nothing was moved before I got there, and strict orders were given that no one should walk upon the paths leading to the house. It was a splendid chance of putting your theories into practice, Mr. Sherlock Holmes. There was really nothing wanting."

"Except Mr. Sherlock Holmes," said my companion, with a somewhat bitter smile. "Well, let us hear about it. What sort of job did you make of it?"

"I must ask you first, Mr. Holmes, to glance at this rough plan, which will give you a general idea of the position of the professor's study and the various points of the case. It will help you in following my investigation."

He unfolded the rough chart, which I here reproduce, and he laid it across Holmes's knee. I rose and, standing behind Holmes, studied it over his shoulder.

"It is very rough, of course, and it only deals with the points which seem to me to be essential. All the rest you will see later for yourself. Now, first of all, presuming that the assassin entered the house, how did he or she come in? Undoubtedly by the garden path and the back door, from which there is direct access to the study. Any other way would have been exceedingly complicated. The escape must have also been made along that line, for of the two other exits from the room one was blocked by Susan as she ran downstairs and the other leads straight to the professor's bedroom. I therefore directed my attention at once to the garden path, which was saturated with recent rain, and would certainly show any footmarks.

"My examination showed me that I was dealing with a cautious and expert criminal. No footmarks were to be found on the path. There could be no question, however, that someone had passed along the grass border which lines the path, and that he had done so in order to avoid leaving a track. I could not find anything in the nature of a distinct impression, but the grass was trodden down, and someone had undoubtedly passed. It could only have been the murderer, since neither the gardener nor anyone else had been there that morning, and the rain had only begun during the night."

"One moment," said Holmes. "Where does this path lead to?"

"To the road."

"How long is it?"

"A hundred yards or so."

"At the point where the path passes through the gate, you could surely pick up the tracks?"

"Unfortunately, the path was tiled at that point."

"Well, on the road itself?"

"No, it was all trodden into mire."

"Tut-tut! Well, then, these tracks upon the grass, were they coming or going?"

"It was impossible to say. There was never any outline."

"A large foot or a small?"

"You could not distinguish."

Holmes gave an ejaculation of impatience.

"It has been pouring rain and blowing a hurricane ever since," said he. "It will be harder to read now than that palimpsest. Well, well, it can't be helped. What did you do, Hopkins, after you had made certain that you had made certain of nothing?"

"I think I made certain of a good deal, Mr. Holmes. I knew that someone had entered the house cautiously from without. I next examined the corridor. It is lined with cocoanut matting and had taken no impression of any kind. This brought me into the study itself. It is a scantily furnished room. The main article is a large writing-table with a fixed bureau. This bureau consists of a double column of drawers, with a central small cupboard between them. The drawers were open, the cupboard locked. The drawers, it seems, were always open, and nothing of value was kept in them. There were some papers of importance in the cupboard, but there were no signs that this had been tampered with, and the professor assures me that nothing was missing. It is certain that no robbery has been committed.

"I come now to the body of the young man. It was found near the bureau, and just to the left of it, as marked upon that chart. The stab was on the right side of the neck and from behind forward, so that it is almost impossible that it could have been self-inflicted."

"Unless he fell upon the knife," said Holmes.

"Exactly. The idea crossed my mind. But we found the knife some feet away from the body, so that seems impossible. Then, of course, there are the man's own dying words. And, finally, there was this very important piece of evidence which was found clasped in the dead man's right hand."

From his pocket Stanley Hopkins drew a small paper packet. He unfolded it and disclosed a golden pince-nez, with two broken ends of black silk cord dangling from the end of it. "Willoughby Smith had excellent sight," he added. "There can be no question that this was snatched from the face or the person of the assassin."

Sherlock Holmes took the glasses into his hand, and examined them with the utmost attention and interest. He held them on his nose, endeavoured to read through them, went to the window and stared up the street with them, looked at them most minutely in the full light of the lamp, and finally, with a chuckle, seated himself at the table and wrote a few lines upon a sheet of paper, which he tossed across to Stanley Hopkins.

"That's the best I can do for you," said he. "It may prove to be of some use."

The astonished detective read the note aloud. It ran as follows:

"Wanted, a woman of good address, attired like a lady. She has a remarkably thick nose, with eyes which are set close upon either side of it. She has a puckered forehead, a peering expression, and probably rounded shoulders. There are indications that she has had recourse to an optician at least twice during the last few months. As her glasses are of remarkable strength, and as opticians are not very numerous, there should be no difficulty in tracing her."

Holmes smiled at the astonishment of Hopkins, which must have been reflected upon my features.

"Surely my deductions are simplicity itself," said he. "It would be difficult to name any articles which afford a finer field for inference than a pair of glasses, especially so remarkable a pair as these. That they belong to a woman I infer from their delicacy, and also, of course, from the last words of the dying man. As to her being a person of refinement and well dressed, they are, as you perceive, handsomely mounted in solid gold, and it is inconceivable that anyone who wore such glasses could be slatternly in other respects. You will find that the clips are too wide for your nose, showing that the lady's nose was very broad at the base. This sort of nose is usually a short and coarse one, but there is a sufficient number of exceptions to prevent me from being dogmatic or from insisting upon this point in my description. My own face is a narrow one, and yet I find that I cannot get my eyes into the centre, nor near the centre, of these glasses. Therefore, the lady's eyes are set very near to the sides of the nose. You will perceive, Watson, that the glasses are concave and of unusual strength. A lady whose vision has been so extremely contracted all her life is sure to have the physical characteristics of such vision, which are seen in the forehead, the eyelids, and the shoulders."

"Yes," I said, "I can follow each of your arguments. I confess, however, that I am unable to understand how you arrive at the double visit to the optician."

Holmes took the glasses in his hand.

"You will perceive," he said, "that the clips are lined with tiny bands of cork to soften the pressure upon the nose. One of these is discoloured and worn to some slight extent, but the other is new. Evidently one has fallen off and been replaced. I should judge that the older of them has not been there more than a few months. They exactly correspond, so I gather that the lady went back to the same establishment for the second."

"By George, it's marvellous!" cried Hopkins, in an ecstasy of admiration. "To think that I had all that evidence in my hand and never knew it! I had intended, however, to go the round of the London opticians."

"Of course you would. Meanwhile, have you anything more to tell us about the case?"

"Nothing, Mr. Holmes. I think that you know as much as I do now— probably more. We have had inquiries made as to any stranger seen on the country roads or at the railway station. We have heard of none. What beats me is the utter want of all object in the crime. Not a ghost of a motive can anyone suggest."

"Ah! there I am not in a position to help you. But I suppose you want us to come out to-morrow?"

"If it is not asking too much, Mr. Holmes. There's a train from Charing Cross to Chatham at six in the morning, and we should be at Yoxley Old Place between eight and nine."

"Then we shall take it. Your case has certainly some features of great interest, and I shall be delighted to look into it. Well, it's nearly one, and we had best get a few hours' sleep. I daresay you can manage all right on the sofa in front of the fire. I'll light my spirit lamp, and give you a cup of coffee before we start."

The gale had blown itself out next day, but it was a bitter morning when we started upon our journey. We saw the cold winter sun rise over the dreary marshes of the Thames and the long, sullen reaches of the river, which I shall ever associate with our pursuit of the Andaman Islander in the earlier days of our career.* After a long and weary journey, we alighted at a small station some miles from Chatham. While a horse was being put into a trap at the local inn, we snatched a hurried breakfast, and so we were all ready for business when we at last arrived at Yoxley Old Place. A constable met us at the garden gate.

"Well, Wilson, any news?"

"No, sir—nothing."

"No reports of any stranger seen?"

"No, sir. Down at the station they are certain that no stranger either came or went yesterday."

"Have you had inquiries made at inns and lodgings?"

"Yes, sir: there is no one that we cannot account for."

"Well, it's only a reasonable walk to Chatham. Anyone might stay there or take a train without being observed. This is the garden path of which I spoke, Mr. Holmes. I'll pledge my word there was no mark on it yesterday."

"On which side were the marks on the grass?"

"This side, sir. This narrow margin of grass between the path and the flowerbed. I can't see the traces now, but they were clear to me then."

"Yes, yes: someone has passed along," said Holmes, stooping over the grass border. "Our lady must have picked her steps carefully, must she not, since on the one side she would leave a track on the path, and on the other an even clearer one on the soft bed?"

"Yes, sir, she must have been a cool hand."

I saw an intent look pass over Holmes's face.

"You say that she must have come back this way?"

"Yes, sir, there is no other."

"On this strip of grass?"

"Certainly, Mr. Holmes."

"Hum! It was a very remarkable performance—very remarkable. Well, I think we have exhausted the path. Let us go farther. This garden door is usually kept open, I suppose? Then this visitor had nothing to do but to walk in. The idea of murder was not in her mind, or she would have

---

*Watson refers to the chase in *The Sign of Four*.

provided herself with some sort of weapon, instead of having to pick this knife off the writing-table. She advanced along this corridor, leaving no traces upon the cocoanut matting. Then she found herself in this study. How long was she there? We have no means of judging."

"Not more than a few minutes, sir. I forgot to tell you that Mrs. Marker, the housekeeper, had been in there tidying not very long before—about a quarter of an hour, she says."

"Well, that gives us a limit. Our lady enters this room, and what does she do? She goes over to the writing-table. What for? Not for anything in the drawers. If there had been anything worth her taking, it would surely have been locked up. No, it was for something in that wooden bureau. Halloa! what is that scratch upon the face of it? Just hold a match, Watson. Why did you not tell me of this, Hopkins?"

The mark which he was examining began upon the brasswork on the righthand side of the keyhole, and extended for about four inches, where it had scratched the varnish from the surface.

"I noticed it, Mr. Holmes, but you'll always find scratches round a keyhole."

"This is recent, quite recent. See how the brass shines where it is cut. An old scratch would be the same colour as the surface. Look at it through my lens. There's the varnish, too, like earth on each side of a furrow. Is Mrs. Marker there?"

A sad-faced, elderly woman came into the room.

"Did you dust this bureau yesterday morning?"

"Yes, sir."

"Did you notice this scratch?"

"No, sir, I did not."

"I am sure you did not, for a duster would have swept away these shreds of varnish. Who has the key of this bureau?"

"The professor keeps it on his watch-chain."

"Is it a simple key?"

"No, sir, it is a Chubb's key."

"Very good. Mrs. Marker, you can go. Now we are making a little progress. Our lady enters the room, advances to the bureau, and either opens it or tries to do so. While she is thus engaged, young Willoughby Smith enters the room. In her hurry to withdraw the key, she makes this scratch upon the door. He seizes her, and she, snatching up the nearest object, which happens to be this knife, strikes at him in order to make him let go his hold. The blow is a fatal one. He falls and she escapes, either with or without the object for which she has come. Is Susan, the maid, there? Could anyone have got away through that door after the time that you heard the cry, Susan?"

"No, sir, it is impossible. Before I got down the stair, I'd have seen anyone in the passage. Besides, the door never opened, or I would have heard it."

"That settles this exit. Then no doubt the lady went out the way she came. I understand that this other passage leads only to the professor's room. There is no exit that way?"

"No, sir."

"We shall go down it and make the acquaintance of the professor. Halloa, Hopkins! this is very important, very important indeed. The professor's corridor is also lined with cocoanut matting."

"Well, sir, what of that?"

"Don't you see any bearing upon the case? Well, well. I don't insist upon it. No doubt I am wrong. And yet it seems to me to be suggestive. Come with me and introduce me."

We passed down the passage, which was of the same length as that which led to the garden. At the end was a short flight of steps ending in a door. Our guide knocked, and then ushered us into the professor's bedroom.

It was a very large chamber, lined with innumerable volumes, which had overflowed from the shelves and lay in piles in the corners, or were stacked all round at the base of the cases. The bed was in the centre of the room, and in it, propped up with pillows, was the owner of the house. I have seldom seen a more remarkable-looking person. It was a gaunt, aquiline face which was turned towards us, with piercing dark eyes, which lurked in deep hollows under overhung and tufted brows. His hair and beard were white, save that the latter was curiously stained with yellow around his mouth. A cigarette glowed amid the tangle of white hair, and the air of the room was fetid with stale tobacco smoke. As he held out his hand to Holmes, I perceived that it was also stained with yellow nicotine.

"A smoker, Mr. Holmes?" said he, speaking in well-chosen English, with a curious little mincing accent. "Pray take a cigarette. And you, sir? I can recommend them, for I have them especially prepared by Ionides, of Alexandria. He sends me a thousand at a time, and I grieve to say that I have to arrange for a fresh supply every fortnight. Bad, sir, very bad, but an old man has few pleasures. Tobacco and my work—that is all that is left to me."

Holmes had lit a cigarette and was shooting little darting glances all over the room.

"Tobacco and my work, but now only tobacco," the old man exclaimed. "Alas! what a fatal interruption! Who could have foreseen such a terrible catastrophe? So estimable a young man! I assure you that, after a few months' training, he was an admirable assistant. What do you think of the matter, Mr. Holmes?"

"I have not yet made up my mind."

"I shall indeed be indebted to you if you can throw a light where all is so dark to us. To a poor bookworm and invalid like myself such a blow is paralyzing. I seem to have lost the faculty of thought. But you are a man of action—you are a man of affairs. It is part of the everyday routine of your life. You can preserve your balance in every emergency. We are fortunate, indeed, in having you at our side."

Holmes was pacing up and down one side of the room whilst the old professor was talking. I observed that he was smoking with extraordinary rapidity. It was evident that he shared our host's liking for the fresh Alexandrian cigarettes.

"Yes, sir, it is a crushing blow," said the old man. "That is my *magnum opus*—the pile of papers on the side table yonder. It is my analysis of the documents found in the Coptic monasteries of Syria and Egypt, a work which will cut deep at the very foundation of revealed religion. With my enfeebled health I do not know whether I shall ever be able to complete it, now that my assistant has been taken from me. Dear me! Mr. Holmes, why, you are even a quicker smoker than I am myself."

Holmes smiled.

"I am a connoisseur," said he, taking another cigarette from the box—his fourth—and lighting it from the stub of that which he had finished. "I will not trouble you with any lengthy cross-examination, Professor Coram, since I gather that you were in bed at the time of the crime, and could know nothing about it. I would only ask this: What do you imagine that this poor fellow meant by his last words: 'The professor—it was she'?"

The professor shook his head.

"Susan is a country girl," said he, "and you know the incredible stupidity of that class. I fancy that the poor fellow murmured some incoherent, delirious words, and that she twisted them into this meaningless message."

"I see. You have no explanation yourself of the tragedy?"

"Possibly an accident, possibly—I only breathe it among ourselves—a suicide. Young men have their hidden troubles—some affair of the heart, perhaps, which we have never known. It is a more probable supposition than murder."

"But the eyeglasses?"

"Ah! I am only a student—a man of dreams. I cannot explain the practical things of life. But still, we are aware, my friend, that love-gages may take strange shapes. By all means take another cigarette. It is a pleasure to see anyone appreciate them so. A fan, a glove, glasses—who knows what article may be carried as a token or treasured when a man puts an end to his life? This gentleman speaks of footsteps in the grass, but, after all, it is easy to be mistaken on such a point. As to the knife, it might well be thrown far from the unfortunate man as he fell. It is possible that I speak as a child, but to me it seems that Willoughby Smith has met his fate by his own hand."

Holmes seemed struck by the theory thus put forward, and he continued to walk up and down for some time, lost in thought and consuming cigarette after cigarette.

"Tell me, Professor Coram," he said, at last, "what is in that cupboard in the bureau?"

"Nothing that would help a thief. Family papers, letters from my poor wife, diplomas of universities which have done me honour. Here is the key. You can look for yourself."

Holmes picked up the key, and looked at it for an instant, then he handed it back.

"No, I hardly think that it would help me," said he. "I should prefer to go quietly down to your garden, and turn the whole matter over in my head. There is something to be said for the theory of suicide which you have put forward. We must apologize for having intruded upon you, Professor Coram, and I promise that we won't disturb you until after lunch. At two o'clock we will come again, and report to you anything which may have happened in the interval."

Holmes was curiously distrait,* and we walked up and down the garden path for some time in silence.

"Have you a clue?" I asked, at last.

"It depends upon those cigarettes that I smoked," said he. "It is possible that I am utterly mistaken. The cigarettes will show me."

"My dear Holmes," I exclaimed, "how on earth—"

"Well, well, you may see for yourself. If not, there's no harm done. Of course, we always have the optician clue to fall back upon, but I take a short cut when I can get it. Ah, here is the good Mrs. Marker! Let us enjoy five minutes of instructive conversation with her."

I may have remarked before that Holmes had, when he liked, a peculiarly ingratiating way with women, and that he very readily established terms of confidence with them. In half the time which he had named, he had captured the housekeeper's goodwill and was chatting with her as if he had known her for years.

"Yes, Mr. Holmes, it is as you say, sir. He does smoke something terrible. All day and sometimes all night, sir. I've seen that room of a morning—well, sir, you'd have thought it was a London fog. Poor young Mr. Smith, he was a smoker also, but not as bad as the professor. His health—well, I don't know that it's better nor worse for the smoking."

"Ah!" said Holmes, "but it kills the appetite."

"Well, I don't know about that, sir."

"I suppose the professor eats hardly anything?"

"Well, he is variable. I'll say that for him."

"I'll wager he took no breakfast this morning, and won't face his lunch after all the cigarettes I saw him consume."

"Well, you're out there, sir, as it happens, for he ate a remarkable big breakfast this morning. I don't know when I've known him make a better one, and he's ordered a good dish of cutlets for his lunch. I'm surprised myself, for since I came into that room yesterday and saw young Mr. Smith lying there on the floor, I couldn't bear to look at food. Well, it takes all sorts to make a world, and the professor hasn't let it take his appetite away."

We loitered the morning away in the garden. Stanley Hopkins had gone down to the village to look into some rumours of a strange woman

---

*Distracted from present concerns; absentminded.

who had been seen by some children on the Chatham Road the previous morning. As to my friend, all his usual energy seemed to have deserted him. I had never known him handle a case in such a half-hearted fashion. Even the news brought back by Hopkins that he had found the children, and that they had undoubtedly seen a woman exactly corresponding with Holmes's description, and wearing either spectacles or eyeglasses, failed to rouse any sign of keen interest. He was more attentive when Susan, who waited upon us at lunch, volunteered the information that she believed Mr. Smith had been out for a walk yesterday morning, and that he had only returned half an hour before the tragedy occurred. I could not myself see the bearing of this incident, but I clearly perceived that Holmes was weaving it into the general scheme which he had formed in his brain. Suddenly he sprang from his chair and glanced at his watch. "Two o'clock, gentlemen," said he. "We must go up and have it out with our friend, the professor."

The old man had just finished his lunch, and certainly his empty dish bore evidence to the good appetite with which his housekeeper had credited him. He was, indeed, a weird figure as he turned his white mane and his glowing eyes towards us. The eternal cigarette smouldered in his mouth. He had been dressed and was seated in an armchair by the fire.

"Well, Mr. Holmes, have you solved this mystery yet?" He shoved the large tin of cigarettes which stood on a table beside him towards my companion. Holmes stretched out his hand at the same moment, and between them they tipped the box over the edge. For a minute or two we were all on our knees retrieving stray cigarettes from impossible places. When we rose again, I observed Holmes's eyes were shining and his cheeks tinged with colour. Only at a crisis have I seen those battle-signals flying.

"Yes," said he, "I have solved it."

Stanley Hopkins and I stared in amazement. Something like a sneer quivered over the gaunt features of the old professor.

"Indeed! In the garden?"

"No, here."

"Here! When?"

"This instant."

"You are surely joking, Mr. Sherlock Holmes. You compel me to tell you that this is too serious a matter to be treated in such a fashion."

"I have forged and tested every link of my chain, Professor Coram, and I am sure that it is sound. What your motives are, or what exact part you play in this strange business, I am not yet able to say. In a few minutes I shall probably hear it from your own lips. Meanwhile I will reconstruct what is past for your benefit, so that you may know the information which I still require.

"A lady yesterday entered your study. She came with the intention of possessing herself of certain documents which were in your bureau. She had a key of her own. I have had an opportunity of examining yours, and I do not find that slight discolouration which the scratch made upon the varnish would have produced. You were not an accessory, therefore, and she came, so far as I can read the evidence, without your knowledge to rob you."

The professor blew a cloud from his lips. "This is most interesting and instructive," said he. "Have you no more to add? Surely, having traced this lady so far, you can also say what has become of her."

"I will endeavour to do so. In the first place she was seized by your secretary, and stabbed him in order to escape. This catastrophe I am inclined to regard as an unhappy accident, for I am convinced that the lady had no intention of inflicting so grievous an injury. An assassin does not come unarmed. Horrified by what she had done, she rushed wildly away from the scene of the tragedy. Unfortunately for her, she had lost her glasses in the scuffle, and as she was extremely shortsighted she was really helpless without them. She ran down a corridor, which she imagined to be that by which she had come—both were lined with cocoanut matting—and it was only when it was too late that she understood that she had taken the wrong passage, and that her retreat was cut off behind her. What was she to do? She could not go back. She could not remain where she was. She must go on. She went on. She mounted a stair, pushed open a door, and found herself in your room."

The old man sat with his mouth open, staring wildly at Holmes. Amazement and fear were stamped upon his expressive features. Now, with an effort, he shrugged his shoulders and burst into insincere laughter.

"All very fine, Mr. Holmes," said he. "But there is one little flaw in your splendid theory. I was myself in my room, and I never left it during the day."

"I am aware of that, Professor Coram."

"And you mean to say that I could lie upon that bed and not be aware that a woman had entered my room?"

"I never said so. You *were* aware of it. You spoke with her. You recognized her. You aided her to escape."

Again the professor burst into high-keyed laughter. He had risen to his feet, and his eyes glowed like embers.

"You are mad!" he cried. "You are talking insanely. I helped her to escape? Where is she now?"

"She is there," said Holmes, and he pointed to a high bookcase in the corner of the room.

I saw the old man throw up his arms, a terrible convulsion passed over his grim face, and he fell back in his chair. At the same instant the bookcase at which Holmes pointed swung round upon a hinge, and a woman rushed out into the room. "You are right!" she cried, in a strange foreign voice. "You are right! I am here."

She was brown with the dust and draped with the cobwebs which had come from the walls of her hiding-place. Her face, too, was streaked with grime, and at the best she could never have been handsome, for she had the exact physical characteristics which Holmes had divined, with, in addition, a long and obstinate chin. What with her natural blindness, and what with the change from dark to light, she stood as one dazed, blinking about her to see where and who we were. And yet, in spite of all these disadvantages, there was a certain nobility in the woman's bearing—a gallantry in the defiant chin and in the upraised head, which compelled something of respect and admiration.

Stanley Hopkins had laid his hand upon her arm and claimed her as his prisoner, but she waved him aside gently, and yet with an over-mastering dignity which compelled obedience. The old man lay back in his chair with a twitching face, and stared at her with brooding eyes.

"Yes, sir, I am your prisoner," she said. "From where I stood I could hear everything, and I know that you have learned the truth. I confess it all. It was I who killed the young man. But you are right—you who say it was an accident. I did not even know that it was a knife which I held in my hand, for in my despair I snatched anything from the table and struck at him to make him let me go. It is the truth that I tell."

"Madam," said Holmes, "I am sure that it is the truth. I fear that you are far from well."

She had turned a dreadful colour, the more ghastly under the dark dust-streaks upon her face. She seated herself on the side of the bed; then she resumed.

"I have only a little time here," she said, "but I would have you to know the whole truth. I am this man's wife. He is not an Englishman. He is a Russian. His name I will not tell."

For the first time the old man stirred. "God bless you, Anna!" he cried. "God bless you!"

She cast a look of the deepest disdain in his direction. "Why should you cling so hard to that wretched life of yours, Sergius?" said she. "It has done harm to many and good to none—not even to yourself. However, it is not for me to cause the frail thread to be snapped before God's time. I have enough already upon my soul since I crossed the threshold of this cursed house. But I must speak or I shall be too late.

"I have said, gentlemen, that I am this man's wife. He was fifty and I a foolish girl of twenty when we married. It was in a city of Russia, a university—I will not name the place."

"God bless you, Anna!" murmured the old man again.

"We were reformers—revolutionists—Nihilists, you understand. He and I and many more. Then there came a time of trouble,* a police officer was killed, many were arrested, evidence was wanted, and in order to save his own life and to earn a great reward, my husband betrayed his own wife and his companions. Yes, we were all arrested upon his confession. Some of us found our way to the gallows, and some to Siberia. I was among these last, but my term was not for life. My husband came to England with his ill-gotten gains and has lived in quiet ever since, knowing

---

*The phrase "time of trouble" or "times of trouble" is found more than a dozen times in the Bible—for example, Psalms 9:9, 10:1, 27:5, 37:39, and 41:1.

well that if the Brotherhood knew where he was not a week would pass before justice would be done."

The old man reached out a trembling hand and helped himself to a cigarette. "I am in your hands, Anna," said he. "You were always good to me."

"I have not yet told you the height of his villainy," said she. "Among our comrades of the Order, there was one who was the friend of my heart. He was noble, unselfish, loving—all that my husband was not. He hated violence. We were all guilty—if that is guilt—but he was not. He wrote forever dissuading us from such a course. These letters would have saved him. So would my diary, in which, from day to day, I had entered both my feelings towards him and the view which each of us had taken. My husband found and kept both diary and letters. He hid them, and he tried hard to swear away the young man's life. In this he failed, but Alexis was sent a convict to Siberia, where now, at this moment, he works in a salt mine. Think of that, you villain, you villain!—now, now, at this very moment, Alexis, a man whose name you are not worthy to speak, works and lives like a slave, and yet I have your life in my hands, and I let you go."

"You were always a noble woman, Anna," said the old man, puffing at his cigarette.

She had risen, but she fell back again with a little cry of pain.

"I must finish," she said. "When my term was over I set myself to get the diary and letters which, if sent to the Russian government, would procure my friend's release. I knew that my husband had come to England. After months of searching I discovered where he was. I knew that he still had the diary, for when I was in Siberia I had a letter from him once, reproaching me and quoting some passages from its pages. Yet I was sure that, with his revengeful nature, he would never give it to me of his own free-will. I must get it for myself. With this object I engaged an agent from a private detective firm, who entered my husband's house as a secretary—it was your second secretary, Sergius, the one who left you so hurriedly. He found that papers were kept in the cupboard, and he got an impression of the key. He would not go farther. He furnished me with a plan of the house, and he told me that in the forenoon the study was always empty, as the secretary was employed up here. So at last I took my courage in both hands, and I came down to get the papers for myself. I succeeded; but at what a cost!

"I had just taken the papers and was locking the cupboard, when the young man seized me. I had seen him already that morning. He had met me on the road, and I had asked him to tell me where Professor Coram lived, not knowing that he was in his employ."

"Exactly! Exactly!" said Holmes. "The secretary came back, and told his employer of the woman he had met. Then, in his last breath, he tried to send a message that it was she—the she whom he had just discussed with him."

"You must let me speak," said the woman, in an imperative voice, and her face contracted as if in pain. "When he had fallen I rushed from the room, chose the wrong door, and found myself in my husband's room. He spoke of giving me up. I showed him that if he did so, his life was in my hands. If he gave me to the law, I could give him to the Brotherhood. It was not that I wished to live for my own sake, but it was that I desired to accomplish my purpose. He knew that I would do what I said—that his own fate was involved in mine. For that reason, and for no other, he shielded me. He thrust me into that dark hiding-place—a relic of old days, known only to himself. He took his meals in his own room, and so was able to give me part of his food. It was agreed that when the police left the house I should slip away by night and come back no more. But in some way you have read our plans." She tore from the bosom of her dress a small packet. "These are my last words," said she; "here is the packet which will save Alexis. I confide it to your honour and to your love of justice. Take it! You will deliver it at the Russian Embassy. Now, I have done my duty, and——"

"Stop her!" cried Holmes. He had bounded across the room and had wrenched a small phial from her hand.

"Too late!" she said, sinking back on the bed. "Too late! I took the poison before I left my hiding-place. My head swims! I am going! I charge you, sir, to remember the packet."

"A simple case, and yet, in some ways, an instructive one," Holmes remarked, as we travelled back to town. "it hinged from the outset upon the pince-nez. But for the fortunate chance of the dying man having seized these, I am not sure that we could ever have reached our solution. It was clear to me, from the strength of the glasses, that the wearer must have been very blind and helpless when deprived of them. When you asked me to believe that she walked along a narrow strip of grass without once making a false step, I remarked, as you may remember, that it was a noteworthy performance. In my mind I set it down as an impossible performance, save in the unlikely case that she had a second pair of glasses. I was forced, therefore, to consider seriously the hypothesis that she had remained within the house. On perceiving the similarity of the two corridors, it became clear that she might very easily have made such a mistake, and, in that case, it was evident that she must have entered the professor's room. I was keenly on the alert, therefore, for whatever would bear out this supposition, and I examined the room narrowly for anything in the shape of a hiding-place. The carpet seemed continuous and firmly nailed, so I dismissed the idea of a trap-door. There might well be a recess behind the books. As you are aware, such devices are common in old libraries. I observed that books were piled on the floor at all other points, but that one bookcase was left clear. This, then, might be the door. I could see no marks to guide me, but the carpet was of a dun colour, which lends itself very well to examination. I therefore smoked a great number of those excellent cigarettes, and I dropped the ash all over the space in front of the suspected bookcase. It was a simple trick, but exceedingly effective. I then went downstairs, and I ascertained, in your presence, Watson, without your perceiving the drift of my remarks, that Professor Coram's consumption of food had increased—as one would expect when he is supplying a second person. We then ascended to the room again, when, by upsetting the cigarette-box, I obtained a very excellent view of the floor, and was able to see quite clearly, from the traces upon the cigarette ash, that the prisoner had in our absence come out from her retreat. Well, Hopkins, here we are at Charing Cross, and I congratulate you on having brought your case to a successful conclusion. You are going to headquarters, no doubt. I think, Watson, you and I will drive together to the Russian Embassy."

THE ADVENTURE OF THE MISSING THREE-QUARTER

We were fairly accustomed to receive weird telegrams at Baker Street, but I have a particular recollection of one which reached us on a gloomy February morning, some seven or eight years ago, and gave Mr. Sherlock Holmes a puzzled quarter of an hour. It was addressed to him, and ran thus:

> Please await me. Terrible misfortune. Right wing three-quarter missing, indispensable to-morrow.
>
> OVERTON.

"Strand postmark, and dispatched ten thirty-six," said Holmes. reading it over and over. "Mr. Overton was evidently considerably excited when he sent it, and somewhat incoherent in consequence. Well, well, he will be here, I daresay, by the time I have looked through the *Times*, and then we shall know all about it. Even the most insignificant problem would be welcome in these stagnant days."

Things had indeed been very slow with us, and I had learned to dread such periods of inaction, for I knew by experience that my companion's brain was so abnormally active that it was dangerous to leave it without material upon which to work. For years I had gradually weaned him from that drug mania which had threatened once to check his remarkable career. Now I knew that under ordinary conditions he no longer craved for this artificial stimulus, but I was well aware that the fiend was not dead but sleeping, and I have known that the sleep was a light one and the waking near when in periods of idleness I have seen the drawn look upon Holmes's ascetic face, and the brooding of his deep-set and inscrutable eyes. Therefore I blessed this Mr. Overton, whoever he might be, since he had come with his enigmatic message to break that dangerous calm which brought more peril to my friend than all the storms of his tempestuous life.

As we had expected, the telegram was soon followed by its sender, and the card of Mr. Cyril Overton, Trinity College, Cambridge, announced the arrival of an enormous young man, sixteen stone of solid bone and muscle, who spanned the doorway with his broad shoulders, and looked from one of us to the other with a comely face which was haggard with anxiety.

"Mr. Sherlock Holmes?"

My companion bowed.

"I've been down to Scotland Yard, Mr. Holmes. I saw Inspector Stanley Hopkins. He advised me to come to you. He said the case, so far as he could see, was more in your line than in that of the regular police."

"Pray sit down and tell me what is the matter."

"It's awful, Mr. Holmes—simply awful! I wonder my hair isn't gray. Godfrey Staunton—you've heard of him, of course? He's simply the hinge that the whole team turns on. I'd rather spare two from the pack, and have Godfrey for my three-quarter line. Whether it's passing, or tackling, or dribbling, there's no one to touch him, and then, he's got the head, and can hold us all together. What am I to do? That's what I ask you, Mr. Holmes. There's Moorhouse, first reserve, but he is trained as a half, and he always edges right in on to the scrum instead of keeping out on the touchline. He's a fine place-kick, it's true, but then he has no judgment, and he can't sprint for nuts. Why, Morton or Johnson, the Oxford fliers, could romp round him. Stevenson is fast enough, but he couldn't drop from the twenty-five line, and a three-quarter who can't either punt or drop isn't worth a place for pace alone. No, Mr. Holmes, we are done unless you can help me to find Godfrey Staunton."

My friend had listened with amused surprise to this long speech, which was poured forth with extraordinary vigour and earnestness, every point being driven home by the slapping of a brawny hand upon the speaker's knee. When our visitor was silent Holmes stretched out his hand and took down letter "S" of his commonplace book. For once he dug in vain into that mine of varied information.

"There is Arthur H. Staunton, the rising young forger," said he, "and there was Henry Staunton, whom I helped to hang, but Godfrey Staunton is a new name to me."

It was our visitor's turn to look surprised.

"Why, Mr. Holmes, I thought you knew things," said he. "I suppose, then, if you have never heard of Godfrey Staunton you don't know Cyril Overton either?"

Holmes shook his head good humouredly.

"Great Scott!" cried the athlete. "Why, I was first reserve for England against Wales, and I've skippered the 'Varsity all this year. But that's nothing! I didn't think there was a soul in England who didn't know Godfrey Staunton, the crack three-quarter, Cambridge, Blackheath, and five Internationals. Good Lord! Mr. Holmes, where *have* you lived?"

Holmes laughed at the young giant's naïve astonishment.

"You live in a different world to me, Mr. Overton—a sweeter and healthier one. My ramifications stretch out into many sections of society, but never, I am happy to say, into amateur sport, which is the best and soundest thing in England. However, your unexpected visit this morning shows me that even in that world of fresh air and fair play, there may be work for me to do. So now, my good sir, I beg you to sit down and to tell me, slowly and quietly, exactly what it is that has occurred, and how you desire that I should help you."

Young Overton's face assumed the bothered look of the man who is more accustomed to using his muscles than his wits, but by degrees, with many repetitions and obscurities which I may omit from his narrative, he laid his strange story before us.

"It's this way, Mr. Holmes. As I have said, I am the skipper of the

Rugger team of Cambridge 'Varsity, and Godfrey Staunton is my best man. To-morrow we play Oxford. Yesterday we all came up, and we settled at Bentley's private hotel. At ten o'clock I went round and saw that all the fellows had gone to roost, for I believe in strict training and plenty of sleep to keep a team fit. I had a word or two with Godfrey before he turned in. He seemed to me to be pale and bothered. I asked him what was the matter. He said he was all right—just a touch of headache. I bade him good-night and left him. Half an hour later, the porter tells me that a rough-looking man with a beard called with a note for Godfrey. He had not gone to bed, and the note was taken to his room. Godfrey read it, and fell back in a chair as if he had been pole-axed.* The porter was so scared that he was going to fetch me, but Godfrey stopped him, had a drink of water, and pulled himself together. Then he went downstairs, said a few words to the man who was waiting in the hall, and the two of them went off together. The last that the porter saw of them, they were almost running down the street in the direction of the Strand. This morning Godfrey's room was empty, his bed had never been slept in, and his things were all just as I had seen them the night before. He had gone off at a moment's notice with this stranger, and no word has come from him since. I don't believe he will ever come back. He was a sportsman, was Godfrey, down to his marrow, and he wouldn't have stopped his training and let in† his skipper if it were not for some cause that was too strong for him. No: I feel as if he were gone for good, and we should never see him again."

Sherlock Holmes listened with the deepest attention to this singular narrative.

"What did you do?" he asked.

"I wired to Cambridge to learn if anything had been heard of him there. I have had an answer. No one has seen him."

"Could he have got back to Cambridge?"

"Yes, there is a late train—quarter-past eleven."

"But, so far as you can ascertain, he did not take it?"

"No, he has not been seen."

"What did you do next?"

"I wired to Lord Mount-James."

"Why to Lord Mount-James?"

"Godfrey is an orphan, and Lord Mount-James is his nearest relative—his uncle, I believe."

"Indeed. This throws new light upon the matter. Lord Mount-James is one of the richest men in England."

"So I've heard Godfrey say."

"And your friend was closely related?"

---

*Hit with a battle-ax having a hammer face opposite the blade.

†Let down, disappoint.

"Yes, he was his heir, and the old boy is nearly eighty—cram full of gout, too. They say he could chalk his billiard-cue with his knuckles. He never allowed Godfrey a shilling in his life, for he is an absolute miser, but it will all come to him right enough."

"Have you heard from Lord Mount-James?"

"No."

"What motive could your friend have in going to Lord Mount-James?"

"Well, something was worrying him the night before, and if it was to do with money it is possible that he would make for his nearest relative, who had so much of it, though from all I have heard he would not have much chance of getting it. Godfrey was not fond of the old man. He would not go if he could help it."

"Well, we can soon determine that. If your friend was going to his relative, Lord Mount-James, you have then to explain the visit of this rough-looking fellow at so late an hour, and the agitation that was caused by his coming."

Cyril Overton pressed his hands to his head. "I can make nothing of it," said he.

"Well, well, I have a clear day, and I shall be happy to look into the matter," said, Holmes. "I should strongly recommend you to make your preparations for your match without reference to this young gentleman. It must, as you say, have been an overpowering necessity which tore him away in such a fashion, and the same necessity is likely to hold him away. Let us step round together to the hotel, and see if the porter can throw any fresh light upon the matter."

Sherlock Holmes was a past-master in the art of putting a humble witness at his ease, and very soon, in the privacy of Godfrey Staunton's abandoned room, he had extracted all that the porter had to tell. The visitor of the night before was not a gentleman, neither was he a workingman. He was simply what the porter described as a "medium-looking chap," a man of fifty, beard grizzled, pale face, quietly dressed. He seemed himself to be agitated. The porter had observed his hand trembling when he had held out the note. Godfrey Staunton had crammed the note into his pocket. Staunton had not shaken hands with the man in the hall. They had exchanged a few sentences, of which the porter had only distinguished the one word "time." Then they had hurried off in the manner described. It was just half-past ten by the hall clock.

"Let me see," said Holmes, seating himself on Staunton's bed. "You are the day porter, are you not?"

"Yes, sir, I go off duty at eleven."

"The night porter saw nothing, I suppose?"

"No, sir, one theatre party came in late. No one else."

"Were you on duty all day yesterday?"

"Yes, sir."

"Did you take any messages to Mr. Staunton?"

"Yes, sir, one telegram."

"Ah! that's interesting. What o'clock was this?"

"About six."

"Where was Mr. Staunton when he received it?"

"Here in his room."

"Were you present when he opened it?"

"Yes, sir, I waited to see if there was an answer."

"Well, was there?"

"Yes, sir, he wrote an answer."

"Did you take it?"

"No, he took it himself."

"But he wrote it in your presence?"

"Yes, sir. I was standing by the door, and he with his back turned to that table. When he had written it he said: 'All right, porter, I will take this myself.' "

"What did he write it with?"

"A pen, sir."

"Was the telegraphic form one of these on the table?"

"Yes, sir, it was the top one."

Holmes rose. Taking the forms, he carried them over to the window and carefully examined that which was uppermost.

"It's a pity he did not write in pencil," said he, throwing them down again with a shrug of disappointment. "As you have no doubt frequently observed, Watson, the impression usually goes through—a fact which has dissolved many a happy marriage. However, I can find no trace here. I rejoice, however, to perceive that he wrote with a broad-pointed quill pen, and I can hardly doubt that we will find some impression upon this blotting-pad. Ah, yes, surely this is the very thing!"

He tore off a strip of the blotting-paper and turned towards us the following hieroglyphic:

Cyril Overton was much excited. "Hold it to the glass!" he cried.

"That is unnecessary," said Holmes. "The paper is thin, and the reverse will give the message. Here it is." He turned it over, and we read:

"So that is the tail end of the telegram which Godfrey Staunton dispatched within a few hours of his disappearance. There are at least six words of the message which have escaped us; but what remains—'Stand by us for God's sake!'—proves that this young man saw a formidable danger which approached him, and from which someone else could protect him. '*Us,*' mark you! Another person was involved. Who should it be but the pale-faced, bearded man, who seemed himself in so nervous a state? What, then, is the connection between Godfrey Staunton and the bearded man? And what is the third source from which each of them sought for help against pressing danger? Our inquiry has already narrowed down to that."

"We have only to find to whom that telegram is addressed," I suggested.

"Exactly, my dear Watson. Your reflection, though profound, had already crossed my mind. But I daresay it may have come to your notice that, if you walk into a postoffice and demand to see the counterfoil of another man's message, there may be some disinclination on the part of the officials to oblige you. There is so much red tape in these matters. However, I have no doubt that with a little delicacy and finesse the end may be attained. Meanwhile, I should like in your presence, Mr. Overton, to go through these papers which have been left upon the table."

There were a number of letters, bills, and notebooks, which Holmes turned over and examined with quick, nervous fingers and darting, penetrating eyes. "Nothing here," he said, at last. "By the way, I suppose your friend was a healthy young fellow—nothing amiss with him?"

"Sound as a bell."

"Have you ever known him ill?"

"Not a day. He has been laid up with a hack, and once he slipped his knee-cap, but that was nothing."

"Perhaps he was not so strong as you suppose. I should think he may have had some secret trouble. With your assent, I will put one or two of these papers in my pocket, in case they should bear upon our future inquiry."

"One moment—one moment!" cried a querulous voice, and we looked up to find a queer little old man, jerking and twitching in the doorway. He was dressed in rusty black, with a very broad-brimmed top-hat and a loose white necktie—the whole effect being that of a very rustic parson or of an undertaker's mute. Yet, in spite of his shabby and even absurd appearance, his voice had a sharp crackle, and his manner a quick intensity which commanded attention.

"Who are you, sir, and by what right do you touch this gentleman's papers?" he asked.

"I am a private detective, and I am endeavouring to explain his disappearance."

"Oh, you are, are you? And who instructed you, eh?"

"This gentleman, Mr. Staunton's friend, was referred to me by Scotland Yard."

"Who are you, sir?"

"I am Cyril Overton."

"Then it is you who sent me a telegram. My name is Lord Mount-James. I came round as quickly as the Bayswater bus would bring me. So you have instructed a detective?"

"Yes, sir."

"And are you prepared to meet the cost?"

"I have no doubt, sir, that my friend Godfrey, when we find him, will be prepared to do that."

"But if he is never found, eh? Answer me that!"

"In that case, no doubt his family——"

"Nothing of the sort, sir!" screamed the little man. "Don't look to me for a penny—not a penny! You understand that, Mr. Detective! I am all the family that this young man has got, and I tell you that I am not responsible. If he has any expectations it is due to the fact that I have never wasted money, and I do not propose to begin to do so now. As to those papers with which you are making so free, I may tell you that in case there should be anything of any value among them, you will be held strictly to account for what you do with them."

"Very good, sir," said Sherlock Holmes. "May I ask, in the meanwhile, whether you have yourself any theory to account for this young man's disappearance?"

"No, sir, I have not. He is big enough and old enough to look after himself, and if he is so foolish as to lose himself, I entirely refuse to accept the responsibility of hunting for him."

"I quite understand your position," said Holmes, with a mischievous twinkle in his eyes. "Perhaps you don't quite understand mine. Godfrey Staunton appears to have been a poor man. If he has been kidnapped, it could not have been for anything which he himself possesses. The fame of your wealth has gone abroad, Lord Mount-James, and it is entirely possible that a gang of thieves have secured your nephew in order to gain from him some information as to your house, your habits, and your treasure."

The face of our unpleasant little visitor turned as white as his neck-cloth.

"Heavens, sir, what an idea! I never thought of such villainy! What inhuman rogues there are in the world! But Godfrey is a fine lad—a staunch lad. Nothing would induce him to give his old uncle away. I'll have the plate* moved over to the bank this evening. In the meantime spare no pains, Mr. Detective! I beg you to leave no stone unturned to bring him safely back. As to money, well, so far as a fiver or even a tenner goes you can always look to me."

Even in his chastened frame of mind, the noble miser could give us no information which could help us, for he knew little of the private life of his nephew. Our only clue lay in the truncated telegram, and with a copy of this in his hand Holmes set forth to find a second link for his chain. We had shaken off Lord Mount-James, and Overton had gone to consult with the other members of his team over the misfortune which had befallen them.

There was a telegraph-office at a short distance from the hotel. We halted outside it.

"It's worth trying, Watson," said Holmes. "Of course, with a warrant we could demand to see the counterfoils, but we have not reached that stage yet. I don't suppose they remember faces in so busy a place. Let us venture it."

"I am sorry to trouble you," said he, in his blandest manner, to the young, woman behind the grating; "there is some small mistake about a telegram I sent yesterday. I have had no answer, and I very much fear that I must have omitted to put my name at the end. Could you tell me if this was so?"

The young woman turned over a sheaf of counterfoils.

"What o'clock was it?" she asked.

"A little after six."

"Whom was it to?"

Holmes put his finger to his lips and glanced at me. "The last words in it were 'for God's sake,'" he whispered, confidentially; "I am very anxious at getting no answer."

The young woman separated one of the forms.

"This is it. There is no name," said she, smoothing it out upon the counter.

"Then that, of course, accounts for my getting no answer," said Holmes. "Dear me, how very stupid of me, to be sure! Good-morning, miss, and many thanks for having relieved my mind." He chuckled and rubbed his hands when we found ourselves in the street once more.

"Well?" I asked.

"We progress, my dear Watson, we progress. I had seven different schemes for getting a glimpse of that telegram, but I could hardly hope to succeed the very first time."

"And what have you gained?"

"A starting-point for our investigation." He hailed a cab. "King's Cross Station," said he.

---

*Household articles plated (covered) with gold or silver.

"We have a journey, then?"

"Yes, I think we must run down to Cambridge together. All the indications seem to me to point in that direction."

"Tell me," I asked, as we rattled up Gray's Inn Road, "have you any suspicion yet as to the cause of the disappearance? I don't think that among all our cases I have known one where the motives are more obscure. Surely you don't really imagine that he may be kidnapped in order to give information against his wealthy uncle?"

"I confess, my dear Watson, that that does not appeal to me as a very probable explanation. It struck me, however, as being the one which was most likely to interest that exceedingly unpleasant old person."

"It certainly did that; but what are your alternatives?"

"I could mention several. You must admit that it is curious and suggestive that this incident should occur on the eve of this important match, and should involve the only man whose presence seems essential to the success of the side. It may, of course, be a coincidence, but it is interesting. Amateur sport is free from betting, but a good deal of outside betting goes on among the public, and it is possible that it might be worth someone's while to get at a player as the ruffians of the turf get at a race-horse. There is one explanation. A second very obvious one is that this young man really is the heir of a great property, however modest his means may at present be, and it is not impossible that a plot to hold him for ransom might be concocted."

"These theories take no account of the telegram."

"Quite true, Watson. The telegram still remains the only solid thing with which we have to deal, and we must not permit our attention to wander away from it. It is to gain light upon the purpose of this telegram that we are now upon our way to Cambridge. The path of our investigation is at present obscure, but I shall be very much surprised if before evening we have not cleared it up, or made a considerable advance along it."

It was already dark when we reached the old university city. Holmes took a cab at the station and ordered the man to drive to the house of Dr. Leslie Armstrong. A few minutes later, we had stopped at a large mansion on the busiest thoroughfare. We were shown in, and after a long wait were at last admitted into the consulting-room, where we found the doctor seated behind his table.

It argues the degree in which I had lost touch with my profession that the name of Leslie Armstrong was unknown to me. Now I am aware that he is not only one of the heads of the medical school of the university, but a thinker of European reputation in more than one branch of science. Yet even without knowing his brilliant record one could not fail to be impressed by a mere glance at the man, the square, massive face, the brooding eyes under the thatched brows, and the granite moulding of the inflexible jaw. A man of deep character, a man with an alert mind, grim, ascetic, self-contained, formidable—so I read Dr. Leslie Armstrong. He held my friend's card in his hand, and he looked up with no very pleased expression upon his dour features.

"I have heard your name, Mr. Sherlock Holmes, and I am aware of your profession—one of which I by no means approve."

"In that, Doctor, you will find yourself in agreement with every criminal in the country," said my friend, quietly.

"So far as your efforts are directed towards the suppression of crime, sir, they must have the support of every reasonable member of the community, though I cannot doubt that the official machinery is amply sufficient for the purpose. Where your calling is more open to criticism is when you pry into the secrets of private individuals, when you rake up family matters which are better hidden, and when you incidentally waste the time of men who are more busy than yourself. At the present moment, for example, I should be writing a treatise instead of conversing with you."

"No doubt, Doctor; and yet the conversation may prove more important than the treatise. Incidentally, I may tell you that we are doing the reverse of what you very justly blame, and that we are endeavouring to prevent anything like public exposure of private matters which must necessarily follow when once the case is fairly in the hands of the official police. You may look upon me simply as an irregular pioneer, who goes in front of the regular forces of the country. I have come to ask you about Mr. Godfrey Staunton."

"What about him?"

"You know him, do you not?"

"He is an intimate friend of mine."

"You are aware that he has disappeared?"

"Ah, indeed!" There was no change of expression in the rugged features of the doctor.

"He left his hotel last night—he has not been heard of."

"No doubt he will return."

"To-morrow is the 'Varsity football match."

"I have no sympathy with these childish games. The young man's fate interests me deeply, since I know him and like him. The football match does not come within my horizon at all."

"I claim your sympathy, then, in my investigation of Mr. Staunton's fate. Do you know where he is?"

"Certainly not."

"You have not seen him since yesterday?"

"No, I have not."

"Was Mr. Staunton a healthy man?"

"Absolutely."

"Did you ever know him ill?"

"Never."

Holmes popped a sheet of paper before the doctor's eyes. "Then perhaps you will explain this receipted bill for thirteen guineas, paid by Mr. Godfrey Staunton last month to Dr. Leslie Armstrong, of Cambridge. I picked it out from among the papers upon his desk."

The doctor flushed with anger.

"I do not feel that there is any reason why I should render an explanation to you, Mr. Holmes."

Holmes replaced the bill in his notebook. "If you prefer a public explanation, it must come sooner or later," said he. "I have already told you that I can hush up that which others will be bound to publish, and you would really be wiser to take me into your complete confidence."

"I know nothing about it."

"Did you hear from Mr. Staunton in London?"

"Certainly not."

"Dear me, dear me—the post office again!" Holmes sighed, wearily. "A most urgent telegram was dispatched to you from London by Godfrey Staunton at six-fifteen yesterday evening—a telegram which is undoubtedly associated with his disappearance—and yet you have not had it. It is most culpable. I shall certainly go down to the office here and register a complaint."

Dr. Leslie Armstrong sprang up from behind his desk, and his dark face was crimson with fury.

"I'll trouble you to walk out of my house, sir," said he. "You can tell your employer, Lord Mount-James, that I do not wish to have anything to do either with him or with his agents. No, sir—not another word!" He rang the bell furiously. "John, show these gentlemen out!" A pompous butler ushered us severely to the door, and we found ourselves in the street. Holmes burst out laughing.

"Dr. Leslie Armstrong is certainly a man of energy and character," said he. "I have not seen a man who, if he turns his talents that way, was more calculated to fill the gap left by the illustrious Moriarty. And now, my poor Watson, here we are, stranded and friendless in this inhospitable town, which we cannot leave without abandoning our case. This little inn just opposite Armstrong's house is singularly adapted to our needs. If you would engage a front room and purchase the necessaries for the night, I may have time to make a few inquiries."

These few inquiries proved, however, to be a more lengthy proceeding than Holmes had imagined, for he did not return to the inn until nearly nine o'clock. He was pale and dejected, stained with dust, and exhausted with hunger and fatigue. A cold supper was ready upon the table, and when his needs were satisfied and his pipe alight he was ready to take that half comic and wholly philosophic view which was natural to him when his affairs were going awry. The sound of carriage wheels caused him to rise and glance out of the window. A brougham and pair of grays, under the glare of a gas-lamp, stood before the doctor's door.

"It's been out three hours," said Holmes; "started at half-past six, and here it is back again. That gives a radius of ten or twelve miles, and he does it once, or sometimes twice, a day."

"No unusual thing for a doctor in practice."

"But Armstrong is not really a doctor in practice. He is a lecturer and a consultant, but he does not care for general practice, which distracts him from his literary work. Why, then, does he make these long journeys, which must be exceedingly irksome to him, and who is it that he visits?"

"His coachman——"

"My dear Watson, can you doubt that it was to him that I first applied? I do not know whether it came from his own innate depravity or from the promptings of his master, but he was rude enough to set a dog at me. Neither dog nor man liked the look of my stick, however, and the matter fell through. Relations were strained after that, and further inquiries out of the question. All that I have learned I got from a friendly native in the yard of our own inn. It was he who told me of the doctor's habits and of his daily journey. At that instant, to give point to his words, the carriage came round to the door."

"Could you not follow it?"

"Excellent, Watson! You are scintillating this evening. The idea did cross my mind. There is, as you may have observed, a bicycle shop next to our inn. Into this I rushed, engaged a bicycle, and was able to get started before the carriage was quite out of sight. I rapidly overtook it, and then, keeping at a discreet distance of a hundred yards or so, I followed its lights until we were clear of the town. We had got well out on the country road, when a somewhat mortifying incident occurred. The carriage stopped, the doctor alighted, walked swiftly back to where I had also halted, and told me in an excellent sardonic fashion that he feared the road was narrow, and that he hoped his carriage did not impede the passage of my bicycle. Nothing could have been more admirable than his way of putting it. I at once rode past the carriage, and, keeping to the main road, I went on for a few miles, and then halted in a convenient place to see if the carriage passed. There was no sign of it, however, and so it became evident that it had turned down one of several side roads which I had observed. I rode back, but again saw nothing of the carriage, and now, as you perceive, it has returned after me. Of course, I had at the outset no particular reason to connect these journeys with the disappearance of Godfrey Staunton, and was only inclined to investigate them on the general grounds that everything which concerns Dr. Armstrong is at present of interest to us, but, now that I find he keeps so keen a look-out upon anyone who may follow him on these excursions, the affair appears more important, and I shall not be satisfied until I have made the matter clear."

"We can follow him tomorrow."

"Can we? It is not so easy as you seem to think. You are not familiar with Cambridgeshire scenery, are you? It does not lend itself to concealment. All this country that I passed over to-night is as flat and clean as the palm of your hand, and the man we are following is no fool, as he very clearly showed to-night. I have wired to Overton to let us know any fresh London developments at this address, and in the meantime we can only concentrate our attention upon Dr. Armstrong, whose name the obliging young lady at the office allowed me to read upon the counterfoil of Staunton's urgent message. He knows where the young man is—to that

I'll swear, and if he knows, then it must be our own fault if we cannot manage to know also. At present it must be admitted that the odd trick is in his possession,* and, as you are aware, Watson, it is not my habit to leave the game in that condition."

And yet the next day brought us no nearer to the solution of the mystery. A note was handed in after breakfast, which Holmes passed across to me with a smile.

SIR [it ran]:

I can assure you that you are wasting your time in dogging my movements. I have, as you discovered last night, a window at the back of my brougham, and if you desire a twenty-mile ride which will lead you to the spot from which you started, you have only to follow me. Meanwhile, I can inform you that no spying upon me can in any way help Mr. Godfrey Staunton, and I am convinced that the best service you can do to that gentleman is to return at once to London and to report to your employer that you are unable to trace him. Your time in Cambridge will certainly be wasted.

Yours faithfully,
LESLIE ARMSTRONG.

"An outspoken, honest antagonist is the doctor," said Holmes. "Well, well, he excites my curiosity, and I must really know before I leave him."

"His carriage is at his door now," said I. "There he is stepping into it. I saw him glance up at our window as he did so. Suppose I try my luck upon the bicycle?"

"No, no, my dear Watson! With all respect for your natural acumen, I do not think that you are quite a match for the worthy doctor. I think that possibly I can attain our end by some independent explorations of my own. I am afraid that I must leave you to your own devices, as the appearance of *two* inquiring strangers upon a sleepy countryside might excite more gossip than I care for. No doubt you will find some sights to amuse you in this venerable city, and I hope to bring back a more favourable report to you before evening."

Once more, however, my friend was destined to be disappointed. He came back at night weary and unsuccessful.

"I have had a blank day, Watson. Having got the doctor's general direction, I spent the day in visiting all the villages upon that side of Cambridge, and comparing notes with publicans and other local news agencies. I have covered some ground. Chesterton, Histon, Waterbeach, and Oakington have each been explored, and have each proved disappointing. The daily appearance of a brougham and pair could hardly have been overlooked in such Sleepy Hollows. The doctor has scored once more. Is there a telegram for me?"

---

*A card game metaphor; means Armstrong currently has the upper hand.

"Yes, I opened it. Here it is:

Ask for Pompey from Jeremy Dixon, Trinity College.

I don't understand it."

"Oh, it is clear enough. It is from our friend Overton, and is in answer to a question from me. I'll just send round a note to Mr. Jeremy Dixon, and then I have no doubt that our luck will turn. By the way, is there any news of the match?"

"Yes, the local evening paper has an excellent account in its last edition. Oxford won by a goal and two tries. The last sentences of the description say:

"The defeat of the Light Blues may be entirely attributed to the unfortunate absence of the crack International, Godfrey Staunton, whose want was felt at every instant of the game. The lack of combination in the three-quarter line and their weakness both in attack and defence more than neutralized the efforts of a heavy and hard-working pack."

"Then our friend Overton's forebodings have been justified," said Holmes. "Personally I am in agreement with Dr. Armstrong, and football does not come within my horizon. Early to bed to-night, Watson, for I foresee that to-morrow may be an eventful day."

I was horrified by my first glimpse of Holmes next morning. for he sat by the fire holding his tiny hypodermic syringe. I associated that instrument with the single weakness of his nature, and I feared the worst when I saw it glittering in his hand. He laughed at my expression of dismay and laid it upon the table.

"No, no, my dear fellow, there is no cause for alarm. It is not upon this occasion the instrument of evil, but it will rather prove to be the key which will unlock our mystery. On this syringe I base all my hopes. I have just returned from a small scouting expedition, and everything is favourable. Eat a good breakfast, Watson, for I propose to get upon Dr. Armstrong's trail to-day, and once on it I will not stop for rest or food until I run him to his burrow."

"In that case," said I, "we had best carry our breakfast with us, for he is making an early start. His carriage is at the door."

"Never mind. Let him go. He will be clever if he can drive where I cannot follow him. When you have finished, come downstairs with me, and I will introduce you to a detective who is a very eminent specialist in the work that lies before us."

When we descended I followed Holmes into the stable yard, where he opened the door of a loose-box* and led out a squat, lop-eared, white-and-tan dog, something between a beagle and a foxhound.

---

*Pen in a stable where a horse is kept without a halter.

"Let me introduce you to Pompey," said he. "Pompey is the pride of the local draghounds—no very great flier, as his build will show, but a staunch hound on a scent. Well, Pompey, you may not be fast, but I expect you will be too fast for a couple of middle-aged London gentlemen. so I will take the liberty of fastening this leather leash to your collar. Now, boy, came along, and show what you can do." He led him across to the doctor's door. The dog sniffed round for an instant, and then with a shrill whine of excitement started off down the street, tugging at his leash in his efforts to go faster. In half an hour, we were clear of the town and hastening down a country road.

"What have you done, Holmes?" I asked.

"A threadbare and venerable device, but useful upon occasion. I walked into the doctor's yard this morning, and shot my syringe full of aniseed over the hind wheel. A draghound will follow aniseed from here to John o' Groat's,* and our friend, Armstrong, would have to drive through the Cam before he would shake Pompey off his trail. Oh, the cunning rascal! This is how he gave me the slip the other night."

The dog had suddenly turned out of the main road into a grass-grown lane. Half a mile farther this opened into another broad road, and the trail turned hard to the right in the direction of the town, which we had just quitted. The road took a sweep to the south of the town, and continued in the opposite direction to that in which we started.

"This *détour* has been entirely for our benefit, then?" said Holmes. "No wonder that my inquiries among those villagers led to nothing. The doctor has certainly played the game for all it is worth, and one would like to know the reason for such elaborate deception. This should be the village of Trumpington to the right of us. And, by Jove! here is the brougham coming round the corner. Quick, Watson—quick, or we are done!"

He sprang through a gate into a field, dragging the reluctant Pompey after him. We had hardly got under the shelter of the hedge when the carriage rattled past. I caught a glimpse of Dr. Armstrong within, his shoulders bowed, his head sunk on his hands, the very image of distress. I could tell by my companion's graver face that he also had seen.

"I fear there is some dark ending to our quest," said he. "It cannot be long before we know it. Come, Pompey! Ah, it is the cottage in the field!"

There could be no doubt that we had reached the end of our journey. Pompey ran about and whined eagerly outside the gate, where the marks of the brougham's wheels were still to be seen. A footpath led across to the lonely cottage. Holmes tied the dog to the hedge, and we hastened onward. My friend knocked at the little rustic door, and knocked again without response. And yet the cottage was not deserted, for a low sound came to our ears—a kind of drone of misery and despair which was indescribably melancholy. Holmes paused irresolute, and then he glanced

*House said to be the northernmost point of Britain.

back at the road which he had just traversed. A brougham was coming down it, and there could be no mistaking those gray horses.

"By Jove, the doctor is coming back!" cried Holmes. "That settles it. We are bound to see what it means before he comes."

He opened the door, and we stepped into the hall. The droning sound swelled louder upon our ears until it became one long, deep wail of distress. It came from upstairs. Holmes darted up, and I followed him. He pushed open a half-closed door, and we both stood appalled at the sight before us.

A woman, young and beautiful, was lying dead upon the bed. Her calm, pale face, with dim, wide-opened blue eyes, looked upward from amid a great tangle of golden hair. At the foot of the bed, half sitting, half kneeling, his face buried in the clothes, was a young man, whose frame was racked by his sobs. So absorbed was he by his bitter grief, that he never looked up until Holmes's hand was on his shoulder.

"Are you Mr. Godfrey Staunton?"

"Yes, yes, I am—but you are too late. She is dead."

The man was so dazed that he could not be made to understand that we were anything but doctors who had been sent to his assistance. Holmes was endeavouring to utter a few words of consolation and to explain the alarm which had been caused to his friends by his sudden disappearance when there was a step upon the stairs, and there was the heavy, stern, questioning face of Dr. Armstrong at the door.

"So, gentlemen," said he, "you have attained your end and have certainly chosen a particularly delicate moment for your intrusion. I would not brawl in the presence of death, but I can assure you that if I were a younger man your monstrous conduct would not pass with impunity."

"Excuse me, Dr. Armstrong, I think we are a little at cross-purposes," said my friend, with dignity. "If you could step downstairs with us, we may each be able to give some light to the other upon this miserable affair."

A minute later, the grim doctor and ourselves were in the sitting-room below.

"Well, sir?" said he.

"I wish you to understand, in the first place, that I am not employed by Lord Mount-James, and that my sympathies in this matter are entirely against that nobleman. When a man is lost it is my duty to ascertain his fate, but having done so the matter ends so far as I am concerned, and so long as there is nothing criminal I am much more anxious to hush up private scandals than to give them publicity. If, as I imagine, there is no breach of the law in this matter, you can absolutely depend upon my discretion and my cooperation in keeping the facts out of the papers."

Dr. Armstrong took a quick step forward and wrung Holmes by the hand.

"You are a good fellow," said he. "I had misjudged you. I thank heaven that my compunction at leaving poor Staunton all alone in this plight caused me to turn my carriage back and so to make your acquaintance. Knowing as much as you do, the situation is very easily explained. A year ago Godfrey Staunton lodged in London for a time and became passionately attached to his landlady's daughter, whom he married. She was as good as she was beautiful and as intelligent as she was good. No man need be ashamed of such a wife. But Godfrey was the heir to this crabbed old nobleman, and it was quite certain that the news of his marriage would have been the end of his inheritance. I knew the lad well, and I loved him for his many excellent qualities. I did all I could to help him to keep things straight. We did our very best to keep the thing from everyone, for, when once such a whisper gets about, it is not long before everyone has heard it. Thanks to this lonely cottage and his own discretion, Godfrey has up to now succeeded. Their secret was known to no one save to me and to one excellent servant, who has at present gone for assistance to Trumpington. But at last there came a terrible blow in the shape of dangerous illness to his wife. It was consumption of the most virulent kind. The poor boy was half crazed with grief, and yet he had to go to London to play this match, for he could not get out of it without explanations which would expose his secret. I tried to cheer him up by wire, and he sent me one in reply, imploring me to do all I could. This was the telegram which you appear in some inexplicable way to have seen. I did not tell him how urgent the danger was, for I knew that he could do no good here, but I sent the truth to the girl's father, and he very injudiciously communicated it to Godfrey. The result was that he came straight away in a state bordering on frenzy, and has remained in the same state, kneeling at the end of her bed, until this morning death put an end to her sufferings. That is all, Mr. Holmes. and I am sure that I can rely upon your discretion and that of your friend."

Holmes grasped the doctor's hand.

"Come, Watson," said he, and we passed from that house of grief into the pale sunlight of the winter day.

THE ADVENTURE OF THE
ABBEY GRANGE

It was on a bitterly cold night and frosty morning, towards the end of the winter of '97, that I was awakened by a tugging at my shoulder. It was Holmes. The candle in his hand shone upon his eager, stooping face, and told me at a glance that something was amiss.

"Come, Watson, come!" he cried. "The game is afoot.* Not a word! Into your clothes and come!"

Ten minutes later we were both in a cab, and rattling through the silent streets on our way to Charing Cross Station. The first faint winter's dawn was beginning to appear, and we could dimly see the occasional figure of an early workman as he passed us, blurred and indistinct in the opalescent London reek. Holmes nestled in silence into his heavy coat, and I was glad to do the same, for the air was most bitter, and neither of us had broken our fast.

It was not until we had consumed some hot tea at the station and taken our places in the Kentish train that we were sufficiently thawed, he to speak and I to listen. Holmes drew a note from his pocket, and read aloud:

> Abbey Grange, Marsham, Kent,
> 3:30 A.M.
>
> "MY DEAR MR. HOLMES:
> I should be very glad of your immediate assistance in what promises to be a most remarkable case. It is something quite in your line. Except for releasing the lady I will see that everything is kept exactly as I have found it, but I beg you not to lose an instant, as it is difficult to leave Sir Eustace there.
>
> Yours faithfully,
> STANLEY HOPKINS."

"Hopkins has called me in seven times, and on each occasion his summons has been entirely justified," said Holmes. "I fancy that every one of his cases has found its way into your collection, and I must admit, Watson, that you have some power of selection, which atones for much which I deplore in your narratives. Your fatal habit of looking at everything from the point of view of a story instead of as a scientific exercise has ruined what might have been an instructive and even classical series of demonstrations. You slur over work of the utmost finesse and delicacy, in

---

*Holmes refers to Shakespeare's *Henry V* (act 3, scene 1): "The game's afoot!"

order to dwell upon sensational details which may excite, but cannot possibly instruct, the reader."

"Why do you not write them yourself?" I said, with some bitterness.

"I will, my dear Watson, I will.* At present I am, as you know, fairly busy, but I propose to devote my declining years to the composition of a textbook, which shall focus the whole art of detection into one volume. Our present research appears to be a case of murder."

"You think this Sir Eustace is dead, then?"

"I should say so. Hopkins's writing shows considerable agitation, and he is not an emotional man. Yes, I gather there has been violence, and that the body is left for our inspection. A mere suicide would not have caused him to send for me. As to the release of the lady, it would appear that she has been locked in her room during the tragedy. We are moving in high life, Watson, crackling paper, 'E. B.' monogram, coat-of-arms, picturesque address. I think that friend Hopkins will live up to his reputation, and that we shall have an interesting morning. The crime was committed before twelve last night."

"How can you possibly tell?"

"By an inspection of the trains, and by reckoning the time. The local police had to be called in, they had to communicate with Scotland Yard, Hopkins had to go out, and he in turn had to send for me. All that makes a fair night's work. Well, here we are at Chiselhurst Station, and we shall soon set our doubts at rest."

A drive of a couple of miles through narrow country lanes brought us to a park gate, which was opened for us by an old lodge-keeper, whose haggard face bore the reflection of some great disaster. The avenue ran through a noble park, between lines of ancient elms, and ended in a low, widespread house, pillared in front after the fashion of Palladio.† The central part was evidently of a great age and shrouded in ivy, but the large windows showed that modern changes had been carried out, and one wing of the house appeared to be entirely new. The youthful figure and alert, eager face of Inspector Stanley Hopkins confronted us in the open doorway.

"I'm very glad you have come, Mr. Holmes. And you, too, Dr. Watson. But, indeed, if I had my time over again, I should not have troubled you, for since the lady has come to herself, she has given so clear an account of the affair that there is not much left for us to do. You remember that Lewisham gang of burglars?"

"What, the three Randalls?"

"Exactly; the father and two sons. It's their work. I have not a doubt of it. They did a job at Sydenham a fortnight ago and were seen and de-

---

*He does; see "The Adventure of the Blanched Soldier" and "The Adventure of the Lion's Mane."

†Andrea Palladio (1508–1580), Italian architect whose style profoundly influenced English architecture.

scribed. Rather cool to do another so soon and so near, but it is they, beyond all doubt. It's a hanging matter this time."

"Sir Eustace is dead, then?"

"Yes, his head was knocked in with his own poker."

"Sir Eustace Brackenstall, the driver tells me."

"Exactly—one of the richest men in Kent—Lady Brackenstall is in the morning-room. Poor lady, she has had a most dreadful experience. She seemed half dead when I saw her first. I think you had best see her and hear her account of the facts. Then we will examine the dining-room together."

Lady Brackenstall was no ordinary person. Seldom have I seen so graceful a figure, so womanly a presence, and so beautiful a face. She was a blonde, golden-haired, blue-eyed, and would no doubt have had the perfect complexion which goes with such colouring, had not her recent experience left her drawn and haggard. Her sufferings were physical as well as mental, for over one eye rose a hideous, plum-coloured swelling, which her maid, a tall, austere woman, was bathing assiduously with vinegar and water. The lady lay back exhausted upon a couch, but her quick, observant gaze, as we entered the room, and the alert expression of her beautiful features, showed that neither her wits nor her courage had been shaken by her terrible experience. She was enveloped in a loose dressing-gown of blue and silver, but a black sequin-covered dinner-dress lay upon the couch beside her.

"I have told you all that happened, Mr. Hopkins," she said, wearily. "Could you not repeat it for me? Well, if you think it necessary, I will tell these gentlemen what occurred. Have they been in the dining-room yet?"

"I thought they had better hear your ladyship's story first."

"I shall be glad when you can arrange matters. It is horrible to me to think of him still lying there." She shuddered and buried her face in her hands. As she did so, the loose gown fell back from her forearms. Holmes uttered an exclamation.

"You have other injuries, madam! What is this?" Two vivid red spots stood out on one of the white, round limbs. She hastily covered it.

"It is nothing. It has no connection with this hideous business to-night. If you and your friend will sit down, I will tell you all I can.

"I am the wife of Sir Eustace Brackenstall. I have been married about a year. I suppose that it is no use my attempting to conceal that our marriage has not been a happy one. I fear that all our neighbours would tell you that, even if I were to attempt to deny it. Perhaps the fault may be partly mine. I was brought up in the freer, less conventional atmosphere of South Australia, and this English life, with its proprieties and its primness, is not congenial to me. But the main reason lies in the one fact, which is notorious to everyone, and that is that Sir Eustace was a confirmed drunkard. To be with such a man for an hour is unpleasant. Can you imagine what it means for a sensitive and high-spirited woman to be tied to him for day and night? It is a sacrilege, a crime, a villainy to hold that such a marriage is binding. I say that these monstrous laws of yours will bring a curse upon the land—God will not let such wickedness endure." For an instant she sat up, her cheeks flushed, and her eyes blazing from under the terrible mark upon her brow. Then the strong, soothing hand of the austere maid drew her head down on to the cushion, and the wild anger died away into passionate sobbing. At last she continued:

"I will tell you about last night. You are aware, perhaps, that in this house all the servants sleep in the modern wing. This central block is made up of the dwelling-rooms, with the kitchen behind and our bedroom above. My maid, Theresa, sleeps above my room. There is no one else, and no sound could alarm those who are in the farther wing. This must have been well known to the robbers, or they would not have acted as they did.

"Sir Eustace retired about half-past ten. The servants had already gone to their quarters. Only my maid was up, and she had remained in her room at the top of the house until I needed her services. I sat until after eleven in this room, absorbed in a book. Then I walked round to see that all was right before I went upstairs. It was my custom to do this myself, for, as I have explained, Sir Eustace was not always to be trusted. I went into the kitchen, the butler's pantry, the gun-room, the billiard-room, the drawing-room, and finally the dining-room. As I approached the window, which is covered with thick curtains, I suddenly felt the wind blow upon my face and realized that it was open. I flung the curtain aside and found myself face to face with a broad-shouldered elderly man, who had just stepped into the room. The window is a long French one, which really forms a door leading to the lawn. I held my bedroom candle lit in my hand, and, by its light, behind the first man I saw two others, who were in the act of entering. I stepped back, but the fellow was on me in an instant. He caught me first by the wrist and then by the throat. I opened my mouth to scream, but he struck me a savage blow with his fist over the eye, and felled me to the ground. I must have been unconscious for a few minutes, for when I came to myself, I found that they had torn down the bell-rope, and had secured me tightly to the oaken chair which stands at the head of the dining-table. I was so firmly bound that I could not move, and a handkerchief round my mouth prevented me from uttering a sound. It was at this instant that my unfortunate husband entered the room. He had evidently heard some suspicious sounds, and he came prepared for such a scene as he found. He was dressed in nightshirt and trousers, with his favourite blackthorn cudgel in his hand. He rushed at the burglars, but another—it was an elderly man—stooped, picked the poker out of the grate and struck him a horrible blow as he passed. He fell with a groan and never moved again. I fainted once more, but again it could only have been for a very few minutes during which I was insensible. When I opened my eyes I found that they had collected the silver from the sideboard, and they had drawn a bottle of wine which stood there. Each of them had a glass in his hand. I have already told you, have I not, that one was elderly, with a beard, and the others young, hairless lads. They might have been a father with his two sons. They talked together in whispers.

Then they came over and made sure that I was securely bound. Finally they withdrew, closing the window after them. It was quite a quarter of an hour before I got my mouth free. When I did so, my screams brought the maid to my assistance. The other servants were soon alarmed, and we sent for the local police, who instantly communicated with London. That is really all that I can tell you, gentlemen, and I trust that it will not be necessary for me to go over so painful a story again."

"Any questions, Mr. Holmes?" asked Hopkins.

"I will not impose any further tax upon Lady Brackenstall's patience and time," said Holmes. "Before I go into the dining-room, I should like to hear your experience." He looked at the maid.

"I saw the men before ever they came into the house," said she. "As I sat by my bedroom window I saw three men in the moonlight down by the lodge gate yonder, but I thought nothing of it at the time. It was more than an hour after that I heard my mistress scream, and down I ran, to find her, poor lamb, just as she says, and him on the floor, with his blood and brains over the room. It was enough to drive a woman out of her wits, tied there, and her very dress spotted with him, but she never wanted courage, did Miss Mary Fraser of Adelaide, and Lady Brackenstall of Abbey Grange hasn't learned new ways. You've questioned her long enough, you gentlemen, and now she is coming to her own room, just with her old Theresa, to get the rest that she badly needs."

With a motherly tenderness the gaunt woman put her arm round her mistress and led her from the room.

"She has been with her all her life," said Hopkins. "Nursed her as a baby, and came with her to England when they first left Australia, eighteen months ago. Theresa Wright is her name, and the kind of maid you don't pick up nowadays. This way, Mr. Holmes, if you please!"

The keen interest had passed out of Holmes's expressive face, and I knew that with the mystery all the charm of the case had departed. There still remained an arrest to be effected, but what were these commonplace rogues that he should soil his hands with them? An abstruse and learned specialist who finds that he has been called in for a case of measles would experience something of the annoyance which I read in my friend's eyes. Yet the scene in the dining-room of the Abbey Grange was sufficiently strange to arrest his attention and to recall his waning interest.

It was a very large and high chamber, with carved oak ceiling, oaken panelling, and a fine array of deer's heads and ancient weapons around the walls. At the further end from the door was the high French window of which we had heard. Three smaller windows on the right-hand side filled the apartment with cold winter sunshine. On the left was a large, deep fireplace, with a massive, overhanging oak mantelpiece. Beside the fireplace was a heavy oaken chair with arms and crossbars at the bottom. In and out through the open woodwork was woven a crimson cord, which was secured at each side to the crosspiece below. In releasing the lady, the cord had been slipped off her, but the knots with which it had been secured still remained. These details only struck our attention afterwards, for our thoughts were entirely absorbed by the terrible object which lay upon the tigerskin hearthrug in front of the fire.

It was the body of a tall, well-made man, about forty years of age. He lay upon his back, his face upturned, with his white teeth grinning through his short, black beard. His two clenched hands were raised above his head, and a heavy, blackthorn stick lay across them. His dark, handsome, aquiline features were convulsed into a spasm of vindictive hatred, which had set his dead face in a terribly fiendish expression. He had evidently been in his bed when the alarm had broken out, for he wore a foppish, embroidered nightshirt, and his bare feet projected from his trousers. His head was horribly injured, and the whole room bore witness to the savage ferocity of the blow which had struck him down. Beside him lay the heavy poker, bent into a curve by the concussion. Holmes examined both it and the indescribable wreck which it had wrought.

"He must be a powerful man, this elder Randall," he remarked.

"Yes," said Hopkins. "I have some record of the fellow, and he is a rough customer."

"You should have no difficulty in getting him."

"Not the slightest. We have been on the look-out for him, and there was some idea that he had got away to America. Now that we know that the gang are here, I don't see how they can escape. We have the news at every seaport already, and a reward will be offered before evening. What beats me is how they could have done so mad a thing, knowing that the lady could describe them and that we could not fail to recognize the description."

"Exactly. One would have expected that they would silence Lady Brackenstall as well."

"They may not have realized," I suggested, "that she had recovered from her faint."

"That is likely enough. If she seemed to be senseless, they would not take her life. What about this poor fellow, Hopkins? I seem to have heard some queer stories about him."

"He was a good-hearted man when he was sober, but a perfect fiend when he was drunk, or rather when he was half drunk, for he seldom really went the whole way. The devil seemed to be in him at such times, and he was capable of anything. From what I hear, in spite of all his wealth and his title, he very nearly came our way once or twice. There was a scandal about his drenching a dog with petroleum and setting it on fire—her ladyship's dog, to make the matter worse—and that was only hushed up with difficulty. Then he threw a decanter at that maid, Theresa Wright—there was trouble about that. On the whole, and between ourselves, it will be a brighter house without him. What are you looking at now?"

Holmes was down on his knees, examining with great attention the knots upon the red cord with which the lady had been secured. Then he carefully scrutinized the broken and frayed end where it had snapped off when the burglar had dragged it down.

"When this was pulled down, the bell in the kitchen must have rung loudly," he remarked.

"No one could hear it. The kitchen stands right at the back of the house."

"How did the burglar know no one would hear it? How dared he pull at a bellrope in that reckless fashion?"

"Exactly, Mr. Holmes, exactly. You put the very question which I have asked myself again and again. There can be no doubt that this fellow must have known the house and its habits. He must have perfectly understood that the servants would all be in bed at that comparatively early hour, and that no one could possibly hear a bell ring in the kitchen. Therefore, he must have been in close league with one of the servants. Surely that is evident. But there are eight servants, and all of good character."

"Other things being equal," said Holmes, "one would suspect the one at whose head the master threw a decanter. And yet that would involve treachery towards the mistress to whom this woman seems devoted. Well, well, the point is a minor one, and when you have Randall you will probably find no difficulty in securing his accomplice. The lady's story certainly seems to be corroborated, if it needed corroboration, by every detail which we see before us." He walked to the French window and threw it open. "There are no signs here, but the ground is iron hard, and one would not expect them. I see that these candles in the mantelpiece have been lighted."

"Yes, it was by their light, and that of the lady's bedroom candle, that the burglars saw their way about."

"And what did they take?"

"Well, they did not take much—only half a dozen articles of plate off the sideboard. Lady Brackenstall thinks that they were themselves so disturbed by the death of Sir Eustace that they did not ransack the house, as they would otherwise have done."

"No doubt that is true, and yet they drank some wine, I understand."

"To steady their nerves."

"Exactly. These three glasses upon the sideboard have been untouched, I suppose?"

"Yes, and the bottle stands as they left it."

"Let us look at it. Halloa, halloa! What is this?"

The three glasses were grouped together, all of them tinged with wine, and one of them containing some dregs of beeswing.* The bottle stood near them, two-thirds full, and beside it lay a long, deeply stained cork. Its appearance and the dust upon the bottle showed that it was no common vintage which the murderers had enjoyed.

A change had come over Holmes's manner. He had lost his listless expression, and again I saw an alert light of interest in his keen, deep-set eyes. He raised the cork and examined it minutely.

*That is, "bees wing": a flaky deposit sometimes found in old bottles of wine.

"How did they draw it?" he asked.

Hopkins pointed to a half-opened drawer. In it lay some table linen and a large corkscrew.

"Did Lady Brackenstall say that screw was used?"

"No, you remember that she was senseless at the moment when the bottle was opened."

"Quite so. As a matter of fact, that screw was *not* used. This bottle was opened by a pocket screw, probably contained in a knife, and not more than an inch and a half long. If you will examine the top of the cork, you will observe that the screw was driven in three times before the cork was extracted. It has never been transfixed. This long screw would have transfixed it and drawn it up with a single pull. When you catch this fellow, you will find that he has one of these multiplex knives in his possession."

"Excellent!" said Hopkins.

"But these glasses do puzzle me, I confess. Lady Brackenstall actually *saw* the three men drinking, did she not?"

"Yes; she was clear about that."

"Then there is an end of it. What more is to be said? And yet, you must admit, that the three glasses are very remarkable. Hopkins. What? You see nothing remarkable? Well, well, let it pass. Perhaps, when a man has special knowledge and special powers like my own, it rather encourages him to seek a complex explanation when a simpler one is at hand. Of course, it must be a mere chance about the glasses. Well, good-morning, Hopkins. I don't see that I can be of any use to you, and you appear to have your case very clear. You will let me know when Randall is arrested, and any further developments which may occur. I trust that I shall soon have to congratulate you upon a successful conclusion. Come, Watson, I fancy that we may employ ourselves more profitably at home."

During our return journey, I could see by Holmes's face that he was much puzzled by something which he had observed. Every now and then, by an effort, he would throw off the impression, and talk as if the matter were clear, but then his doubts would settle down upon him again, and his knitted brows and abstracted eyes would show that his thoughts had gone back once more to the great dining-room of the Abbey Grange, in which this midnight tragedy had been enacted. At last, by a sudden impulse, just as our train was crawling out of a suburban station, he sprang on to the platform and pulled me out after him.

"Excuse me, my dear fellow," said he, as we watched the rear carriages of our train disappearing round a curve, "I am sorry to make you the victim of what may seem a mere whim, but on my life, Watson, I simply *can't* leave that case in this condition. Every instinct that I possess cries out against it. It's wrong—it's all wrong—I'll swear that it's wrong. And yet the lady's story was complete, the maid's corroboration was sufficient, the detail was fairly exact. What have I to put up against that? Three wine-glasses, that is all. But if I had not taken things for granted, if I had examined everything with care which I should have shown had we approached the case *de novo* and had no cut-and-dried story to warp my mind, should I not then have found something more definite to go upon? Of course I should. Sit down on this bench, Watson, until a train for Chiselhurst arrives, and allow me to lay the evidence before you, imploring you in the first instance to dismiss from your mind the idea that anything which the maid or her mistress may have said must necessarily be true. The lady's charming personality must not be permitted to warp our judgment.

"Surely there are details in her story which, if we looked at in cold blood, would excite our suspicion. These burglars made a considerable haul at Sydenham a fortnight ago. Some account of them and of their appearance was in the papers, and would naturally occur to anyone who wished to invent a story in which imaginary robbers should play a part. As a matter of fact, burglars who have done a good stroke of business are, as a rule, only too glad to enjoy the proceeds in peace and quiet without embarking on another perilous undertaking. Again, it is unusual for burglars to operate at so early an hour, it is unusual for burglars to strike a lady to prevent her screaming, since one would imagine that was the sure way to make her scream, it is unusual for them to commit murder when their numbers are sufficient to overpower one man, it is unusual for them to be content with a limited plunder when there was much more within their reach, and finally, I should say, that it was very unusual for such men to leave a bottle half empty. How do all these unusuals strike you, Watson?"

"Their cumulative effect is certainly considerable, and yet each of them is quite possible in itself. The most unusual thing of all, as it seems to me, is that the lady should be tied to the chair."

"Well, I am not so clear about that, Watson, for it is evident that they must either kill her or else secure her in such a way that she could not give immediate notice of their escape. But at any rate I have shown, have I not, that there is a certain element of improbability about the lady's story? And now, on the top of this, comes the incident of the wineglasses."

"What about the wineglasses?"

"Can you see them in your mind's eye?"

"I see them clearly."

"We are told that three men drank from them. Does that strike you as likely?"

"Why not? There was wine in each glass."

"Exactly, but there was beeswing only in one glass. You must have noticed that fact. What does that suggest to your mind?"

"The last glass filled would be most likely to contain beeswing."

"Not at all. The bottle was full of it, and it is inconceivable that the first two glasses were clear and the third heavily charged with it. There are two possible explanations, and only two. One is that after the second glass was filled the bottle was violently agitated, and so the third glass received the beeswing. That does not appear probable. No, no, I am sure that I am right."

"What, then, do you suppose?"

"That only two glasses were used, and that the dregs of both were poured into a third glass, so as to give the false impression that three people had been here. In that way all the beeswing would be in the last glass, would it not? Yes. I am convinced that this is so. But if I have hit upon the true explanation of this one small phenomenon, then in an instant the case rises from the commonplace to the exceedingly remarkable, for it can only mean that Lady Brackenstall and her maid have deliberately lied to us, that not one word of their story is to be believed, that they have some very strong reason for covering the real criminal, and that we must construct our case for ourselves without any help from them. That is the mission which now lies before us, and here, Watson, is the Sydenham train."

The household at the Abbey Grange were much surprised at our return, but Sherlock Holmes, finding that Stanley Hopkins had gone off to report to headquarters, took possession of the dining-room, locked the door upon the inside, and devoted himself for two hours to one of those minute and laborious investigations which form the solid basis on which his brilliant edifices of deduction were reared. Seated in a corner like an interested student who observes the demonstration of his professor, I followed every step of that remarkable research. The window, the curtains, the carpet, the chair, the rope—each in turn was minutely examined and duly pondered. The body of the unfortunate baronet had been removed, and all else remained as we had seen it in the morning. Finally, to my astonishment, Holmes climbed up on to the massive mantelpiece. Far above his head hung the few inches of red cord which were still attached to the wire. For a long time he gazed upward at it, and then in an attempt to get nearer to it he rested his knee upon a wooden bracket on the wall. This brought his hand within a few inches of the broken end of the rope, but it was not this so much as the bracket itself which seemed to engage his attention. Finally, he sprang down with an ejaculation of satisfaction.

"It's all right, Watson," said he. "We have got our case—one of the most remarkable in our collection. But, dear me, how slow-witted I have been, and how nearly I have committed the blunder of my lifetime! Now, I think that, with a few missing links, my chain is almost complete."

"You have got your men?"

"Man, Watson, man. Only one, but a very formidable person. Strong as a lion—witness the blow that bent that poker! Six foot three in height, active as a squirrel, dexterous with his fingers, finally, remarkably quick-witted, for this whole ingenious story is of his concoction. Yes, Watson, we have come upon the handiwork of a very remarkable individual. And yet, in that bell-rope, he has given us a clue which should not have left us a doubt."

"Where was the clue?"

"Well, if you were to pull down a bell-rope, Watson, where would you expect it to break? Surely at the spot where it is attached to the wire. Why should it break three inches from the top, as this one has done?"

"Because it is frayed there?"

"Exactly. This end, which we can examine, is frayed. He was cunning enough to do that with his knife. But the other end is not frayed. You could not observe that from here, but if you were on the mantelpiece you would see that it is cut clean off without any mark of fraying whatever. You can reconstruct what occurred. The man needed the rope. He would not tear it down for fear of giving the alarm by ringing the bell. What did he do? He sprang up on the mantelpiece, could not quite reach it, put his knee on the bracket—you will see the impression in the dust—and so got his knife to bear upon the cord. I could not reach the place by at least three inches—from which I infer that he is at least three inches a bigger man than I. Look at that mark upon the seat of the oaken chair! What is it?"

"Blood."

"Undoubtedly it is blood. This alone puts the lady's story out of court. If she were seated on the chair when the crime was done, how comes that mark? No, no, she was placed in the chair *after* the death of her husband. I'll wager that the black dress shows a corresponding mark to this. We have not yet met our Waterloo, Watson, but this is our Marengo,[1] for it begins in defeat and ends in victory. I should like now to have a few words with the nurse, Theresa. We must be wary for a while, if we are to get the information which we want."

She was an interesting person, this stern Australian nurse—taciturn, suspicious, ungracious, it took some time before Holmes's pleasant manner and frank acceptance of all that she said thawed her into a corresponding amiability. She did not attempt to conceal her hatred for her late employer.

"Yes, sir, it is true that he threw the decanter at me. I heard him call my mistress a name, and I told him that he would not dare to speak so if her brother had been there. Then it was that he threw it at me. He might have thrown a dozen if he had but left my bonny bird alone. He was forever ill-treating her, and she too proud to complain. She will not even tell me all that he has done to her. She never told me of those marks on her arm that you saw this morning, but I know very well that they come from a stab with a hatpin. The sly devil—God forgive me that I should speak of him so, now that he is dead! But a devil he was, if ever one walked the earth. He was all honey when first we met him—only eighteen months ago, and we both feel as if it were eighteen years. She had only just arrived in London. Yes, it was her first voyage—she had never been from home before. He won her with his title and his money and his false London ways. If she made a mistake she has paid for it, if ever a woman did. What month did we meet him? Well, I tell you it was just after we arrived. We arrived in June, and it was July. They were married in January of last year. Yes, she is down in the morning-room again, and I have no doubt she will see you, but you must not ask too much of her, for she has gone through all that flesh and blood will stand."

Lady Brackenstall was reclining on the same couch, but looked brighter than before. The maid had entered with us, and began once more to foment the bruise upon her mistress's brow.

"I hope," said the lady, "that you have not come to cross-examine me again?"

"No," Holmes answered, in his gentlest voice, "I will not cause you any unnecessary trouble, Lady Brackenstall, and my whole desire is to make things easy for you, for I am convinced that you are a much-tried woman. If you will treat me as a friend and trust me, you may find that I will justify your trust."

"What do you want me to do?"

"To tell me the truth."

"Mr. Holmes!"

"No, no, Lady Brackenstall—it is no use. You may have heard of any little reputation which I possess. I will stake it all on the fact that your story is an absolute fabrication."

Mistress and maid were both staring at Holmes with pale faces and frightened eyes.

"You are an impudent fellow!" cried Theresa. "Do you mean to say that my mistress has told a lie?"

Holmes rose from his chair.

"Have you nothing to tell me?"

"I have told you everything."

"Think once more, Lady Brackenstall. Would it not be better to be frank?"

For an instant there was hesitation in her beautiful face. Then some new strong thought caused it to set like a mask.

"I have told you all I know."

Holmes took his hat and shrugged his shoulders. "I am sorry," he said, and without another word we left the room and the house. There was a pond in the park, and to this my friend led the way. It was frozen over, but a single hole was left for the convenience of a solitary swan. Holmes gazed at it, and then passed on to the lodge gate. There he scribbled a short note for Stanley Hopkins, and left it with the lodge-keeper.

"It may be a hit, or it may be a miss, but we are bound to do something for friend Hopkins, just to justify this second visit," said he. "I will not quite take him into my confidence yet. I think our next scene of operations must be the shipping office of the Adelaide-Southampton line, which stands at the end of Pall Mall, if I remember right. There is a second line of steamers which connect South Australia with England, but we will draw the larger cover first."

Holmes's card sent in to the manager ensured instant attention, and he was not long in acquiring all the information he needed. In June of '95, only one of their line had reached a home port. It was the *Rock of Gibraltar*, their largest and best boat. A reference to the passenger list showed that Miss Fraser, of Adelaide, with her maid had made the voyage in her. The boat was now somewhere south of the Suez Canal on her way to Australia. Her officers were the same as in '95, with one exception. The first officer, Mr. Jack Crocker, had been made a captain and was to take charge of their new ship, the *Bass Rock*, sailing in two days' time from Southampton. He lived at Sydenham, but he was likely to be in that morning for instructions, if we cared to wait for him.

No, Mr. Holmes had no desire to see him, but would be glad to know more about his record and character.

His record was magnificent. There was not an officer in the fleet to touch him. As to his character, he was reliable on duty, but a wild, desperate fellow off the deck of his ship—hot-headed, excitable, but loyal, honest, and kind-hearted. That was the pith of the information with which Holmes left the office of the Adelaide-Southampton company. Thence he drove to Scotland Yard, but, instead of entering, he sat in his cab with his brows drawn down, lost in profound thought. Finally he drove round to the Charing Cross telegraph office, sent off a message, and then, at last, we made for Baker Street once more.

"No, I couldn't do it, Watson," said he, as we reëntered our room. "Once that warrant was made out, nothing on earth would save him. Once or twice in my career I feel that I have done more real harm by my discovery of the criminal than ever he had done by his crime. I have learned caution now, and I had rather play tricks with the law of England than with my own conscience. Let us know a little more before we act."

Before evening, we had a visit from Inspector Stanley Hopkins. Things were not going very well with him.

"I believe that you are a wizard, Mr. Holmes. I really do sometimes think that you have powers that are not human. Now, how on earth could you know that the stolen silver was at the bottom of that pond?"

"I didn't know it."

"But you told me to examine it."

"You got it, then?"

"Yes, I got it."

"I am very glad if I have helped you."

"But you haven't helped me. You have made the affair far more difficult. What sort of burglars are they who steal silver and then throw it into the nearest pond?"

"It was certainly rather eccentric behaviour. I was merely going on the idea that if the silver had been taken by persons who did not want it— who merely took it for a blind, as it were—then they would naturally be anxious to get rid of it."

"But why should such an idea cross your mind?"

"Well, I thought it was possible. When they came out through the French window, there was the pond with one tempting little hole in the ice, right in front of their noses. Could there be a better hiding-place?"

"Ah, a hiding-place—that is better!" cried Stanley Hopkins. "Yes, yes, I see it all now! It was early, there were folk upon the roads, they were afraid of being seen with the silver, so they sank it in the pond, intending to return for it when the coast was clear. Excellent, Mr. Holmes—that is better than your idea of a blind."

"Quite so, you have got an admirable theory. I have no doubt that my own ideas were quite wild, but you must admit that they have ended in discovering the silver."

"Yes, sir—yes. It was all your doing. But I have had a bad setback."

"A setback?"

"Yes, Mr. Holmes. The Randall gang were arrested in New York this morning."

"Dear me, Hopkins! That is certainly rather against your theory that they committed a murder in Kent last night."

"It is fatal, Mr. Holmes—absolutely fatal. Still, there are other gangs of three besides the Randalls, or it may be some new gang of which the police have never heard."

"Quite so, it is perfectly possible. What, are you off?"

"Yes, Mr. Holmes, there is no rest for me until I have got to the bottom of the business. I suppose you have no hint to give me?"

"I have given you one."

"Which?"

"Well, I suggested a blind."

"But why, Mr. Holmes, why?"

"Ah, that's the question, of course. But I commend the idea to your mind. You might possibly find that there was something in it. You won't stop for dinner? Well, good-bye, and let us know how you get on."

Dinner was over, and the table cleared before Holmes alluded to the matter again. He had lit his pipe and held his slippered feet to the cheerful blaze of the fire. Suddenly he looked at his watch.

"I expect developments, Watson."

"When?"

"Now—within a few minutes. I dare say you thought I acted rather badly to Stanley Hopkins just now?"

"I trust your judgment."

"A very sensible reply, Watson. You must look at it this way: what I know is unofficial, what he knows is official. I have the right to private judgment, but he has none. He must disclose all, or he is a traitor to his service. In a doubtful case I would not put him in so painful a position, and so I reserve my information until my own mind is clear upon the matter."

"But when will that be?"

"The time has come. You will now be present at the last scene of a remarkable little drama."

There was a sound upon the stairs, and our door was opened to admit as fine a specimen of manhood as ever passed through it. He was a very tall young man, golden-moustached, blue-eyed, with a skin which had been burned by tropical suns, and a springy step, which showed that the huge frame was as active as it was strong. He closed the door behind him, and then he stood with clenched hands and heaving breast, choking down some overmastering emotion.

"Sit down, Captain Crocker. You got my telegram?"

Our visitor sank into an armchair and looked from one to the other of us with questioning eyes.

"I got your telegram, and I came at the hour you said. I heard that you had been down to the office. There was no getting away from you. Let's hear the worst. What are you going to do with me? Arrest me? Speak out, man! You can't sit there and play with me like a cat with a mouse."

"Give him a cigar," said Holmes. "Bite on that, Captain Crocker, and don't let your nerves run away with you. I should not sit here smoking with you if I thought that you were a common criminal, you may be sure of that. Be frank with me and we may do some good. Play tricks with me, and I'll crush you."

"What do you wish me to do?"

"To give me a true account of all that happened at the Abbey Grange last night—a *true* account, mind you, with nothing added and nothing taken off. I know so much already that if you go one inch off the straight, I'll blow this police whistle from my window and the affair goes out of my hands forever."

The sailor thought for a little. Then he struck his leg with his great sunburned hand.

"I'll chance it," he cried. "I believe you are a man of your word, and a white man, and I'll tell you the whole story. But one thing I will say first. So far as I am concerned, I regret nothing and I fear nothing, and I would do it all again and be proud of the job. Damn the beast, if he had as many lives as a cat, he would owe them all to me! But it's the lady, Mary—Mary Fraser—for never will I call her by that accursed name. When I think of getting her into trouble, I who would give my life just to bring one smile to her dear face, it's that that turns my soul into water. And yet—and yet—what less could I do? I'll tell you my story, gentlemen, and then I'll ask you, as man to man, what less could I do?

"I must go back a bit. You seem to know everything, so I expect that you know that I met her when she was a passenger and I was first officer of the *Rock of Gibraltar*. From the first day I met her, she was the only woman to me. Every day of that voyage I loved her more, and many a time since have I kneeled down in the darkness of the night watch and kissed the deck of that ship because I knew her dear feet had trod it. She was never engaged to me. She treated me as fairly as ever a woman treated a man. I have no complaint to make. It was all love on my side, and all good comradeship and friendship on hers. When we parted she was a free woman, but I could never again be a free man.

"Next time I came back from sea, I heard of her marriage. Well, why shouldn't she marry whom she liked? Title and money—who could carry them better than she? She was born for all that is beautiful and dainty. I didn't grieve over her marriage. I was not such a selfish hound as that. I just rejoiced that good luck had come her way, and that she had not thrown herself away on a penniless sailor. That's how I loved Mary Fraser.

"Well, I never thought to see her again, but last voyage I was promoted, and the new boat was not yet launched, so I had to wait for a couple of months with my people at Sydenham. One day out in a country lane I met Theresa Wright, her old maid. She told me all about her, about him, about everything. I tell you, gentlemen, it nearly drove me mad. This drunken hound, that he should dare to raise his hand to her, whose boots he was not worthy to lick! I met Theresa again. Then I met Mary herself—and met her again. Then she would meet me no more. But the other day I had a notice that I was to start on my voyage within a week, and I determined that I would see her once before I left. Theresa was always my friend, for she loved Mary and hated this villain almost as much as I did. From her I learned the ways of the house. Mary used to sit up reading in her own little room downstairs. I crept round there last night and scratched at the window. At first she would not open to me, but in her heart I know that now she loves me, and she could not leave me in the frosty night. She whispered to me to come round to the big front window, and I found it open before me, so as to let me into the dining-room. Again I heard from her own lips things that made my blood boil, and again I cursed this brute who mishandled the woman I loved. Well, gentlemen, I was standing with her just inside the window, in all innocence, as God is my judge, when he rushed like a madman into the room, called her the vilest name that a man could use to a woman, and welted her across the face with the stick he had in his hand. I had sprung for the poker, and it was a fair fight between us. See here, on my arm, where his first blow fell. Then it was my turn, and I went through him as if he had been a rotten pumpkin. Do you think I was sorry? Not I! It was his life or mine, but far more than that, it was his life or hers, for how could I leave her in the power of this madman? That was how I killed him. Was I wrong? Well, then, what would either of you gentlemen have done, if you had been in my position?"

"She had screamed when he struck her, and that brought old Theresa down from the room above. There was a bottle of wine on the sideboard, and I opened it and poured a little between Mary's lips, for she was half dead with shock. Then I took a drop myself. Theresa was as cool as ice, and it was her plot as much as mine. We must make it appear that burglars had done the thing. Theresa kept on repeating our story to her mistress, while I swarmed up and cut the rope of the bell. Then I lashed her in her chair, and frayed out the end of the rope to make it look natural, else they would wonder how in the world a burglar could have got up there to cut it. Then I gathered up a few plates and pots of silver, to carry out the idea of the robbery, and there I left them, with orders to give the alarm when I had a quarter of an hour's start. I dropped the silver into the pond, and made off for Sydenham, feeling that for once in my life I had done a real good night's work. And that's the truth and the whole truth, Mr. Holmes, if it costs me my neck."

Holmes smoked for some time in silence. Then he crossed the room, and shook our visitor by the hand.

"That's what I think," said he. "I know that every word is true, for you have hardly said a word which I did not know. No one but an acrobat or a sailor could have got up to that bell-rope from the bracket, and no one but a sailor could have made the knots with which the cord was fastened to the chair. Only once had this lady been brought into contact with sailors, and that was on her voyage, and it was someone of her own class of life, since she was trying hard to shield him, and so showing that she loved him. You see how easy it was for me to lay my hands upon you when once I had started upon the right trail."

"I thought the police never could have seen through our dodge."

"And the police haven't, nor will they, to the best of my belief. Now, look here, Captain Crocker, this is a very serious matter, though I am willing to admit that you acted under the most extreme provocation to which any man could be subjected. I am not sure that in defence of your own life your action will not be pronounced legitimate. However, that is for a British jury to decide. Meanwhile I have so much sympathy for you that, if you choose to disappear in the next twenty-four hours. I will promise you that no one will hinder you."

"And then it will all come out?"

"Certainly it will come out."

The sailor flushed with anger.

"What sort of proposal is that to make a man? I know enough of law to understand that Mary would be held as accomplice. Do you think I would leave her alone to face the music while I slunk away? No, sir, let them do their worst upon me, but for heaven's sake, Mr. Holmes, find some way of keeping my poor Mary out of the courts."

Holmes for a second time held out his hand to the sailor.

"I was only testing you, and you ring true every time. Well, it is a great responsibility that I take upon myself, but I have given Hopkins an excellent hint, and if he can't avail himself of it I can do no more. See here, Captain Crocker, we'll do this in due form of law. You are the prisoner. Watson, you are a British jury, and I never met a man who was more eminently fitted to represent one. I am the judge. Now, gentleman of the jury, you have heard the evidence. Do you find the prisoner guilty or not guilty?"

"Not guilty, my lord," said I.

"*Vox populi, vox Dei.** You are acquitted, Captain Crocker. So long as the law does not find some other victim you are safe from me. Come back to this lady in a year, and may her future and yours justify us in the judgment which we have pronounced this night!"

---

*The voice of the people is the voice of God (Latin); attributed to English scholar Alcuin (c. 735–804).

THE ADVENTURE OF THE
SECOND STAIN

I had intended "The Adventure of the Abbey Grange" to be the last of those exploits of my friend, Mr. Sherlock Holmes, which I should ever communicate to the public. This resolution of mine was not due to any lack of material, since I have notes of many hundreds of cases to which I have never alluded, nor was it caused by any waning interest on the part of my readers in the singular personality and unique methods of this remarkable man. The real reason lay in the reluctance which Mr. Holmes has shown to the continued publication of his experiences. So long as he was in actual professional practice the records of his successes were of some practical value to him, but since he has definitely retired from London and betaken himself to study and bee-farming on the Sussex Downs, notoriety has become hateful to him, and he has peremptorily requested that his wishes in this matter should be strictly observed. It was only upon my representing to him that I had given a promise that "The Adventure of the Second Stain" should be published when the times were ripe, and pointing out to him that it is only appropriate that this long series of episodes should culminate in the most important international case which he has ever been called upon to handle, that I at last succeeded in obtaining his consent that a carefully guarded account of the incident should at last be laid before the public. If in telling the story I seem to be somewhat vague in certain details, the public will readily understand that there is an excellent reason for my reticence.

It was, then, in a year, and even in a decade, that shall be nameless, that upon one Tuesday morning in autumn we found two visitors of European fame within the walls of our humble room in Baker Street. The one, austere, high-nosed, eagle-eyed, and dominant, was none other than the illustrious Lord Bellinger, twice Premier of Britain. The other, dark, clear-cut, and elegant, hardly yet of middle age, and endowed with every beauty of body and of mind, was the Right Honourable Trelawney Hope, Secretary for European Affairs, and the most rising statesman in the country. They sat side by side upon our paper-littered settee, and it was easy to see from their worn and anxious faces that it was business of the most pressing importance which had brought them. The Premier's thin, blue-veined hands were clasped tightly over the ivory head of his umbrella, and his gaunt, ascetic face looked gloomily from Holmes to me. The European Secretary pulled nervously at his moustache and fidgeted with the seals of his watch-chain.

"When I discovered my loss, Mr. Holmes, which was at eight o'clock this morning, I at once informed the Prime Minister. It was at his suggestion that we have both come to you."

"Have you informed the police?"

"No, sir," said the Prime Minister, with the quick, decisive manner for which he was famous. "We have not done so, nor is it possible that we should do so. To inform the police must, in the long run, mean to inform the public. This is what we particularly desire to avoid."

"And why, sir?"

"Because the document in question is of such immense importance that its publication might very easily—I might almost say probably—lead to European complications of the utmost moment. It is not too much to say that peace or war may hang upon the issue. Unless its recovery can be attended with the utmost secrecy, then it may as well not be recovered at all, for all that is aimed at by those who have taken it is that its contents should be generally known."

"I understand. Now, Mr. Trelawney Hope, I should be much obliged if you would tell me exactly the circumstances under which this document disappeared."

"That can be done in a very few words, Mr. Holmes. The letter—for it was a letter from a foreign potentate—was received six days ago. It was of such importance that I have never left it in my safe, but I have taken it across each evening to my house in Whitehall Terrace, and kept it in my bedroom in a locked despatch-box. It was there last night. Of that I am certain. I actually opened the box while I was dressing for dinner and saw the document inside. This morning it was gone. The despatch-box had stood beside the glass upon my dressing-table all night. I am a light sleeper, and so is my wife. We are both prepared to swear that no one could have entered the room during the night. And yet I repeat that the paper is gone."

"What time did you dine?"

"Half-past seven."

"How long was it before you went to bed?"

"My wife had gone to the theatre. I waited up for her. It was half-past eleven before we went to our room."

"Then for four hours the despatch-box had lain unguarded?"

"No one is ever permitted to enter that room save the house-maid in the morning, and my valet, or my wife's maid, during the rest of the day. They are both trusty servants who have been with us for some time. Besides, neither of them could possibly have known that there was anything more valuable than the ordinary departmental papers in my despatch-box."

"Who did know of the existence of that letter?"

"No one in the house."

"Surely your wife knew?"

"No, sir. I had said nothing to my wife until I missed the paper this morning."

The Premier nodded approvingly.

"I have long known, sir, how high is your sense of public duty," said he. "I am convinced that in the case of a secret of this importance it would rise superior to the most intimate domestic ties."

The European Secretary bowed.

"You do me no more than justice, sir. Until this morning I have never breathed one word to my wife upon this matter."

"Could she have guessed?"

"No, Mr. Holmes, she could not have guessed—nor could anyone have guessed."

"Have you lost any documents before?"

"No, sir."

"Who is there in England who did know of the existence of this letter?"

"Each member of the Cabinet was informed of it yesterday, but the pledge of secrecy which attends every Cabinet meeting was increased by the solemn warning which was given by the Prime Minister. Good heavens, to think that within a few hours I should myself have lost it!" His handsome face was distorted with a spasm of despair, and his hands tore at his hair. For a moment we caught a glimpse of the natural man, impulsive, ardent, keenly sensitive. The next the aristocratic mask was replaced, and the gentle voice had returned. "Besides the members of the Cabinet there are two, or possibly three, departmental officials who know of the letter. No one else in England, Mr. Holmes, I assure you."

"But abroad?"

"I believe that no one abroad has seen it save the man who wrote it. I am well convinced that his Ministers—that the usual official channels have not been employed."

Holmes considered for some little time.

"Now, sir, I must ask you more particularly what this document is, and why its disappearance should have such momentous consequences?"

The two statesmen exchanged a quick glance and the Premier's shaggy eyebrows gathered in a frown.

"Mr. Holmes, the envelope is a long, thin one of pale blue colour. There is a seal of red wax stamped with a crouching lion. It is addressed in large, bold handwriting to——"

"I fear, sir," said Holmes, "that, interesting and indeed essential as these details are, my inquiries must go more to the root of things. What *was* the letter?"

"That is a State secret of the utmost importance, and I fear that I cannot tell you, nor do I see that it is necessary. If by the aid of the powers which you are said to possess you can find such an envelope as I describe with its enclosure, you will have deserved well of your country, and earned any reward which it lies in our power to bestow."

Sherlock Holmes rose with a smile.

"You are two of the most busy men in the country," said he, "and in my own small way I have also a good many calls upon me. I regret exceedingly that I cannot help you in this matter, and any continuation of this interview would be a waste of time."

The Premier sprang to his feet with that quick, fierce gleam of his deep-set eyes before which a Cabinet has cowered. "I am not accustomed, sir," he began, but mastered his anger and resumed his seat. For a minute or more we all sat in silence. Then the old statesman shrugged his shoulders.

"We must accept your terms, Mr. Holmes. No doubt you are right, and it is unreasonable for us to expect you to act unless we give you our entire confidence."

"I agree with you," said the younger statesman.

"Then I will tell you, relying entirely upon your honour and that of your colleague, Dr. Watson. I may appeal to your patriotism also, for I could not imagine a greater misfortune for the country than that this affair should come out."

"You may safely trust us."

"The letter, then, is from a certain foreign potentate who has been ruffled by some recent Colonial developments of this country. It has been written hurriedly and upon his own responsibility entirely. Inquiries have shown that his Ministers know nothing of the matter. At the same time it is couched in so unfortunate a manner, and certain phrases in it are of so provocative a character, that its publication would undoubtedly lead to a most dangerous state of feeling in this country. There would be such a ferment, sir, that I do not hesitate to say that within a week of the publication of that letter this country would be involved in a great war."

Holmes wrote a name upon a slip of paper and handed it to the Premier.

"Exactly. It was he. And it is this letter—this letter which may well mean the expenditure of a thousand millions and the lives of a hundred thousand men—which has become lost in this unaccountable fashion."

"Have you informed the sender?"

"Yes, sir, a cipher telegram has been despatched."

"Perhaps he desires the publication of the letter."

"No, sir, we have strong reason to believe that he already understands that he has acted in an indiscreet and hot-headed manner. It would be a greater blow to him and to his country than to us if this letter were to come out."

"If this is so, whose interest is it that the letter should come out? Why should anyone desire to steal it or to publish it?"

"There, Mr. Holmes, you take me into regions of high international politics. But if you consider the European situation you will have no difficulty in perceiving the motive. The whole of Europe is an armed camp. There is a double league which makes a fair balance of military power. Great Britain holds the scales. If Britain were driven into war with one confederacy, it would assure the supremacy of the other confederacy, whether they joined in the war or not. Do you follow?"

"Very clearly. It is then the interest of the enemies of this potentate to secure and publish this letter, so as to make a breach between his country and ours?"

"Yes, sir."

"And to whom would this document be sent if it fell into the hands of an enemy?"

"To any of the great Chancelleries of Europe. It is probably speeding on its way thither at the present instant as fast as steam can take it."

Mr. Trelawney Hope dropped his head on his chest and groaned aloud. The Premier placed his hand kindly upon his shoulder.

"It is your misfortune, my dear fellow. No one can blame you. There is no precaution which you have neglected. Now, Mr. Holmes, you are in full possession of the facts. What course do you recommend?"

Holmes shook his head mournfully.

"You think, sir, that unless this document is recovered there will be war?"

"I think it is very probable."

"Then, sir, prepare for war."

"That is a hard saying, Mr. Holmes."

"Consider the facts, sir. It is inconceivable that it was taken after eleven-thirty at night, since I understand that Mr. Hope and his wife were both in the room from that hour until the loss was found out. It was taken, then, yesterday evening between seven-thirty and eleven-thirty, probably near the earlier hour, since whoever took it evidently knew that it was there and would naturally secure it as early as possible. Now, sir, if a document of this importance were taken at that hour, where can it be now? No one has any reason to retain it. It has been passed rapidly on to those who need it. What chance have we now to overtake or even to trace it? It is beyond our reach."

The Prime Minister rose from the settee.

"What you say is perfectly logical, Mr. Holmes. I feel that the matter is indeed out of our hands."

"Let us presume, for argument's sake, that the document was taken by the maid or by the valet——"

"They are both old and tried servants."

"I understand you to say that your room is on the second floor, that there is no entrance from without, and that from within no one could go up unobserved. It must, then, be somebody in the house who has taken it. To whom would the thief take it? To one of several international spies and secret agents, whose names are tolerably familiar to me. There are three who may be said to be the heads of their profession. I will begin my research by going round and finding if each of them is at his post. If one is missing—especially if he has disappeared since last night—we will have some indication as to where the document has gone."

"Why should he be missing?" asked the European Secretary. "He would take the letter to an Embassy in London, as likely as not."

"I fancy not. These agents work independently, and their relations with the Embassies are often strained."

The Prime Minister nodded his acquiescence.

"I believe you are right, Mr. Holmes. He would take so valuable a prize to headquarters with his own hands. I think that your course of action is an excellent one. Meanwhile, Hope, we cannot neglect all our other duties on account of this one misfortune. Should there be any fresh developments during the day we shall communicate with you, and you will no doubt let us know the results of your own inquiries."

The two statesmen bowed and walked gravely from the room. When our illustrious visitors had departed Holmes lit his pipe in silence and sat for some time lost in the deepest thought. I had opened the morning paper and was immersed in a sensational crime which had occurred in London the night before, when my friend gave an exclamation, sprang to his feet, and laid his pipe down upon the mantelpiece.

"Yes," said he, "there is no better way of approaching it. The situation is desperate, but not hopeless. Even now, if we could be sure which of them has taken it, it is just possible that it has not yet passed out of his hands. After all, it is a question of money with these fellows, and I have the British treasury behind me. If it's on the market I'll buy it—if it means another penny on the income-tax. It is conceivable that the fellow might hold it back to see what bids come from this side before he tries his luck on the other. There are only those three capable of playing so bold a game—there are Oberstein, La Rothiere, and Eduardo Lucas. I will see each of them."

I glanced at my morning paper.

"Is that Eduardo Lucas of Godolphin Street?"

"Yes."

"You will not see him."

"Why not?"

"He was murdered in his house last night."

My friend has so often astonished me in the course of our adventures that it was with a sense of exultation that I realized how completely I had astonished him. He stared in amazement, and then snatched the paper from my hands. This was the paragraph which I had been engaged in reading when he rose from his chair.

MURDER IN WESTMINSTER

A crime of mysterious character was committed last night at 16 Godolphin Street, one of the old-fashioned and secluded rows of eighteenth-century houses which lie between the river and the Abbey, almost in the shadow of the great Tower of the Houses of Parliament. This small but select mansion has been inhabited for some years by Mr. Eduardo Lucas, well known in society circles both on account of his charming personality and because he has the well-deserved reputation of being one of the best amateur tenors in the country. Mr. Lucas is an unmarried man, thirty-four years of age, and his establishment consists of Mrs. Pringle, an elderly housekeeper, and of Mitton, his valet. The former retires early and sleeps at the top of the house. The valet was out for the evening, visiting a friend at Hammersmith. From ten o'clock onward Mr. Lucas had the house to himself. What occurred during that time has not yet transpired, but at a quarter to twelve Police-constable Barrett, passing along Godolphin Street, observed that the door of No. 16 was ajar. He knocked, but received no answer. Perceiving a light in the front room, he advanced into the passage and again knocked, but without reply. He then pushed open the door and entered. The room was in a state of wild disorder, the furniture being all swept to one side, and one chair lying on its back in the centre. Beside this chair, and still grasping one of its legs, lay the unfortunate tenant of the house. He had been stabbed to the heart and must have died instantly. The knife with which the crime had been committed was a curved Indian dagger, plucked down from a trophy of Oriental arms which adorned one of the walls. Robbery does not appear to have been the motive of the crime, for there had been no attempt to remove the valuable contents of the room. Mr. Eduardo Lucas was so well known and popular that his violent and mysterious fate will arouse painful interest and intense sympathy in a widespread circle of friends.

"Well, Watson, what do you make of this?" asked Holmes, after a long pause.

"It is an amazing coincidence."

"A coincidence! Here is one of the three men whom we had named as possible actors in this drama, and he meets a violent death during the very hours when we know that that drama was being enacted. The odds are enormous against its being coincidence. No figures could express them. No, my dear Watson, the two events are connected—*must* be connected. It is for us to find the connection."

"But now the official police must know all."

"Not at all. They know all they see at Godolphin Street. They know—and shall know—nothing of Whitehall Terrace. Only *we* know of both events, and can trace the relation between them. There is one obvious point which would, in any case, have turned my suspicions against Lucas. Godolphin Street, Westminster, is only a few minutes' walk from Whitehall Terrace. The other secret agents whom I have named live in the extreme West End. It was easier, therefore, for Lucas than for the others to establish a connection or receive a message from the European Secretary's household—a small thing, and yet where events are compressed into a few hours it may prove essential. Halloa! what have we here?"

Mrs. Hudson had appeared with a lady's card upon her salver. Holmes glanced at it, raised his eyebrows, and handed it over to me.

"Ask Lady Hilda Trelawney Hope if she will be kind enough to step up," said he.

A moment later our modest apartment, already so distinguished that morning, was further honoured by the entrance of the most lovely woman in London. I had often heard of the beauty of the youngest daughter of the Duke of Belminster, but no description of it, and no contemplation of colourless photographs, had prepared me for the subtle, delicate charm and the beautiful colouring of that exquisite head. And yet as we saw it that autumn morning, it was not its beauty which would be the first thing to impress the observer. The cheek was lovely but it was paled with emotion, the eyes were bright, but it was the brightness of fever, the sensitive mouth was tight and drawn in an effort after self-command. Terror—not beauty—was what sprang first to the eye as our fair visitor stood framed for an instant in the open door.

"Has my husband been here, Mr. Holmes?"

"Yes, madam, he has been here."

"Mr. Holmes, I implore you not to tell him that I came here." Holmes bowed coldly, and motioned the lady to a chair.

"Your ladyship places me in a very delicate position. I beg that you will sit down and tell me what you desire, but I fear that I cannot make any unconditional promise."

She swept across the room and seated herself with her back to the window. It was a queenly presence—tall, graceful, and intensely womanly.

"Mr. Holmes," she said—and her white-gloved hands clasped and unclasped as she spoke—"I will speak frankly to you in the hopes that it may induce you to speak frankly in return. There is complete confidence between my husband and me on all matters save one. That one is politics. On this his lips are sealed. He tells me nothing. Now, I am aware that there was a most deplorable occurrence in our house last night. I know that a paper has disappeared. But because the matter is political my husband refuses to take me into his complete confidence. Now it is essential—essential, I say—that I should thoroughly understand it. You are the only other person, save only these politicians, who knows the true facts. I beg you then, Mr. Holmes, to tell me exactly what has happened and what it will lead to. Tell me all, Mr. Holmes. Let no regard for your client's interests keep you silent, for I assure you that his interests, if he would only see it, would be best served by taking me into his complete confidence. What was this paper which was stolen?"

"Madam, what you ask me is really impossible."

She groaned and sank her face in her hands.

"You must see that this is so, madam. If your husband thinks fit to keep you in the dark over this matter, is it for me, who has only learned the true facts under the pledge of professional secrecy, to tell what he has withheld? It is not fair to ask it. It is him whom you must ask."

"I have asked him. I come to you as a last resource. But without your telling me anything definite, Mr. Holmes, you may do a great service if you would enlighten me on one point."

"What is it, madam?"

"Is my husband's political career likely to suffer through this incident?"

"Well, madam, unless it is set right it may certainly have a very unfortunate effect."

"Ah!" She drew in her breath sharply as one whose doubts are resolved.

"One more question, Mr. Holmes. From an expression which my husband dropped in the first shock of this disaster I understood that terrible public consequences might arise from the loss of this document."

"If he said so, I certainly cannot deny it."

"Of what nature are they?"

"Nay, madam, there again you ask me more than I can possibly answer."

"Then I will take up no more of your time. I cannot blame you, Mr. Holmes, for having refused to speak more freely, and you on your side will not, I am sure, think the worse of me because I desire, even against his will, to share my husband's anxieties. Once more I beg that you will say nothing of my visit."

She looked back at us from the door, and I had a last impression of that beautiful haunted face, the startled eyes, and the drawn mouth. Then she was gone.

"Now, Watson, the fair sex is your department," said Holmes, with a smile, when the dwindling frou-frou of skirts had ended in the slam of the front door. "What was the fair lady's game? What did she really want?"

"Surely her own statement is clear and her anxiety very natural."

"Hum! Think of her appearance, Watson—her manner, her suppressed excitement, her restlessness, her tenacity in asking questions. Remember that she comes of a caste who do not lightly show emotion."

"She was certainly much moved."

"Remember also the curious earnestness with which she assured us that it was best for her husband that she should know all. What did she mean by that? And you must have observed, Watson, how she manoeuvred to have the light at her back. She did not wish us to read her expression."

"Yes, she chose the one chair in the room."

"And yet the motives of women are so inscrutable. You remember the woman at Margate whom I suspected for the same reason. No powder on her nose—that proved to be the correct solution. How can you build on such a quicksand? Their most trivial action may mean volumes, or their most extraordinary conduct may depend upon a hairpin or a curling tongs. Good-morning, Watson."

"You are off?"

"Yes, I will while away the morning at Godolphin Street with our friends of the regular establishment. With Eduardo Lucas lies the solution of our problem, though I must admit that I have not an inkling as to what form it may take. It is a capital mistake to theorize in advance of the facts. Do you stay on guard, my good Watson, and receive any fresh visitors. I'll join you at lunch if I am able."

All that day and the next and the next Holmes was in a mood which his friends would call taciturn, and others morose. He ran out and ran in, smoked incessantly, played snatches on his violin, sank into reveries, devoured sandwiches at irregular hours, and hardly answered the casual questions which I put to him. It was evident to me that things were not going well with him or his quest. He would say nothing of the case, and it was from the papers that I learned the particulars of the inquest, and the arrest with the subsequent release of John Mitton, the valet of the deceased. The coroner's jury brought in the obvious Wilful Murder, but the parties remained as unknown as ever. No motive was suggested. The room was full of articles of value, but none had been taken. The dead man's papers had not been tampered with. They were carefully examined, and showed that he was a keen student of international politics, an indefatigable gossip, a remarkable linguist, and an untiring letter writer. He had been on intimate terms with the leading politicians of several countries. But nothing sensational was discovered among the documents which filled his drawers. As to his relations with women, they appeared to have been promiscuous but superficial. He had many acquaintances among them, but few friends, and no one whom he loved. His habits were regular, his conduct inoffensive. His death was an absolute mystery and likely to remain so.

As to the arrest of John Mitton, the valet, it was a council of despair as an alternative to absolute inaction. But no case could be sustained against him. He had visited friends in Hammersmith that night. The *alibi* was complete. It is true that he started home at an hour which should have brought him to Westminster before the time when the crime was discovered, but his own explanation that he had walked part of the way seemed probable enough in view of the fineness of the night. He had actually arrived at twelve o'clock, and appeared to be overwhelmed by the unexpected tragedy. He had always been on good terms with his master. Several of the dead man's possessions—notably a small case of razors—had been found in the valet's boxes, but he explained that they had been presents from the deceased, and the housekeeper was able to corroborate the story. Mitton had been in Lucas's employment for three years. It was noticeable that Lucas did not take Mitton on the Continent with him. Sometimes he visited Paris for three months on end, but Mitton was left in charge of the Godolphin Street house. As to the housekeeper, she had heard nothing on the night of the crime. If her master had a visitor he had himself admitted him.

So for three mornings the mystery remained, so far as I could follow it in the papers. If Holmes knew more, he kept his own counsel, but, as he told me that Inspector Lestrade had taken him into his confidence in the case, I knew that he was in close touch with every development. Upon the fourth day there appeared a long telegram from Paris which seemed to solve the whole question.

A discovery has just been made by the Parisian police [said the *Daily Telegraph*] which raises the veil which hung round the tragic fate of Mr. Eduardo Lucas, who met his death by violence last Monday night at Godolphin Street, Westminster. Our readers will remember that the deceased gentleman was found stabbed in his room, and that some suspicion attached to his valet, but that the case broke down on an *alibi*. Yesterday a lady, who has been known as Mme. Henri Four-

naye, occupying a small villa in the Rue Austerlitz, was reported to
the authorities by her servants as being insane. An examination
showed she had indeed developed mania of a dangerous and permanent form. On inquiry, the police have discovered that Mme. Henri
Fournaye only returned from a journey to London on Tuesday last,
and there is evidence to connect her with the crime at Westminster. A
comparison of photographs has proved conclusively that M. Henri
Fournaye and Eduardo Lucas were really one and the same person,
and that the deceased had for some reason lived a double life in London and Paris. Mme. Fournaye, who is of Creole origin, is of an extremely excitable nature, and has suffered in the past from attacks of
jealousy which have amounted to frenzy. It is conjectured that it was
in one of these that she committed the terrible crime which has caused
such a sensation in London. Her movements upon the Monday night
have not yet been traced, but it is undoubted that a woman answering
to her description attracted much attention at Charing Cross Station
on Tuesday morning by the wildness of her appearance and the violence of her gestures. It is probable, therefore, that the crime was either committed when insane, or that its immediate effect was to drive
the unhappy woman out of her mind. At present she is unable to give
any coherent account of the past, and the doctors hold out no hopes
of the reëstablishment of her reason. There is evidence that a woman,
who might have been Mme. Fournaye, was seen for some hours upon
Monday night watching the house in Godolphin Street.

"What do you think of that, Holmes?" I had read the account aloud to
him, while he finished his breakfast.

"My dear Watson," said he, as he rose from the table and paced up and
down the room, "you are most long-suffering, but if I have told you nothing in the last three days, it is because there is nothing to tell. Even now
this report from Paris does not help us much."

"Surely it is final as regards the man's death."

"The man's death is a mere incident—a trivial episode—in comparison
with our real task, which is to trace this document and save a European
catastrophe. Only one important thing has happened in the last three
days, and that is that nothing has happened. I get reports almost hourly
from the government, and it is certain that nowhere in Europe is there
any sign of trouble. Now, if this letter were loose—no, it *can't* be loose—
but if it isn't loose, where can it be? Who has it? Why is it held back?
That's the question that beats in my brain like a hammer. Was it, indeed,
a coincidence that Lucas should meet his death on the night when the letter disappeared? Did the letter ever reach him? If so, why is it not among
his papers? Did this mad wife of his carry it off with her? If so, is it in her
house in Paris? How could I search for it without the French police having their suspicions aroused? It is a case, my dear Watson, where the law
is as dangerous to us as the criminals are. Every man's hand is against us,
and yet the interests at stake are colossal. Should I bring it to a successful

conclusion, it will certainly represent the crowning glory of my career. Ah, here is my latest from the front!" He glanced hurriedly at the note which had been handed in. "Halloa! Lestrade seems to have observed something of interest. Put on your hat, Watson, and we will stroll down together to Westminster."

It was my first visit to the scene of the crime—a high, dingy, narrow-chested house, prim, formal, and solid, like the century which gave it birth. Lestrade's bulldog features gazed out at us from the front window, and he greeted us warmly when a big constable had opened the door and let us in. The room into which we were shown was that in which the crime had been committed, but no trace of it now remained save an ugly, irregular stain upon the carpet. This carpet was a small square drugget* in the centre of the room, surrounded by a broad expanse of beautiful, old-fashioned wood-flooring in square blocks, highly polished. Over the fireplace was a magnificent trophy of weapons, one of which had been used on that tragic night. In the window was a sumptuous writing-desk, and every detail of the apartment, the pictures, the rugs, and the hangings, all pointed to a taste which was luxurious to the verge of effeminacy.

"Seen the Paris news?" asked Lestrade.

Holmes nodded.

"Our French friends seem to have touched the spot this time. No doubt it's just as they say. She knocked at the door—surprise visit, I guess, for he kept his life in water-tight compartments—he let her in, couldn't keep her in the street. She told him how she had traced him, reproached him. One thing led to another, and then with that dagger so handy the end soon came. It wasn't all done in an instant, though, for these chairs were all swept over yonder, and he had one in his hand as if he had tried to hold her off with it. We've got it all clear as if we had seen it."

Holmes raised his eyebrows.

"And yet you have sent for me?"

"Ah, yes, that's another matter—a mere trifle, but the sort of thing you take an interest in—queer, you know, and what you might call freakish. It has nothing to do with the main fact—can't have, on the face of it."

"What is it, then?"

"Well, you know, after a crime of this sort we are very careful to keep things in their position. Nothing has been moved. Officer in charge here day and night. This morning, as the man was buried and the investigation over—so far as this room is concerned—we thought we could tidy up a bit. This carpet. You see, it is not fastened down, only just laid there. We had occasion to raise it. We found——"

"Yes? You found——"

Holmes's face grew tense with anxiety.

"Well, I'm sure you would never guess in a hundred years what we did

---

*Rug made in India of coarse wool and cotton.

find. You see that stain on the carpet? Well, a great deal must have soaked through, must it not?"

"Undoubtedly it must."

"Well, you will be surprised to hear that there is no stain on the white woodwork to correspond."

"No stain! But there must——"

"Yes, so you would say. But the fact remains that there isn't."

He took the corner of the carpet in his hand and, turning it over, he showed that it was indeed as he said.

"But the under side is as stained as the upper. It must have left a mark."

Lestrade chuckled with delight at having puzzled the famous expert.

"Now, I'll show you the explanation. There *is* a second stain, but it does not correspond with the other. See for yourself." As he spoke he turned over another portion of the carpet, and there, sure enough, was a great crimson spill upon the square white facing of the old-fashioned floor. "What do you make of that, Mr. Holmes?"

"Why, it is simple enough. The two stains did correspond, but the carpet has been turned round. As it was square and unfastened it was easily done."

"The official police don't need you, Mr. Holmes, to tell them that the carpet must have been turned round. That's clear enough, for the stains lie above each other—if you lay it over this way. But what I want to know is, who shifted the carpet, and why?"

I could see from Holmes's rigid face that he was vibrating with inward excitement.

"Look here, Lestrade," said he, "has that constable in the passage been in charge of the place all the time?"

"Yes, he has."

"Well, take my advice. Examine him carefully. Don't do it before us. We'll wait here. You take him into the back room. You'll be more likely to get a confession out of him alone. Ask him how he dared to admit people and leave them alone in this room. Don't ask him if he has done it. Take it for granted. Tell him you *know* someone has been here. Press him. Tell him that a full confession is his only chance of forgiveness. Do exactly what I tell you!"

"By George, if he knows I'll have it out of him!" cried Lestrade. He darted into the hall, and a few moments later his bullying voice sounded from the back room.

"Now, Watson, now!" cried Holmes with frenzied eagerness. All the demoniacal force of the man masked behind that listless manner burst out in a paroxysm of energy. He tore the drugget from the floor, and in an instant was down on his hands and knees clawing at each of the squares of wood beneath it. One turned sideways as he dug his nails into the edge of it. It hinged back like the lid of a box. A small black cavity opened beneath it. Holmes plunged his eager hand into it and drew it out with a bitter snarl of anger and disappointment. It was empty.

"Quick, Watson, quick! Get it back again!" The wooden lid was replaced, and the drugget had only just been drawn straight when Lestrade's voice was heard in the passage. He found Holmes leaning languidly against the mantelpiece, resigned and patient, endeavouring to conceal his irrepressible yawns.

"Sorry to keep you waiting, Mr. Holmes. I can see that you are bored to death with the whole affair. Well, he has confessed, all right. Come in here, MacPherson. Let these gentlemen hear of your most inexcusable conduct."

The big constable, very hot and penitent, sidled into the room.

"I meant no harm, sir, I'm sure. The young woman came to the door last evening—mistook the house, she did. And then we got talking. It's lonesome, when you're on duty here all day."

"Well, what happened then?"

"She wanted to see where the crime was done—had read about it in the papers, she said. She was a very respectable, well-spoken young woman, sir, and I saw no harm in letting her have a peep. When she saw that mark on the carpet, down she dropped on the floor, and lay as if she were dead. I ran to the back and got some water, but I could not bring her to. Then I went round the corner to the Ivy Plant for some brandy, and by the time I had brought it back the young woman had recovered and was off—ashamed of herself, I daresay, and dared not face me."

"How about moving that drugget?"

"Well, sir, it was a bit rumpled, certainly, when I came back. You see, she fell on it and it lies on a polished floor with nothing to keep it in place. I straightened it out afterwards."

"It's a lesson to you that you can't deceive me, Constable MacPherson," said Lestrade, with dignity. "No doubt you thought that your breach of duty could never be discovered, and yet a mere glance at that drugget was enough to convince me that someone had been admitted to the room. It's lucky for you, my man, that nothing is missing, or you would find yourself in Queer Street.* I'm sorry to have called you down over such a petty business, Mr. Holmes, but I thought the point of the second stain not corresponding with the first would interest you."

"Certainly, it was most interesting. Has this woman only been here once, constable?"

"Yes, sir, only once."

"Who was she?"

"Don't know the name, sir. Was answering an advertisement about typewriting and came to the wrong number—very pleasant, genteel young woman, sir."

"Tall? Handsome?"

"Yes, sir, she was a well-grown young woman. I suppose you might say she was handsome. Perhaps some would say she was very handsome. 'Oh,

---

*In uncomfortable circumstances, especially financial trouble.

officer, do let me have a peep!' says she. She had pretty, coaxing ways, as you might say, and I thought there was no harm in letting her just put her head through the door."

"How was she dressed?"

"Quiet, sir—a long mantle down to her feet."

"What time was it?"

"It was just growing dusk at the time. They were lighting the lamps as I came back with the brandy."

"Very good," said Holmes. "Come, Watson, I think that we have more important work elsewhere."

As we left the house Lestrade remained in the front room, while the repentant constable opened the door to let us out. Holmes turned on the step and held up something in his hand. The constable stared intently.

"Good Lord, sir!" he cried, with amazement on his face. Holmes put his finger on his lips, replaced his hand in his breast pocket, and burst out laughing as we turned down the street. "Excellent!" said he. "Come, friend Watson, the curtain rings up for the last act. You will be relieved to hear that there will be no war, that the Right Honourable Trelawney Hope will suffer no setback in his brilliant career, that the indiscreet Sovereign will receive no punishment for his indiscretion, that the Prime Minister will have no European complication to deal with, and that with a little tact and management upon our part nobody will be a penny the worse for what might have been a very ugly incident."

My mind filled with admiration for this extraordinary man.

"You have solved it!" I cried.

"Hardly that, Watson. There are some points which are as dark as ever. But we have so much that it will be our own fault if we cannot get the rest. We will go straight to Whitehall Terrace and bring the matter to a head."

When we arrived at the residence of the European Secretary it was for Lady Hilda Trelawney Hope that Sherlock Holmes inquired. We were shown into the morning-room.

"Mr. Holmes!" said the lady, and her face was pink with her indignation. "This is surely most unfair and ungenerous upon your part. I desired, as I have explained, to keep my visit to you a secret, lest my husband should think that I was intruding into his affairs. And yet you compromise me by coming here and so showing that there are business relations between us."

"Unfortunately, madam, I had no possible alternative. I have been commissioned to recover this immensely important paper. I must therefore ask you, madam, to be kind enough to place it in my hands."

The lady sprang to her feet, with the colour all dashed in an instant from her beautiful face. Her eyes glazed—she tottered—I thought that she would faint. Then with a grand effort she rallied from the shock, and a supreme astonishment and indignation chased every other expression from her features.

"You—you insult me, Mr. Holmes."

"Come, come, madam, it is useless. Give up the letter."

She darted to the bell.

"The butler shall show you out."

"Do not ring, Lady Hilda. If you do, then all my earnest efforts to avoid a scandal will be frustrated. Give up the letter and all will be set right. If you will work with me I can arrange everything. If you work against me I must expose you."

She stood grandly defiant, a queenly figure, her eyes fixed upon his as if she would read his very soul. Her hand was on the bell, but she had forborne to ring it.

"You are trying to frighten me. It is not a very manly thing, Mr. Holmes, to come here and browbeat a woman. You say that you know something. What is it that you know?"

"Pray sit down, madam. You will hurt yourself there if you fall. I will not speak until you sit down. Thank you."

"I give you five minutes, Mr. Holmes."

"One is enough, Lady Hilda. I know of your visit to Eduardo Lucas, of your giving him this document, of your ingenious return to the room last night, and of the manner in which you took the letter from the hiding-place under the carpet."

She stared at him with an ashen face and gulped twice before she could speak.

"You are mad, Mr. Holmes—you are mad!" she cried, at last.

He drew a small piece of cardboard from his pocket. It was the face of a woman cut out of a portrait.

"I have carried this because I thought it might be useful," said he. "The policeman has recognized it."

She gave a gasp, and her head dropped back in the chair.

"Come, Lady Hilda. You have the letter. The matter may still be adjusted. I have no desire to bring trouble to you. My duty ends when I have returned the lost letter to your husband. Take my advice and be frank with me. It is your only chance."

Her courage was admirable. Even now she would not own defeat.

"I tell you again, Mr. Holmes, that you are under some absurd illusion."

Holmes rose from his chair.

"I am sorry for you, Lady Hilda. I have done my best for you. I can see that it is all in vain."

He rang the bell. The butler entered.

"Is Mr. Trelawney Hope at home?"

"He will be home, sir, at a quarter to one."

Holmes glanced at his watch.

"Still a quarter of an hour," said he. "Very good, I shall wait."

The butler had hardly closed the door behind him when Lady Hilda was down on her knees at Holmes's feet, her hands outstretched, her beautiful face upturned and wet with her tears.

"Oh, spare me, Mr. Holmes! Spare me!" she pleaded, in a frenzy of supplication. "For heaven's sake, don't tell him! I love him so! I would not bring one shadow on his life, and this I know would break his noble heart."

Holmes raised the lady. "I am thankful, madam, that you have come to your senses even at this last moment! There is not an instant to lose. Where is the letter?"

She darted across to a writing-desk, unlocked it, and drew out a long blue envelope.

"Here it is, Mr. Holmes. Would to heaven I had never seen it!"

"How can we return it?" Holmes muttered. "Quick, quick, we must think of some way! Where is the despatch-box?"

"Still in his bedroom."

"What a stroke of luck! Quick, madam, bring it here!"

A moment later she had appeared with a red flat box in her hand.

"How did you open it before? You have a duplicate key? Yes, of course you have. Open it!"

From out of her bosom Lady Hilda had drawn a small key. The box flew open. It was stuffed with papers. Holmes thrust the blue envelope deep down into the heart of them, between the leaves of some other document. The box was shut, locked, and returned to the bedroom.

"Now we are ready for him," said Holmes. "We have still ten minutes. I am going far to screen you, Lady Hilda. In return you will spend the time in telling me frankly the real meaning of this extraordinary affair."

"Mr. Holmes, I will tell you everything," cried the lady. "Oh, Mr. Holmes, I would cut off my right hand before I gave him a moment of sorrow! There is no woman in all London who loves her husband as I do, and yet if he knew how I have acted—how I have been compelled to act—he would never forgive me. For his own honour stands so high that he could not forget or pardon a lapse in another. Help me, Mr. Holmes! My happiness, his happiness, our very lives are at stake!"

"Quick, madam, the time grows short!"

"It was a letter of mine, Mr. Holmes, an indiscreet letter written before my marriage—a foolish letter, a letter of an impulsive, loving girl. I meant no harm, and yet he would have thought it criminal. Had he read that letter his confidence would have been forever destroyed. It is years since I wrote it. I had thought that the whole matter was forgotten. Then at last I heard from this man, Lucas, that it had passed into his hands, and that he would lay it before my husband. I implored his mercy. He said that he would return my letter if I would bring him a certain document which he described in my husband's despatch-box. He had some spy in the office who had told him of its existence. He assured me that no harm could come to my husband. Put yourself in my position, Mr. Holmes! What was I to do?"

"Take your husband into your confidence."

"I could not, Mr. Holmes, I could not! On the one side seemed certain ruin, on the other, terrible as it seemed to take my husband's paper, still in a matter of politics I could not understand the consequences, while in a matter of love and trust they were only too clear to me. I did it, Mr. Holmes! I took an impression of his key. This man, Lucas, furnished a duplicate. I opened his despatch-box, took the paper, and conveyed it to Godolphin Street."

"What happened there, madam?"

"I tapped at the door as agreed. Lucas opened it. I followed him into his room, leaving the hall door ajar behind me, for I feared to be alone with the man. I remember that there was a woman outside as I entered. Our business was soon done. He had my letter on his desk, I handed him the document. He gave me the letter. At this instant there was a sound at the door. There were steps in the passage. Lucas quickly turned back the drugget, thrust the document into some hiding-place there, and covered it over.

"What happened after that is like some fearful dream. I have a vision of a dark, frantic face, of a woman's voice, which screamed in French, 'My waiting is not in vain. At last, at last I have found you with her!' There was a savage struggle. I saw him with a chair in his hand, a knife gleamed in hers. I rushed from the horrible scene, ran from the house, and only next morning in the paper did I learn the dreadful result. That night I was happy, for I had my letter, and I had not seen yet what the future would bring.

"It was the next morning that I realized that I had only exchanged one trouble for another. My husband's anguish at the loss of his paper went to my heart. I could hardly prevent myself from there and then kneeling down at his feet and telling him what I had done. But that again would mean a confession of the past. I came to you that morning in order to understand the full enormity of my offence. From the instant that I grasped it my whole mind was turned to the one thought of getting back my husband's paper. It must still be where Lucas had placed it, for it was concealed before this dreadful woman entered the room. If it had not been for her coming, I should not have known where his hiding-place was. How was I to get into the room? For two days I watched the place, but the door was never left open. Last night I made a last attempt. What I did and how I succeeded, you have already learned. I brought the paper back with me, and thought of destroying it, since I could see no way of returning it without confessing my guilt to my husband. Heavens, I hear his step upon the stair!"

The European Secretary burst excitedly into the room.

"Any news, Mr. Holmes, any news?" he cried.

"I have some hopes."

"Ah, thank heaven!" His face became radiant. "The Prime Minister is lunching with me. May he share your hopes? He has nerves of steel, and yet I know that he has hardly slept since this terrible event. Jacobs, will you ask the Prime Minister to come up? As to you, dear, I fear that this is a matter of politics. We will join you in a few minutes in the dining-room."

The Prime Minister's manner was subdued, but I could see by the gleam of his eyes and the twitchings of his bony hands that he shared the excitement of his young colleague.

"I understand that you have something to report, Mr. Holmes?"

"Purely negative as yet," my friend answered. "I have inquired at every point where it might be, and I am sure that there is no danger to be apprehended."

"But that is not enough, Mr. Holmes. We cannot live forever on such a volcano. We must have something definite."

"I am in hopes of getting it. That is why I am here. The more I think of the matter the more convinced I am that the letter has never left this house."

"Mr. Holmes!"

"If it had it would certainly have been public by now."

"But why should anyone take it in order to keep it in his house?"

"I am not convinced that anyone did take it."

"Then how could it leave the despatch-box?"

"I am not convinced that it ever did leave the despatch-box."

"Mr. Holmes, this joking is very ill-timed. You have my assurance that it left the box."

"Have you examined the box since Tuesday morning?"

"No. It was not necessary."

"You may conceivably have overlooked it."

"Impossible, I say."

"But I am not convinced of it. I have known such things to happen. I presume there are other papers there. Well, it may have got mixed with them."

"It was on the top."

"Someone may have shaken the box and displaced it."

"No, no, I had everything out."

"Surely it is easily decided, Hope," said the Premier. "Let us have the despatch-box brought in."

The Secretary rang the bell.

"Jacobs, bring down my despatch-box. This is a farcical waste of time, but still, if nothing else will satisfy you, it shall be done. Thank you, Jacobs, put it here. I have always had the key on my watch-chain. Here are the papers, you see. Letter from Lord Merrow, report from Sir Charles Hardy, memorandum from Belgrade, note on the Russo-German grain taxes, letter from Madrid, note from Lord Flowers——Good heavens! what is this? Lord Bellinger! Lord Bellinger!"

The Premier snatched the blue envelope from his hand.

"Yes, it is it—and the letter is intact. Hope, I congratulate you."

"Thank you! Thank you! What a weight from my heart. But this is inconceivable—impossible. Mr. Holmes, you are a wizard, a sorcerer! How did you know it was there?"

"Because I knew it was nowhere else."

"I cannot believe my eyes!" He ran wildly to the door. "Where is my wife? I must tell her that all is well. Hilda! Hilda!" we heard his voice on the stairs.

The Premier looked at Holmes with twinkling eyes.

"Come, sir," said he. "There is more in this than meets the eye. How came the letter back in the box?"

Holmes turned away smiling from the keen scrutiny of those wonderful eyes.

"We also have our diplomatic secrets," said he and, picking up his hat, he turned to the door.

THE VALLEY OF FEAR

Part 1

THE TRAGEDY OF
BIRLSTONE

CHAPTER 1

The Warning

"I am inclined to think——" said I.

"I should do so," Sherlock Holmes remarked impatiently.

I believe that I am one of the most long-suffering of mortals; but I'll admit that I was annoyed at the sardonic interruption. "Really, Holmes," said I severely, "you are a little trying at times."

He was too much absorbed with his own thoughts to give any immediate answer to my remonstrance. He leaned upon his hand, with his untasted breakfast before him, and he stared at the slip of paper which he had just drawn from its envelope. Then he took the envelope itself, held it up to the light, and very carefully studied both the exterior and the flap.

"It is Porlock's[2] writing," said he thoughtfully. "I can hardly doubt that it is Porlock's writing, though I have seen it only twice before. The Greek *e* with the peculiar top flourish is distinctive. But if it is Porlock then it must be something of the very first importance."

He was speaking to himself rather than to me; but my vexation disappeared in the interest which the words awakened.

"Who then is Porlock?" I asked.

"Porlock, Watson, is a nom-de-plume, a mere identification mark; but behind it lies a shifty and evasive personality. In a former letter he frankly informed me that the name was not his own, and defied me ever to trace him among the teeming millions of this great city. Porlock is important, not for himself, but for the great man with whom he is in touch. Picture to yourself the pilot fish with the shark, the jackal with the lion—anything that is insignificant in companionship with what is formidable: not only formidable, Watson, but sinister—in the highest degree sinister. That is where he comes within my purview. You have heard me speak of Professor Moriarty?"

"The famous scientific criminal, as famous among crooks as——"

"My blushes, Watson!" Holmes murmured in a deprecating voice.

"I was about to say, as he is unknown to the public."

"A touch! A distinct touch!" cried Holmes. "You are developing a certain unexpected vein of pawky* humour, Watson, against which I must learn to guard myself. But in calling Moriarty a criminal you are uttering libel in the eyes of the law—and there lie the glory and the wonder of it! The greatest schemer of all time, the organizer of every deviltry, the controlling brain of the underworld, a brain which might have made or

---

*Matter-of-factly humorous.

marred the destiny of nations—that's the man! But so aloof is he from general suspicion, so immune from criticism, so admirable in his management and self-effacement, that for those very words that you have uttered he could hale you to a court and emerge with your year's pension as a solatium* for his wounded character. Is he not the celebrated author of *The Dynamics of an Asteroid*, a book which ascends to such rarefied heights of pure mathematics that it is said that there was no man in the scientific press capable of criticizing it? Is this a man to traduce? Foul-mouthed doctor and slandered professor—such would be your respective rôles! That's genius, Watson. But if I am spared by lesser men, our day will surely come."

"May I be there to see!" I exclaimed devoutly. "But you were speaking of this man Porlock."

"Ah, yes—the so-called Porlock is a link in the chain some little way from its great attachment. Porlock is not quite a sound link between ourselves. He is the only flaw in that chain so far as I have been able to test it."

"But no chain is stronger than its weakest link."

"Exactly, my dear Watson! Hence the extreme importance of Porlock. Led on by some rudimentary aspirations towards right, and encouraged by the judicious stimulation of an occasional ten-pound note sent to him by devious methods, he has once or twice given me advance information which has been of value—that highest value which anticipates and prevents rather than avenges crime. I cannot doubt that, if we had the cipher, we should find that this communication is of the nature that I indicate."

Again Holmes flattened out the paper upon his unused plate. I rose and, leaning over him, stared down at the curious inscription, which ran as follows:

534	C2	13	127	36	31	4	17	21	41
	DOUGLAS	109	293	5	37	BIRLSTONE			
	26	BIRLSTONE	9	47	171				

"What do you make of it, Holmes?"

"It is obviously an attempt to convey secret information."

"But what is the use of a cipher message without the cipher?"

"In this instance, none at all."

"Why do you say 'in this instance'?"

"Because there are many ciphers which I would read as easily as I do the apocrypha of the agony column:[3] such crude devices amuse the intelligence without fatiguing it. But this is different. It is clearly a reference to the words in a page of some book. Until I am told which page and which book I am powerless."

"But why 'Douglas' and 'Birlstone'?"

---

*Damages awarded by a court for injury to feelings.

"Clearly because those are words which were not contained in the page in question."

"Then why has he not indicated the book?"

"Your native shrewdness, my dear Watson, that innate cunning which is the delight of your friends, would surely prevent you from inclosing cipher and message in the same envelope. Should it miscarry, you are undone. As it is, both have to go wrong before any harm comes from it. Our second post is now overdue, and I shall be surprised if it does not bring us either a further letter of explanation, or, as is more probable, the very volume to which these figures refer."

Holmes's calculation was fulfilled within a very few minutes by the appearance of Billy, the page, with the very letter which we were expecting.

"The same writing," remarked Holmes, as he opened the envelope, "and actually signed," he added in an exultant voice as he unfolded the epistle. "Come, we are getting on, Watson." His brow clouded, however, as he glanced over the contents.

"Dear me, this is very disappointing! I fear, Watson, that all our expectations come to nothing. I trust that the man Porlock will come to no harm.

"DEAR MR. HOLMES [he says]:
I will go no further in this matter. It is too dangerous—he suspects me. I can see that he suspects me. He came to me quite unexpectedly after I had actually addressed this envelope with the intention of sending you the key to the cipher. I was able to cover it up. If he had seen it, it would have gone hard with me. But I read suspicion in his eyes. Please burn the cipher message, which can now be of no use to you.

FRED PORLOCK."

Holmes sat for some little time twisting this letter between his fingers, and frowning, as he stared into the fire.

"After all," he said at last, "there may be nothing in it. It may be only his guilty conscience. Knowing himself to be a traitor, he may have read the accusation in the other's eyes."

"The other being, I presume, Professor Moriarty."

"No less! When any of that party talk about 'He' you know whom they mean. There is one predominant. 'He' for all of them."

"But what can he do?"

"Hum! That's a large question. When you have one of the first brains of Europe up against you, and all the powers of darkness at his back, there are infinite possibilities. Anyhow, Friend Porlock is evidently scared out of his senses—kindly compare the writing in the note to that upon its envelope; which was done, he tells us, before this ill-omened visit. The one is clear and firm. The other hardly legible."

"Why did he write at all? Why did he not simply drop it?"

"Because he feared I would make some inquiry after him in that case, and possibly bring trouble on him."

"No doubt," said I. "Of course." I had picked up the original cipher message and was bending my brows over it. "It's pretty maddening to think that an important secret may lie here on this slip of paper, and that it is beyond human power to penetrate it.

Sherlock Holmes had pushed away his untasted breakfast and lit the unsavoury pipe which was the companion of his deepest meditations. "I wonder!" said he, leaning back and staring at the ceiling. "Perhaps there are points which have escaped your Machiavellian[4] intellect. Let us consider the problem in the light of pure reason. This man's reference is to a book. That is our point of departure."

"A somewhat vague one."

"Let us see then if we can narrow it down. As I focus my mind upon it, it seems rather less impenetrable. What indications have we as to this book?"

"None."

"Well, well, it is surely not quite so bad as that. The cipher message begins with a large 534, does it not? We may take it as a working hypothesis that 534 is the particular page to which the cipher refers. So our book has already become a *large* book, which is surely something gained. What other indications have we as to the nature of this large book? The next sign is C2. What do you make of that, Watson?"

"Chapter the second, no doubt."

"Hardly that, Watson. You will, I am sure, agree with me that if the page be given, the number of the chapter is immaterial. Also that if page 534 finds us only in the second chapter, the length of the first one must have been really intolerable."

"Column!" I cried.

"Brilliant, Watson. You are scintillating this morning. If it is not column, then I am very much deceived. So now, you see, we begin to visualize a large book, printed in double columns, which are each of a considerable length, since one of the words is numbered in the document as the two hundred and ninety-third. Have we reached the limits of what reason can supply?"

"I fear that we have."

"Surely you do yourself an injustice. One more coruscation, my dear Watson—yet another brain-wave! Had the volume been an unusual one, he would have sent it to me. Instead of that, he had intended, before his plans were nipped, to send me the clue in this envelope. He says so in his note. This would seem to indicate that the book is one which he thought I would have no difficulty in finding for myself. He had it—and he imagined that I would have it, too. In short, Watson, it is a very common book."

"What you say certainly sounds plausible."

"So we have contracted our field of search to a large book, printed in double columns and in common use."

"The Bible!" I cried triumphantly.

"Good, Watson, good! But not, if I may say so, quite good enough! Even if I accepted the compliment for myself, I could hardly name any volume which would be less likely to lie at the elbow of one of Moriarty's associates. Besides, the editions of Holy Writ are so numerous that he could hardly suppose that two copies would have the same pagination. This is clearly a book which is standardized. He knows for certain that his page 534 will exactly agree with my page 534."

"But very few books would correspond with that."

"Exactly. Therein lies our salvation. Our search is narrowed down to standardized books which anyone may be supposed to possess."

"Bradshaw!"*

"There are difficulties, Watson. The vocabulary of Bradshaw is nervous and terse, but limited. The selection of words would hardly lend itself to the sending of general messages. We will eliminate Bradshaw. The dictionary is, I fear, inadmissible for the same reason. What then is left?"

"An almanac!"

"Excellent, Watson! I am very much mistaken if you have not touched the spot. An almanac! Let us consider the claims of Whitaker's Almanac. It is in common use. It has the requisite number of pages. It is in double column. Though reserved in its earlier vocabulary, it becomes, if I remember right, quite garrulous towards the end." He picked the volume from his desk. "Here is page 534, column two, a substantial block of print dealing, I perceive, with the trade and resources of British India. Jot down the words, Watson! Number thirteen is 'Mahratta.' Not, I fear, a very auspicious beginning. Number one hundred and twenty-seven is 'Government'; which at least makes sense, though somewhat irrelevant to ourselves and Professor Moriarty. Now let us try again. What does the Mahratta government do? Alas! the next word is 'pig's-bristles.' We are undone, my good Watson! It is finished!"

He had spoken in jesting vein,[5] but the twitching of his bushy eyebrows bespoke his disappointment and irritation. I sat helpless and unhappy, staring into the fire. A long silence was broken by a sudden exclamation from Holmes, who dashed at a cupboard, from which he emerged with a second yellow-covered volume in his hand.

"We pay the price, Watson, for being too up-to-date!" he cried. "We are before our time, and suffer the usual penalties. Being the seventh of January, we have very properly laid in the new almanac. It is more than likely that Porlock took his message from the old one. No doubt he would have told us so had his letter of explanation been written. Now let us see what page 534 has in store for us. Number thirteen is 'There,' which is much more promising. Number one hundred and twenty-seven is 'is'— 'There is' "—Holmes's eyes were gleaming with excitement, and his thin,

---

*Bradshaw's Monthly Railway Guide, first devised by George Bradshaw (1801–1853).

nervous fingers twitched as he counted the words—" 'danger.' Ha! Ha! Capital! Put that down, Watson. 'There is danger—may—come—very—soon—one.' Then we have the name 'Douglas'—'rich—country—now—at—Birlstone—confidence—is—pressing.' There, Watson! What do you think of pure reason and its fruit? If the green-grocer had such a thing as a laurel wreath,* I should send Billy round for it."

I was staring at the strange message which I had scrawled, as he deciphered it, upon a sheet of foolscap† on my knee.

"What a queer, scrambling way of expressing his meaning!" said I.

"On the contrary, he has done quite remarkably well," said Holmes. "When you search a single column for words with which to express your meaning, you can hardly expect to get everything you want. You are bound to leave something to the intelligence of your correspondent. The purport is perfectly clear. Some deviltry is intended against one Douglas, whoever he may be, residing as stated, a rich country gentleman. He is sure—'confidence' was as near as he could get to 'confident' that it is pressing. There is our result—and a very workmanlike little bit of analysis it was!"

Holmes had the impersonal joy of the true artist in his better work, even as he mourned darkly when it fell below the high level to which he aspired. He was still chuckling over his success when Billy swung open the door and Inspector MacDonald of Scotland Yard was ushered into the room.

Those were the early days at the end of the '80's, when Alec MacDonald was far from having attained the national fame which he has now achieved. He was a young but trusted member of the detective force, who had distinguished himself in several cases which had been intrusted to him. His tall, bony figure gave promise of exceptional physical strength, while his great cranium and deep-set, lustrous eyes spoke no less clearly of the keen intelligence which twinkled out from behind his bushy eyebrows. He was a silent, precise man with a dour nature and a hard Aberdonian accent.

Twice already in his career had Holmes helped him to attain success, his own sole reward being the intellectual joy of the problem. For this reason the affection and respect of the Scotchman for his amateur colleague were profound, and he showed them by the frankness with which he consulted Holmes in every difficulty. Mediocrity knows nothing higher than itself; but talent instantly recognizes genius, and MacDonald had talent enough for his profession to enable him to perceive that there was no humiliation in seeking the assistance of one who already stood alone in Europe, both in his gifts and in his experience. Holmes was not prone to

---

*Given to victors of the ancient Greek contests called the Pythian games, and sometimes to victorious generals.

†Writing paper; so called because its watermark shows a jester's cap and bells.

friendship, but he was tolerant of the big Scotchman, and smiled at the sight of him.

"You are an early bird, Mr. Mac," said he. "I wish you luck with your worm. I fear this means that there is some mischief afoot."

"If you said 'hope' instead of 'fear,' it would be nearer the truth, I'm thinking, Mr. Holmes," the inspector answered, with a knowing grin. "Well, maybe a wee nip would keep out the raw morning chill. No, I won't smoke, I thank you. I'll have to be pushing on my way; for the early hours of a case are the precious ones, as no man knows better than your own self. But—but——"

The inspector had stopped suddenly, and was staring with a look of absolute amazement at a paper upon the table. It was the sheet upon which I had scrawled the enigmatic message.

"Douglas!" he stammered. "Birlstone! What's this, Mr. Holmes? Man, it's witchcraft! Where in the name of all that is wonderful did you get those names?"

"It is a cipher that Dr. Watson and I have had occasion to solve. But why—what's amiss with the names?"

The inspector looked from one to the other of us in dazed astonishment. "Just this," said he, "that Mr. Douglas of Birlstone Manor House was horribly murdered last night!"

CHAPTER 2

Sherlock Holmes Discourses

It was one of those dramatic moments for which my friend existed. It would be an overstatement to say that he was shocked or even excited by the amazing announcement. Without having a tinge of cruelty in his singular composition, he was undoubtedly callous from long over-stimulation. Yet, if his emotions were dulled, his intellectual perceptions were exceedingly active. There was no trace then of the honour which I had myself felt at this curt declaration; but his face showed rather the quiet and interested composure of the chemist who sees the crystals falling into position from his oversaturated solution.

"Remarkable!" said he. "Remarkable!"

"You don't seem surprised."

"Interested, Mr. Mac, but hardly surprised. Why should I be surprised? I receive an anonymous communication from a quarter which I know to be important, warning me that danger threatens a certain person. Within an hour I learn that this danger has actually materialized and that the person is dead. I am interested; but, as you observe, I am not surprised."

In a few short sentences he explained to the inspector the facts about the letter and the cipher. MacDonald sat with his chin on his hands and his great sandy eyebrows bunched into a yellow tangle.

"I was going down to Birlstone this morning," said he. "I had come to ask you if you cared to come with me—you and your friend here. But from what you say we might perhaps be doing better work in London."

"I rather think not," said Holmes.

"Hang it all, Mr. Holmes!" cried the inspector. "The papers will be full of the Birlstone mystery in a day or two; but where's the mystery if there is a man in London who prophesied the crime before ever it occurred? We have only to lay our hands on that man, and the rest will follow."

"No doubt, Mr. Mac. But how do you propose to lay your hands on the so-called Porlock?"

MacDonald turned over the letter which Holmes had handed him. "Posted in Camberwell—that doesn't help us much. Name, you say, is assumed. Not much to go on, certainly. Didn't you say that you have sent him money?"

"Twice."

"And how?"

"In notes to Camberwell postoffice."

"Did you ever trouble to see who called for them?"

"No."

The inspector looked surprised, and a little shocked. "Why not?"

"Because I always keep faith. I had promised when he first wrote that I would not try to trace him."

"You think there is someone behind him?"

"I know there is."

"This professor that I've heard you mention?"

"Exactly!"

Inspector MacDonald smiled, and his eyelid quivered as he glanced towards me. "I won't conceal from you, Mr. Holmes, that we think in the C. I. D.* that you have a wee bit of a bee in your bonnet† over this professor. I made some inquiries myself about the matter. He seems to be a very respectable, learned, and talented sort of man."

"I'm glad you've got so far as to recognize the talent."

"Man, you can't but recognize it! After I heard your view I made it my business to see him. I had a chat with him on eclipses. How the talk got that way I canna think; but he had out a reflector lantern and a globe, and made it all clear in a minute. He lent me a book; but I don't mind saying that it was a bit above my head, though I had a good Aberdeen upbringing. He'd have made a grand meenister with his thin face and gray hair and solemn-like way of talking. When he put his hand on my shoulder as we were parting, it was like a father's blessing before you go out into the cold, cruel world."

Holmes chuckled and rubbed his hands. "Great!" he said. "Great! Tell me, Friend MacDonald, this pleasing and touching interview was, I suppose, in the professor's study?"

"That's so."

"A fine room, is it not?"

"Very fine—very handsome indeed, Mr. Holmes."

"You sat in front of his writing desk?"

"Just so."

"Sun in your eyes and his face in the shadow?"

"Well, it was evening; but I mind that the lamp was turned on my face."

"It would be. Did you happen to observe a picture over the professor's head?"

"I don't miss much, Mr. Holmes. Maybe I learned that from you. Yes, I saw the picture—a young woman with her head on her hands, peeping at you sideways."

"That painting was by Jean Baptiste Greuze."

The inspector endeavoured to look interested.

"Jean Baptiste Greuze," Holmes continued, joining his finger tips and leaning well back in his chair, "was a French artist who flourished be-

---

*Criminal Investigation Department of Scotland Yard.

†That is, you are unnaturally obsessed with something. Also reminds us that Holmes will retire as a beekeeper.

tween the years 1750 and 1800. I allude, of course, to his working career. Modern criticism has more than indorsed the high opinion formed of him by his contemporaries."

The inspector's eyes grew abstracted. "Hadn't we better——" he said.

"We are doing so," Holmes interrupted. "All that I am saying has a very direct and vital bearing upon what you have called the Birlstone Mystery. In fact, it may in a sense be called the very centre of it."

MacDonald smiled feebly, and looked appealingly to me. "Your thoughts move a bit too quick for me, Mr. Holmes. You leave out a link or two, and I can't get over the gap. What in the whole wide world can be the connection between this dead painting man and the affair at Birlstone?"

"All knowledge comes useful to the detective," remarked Holmes. "Even the trivial fact that in the year 1865 a picture by Greuze entitled La Jeune Fille à l'Agneau* fetched one million two hundred thousand francs—more than forty thousand pounds—at the Portalis sale may start a train of reflection in your mind."

It was clear that it did. The inspector looked honestly interested.

"I may remind you," Holmes continued, "that the professor's salary can be ascertained in several trustworthy books of reference. It is seven hundred a year."

"Then how could he buy——"

"Quite so! How could he?"

"Ay, that's remarkable," said the inspector thoughtfully. "Talk away, Mr. Holmes. I'm just loving it. It's fine!"

Holmes smiled. He was always warmed by genuine admiration—the characteristic of the real artist. "What about Birlstone?" he asked.

"We've time yet," said the inspector, glancing at his watch. "I've a cab at the door, and it won't take us twenty minutes to Victoria. But about this picture: I thought you told me once, Mr. Holmes, that you had never met Professor Moriarty."

"No, I never have."

"Then how do you know about his rooms?"

"Ah, that's another matter. I have been three times in his rooms, twice waiting for him under different pretexts and leaving before he came. Once—well, I can hardly tell about the once to an official detective. It was on the last occasion that I took the liberty of running over his papers—with the most unexpected results."

"You found something compromising?"

"Absolutely nothing. That was what amazed me. However, you have now seen the point of the picture. It shows him to be a very wealthy man. How did he acquire wealth? He is unmarried. His younger brother is a station master in the west of England. His chair is worth seven hundred a year. And he owns a Greuze."

---

*Young Girl with a Lamb (French).

"Well?"

"Surely the inference is plain."

"You mean that he has a great income and that he must earn it in an illegal fashion?"

"Exactly. Of course I have other reasons for thinking so—dozens of exiguous threads which lead vaguely up towards the centre of the web where the poisonous, motionless creature is lurking. I only mention the Greuze because it brings the matter within the range of your own observation."

"Well, Mr. Holmes, I admit that what you say is interesting: it's more than interesting—it's just wonderful. But let us have it a little clearer if you can. Is it forgery, coining, burglary—where does the money come from?"

"Have you ever read of Jonathan Wild?"

"Well, the name has a familiar sound. Someone in a novel, was he not? I don't take much stock of detectives in novels—chaps that do things and never let you see how they do them. That's just inspiration: not business."

"Jonathan Wild wasn't a detective, and he wasn't in a novel. He was a master criminal, and he lived last century—1750 or thereabouts."

"Then he's no use to me. I'm a practical man."

"Mr. Mac, the most practical thing that you ever did in your life would be to shut yourself up for three months and read twelve hours a day at the annals of crime. Everything comes in circles—even Professor Moriarty. Jonathan Wild was the hidden force of the London criminals, to whom he sold his brains and his organization on a fifteen per cent commission. The old wheel turns, and the same spoke comes up. It's all been done before, and will be again. I'll tell you one or two things about Moriarty which may interest you."

"You'll interest me, right enough."

"I happen to know who is the first link in his chain—a chain with this Napoleon-gone-wrong at one end, and a hundred broken fighting men, pickpockets, blackmailers, and card sharpers at the other, with every sort of crime in between. His chief of staff is Colonel Sebastian Moran,* as aloof and guarded and inaccessible to the law as himself. What do you think he pays him?"

"I'd like to hear."

"Six thousand a year. That's paying for brains, you see—the American business principle. I learned that detail quite by chance. It's more than the Prime Minister gets. That gives you an idea of Moriarty's gains and of the scale on which he works. Another point: I made it my business to hunt down some of Moriarty's checks lately—just common innocent checks that he pays his household bills with. They were drawn on six different banks. Does that make any impression on your mind?"

---

*The grim Colonel appears as a principal in "The Adventure of the Empty House" and is mentioned in "The Adventure of the Illustrious Client" and "His Last Bow."

"Queer, certainly! But what do you gather from it?"

"That he wanted no gossip about his wealth. No single man should know what he had. I have no doubt that he has twenty banking accounts; the bulk of his fortune abroad in the Deutsche Bank or the Crédit Lyonnais as likely as not. Sometime when you have a year or two to spare I commend to you the study of Professor Moriarty."

Inspector MacDonald had grown steadily more impressed as the conversation proceeded. He had lost himself in his interest. Now his practical Scotch intelligence brought him back with a snap to the matter in hand.

"He can keep, anyhow," said he. "You've got us side-tracked with your interesting anecdotes, Mr. Holmes. What really counts is your remark that there is some connection between the professor and the crime. That you get from the warning received through the man Porlock. Can we for our present practical needs get any further than that?"

"We may form some conception as to the motives of the crime. It is, as I gather from your original remarks, an inexplicable, or at least an unexplained, murder. Now, presuming that the source of the crime is as we suspect it to be, there might be two different motives. In the first place, I may tell you that Moriarty rules with a rod of iron over his people. His discipline is tremendous. There is only one punishment in his code. It is death. Now we might suppose that this murdered man—this Douglas whose approaching fate was known by one of the arch-criminal's subordinates—had in some way betrayed the chief. His punishment followed, and would be known to all—if only to put the fear of death into them."

"Well, that is one suggestion, Mr. Holmes."

"The other is that it has been engineered by Moriarty in the ordinary course of business. Was there any robbery?"

"I have not heard."

"If so, it would, of course, be against the first hypothesis and in favour of the second. Moriarty may have been engaged to engineer it on a promise of part spoils, or he may have been paid so much down to manage it. Either is possible. But whichever it may be, or if it is some third combination, it is down at Birlstone that we must seek the solution. I know our man too well to suppose that he has left anything up here which may lead us to him."

"Then to Birlstone we must go!" cried MacDonald, jumping from his chair. "My word! it's later than I thought. I can give you, gentlemen, five minutes for preparation, and that is all."

"And ample for us both," said Holmes, as he sprang up and hastened to change from his dressing gown to his coat. "While we are on our way, Mr. Mac, I will ask you to be good enough to tell me all about it."

"All about it" proved to be disappointingly little, and yet there was enough to assure us that the case before us might well be worthy of the expert's closest attention. He brightened and rubbed his thin hands together as he listened to the meagre but remarkable details. A long series of sterile weeks lay behind us, and here at last there was a fitting object for those remarkable powers which, like all special gifts, become irksome to their owner when they are not in use. That razor brain blunted and rusted with inaction.

Sherlock Holmes's eyes glistened, his pale cheeks took a warmer hue, and his whole eager face shone with an inward light when the call for work reached him. Leaning forward in the cab, he listened intently to MacDonald's short sketch of the problem which awaited us in Sussex. The inspector was himself dependent, as he explained to us, upon a scribbled account forwarded to him by the milk train in the early hours of the morning. White Mason, the local officer, was a personal friend, and hence MacDonald had been notified much more promptly than is usual at Scotland Yard when provincials need their assistance. It is a very cold scent upon which the Metropolitan expert is generally asked to run.

DEAR INSPECTOR MACDONALD [said the letter which he read to us]:
Official requisition for your services is in separate envelope. This is for your private eye. Wire me what train in the morning you can get for Birlstone, and I will meet it—or have it met if I am too occupied. This case is a snorter. Don't waste a moment in getting started. If you can bring Mr. Holmes, please do so; for he will find something after his own heart. We would think the whole thing had been fixed up for theatrical effect if there wasn't a dead man in the middle of it. My word! it *is* a snorter.

"Your friend seems to be no fool," remarked Holmes.

"No, sir, White Mason is a very live man, if I am any judge."

"Well, have you anything more?"

"Only that he will give us every detail when we meet."

"Then how did you get at Mr. Douglas and the fact that he had been horribly murdered?"

"That was in the inclosed official report. It didn't say 'horrible': that's not a recognized official term. It gave the name John Douglas. It mentioned that his injuries had been in the head, from the discharge of a shotgun. It also mentioned the hour of the alarm, which was close on to midnight last night. It added that the case was undoubtedly one of murder, but that no arrest had been made, and that the case was one which presented some very perplexing and extraordinary features. That's absolutely all we have at present, Mr. Holmes."

"Then, with your permission, we will leave it at that, Mr. Mac. The temptation to form premature theories upon insufficient data is the bane of our profession. I can see only two things for certain at present—a great brain in London, and a dead man in Sussex. It's the chain between that we are going to trace."

CHAPTER 3

The Tragedy of Birlstone

Now for a moment I will ask leave to remove my own insignificant personality and to describe events which occurred before we arrived upon the scene by the light of knowledge which came to us afterwards. Only in this way can I make the reader appreciate the people concerned and the strange setting in which their fate was cast.

The village of Birlstone is a small and very ancient cluster of half-timbered cottages on the northern border of the county of Sussex. For centuries it had remained unchanged; but within the last few years its picturesque appearance and situation have attracted a number of well-to-do residents, whose villas peep out from the woods around. These woods are locally supposed to be the extreme fringe of the great Weald forest, which thins away until it reaches the northern chalk downs. A number of small shops have come into being to meet the wants of the increased population; so there seems some prospect that Birlstone may soon grow from an ancient village into a modern town. It is the centre for a considerable area of country, since Tunbridge Wells, the nearest place of importance, is ten or twelve miles to the eastward, over the borders of Kent.

About half a mile from the town, standing in an old park famous for its huge beech trees, is the ancient Manor House of Birlstone. Part of this venerable building dates back to the time of the first crusade, when Hugo de Capus built a fortalice in the centre of the estate, which had been granted to him by the Red King.[6] This was destroyed by fire in 1543, and some of its smoke-blackened corner stones were used when, in Jacobean* times, a brick country house rose upon the ruins of the feudal castle.

The Manor House, with its many gables and its small diamond-paned windows, was still much as the builder had left it in the early seventeenth century. Of the double moats which had guarded its more warlike predecessor, the outer had been allowed to dry up, and served the humble function of a kitchen garden. The inner one was still there, and lay forty feet in breadth, though now only a few feet in depth, round the whole house. A small stream fed it and continued beyond it, so that the sheet of water, though turbid, was never ditchlike or unhealthy. The ground floor windows were within a foot of the surface of the water.

The only approach to the house was over a drawbridge, the chains and windlass of which had long been rusted and broken. The latest tenants of the Manor House had, however, with characteristic energy, set this right,

---

*The times of James I, king of England from 1603 to 1625; Jacob is the Latin form of James.

and the drawbridge was not only capable of being raised, but actually was raised every evening and lowered every morning. By thus renewing the custom of the old feudal days the Manor House was converted into an island during the night—a fact which had a very direct bearing upon the mystery which was soon to engage the attention of all England.

The house had been untenanted for some years and was threatening to moulder into a picturesque decay when the Douglases took possession of it. This family consisted of only two individuals: John Douglas and his wife. Douglas was a remarkable man, both in character and in person. In age he may have been about fifty, with a strong-jawed, rugged face, a grizzling moustache, peculiarly keen gray eyes, and a wiry, vigorous figure which had lost nothing of the strength and activity of youth. He was cheery and genial to all, but somewhat offhand in his manners, giving the impression that he had seen life in social strata on some far lower horizon than the county society of Sussex.

Yet, though looked at with some curiosity and reserve by his more cultivated neighbours, he soon acquired a great popularity among the villagers, subscribing handsomely to all local objects, and attending their smoking concerts and other functions, where, having a remarkably rich tenor voice, he was always ready to oblige with an excellent song. He appeared to have plenty of money, which was said to have been gained in the California gold fields, and it was clear from his own talk and that of his wife that he had spent a part of his life in America.

The good impression which had been produced by his generosity and by his democratic manners was increased by a reputation gained for utter indifference to danger. Though a wretched rider, he turned out at every meet, and took the most amazing falls in his determination to hold his own with the best. When the vicarage caught fire he distinguished himself also by the fearlessness with which he reentered the building to save property, after the local fire brigade had given it up as impossible. Thus it came about that John Douglas of the Manor House had within five years won himself quite a reputation in Birlstone.

His wife, too, was popular with those who had made her acquaintance; though, after the English fashion, the callers upon a stranger who settled in the county without introductions were few and far between. This mattered the less to her, as she was retiring by disposition, and very much absorbed, to all appearance, in her husband and her domestic duties. It was known that she was an English lady who had met Mr. Douglas in London, he being at that time a widower. She was a beautiful woman, tall, dark, and slender, some twenty years younger than her husband; a disparity which seemed in no wise to mar the contentment of their family life.

It was remarked sometimes, however, by those who knew them best, that the confidence between the two did not appear to be complete, since the wife was either very reticent about her husband's past life, or else, as seemed more likely, was imperfectly informed about it. It had also been noted and commented upon by a few observant people that there were signs sometimes of some nerve-strain upon the part of Mrs. Douglas, and that she would display acute uneasiness if her absent husband should ever be particularly late in his return. On a quiet countryside, where all gossip is welcome, this weakness of the lady of the Manor House did not pass without remark, and it bulked larger upon people's memory when the events arose which gave it a very special significance.

There was yet another individual whose residence under that roof was, it is true, only an intermittent one, but whose presence at the time of the strange happenings which will now be narrated brought his name prominently before the public. This was Cecil James Barker, of Hales Lodge, Hampstead.

Cecil Barker's tall, loose-jointed figure was a familiar one in the main street of Birlstone village; for he was a frequent and welcome visitor at the Manor House. He was the more noticed as being the only friend of the past unknown life of Mr. Douglas who was ever seen in his new English surroundings. Barker was himself an undoubted Englishman; but by his remarks it was clear that he had first known Douglas in America and had there lived on intimate terms with him. He appeared to be a man of considerable wealth, and was reputed to be a bachelor.

In age he was rather younger than Douglas—forty-five at the most—a tall, straight, broad-chested fellow with a clean-shaved, prize-fighter face, thick, strong, black eyebrows, and a pair of masterful black eyes which might, even without the aid of his very capable hands, clear a way for him through a hostile crowd. He neither rode nor shot, but spent his days in wandering round the old village with his pipe in his mouth, or in driving with his host, or in his absence with his hostess, over the beautiful countryside. "An easy-going, free-handed gentleman," said Ames, the butler. "But, my word! I had rather not be the man that crossed him!" He was cordial and intimate with Douglas, and he was no less friendly with his wife—a friendship which more than once seemed to cause some irritation to the husband, so that even the servants were able to perceive his annoyance. Such was the third person who was one of the family when the catastrophe occurred.

As to the other denizens of the old building, it will suffice out of a large household to mention the prim, respectable, and capable Ames, and Mrs. Allen, a buxom and cheerful person, who relieved the lady of some of her household cares. The other six servants in the house bear no relation to the events of the night of January 6th.

It was at eleven forty-five that the first alarm reached the small local police station, in charge of Sergeant Wilson of the Sussex Constabulary. Cecil Barker, much excited, had rushed up to the door and pealed furiously upon the bell. A terrible tragedy had occurred at the Manor House, and John Douglas had been murdered. That was the breathless burden of his message. He had hurried back to the house, followed within a few minutes by the police sergeant, who arrived at the scene of the crime a little after twelve o'clock, after taking prompt steps to warn the county authorities that something serious was afoot.

On reaching the Manor House, the sergeant had found the drawbridge down, the windows lighted up, and the whole household in a state of wild confusion and alarm. The white-faced servants were huddling together in the hall, with the frightened butler wringing his hands in the doorway. Only Cecil Barker seemed to be master of himself and his emotions; he had opened the door which was nearest to the entrance and he had beckoned to the sergeant to follow him. At that moment there arrived Dr. Wood, a brisk and capable general practitioner from the village. The three men entered the fatal room together, while the horror-stricken butler followed at their heels, closing the door behind him to shut out the terrible scene from the maid servants.

The dead man lay on his back, sprawling with outstretched limbs in the centre of the room. He was clad only in a pink dressing gown, which covered his night clothes. There were carpet slippers on his bare feet. The doctor knelt beside him and held down the hand lamp which had stood on the table. One glance at the victim was enough to show the healer that his presence could be dispensed with. The man had been horribly injured. Lying across his chest was a curious weapon, a shotgun with the barrel sawed off a foot in front of the triggers. It was clear that this had been fired at close range and that he had received the whole charge in the face, blowing his head almost to pieces. The triggers had been wired together, so as to make the simultaneous discharge more destructive.

The country policeman was unnerved and troubled by the tremendous responsibility which had come so suddenly upon him. "We will touch nothing until my superiors arrive," he said in a hushed voice, staring in horror at the dreadful head.

"Nothing has been touched up to now," said Cecil Barker. "I'll answer for that. You see it all exactly as I found it."

"When was that?" The sergeant had drawn out his notebook.

"It was just half-past eleven. I had not begun to undress, and I was sitting by the fire in my bedroom when I heard the report.* It was not very loud—it seemed to be muffled. I rushed down—I don't suppose it was thirty seconds before I was in the room."

"Was the door open?"

"Yes, it was open. Poor Douglas was lying as you see him. His bedroom candle was burning on the table. It was I who lit the lamp some minutes afterward."

"Did you see no one?"

"No. I heard Mrs. Douglas coming down the stair behind me, and I rushed out to prevent her from seeing this dreadful sight. Mrs. Allen, the housekeeper, came and took her away. Ames had arrived, and we ran back into the room once more."

"But surely I have heard that the drawbridge is kept up all night."

"Yes, it was up until I lowered it."

---

*Explosive noise of the rifle.

"Then how could any murderer have got away? It is out of the question! Mr. Douglas must have shot himself."

"That was our first idea. But see!" Barker drew aside the curtain, and showed that the long, diamond-paned window was open to its full extent. "And look at this!" He held the lamp down and illuminated a smudge of blood like the mark of a boot-sole upon the wooden sill. "Someone has stood there in getting out."

"You mean that someone waded across the moat?"

"Exactly!"

"Then if you were in the room within half a minute of the crime, he must have been in the water at that very moment."

"I have not a doubt of it. I wish to heaven that I had rushed to the window! But the curtain screened it, as you can see, and so it never occurred to me. Then I heard the step of Mrs. Douglas, and I could not let her enter the room. It would have been too horrible."

"Horrible enough!" said the doctor, looking at the shattered head and the terrible marks which surrounded it. "I've never seen such injuries since the Birlstone railway smash."

"But, I say," remarked the police sergeant, whose slow, bucolic common sense was still pondering the open window. "It's all very well your saying that a man escaped by wading this moat, but what I ask you is, how did he ever get into the house at all if the bridge was up?"

"Ah, that's the question," said Barker.

"At what o'clock was it raised?"

"It was nearly six o'clock," said Ames, the butler.

"I've heard," said the sergeant, "that it was usually raised at sunset. That would be nearer half-past four than six at this time of year."

"Mrs. Douglas had visitors to tea," said Ames. "I couldn't raise it until they went. Then I wound it up myself."

"Then it comes to this," said the sergeant: "If anyone came from outside—*if* they did—they must have got in across the bridge before six and been in hiding ever since, until Mr. Douglas came into the room after eleven."

"That is so! Mr. Douglas went round the house every night the last thing before he turned in to see that the lights were right. That brought him in here. The man was waiting and shot him. Then he got away through the window and left his gun behind him. That's how I read it; for nothing else will fit the facts."

The sergeant picked up a card which lay beside the dead man on the floor. The initials V. V. and under them the number 341 were rudely scrawled in ink upon it.

"What's this?" he asked, holding it up.

Barker looked at it with curiosity. "I never noticed it before," he said. "The murderer must have left it behind him."

"V. V.—341. I can make no sense of that."

The sergeant kept turning it over in his big fingers. "What's V. V.? Somebody's initials, maybe. What have you got there, Dr. Wood?"

It was a good-sized hammer which had been lying on the rug in front of the fireplace—a substantial, workmanlike hammer. Cecil Barker pointed to a box of brass-headed nails upon the mantelpiece.

"Mr. Douglas was altering the pictures yesterday," he said. "I saw him myself, standing upon that chair and fixing the big picture above it. That accounts for the hammer."

"We'd best put it back on the rug where we found it," said the sergeant, scratching his puzzled head in his perplexity. "It will want the best brains in the force to get to the bottom of this thing. It will be a London job before it is finished." He raised the hand lamp and walked slowly round the room. "Hullo!" he cried, excitedly, drawing the window curtain to one side. "What o'clock were those curtains drawn?"

"When the lamps were lit," said the butler. "It would be shortly after four."

"Someone had been hiding here, sure enough." He held down the light, and the marks of muddy boots were very visible in the corner. "I'm bound to say this bears out your theory, Mr. Barker. It looks as if the man got into the house after four when the curtains were drawn, and before six when the bridge was raised. He slipped into this room, because it was the first that he saw. There was no other place where he could hide, so he popped in behind this curtain. That all seems clear enough. It is likely that his main idea was to burgle the house; but Mr. Douglas chanced to come upon him, so he murdered him and escaped."

"That's how I read it," said Barker. "But, I say, aren't we wasting precious time? Couldn't we start out and scour the country before the fellow gets away?"

The sergeant considered for a moment.

"There are no trains before six in the morning; so he can't get away by rail. If he goes by road with his legs all dripping, it's odds that someone will notice him. Anyhow, I can't leave here myself until I am relieved. But I think none of you should go until we see more clearly, how we all stand."

The doctor had taken the lamp and was narrowly scrutinizing the body. "What's this mark?" he asked. "Could this have any connection with the crime?"

The dead man's right arm was thrust out from his dressing gown, and exposed as high as the elbow. About halfway up the forearm was a curious brown design, a triangle inside a circle, standing out in vivid relief upon the lard-coloured skin.

"It's not tattooed," said the doctor, peering through his glasses. I never saw anything like it. The man has been branded at some time as they brand cattle. What is the meaning of this?"

"I don't profess to know the meaning of it," said Cecil Barker; "but I have seen the mark on Douglas many times this last ten years."

"And so have I," said the butler. "Many a time when the master has rolled up his sleeves I have noticed that very mark. I've often wondered what it could be."

"Then it has nothing to do with the crime, anyhow," said the sergeant. "But it's a rum* thing all the same. Everything about this case is rum. Well, what is it now?"

The butler had given an exclamation of astonishment and was pointing at the dead man's outstretched hand.

"They've taken his wedding ring!" he gasped.

"What!"

"Yes, indeed. Master always wore his plain gold wedding ring on the little finger of his left hand. That ring with the rough nugget on it was above it, and the twisted snake ring on the third finger. There's the nugget and there's the snake, but the wedding ring is gone."

"He's right," said Barker.

"Do you tell me," said the sergeant, "that the wedding ring was *below* the other?"

"Always!"

"Then the murderer or whoever it was, first took off this ring you call the nugget ring, then the wedding ring, and afterwards put the nugget ring back again."

"That is so!"

The worthy country policeman shook his head. "Seems to me the sooner we get London on to this case the better," said he. "White Mason is a smart man. No local job has ever been too much for White Mason. It won't be long now before he is here to help us. But I expect we'll have to look to London before we are through. Anyhow, I'm not ashamed to say that it is a deal too thick for the likes of me."

---

* Slang for "odd" or "strange."

CHAPTER 4

Darkness

At three in the morning the chief Sussex detective, obeying the urgent call from Sergeant Wilson of Birlstone, arrived from headquarters in a light dog-cart behind a breathless trotter. By the five-forty train in the morning he had sent his message to Scotland Yard, and he was at the Birlstone station at twelve o'clock to welcome us. White Mason was a quiet, comfortable-looking person in a loose tweed suit, with a clean-shaved, ruddy face, a stoutish body, and powerful bandy legs adorned with gaiters, looking like a small farmer, a retired gamekeeper, or anything upon earth except a very favourable specimen of the provincial criminal officer.

"A real downright snorter, Mr. MacDonald!" he kept repeating. "We'll have the pressmen down like flies when they understand it. I'm hoping we will get our work done before they get poking their noses into it and messing up all the trails. There has been nothing like this that I can remember. There are some bits that will come home to you, Mr. Holmes, or I am mistaken. And you also, Dr. Watson; for the medicos will have a word to say before we finish. Your room is at the Westville Arms. There's no other place; but I hear that it is clean and good. The man will carry your bags. This way, gentlemen, if you please."

He was a very bustling and genial person, this Sussex detective. In ten minutes we had all found our quarters. In ten more we were seated in the parlour of the inn and being treated to a rapid sketch of those events which have been outlined in the previous chapter. MacDonald made an occasional note; while Holmes sat absorbed, with the expression of surprised and reverent admiration with which the botanist surveys the rare and precious bloom.

"Remarkable!" he said, when the story was unfolded, "most remarkable! I can hardly recall any case where the features have been more peculiar."

"I thought you would say so, Mr. Holmes," said White Mason in great delight. "We're well up with the times in Sussex. I've told you now how matters were, up to the time when I took over from Sergeant Wilson between three and four this morning. My word! I made the old mare go! But I need not have been in such a hurry, as it turned out; for there was nothing immediate that I could do. Sergeant Wilson had all the facts. I checked them and considered them and maybe added a few of my own."

"What were they?" asked Holmes eagerly.

"Well, I first had the hammer examined. There was Dr. Wood there to help me. We found no signs of violence upon it. I was hoping that if Mr.

Douglas defended himself with the hammer, he might have left his mark upon the murderer before he dropped it on the mat. But there was no stain."

"That, of course, proves nothing at all," remarked Inspector MacDonald. "There has been many a hammer murder and no trace on the hammer."

"Quite so. It doesn't prove it wasn't used. But there might have been stains, and that would have helped us. As a matter of fact there were none. Then I examined the gun. They were buckshot cartridges, and, as Sergeant Wilson pointed out, the triggers were wired together so that, if you pulled on the hinder one, both barrels were discharged. Whoever fixed that up had made up his mind that he was going to take no chances of missing his man. The sawed gun was not more than two foot long—one could carry it easily under one's coat. There was no complete maker's name; but the printed letters P-E-N were on the fluting between the barrels, and the rest of the name had been cut off by the saw."

"A big P with a flourish above it, E and N smaller?" asked Holmes.

"Exactly."

"Pennsylvania Small Arms Company—well-known American firm," said Holmes.

White Mason gazed at my friend as the little village practitioner looks at the Harley Street specialist who by a word can solve the difficulties that perplex him.

"That is very helpful, Mr. Holmes. No doubt you are right. Wonderful! Wonderful! Do you carry the names of all the gun makers in the world in your memory?"

Holmes dismissed the subject with a wave.

"No doubt it is an American shotgun," White Mason continued. "I seem to have read that a sawed-off shotgun is a weapon used in some parts of America. Apart from the name upon the barrel, the idea had occurred to me. There is some evidence, then, that this man who entered the house and killed its master was an American."

MacDonald shook his head. "Man, you are surely travelling overfast," said he. "I have heard no evidence yet that any stranger was ever in the house at all."

"The open window, the blood on the sill, the queer card, the marks of boots in the corner, the gun!"

"Nothing there that could not have been arranged. Mr. Douglas was an American, or had lived long in America. So had Mr. Barker. You don't need to import an American from outside in order to account for American doings."

"Ames, the butler——"

"What about him? Is he reliable?"

"Ten years with Sir Charles Chandos—as solid as a rock. He has been with Douglas ever since he took the Manor House five years ago. He has never seen a gun of this sort in the house."

"The gun was made to conceal. That's why the barrels were sawed. It would fit into any box. How could he swear there was no such gun in the house?"

"Well, anyhow, he had never seen one."

MacDonald shook his obstinate Scotch head. "I'm not convinced yet that there was ever anyone in the house," said he. "I'm asking you to con-seedar" (his accent became more Aberdonian as he lost himself in his argument) "I'm asking you to conseedar what it involves if you suppose that this gun was ever brought into the house, and that all these strange things were done by a person from outside. Oh, man, it's just inconceivable! It's clean against common sense! I put it to you, Mr. Holmes, judging it by what we have heard."

"Well, state your case, Mr. Mac," said Holmes in his most judicial style.

"The man is not a burglar, supposing that he ever existed. The ring business and the card point to premeditated murder for some private reason. Very good. Here is a man who slips into a house with the deliberate intention of committing murder. He knows, if he knows anything, that he will have a deeficulty in making his escape, as the house is surrounded with water. What weapon would he choose? You would say the most silent in the world. Then he could hope when the deed was done to slip quickly from the window, to wade the moat, and to get away at his leisure. That's understandable. But is it understandable that he should go out of his way to bring with him the most noisy weapon he could select, knowing well that it will fetch every human being in the house to the spot as quick as they can run, and that it is all odds that he will be seen before he can get across the moat? Is that credible, Mr. Holmes?"

"Well, you put the case strongly," my friend replied thoughtfully. "It certainly needs a good deal of justification. May I ask, Mr. White Mason, whether you examined the farther side of the moat at once, to see if there were any signs of the man having climbed out from the water?"

"There were no signs, Mr. Holmes. But it is a stone ledge, and one could hardly expect them."

"No tracks or marks?"

"None."

"Ha! Would there be any objection, Mr. White Mason, to our going down to the house at once? There may possibly be some small point which might be suggestive."

"I was going to propose it, Mr. Holmes; but I thought it well to put you in touch with all the facts before we go. I suppose if anything should strike you——" White Mason looked doubtfully at the amateur.

"I have worked with Mr. Holmes before," said Inspector MacDonald. "He plays the game."

"My own idea of the game, at any rate," said Holmes, with a smile. "I go into a case to help the ends of justice and the work of the police. If I have ever separated myself from the official force, it is because they have first separated themselves from me. I have no wish ever to score at their expense. At the same time, Mr. White Mason, I claim the right to work in my own way and give my results at my own time—complete rather than in stages."

"I am sure we are honoured by your presence and to show you all we know," said White Mason cordially. "Come along, Dr. Watson, and when the time comes we'll all hope for a place in your book."

We walked down the quaint village street with a row of pollarded elms* on each side of it. Just beyond were two ancient stone pillars, weather-stained and lichen-blotched, bearing upon their summits a shapeless something which had once been the rampant lion of Capus of Birlstone. A short walk along the winding drive with such sward and oaks around it as one only sees in rural England, then a sudden turn, and the long, low Jacobean house of dingy, liver-coloured brick lay before us, with an old-fashioned garden of cut yews on each side of it. As we approached it, there was the wooden drawbridge and the beautiful broad moat as still and luminous as quicksilver in the cold, winter sunshine.

Three centuries had flowed past the old Manor House, centuries of births and of homecomings, of country dances and of the meetings of fox hunters. Strange that now in its old age this dark business should have cast its shadow upon the venerable walls! And yet those strange, peaked roofs and quaint, overhung gables were a fitting covering to grim and terrible intrigue. As I looked at the deep-set windows and the long sweep of the dull-coloured, water-lapped front, I felt that no more fitting scene could be set for such a tragedy.

"That's the window," said White Mason, "that one on the immediate right of the drawbridge. It's open just as it was found last night."

"It looks rather narrow for a man to pass."

"Well, it wasn't a fat man, anyhow. We don't need your deductions, Mr. Holmes, to tell us that. But you or I could squeeze through all right."

Holmes walked to the edge of the moat and looked across. Then he examined the stone ledge and the grass border beyond it.

"I've had a good look, Mr. Holmes," said White Mason. "There is nothing there, no sign that anyone has landed—but why should he leave any sign?"

"Exactly. Why should he? Is the water always turbid?"

"Generally about this colour. The stream brings down the clay."

"How deep is it?"

"About two feet at each side and three in the middle."

"So we can put aside all idea of the man having been drowned in crossing."

"No, a child could not be drowned in it."

We walked across the drawbridge, and were admitted by a quaint, gnarled, dried-up person, who was the butler, Ames. The poor old fellow was white and quivering from the shock. The village sergeant, a tall, for-

---

*Trees whose top branches have been pruned so that they will produce dense growths of new shoots.

mal, melancholy man, still held his vigil in the room of Fate. The doctor had departed.

"Anything fresh, Sergeant Wilson?" asked White Mason.

"No, sir."

"Then you can go home. You've had enough. We can send for you if we want you. The butler had better wait outside. Tell him to warn Mr. Cecil Barker, Mrs. Douglas, and the housekeeper that we may want a word with them presently. Now, gentlemen, perhaps you will allow me to give you the views I have formed first, and then you will be able to arrive at your own."

He impressed me, this country specialist. He had a solid grip of fact and a cool, clear, common-sense brain, which should take him some way in his profession. Holmes listened to him intently, with no sign of that impatience which the official exponent too often produced.

"Is it suicide, or is it murder—that's our first question, gentlemen, is it not? If it were suicide, then we have to believe that this man began by taking off his wedding ring and concealing it; that he then came down here in his dressing gown, trampled mud into a corner behind the curtain in order to give the idea someone had waited for him, opened the window, put blood on the——"

"We can surely dismiss that," said MacDonald.

"So I think. Suicide is out of the question. Then a murder has been done. What we have to determine is, whether it was done by someone outside or inside the house."

"Well, let's hear the argument."

"There are considerable difficulties both ways, and yet one or the other it must be. We will suppose first that some person or persons inside the house did the crime. They got this man down here at a time when everything was still and yet no one was asleep. They then did the deed with the queerest and noisiest weapon in the world so as to tell everyone what had happened—a weapon that was never seen in the house before. That does not seem a very likely start, does it?"

"No, it does not."

"Well, then, everyone is agreed that after the alarm was given only a minute at the most had passed before the whole household—not Mr. Cecil Barker alone, though he claims to have been the first, but Ames and all of them were on the spot. Do you tell me that in that time the guilty person managed to make footmarks in the corner, open the window, mark the sill with blood, take the wedding ring off the dead man's finger, and all the rest of it? It's impossible!"

"You put it very clearly," said Holmes. "I am inclined to agree with you."

"Well, then, we are driven back to the theory that it was done by someone from outside. We are still faced with some big difficulties; but anyhow they have ceased to be impossibilities. The man got into the house between four-thirty and six; that is to say, between dusk and the time when the bridge was raised. There had been some visitors, and

the door was open; so there was nothing to prevent him. He may have
been a common burglar, or he may have had some private grudge against
Mr. Douglas. Since Mr. Douglas has spent most of his life in America, and
this shotgun seems to be an American weapon, it would seem that the private grudge is the more likely theory. He slipped into this room because
it was the first he came to, and he hid behind the curtain. There he remained until past eleven at night. At that time Mr. Douglas entered the
room. It was a short interview, if there were any interview at all; for Mrs.
Douglas declares that her husband had not left her more than a few minutes when she heard the shot."

"The candle shows that," said Holmes.

"Exactly. The candle, which was a new one, is not burned more than
half an inch. He must have placed it on the table before he was attacked;
otherwise, of course, it would have fallen when he fell. This shows that he
was not attacked the instant that he entered the room. When Mr. Barker
arrived the candle was lit and the lamp was out."

"That's all clear enough."

"Well, now, we can reconstruct things on those lines. Mr. Douglas enters the room. He puts down the candle. A man appears from behind the
curtain. He is armed with this gun. He demands the wedding ring—
Heaven only knows why, but so it must have been. Mr. Douglas gave it
up. Then either in cold blood or in the course of a struggle—Douglas may
have gripped the hammer that was found upon the mat—he shot Douglas
in this horrible way. He dropped his gun and also it would seem this queer
card—V. V. 341, whatever that may mean—and he made his escape
through the window and across the moat at the very moment when Cecil
Barker was discovering the crime. How's that, Mr. Holmes?"

"Very interesting, but just a little unconvincing."

"Man, it would be absolute nonsense if it wasn't that anything else is
even worse!" cried MacDonald. "Somebody killed the man, and whoever
it was I could clearly prove to you that he should have done it some other
way. What does he mean by allowing his retreat to be cut off like that?
What does he mean by using a shotgun when silence was his one chance
of escape? Come, Mr. Holmes, it's up to you to give us a lead, since you
say Mr. White Mason's theory is unconvincing."

Holmes had sat intently observant during this long discussion, missing
no word that was said, with his keen eyes darting to right and to left, and
his forehead wrinkled with speculation.

"I should like a few more facts before I get so far as a theory, Mr.
Mac," said he, kneeling down beside the body. "Dear me! these injuries
are really appalling. Can we have the butler in for a moment? . . . Ames,
I understand that you have often seen this very unusual mark—a branded
triangle inside a circle—upon Mr. Douglas's forearm?"

"Frequently, sir."

"You never heard any speculation as to what it meant?"

"No, sir."

"It must have caused great pain when it was inflicted. It is undoubtedly a burn. Now, I observe, Ames, that there is a small piece of plaster at the angle of Mr. Douglas's jaw. Did you observe that in life?"

"Yes, sir, he cut himself in shaving yesterday morning."

"Did you ever know him to cut himself in shaving before?"

"Not for a very long time, sir."

"Suggestive!" said Holmes. "It may, of course, be a mere coincidence, or it may point to some nervousness which would indicate that he had reason to apprehend danger. Had you noticed anything unusual in his conduct, yesterday, Ames?"

"It struck me that he was a little restless and excited, sir."

"Ha! The attack may not have been entirely unexpected. We do seem to make a little progress, do we not? Perhaps you would rather do the questioning. Mr. Mac?"

"No, Mr. Holmes, it's in better hands than mine."

"Well, then, we will pass to this card—V. V. 341. It is rough cardboard. Have you any of the sort in the house?"

"I don't think so."

Holmes walked across to the desk and dabbed a little ink from each bottle on to the blotting paper. "It was not printed in this room," he said; "this is black ink and the other purplish. It was done by a thick pen, and these are fine. No, it was done elsewhere, I should say. Can you make anything of the inscription, Ames?"

"No, sir, nothing."

"What do you think, Mr. Mac?"

"It gives me the impression of a secret society of some sort; the same with his badge upon the forearm."

"That's my idea, too," said White Mason.

"Well, we can adopt it as a working hypothesis and then see how far our difficulties disappear. An agent from such a society makes his way into the house, waits for Mr. Douglas, blows his head nearly off with this weapon, and escapes by wading the moat, after leaving a card beside the dead man, which will, when mentioned in the papers, tell other members of the society that vengeance has been done. That all hangs together. But why this gun, of all weapons?"

"Exactly."

"And why the missing ring?"

"Quite so."

"And why no arrest? It's past two now. I take it for granted that since dawn every constable within forty miles has been looking out for a wet stranger?"

"That is so, Mr. Holmes."

"Well, unless he has a burrow close by or a change of clothes ready, they can hardly miss him. And yet they *have* missed him up to now!" Holmes had gone to the window and was examining with his lens the blood mark on the sill. "It is clearly the tread of a shoe. It is remarkably broad; a splay-foot, one would say. Curious, because, so far as one can trace any footmark in this mud-stained corner, one would say it was a more shapely sole. However, they are certainly very indistinct. What's this under the side table?"

"Mr. Douglas's dumb-bells," said Ames.

"Dumb-bell—there's only one. Where's the other?"

"I don't know, Mr. Holmes. There may have been only one. I have not noticed them for months."

"One dumb-bell——" Holmes said seriously; but his remarks were interrupted by a sharp knock at the door.

A tall, sunburned, capable-looking, clean-shaved man looked in at us. I had no difficulty in guessing that it was the Cecil Barker of whom I had heard. His masterful eyes travelled quickly with a questioning glance from face to face.

"Sorry to interrupt your consultation," said he, "but you should hear the latest news."

"An arrest?"

"No such luck. But they've found his bicycle. The fellow left his bicycle behind him. Come and have a look. It is within a hundred yards of the hall door."

We found three or four grooms and idlers standing in the drive inspecting a bicycle which had been drawn out from a clump of evergreens in which it had been concealed. It was a well used Rudge-Whitworth, splashed as from a considerable journey. There was a saddlebag with spanner* and oilcan, but no clue as to the owner.

"It would be a grand help to the police," said the inspector, "if these things were numbered and registered. But we must be thankful for what we've got. If we can't find where he went to, at least we are likely to get where he came from. But what in the name of all that is wonderful made the fellow leave it behind? And how in the world has he got away without it? We don't seem to get a gleam of light in the case, Mr. Holmes."

"Don't we?" my friend answered thoughtfully. "I wonder!"

---

*Adjustable wrench.

CHAPTER 5

The People of the Drama

"Have you seen all you want of the study?" asked White Mason as we reëntered the house.

"For the time," said the inspector, and Holmes nodded.

"Then perhaps you would now like to hear the evidence of some of the people in the house. We could use the dining-room, Ames. Please come yourself first and tell us what you know."

The butler's account was a simple and a clear one, and he gave a convincing impression of sincerity. He had been engaged five years before, when Douglas first came to Birlstone. He understood that Mr. Douglas was a rich gentleman who had made his money in America. He had been a kind and considerate employer—not quite what Ames was used to, perhaps; but one can't have everything. He never saw any signs of apprehension in Mr. Douglas: on the contrary, he was the most fearless man he had ever known. He ordered the drawbridge to be pulled up every night because it was the ancient custom of the old house, and he liked to keep the old ways up.

Mr. Douglas seldom went to London or left the village; but on the day before the crime he had been shopping at Tunbridge Wells. He (Ames) had observed some restlessness and excitement on the part of Mr. Douglas that day; for he had seemed impatient and irritable, which was unusual with him. He had not gone to bed that night; but was in the pantry at the back of the house, putting away the silver, when he heard the bell ring violently. He heard no shot; but it was hardly possible he would, as the pantry and kitchens were at the very back of the house and there were several closed doors and a long passage between. The housekeeper had come out of her room, attracted by the violent ringing of the bell. They had gone to the front of the house together.

As they reached the bottom of the stair he had seen Mrs. Douglas coming down it. No, she was not hurrying; it did not seem to him that she was particularly agitated. Just as she reached the bottom of the stair Mr. Barker had rushed out of the study. He had stopped Mrs. Douglas and begged her to go back.

"For God's sake, go back to your room!" he cried. "Poor Jack is dead! You can do nothing. For God's sake, go back!"

After some persuasion upon the stairs Mrs. Douglas had gone back. She did not scream. She made no outcry whatever. Mrs. Allen, the housekeeper, had taken her upstairs and stayed with her in the bedroom. Ames and Mr. Barker had then returned to the study, where they had found everything exactly as the police had seen it. The candle was not lit at that time; but the lamp was burning. They had looked out of the window; but the night was very dark and nothing could be seen or heard. They had then rushed out into the hall, where Ames had turned the windlass which lowered the drawbridge. Mr. Barker had then hurried off to get the police.

Such, in its essentials, was the evidence of the butler.

The account of Mrs. Allen, the housekeeper, was, so far as it went, a corroboration of that of her fellow servant. The housekeeper's room was rather nearer to the front of the house than the pantry in which Ames had been working. She was preparing to go to bed when the loud ringing of the bell had attracted her attention. She was a little hard of hearing. Perhaps that was why she had not heard the shot; but in any case the study was a long way off. She remembered hearing some sound which she imagined to be the slamming of a door. That was a good deal earlier—half an hour at least before the ringing of the bell. When Mr. Ames ran to the front she went with him. She saw Mr. Barker, very pale and excited, come out of the study. He intercepted Mrs. Douglas, who was coming down the stairs. He entreated her to go back, and she answered him, but what she said could not be heard.

"Take her up! Stay with her!" he had said to Mrs. Allen.

She had therefore taken her to the bedroom, and endeavoured to soothe her. She was greatly excited, trembling all over, but made no other attempt to go downstairs. She just sat in her dressing gown by her bedroom fire, with her head sunk in her hands. Mrs. Allen stayed with her most of the night. As to the other servants, they had all gone to bed, and the alarm did not reach them until just before the police arrived. They slept at the extreme back of the house, and could not possibly have heard anything.

So far the housekeeper could add nothing on cross-examination save lamentations and expressions of amazement.

Cecil Barker succeeded Mrs. Allen as a witness. As to the occurrences of the night before, he had very little to add to what he had already told the police. Personally, he was convinced that the murderer had escaped by the window. The bloodstain was conclusive, in his opinion, on that point. Besides, as the bridge was up. there was no other possible way of escaping. He could not explain what had become of the assassin or why he had not taken his bicycle, if it were indeed his. He could not possibly have been drowned in the moat, which was at no place more than three feet deep.

In his own mind he had a very definite theory about the murder. Douglas was a reticent man, and there were some chapters in his life of which he never spoke. He had emigrated to America when he was a very young man. He had prospered well, and Barker had first met him in California, where they had become partners in a successful mining claim at a place called Benito Cañon. They had done very well; but Douglas had suddenly sold out and started for England. He was a widower at that time. Barker had afterwards realized his money and come to live in London. Thus they had renewed their friendship.

Douglas had given him the impression that some danger was hanging over his head, and he had always looked upon his sudden departure from California, and also his renting a house in so quiet a place in England, as being connected with this peril. He imagined that some secret society, some implacable organization, was on Douglas's track, which would never rest until it killed him. Some remarks of his had given him this idea; though he had never told him what the society was, nor how he had come to offend it. He could only suppose that the legend upon the placard had some reference to this secret society.

"How long were you with Douglas in California?" asked Inspector MacDonald.

"Five years altogether."

"He was a bachelor, you say?"

"A widower."

"Have you ever heard where his first wife came from?"

"No, I remember his saying that she was of German extraction, and I have seen her portrait. She was a very beautiful woman. She died of typhoid the year before I met him."

"You don't associate his past with any particular part of America?"

"I have heard him talk of Chicago. He knew that city well and had worked there. I have heard him talk of the coal and iron districts. He had travelled a good deal in his time."

"Was he a politician? Had this secret society to do with politics?"

"No, he cared nothing about politics."

"You have no reason to think it was criminal?"

"On the contrary, I never met a straighter man in my life."

"Was there anything curious about his life in California?"

"He liked best to stay and to work at our claim in the mountains. He would never go where other men were if he could help it. That's why I first thought that someone was after him. Then when he left so suddenly for Europe I made sure that it was so. I believe that he had a warning of some sort. Within a week of his leaving half a dozen men were inquiring for him."

"What sort of men?"

"Well, they were a mighty hard-looking crowd. They came up to the claim and wanted to know where he was. I told them that he was gone to Europe and that I did not know where to find him. They meant him no good—it was easy to see that."

"Were these men Americans—Californians?"

"Well, I don't know about Californians. They were Americans, all right. But they were not miners. I don't know what they were, and was very glad to see their backs."

"That was six years ago?"

"Nearer seven."

"And then you were together five years in California, so that this business dates back not less than eleven years at the least?"

"That is so."

"It must be a very serious feud that would be kept up with such earnestness for as long as that. It would be no light thing that would give rise to it."

"I think it shadowed his whole life. It was never quite out of his mind."

"But if a man had a danger hanging over him, and knew what it was, don't you think he would turn to the police for protection?"

"Maybe it was some danger that he could not be protected against. There's one thing you should know. He always went about armed. His revolver was never out of his pocket. But, by bad luck, he was in his dressing gown and had left it in the bedroom last night. Once the bridge was up, I guess he thought he was safe."

"I should like these dates a little clearer," said MacDonald. "It is quite six years since Douglas left California. You followed him next year, did you not?"

"That is so."

"And he had been married five years. You must have returned about the time of his marriage."

"About a month before. I was his best man."

"Did you know Mrs. Douglas before her marriage?"

"No, I did not. I had been away from England for ten years."

"But you have seen a good deal of her since."

Barker looked sternly at the detective. "I have seen a good deal of *him* since," he answered. "If I have seen her, it is because you cannot visit a man without knowing his wife. If you imagine there is any connection——"

"I imagine nothing, Mr. Barker. I am bound to make every inquiry which can bear upon the case. But I mean no offense."

"Some inquiries are offensive," Barker answered angrily.

"It's only the facts that we want. It is in your interest and everyone's interest that they should be cleared up. Did Mr. Douglas entirely approve your friendship with his wife?"

Barker grew paler, and his great, strong hands were clasped convulsively together. "You have no right to ask such questions!" he cried. "What has this to do with the matter you are investigating?"

"I must repeat the question."

"Well, I refuse to answer."

"You can refuse to answer; but you must be aware that your refusal is in itself an answer, for you would not refuse if you had not something to conceal."

Barker stood for a moment with his face set grimly and his strong black eyebrows drawn low in intense thought. Then he looked up with a smile. "Well, I guess you gentlemen are only doing your clear duty after all, and I have no right to stand in the way of it. I'd only ask you not to worry Mrs. Douglas over this matter; for she has enough upon her just now. I may tell you that poor Douglas had just one fault in the world, and that was his jealousy. He was fond of me—no man could be fonder of a friend. And he was devoted to his wife. He loved me to come here, and was forever sending for me. And yet if his wife and I talked together or there seemed any sympathy between us, a kind of wave of jealousy would pass over him, and he would be off the handle and saying the wildest things in a moment. More than once I've sworn off coming for that reason, and then he would write me such penitent, imploring letters that I just had to. But you can take it from me, gentlemen, if it was my last word, that no man ever had a more loving, faithful wife—and I can say also no friend could be more loyal than I!"

It was spoken with fervour and feeling, and yet Inspector MacDonald could not dismiss the subject.

"You are aware," said he, "that the dead man's wedding ring has been taken from his finger?"

"So it appears," said Barker.

"What do you mean by 'appears'? You know it as a fact."

The man seemed confused and undecided. "When I said 'appears' I meant that it was conceivable that he had himself taken off the ring."

"The mere fact that the ring should be absent, whoever may have removed it, would suggest to anyone's mind, would it not, that the marriage and the tragedy were connected?"

Barker shrugged his broad shoulders. "I can't profess to say what it means," he answered. "But if you mean to hint that it could reflect in any way upon this lady's honour"—his eyes blazed for an instant, and then with an evident effort he got a grip upon his own emotions—"well, you are on the wrong track, that's all."

"I don't know that I've anything else to ask you at present," said Mac-Donald, coldly.

"There was one small point," remarked Sherlock Holmes. "When you entered the room there was only a candle lighted on the table, was there not?"

"Yes, that was so."

"By its light you saw that some terrible incident had occurred?"

"Exactly."

"You at once rang for help?"

"Yes."

"And it arrived very speedily?"

"Within a minute or so."

"And yet when they arrived they found that the candle was out and that the lamp had been lighted. That seems very remarkable."

Again Barker showed some signs of indecision. "I don't see that it was remarkable, Mr. Holmes," he answered after a pause. "The candle threw a very bad light. My first thought was to get a better one. The lamp was on the table; so I lit it."

"And blew out the candle?"

"Exactly."

Holmes asked no further question, and Barker, with a deliberate look from one to the other of us, which had, as it seemed to me, something of defiance in it, turned and left the room.

Inspector MacDonald had sent up a note to the effect that he would wait upon Mrs. Douglas in her room; but she had replied that she would meet us in the dining room. She entered now, a tall and beautiful woman of thirty, reserved and self-possessed to a remarkable degree, very different from the tragic and distracted figure I had pictured. It is true that her face was pale and drawn, like that of one who has endured a great shock; but her manner was composed, and the finely moulded hand which she rested upon the edge of the table was as steady as my own. Her sad, appealing eyes travelled from one to the other of us with a curiously inquisitive expression. That questioning gaze transformed itself suddenly into abrupt speech.

"Have you found anything out yet?" she asked.

Was it my imagination that there was an undertone of fear rather than of hope in the question?

"We have taken every possible step, Mrs. Douglas," said the inspector. "You may rest assured that nothing will be neglected."

"Spare no money," she said in a dead, even tone. "It is my desire that every possible effort should be made."

"Perhaps you can tell us something which may throw some light upon the matter."

"I fear not; but all I know is at your service."

"We have heard from Mr. Cecil Barker that you did not actually see— that you were never in the room where the tragedy occurred?"

"No, he turned me back upon the stairs. He begged me to return to my room."

"Quite so. You had heard the shot, and you had at once come down."

"I put on my dressing gown and then came down."

"How long was it after hearing the shot that you were stopped on the stair by Mr. Barker?"

"It may have been a couple of minutes. It is so hard to reckon time at such a moment. He implored me not to go on. He assured me that I could do nothing. Then Mrs. Allen, the housekeeper, led me upstairs again. It was all like some dreadful dream."

"Can you give us any idea how long your husband had been downstairs before you heard the shot?"

"No, I cannot say. He went from his dressing room, and I did not hear him go. He did the round of the house every night, for he was nervous of fire. It is the only thing that I have ever known him nervous of."

"That is just the point which I want to come to, Mrs. Douglas. You have known your husband only in England, have you not?"

"Yes, we have been married five years."

"Have you heard him speak of anything which occurred in America and might bring some danger upon him?"

Mrs. Douglas thought earnestly before she answered. "Yes," she said at last, "I have always felt that there was a danger hanging over him. He refused to discuss it with me. It was not from want of confidence in me—there was the most complete love and confidence between us—but it was out of his desire to keep all alarm away from me. He thought I should brood over it if I knew all, and so he was silent."

"How did you know it, then?"

Mrs. Douglas's face lit with a quick smile. "Can a husband ever carry about a secret all his life and a woman who loves him have no suspicion of it? I knew it by his refusal to talk about some episodes in his American life. I knew it by certain precautions he took. I knew it by certain words he let fall. I knew it by the way he looked at unexpected strangers. I was perfectly certain that he had some powerful enemies, that he believed they were on his track, and that he was always on his guard against them. I was so sure of it that for years I have been terrified if ever he came home later than was expected."

"Might I ask," asked Holmes, "what the words were which attracted your attention?"

"The Valley of Fear," the lady answered. "That was an expression he has used when I questioned him. 'I have been in the Valley of Fear. I am not out of it yet.'—'Are we never to get out of the Valley of Fear?' I have asked him when I have seen him more serious than usual. 'Sometimes I think that we never shall,' he has answered."

"Surely you asked him what he meant by the Valley of Fear?"

"I did; but his face would become very grave and he would shake his head. 'It is bad enough that one of us should have been in its shadow,' he said. 'Please God it shall never fall upon you!' It was some real valley in which he had lived and in which something terrible had occurred to him, of that I am certain; but I can tell you no more."

"And he never mentioned any names?"

"Yes, he was delirious with fever once when he had his hunting accident three years ago. Then I remember that there was a name that came continually to his lips. He spoke it with anger and a sort of horror. McGinty was the name—Bodymaster* McGinty. I asked him when he recovered who Bodymaster McGinty was, and whose body he was master of. 'Never of mine, thank God!' he answered with a laugh, and that was all I could get from him. But there is a connection between Bodymaster McGinty and the Valley of Fear."

"There is one other point," said Inspector MacDonald. "You met Mr. Douglas in a boarding house in London, did you not, and became engaged to him there? Was there any romance, anything secret or mysterious, about the wedding?"

"There was romance. There is always romance. There was nothing mysterious."

"He had no rival?"

---

*Term denoting the head of a lodge.

"No, I was quite free."

"You have heard, no doubt, that his wedding ring has been taken. Does that suggest anything to you? Suppose that some enemy of his old life had tracked him down and committed this crime, what possible reason could he have for taking his wedding ring?"

For an instant I could have sworn that the faintest shadow of a smile flickered over the woman's lips.

"I really cannot tell," she answered. "It is certainly a most extraordinary thing."

"Well, we will not detain you any longer, and we are sorry to have put you to this trouble at such a time," said the inspector. "There are some other points, no doubt; but we can refer to you as they arise."

She rose, and I was again conscious of that quick, questioning glance with which she had just surveyed us. "What impression has my evidence made upon you?" The question might as well have been spoken. Then, with a bow, she swept from the room.

"She's a beautiful woman—a very beautiful woman," said MacDonald thoughtfully, after the door had closed behind her. "This man Barker has certainly been down here a good deal. He is a man who might be attractive to a woman. He admits that the dead man was jealous, and maybe he knew best himself what cause he had for jealousy. Then there's that wedding ring. You can't get past that. The man who tears a wedding ring off a dead man's——What do you say to it, Mr. Holmes?"

My friend had sat with his head upon his hands, sunk in the deepest thought. Now he rose and rang the bell. "Ames," he said, when the butler entered, "where is Mr. Cecil Barker now?"

"I'll see, sir."

He came back in a moment to say that Barker was in the garden.

"Can you remember, Ames, what Mr. Barker had on his feet last night when you joined him in the study?"

"Yes, Mr. Holmes. He had a pair of bedroom slippers. I brought him his boots when he went for the police."

"Where are the slippers now?"

"They are still under the chair in the hall."

"Very good, Ames. It is, of course, important for us to know which tracks may be Mr. Barker's and which from outside."

"Yes, sir. I may say that I noticed that the slippers were stained with blood—so indeed were my own."

"That is natural enough, considering the condition of the room. Very good, Ames. We will ring if we want you."

A few minutes later we were in the study. Holmes had brought with him the carpet slippers from the hall. As Ames had observed, the soles of both were dark with blood.

"Strange!" murmured Holmes, as he stood in the light of the window and examined them minutely. "Very strange indeed!"

Stooping with one of his quick feline pounces, he placed the slipper upon the blood mark on the sill. It exactly corresponded. He smiled in silence at his colleagues.

The inspector was transfigured with excitement. His native accent rattled like a stick upon railings.

"Man," he cried, "there's not a doubt of it! Barker has just marked the window himself. It's a good deal broader than any bootmark. I mind that you said it was a splay-foot, and here's the explanation. But what's the game, Mr. Holmes—what's the game?"

"Ay, what's the game?" my friend repeated thoughtfully.

White Mason chuckled and rubbed his fat hands together in his professional satisfaction. "I said it was a snorter!" he cried. "And a real snorter it is!"

CHAPTER 6

A Dawning Light

The three detectives had many matters of detail into which to inquire; so I returned alone to our modest quarters at the village inn. But before doing so I took a stroll in the curious old-world garden which flanked the house. Rows of very ancient yew trees cut into strange designs girded it round. Inside was a beautiful stretch of lawn with an old sundial in the middle, the whole effect so soothing and restful that it was welcome to my somewhat jangled nerves.

In that deeply peaceful atmosphere one could forget, or remember only as some fantastic nightmare, that darkened study with the sprawling, bloodstained figure on the floor. And yet, as I strolled round it and tried to steep my soul in its gentle balm, a strange incident occurred, which brought me back to the tragedy and left a sinister impression in my mind.

I have said that a decoration of yew trees circled the garden. At the end farthest from the house they thickened into a continuous hedge. On the other side of this hedge, concealed from the eyes of anyone approaching from the direction of the house, there was a stone seat. As I approached the spot I was aware of voices, some remark in the deep tones of a man, answered by a little ripple of feminine laughter.

An instant later I had come round the end of the hedge and my eyes lit upon Mrs. Douglas and the man Barker before they were aware of my presence. Her appearance gave me a shock. In the dining-room she had been demure and discreet. Now all pretense of grief had passed away from her. Her eyes shone with the joy of living, and her face still quivered with amusement at some remark of her companion. He sat forward, his hands clasped and his forearms on his knees, with an answering smile upon his bold, handsome face. In an instant—but it was just one instant too late—they resumed their solemn masks as my figure came into view. A hurried word or two passed between them, and then Barker rose and came towards me.

"Excuse me, sir," said he, "but am I addressing Dr. Watson?"

I bowed with a coldness which showed, I dare say, very plainly the impression which had been produced upon my mind.

"We thought that it was probably you, as your friendship with Mr. Sherlock Holmes is so well known. Would you mind coming over and speaking to Mrs. Douglas for one instant?"

I followed him with a dour face. Very clearly I could see in my mind's eye that shattered figure on the floor. Here within a few hours of the tragedy were his wife and his nearest friend laughing together behind a bush in the garden which had been his. I greeted the lady with reserve. I had grieved with her grief in the dining-room. Now I met her appealing gaze with an unresponsive eye.

"I fear that you think me callous and hard-hearted," said she.

I shrugged my shoulders. "It is no business of mine," said I.

"Perhaps some day you will do me justice. If you only realized——"

"There is no need why Dr. Watson should realize," said Barker quickly. "As he has himself said, it is no possible business of his."

"Exactly," said I, "and so I will beg leave to resume my walk."

"One moment, Dr. Watson," cried the woman in a pleading voice. "There is one question which you can answer with more authority than anyone else in the world, and it may make a very great difference to me. You know Mr. Holmes and his relations with the police better than anyone else can. Supposing that a matter were brought confidentially to his knowledge, is it absolutely necessary that he should pass it on to the detectives?"

"Yes, that's it," said Barker eagerly. "Is he on his own or is he entirely in with them?"

"I really don't know that I should be justified in discussing such a point."

"I beg—I implore that you will, Dr. Watson! I assure you that you will be helping us—helping me greatly if you will guide us on that point."

There was such a ring of sincerity in the woman's voice that for the instant I forgot all about her levity and was moved only to do her will.

"Mr. Holmes is an independent investigator," I said. "He is his own master, and would act as his own judgment directed. At the same time, he would naturally feel loyalty towards the officials who were working on the same case, and he would not conceal from them anything which would help them in bringing a criminal to justice. Beyond this I can say nothing, and I would refer you to Mr. Holmes himself if you wanted fuller information."

So saying I raised my hat and went upon my way, leaving them still seated behind that concealing hedge. I looked back as I rounded the far end of it, and saw that they were still talking very earnestly together, and, as they were gazing after me, it was clear that it was our interview that was the subject of their debate.

"I wish none of their confidences," said Holmes, when I reported to him what had occurred. He had spent the whole afternoon at the Manor House in consultation with his two colleagues, and returned about five with a ravenous appetite for a high tea which I had ordered for him. "No confidences, Watson; for they are mighty awkward if it comes to an arrest for conspiracy and murder."

"You think it will come to that?"

He was in his most cheerful and debonair humour. "My dear Watson, when I have exterminated that fourth egg I shall be ready to put you in touch with the whole situation. I don't say that we have fathomed it—far from it—but when we have traced the missing dumb-bell——"

"The dumb-bell!"

"Dear me, Watson, is it possible that you have not penetrated the fact that the case hangs upon the missing dumb-bell? Well, well, you need not be downcast; for between ourselves I don't think that either Inspector Mac or the excellent local practitioner has grasped the overwhelming importance of this incident. One dumb-bell, Watson! Consider an athlete with one dumb-bell! Picture to yourself the unilateral development, the imminent danger of a spinal curvature. Shocking, Watson, shocking!"[7]

He sat with his mouth full of toast and his eyes sparkling with mischief, watching my intellectual entanglement. The mere sight of his excellent appetite was an assurance of success; for I had very clear recollections of days and nights without a thought of food, when his baffled mind had chafed before some problem while his thin, eager features became more attenuated with the asceticism of complete mental concentration. Finally he lit his pipe, and sitting in the inglenook* of the old village inn he talked slowly and at random about his case, rather as one who thinks aloud than as one who makes a considered statement.

"A lie, Watson—a great, big, thumping, obtrusive, uncompromising lie—that's what meets us on the threshold! There is our starting point. The whole story told by Barker is a lie. But Barker's story is corroborated by Mrs. Douglas. Therefore she is lying also. They are both lying, and in a conspiracy. So now we have the clear problem. Why are they lying, and what is the truth which they are trying so hard to conceal? Let us try. Watson, you and I, if we can get behind the lie and reconstruct the truth.

"How do I know that they are lying? Because it is a clumsy fabrication which simply could not be true. Consider! According to the story given to us, the assassin had less than a minute after the murder had been committed to take that ring, which was under another ring, from the dead man's finger, to replace the other ring—a thing which he would surely never have done—and to put that singular card beside his victim. I say that this was obviously impossible.

"You may argue—but I have too much respect for your judgment, Watson, to think that you will do so—that the ring may have been taken before the man was killed. The fact that the candle had been lit only a short time shows that there had been no lengthy interview. Was Douglas, from what we hear of his fearless character, a man who would be likely to give up his wedding ring at such short notice, or could we conceive of his giving it up at all? No, no, Watson, the assassin was alone with the dead man for some time with the lamp lit. Of that I have no doubt at all.

"But the gunshot was apparently the cause of death. Therefore the shot must have been fired some time earlier than we are told. But there could be no mistake about such a matter as that. We are in the presence, therefore, of a deliberate conspiracy upon the part of the two people who heard the gunshot—of the man Barker and of the woman Douglas. When on the top of this I am able to show that the blood mark on the windowsill

---

*Nook or corner near the ingle (fireplace).

was deliberately placed there by Barker, in order to give a false clue to the police, you will admit that the case grows dark against him.

"Now we have to ask ourselves at what hour the murder actually did occur. Up to half-past ten the servants were moving about the house; so it was certainly not before that time. At a quarter to eleven they had all gone to their rooms with the exception of Ames, who was in the pantry. I have been trying some experiments after you left us this afternoon, and I find that no noise which MacDonald can make in the study can penetrate to me in the pantry when the doors are all shut.

"It is otherwise, however, from the housekeeper's room. It is not so far down the corridor, and from it I could vaguely hear a voice when it was very loudly raised. The sound from a shotgun is to some extent muffled when the discharge is at very close range, as it undoubtedly was in this instance. It would not be very loud, and yet in the silence of the night it should have easily penetrated to Mrs. Allen's room. She is, as she has told us, somewhat deaf; but none the less she mentioned in her evidence that she did hear something like a door slamming half an hour before the alarm was given. Half an hour before the alarm was given would be a quarter to eleven. I have no doubt that what she heard was the report of the gun, and that this was the real instant of the murder.

"If this is so, we have now to determine what Barker and Mrs. Douglas, presuming that they are not the actual murderers, could have been doing from quarter to eleven, when the sound of the shot brought them down, until quarter past eleven, when they rang the bell and summoned the servants. What were they doing, and why did they not instantly give the alarm? That is the question which faces us, and when it has been answered we shall surely have gone some way to solve our problem."

"I am convinced myself," said I, "that there is an understanding between those two people. She must be a heartless creature to sit laughing at some jest within a few hours of her husband's murder."

"Exactly. She does not shine as a wife even in her own account of what occurred. I am not a whole-souled admirer of womankind, as you are aware, Watson, but my experience of life has taught me that there are few wives, having any regard for their husbands, who would let any man's spoken word stand between them and that husband's dead body. Should I ever marry, Watson, I should hope to inspire my wife with some feeling which would prevent her from being walked off by a housekeeper when my corpse was lying within a few yards of her. It was badly stage-managed; for even the rawest investigators must be struck by the absence of the usual feminine ululation. If there had been nothing else, this incident alone would have suggested a prearranged conspiracy to my mind."

"You think then, definitely, that Barker and Mrs. Douglas are guilty of the murder?"

"There is an appalling directness about your questions, Watson, said Holmes, shaking his pipe at me. "They come at me like bullets. If you put it that Mrs. Douglas and Barker know the truth about the murder, and are conspiring to conceal it, then I can give you a whole-souled answer. I am sure they do. But your more deadly proposition is not so clear. Let us for a moment consider the difficulties which stand in the way.

"We will suppose that this couple are united by the bonds of a guilty love, and that they have determined to get rid of the man who stands between them. It is a large supposition; for discreet inquiry among servants and others has failed to corroborate it in any way. On the contrary, there is a good deal of evidence that the Douglases were very attached to each other."

"That, I am sure, cannot be true," said I, thinking of the beautiful smiling face in the garden.

"Well, at least they gave that impression. However, we will suppose that they are an extraordinarily astute couple, who deceive everyone upon this point, and conspire to murder the husband. He happens to be a man over whose head some danger hangs——"

"We have only their word for that."

Holmes looked thoughtful. "I see, Watson. You are sketching out a theory by which everything they say from the beginning is false. According to your idea, there was never any hidden menace, or secret society, or Valley of Fear, or Boss MacSomebody, or anything else. Well, that is a good sweeping generalization. Let us see what that brings us to. They invent this theory to account for the crime. They then play up to the idea by leaving this bicycle in the park as proof of the existence of some outsider. The stain on the windowsill conveys the same idea. So does the card on the body, which might have been prepared in the house. That all fits into your hypothesis, Watson. But now we come on the nasty, angular, uncompromising bits which won't slip into their places. Why a cut-off shotgun of all weapons—and an American one at that? How could they be so sure that the sound of it would not bring someone on to them? It's a mere chance as it is that Mrs. Allen did not start out to inquire for the slamming door. Why did your guilty couple do all this, Watson?"

"I confess that I can't explain it."

"Then again, if a woman and her lover conspire to murder a husband, are they going to advertise their guilt by ostentatiously removing his wedding ring after his death? Does that strike you as very probable, Watson?"

"No, it does not."

"And once again, if the thought of leaving a bicycle concealed outside had occurred to you, would it really have seemed worth doing when the dullest detective would naturally say this is an obvious blind, as the bicycle is the first thing which the fugitive needed in order to make his escape."

"I can conceive of no explanation."

"And yet there should be no combination of events for which the wit of man cannot conceive an explanation. Simply as a mental exercise, without any assertion that it is true, let me indicate a possible line of thought. It is, I admit, mere imagination; but how often is imagination the mother of truth?

"We will suppose that there was a guilty secret, a really shameful secret in the life of this man Douglas. This leads to his murder by someone who is, we will suppose, an avenger, someone from outside. This avenger, for some reason which I confess I am still at a loss to explain, took the dead man's wedding ring. The vendetta might conceivably date back to the man's first marriage, and the ring be taken for some such reason.

"Before this avenger got away, Barker and the wife had reached the room. The assassin convinced them that any attempt to arrest him would lead to the publication of some hideous scandal. They were converted to this idea, and preferred to let him go. For this purpose they probably lowered the bridge, which can be done quite noiselessly, and then raised it again. He made his escape, and for some reason thought that he could do so more safely on foot than on the bicycle. He therefore left his machine where it would not be discovered until he had got safely away. So far we are within the bounds of possibility, are we not?"

"Well, it is possible, no doubt," said I, with some reserve.

"We have to remember, Watson, that whatever occurred is certainly something very extraordinary. Well, now, to continue our supposititious case, the couple—not necessarily a guilty couple—realize after the murderer is gone that they have placed themselves in a position in which it may be difficult for them to prove that they did not themselves either do the deed or connive at it. They rapidly and rather clumsily met the situation. The mark was put by Barker's bloodstained slipper upon the window-sill to suggest how the fugitive got away. They obviously were the two who must have heard the sound of the gun; so they gave the alarm exactly as they would have done, but a good half hour after the event."

"And how do you propose to prove all this?"

"Well, if there were an outsider, he may be traced and taken. That would be the most effective of all proofs. But if not—well, the resources of science are far from being exhausted. I think that an evening alone in that study would help me much."

"An evening alone!"

"I propose to go up there presently. I have arranged it with the estimable Ames, who is by no means whole-hearted about Barker. I shall sit in that room and see if its atmosphere brings me inspiration. I'm a believer in the genius loci.* You smile, Friend Watson. Well, we shall see. By the way, you have that big umbrella of yours, have you not?"

"It is here."

"Well, I'll borrow that if I may."

"Certainly—but what a wretched weapon! If there is danger——"

"Nothing serious, my dear Watson, or I should certainly ask for your assistance. But I'll take the umbrella. At present I am only awaiting the return of our colleagues from Tunbridge Wells, where they are at present engaged in trying for a likely owner to the bicycle."

---

*Spirit of a place (Latin).

It was nightfall before Inspector MacDonald and White Mason came back from their expedition, and they arrived exultant, reporting a great advance in our investigation.

"Man, I'll admeet that I had my doubts if there was ever an outsider," said MacDonald; "but that's all past now. We've had the bicycle identified, and we have a description of our man; so that's a long step on our journey."

"It sounds to me like the beginning of the end," said Holmes. "I'm sure I congratulate you both with all my heart."

"Well, I started from the fact that Mr. Douglas had seemed disturbed since the day before, when he had been at Tunbridge Wells. It was at Tunbridge Wells then that he had become conscious of some danger. It was clear, therefore, that if a man had come over with a bicycle it was from Tunbridge Wells that he might be expected to have come. We took the bicycle over with us and showed it at the hotels. It was identified at once by the manager of the Eagle Commercial as belonging to a man named Hargrave, who had taken a room there two days before. This bicycle and a small valise were his whole belongings. He had registered his name as coming from London, but had given no address. The valise was London made, and the contents were British; but the man himself was undoubtedly an American."

"Well, well," said Holmes gleefully, "you have indeed done some solid work while I have been sitting spinning theories with my friend! It's a lesson in being practical, Mr. Mac."

"Ay, it's just that, Mr. Holmes," said the inspector with satisfaction.

"But this may all fit in with your theories," I remarked.

"That may or may not be. But let us hear the end, Mr. Mac. Was there nothing to identify this man?"

"So little that it was evident that he had carefully guarded himself against identification. There were no papers or letters, and no marking upon the clothes. A cycle map of the county lay on his bedroom table. He had left the hotel after breakfast yesterday morning on his bicycle, and no more was heard of him until our inquiries."

"That's what puzzles me, Mr. Holmes," said White Mason. "If the fellow did not want the hue and cry raised over him, one would imagine that he would have returned and remained at the hotel as an inoffensive tourist. As it is, he must know that he will be reported to the police by the hotel manager and that his disappearance will be connected with the murder."

"So one would imagine. Still, he has been justified of his wisdom up to date, at any rate, since he has not been taken. But his description—what of that?"

MacDonald referred to his notebook. "Here we have it so far as they could give it. They don't seem to have taken any very particular stock of him; but still the porter, the clerk, and the chambermaid are all agreed that this about covers the points. He was a man about five foot nine in height, fifty or so of age, his hair slightly grizzled, a grayish moustache, a curved nose, and a face which all of them described as fierce and forbidding."

"Well, bar the expression, that might almost be a description of Douglas himself," said Holmes. "He is just over fifty, with grizzled hair and moustache, and about the same height. Did you get anything else?"

"He was dressed in a heavy gray suit with a reefer jacket, and he wore a short yellow overcoat and a soft cap."

"What about the shotgun?"

"It is less than two feet long. It could very well have fitted into his valise. He could have carried it inside his overcoat without difficulty."

"And how do you consider that all this bears upon the general case?"

"Well, Mr. Holmes," said MacDonald, "when we have got our man—and you may be sure that I had his description on the wires within five minutes of hearing it—we shall be better able to judge. But, even as it stands, we have surely gone a long way. We know that an American calling himself Hargrave came to Tunbridge Wells two days ago with bicycle and valise. In the latter was a sawed-off shotgun; so he came with the deliberate purpose of crime. Yesterday morning he set off for this place on his bicycle, with his gun concealed in his overcoat. No one saw him arrive, so far as we can learn; but he need not pass through the village to reach the park gates, and there are many cyclists upon the road. Presumably he at once concealed his cycle among the laurels where it was found, and possibly lurked there himself, with his eye on the house, waiting for Mr. Douglas to come out. The shotgun is a strange weapon to use inside a house; but he had intended to use it outside, and there it has very obvious advantages, as it would be impossible to miss with it, and the sound of shots is so common in an English sporting neighbourhood that no particular notice would be taken."

"That is all very clear," said Holmes.

"Well, Mr. Douglas did not appear. What was he to do next? He left his bicycle and approached the house in the twilight. He found the bridge down and no one about. He took his chance, intending, no doubt, to make some excuse if he met anyone. He met no one. He slipped into the first room that he saw, and concealed himself behind the curtain. Thence he could see the drawbridge go up, and he knew that his only escape was through the moat. He waited until quarter-past eleven, when Mr. Douglas upon his usual nightly round came into the room. He shot him and escaped, as arranged. He was aware that the bicycle would be described by the hotel people and be a clue against him; so he left it there and made his way by some other means to London or to some safe hiding place which he had already arranged. How is that, Mr. Holmes?"

"Well, Mr. Mac, it is very good and very clear so far as it goes. That is your end of the story. My end is that the crime was committed half an hour earlier than reported; that Mrs. Douglas and Barker are both in a conspiracy to conceal something; that they aided the murderer's escape—or at least that they reached the room before he escaped—and that they fabricated evidence of his escape through the window, whereas in all probability they had themselves let him go by lowering the bridge. That's my reading of the first half."

The two detectives shook their heads.

"Well, Mr. Holmes, if this is true, we only tumble out of one mystery into another," said the London inspector.

"And in some ways a worse one," added White Mason. "The lady has never been in America in all her life. What possible connection could she have with an American assassin which would cause her to shelter him?"

"I freely admit the difficulties," said Holmes. "I propose to make a little investigation of my own to-night, and it is just possible that it may contribute something to the common cause."

"Can we help you, Mr. Holmes?"

"No, no! Darkness and Dr. Watson's umbrella—my wants are simple. And Ames, the faithful Ames, no doubt he will stretch a point for me. All my lines of thought lead me back invariably to the one basic question—why should an athletic man develop his frame upon so unnatural an instrument as a single dumb-bell?"

It was late that night when Holmes returned from his solitary excursion. We slept in a double-bedded room, which was the best that the little country inn could do for us. I was already asleep when I was partly awakened by his entrance.

"Well, Holmes," I murmured, "have you found anything out?"

He stood beside me in silence, his candle in his hand. Then the tall, lean figure inclined towards me. "I say, Watson," he whispered, "would you be afraid to sleep in the same room with a lunatic, a man with softening of the brain, an idiot whose mind has lost its grip?"

"Not in the least," I answered in astonishment.

"Ah, that's lucky," he said, and not another word would he utter that night.

CHAPTER 7

The Solution

Next morning, after breakfast, we found Inspector MacDonald and White Mason seated in close consultation in the small parlour of the local police sergeant. On the table in front of them were piled a number of letters and telegrams, which they were carefully sorting and docketing. Three had been placed on one side.

"Still on the track of the elusive bicyclist?" Holmes asked cheerfully. "What is the latest news of the ruffian?"

MacDonald pointed ruefully to his heap of correspondence.

"He is at present reported from Leicester, Nottingham, Southampton, Derby, East Ham, Richmond, and fourteen other places. In three of them—East Ham, Leicester, and Liverpool—there is a clear case against him, and he has actually been arrested. The country seems to be full of the fugitives with yellow coats."

"Dear me!" said Holmes sympathetically. "Now, Mr. Mac, and you, Mr. White Mason, I wish to give you a very earnest piece of advice. When I went into this case with you I bargained, as you will no doubt remember, that I should not present you with half-proved theories, but that I should retain and work out my own ideas until I had satisfied myself that they were correct. For this reason I am not at the present moment telling you all that is in my mind. On the other hand, I said that I would play the game fairly by you, and I do not think it is a fair game to allow you for one unnecessary moment to waste your energies upon a profitless task. Therefore I am here to advise you this morning, and my advice to you is summed up in three words—abandon the case."

MacDonald and White Mason stared in amazement at their celebrated colleague.

"You consider it hopeless!" cried the inspector.

"I consider your case to be hopeless. I do not consider that it is hopeless to arrive at the truth."

"But this cyclist. He is not an invention. We have his description, his valise, his bicycle. The fellow must be somewhere. Why should we not get him?"

"Yes, yes, no doubt he is somewhere, and no doubt we shall get him; but I would not have you waste your energies in East Ham or Liverpool. I am sure that we can find some shorter cut to a result."

"You are holding something back. It's hardly fair of you, Mr. Holmes." The inspector was annoyed.

"You know my methods of work, Mr. Mac. But I will hold it back for the shortest time possible. I only wish to verify my details in one way, which can very readily be done, and then I make my bow and return to London, leaving my results entirely at your service. I owe you too much to act otherwise; for in all my experience I cannot recall any more singular and interesting study."

"This is clean beyond me, Mr. Holmes. We saw you when we returned from Tunbridge Wells last night, and you were in general agreement with our results. What has happened since then to give you a completely new idea of the case?"

"Well, since you ask me, I spent, as I told you that I would, some hours last night at the Manor House."

"Well, what happened?"

"Ah, I can only give you a very general answer to that for the moment. By the way, I have been reading a short but clear and interesting account of the old building, purchasable at the modest sum of one penny from the local tobacconist."

Here Holmes drew a small tract, embellished with a rude engraving of the ancient Manor House, from his waistcoat pocket.

"It immensely adds to the zest of an investigation, my dear Mr. Mac, when one is in conscious sympathy with the historical atmosphere of one's surroundings. Don't look so impatient; for I assure you that even so bald an account as this raises some sort of picture of the past in one's mind. Permit me to give you a sample. 'Erected in the fifth year of the reign of James I,* and standing upon the site of a much older building, the Manor House of Birlstone presents one of the finest surviving examples of the moated Jacobean residence——'"

"You are making fools of us, Mr. Holmes!"

"Tut, tut, Mr. Mac!—the first sign of temper I have detected in you. Well, I won't read it verbatim, since you feel so strongly upon the subject. But when I tell you that there is some account of the taking of the place by a parliamentary colonel in 1644, of the concealment of Charles for several days in the course of the Civil War, and finally of a visit there by the second George,[8] you will admit that there are various associations of interest connected with this ancient house."

"I don't doubt it, Mr. Holmes; but that is no business of ours."

"Is it not? Is it not? Breadth of view, my dear Mr. Mac, is one of the essentials of our profession. The interplay of ideas and the oblique uses of knowledge are often of extraordinary interest. You will excuse these remarks from one who, though a mere connoisseur of crime, is still rather older and perhaps more experienced than yourself."

"I'm the first to admit that," said the detective heartily. "You get to your point, I admit; but you have such a deuced round-the-corner way of doing it."

"Well, well, I'll drop past history and get down to present-day facts. I

---

*James I reigned from 1603 until 1625; thus 1607.

called last night, as I have already said, at the Manor House. I did not see either Barker or Mrs. Douglas. I saw no necessity to disturb them; but I was pleased to hear that the lady was not visibly pining and that she had partaken of an excellent dinner. My visit was specially made to the good Mr. Ames, with whom I exchanged some amiabilities, which culminated in his allowing me, without reference to anyone else, to sit alone for a time in the study."

"What! With that?" I ejaculated.

"No, no, everything is now in order. You gave permission for that, Mr. Mac, as I am informed. The room was in its normal state, and in it I passed an instructive quarter of an hour."

"What were you doing?"

"Well, not to make a mystery of so simple a matter, I was looking for the missing dumb-bell. It has always bulked rather large in my estimate of the case. I ended by finding it."

"Where?"

"Ah, there we come to the edge of the unexplored. Let me go a little further, a very little further, and I will promise that you shall share everything that I know."

"Well, we're bound to take you on your own terms," said the inspector; "but when it comes to telling us to abandon the case—why in the name of goodness should we abandon the case?"

"For the simple reason, my dear Mr. Mac, that you have not got the first idea what it is that you are investigating."

"We are investigating the murder of Mr. John Douglas of Birlstone Manor."

"Yes, yes, so you are. But don't trouble to trace the mysterious gentleman upon the bicycle. I assure you that it won't help you."

"Then what do you suggest that we do?"

"I will tell you exactly what to do, if you will do it."

"Well, I'm bound to say I've always found you had reason behind all your queer ways. I'll do what you advise."

"And you, Mr. White Mason?"

The country detective looked helplessly from one to the other. Holmes and his methods were new to him. "Well, if it is good enough for the inspector, it is good enough for me," he said at last.

"Capital!" said Holmes. "Well, then, I should recommend a nice, cheery country walk for both of you. They tell me that the views from Birlstone Ridge over the Weald are very remarkable. No doubt lunch could be got at some suitable hostelry; though my ignorance of the country prevents me from recommending one. In the evening, tired but happy——"

"Man, this is getting past a joke!" cried MacDonald, rising angrily from his chair.

"Well, well, spend the day as you like," said Holmes, patting him cheerfully upon the shoulder. "Do what you like and go where you will, but meet me here before dusk without fail—without fail, Mr. Mac."

"That sounds more like sanity."

"All of it was excellent advice; but I don't insist, so long as you are here when I need you. But now, before we part, I want you to write a note to Mr. Barker."

"Well?"

"I'll dictate it, if you like. Ready?

"DEAR SIR:

It has struck me that it is our duty to drain the moat, in the hope that we may find some——"

"It's impossible," said the inspector. "I've made inquiry."

"Tut, tut! My dear sir, please do what I ask you."

"Well, go on."

"——in the hope that we may find something which may bear upon our investigation. I have made arrangements, and the workmen will be at work early to-morrow morning diverting the stream——"

"Impossible!"

"——diverting the stream; so I thought it best to explain matters before-hand.

Now sign that, and send it by hand about four o'clock. At that hour we shall meet again in this room. Until then we may each do what we like; for I can assure you that this inquiry has come to a definite pause."

Evening was drawing in when we reassembled. Holmes was very serious in his manner, myself curious, and the detectives obviously critical and annoyed.

"Well, gentlemen," said my friend gravely, "I am asking you now to put everything to the test with me, and you will judge for yourselves whether the observations I have made justify the conclusions to which I have come. It is a chill evening, and I do not know how long our expedition may last; so I beg that you will wear your warmest coats. It is of the first importance that we should be in our places before it grows dark; so with your permission we shall get started at once."

We passed along the outer bounds of the Manor House park until we came to a place where there was a gap in the rails which fenced it. Through this we slipped, and then in the gathering gloom we followed Holmes until we had reached a shrubbery which lies nearly opposite to the main door and the drawbridge. The latter had not been raised. Holmes crouched down behind the screen of laurels, and we all three followed his example.

"Well, what are we to do now?" asked MacDonald with some gruffness.

"Possess our souls in patience* and make as little noise as possible," Holmes answered.

---

*Reference to the Bible, Luke 21:19: "In your patience possess ye your souls" (King James Version; henceforth, KJV).

"What are we here for at all? I really think that you might treat us with more frankness"

Holmes laughed. "Watson insists that I am the dramatist in real life," said he. "Some touch of the artist wells up within me, and calls insistently for a well-staged performance. Surely our profession, Mr. Mac, would be a drab and sordid one if we did not sometimes set the scene so as to glorify our results. The blunt accusation, the brutal tap upon the shoulder— what can one make of such a *dénouement*? But the quick inference, the subtle trap, the clever forecast of coming events, the triumphant vindication of bold theories—are these not the pride and the justification of our life's work? At the present moment you thrill with the glamour of the situation and the anticipation of the hunt. Where would be that thrill if I had been as definite as a timetable? I only ask a little patience, Mr. Mac, and all will be clear to you."

"Well, I hope the pride and justification and the rest of it will come before we all get our death of cold," said the London detective with comic resignation.

We all had good reason to join in the aspiration; for our vigil was a long and bitter one. Slowly the shadows darkened over the long, sombre face of the old house. A cold, damp reek from the moat chilled us to the bones and set our teeth chattering. There was a single lamp over the gateway and a steady globe of light in the fatal study. Everything else was dark and still.

"How long is this to last?" asked the inspector finally. "And what is it we are watching for?"

"I have no more notion than you how long it is to last," Holmes answered with some asperity. "If criminals would always schedule their movements like railway trains, it would certainly be more convenient for all of us. As to what it is we——Well, *that's* what we are watching for!"

As he spoke the bright, yellow light in the study was obscured by somebody passing to and fro before it. The laurels among which we lay were immediately opposite the window and not more than a hundred feet from it. Presently it was thrown open with a whining of hinges, and we could dimly see the dark outline of a man's head and shoulders looking out into the gloom. For some minutes he peered forth in furtive, stealthy fashion, as one who wishes to be assured that he is unobserved. Then he leaned forward, and in the intense silence we were aware of the soft lapping of agitated water. He seemed to be stirring up the moat with something which he held in his hand. Then suddenly he hauled something in as a fisherman lands a fish—some large, round object which obscured the light as it was dragged through the open casement.

"Now!" cried Holmes. "Now!"

We were all upon our feet, staggering after him with our stiffened limbs, while he ran swiftly across the bridge and rang violently at the bell. There was the rasping of bolts from the other side, and the amazed Ames stood in the entrance. Holmes brushed him aside without a word and, followed by all of us, rushed into the room which had been occupied by the man whom we had been watching.

The oil lamp on the table represented the glow which we had seen from outside. It was now in the hand of Cecil Barker, who held it towards us as we entered. Its light shone upon his strong, resolute, clean-shaved face and his menacing eyes.

"What the devil is the meaning of all this?" he cried. "What are you after, anyhow?"

Holmes took a swift glance round, and then pounced upon a sodden bundle tied together with cord which lay where it had been thrust under the writing table.

"This is what we are after, Mr. Barker—this bundle, weighted with a dumb-bell, which you have just raised from the bottom of the moat."

Barker stared at Holmes with amazement in his face. "How in thunder came you to know anything about it?" he asked.

"Simply that I put it there."

"You put it there! You!"

"Perhaps I should have said 'replaced it there,'" said Holmes. "You will remember, Inspector MacDonald, that I was somewhat struck by the absence of a dumb-bell. I drew your attention to it; but with the pressure of other events you had hardly the time to give it the consideration which would have enabled you to draw deductions from it. When water is near and a weight is missing it is not a very far-fetched supposition that something has been sunk in the water. The idea was at least worth testing; so with the help of Ames, who admitted me to the room, and the crook of Dr. Watson's umbrella, I was able last night to fish up and inspect this bundle.

"It was of the first importance, however, that we should be able to prove who placed it there. This we accomplished by the very obvious device of announcing that the moat would be dried to-morrow, which had, of course, the effect that whoever had hidden the bundle would most certainly withdraw it the moment that darkness enabled him to do so. We have no less than four witnesses as to who it was who took advantage of the opportunity, and so, Mr. Barker, I think the word lies now with you."

Sherlock Holmes put the sopping bundle upon the table beside the lamp and undid the cord which bound it. From within he extracted a dumb-bell, which he tossed down to its fellow in the corner. Next he drew forth a pair of boots. "American, as you perceive," he remarked, pointing to the toes. Then he laid upon the table a long, deadly, sheathed knife. Finally he unravelled a bundle of clothing, comprising a complete set of underclothes, socks, a gray tweed suit, and a short yellow overcoat.

"The clothes are commonplace," remarked Holmes, "save only the overcoat, which is full of suggestive touches." He held it tenderly towards the light. "Here, as you perceive, is the inner pocket prolonged into the lining in such fashion as to give ample space for the truncated fowling piece. The tailor's tab is on the neck—'Neal, Outfitter, Vermissa, U. S. A.' I have spent an instructive afternoon in the rector's library, and have en-

larged my knowledge by adding the fact that Vermissa is a flourishing little town at the head of one of the best known coal and iron valleys in the
United States. I have some recollection, Mr. Barker, that you associated
the coal districts with Mr. Douglas's first wife, and it would surely not be
too far-fetched an inference that the V. V. upon the card by the dead body
might stand for Vermissa Valley, or that this very valley which sends forth
emissaries of murder may be that Valley of Fear of which we have heard.
So much is fairly clear. And now, Mr. Barker, I seem to be standing rather
in the way of your explanation."

It was a sight to see Cecil Barker's expressive face during this exposi-
tion of the great detective. Anger, amazement, consternation, and indecision swept over it in turn. Finally he took refuge in a somewhat acrid
irony.

"You know such a lot, Mr. Holmes, perhaps you had better tell us
some more," he sneered.

"I have no doubt that I could tell you a great deal more, Mr. Barker;
but it would come with a better grace from you."

"Oh, you think so, do you? Well, all I can say is that if there's any secret here it is not my secret, and I am not the man to give it away."

"Well, if you take that line, Mr. Barker," said the inspector quietly, "we
must just keep you in sight until we have the warrant and can hold you."

"You can do what you damn please about that," said Barker defiantly.

The proceedings seemed to have come to a definite end so far as he
was concerned; for one had only to look at that granite face to realize that
no *peine forte et dure** would ever force him to plead against his will. The
deadlock was broken, however, by a woman's voice. Mrs. Douglas had
been standing listening at the half opened door, and now she entered the
room.

"You have done enough for now, Cecil," said she. "Whatever comes of
it in the future, you have done enough."

"Enough and more than enough," remarked Sherlock Holmes gravely.
"I have every sympathy with you, madam, and I should strongly urge you
to have some confidence in the common sense of our jurisdiction and to
take the police voluntarily into your complete confidence. It may be that
I am myself at fault for not following up the hint which you conveyed to
me through my friend, Dr. Watson; but, at that time I had every reason to
believe that you were directly concerned in the crime. Now I am assured
that this is not so. At the same time, there is much that is unexplained,
and I should strongly recommend that you ask Mr. Douglas to tell us his
own story."

Mrs. Douglas gave a cry of astonishment at Holmes's words. The detectives and I must have echoed it, when we were aware of a man who
seemed to have emerged from the wall, who advanced now from the
gloom of the corner in which he had appeared. Mrs. Douglas turned, and

---

*Strong and hard punishment (French).

in an instant her arms were round him. Barker had seized his outstretched hand.

"It's best this way, Jack," his wife repeated; "I am sure that it is best."

"Indeed, yes, Mr. Douglas," said Sherlock Holmes, "I am sure that you will find it best."

The man stood blinking at us with the dazed look of one who comes from the dark into the light. It was a remarkable face, bold gray eyes, a strong, short-clipped, grizzled moustache, a square, projecting chin, and a humorous mouth. He took a good look at us all, and then to my amazement he advanced to me and handed me a bundle of paper.

"I've heard of you," said he in a voice which was not quite English and not quite American, but was altogether mellow and pleasing. "You are the historian of this bunch. Well, Dr. Watson, you've never had such a story as that pass through your hands before, and I'll lay my last dollar on that. Tell it your own way; but there are the facts, and you can't miss the public so long as you have those. I've been cooped up two days, and I've spent the daylight hours—as much daylight as I could get in that rat trap—in putting the thing into words. You're welcome to them—you and your public. There's the story of the Valley of Fear."

"That's the past, Mr. Douglas," said Sherlock Holmes quietly. "What we desire now is to hear your story of the present."

"You'll have it, sir," said Douglas. "May I smoke as I talk? Well, thank you, Mr. Holmes. You're a smoker yourself, if I remember right, and you'll guess what it is to be sitting for two days with tobacco in your pocket and afraid that the smell will give you away." He leaned against the mantelpiece and sucked at the cigar which Holmes had handed him. "I've heard of you, Mr. Holmes. I never guessed that I should meet you. But before you are through with that," he nodded at my papers, "you will say I've brought you something fresh."

Inspector MacDonald had been staring at the newcomer with the greatest amazement. "Well, this fairly beats me!" he cried at last. "If you are Mr. John Douglas of Birlstone Manor, then whose death have we been investigating for these two days, and where in the world have you sprung from now? You seemed to me to come out of the floor like a jack-in-a-box."

"Ah, Mr. Mac," said Holmes, shaking a reproving forefinger, "you would not read that excellent local compilation which described the concealment of King Charles. People did not hide in those days without excellent hiding places, and the hiding place that has once been used may be again. I had persuaded myself that we should find Mr. Douglas under this roof."

"And how long have you been playing this trick upon us, Mr. Holmes?" said the inspector angrily. "How long have you allowed us to waste ourselves upon a search that you knew to be an absurd one?"

"Not one instant, my dear Mr. Mac. Only last night did I form my views of the case. As they could not be put to the proof until this evening, I invited you and your colleague to take a holiday for the day. Pray what more could I do? When I found the suit of clothes in the moat, it at once became apparent to me that the body we had found could not have been the body of Mr. John Douglas at all, but must be that of the bicyclist from Tunbridge Wells. No other conclusion was possible. Therefore I had to determine where Mr. John Douglas himself could be, and the balance of probability was that with the connivance of his wife and his friend he was concealed in a house which had such conveniences for a fugitive, and awaiting quieter times when he could make his final escape."

"Well, you figured it out about right," said Douglas approvingly. "I thought I'd dodge your British law; for I was not sure how I stood under it, and also I saw my chance to throw these hounds once for all off my track. Mind you, from first to last I have done nothing to be ashamed of, and nothing that I would not do again; but you'll judge that for yourselves when I tell you my story. Never mind warning me, Inspector: I'm ready to stand pat upon the truth.

"I'm not going to begin at the beginning. That's all there," he indicated my bundle of papers, "and a mighty queer yarn you'll find it. It all comes down to this: That there are some men that have good cause to hate me and would give their last dollar to know that they had got me. So long as I am alive and they are alive, there is no safety in this world for me. They hunted me from Chicago to California, then they chased me out of America; but when I married and settled down in this quiet spot I thought my last years were going to be peaceable.

"I never explained to my wife how things were. Why should I pull her into it? She would never have a quiet moment again; but would always be imagining trouble. I fancy she knew something, for I may have dropped a word here or a word there; but until yesterday, after you gentlemen had seen her, she never knew the rights of the matter. She told you all she knew, and so did Barker here; for on the night when this thing happened there was mighty little time for explanations. She knows everything now, and I would have been a wiser man if I had told her sooner. But it was a hard question, dear," he took her hand for an instant in his own, "and I acted for the best.

"Well, gentlemen, the day before these happenings I was over in Tunbridge Wells, and I got a glimpse of a man in the street. It was only a glimpse; but I have a quick eye for these things, and I never doubted who it was. It was the worst enemy I had among them all—one who has been after me like a hungry wolf after a caribou all these years. I knew there was trouble coming, and I came home and made ready for it. I guessed I'd fight through it all right on my own, my luck was a proverb in the States about '76. I never doubted that it would be with me still.

"I was on my guard all that next day, and never went out into the park. It's as well, or he'd have had the drop on me with that buckshot gun of his before ever I could draw on him. After the bridge was up—my mind was always more restful when that bridge was up in the evenings—I put the thing clear out of my head. I never dreamed of his getting into the house and waiting for me. But when I made my round in my dressing gown, as was my habit, I had no sooner entered the study than I scented danger. I guess when a man has had dangers in his life—and I've had more than most in my time—there is a kind of sixth sense that waves the red flag. I saw the signal clear enough, and yet I couldn't tell you why. Next instant I spotted a boot under the window curtain, and then I saw why plain enough.

"I'd just the one candle that was in my hand; but there was a good light from the hall lamp through the open door. I put down the candle and jumped for a hammer that I'd left on the mantel. At the same moment he sprang at me. I saw the glint of a knife, and I lashed at him with the hammer. I got him somewhere; for the knife tinkled down on the floor. He dodged round the table as quick as an eel, and a moment later he'd got his gun from under his coat. I heard him cock it; but I had got hold of it before he could fire. I had it by the barrel, and we wrestled for it all ends up for a minute or more. It was death to the man that lost his grip.

"He never lost his grip; but he got it butt downward for a moment too long. Maybe it was I that pulled the trigger. Maybe we just jolted it off between us. Anyhow, he got both barrels in the face, and there I was, staring down at all that was left of Ted Baldwin. I'd recognized him in the township, and again when he sprang for me; but his own mother wouldn't recognize him as I saw him then. I'm used to rough work; but I fairly turned sick at the sight of him.

"I was hanging on the side of the table when Barker came hurrying down. I heard my wife coming, and I ran to the door and stopped her. It was no sight for a woman. I promised I'd come to her soon. I said a word or two to Barker—he took it all in at a glance and we waited for the rest to come along. But there was no sign of them. Then we understood that they could hear nothing, and that all that had happened was known only to ourselves.

"It was at that instant that the idea came to me. I was fairly dazzled by the brilliance of it. The man's sleeve had slipped up and there was the branded mark of the lodge upon his forearm. See here!"

The man whom we had known as Douglas turned up his own coat and cuff to show a brown triangle within a circle exactly like that which we had seen upon the dead man.

"It was the sight of that which started me on it. I seemed to see it all clear at a glance. There were his height and hair and figure, about the same as my own. No one could swear to his face, poor devil! I brought down this suit of clothes, and in a quarter of an hour Barker and I had put my dressing gown on him and he lay as you found him. We tied all his things into a bundle, and I weighted them with the only weight I could find and put them through the window. The card he had meant to lay upon my body was lying beside his own.

"My rings were put on his finger; but when it came to the wedding ring," he held out his muscular hand, "you can see for yourselves that I had struck the limit. I have not moved it since the day I was married, and it would have taken a file to get it off. I don't know, anyhow, that I should have cared to part with it; but if I had wanted to I couldn't. So we just had to leave that detail to take care of itself. On the other hand, I brought a bit of plaster down and put it where I am wearing one myself at this instant. You slipped up there, Mr. Holmes, clever as you are; for if you had chanced to take off that plaster you would have found no cut underneath it.

"Well, that was the situation. If I could lie low for a while and then get away where I could be joined by my 'widow' we should have a chance at last of living in peace for the rest of our lives. These devils would give me no rest so long as I was above ground; but if they saw in the papers that Baldwin had got his man, there would be an end of all my troubles. I hadn't much time to make it all clear to Barker and to my wife; but they understood enough to be able to help me. I knew all about this hiding place, so did Ames; but it never entered his head to connect it with the matter. I retired into it, and it was up to Barker to do the rest.

"I guess you can fill in for yourselves what he did. He opened the window and made the mark on the sill to give an idea of how the murderer escaped. It was a tall order, that; but as the bridge was up there was no other way. Then, when everything was fixed, he rang the bell for all he was worth. What happened afterward you know. And so, gentlemen, you can do what you please; but I've told you the truth and the whole truth, so help me God! What I ask you now is how do I stand by the English law?"

There was a silence which was broken by Sherlock Holmes.

"The English law is in the main a just law. You will get no worse than your deserts from that, Mr. Douglas. But I would ask you how did this man know that you lived here, or how to get into your house, or where to hide to get you?"

"I know nothing of this."

Holmes's face was very white and grave. "The story is not over yet, I fear," said he. "You may find worse dangers than the English law, or even than your enemies from America. I see trouble before you, Mr. Douglas. You'll take my advice and still be on your guard."

And now, my long-suffering readers, I will ask you to come away with me for a time, far from the Sussex Manor House of Birlstone, and far also from the year of grace in which we made our eventful journey which ended with the strange story of the man who had been known as John Douglas. I wish you to journey back some twenty years in time, and westward some thousands of miles in space, that I may lay before you a singular and terrible narrative—so singular and so terrible that you may find it hard to believe that even as I tell it, even so did it occur.

Do not think that I intrude one story before another is finished. As you read on you will find that this is not so. And when I have detailed those distant events and you have solved this mystery of the past, we shall meet once more in those rooms on Baker Street, where this, like so many other wonderful happenings, will find its end.

Part 2

THE SCOWRERS

CHAPTER 1

The Man

It was the fourth of February in the year 1875. It had been a severe winter, and the snow lay deep in the gorges of the Gilmerton Mountains. The steam ploughs had, however, kept the railroad open, and the evening train which connects the long line of coal-mining and iron-working settlements was slowly groaning its way up the steep gradients which lead from Stagville on the plain to Vermissa, the central township which lies at the head of Vermissa Valley. From this point the track sweeps downward to Bartons Crossing, Helmdale, and the purely agricultural county of Merton. It was a single-track railroad; but at every siding—and they were numerous—long lines of trucks piled with coal and iron ore told of the hidden wealth which had brought a rude population and a bustling life to this most desolate corner of the United States of America.

For desolate it was! Little could the first pioneer who had traversed it have ever imagined that the fairest prairies and the most lush water pastures were valueless compared to this gloomy land of black crag and tangled forest. Above the dark and often scarcely penetrable woods upon their flanks, the high, bare crowns of the mountains, white snow, and jagged rock towered upon each flank, leaving a long, winding, tortuous valley in the centre. Up this the little train was slowly crawling.

The oil lamps had just been lit in the leading passenger car, a long, bare carriage in which some twenty or thirty people were seated. The greater number of these were workmen returning from their day's toil in the lower part of the valley. At least a dozen, by their grimed faces and the safety lanterns which they carried, proclaimed themselves miners. These sat smoking in a group and conversed in low voices, glancing occasionally at two men on the opposite side of the car, whose uniforms and badges showed them to be policemen.

Several women of the labouring class and one or two travellers who might have been small local storekeepers made up the rest of the company, with the exception of one young man in a corner by himself. It is with this man that we are concerned. Take a good look at him; for he is worth it.

He is a fresh-complexioned, middle-sized young man, not far, one would guess, from his thirtieth year. He has large, shrewd, humorous gray eyes which twinkle inquiringly from time to time as he looks round through his spectacles at the people about him. It is easy to see that he is of a sociable and possibly simple disposition, anxious to be friendly to all men. Anyone could pick him at once as gregarious in his habits and communicative in his nature, with a quick wit and a ready smile. And yet the man who studied him more closely might discern a certain firmness of jaw and grim tightness about the lips which would warn him that there were depths beyond, and that this pleasant, brown-haired young Irishman might conceivably leave his mark for good or evil upon any society to which he was introduced.

Having made one or two tentative remarks to the nearest miner, and receiving only short, gruff replies, the traveller resigned himself to uncongenial silence, staring moodily out of the window at the fading landscape.

It was not a cheering prospect. Through the growing gloom there pulsed the red glow of the furnaces on the sides of the hills. Great heaps of slag and dumps of cinders loomed up on each side, with the high shafts of the collieries towering above them. Huddled groups of mean, wooden houses, the windows of which were beginning to outline themselves in light, were scattered here and there along the line, and the frequent halting places were crowded with their swarthy inhabitants.

The iron and coal valleys of the Vermissa district were no resorts for the leisured or the cultured. Everywhere there were stern signs of the crudest battle of life, the rude work to be done, and the rude, strong workers who did it.

The young traveller gazed out into this dismal country with a face of mingled repulsion and interest, which showed that the scene was new to him. At intervals he drew from his pocket a bulky letter to which he referred, and on the margins of which he scribbled some notes. Once from the back of his waist he produced something which one would hardly have expected to find in the possession of so mild-mannered a man. It was a navy revolver of the largest size. As he turned it slantwise to the light, the glint upon the rims of the copper shells within the drum showed that it was fully loaded. He quickly restored it to his secret pocket, but not before it had been observed by a working man who had seated himself upon the adjoining bench.

"Hullo, mate!" said he. "You seem heeled and ready."

The young man smiled with an air of embarrassment.

"Yes," said he, "we need them sometimes in the place I come from."

"And where may that be?"

"I'm last from Chicago."

"A stranger in these parts?"

"Yes."

"You may find you need it here," said the workman.

"Ah! is that so?" The young man seemed interested.

"Have you heard nothing of doings hereabouts?"

"Nothing out of the way."

"Why, I thought the country was full of it. You'll hear quick enough. What made you come here?"

"I heard there was always work for a willing man."

"Are you a member of the union?"

"Sure."

"Then you'll get your job, I guess. Have you any friends?"

"Not yet; but I have the means of making them."

"How's that, then?"

"I am one of the Eminent Order of Freemen. There's no town without a lodge, and where there is a lodge I'll find my friends."

The remark had a singular effect upon his companion. He glanced round suspiciously at the others in the car. The miners were still whispering among themselves. The two police officers were dozing. He came across, seated himself close to the young traveller, and held out his hand.

"Put it there," he said.

A hand-grip passed between the two.

"I see you speak the truth," said the workman. "But it's well to make certain." He raised his right hand to his right eyebrow. The traveller at once raised his left hand to his left eyebrow.

"Dark nights are unpleasant," said the workman.

"Yes, for strangers to travel," the other answered.

"That's good enough. I'm Brother Scanlan, Lodge 341, Vermissa Valley. Glad to see you in these parts."

"Thank you. I'm Brother John McMurdo, Lodge 29, Chicago. Bodymaster J. H. Scott. But I am in luck to meet a brother so early."

"Well, there are plenty of us about. You won't find the order more flourishing anywhere in the States than right here in Vermissa Valley. But we could do with some lads like you. I can't understand a spry man of the union finding no work to do in Chicago."

"I found plenty of work to do," said McMurdo.

"Then why did you leave?"

McMurdo nodded towards the policemen and smiled. "I guess those chaps would be glad to know," he said.

Scanlan groaned sympathetically. "In trouble?" he asked in a whisper.

"Deep."

"A penitentiary job?"

"And the rest."

"Not a killing!"

"It's early days to talk of such things," said McMurdo with the air of a man who had been surprised into saying more than he intended. "I've my own good reasons for leaving Chicago, and let that be enough for you. Who are you that you should take it on yourself to ask such things?" His gray eyes gleamed with sudden and dangerous anger from behind his glasses.

"All right, mate, no offense meant. The boys will think none the worse of you, whatever you may have done. Where are you bound for now?"

"Vermissa."

"That's the third halt down the line. Where are you staying?"

McMurdo took out an envelope and held it close to the murky oil lamp. "Here is the address—Jacob Shafter, Sheridan Street. It's a boarding house that was recommended by a man I knew in Chicago."

"Well, I don't know it; but Vermissa is out of my beat. I live at Hobson's

Patch, and that's here where we are drawing up. But, say, there's one bit of advice I'll give you before we part: If you're in trouble in Vermissa, go straight to the Union House and see Boss McGinty. He is the Bodymaster of Vermissa Lodge, and nothing can happen in these parts unless Black Jack McGinty wants it. So long, mate! Maybe we'll meet in lodge one of these evenings. But mind my words: If you are in trouble, go to Boss McGinty."

Scanlan descended, and McMurdo was left once again to his thoughts. Night had now fallen, and the flames of the frequent furnaces were roaring and leaping in the darkness. Against their lurid background dark figures were bending and straining, twisting and turning, with the motion of winch or of windlass, to the rhythm of an eternal clank and roar.

"I guess hell must look something like that," said a voice.

McMurdo turned and saw that one of the policemen had shifted in his seat and was staring out into the fiery waste.

"For that matter," said the other policeman, "I allow that hell must *be* something like that. If there are worse devils down yonder than some we could name, it's more than I'd expect. I guess you are new to this part, young man?"

"Well, what if I am?" McMurdo answered in a surly voice.

"Just this, mister, that I should advise you to be careful in choosing your friends. I don't think I'd begin with Mike Scanlan or his gang if I were you."

"What the hell is it to you who are my friends?" roared McMurdo in a voice which brought every head in the carriage round to witness the altercation. "Did I ask you for your advice, or did you think me such a sucker that I couldn't move without it? You speak when you are spoken to, and by the Lord you'd have to wait a long time if it was me!" He thrust out his face and grinned at the patrolmen like a snarling dog.

The two policemen, heavy, good-natured men, were taken aback by the extraordinary vehemence with which their friendly advances had been rejected.

"No offense, stranger," said one. "It was a warning for your own good, seeing that you are, by your own showing, new to the place."

"I'm new to the place; but I'm not new to you and your kind!" cried McMurdo in cold fury. "I guess you're the same in all places, shoving your advice in when nobody asks for it."

"Maybe we'll see more of you before very long," said one of the patrolmen with a grin. "You're a real hand-picked one, if I am a judge."

"I was thinking the same," remarked the other. "I guess we may meet again."

"I'm not afraid of you, and don't you think it!" cried McMurdo. "My name's Jack McMurdo—see? If you want me, you'll find me at Jacob Shafter's on Sheridan Street, Vermissa; so I'm not hiding from you, am I? Day or night I dare to look the like of you in the face—don't make any mistake about that!"

There was a murmur of sympathy and admiration from the miners at the dauntless demeanour of the newcomer, while the two policemen shrugged their shoulders and renewed a conversation between themselves.

A few minutes later the train ran into the ill-lit station, and there was a general clearing; for Vermissa was by far the largest town on the line. McMurdo picked up his leather gripsack and was about to start off into the darkness, when one of the miners accosted him.

"By Gar, mate! you know how to speak to the cops," he said in a voice, of awe. "It was grand to hear you. Let me carry your grip and show you the road. I'm passing Shafter's on the way to my own shack."

There was a chorus of friendly "Good-nights" from the other miners as they passed from the platform. Before ever he had set foot in it, Mc-Murdo the turbulent had become a character in Vermissa.

The country had been a place of terror; but the town was in its way even more depressing. Down that long valley there was at least a certain gloomy grandeur in the huge fires and the clouds of drifting smoke, while the strength and industry of man found fitting monuments in the hills which he had spilled by the side of his monstrous excavations. But the town showed a dead level of mean ugliness and squalor. The broad street was churned up by the traffic into a horrible rutted paste of muddy snow. The sidewalks were narrow and uneven. The numerous gas-lamps served only to show more clearly a long line of wooden houses, each with its veranda facing the street, unkempt and dirty.

As they approached the centre of the town the scene was brightened by a row of well-lit stores, and even more by a cluster of saloons and gaming houses, in which the miners spent their hard-earned but generous wages.

"That's the Union House," said the guide, pointing to one saloon which rose almost to the dignity of being a hotel. "Jack McGinty is the boss there."

"What sort of a man is he?" McMurdo asked.

"What! have you never heard of the boss?"

"How could I have heard of him when you know that I am a stranger in these parts?"

"Well, I thought his name was known clear across the country. It's been in the papers often enough."

"What for?"

"Well," the miner lowered his voice—"over the affairs."

"What affairs?"

"Good Lord, mister! you are queer, if I must say it without offense. There's only one set of affairs that you'll hear of in these parts, and that's the affairs of the Scowrers."

"Why, I seem to have read of the Scowrers in Chicago. A gang of murderers, are they not?"

"Hush, on your life!" cried the miner, standing still in alarm, and gazing in amazement at his companion. "Man, you won't live long in these parts if you speak in the open street like that. Many a man has had the life beaten out of him for less."

"Well, I know nothing about them. It's only what I have read."

"And I'm not saying that you have not read the truth." The man looked nervously round him as he spoke, peering into the shadows as if he feared to see some lurking danger. "If killing is murder, then God knows there is murder and to spare. But don't you dare to breathe the name of Jack McGinty in connection with it, stranger; for every whisper goes back to him, and he is not one that is likely to let it pass. Now, that's the house you're after, that one standing back from the street. You'll find old Jacob Shafter that runs it as honest a man as lives in this township."

"I thank you," said McMurdo, and shaking hands with his new acquaintance he plodded, gripsack in hand, up the path which led to the dwelling house, at the door of which he gave a resounding knock.

It was opened at once by someone very different from what he had expected. It was a woman, young and singularly beautiful. She was of the German type, blonde and fair-haired, with the piquant contrast of a pair of beautiful dark eyes with which she surveyed the stranger with surprise and a pleasing embarrassment which brought a wave of colour over her pale face. Framed in the bright light of the open doorway, it seemed to McMurdo that he had never seen a more beautiful picture; the more attractive for its contrast with the sordid and gloomy surroundings. A lovely violet growing upon one of those black slag-heaps of the mines would not have seemed more surprising. So entranced was he that he stood staring without a word, and it was she who broke the silence.

"I thought it was father," said she with a pleasing little touch of a German accent. "Did you come to see him? He is downtown. I expect him back every minute."

McMurdo continued to gaze at her in open admiration until her eyes dropped in confusion before this masterful visitor.

"No, miss," he said at last, "I'm in no hurry to see him. But your house was recommended to me for board. I thought it might suit me—and now I know it will."

"You are quick to make up your mind," said she with a smile.

"Anyone but a blind man could do as much," the other answered.

She laughed at the compliment. "Come right in, sir," she said. "I'm Miss Ettie Shafter, Mr. Shafter's daughter. My mother's dead, and I run the house. You can sit down by the stove in the front room until father comes along——Ah, here he is! So you can fix things with him right away."

A heavy, elderly man came plodding up the path. In a few words McMurdo explained his business. A man of the name of Murphy had given him the address in Chicago. He in turn had had it from someone else. Old Shafter was quite ready. The stranger made no bones about terms, agreed at once to every condition, and was apparently fairly flush of money. For seven dollars a week paid in advance he was to have board and lodging.

So it was that McMurdo, the self-confessed fugitive from justice, took up his abode under the roof of the Shafters, the first step which was to lead to so long and dark a train of events, ending in a far distant land.

CHAPTER 2

The Bodymaster

McMurdo was a man who made his mark quickly. Wherever he was the folk around soon knew it. Within a week he had become infinitely the most important person at Shafter's. There were ten or a dozen boarders there; but they were honest foremen or commonplace clerks from the stores, of a very different calibre from the young Irishman. Of an evening when they gathered together his joke was always the readiest, his conversation the brightest, and his song the best. He was a born boon companion, with a magnetism which drew good humour from all around him.

And yet he showed again and again, as he had shown in the railway carriage, a capacity for sudden, fierce anger, which compelled the respect and even the fear of those who met him. For the law, too, and all who were connected with it, he exhibited a bitter contempt which delighted some and alarmed others of his fellow boarders.

From the first he made it evident, by his open admiration, that the daughter of the house had won his heart from the instant that he had set eyes upon her beauty and her grace. He was no backward suitor. On the second day he told her that he loved her, and from then onward he repeated the same story with an absolute disregard of what she might say to discourage him.

"Someone else?" he would cry. "Well, the worse luck for someone else! Let him look out for himself! Am I to lose my life's chance and all my heart's desire for someone else? You can keep on saying no, Ettie: the day will come when you will say yes, and I'm young enough to wait."

He was a dangerous suitor, with his glib Irish tongue, and his pretty, coaxing ways. There was about him also that glamour of experience and of mystery which attracts a woman's interest, and finally her love. He could talk of the sweet valleys of County Monaghan from which he came, of the lovely, distant island, the low hills and green meadows of which seemed the more beautiful when imagination viewed them from this place of grime and snow.

Then he was versed in the life of the cities of the North, of Detroit, and the lumber camps of Michigan, and finally of Chicago, where he had worked in a planing mill. And afterwards came the hint of romance, the feeling that strange things had happened to him in that great city, so strange and so intimate that they might not be spoken of. He spoke wistfully of a sudden leaving, a breaking of old ties, a flight into a strange world, ending in this dreary valley, and Ettie listened, her dark eyes gleaming with pity and with sympathy—those two qualities which may turn so rapidly and so naturally to love.

McMurdo had obtained a temporary job as bookkeeper; for he was a well-educated man. This kept him out most of the day, and he had not found occasion yet to report himself to the head of the lodge of the Eminent Order of Freemen. He was reminded of his omission, however, by a visit one evening from Mike Scanlan, the fellow member whom he had met in the train. Scanlan, the small, sharp-faced, nervous, black-eyed man, seemed glad to see him once more. After a glass or two of whisky he broached the object of his visit.

"Say, McMurdo," said he, "I remembered your address, so I made bold to call. I'm surprised that you've not reported to the Bodymaster. Why haven't you seen Boss McGinty yet?"

"Well, I had to find a job. I have been busy."

"You must find time for him if you have none for anything else. Good Lord, man! you're a fool not to have been down to the Union House and registered your name the first morning after you came here! If you run against him—well, you mustn't, that's all!"

McMurdo showed mild surprise. "I've been a member of the lodge for over two years, Scanlan, but I never heard that duties were so pressing as all that."

"Maybe not in Chicago."

"Well, it's the same society here."

"Is it?"

Scanlan looked at him long and fixedly. There was something sinister in his eyes.

"Isn't it?"

"You'll tell me that in a month's time. I hear you had a talk with the patrolmen after I left the train."

"How did you know that?"

"Oh, it got about—things do get about for good and for bad in this district."

"Well, yes. I told the hounds what I thought of them."

"By the Lord, you'll be a man after McGinty's heart!"

"What, does he hate the police too?"

Scanlan burst out laughing. "You go and see him, my lad," said he as he took his leave. "It's not the police but you that he'll hate if you don't! Now, take a friend's advice and go at once!"

It chanced that on the same evening McMurdo had another more pressing interview which urged him in the same direction. It may have been that his attentions to Ettie had been more evident than before, or that they had gradually obtruded themselves into the slow mind of his good German host; but, whatever the cause, the boarding-house keeper beckoned the young man into his private room and started on the subject without any circumlocution.

"It seems to me, mister," said he, "that you are gettin' set on my Ettie. Ain't that so, or am I wrong?"

"Yes, that is so," the young man answered.

"Vell, I vant to tell you right now that it ain't no manner of use. There's someone slipped in afore you."

"She told me so."

"Vell, you can lay that she told you truth. But did she tell you who it vas?"

"No, I asked her; but she wouldn't tell."

"I dare say not, the leetle baggage! Perhaps she did not vish to frighten you avay."

"Frighten!" McMurdo was on fire in a moment.

"Ah, yes, my friend! You need not be ashamed to be frightened of him. It is Teddy Baldwin."

"And who the devil is he?"

"He is a boss of Scowrers."

"Scowrers! I've heard of them before. It's Scowrers here and Scowrers there, and always in a whisper! What are you all afraid of? Who are the Scowrers?"

The boarding-house keeper instinctively sank his voice, as everyone did who talked about that terrible society. "The Scowrers," said he, "are the Eminent Order of Freemen!"

The young man stared. "Why, I am a member of that order myself."

"You! I vould never have had you in my house if I had known it—not if you vere to pay me a hundred dollar a veek."

"What's wrong with the order? It's for charity and good fellowship. The rules say so."

"Maybe in some places. Not here!"

"What is it here?"

"It's a murder society, that's vat it is."

McMurdo laughed incredulously. "How can you prove that?" he asked.

"Prove it! Are there not fifty murders to prove it? Vat about Milman and Van Shorst, and the Nicholson family, and old Mr. Hyam, and little Billy James, and the others? Prove it! Is there a man or a voman in this valley vat does not know it?"

"See here!" said McMurdo earnestly. "I want you to take back what you've said, or else make it good. One or the other you must do before I quit this room. Put yourself in my place. Here am I, a stranger in the town. I belong to a society that I know only as an innocent one. You'll find it through the length and breadth of the States; but always as an innocent one. Now, when I am counting upon joining it here, you tell me that it is the same as a murder society called the Scowrers. I guess you owe me either an apology or else an explanation, Mr. Shafter."

"I can but tell you vat the whole vorld knows, mister. The bosses of the one are the bosses of the other. If you offend the one, it is the other vat vill strike you. We have proved it too often."

"That's just gossip—I want proof!" said McMurdo.

"If you live here long you vill get your proof. But I forget that you are yourself one of them. You vill soon be as bad as the rest. But you vill find other lodgings, mister. I cannot have you here. Is it not bad enough that one of these people come courting my Ettie, and that I dare not turn him down, but that I should have another for my boarder? Yes, indeed, you shall not sleep here after to-night!"

McMurdo found himself under sentence of banishment both from his comfortable quarters and from the girl whom he loved. He found her alone in the sitting-room that same evening, and he poured his troubles into her ear.

"Sure, your father is after giving me notice," he said. "It's little I would care if it was just my room, but indeed, Ettie, though it's only a week that I've known you, you are the very breath of life to me, and I can't live without you!"

"Oh, hush, Mr. McMurdo, don't speak so!" said the girl. "I have told you, have I not, that you are too late? There is another, and if I have not promised to marry him at once, at least I can promise no one else."

"Suppose I had been first, Ettie, would I have had a chance?"

The girl sank her face into her hands. "I wish to heaven that you had been first!" she sobbed.

McMurdo was down on his knees before her in an instant. "For God's sake, Ettie, let it stand at that!" he cried. "Will you ruin your life and my own for the sake of this promise? Follow your heart, acushla!* 'Tis a safer guide than any promise before you knew what it was that you were saying."

He had seized Ettie's white hand between his own strong brown ones.

"Say that you will be mine, and we will face it out together!"

"Not here?"

"Yes, here."

"No, no, Jack!" His arms were round her now. "It could not be here. Could you take me away?"

A struggle passed for a moment over McMurdo's face; but it ended by setting like granite. "No, here," he said. "I'll hold you against the world, Ettie, right here where we are!"

"Why should we not leave together?"

"No, Ettie, I can't leave here."

"But why?"

"I'd never hold my head up again if I felt that I had been driven out. Besides, what is there to be afraid of? Are we not free folks in a free country? If you love me, and I you, who will dare to come between?"

---

*Conan Doyle's mangled attempt to recreate an Irish endearment; what this word actually means is "O diarrhea" (per the Oxford edition of *The Valley of Fear*).

"You don't know, Jack. You've been here too short a time. You don't know this Baldwin. You don't know McGinty and his Scowrers."

"No, I don't know them, and I don't fear them, and I don't believe in them!" said McMurdo. "I've lived among rough men, my darling, and instead of fearing them it has always ended that they have feared me—always, Ettie. It's mad on the face of it! If these men, as your father says, have done crime after crime in the valley, and if everyone knows them by name, how comes it that none are brought to justice? You answer me that, Ettie!"

"Because no witness dares to appear against them. He would not live a month if he did. Also because they have always their own men to swear that the accused one was far from the scene of the crime. But surely, Jack, you must have read all this. I had understood that every paper in the United States was writing about it."

"Well, I have read something, it is true; but I had thought it was a story. Maybe these men have some reason in what they do. Maybe they are wronged and have no other way to help themselves."

"Oh, Jack, don't let me hear you speak so! That is how he speaks—the other one!"

"Baldwin—he speaks like that, does he?"

"And that is why I loathe him so. Oh, Jack, now I can tell you the truth. I loathe him with all my heart; but I fear him also. I fear him for myself; but above all I fear him for father. I know that some great sorrow would come upon us if I dared to say what I really felt. That is why I have put him off with half-promises. It was in real truth our only hope. But if you would fly with me, Jack, we could take father with us and live forever far from the power of these wicked men."

Again there was the struggle upon McMurdo's face, and again it set like granite. "No harm shall come to you, Ettie—nor to your father either. As to wicked men, I expect you may find that I am as bad as the worst of them before we're through."

"No, no, Jack! I would trust you anywhere."

McMurdo laughed bitterly. "Good Lord! how little you know of me! Your innocent soul, my darling, could not even guess what is passing in mine. But, hullo, who's the visitor?"

The door had opened suddenly, and a young fellow came swaggering in with the air of one who is the master. He was a handsome, dashing young man of about the same age and build as McMurdo himself. Under his broad-brimmed black felt hat, which he had not troubled to remove, a handsome face with fierce, domineering eyes and a curved hawk-bill of a nose looked savagely at the pair who sat by the stove.

Ettie had jumped to her feet full of confusion and alarm. "I'm glad to see you, Mr. Baldwin," said she. "You're earlier than I had thought. Come and sit down."

Baldwin stood with his hands on his hips looking at McMurdo. "Who is this?" he asked curtly.

"It's a friend of mine, Mr. Baldwin, a new boarder here. Mr. McMurdo, may I introduce you to Mr. Baldwin?"

The young men nodded in surly fashion to each other.

"Maybe Miss Ettie has told you how it is with us?" said Baldwin.

"I didn't understand that there was any relation between you."

"Didn't you? Well, you can understand it now. You can take it from me that this young lady is mine, and you'll find it a very fine evening for a walk."

"Thank you, I am in no humour for a walk."

"Aren't you?" The man's savage eyes were blazing with anger. "Maybe you are in a humour for a fight, Mr. Boarder!"

"That I am!" cried McMurdo, springing to his feet. "You never said a more welcome word."

"For God's sake, Jack! Oh, for God's sake!" cried poor, distracted Ettie. "Oh, Jack, Jack, he will hurt you!"

"Oh, it's Jack, is it?" said Baldwin with an oath. "You've come to that already, have you?"

"Oh, Ted, be reasonable—be kind! For my sake, Ted, if ever you loved me, be big-hearted and forgiving!"

"I think, Ettie, that if you were to leave us alone we could get this thing settled," said McMurdo quietly. "Or maybe, Mr. Baldwin, you will take a turn down the street with me. It's a fine evening, and there's some open ground beyond the next block."

"I'll get even with you without needing to dirty my hands," said his enemy. "You'll wish you had never set foot in this house before I am through with you!"

"No time like the present," cried McMurdo.

"I'll choose my own time, mister. You can leave the time to me. See here!" He suddenly rolled up his sleeve and showed upon his forearm a peculiar sign which appeared to have been branded there. It was a circle with a triangle within it. "D'you know what that means?"

"I neither know nor care!"

"Well, you will know, I'll promise you that. You won't be much older, either. Perhaps Miss Ettie can tell you something about it. As to you, Ettie, you'll come back to me on your knees—d'ye hear, girl?—on your knees—and then I'll tell you what your punishment may be. You've sowed—and by the Lord, I'll see that you reap!"* He glanced at them both in fury. Then he turned upon his heel, and an instant later the outer door had banged behind him.

For a few moments McMurdo and the girl stood in silence. Then she threw her arms around him.

"Oh, Jack, how brave you were! But it is no use, you must fly! To-night—Jack—to-night! It's your only hope. He will have your life. I read

---

*Reference to the Bible, Galatians 6:7: "Whatsoever a man soweth, that shall he also reap" (KJV).

it in his horrible eyes. What chance have you against a dozen of them, with Boss McGinty and all the power of the lodge behind them?"

McMurdo disengaged her hands, kissed her, and gently pushed her back into a chair. "There, acushla, there! Don't be disturbed or fear for me. I'm a Freeman myself. I'm after telling your father about it. Maybe I am no better than the others; so don't make a saint of me. Perhaps you hate me too, now that I've told you as much?"

"Hate you, Jack? While life lasts I could never do that! I've heard that there is no harm in being a Freeman anywhere but here; so why should I think the worse of you for that? But if you are a Freeman, Jack, why should you not go down and make a friend of Boss McGinty? Oh, hurry, Jack, hurry! Get your word in first, or the hounds will be on your trail."

"I was thinking the same thing," said McMurdo. "I'll go right now and fix it. You can tell your father that I'll sleep here to-night and find some other quarters in the morning."

The bar of McGinty's saloon was crowded as usual; for it was the favourite loafing place of all the rougher elements of the town. The man was popular; for he had a rough, jovial disposition which formed a mask, covering a great deal which lay behind it. But apart from this popularity, the fear in which he was held throughout the township, and indeed down the whole thirty miles of the valley and past the mountains on each side of it, was enough in itself to fill his bar; for none could afford to neglect his good will.

Besides those secret powers which it was universally believed that he exercised in so pitiless a fashion, he was a high public official, a municipal councillor, and a commissioner of roads, elected to the office through the votes of the ruffians who in turn expected to receive favours at his hands. Assessments and taxes were enormous; the public works were notoriously neglected, the accounts were slurred over by bribed auditors, and the decent citizen was terrorized into paying public blackmail, and holding his tongue lest some worse thing befall him.

Thus it was that, year by year, Boss McGinty's diamond pins became more obtrusive, his gold chains more weighty across a more gorgeous vest, and his saloon stretched farther and farther, until it threatened to absorb one whole side of the Market Square.

McMurdo pushed open the swinging door of the saloon and made his way amid the crowd of men within, through an atmosphere blurred with tobacco smoke and heavy with the smell of spirits. The place was brilliantly lighted, and the huge, heavily gilt minors upon every wall reflected and multiplied the garish illumination. There were several bartenders in their shirt sleeves, hard at work mixing drinks for the loungers who fringed the broad, brass-trimmed counter.

At the far end, with his body resting upon the bar and a cigar stuck at an acute angle from the corner of his mouth, stood a tall, strong, heavily built man who could be none other than the famous McGinty himself. He was a black-maned giant, bearded to the cheek-bones, and with a shock of raven hair which fell to his collar. His complexion was as swarthy as that of an Italian, and his eyes were of a strange dead black, which, combined with a slight squint, gave them a particularly sinister appearance.

All else in the man—his noble proportions, his fine features, and his frank bearing—fitted in with that jovial, man-to-man manner which he affected. Here, one would say, is a bluff, honest fellow, whose heart would be sound however rude his outspoken words might seem. It was only when those dead, dark eyes, deep and remorseless, were turned upon a man that he shrank within himself, feeling that he was face to face with an infinite possibility of latent evil, with a strength and courage and cunning behind it which made it a thousand times more deadly.

Having had a good look at his man, McMurdo elbowed his way forward with his usual careless audacity, and pushed himself through the little group of courtiers who were fawning upon the powerful boss, laughing uproariously at the smallest of his jokes. The young stranger's bold gray eyes looked back fearlessly through their glasses at the deadly black ones which turned sharply upon him.

"Well, young man, I can't call your face to mind."

"I'm new here, Mr. McGinty."

"You are not so new that you can't give a gentleman his proper title."

"He's Councillor McGinty, young man," said a voice from the group.

"I'm sorry, Councillor. I'm strange to the ways of the place. But I was advised to see you."

"Well, you see me. This is all there is. What d'you think of me?"

"Well, it's early days. If your heart is as big as your body, and your soul as fine as your face, then I'd ask for nothing better," said McMurdo.

"By Gar! you've got an Irish tongue in your head anyhow," cried the saloon-keeper, not quite certain whether to humour this audacious visitor or to stand upon his dignity.

"So you are good enough to pass my appearance?"

"Sure," said McMurdo.

"And you were told to see me?"

"I was."

"And who told you?"

"Brother Scanlan of Lodge 341, Vermissa. I drink your health, Councillor, and to our better acquaintance." He raised a glass with which he had been served to his lips and elevated his little finger as he drank it.

McGinty, who had been watching him narrowly, raised his thick black eyebrows. "Oh, it's like that, is it?" said he. "I'll have to look a bit closer into this, Mister——"

"McMurdo."

"A bit closer, Mr. McMurdo; for we don't take folk on trust in these parts, nor believe all we're told neither. Come in here for a moment, behind the bar."

There was a small room there, lined with barrels. McGinty carefully closed the door, and then seated himself on one of them, biting thoughtfully on his cigar and surveying his companion with those disquieting eyes. For a couple of minutes he sat in complete silence. McMurdo bore the inspection cheerfully, one hand in his coat pocket, the other twisting his brown moustache. Suddenly McGinty stooped and produced a wicked-looking revolver.

"See here, my joker," said he, "if I thought you were playing any game on us, it would be short work for you."

"This is a strange welcome," McMurdo answered with some dignity, "for the Bodymaster of a lodge of Freemen to give to a stranger brother."

"Ay, but it's just that same that you have to prove," said McGinty, "and God help you if you fail! Where were you made?"

"Lodge 29, Chicago."

"When?"

"June 24, 1872."

"What Bodymaster?"

"James H. Scott."

"Who is your district ruler?"

"Bartholomew Wilson."

"Hum! You seem glib enough in your tests. What are you doing here?"

"Working, the same as you—but a poorer job."

"You have your back answer quick enough."

"Yes, I was always quick of speech."

"Are you quick of action?"

"I have had that name among those that knew me best."

"Well, we may try you sooner than you think. Have you heard anything of the lodge in these parts?"

"I've heard that it takes a man to be a brother."

"True for you, Mr. McMurdo. Why did you leave Chicago?"

"I'm damned if I tell you that!"

McGinty opened his eyes. He was not used to being answered in such fashion, and it amused him. "Why won't you tell me?"

"Because no brother may tell another a lie."

"Then the truth is too bad to tell?"

"You can put it that way if you like."

"See here, mister, you can't expect me, as Bodymaster, to pass into the lodge a man for whose past he can't answer."

McMurdo looked puzzled. Then he took a worn newspaper cutting from an inner pocket.

"You wouldn't squeal on a fellow?" said he.

"I'll wipe my hand across your face if you say such words to me!" cried McGinty hotly.

"You are right, Councillor," said McMurdo meekly. "I should apologize. I spoke without thought. Well, I know that I am safe in your hands. Look at that clipping."

McGinty glanced his eyes over the account of the shooting of one Jonas Pinto, in the Lake Saloon, Market Street, Chicago, in the New Year week of 1874.

"Your work?" he asked, as he handed back the paper.

McMurdo nodded.

"Why did you shoot him?"

"I was helping Uncle Sam to make dollars. Maybe mine were not as good gold as his, but they looked as well and were cheaper to make. This man Pinto helped me to shove the queer——"

"To do what?"

"Well, it means to pass the dollars out into circulation. Then he said he would split. Maybe he did split. I didn't wait to see. I just killed him and lighted out for the coal country."

"Why the coal country?"

" 'Cause I'd read in the papers that they weren't too particular in those parts."

McGinty laughed. "You were first a coiner and then a murderer, and you came to these parts because you thought you'd be welcome."

"That's about the size of it," McMurdo answered.

"Well, I guess you'll go far. Say, can you make those dollars yet?"

McMurdo took half a dozen from his pocket. "Those never passed the Philadelphia mint," said he.

"You don't say!" McGinty held them to the light in his enormous hand, which was hairy as a gorilla's. "I can see no difference. Gar! you'll be a mighty useful brother, I'm thinking! We can do with a bad man or two among us, Friend McMurdo: for there are times when we have to take our own part. We'd soon be against the wall if we didn't shove back at those that were pushing us."

"Well, I guess I'll do my share of shoving with the rest of the boys."

"You seem to have a good nerve. You didn't squirm when I shoved this gun at you."

"It was not me that was in danger."

"Who then?"

"It was you, Councillor." McMurdo drew a cocked pistol from the side pocket of his pea-jacket. "I was covering you all the time. I guess my shot would have been as quick as yours."

"By Gar!" McGinty flushed an angry red and then burst into a roar of laughter. "Say, we've had no such holy terror come to hand this many a year. I reckon the lodge will learn to be proud of you. . . . Well, what the hell do you want? And can't I speak alone with a gentleman for five minutes but you must butt in on us?"

The bartender stood abashed. "I'm sorry, Councillor, but it's Ted Baldwin. He says he must see you this very minute."

The message was unnecessary; for the set, cruel face of the man himself was looking over the servant's shoulder. He pushed the bartender out and closed the door on him.

"So," said he with a furious glance at McMurdo, "you got here first, did you? I've a word to say to you, Councillor, about this man."

"Then say it here and now before my face," cried McMurdo.

"I'll say it at my own time, in my own way."

"Tut! Tut!" said McGinty, getting off his barrel. "This will never do.

We have a new brother here, Baldwin, and it's not for us to greet him in such fashion. Hold out your hand, man, and make it up!"

"Never!" cried Baldwin in a fury.

"I've offered to fight him if he thinks I have wronged him," said Mc-Murdo. "I'll fight him with fists, or, if that won't satisfy him, I'll fight him any other way he chooses. Now, I'll leave it to you, Councillor, to judge between us as a Bodymaster should."

"What is it, then?"

"A young lady. She's free to choose for herself."

"Is she?" cried Baldwin.

"As between two brothers of the lodge I should say that she was," said the Boss.

"Oh, that's your ruling, is it?"

"Yes, it is, Ted Baldwin," said McGinty, with a wicked stare. "Is it you that would dispute it?"

"You would throw over one that has stood by you this five years in favour of a man that you never saw before in your life? You're not Body-master for life, Jack McGinty, and by God! when next it comes to a vote——"

The Councillor sprang at him like a tiger. His hand closed round the other's neck, and he hurled him back across one of the barrels. In his mad fury he would have squeezed the life out of him if McMurdo had not interfered.

"Easy, Councillor! For heaven's sake, go easy!" he cried, as he dragged him back.

McGinty released his hold, and Baldwin, cowed and shaken, gasping for breath, and shivering in every limb, as one who has looked over the very edge of death, sat up on the barrel over which he had been hurled.

"You've been asking for it this many a day, Ted Baldwin—now you've got it!" cried McGinty, his huge chest rising and falling. "Maybe you think if I was voted down from Bodymaster you would find yourself in my shoes. It's for the lodge to say that. But so long as I am the chief I'll have no man lift his voice against me or my rulings."

"I have nothing against you," mumbled Baldwin, feeling his throat.

"Well, then," cried the other, relapsing in a moment into a bluff joviality, "we are all good friends again and there's an end of the matter."

He took a bottle of champagne down from the shelf and twisted out the cork.

"See now," he continued, as he filled three high glasses. "Let us drink the quarrelling toast of the lodge. After that, as you know, there can be no bad blood between us. Now, then, the left hand on the apple of my throat. I say to you, Ted Baldwin, what is the offense, sir?"

"The clouds are heavy," answered Baldwin.

"But they will forever brighten."

"And this I swear!"

The men drank their glasses, and the same ceremony was performed between Baldwin and McMurdo.

"There!" cried McGinty, rubbing his hands. "That's the end of the black blood. You come under lodge discipline if it goes further, and that's a heavy hand in these parts, as Brother Baldwin knows—and as you will damn soon find out, Brother McMurdo, if you ask for trouble!"

"Faith, I'd be slow to do that," said McMurdo. He held out his hand to Baldwin. "I'm quick to quarrel and quick to forgive. It's my hot Irish blood, they tell me. But it's over for me, and I bear no grudge."

Baldwin had to take the proffered hand, for the baleful eye of the terrible Boss was upon him. But his sullen face showed how little the words of the other had moved him.

McGinty clapped them both on the shoulders. "Tut! These girls! These girls!" he cried. "To think that the same petticoats should come between two of my boys! It's the devil's own luck! Well, it's the colleen* inside of them that must settle the question; for it's outside the jurisdiction of a Bodymaster—and the Lord be praised for that! We have enough on us, without the women as well. You'll have to be affiliated to Lodge 341, Brother McMurdo. We have our own ways and methods, different from Chicago. Saturday night is our meeting, and if you come then, we'll make you free forever of the Vermissa Valley."

---

*An Irish girl.

CHAPTER 3

Lodge 341, Vermissa

On the day following the evening which had contained so many exciting events, McMurdo moved his lodgings from old Jacob Shafter's and took up his quarters at the Widow MacNamara's on the extreme outskirts of the town. Scanlan, his original acquaintance aboard the train, had occasion shortly afterwards to move into Vermissa, and the two lodged together. There was no other boarder, and the hostess was an easy-going old Irishwoman who left them to themselves; so that they had a freedom for speech and action welcome to men who had secrets in common.

Shafter had relented to the extent of letting McMurdo come to his meals there when he liked; so that his intercourse* with Ettie was by no means broken. On the contrary, it drew closer and more intimate as the weeks went by.

In his bedroom at his new abode McMurdo felt it safe to take out the coining moulds, and under many a pledge of secrecy a number of brothers from the lodge were allowed to come in and see them, each carrying away in his pocket some examples of the false money, so cunningly struck that there was never the slightest difficulty or danger in passing it. Why, with such a wonderful art at his command, McMurdo should condescend to work at all was a perpetual mystery to his companions; though he made it clear to anyone who asked him that if he lived without any visible means it would very quickly bring the police upon his track.

One policeman was indeed after him already; but the incident, as luck would have it, did the adventurer a great deal more good than harm. After the first introduction there were few evenings when he did not find his way to McGinty's saloon, there to make closer acquaintance with "the boys," which was the jovial title by which the dangerous gang who infested the place were known to one another. His dashing manner and fearlessness of speech made him a favourite with them all; while the rapid and scientific way in which he polished off his antagonist in an "all in" bar-room scrap earned the respect of that rough community. Another incident, however, raised him even higher in their estimation.

Just at the crowded hour one night, the door opened and a man entered with the quiet blue uniform and peaked cap of the mine police. This was a special body raised by the railways and colliery owners to supplement the efforts of the ordinary civil police, who were perfectly helpless in the face of the organized ruffianism which terrorized the district. There

---

*Daily exchanges; at the time the word carried no sexual connotation.

was a hush as he entered, and many a curious glance was cast at him; but the relations between policemen and criminals are peculiar in some parts of the States, and McGinty himself, standing behind his counter, showed no surprise when the policeman enrolled himself among his customers.

"A straight whisky, for the night is bitter," said the police officer. "I don't think we have met before, Councillor?"

"You'll be the new captain?" said McGinty.

"That's so. We're looking to you, Councillor, and to the other leading citizens, to help us in upholding law and order in this township. Captain Marvin is my name."

"We'd do better without you, Captain Marvin," said McGinty coldly; "for we have our own police of the township, and no need for any imported goods. What are you but the paid tool of the capitalists, hired by them to club or shoot your poorer fellow citizen?"

"Well, well, we won't argue about that," said the police officer good-humouredly. "I expect we all do our duty same as we see it; but we can't all see it the same." He had drunk off his glass and had turned to go, when his eyes fell upon the face of Jack McMurdo, who was scowling at his elbow. "Hullo! Hullo!" he cried, looking him up and down. "Here's an old acquaintance!"

McMurdo shrank away from him. "I was never a friend to you nor any other cursed copper in my life," said he.

"An acquaintance isn't always a friend," said the police captain, grinning. "You're Jack McMurdo of Chicago, right enough, and don't you deny it!"

McMurdo shrugged his shoulders. "I'm not denying it," said he. "D'ye think I'm ashamed of my own name?"

"You've got good cause to be, anyhow."

"What the devil d'you mean by that?" he roared with his fists clenched.

"No, no, Jack, bluster won't do with me. I was an officer in Chicago before ever I came to this darned coal bunker, and I know a Chicago crook when I see one."

McMurdo's face fell. "Don't tell me that you're Marvin of the Chicago Central!" he cried.

"Just the same old Teddy Marvin, at your service. We haven't forgotten the shooting of Jonas Pinto up there."

"I never shot him."

"Did you not? That's good impartial evidence, ain't it? Well, his death came in uncommon handy for you, or they would have had you for shoving the queer. Well, we can let that be bygones; for, between you and me—and perhaps I'm going further than my duty in saying it—they could get no clear case against you, and Chicago's open to you to-morrow."

"I'm very well where I am."

"Well, I've given you the pointer, and you're a sulky dog not to thank me for it."

"Well, I suppose you mean well, and I do thank you," said McMurdo in no very gracious manner.

"It's mum with me so long as I see you living on the straight," said the captain. "But, by the Lord! if you get off after this, it's another story! So good-night to you—and good-night, Councillor."

He left the bar-room; but not before he had created a local hero. McMurdo's deeds in far Chicago had been whispered before. He had put off all questions with a smile, as one who did not wish to have greatness thrust upon him.* But now the thing was officially confirmed. The bar loafers crowded round him and shook him heartily by the hand. He was free of the community from that time on. He could drink hard and show little trace of it; but that evening, had his mate Scanlan not been at hand to lead him home, the fêted hero would surely have spent his night under the bar.

On a Saturday night McMurdo was introduced to the lodge. He had thought to pass in without ceremony as being an initiate of Chicago; but there were particular rites in Vermissa of which they were proud, and these had to be undergone by every postulant.† The assembly met in a large room reserved for such purposes at the Union House. Some sixty members assembled at Vermissa; but that by no means represented the full strength of the organization, for there were several other lodges in the valley, and others across the mountains on each side, who exchanged members when any serious business was afoot, so that a crime might be done by men who were strangers to the locality. Altogether there were not less than five hundred scattered over the coal district.

In the bare assembly room the men were gathered round a long table. At the side was a second one laden with bottles and glasses, on which some members of the company were already turning their eyes. McGinty sat at the head with a flat black velvet cap upon his shock of tangled black hair, and a coloured purple stole round his neck, so that he seemed to be a priest presiding over some diabolical ritual. To right and left of him were the higher lodge officials, the cruel, handsome face of Ted Baldwin among them. Each of these wore some scarf or medallion as emblem of his office.

They were, for the most part, men of mature age; but the rest of the company consisted of young fellows from eighteen to twenty-five, the ready and capable agents who carried out the commands of their seniors. Among the older men were many whose features showed the tigerish, lawless souls within; but looking at the rank and file it was difficult to believe that these eager and open-faced young fellows were in very truth a dangerous gang of murderers, whose minds had suffered such complete moral perversion that they took a horrible pride in their proficiency at the business, and looked with deepest respect at the man who had the reputation of making what they called "a clean job."

---

*Reference to Shakespeare's *Twelfth Night* (act 2, scene 5): "Some are born great, some achieve greatness, and some have greatness thrust upon 'em."
†Candidate for admission to an order or fraternity.

To their contorted natures it had become a spirited and chivalrous thing to volunteer for service against some man who had never injured them, and whom in many cases they had never seen in their lives. The crime committed, they quarrelled as to who had actually struck the fatal blow, and amused one another and the company by describing the cries and contortions of the murdered man.

At first they had shown some secrecy in their arrangements; but at the time which this narrative describes their proceedings were extraordinarily open, for the repeated failures of the law had proved to them that, on the one hand, no one would dare to witness against them, and on the other they had an unlimited number of staunch witnesses upon whom they could call, and a well-filled treasure chest from which they could draw the funds to engage the best legal talent in the state. In ten long years of outrage there had been no single conviction, and the only danger that ever threatened the Scowrers lay in the victim himself—who, however outnumbered and taken by surprise, might and occasionally did leave his mark upon his assailants.

McMurdo had been warned that some ordeal lay before him; but no one would tell him in what it consisted. He was led now into an outer room by two solemn brothers. Through the plank partition he could hear the murmur of many voices from the assembly within. Once or twice he caught the sound of his own name, and he knew that they were discussing his candidacy. Then there entered an inner guard with a green and gold sash across his chest.

"The Bodymaster orders that he shall be trussed, blinded, and entered," said he.

The three of them removed his coat, turned up the sleeve of his right arm, and finally passed a rope round above the elbows and made it fast. They next placed a thick black cap right over his head and the upper part of his face, so that he could see nothing. He was then led into the assembly hall.

It was pitch dark and very oppressive under his hood. He heard the rustle and murmur of the people round him, and then the voice of McGinty sounded dull and distant through the covering of his ears.

"John McMurdo," said the voice, "are you already a member of the Ancient Order of Freemen?"

He bowed in assent.

"Is your lodge No. 29, Chicago?"

He bowed again.

"Dark nights are unpleasant," said the voice.

"Yes, for strangers to travel," he answered.

"The clouds are heavy."

"Yes, a storm is approaching."

"Are the brethren satisfied?" asked the Bodymaster.

There was a general murmur of assent.

"We know, Brother, by your sign and by your countersign that you are indeed one of us," said McGinty. "We would have you know, however, that in this county and in other counties of these parts we have certain rites, and also certain duties of our own which call for good men. Are you ready to be tested?"

"I am."

"Are you of stout heart?"

"I am."

"Take a stride forward to prove it."

As the words were said he felt two hard points in front of his eyes, pressing upon them so that it appeared as if he could not move forward without a danger of losing them. None the less, he nerved himself to step resolutely out, and as he did so the pressure melted away. There was a low murmur of applause.

"He is of stout heart," said the voice. "Can you bear pain?"

"As well as another," he answered.

"Test him!"

It was all he could do to keep himself from screaming out, for an agonizing pain shot through his forearm. He nearly fainted at the sudden shock of it; but he bit his lip and clenched his hands to hide his agony.

"I can take more than that," said he.

This time there was loud applause. A finer first appearance had never been made in the lodge. Hands clapped him on the back, and the hood was plucked from his head. He stood blinking and smiling amid the congratulations of the brothers.

"One last word, Brother McMurdo," said McGinty. "You have already sworn the oath of secrecy and fidelity, and you are aware that the punishment for any breach of it is instant and inevitable death?"

"I am," said McMurdo.

"And you accept the rule of the Bodymaster for the time being under all circumstances?"

"I do."

"Then in the name of Lodge 341, Vermissa, I welcome you to its privileges and debates. You will put the liquor on the table, Brother Scanlan, and we will drink to our worthy brother."

McMurdo's coat had been brought to him; but before putting it on he examined his right arm, which still smarted heavily. There on the flesh of the forearm was a circle with a triangle within it, deep and red, as the branding iron had left it. One or two of his neighbours pulled up their sleeves and showed their own lodge marks.

"We've all had it," said one; "but not all as brave as you over it."

"Tut! It was nothing," said he; but it burned and ached all the same.

When the drinks which followed the ceremony of initiation had all been disposed of, the business of the lodge proceeded. McMurdo, accustomed only to the prosaic performances of Chicago, listened with open ears and more surprise than he ventured to show to what followed.

"The first business on the agenda paper," said McGinty, "is to read the following letter from Division Master Windle of Merton County Lodge 249. He says:

"DEAR SIR:

There is a job to be done on Andrew Rae of Rae & Sturmash, coal owners near this place. You will remember that your lodge owes us a return, having had the service of two brethren in the matter of the patrolman last fall. You will send two good men, they will be taken charge of by Treasurer Higgins of this lodge, whose address you know. He will show them when to act and where. Yours in freedom,

J. W. WINDLE, D. M. A. O. F.*

"Windle has never refused us when we have had occasion to ask for the loan of a man or two, and it is not for us to refuse him." McGinty paused and looked round the room with his dull, malevolent eyes. "Who will volunteer for the job?"

Several young fellows held up their hands. The Bodymaster looked at them with an approving smile.

"You'll do, Tiger Cormac. If you handle it as well as you did the last, you won't be wrong. And you, Wilson."

"I've no pistol," said the volunteer, a mere boy in his teens.

"It's your first, is it not? Well, you have to be blooded some time. It will be a great start for you. As to the pistol, you'll find it waiting for you, or I'm mistaken. If you report yourselves on Monday, it will be time enough. You'll get a great welcome when you return."

"Any reward this time?" asked Cormac, a thick-set, dark-faced, brutal-looking young man, whose ferocity had earned him the nickname of "Tiger."

"Never mind the reward. You just do it for the honour of the thing. Maybe when it is done there will be a few odd dollars at the bottom of the box."

"What has the man done?" asked young Wilson.

"Sure, it's not for the likes of you to ask what the man has done. He has been judged over there. That's no business of ours. All we have to do is to carry it out for them, same as they would for us. Speaking of that, two brothers from the Merton lodge are coming over to us next week to do some business in this quarter."

"Who are they?" asked someone.

"Faith, it is wiser not to ask. If you know nothing, you can testify nothing, and no trouble can come of it. But they are men who will make a clean job when they are about it."

"And time, too!" cried Ted Baldwin. "Folk are gettin' out of hand in these parts. It was only last week that three of our men were turned off by Foreman Blaker. It's been owing him a long time, and he'll get it full and proper."

---

*Division Master of Ancient Order of Freemen; the organization is probably part of or related to the secret fraternal order the Ancient Free and Accepted Masons.

"Get what?" McMurdo whispered to his neighbour.

"The business end of a buckshot cartridge!" cried the man with a loud laugh. "What think you of our ways, Brother?"

McMurdo's criminal soul seemed to have already absorbed the spirit of the vile association of which he was now a member. "I like it well," said he. " 'Tis a proper place for a lad of mettle."

Several of those who sat around heard his words and applauded them.

"What's that?" cried the black-maned Bodymaster from the end of the table.

" 'Tis our new brother, sir, who finds our ways to his taste."

McMurdo rose to his feet for an instant. "I would say, Eminent Body-master, that if a man should be wanted I should take it as an honour to be chosen to help the lodge."

There was great applause at this. It was felt that a new sun was push-ing its rim above the horizon. To some of the elders it seemed that the progress was a little too rapid.

"I would move," said the secretary, Harraway, a vulture-faced old graybeard who sat near the chairman, "that Brother McMurdo should wait until it is the good pleasure of the lodge to employ him."

"Sure, that was what I meant; I'm in your hands," said McMurdo.

"Your time will come, Brother," said the chairman. "We have marked you down as a willing man, and we believe that you will do good work in these parts. There is a small matter to-night in which you may take a hand if it so please you."

"I will wait for something that is worth while."

"You can come to-night, anyhow, and it will help you to know what we stand for in this community. I will make the announcement later. Mean-while," he glanced at his agenda paper, "I have one or two more points to bring before the meeting. First of all, I will ask the treasurer as to our bank balance. There is the pension to Jim Carnaway's widow. He was struck down doing the work of the lodge, and it is for us to see that she is not the loser."

"Jim was shot last month when they tried to kill Chester Wilcox of Marley Creek," McMurdo's neighbour informed him.

"The funds are good at the moment," said the treasurer, with the bankbook in front of him. "The firms have been generous of late. Max Linder & Co. paid five hundred to be left alone. Walker Brothers sent in a hundred; but I took it on myself to return it and ask for five. If I do not hear by Wednesday, their winding gear may get out of order. We had to burn their breaker last year before they became reasonable. Then the West Section Coaling Company has paid its annual contribution. We have enough on hand to meet any obligations."

"What about Archie Swindon?" asked a brother.

"He has sold out and left the district. The old devil left a note for us to say that he had rather be a free crossing sweeper in New York than a large mine owner under the power of a ring of blackmailers. By Gar! it was as well that he made a break for it before the note reached us! I guess he won't show his face in this valley again."

An elderly, clean-shaved man with a kindly face and a good brow rose from the end of the table which faced the chairman. "Mr. Treasurer," he asked, "may I ask who has bought the property of this man that we have driven out of the district?"

"Yes, Brother Morris. It has been bought by the State & Merton County Railroad Company."

"And who bought the mines of Todman and of Lee that came into the market in the same way last year?"

"The same company, Brother Morris."

"And who bought the ironworks of Manson and of Shuman, and of Van Deher and of Atwood, which have all been given up of late?"

"They were all bought by the West Gilmerton General Mining Company."

"I don't see, Brother Morris," said the chairman, "that it matters to us who buys them, since they can't carry them out of the district."

"With all respect to you, Eminent Bodymaster, I think it may matter very much to us. This process has been going on now for ten long years. We are gradually driving all the small men out of trade. What is the result? We find in their places great companies like the Railroad or the General Iron, who have their directors in New York or Philadelphia, and care nothing for our threats. We can take it out of their local bosses; but it only means that others will be sent in their stead. And we are making it dangerous for ourselves. The small men could not harm us. They had not the money nor the power. So long as we did not squeeze them too dry, they would stay on under our power. But if these big companies find that we stand between them and their profits, they will spare no pains and no expense to hunt us down and bring us to court."

There was a hush at these ominous words, and every face darkened as gloomy looks were exchanged. So omnipotent and unchallenged had they been that the very thought that there was possible retribution in the background had been banished from their minds. And yet the idea struck a chill to the most reckless of them.

"It is my advice," the speaker continued, "that we go easier upon the small men. On the day that they have all been driven out the power of this society will have been broken."

Unwelcome truths are not popular. There were angry cries as the speaker resumed his seat. McGinty rose with gloom upon his brow.

"Brother Morris," said he, "you were always a croaker. So long as the members of this lodge stand together there is no power in the United States that can touch them. Sure, have we not tried it often enough in the law courts? I expect the big companies will find it easier to pay than to fight, same as the little companies do. And now, Brethren," McGinty took off his black velvet cap and his stole as he spoke, "this lodge has finished its business for the evening, save for one small matter which may be mentioned when we are parting. The time has now come for fraternal refreshment and for harmony."

Strange indeed is human nature. Here were these men, to whom murder was familiar, who again and again had struck down the father of the family, some man against whom they had no personal feeling, without one thought of compunction or of compassion for his weeping wife or helpless children, and yet the tender or pathetic in music could move them to tears. McMurdo had a fine tenor voice, and if he had failed to gain the good will of the lodge before, it could no longer have been withheld after he had thrilled them with "I'm Sitting on the Stile, Mary," and "On the Banks of Allan Water."

In his very first night the new recruit had made himself one of the most popular of the brethren, marked already for advancement and high office. There were other qualities needed, however, besides those of good fellowship, to make a worthy Freeman, and of these he was given an example before the evening was over. The whisky bottle had passed round many times, and the men were flushed and ripe for mischief when their Bodymaster rose once more to address them.

"Boys," said he, "there's one man in this town that wants trimming up, and it's for you to see that he gets it. I'm speaking of James Stanger of the *Herald*. You've seen how he's been opening his mouth against us again?"

There was a murmur of assent, with many a muttered oath. McGinty took a slip of paper from his waistcoat pocket.

"LAW AND ORDER!"

That's how he heads it.

"REIGN OF TERROR IN THE COAL AND IRON DISTRICT"
Twelve years have now elapsed since the first assassinations which proved the existence of a criminal organization in our midst. From that day these outrages have never ceased, until now they have reached a pitch which makes us the opprobrium of the civilized world. Is it for such results as this that our great country welcomes to its bosom the alien who flies from the despotisms of Europe? Is it that they shall themselves become tyrants over the very men who have given them shelter, and that a state of terrorism and lawlessness should be established under the very shadow of the sacred folds of the starry Flag of Freedom which would raise horror in our minds if we read of it as existing under the most effete monarchy of the East? The men are known. The organization is patent and public. How long are we to endure it? Can we forever live——

"Sure, I've read enough of the slush!" cried the chairman, tossing the paper down upon the table. "That's what he says of us. The question I'm asking you is what shall we say to him?"

"Kill him!" cried a dozen fierce voices.

"I protest against that," said Brother Morris, the man of the good brow and shaved face. "I tell you, Brethren, that our hand is too heavy in this valley, and that there will come a point where in self-defense every man will unite to crush us out. James Stanger is an old man. He is respected in the township and the district. His paper stands for all that is solid in the valley. If that man is struck down, there will be a stir through this state that will only end with our destruction."

"And how would they bring about our destruction, Mr. Standback?" cried McGinty. "Is it by the police? Sure, half of them are in our pay and half of them afraid of us. Or is it by the law courts and the judge? Haven't we tried that before now, and what ever came of it?"

"There is a Judge Lynch that might try the case," said Brother Morris.

A general shout of anger greeted the suggestion.

"I have but to raise my finger," cried McGinty, "and I could put two hundred men into this town that would clear it out from end to end." Then suddenly raising his voice and bending his huge black brows into a terrible frown, "See here, Brother Morris, I have my eye on you, and have had for some time! You've no heart yourself, and you try to take the heart out of others. It will be an ill day for you, Brother Morris, when your own name comes on our agenda paper, and I'm thinking that it's just there that I ought to place it."

Morris had turned deadly pale, and his knees seemed to give way under him as he fell back into his chair. He raised his glass in his trembling hand and drank before he could answer. "I apologize, Eminent Bodymaster, to you and to every brother in this lodge if I have said more than I should. I am a faithful member—you all know that—and it is my fear lest evil come to the lodge which makes me speak in anxious words. But I have greater trust in your judgment than in my own, Eminent Bodymaster, and I promise you that I will not offend again."

The Bodymaster's scowl relaxed as he listened to the humble words. "Very good, Brother Morris. It's myself that would be sorry if it were needful to give you a lesson. But so long as I am in this chair we shall be a united lodge in word and in deed. And now, boys," he continued, looking round at the company, "I'll say this much, that if Stanger got his full deserts there would be more trouble than we need ask for. These editors hang together, and every journal in the state would be crying out for police and troops. But I guess you can give him a pretty severe warning. Will you fix it, Brother Baldwin?"

"Sure!" said the young man eagerly.

"How many will you take?"

"Half a dozen, and two to guard the door. You'll come, Gower, and you, Mansel, and you, Scanlan, and the two Willabys."

"I promised the new brother he should go," said the chairman.

Ted Baldwin looked at McMurdo with eyes which showed that he had not forgotten nor forgiven. "Well, he can come if he wants," he said in a surly voice. "That's enough. The sooner we get to work the better."

The company broke up with shouts and yells and snatches of drunken song. The bar was still crowded with revellers, and many of the brethren remained there. The little band who had been told off for duty passed out into the street, proceeding in twos and threes along the sidewalk so as not to provoke attention. It was a bitterly cold night, with a half-moon shining brilliantly in a frosty, star-spangled sky. The men stopped and gathered in a yard which faced a high building. The words "Vermissa Herald" were printed in gold lettering between the brightly lit windows. From within came the clanking of the printing press.

"Here, you," said Baldwin to McMurdo, "you can stand below at the door and see that the road is kept open for us. Arthur Willaby can stay with you. You others come with me. Have no fears, boys; for we have a dozen witnesses that we are in the Union Bar at this very moment."

It was nearly midnight, and the street was deserted save for one or two revellers upon their way home. The party crossed the road, and, pushing open the door of the newspaper office, Baldwin and his men rushed in and up the stair which faced them. McMurdo and another remained below. From the room above came a shout, a cry for help, and then the sound of trampling feet and of falling chairs. An instant later a gray-haired man rushed out on the landing.

He was seized before he could get farther, and his spectacles came tinkling down to McMurdo's feet. There was a thud and a groan. He was on his face, and half a dozen sticks were clattering together as they fell upon him. He writhed, and his long, thin limbs quivered under the blows. The others ceased at last; but Baldwin, his cruel face set in an infernal smile, was hacking at the man's head, which he vainly endeavoured to defend with his arms. His white hair was dabbled with patches of blood. Baldwin was still stooping over his victim, putting in a short, vicious blow whenever he could see a part exposed, when McMurdo dashed up the stair and pushed him back.

"You'll kill the man," said he. "Drop it!"

Baldwin looked at him in amazement. "Curse you!" he cried. "Who are you to interfere—you that are new to the lodge? Stand back!" He raised his stick; but McMurdo had whipped his pistol out of his hip pocket.

"Stand back yourself!" he cried. "I'll blow your face in if you lay a hand on me. As to the lodge, wasn't it the order of the Bodymaster that the man was not to be killed—and what are you doing but killing him?"

"It's truth he says," remarked one of the men.

"By Gar! you'd best hurry yourselves!" cried the man below. "The windows are all lighting up, and you'll have the whole town here inside of five minutes."

There was indeed the sound of shouting in the street, and a little group of compositors and pressmen was forming in the hall below and nerving itself to action. Leaving the limp and motionless body of the editor at the head of the stair, the criminals rushed down and made their way swiftly along the street. Having reached the Union House, some of them mixed with the crowd in McGinty's saloon, whispering across the bar to the Boss that the job had been well carried through. Others, and among them McMurdo, broke away into side streets, and so by devious paths to their own homes.

CHAPTER 4

The Valley of Fear

When McMurdo awoke next morning he had good reason to remember his initiation into the lodge. His head ached with the effect of the drink, and his arm, where he had been branded, was hot and swollen. Having his own peculiar source of income, he was irregular in his attendance at his work; so he had a late breakfast, and remained at home for the morning writing a long letter to a friend. Afterwards he read the *Daily Herald*. In a special column put in at the last moment he read:

OUTRAGE AT THE HERALD OFFICE—EDITOR
SERIOUSLY INJURED.

It was a short account of the facts with which he was himself more familiar than the writer could have been. It ended with the statement:

The matter is now in the hands of the police; but it can hardly be hoped that their exertions will be attended by any better results than in the past. Some of the men were recognized, and there is hope that a conviction may be obtained. The source of the outrage was, it need hardly be said, that infamous society which has held this community in bondage for so long a period, and against which the *Herald* has taken so uncompromising a stand. Mr. Stanger's many friends will rejoice to hear that, though he has been cruelly and brutally beaten, and though he has sustained severe injuries about the head, there is no immediate danger to his life.

Below it stated that a guard of police, armed with Winchester rifles, had been requisitioned for the defense of the office.

McMurdo had laid down the paper, and was lighting his pipe with a hand which was shaky from the excesses of the previous evening, when there was a knock outside, and his landlady brought to him a note which had just been handed in by a lad. It was unsigned, and ran thus:

I should wish to speak to you; but would rather not do so in your house. You will find me beside the flagstaff upon Miller Hill. If you will come there now, I have something which it is important for you to hear and for me to say.

McMurdo read the note twice with the utmost surprise; for he could not imagine what it meant or who was the author of it. Had it been in a feminine hand, he might have imagined that it was the beginning of one of those adventures which had been familiar enough in his past life. But it was the writing of a man, and of a well educated one, too. Finally, after some hesitation, he determined to see the matter through.

Miller Hill is an ill-kept public park in the very centre of the town. In summer it is a favourite resort of the people; but in winter it is desolate enough. From the top of it one has a view not only of the whole straggling, grimy town, but of the winding valley beneath, with its scattered mines and factories blackening the snow on each side of it, and of the wooded and white-capped ranges flanking it.

McMurdo strolled up the winding path hedged in with evergreens until he reached the deserted restaurant which forms the centre of summer gaiety. Beside it was a bare flagstaff, and underneath it a man, his hat drawn down and the collar of his overcoat turned up. When he turned his face McMurdo saw that it was Brother Morris, he who had incurred the anger of the Bodymaster the night before. The lodge sign was given and exchanged as they met.

"I wanted to have a word with you, Mr. McMurdo," said the older man, speaking with a hesitation which showed that he was on delicate ground. "It was kind of you to come."

"Why did you not put your name to the note?"

"One has to be cautious, mister. One never knows in times like these how a thing may come back to one. One never knows either who to trust or who not to trust."

"Surely one may trust brothers of the lodge."

"No, no, not always," cried Morris with vehemence. "Whatever we say, even what we think, seems to go back to that man McGinty."

"Look here!" said McMurdo sternly. "It was only last night, as you know well, that I swore good faith to our Bodymaster. Would you be asking me to break my oath?"

"If that is the view you take," said Morris sadly, "I can only say that I am sorry I gave you the trouble to come and meet me. Things have come to a bad pass when two free citizens cannot speak their thoughts to each other."

McMurdo, who had been watching his companion very narrowly, relaxed somewhat in his bearing. "Sure I spoke for myself only," said he. "I am a newcomer, as you know, and I am strange to it all. It is not for me to open my mouth, Mr. Morris, and if you think well to say anything to me I am here to hear it."

"And to take it back to Boss McGinty!" said Morris bitterly.

"Indeed, then, you do me injustice there," cried McMurdo. "For myself I am loyal to the lodge, and so I tell you straight; but I would be a poor creature if I were to repeat to any other what you might say to me in confidence. It will go no further than me; though I warn you that you may get neither help nor sympathy."

"I have given up looking for either the one or the other," said Morris. "I may be putting my very life in your hands by what I say; but, bad as you are—and it seemed to me last night that you were shaping to be as bad as the worst—still you are new to it, and your conscience cannot yet be as hardened as theirs. That was why I thought to speak with you."

"Well, what have you to say?"

"If you give me away, may a curse be on you!"

"Sure, I said I would not."

"I would ask you, then, when you joined the Freeman's society in Chicago and swore vows of charity and fidelity, did ever it cross your mind that you might find it would lead you to crime?"

"If you call it crime," McMurdo answered.

"Call it crime!" cried Morris, his voice vibrating with passion. "You have seen little of it if you can call it anything else. Was it crime last night when a man old enough to be your father was beaten till the blood dripped from his white hairs? Was that crime—or what else would you call it?"

"There are some would say it was war," said McMurdo. "a war of two classes with all in, so that each struck as best it could."

"Well, did you think of such a thing when you joined the Freeman's society at Chicago?"

"No, I'm bound to say I did not."

"Nor did I when I joined it at Philadelphia. It was just a benefit club and a meeting place for one's fellows. Then I heard of this place—curse the hour that the name first fell upon my ears!—and I came to better myself! My God! to better myself! My wife and three children came with me. I started a drygoods store on Market Square, and I prospered well. The word had gone round that I was a Freeman, and I was forced to join the local lodge, same as you did last night. I've the badge of shame on my forearm and something worse branded on my heart. I found that I was under the orders of a black villain and caught in a meshwork of crime. What could I do? Every word I said to make things better was taken as treason, same as it was last night. I can't get away; for all I have in the world is in my store. If I leave the society, I know well that it means murder to me, and God knows what to my wife and children. Oh, man, it is awful—awful!" He put his hands to his face, and his body shook with convulsive sobs.

McMurdo shrugged his shoulders. "You were too soft for the job," said he. "You are the wrong sort for such work."

"I had a conscience and a religion; but they made me a criminal among them. I was chosen for a job. If I backed down, I knew well what would come to me. Maybe I'm a coward. Maybe it's the thought of my poor little woman and the children that makes me one. Anyhow I went. I guess it will haunt me forever.

"It was a lonely house, twenty miles from here, over the range yonder. I was told off for the door, same as you were last night. They could not trust me with the job. The others went in. When they came out their

hands were crimson to the wrists. As we turned away a child was screaming out of the house behind us. It was a boy of five who had seen his father murdered. I nearly fainted with the horror of it, and yet I had to keep
a bold and smiling face; for well I knew that if I did not it would be out of
my house that they would come next with their bloody hands, and it
would be my little Fred that would be screaming for his father.

"But I was a criminal then, part sharer in a murder, lost forever in this
world, and lost also in the next. I am a good Catholic; but the priest would
have no word with me when he heard I was a Scowrer, and I am excom-
municated from my faith. That's how it stands with me. And I see you
going down the same road, and I ask you what the end is to be. Are you
ready to be a cold-blooded murderer also, or can we do anything to stop
it?"

"What would you do?" asked McMurdo abruptly. "You would not inform?"

"God forbid!" cried Morris. "Sure, the very thought would cost me my
life."

"That's well," said McMurdo. "I'm thinking that you are a weak man
and that you make too much of the matter."

"Too much! Wait till you have lived here, longer. Look down the valley! See the cloud of a hundred chimneys that overshadows it! I tell you
that the cloud of murder hangs thicker and lower than that over the heads
of the people. It is the Valley of Fear, the Valley of Death. The terror is
in the hearts of the people from the dusk to the dawn. Wait, young man,
and you will learn for yourself."

"Well, I'll let you know what I think when I have seen more," said Mc-
Murdo carelessly. "What is very clear is that you are not the man for the
place, and that the sooner you sell out—if you only get a dime a dollar for
what the business is worth—the better it will be for you. What you have
said is safe with me; but, by Gar! if I thought you were an informer——"

"No, no!" cried Morris piteously.

"Well, let it rest at that. I'll bear what you have said in mind, and
maybe some day I'll come back to it. I expect you meant kindly by speaking to me like this. Now I'll be getting home."

"One word before you go," said Morris. "We may have been seen together. They may want to know what we have spoken about."

"Ah! that's well thought of."

"I offer you a clerkship in my store."

"And I refuse it. That's our business. Well, so long, Brother Morris,
and may you find things go better with you in the future."

That same afternoon, as McMurdo sat smoking, lost in thought, beside
the stove of his sitting-room, the door swung open and its framework was
filled with the huge figure of Boss McGinty. He passed the sign, and then
seating himself opposite to the young man he looked at him steadily for
some time, a look which was as steadily returned.

"I'm not much of a visitor, Brother McMurdo," he said at last. "I guess

I am too busy over the folk that visit me. But I thought I'd stretch a point and drop down to see you in your own house."

"I'm proud to see you here, Councillor," McMurdo answered heartily, bringing his whisky bottle out of the cupboard. "it's an honour that I had not expected."

"How's the arm?" asked the Boss.

McMurdo made a wry face. "Well, I'm not forgetting it," he said; "but it's worth it."

"Yes, it's worth it," the other answered, "to those that are loyal and go through with it and are a help to the lodge. What were you speaking to Brother Morris about on Miller Hill this morning?"

The question came so suddenly that it was well that he had his answer prepared. He burst into a hearty laugh. "Morris didn't know I could earn a living here at home. He shan't know either; for he has got too much conscience for the likes of me. But he's a good-hearted old chap. It was his idea that I was at a loose end, and that he would do me a good turn by offering me a clerkship in a drygoods store."

"Oh, that was it?"

"Yes, that was it."

"And you refused it?"

"Sure. Couldn't I earn ten times as much in my own bedroom with four hours' work?"

"That's so. But I wouldn't get about too much with Morris."

"Why not?"

"Well, I guess because I tell you not. That's enough for most folk in these parts."

"It may be enough for most folk; but it ain't enough for me, Councillor," said McMurdo boldly. "If you are a judge of men, you'll know that."

The swarthy giant glared at him, and his hairy paw closed for an instant round the glass as though he would hurl it at the head of his companion. Then he laughed in his loud, boisterous, insincere fashion.

"You're a queer card, for sure," said he. "Well, if you want reasons, I'll give them. Did Morris say nothing to you against the lodge?"

"No."

"Nor against me?"

"No."

"Well, that's because he daren't trust you. But in his heart he is not a loyal brother. We know that well. So we watch him and we wait for the time to admonish him. I'm thinking that the time is drawing near. There's no room for scabby sheep in our pen. But if you keep company with a disloyal man, we might think that you were disloyal, too. See?"

"There's no chance of my keeping company with him; for I dislike the man," McMurdo answered. "As to being disloyal, if it was any man but you he would not use the word to me twice."

"Well, that's enough," said McGinty, draining off his glass. "I came down to give you a word in season, and you've had it."

"I'd like to know," said McMurdo, "how you ever came to learn that I had spoken with Morris at all?"

McGinty laughed. "It's my business to know what goes on in this township," said he. "I guess you'd best reckon on my hearing all that passes. Well, time's up, and I'll just say——"

But his leavetaking was cut short in a very unexpected fashion. With a sudden crash the door flew open, and three frowning, intent faces glared in at them from under the peaks of police caps. McMurdo sprang to his feet and half drew his revolver; but his arm stopped midway as he became conscious that two Winchester rifles were levelled at his head. A man in uniform advanced into the room, a six-shooter in his hand. It was Captain Marvin, once of Chicago, and now, of the Mine Constabulary. He shook his head with a half-smile at McMurdo.

"I thought you'd be getting into trouble, Mr. Crooked McMurdo of Chicago," said he. "Can't keep out of it, can you? Take your hat and come along with us."

"I guess you'll pay for this, Captain Marvin," said McGinty. "Who are you, I'd like to know, to break into a house in this fashion and molest honest, law-abiding men?"

"You're standing out in this deal, Councillor McGinty," said the police captain. "We are not out after you, but after this man McMurdo. It is for you to help, not to hinder us in our duty."

"He is a friend of mine, and I'll answer for his conduct," said the Boss.

"By all accounts, Mr. McGinty, you may have to answer for your own conduct some of these days," the captain answered. "This man McMurdo was a crook before ever he came here, and he's a crook still. Cover him, Patrolman, while I disarm him."

"There's my pistol," said McMurdo coolly. "Maybe, Captain Marvin, if you and I were alone and face to face you would not take me so easily."

"Where's your warrant?" asked McGinty. "By Gar! a man might as well live in Russia* as in Vermissa while folk like you are running the police. It's capitalist outrage, and you'll hear more of it, I reckon."

"You do what you think is your duty the best way you can. Councillor. We'll look after ours."

"What am I accused of?" asked McMurdo.

"Of being concerned in the beating of old Editor Stanger at the *Herald* office. It wasn't your fault that it isn't a murder charge."

"Well, if that's all you have against him," cried McGinty with a laugh, "you can save yourself a deal of trouble by dropping it right now. This man was with me in my saloon playing poker up to midnight, and I can bring a dozen to prove it."

"That's your affair, and I guess you can settle it in court to-morrow. Meanwhile, come on, McMurdo, and come quietly if you don't want a gun

---

*That is, live under the oppressive tyranny of Czar Alexander II.

across your head. You stand wide, Mr. McGinty; for I warn you I will
stand no resistance when I am on duty!"

So determined was the appearance of the captain that both McMurdo
and his boss were forced to accept the situation. The latter managed to
have a few whispered words with the prisoner before they parted.

"What about——" he jerked his thumb upward to signify the coining
plant.

"All right," whispered McMurdo, who had devised a safe hiding place
under the floor.

"I'll bid you good-bye," said the Boss, shaking hands. "I'll see Reilly
the lawyer and take the defense upon myself. Take my word for it that
they won't be able to hold you."

"I wouldn't bet on that. Guard the prisoner, you two, and shoot him if
he tries any games. I'll search the house before I leave."

He did so; but apparently found no trace of the concealed plant. When
he had descended he and his men escorted McMurdo to headquarters.
Darkness had fallen, and a keen blizzard was blowing so that the streets
were nearly deserted; but a few loiterers followed the group, and em-
boldened by invisibility shouted imprecations at the prisoner.

"Lynch the cursed Scowrer!" they cried. "Lynch him!" They laughed
and jeered as he was pushed into the police station. After a short, formal
examination from the inspector in charge he was put into the common
cell. Here he found Baldwin and three other criminals of the night before,
all arrested that afternoon and waiting their trial next morning.

But even within this inner fortress of the law the long arm of the
Freemen was able to extend. Late at night there came a jailer with a straw
bundle for their bedding, out of which he extracted two bottles of whisky,
some glasses, and a pack of cards. They spent a hilarious night, without
an anxious thought as to the ordeal of the morning.

Nor had they cause, as the result was to show. The magistrate could
not possibly, on the evidence, have held them for a higher court. On the
one hand the compositors and pressmen were forced to admit that the
light was uncertain, that they were themselves much perturbed, and that
it was difficult for them to swear to the identity of the assailants; although
they believed that the accused were among them. Cross examined by the
clever attorney who had been engaged by McGinty, they were even more
nebulous in their evidence.

The injured man had already deposed that he was so taken by surprise
by the suddenness of the attack that he could state nothing beyond the
fact that the first man who struck him wore a moustache. He added that
he knew them to be Scowrers, since no one else in the community could
possibly have any enmity to him, and he had long been threatened on account of his outspoken editorials. On the other hand, it was clearly shown
by the united and unfaltering evidence of six citizens, including that high
municipal official, Councillor McGinty, that the men had been at a card
party at the Union House until an hour very much later than the commission of the outrage.

Needless to say that they were discharged with something very near to an apology from the bench for the inconvenience to which they had been put, together with an implied censure of Captain Marvin and the police for their officious zeal.

The verdict was greeted with loud applause by a court in which McMurdo saw many familiar faces. Brothers of the lodge smiled and waved. But there were others who sat with compressed lips and brooding eyes as the men filed out of the dock. One of them, a little, dark-bearded, resolute fellow, put the thoughts of himself and comrades into words as the ex-prisoners passed him.

"You damned murderers!" he said. "We'll fix you yet!"

CHAPTER 5

The Darkest Hour

If anything had been needed to give an impetus to Jack McMurdo's popularity among his fellows it would have been his arrest and acquittal. That a man on the very night of joining the lodge should have done something which brought him before the magistrate was a new record in the annals of the society. Already he had earned the reputation of a good boon companion, a cheery reveller, and withal a man of high temper, who would not take an insult even from the all-powerful Boss himself. But in addition to this he impressed his comrades with the idea that among them all there was not one whose brain was so ready to devise a bloodthirsty scheme, or whose hand would be more capable of carrying it out. "He'll be the boy for the clean job," said the oldsters to one another, and waited their time until they could set him to his work.

McGinty had instruments enough already; but he recognized that this was a supremely able one. He felt like a man holding a fierce bloodhound in leash. There were curs to do the smaller work; but some day he would slip this creature upon its prey. A few members of the lodge, Ted Baldwin among them, resented the rapid rise of the stranger and hated him for it; but they kept clear of him, for he was as ready to fight as to laugh.

But if he gained favour with his fellows, there was another quarter, one which had become even more vital to him, in which he lost it. Ettie Shafter's father would have nothing more to do with him, nor would he allow him to enter the house. Ettie herself was too deeply in love to give him up altogether, and yet her own good sense warned her of what would come from a marriage with a man who was regarded as a criminal.

One morning after a sleepless night she determined to see him, possibly for the last time, and make one strong endeavour to draw him from those evil influences which were sucking him down. She went to his house, as he had often begged her to do, and made her way into the room which he used as his sitting-room. He was seated at a table, with his back turned and a letter in front of him. A sudden spirit of girlish mischief came over her—she was still only nineteen. He had not heard her when she pushed open the door. Now she tiptoed forward and laid her hand lightly upon his bended shoulders.

If she had expected to startle him, she certainly succeeded; but only in turn to be startled herself. With a tiger spring he turned on her, and his right hand was feeling for her throat. At the same instant with the other hand he crumpled up the paper that lay before him. For an instant he stood glaring. Then astonishment and joy took the place of the ferocity which had convulsed his features—a ferocity which had sent her shrinking back in horror as from something which had never before intruded into her gentle life.

"It's you!" said he, mopping his brow. "And to think that you should come to me, heart of my heart, and I should find nothing better to do than to want to strangle you! Come then, darling," and he held out his arms, "let me make it up to you."

But she had not recovered from that sudden glimpse of guilty fear which she had read in the man's face. All her woman's instinct told her that it was not the mere fright of a man who is startled. Guilt—that was it—guilt and fear!

"What's come over you, Jack?" she cried. "Why were you so scared of me? Oh, Jack, if your conscience was at ease, you would not have looked at me like that!"

"Sure, I was thinking of other things, and when you came tripping so lightly on those fairy feet of yours——"

"No, no, it was more than that, Jack." Then a sudden suspicion seized her. "Let me see that letter you were writing."

"Ah, Ettie, I couldn't do that."

Her suspicions became certainties. "It's to another woman," she cried. "I know it! Why else should you hold it from me? Was it to your wife that you were writing? How am I to know that you are not a married man—you, a stranger, that nobody knows?"

"I am not married, Ettie. See now, I swear it! You're the only one woman on earth to me. By the cross of Christ I swear it!"

He was so white with passionate earnestness that she could not but believe him.

"Well, then," she cried, "why will you not show me the letter?"

"I'll tell you, acushla," said he. "I'm under oath not to show it, and just as I wouldn't break my word to you so I would keep it to those who hold my promise. It's the business of the lodge, and even to you it's secret. And if I was scared when a hand fell on me, can't you understand it when it might have been the hand of a detective?"

She felt that he was telling the truth. He gathered her into his arms and kissed away her fears and doubts.

"Sit here by me, then. It's a queer throne for such a queen; but it's the best your poor lover can find. He'll do better for you some of these days, I'm thinking. Now your mind is easy once again, is it not?"

"How can it ever be at ease, Jack, when I know that you are a criminal among criminals, when I never know the day that I may hear you are in court for murder? 'McMurdo the Scowrer,' that's what one of our boarders called you yesterday. It went through my heart like a knife."

"Sure, hard words break no bones."

"But they were true."

"Well, dear, it's not so bad as you think. We are but poor men that are trying in our own way to get our rights."

Ettie threw her arms round her lover's neck. "Give it up, Jack! For my sake, for God's sake, give it up! It was to ask you that I came here to-day.

Oh, Jack, see—I beg it of you on my bended knees! Kneeling here before you I implore you to give it up!"

He raised her and soothed her with her head against his breast.

"Sure, my darlin', you don't know what it is you are asking. How could I give it up when it would be to break my oath and to desert my comrades? If you could see how things stand with me you could never ask it of me. Besides, if I wanted to, how could I do it? You don't suppose that the lodge would let a man go free with all its secrets?"

"I've thought of that, Jack. I've planned it all. Father has saved some money. He is weary of this place where the fear of these people darkens our lives. He is ready to go. We would fly together to Philadelphia or New York, where we would be safe from them."

McMurdo laughed. "The lodge has a long arm. Do you think it could not stretch from here to Philadelphia or New York?"

"Well, then, to the West, or to England, or to Germany, where father came from—anywhere to get away from this Valley of Fear!"

McMurdo thought of old Brother Morris. "Sure, it is the second time I have heard the valley so named," said he. "The shadow does indeed seem to lie heavy on some of you."

"It darkens every moment of our lives. Do you suppose that Ted Baldwin has ever forgiven us? If it were not that he fears you, what do you suppose our chances would be? If you saw the look in those dark, hungry eyes of his when they fall on me!"

"By Gar! I'd teach him better manners if I caught him at it! But see here, little girl. I can't leave here. I can't—take that from me once and for all. But if you will leave me to find my own way, I will try to prepare a way of getting honourably out of it."

"There is no honour in such a matter."

"Well, well, it's just how you look at it. But if you'll give me six months, I'll work it so that I can leave without being ashamed to look others in the face."

The girl laughed with joy. "Six months!" she cried. "Is it a promise?"

"Well, it may be seven or eight. But within a year at the furthest we will leave the valley behind us."

It was the most that Ettie could obtain, and yet it was something. There was this distant light to illuminate the gloom of the immediate future. She returned to her father's house more light-hearted than she had ever been since Jack McMurdo had come into her life.

It might be thought that as a member, all the doings of the society would be told to him; but he was soon to discover that the organization was wider and more complex than the simple lodge. Even Boss McGinty was ignorant as to many things; for there was an official named the County Delegate, living at Hobson's Patch farther down the line, who had power over several different lodges which he wielded in a sudden and arbitrary way. Only once did McMurdo see him, a sly, little gray-haired rat of a man, with a slinking gait and a sidelong glance which was charged with malice. Evans Pott was his name, and even the great Boss of Vermissa felt towards him something of the repulsion and fear which the huge Danton may have felt for the puny but dangerous Robespierre.[9]

One day Scanlan, who was McMurdo's fellow boarder, received a note from McGinty inclosing one from Evans Pott, which informed him that he was sending over two good men, Lawler and Andrews, who had instructions to act in the neighbourhood; though it was best for the cause that no particulars as to their objects should be given. Would the Bodymaster see to it that suitable arrangements be made for their lodgings and comfort until the time for action should arrive? McGinty added that it was impossible for anyone to remain secret at the Union House, and that, therefore, he would be obliged if McMurdo and Scanlan would put the strangers up for a few days in their boarding house.

The same evening the two men arrived, each carrying his gripsack. Lawler was an elderly man, shrewd, silent, and self-contained, clad in an old black frock coat, which with his soft felt hat and ragged, grizzled beard gave him a general resemblance to an itinerant preacher. His companion Andrews was little more than a boy, frank-faced and cheerful, with the breezy manner of one who is out for a holiday and means to enjoy every minute of it. Both men were total abstainers, and behaved in all ways as exemplary members of the society, with the one simple exception that they were assassins who had often proved themselves to be most capable instruments for this association of murder. Lawler had already carried out fourteen commissions of the kind, and Andrews three.

They were, as McMurdo found, quite ready to converse about their deeds in the past, which they recounted with the half-bashful pride of men who had done good and unselfish service for the community. They were reticent, however, as to the immediate job in hand.

"They chose us because neither I nor the boy here drink," Lawler explained. "They can count on us saying no more than we should. You must not take it amiss, but it is the orders of the County Delegate that we obey."

"Sure, we are all in it together," said Scanlan, McMurdo's mate, as the four sat together at supper.

"That's true enough, and we'll talk till the cows come home of the killing of Charlie Williams or of Simon Bird, or any other job in the past. But till the work is done we say nothing."

"There are half a dozen about here that I have a word to say to," said McMurdo, with an oath. "I suppose it isn't Jack Knox of Ironhill that you are after. I'd go some way to see him get his deserts."

"No, it's not him yet."

"Or Herman Strauss?"

"No, nor him either."

"Well, if you won't tell us we can't make you; but I'd be glad to know."

Lawler smiled and shook his head. He was not to be drawn.

In spite of the reticence of their guests, Scanlan and McMurdo were quite determined to be present at what they called "the fun." When, therefore, at an early hour one morning McMurdo heard them creeping down the stairs he awakened Scanlan, and the two hurried on their clothes. When they were dressed they found that the others had stolen out, leaving the door open behind them. It was not yet dawn, and by the light of the lamps they could see the two men some distance down the street. They followed them warily, treading noiselessly in the deep snow.

The boarding house was near the edge of the town, and soon they were at the crossroads which is beyond its boundary. Here three men were waiting, with whom Lawler and Andrews held a short, eager conversation. Then they all moved on together. It was clearly some notable job which needed numbers. At this point there are several trails which lead to various mines. The strangers took that which led to the Crow Hill, a huge business which was in strong hands which had been able, thanks to their energetic and fearless New England manager, Josiah H. Dunn, to keep some order and discipline during the long reign of terror.

Day was breaking now, and a line of workmen were slowly making their way, singly and in groups, along the blackened path.

McMurdo and Scanlan strolled on with the others, keeping in sight of the men whom they followed. A thick mist lay over them, and from the heart of it there came the sudden scream of a steam whistle. It was the ten-minute signal before the cages descended and the day's labour began.

When they reached the open space round the mine shaft there were a hundred miners waiting, stamping their feet and blowing on their fingers; for it was bitterly cold. The strangers stood in a little group under the shadow of the engine house. Scanlan and McMurdo climbed a heap of slag from which the whole scene lay before them. They saw the mine engineer, a great bearded Scotchman named Menzies, come out of the engine house and blow his whistle for the cages to be lowered.

At the same instant a tall, loose-framed young man with a clean-shaved, earnest face advanced eagerly towards the pit head. As he came forward his eyes fell upon the group, silent and motionless, under the engine house. The men had drawn down their hats and turned up their collars to screen their faces. For a moment the presentiment of Death laid its cold hand upon the manager's heart. At the next he had shaken it off and saw only his duty towards intrusive strangers.

"Who are you?" he asked as he advanced. "What are you loitering there for?"

There was no answer; but the lad Andrews stepped forward and shot him in the stomach. The hundred waiting miners stood as motionless and helpless as if they were paralyzed. The manager clapped his two hands to the wound and doubled himself up. Then he staggered away; but another of the assassins fired, and he went down sidewise, kicking and clawing among a heap of clinkers. Menzies, the Scotchman, gave a roar of rage at the sight and rushed with an iron spanner at the murderers; but was met by two balls in the face which dropped him dead at their very feet.

There was a surge forward of some of the miners, and an inarticulate cry of pity and of anger; but a couple of the strangers emptied their six-shooters over the heads of the crowd, and they broke and scattered, some of them rushing wildly back to their homes in Vermissa.

When a few of the bravest had rallied, and there was a return to the mine, the murderous gang had vanished in the mists of morning, without a single witness being able to swear to the identity of these men who in front of a hundred spectators had wrought this double crime.

Scanlan and McMurdo made their way back; Scanlan somewhat subdued, for it was the first murder job that he had seen with his own eyes, and it appeared less funny than he had been led to believe. The horrible screams of the dead manager's wife pursued them as they hurried to the town. McMurdo was absorbed and silent; but he showed no sympathy for the weakening of his companion.

"Sure, it is like a war," he repeated. "What is it but a war between us and them, and we hit back where we best can."

There was high revel in the lodge room at the Union House that night, not only over the killing of the manager and engineer of the Crow Hill mine, which would bring this organization into line with the other blackmailed and terror-stricken companies of the district, but also over a distant triumph which had been wrought by the hands of the lodge itself.

It would appear that when the County Delegate had sent over five good men to strike a blow in Vermissa, he had demanded that in return three Vermissa men should be secretly selected and sent across to kill William Hales of Stake Royal, one of the best known and most popular mine owners in the Gilmerton district, a man who was believed not to have an enemy in the world; for he was in all ways a model employer. He had insisted, however, upon efficiency in the work, and had, therefore, paid off certain drunken and idle employees who were members of the all-powerful society. Coffin notices hung outside his door had not weakened his resolution, and so in a free, civilized country he found himself condemned to death.

The execution had now been duly carried out. Ted Baldwin, who sprawled now in the seat of honour beside the Bodymaster, had been chief of the party. His flushed face and glazed, blood-shot eyes told of sleeplessness and drink. He and his two comrades had spent the night before among the mountains. They were unkempt and weather-stained. But no heroes, returning from a forlorn hope, could have had a warmer welcome from their comrades.

The story was told and retold amid cries of delight and shouts of laughter. They had waited for their man as he drove home at nightfall, taking their station at the top of a steep hill, where his horse must be at a walk. He was so furred to keep out the cold that he could not lay his hand on his pistol. They had pulled him out and shot him again and again. He had screamed for mercy. The screams were repeated for the amusement of the lodge.

"Let's hear again how he squealed," they cried.

None of them knew the man; but there is eternal drama in a killing, and they had shown the Scowrers of Gilmerton that the Vermissa men were to be relied upon.

There had been one contretemps; for a man and his wife had driven up while they were still emptying their revolvers into the silent body. It had been suggested that they should shoot them both; but they were harmless folk who were not connected with the mines, so they were sternly bidden to drive on and keep silent, lest a worse thing befall them. And so the blood-mottled figure had been left as a warning to all such hard-hearted employers, and the three noble avengers had hurried off into the mountains where unbroken nature comes down to the very edge of the furnaces and the slag heaps. Here they were, safe and sound, their work well done, and the plaudits of their companions in their ears.

It had been a great day for the Scowrers. The shadow had fallen even darker over the valley. But as the wise general chooses the moment of victory in which to redouble his efforts, so that his foes may have no time to steady themselves after disaster, so Boss McGinty, looking out upon the scene of his operations with his brooding and malicious eyes, had devised a new attack upon those who opposed him. That very night, as the half-drunken company broke up, he touched McMurdo on the arm and led him aside into that inner room where they had their first interview.

"See here, my lad," said he, "I've got a job that's worthy of you at last. You'll have the doing of it in your own hands."

"Proud I am to hear it," McMurdo answered.

"You can take two men with you—Manders and Reilly. They have been warned for service. We'll never be right in this district until Chester Wilcox has been settled, and you'll have the thanks of every lodge in the coal fields if you can down him."

"I'll do my best, anyhow. Who is he, and where shall I find him?"

McGinty took his eternal half-chewed, half-smoked cigar from the corner of his mouth, and proceeded to draw a rough diagram on a page torn from his notebook.

"He's the chief foreman of the Iron Dike Company. He's a hard citizen, an old colour sergeant of the war, all scars and grizzle. We've had two tries at him; but had no luck, and Jim Carnaway lost his life over it. Now it's for you to take it over. That's the house—all alone at the Iron Dike crossroad, same as you see here on the map—without another within earshot. It's no good by day. He's armed and shoots quick and straight, with no questions asked. But at night—well, there he is with his wife, three children, and a hired help. You can't pick or choose. It's all or none. If you could get a bag of blasting powder at the front door with a slow match to it——"

"What's the man done?"

"Didn't I tell you he shot Jim Carnaway?"

"Why did he shoot him?"

"What in thunder has that to do with you? Carnaway was about his house at night, and he shot him. That's enough for me and you. You've got to settle the thing right."

"There's these two women and the children. Do they go up too?"

"They have to—else how can we get him?"

"It seems hard on them; for they've done nothing."

"What sort of fool's talk is this? Do you back out?"

"Easy, Councillor, easy! What have I ever said or done that you should think I would be after standing back from an order of the Bodymaster of my own lodge? If it's right or if it's wrong, it's for you to decide."

"You'll do it, then?"

"Of course I will do it."

"When?"

"Well, you had best give me a night or two that I may see the house and make my plans. Then——"

"Very good," said McGinty, shaking him by the hand. "I leave it with you. It will be a great day when you bring us the news. It's just the last stroke that will bring them all to their knees."

McMurdo thought long and deeply over the commission which had been so suddenly placed in his hands. The isolated house in which Chester Wilcox lived was about five miles off in an adjacent valley. That very night he started off all alone to prepare for the attempt. It was daylight before he returned from his reconnaissance. Next day he interviewed his two subordinates, Manders and Reilly, reckless youngsters who were as elated as if it were a deer-hunt.

Two nights later they met outside the town, all three armed, and one of them carrying a sack stuffed with the powder which was used in the quarries. It was two in the morning before they came to the lonely house. The night was a windy one, with broken clouds drifting swiftly across the face of a three-quarter moon. They had been warned to be on their guard against bloodhounds; so they moved forward cautiously, with their pistols cocked in their hands. But there was no sound save the howling of the wind, and no movement but the swaying branches above them.

McMurdo listened at the door of the lonely house; but all was still within. Then he leaned the powder bag against it, ripped a hole in it with his knife, and attached the fuse. When it was well alight he and his two companions took to their heels, and were some distance off, safe and snug in a sheltering ditch, before the shattering roar of the explosion, with the low, deep rumble of the collapsing building, told them that their work was done. No cleaner job had ever been carried out in the bloodstained annals of the society.

But alas that work so well organized and boldly carried out should all have gone for nothing! Warned by the fate of the various victims, and knowing that he was marked down for destruction, Chester Wilcox had moved himself and his family only the day before to some safer and less known quarters, where a guard of police should watch over them. It was an empty house which had been torn down by the gunpowder, and the grim old colour sergeant of the war was still teaching discipline to the miners of Iron Dike.

"Leave him to me, said McMurdo. "He's my man, and I'll get him sure if I have to wait a year for him."

A vote of thanks and confidence was passed in full lodge, and so for the time the matter ended. When a few weeks later it was reported in the papers that Wilcox had been shot at from an ambuscade, it was an open secret that McMurdo was still at work upon his unfinished job.

Such were the methods of the Society of Freemen, and such were the deeds of the Scowrers by which they spread their rule of fear over the great and rich district which was for so long a period haunted by their terrible presence. Why should these pages be stained by further crimes? Have I not said enough to show the men and their methods?

These deeds are written in history, and there are records wherein one may read the details of them. There one may learn of the shooting of Policemen Hunt and Evans because they had ventured to arrest two members of the society—a double outrage planned at the Vermissa lodge and carried out in cold blood upon two helpless and disarmed men. There also one may read of the shooting of Mrs. Larbey when she was nursing her husband, who had been beaten almost to death by orders of Boss McGinty. The killing of the elder Jenkins, shortly followed by that of his brother, the mutilation of James Murdoch, the blowing up of the Staphouse family, and the murder of the Stendals all followed hard upon one another in the same terrible winter.

Darkly the shadow lay upon the Valley of Fear. The spring had come with running brooks and blossoming trees. There was hope for all Nature bound so long in an iron grip; but nowhere was there any hope for the men and women who lived under the yoke of the terror. Never had the cloud above them been so dark and hopeless as in the early summer of the year 1875.

CHAPTER 6

Danger

It was the height of the reign of terror. McMurdo, who had already been appointed Inner Deacon, with every prospect of some day succeeding McGinty as Bodymaster, was now so necessary to the councils of his comrades that nothing was done without his help and advice. The more popular he became, however, with the Freemen, the blacker were the scowls which greeted him as he passed along the streets of Vermissa. In spite of their terror the citizens were taking heart to band themselves together against their oppressors. Rumours had reached the lodge of secret gatherings in the *Herald* office and of distribution of firearms among the law-abiding people. But McGinty and his men were undisturbed by such reports. They were numerous, resolute, and well armed. Their opponents were scattered and powerless. It would all end, as it had done in the past, in aimless talk and possibly in impotent arrests. So said McGinty, McMurdo, and all the bolder spirits.

It was a Saturday evening in May. Saturday was always the lodge night, and McMurdo was leaving his house to attend it when Morris, the weaker brother of the order, came to see him. His brow was creased with care, and his kindly face was drawn and haggard.

"Can I speak with you freely, Mr. McMurdo?"

"Sure."

"I can't forget that I spoke my heart to you once, and that you kept it to yourself, even though the Boss himself came to ask you about it."

"What else could I do if you trusted me? It wasn't that I agreed with what you said."

"I know that well. But you are the one that I can speak to and be safe. I've a secret here," he put his hand to his breast, "and it is just burning the life out of me. I wish it had come to any one of you but me. If I tell it, it will mean murder, for sure. If I don't, it may bring the end of us all. God help me, but I am near out of my wits over it!"

McMurdo looked at the man earnestly. He was trembling in every limb. He poured some whisky into a glass and handed it to him. "That's the physic* for the likes of you," said he. "Now let me hear of it."

Morris drank, and his white face took a tinge of colour. "I can tell it to you all in one sentence," said he. "There's a detective on our trail."

McMurdo stared at him in astonishment. "Why, man, you're crazy," he

---

*Medicine; remedy.

said. "Isn't the place full of police and detectives, and what harm did they ever do us?"

"No, no, it's no man of the district. As you say, we know them, and it is little that they can do. But you've heard of Pinkerton's?"[10]

"I've read of some folk of that name."

"Well, you can take it from me you've no show when they are on your trail. It's not a take-it-or-miss-it government concern. It's a dead earnest business proposition that's out for results and keeps out till by hook or crook it gets them. If a Pinkerton man is deep in this business, we are all destroyed."

"We must kill him."

"Ah, it's the first thought that came to you! So it will be up at the lodge. Didn't I say to you that it would end in murder?"

"Sure, what is murder? Isn't it common enough in these parts?"

"It is, indeed; but it's not for me to point out the man that is to be murdered. I'd never rest easy again. And yet it's our own necks that may be at stake. In God's name what shall I do?" He rocked to and fro in his agony of indecision.

But his words had moved McMurdo deeply. It was easy to see that he shared the other's opinion as to the danger, and the need for meeting it. He gripped Morris's shoulder and shook him in his earnestness.

"See here, man," he cried, and he almost screeched the words in his excitement, "you won't gain anything by sitting keening* like an old wife at a wake. Let's have the facts. Who is the fellow? Where is he? How did you hear of him? Why did you come to me?"

"I came to you; for you are the one man that would advise me. I told you that I had a store in the East before I came here. I left good friends behind me, and one of them is in the telegraph service. Here's a letter that I had from him yesterday. It's this part from the top of the page. You can read it yourself."

This was what McMurdo read:

How are the Scowrers getting on in your parts? We read plenty of them in the papers. Between you and me I expect to hear news from you before long. Five big corporations and the two railroads have taken the thing up in dead earnest. They mean it, and you can bet they'll get there! They are right deep down into it. Pinkerton has taken hold under their orders, and his best man, Birdy Edwards, is operating. The thing has got to be stopped right now.

"Now read the postscript."

Of course, what I give you is what I learned in business; so it goes no further. It's a queer cipher that you handle by the yard every day and can get no meaning from.

---

*Loud wailing over the dead.

McMurdo sat in silence for some time, with the letter in his listless hands. The mist had lifted for a moment, and there was the abyss before him.

"Does anyone else know of this?" he asked.

"I have told no one else."

"But this man—your friend—has he any other person that he would be likely to write to?"

"Well, I dare say he knows one or two more."

"Of the lodge?"

"It's likely enough."

"I was asking because it is likely that he may have given some description of this fellow Birdy Edwards—then we could get on his trail."

"Well, it's possible. But I should not think he knew him. He is just telling me the news that came to him by way of business. How would he know this Pinkerton man?"

McMurdo gave a violent start.

"By Gar!" he cried, "I've got him. What a fool I was not to know it. Lord! but we're in luck! We will fix him before he can do any harm. See here, Morris, will you leave this thing in my hands?"

"Sure, if you will only take it off mine."

"I'll do that. You can stand right back and let me run it. Even your name need not be mentioned. I'll take it all on myself, as if it were to me that this letter has come. Will that content you?"

"It's just what I would ask."

"Then leave it at that and keep your head shut. Now I'll get down to the lodge, and we'll soon make old man Pinkerton sorry for himself."

"You wouldn't kill this man?"

"The less you know, Friend Morris, the easier your conscience will be, and the better you will sleep. Ask no questions, and let these things settle themselves. I have hold of it now."

Morris shook his head sadly as he left. "I feel that his blood is on my hands," he groaned.

"Self-protection is no murder, anyhow," said McMurdo, smiling grimly. "It's him or us. I guess this man would destroy us all if we left him long in the valley. Why, Brother Morris, we'll have to elect you Bodymaster yet; for you've surely saved the lodge."

And yet it was clear from his actions that he thought more seriously of this new intrusion than his words would show. It may have been his guilty conscience, it may have been the reputation of the Pinkerton organization, it may have been the knowledge that great, rich corporations had set themselves the task of clearing out the Scowrers; but, whatever his reason, his actions were those of a man who is preparing for the worst. Every paper which would incriminate him was destroyed before he left the house. After that he gave a long sigh of satisfaction; for it seemed to him that he was safe. And yet the danger must still have pressed somewhat upon him; for on his way to the lodge he stopped at old man Shafter's. The house was forbidden him; but when he tapped at the window Ettie came out to him. The dancing Irish deviltry had gone from her lover's eyes. She read his danger in his earnest face.

"Something has happened!" she cried. "Oh, Jack, you are in danger!"

"Sure, it is not very bad, my sweetheart. And yet it may be wise that we make a move before it is worse."

"Make a move?"

"I promised you once that I would go some day. I think the time is coming. I had news to-night, bad news, and I see trouble coming."

"The police?"

"Well, a Pinkerton. But, sure, you wouldn't know what that is, acushla, nor what it may mean to the likes of me. I'm too deep in this thing, and I may have to get out of it quick. You said you would come with me if I went."

"Oh, Jack, it would be the saving of you!"

"I'm an honest man in some things, Ettie. I wouldn't hurt a hair of your bonny head for all that the world can give, nor ever pull you down one inch from the golden throne above the clouds where I always see you. Would you trust me?"

She put her hand in his without a word. "Well, then, listen to what I say, and do as I order you; for indeed it's the only way for us. Things are going to happen in this valley. I feel it in my bones. There may be many of us that will have to look out for ourselves. I'm one, anyhow. If I go, by day or night, it's you that must come with me!"

"I'd come after you, Jack."

"No, no, you shall come *with* me. If this valley is closed to me and I can never come back, how can I leave you behind, and me perhaps in hiding from the police with never a chance of a message? It's with me you must come. I know a good woman in the place I come from, and it's there I'd leave you till we can get married. Will you come?"

"Yes, Jack, I will come."

"God bless you for your trust in me! It's a fiend out of hell that I should be if I abused it. Now, mark you, Ettie, it will be just a word to you, and when it reaches you, you will drop everything and come right down to the waiting room at the depot and stay there till I come for you."

"Day or night, I'll come at the word, Jack."

Somewhat eased in mind, now that his own preparations for escape had been begun, McMurdo went on to the lodge. It had already assembled, and only by complicated signs and counter-signs could he pass through the outer guard and inner guard who close-tiled it. A buzz of pleasure and welcome greeted him as he entered. The long room was crowded, and through the haze of tobacco smoke he saw the tangled black mane of the Bodymaster, the cruel, unfriendly features of Baldwin, the vulture face of Harraway, the secretary, and a dozen more who were among the leaders of the lodge. He rejoiced that they should all be there to take counsel over his news.

"Indeed, it's glad we are to see you, Brother!" cried the chairman. "There's business here that wants a Solomon in judgment to set it right."

"It's Lander and Egan," explained his neighbour as he took his seat. "They both claim the head money given by the lodge for the shooting of old man Crabbe over at Stylestown, and who's to say which fired the bullet?"

McMurdo rose in his place and raised his hand. The expression of his face froze the attention of the audience. There was a dead hush of expectation.

"Eminent Bodymaster," he said, in a solemn voice, "I claim urgency!"

"Brother McMurdo claims urgency," said McGinty. "It's a claim that by the rules of this lodge takes precedence. Now, Brother, we attend you."

McMurdo took the letter from his pocket.

"Eminent Bodymaster and Brethren," he said, "I am the bearer of ill news this day; but it is better that it should be known and discussed, than that a blow should fall upon us without warning which would destroy us all. I have information that the most powerful and richest organizations in this state have bound themselves together for our destruction, and that at this very moment there is a Pinkerton detective, one Birdy Edwards, at work in the valley collecting the evidence which may put a rope round the necks of many of us, and send every man in this room into a felon's cell. That is the situation for the discussion of which I have made a claim of urgency."

There was a dead silence in the room. It was broken by the chairman.

"What is your evidence for this, Brother McMurdo?" he asked.

"It is in this letter which has come into my hands," said McMurdo. He read the passage aloud. "It is a matter of honour with me that I can give no further particulars about the letter, nor put it into your hands; but I assure you that there is nothing else in it which can affect the interests of the lodge. I put the case before you as it has reached me."

"Let me say, Mr. Chairman," said one of the older brethren, "that I have heard of Birdy Edwards, and that he has the name of being the best man in the Pinkerton service."

"Does anyone know him by sight?" asked McGinty.

"Yes," said McMurdo, "I do."

There was a murmur of astonishment through the hall.

"I believe we hold him in the hollow of our hands," he continued with an exulting smile upon his face. "If we act quickly and wisely, we can cut this thing short. If I have your confidence and your help, it is little that we have to fear."

"What have we to fear, anyhow? What can he know of our affairs?"

"You might say so if all were as stanch as you, Councillor. But this man has all the millions of the capitalists at his back. Do you think there is no weaker brother among all our lodges that could not be bought? He will get at our secrets—maybe has got them already. There's only one sure cure."

"That he never leaves the valley," said Baldwin.

McMurdo nodded. "Good for you, Brother Baldwin," he said. "You and I have had our differences, but you have said the true word to-night."

"Where is he, then? Where shall we know him?"

"Eminent Bodymaster," said McMurdo, earnestly, "I would put it to you that this is too vital a thing for us to discuss in open lodge. God forbid that I should throw a doubt on anyone here; but if so much as a word of gossip got to the ears of this man, there would be an end of any chance of our getting him. I would ask the lodge to choose a trusty committee, Mr. Chairman—yourself, if I might suggest it, and Brother Baldwin here, and five more. Then I can talk freely of what I know and of what I advise should be done."

The proposition was at once adopted, and the committee chosen. Besides the chairman and Baldwin there were the vulture-faced secretary, Harraway, Tiger Cormac, the brutal young assassin, Carter, the treasurer, and the brothers Willaby, fearless and desperate men who would stick at nothing.

The usual revelry of the lodge was short and subdued: for there was a cloud upon the men's spirits, and many there for the first time began to see the cloud of avenging Law drifting up in that serene sky under which they had dwelt so long. The horrors they had dealt out to others had been so much a part of their settled lives that the thought of retribution had become a remote one, and so seemed the more startling now that it came so closely upon them. They broke up early and left their leaders to their council.

"Now, McMurdo!" said McGinty when they were alone. The seven men sat frozen in their seats.

"I said just now that I knew Birdy Edwards," McMurdo explained. "I need not tell you that he is not here under that name. He's a brave man, but not a crazy one. He passes under the name of Steve Wilson, and he is lodging at Hobson's Patch."

"How do you know this?"

"Because I fell into talk with him. I thought little of it at the time, nor would have given it a second thought but for this letter; but now I'm sure it's the man. I met him on the cars when I went down the line on Wednesday—a hard case if ever there was one. He said he was a reporter. I believed it for the moment. Wanted to know all he could about the Scowrers and what he called 'the outrages' for a New York paper. Asked me every kind of question so as to get something. You bet I was giving nothing away. 'I'd pay for it and pay well,' said he, 'if I could get some stuff that would suit my editor.' I said what I thought would please him best, and he handed me a twenty-dollar bill for my information. 'There's ten times that for you,' said he, 'if you can find me all that I want.'"

"What did you tell him, then?"

"Any stuff I could make up."

"How do you know he wasn't a newspaper man?"

"I'll tell you. He got out at Hobson's Patch, and so did I. I chanced into the telegraph bureau, and he was leaving it.

" 'See here,' said the operator after he'd gone out, 'I guess we should charge double rates for this.'—'I guess you should,' said I. He had filled the form with stuff that might have been Chinese, for all we could make of it. 'He fires a sheet of this off every day,' said the clerk. 'Yes,' said I; 'it's special news for his paper, and he's scared that the others should tap it.' That was what the operator thought and what I thought at the time; but I think differently now."

"By Gar! I believe you are right," said McGinty. "But what do you allow that we should do about it?"

"Why not go right down now and fix him?" someone suggested.

"Ay, the sooner the better."

"I'd start this next minute if I knew where we could find him," said McMurdo. "He's in Hobson's Patch; but I don't know the house. I've got a plan, though, if you'll only take my advice."

"Well, what is it?"

"I'll go to the Patch to-morrow morning. I'll find him through the operator. He can locate him, I guess. Well, then I'll tell him that I'm a Freeman myself. I'll offer him all the secrets of the lodge for a price. You bet he'll tumble to it. I'll tell him the papers are at my house, and that it's as much as my life would be worth to let him come while folk were about. He'll see that that's horse sense. Let him come at ten o'clock at night, and he shall see everything. That will fetch him sure."

"Well?"

"You can plan the rest for yourselves. Widow MacNamara's is a lonely house. She's as true as steel and as deaf as a post. There's only Scanlan and me in the house. If I get his promise—and I'll let you know if I do— I'd have the whole seven of you come to me by nine o'clock. We'll get him in. If ever he gets out alive—well, he can talk of Birdy Edwards's luck for the rest of his days!"

"There's going to be a vacancy at Pinkerton's or I'm mistaken. Leave it at that, McMurdo. At nine to-morrow we'll be with you. You once get the door shut behind him, and you can leave the rest with us."

CHAPTER 7

The Trapping of Birdy Edwards

As McMurdo had said, the house in which he lived was a lonely one and very well suited for such a crime as they had planned. It was on the extreme fringe of the town and stood well back from the road. In any other case the conspirators would have simply called out their man, as they had many a time before, and emptied their pistols into his body; but in this instance it was very necessary to find out how much he knew, how he knew it, and what had been passed on to his employers.

It was possible that they were already too late and that the work had been done. If that was indeed so, they could at least have their revenge upon the man who had done it. But they were hopeful that nothing of great importance had yet come to the detective's knowledge, as otherwise, they argued, he would not have troubled to write down and forward such trivial information as McMurdo claimed to have given him. However, all this they would learn from his own lips. Once in their power, they would find a way to make him speak. It was not the first time that they had handled an unwilling witness.

McMurdo went to Hobson's Patch as agreed. The police seemed to take particular interest in him that morning, and Captain Marvin—he who had claimed the old acquaintance with him at Chicago—actually addressed him as he waited at the station. McMurdo turned away and refused to speak with him. He was back from his mission in the afternoon, and saw McGinty at the Union House.

"He is coming," he said.

"Good!" said McGinty. The giant was in his shirt sleeves, with chains and seals gleaming athwart his ample waistcoat and a diamond twinkling through the fringe of his bristling beard. Drink and politics had made the Boss a very rich as well as powerful man. The more terrible, therefore, seemed that glimpse of the prison or the gallows which had risen before him the night before.

"Do you reckon he knows much?" he asked anxiously.

McMurdo shook his head gloomily. "He's been here some time—six weeks at the least. I guess he didn't come into these parts to look at the prospect. If he has been working among us all that time with the railroad money at his back, I should expect that he has got results, and that he has passed them on."

"There's not a weak man in the lodge," cried McGinty. "True as steel, every man of them. And yet, by the Lord! there is that skunk Morris. What about him? If any man gives us away, it would be he. I've a mind to send a couple of the boys round before evening to give him a beating up and see what they can get from him."

"Well, there would be no harm in that," McMurdo answered. "I won't deny that I have a liking for Morris and would be sorry to see him come to harm. He has spoken to me once or twice over lodge matters, and though he may not see them the same as you or I, he never seemed the sort that squeals. But still it is not for me to stand between him and you."

"I'll fix the old devil!" said McGinty with an oath. "I've had my eye on him this year past."

"Well, you know best about that," McMurdo answered. "But whatever you do must be to-morrow; for we must lie low until the Pinkerton affair is settled up. We can't afford to set the police buzzing, to-day of all days."

"True for you," said McGinty. "And we'll learn from Birdy Edwards himself where he got his news if we have to cut his heart out first. Did he seem to scent a trap?"

McMurdo laughed. "I guess I took him on his weak point," he said. "If he could get on a good trail of the Scowrers, he's ready to follow it into hell. I took his money," McMurdo grinned as he produced a wad of dollar notes, "and as much more when he has seen all my papers."

"What papers?"

"Well, there are no papers. But I filled him up about constitutions and books of rules and forms of membership. He expects to get right down to the end of everything before he leaves."

"Faith, he's right there," said McGinty grimly. "Didn't he ask you why you didn't bring him the papers?"

"As if I would carry such things, and me a suspected man, and Captain Marvin after speaking to me this very day at the depot!"

"Ay, I heard of that," said McGinty. "I guess the heavy end of this business is coming on to you. We could put him down an old shaft when we've done with him; but however we work it we can't get past the man living at Hobson's Patch and you being there to-day."

McMurdo shrugged his shoulders. "If we handle it right, they can never prove the killing," said he. "No one can see him come to the house after dark, and I'll lay to it that no one will see him go. Now see here, Councillor, I'll show you my plan and I'll ask you to fit the others into it. You will all come in good time. Very well. He comes at ten. He is to tap three times, and me to open the door for him. Then I'll get behind him and shut it. He's our man then."

"That's all easy and plain."

"Yes; but the next step wants considering. He's a hard proposition. He's heavily armed. I've fooled him proper, and yet he is likely to be on his guard. Suppose I show him right into a room with seven men in it where he expected to find me alone. There is going to be shooting, and somebody is going to be hurt."

"That's so."

"And the noise is going to bring every damned copper in the township on top of it."

"I guess you are right."

"This is how I should work it. You will all be in the big room—same as you saw when you had a chat with me. I'll open the door for him, show him into the parlour beside the door, and leave him there while I get the papers. That will give me the chance of telling you how things are shaping. Then I will go back to him with some faked papers. As he is reading them I will jump for him and get my grip on his pistol arm. You'll hear me call and in you will rush. The quicker the better; for he is as strong a man as I, and I may have more than I can manage. But I allow that I can hold till you come."

"It's a good plan," said McGinty. "The lodge will owe you a debt for this. I guess when I move out of the chair I can put a name to the man that's coming after me."

"Sure, Councillor, I am little more than a recruit," said McMurdo; but his face showed what he thought of the great man's compliment.

When he had returned home he made his own preparations for the grim evening in front of him. First he cleaned, oiled, and loaded his Smith & Wesson revolver. Then he surveyed the room in which the detective was to be trapped. It was a large apartment, with a long deal table in the centre, and the big stove at one side. At each of the other sides were windows. There were no shutters on these: only light curtains which drew across. McMurdo examined these attentively. No doubt it must have struck him that the apartment was very exposed for so secret a meeting. Yet its distance from the road made it of less consequence. Finally he discussed the matter with his fellow lodger. Scanlan, though a Scowrer, was an inoffensive little man who was too weak to stand against the opinion of his comrades, but was secretly horrified by the deeds of blood at which he had sometimes been forced to assist. McMurdo told him shortly what was intended.

"And if I were you, Mike Scanlan, I would take a night off and keep clear of it. There will be bloody work here before morning."

"Well, indeed then, Mac," Scanlan answered. "It's not the will but the nerve that is wanting in me. When I saw Manager Dunn go down at the colliery yonder it was just more than I could stand. I'm not made for it, same as you or McGinty. If the lodge will think none the worse of me, I'll just do as you advise and leave you to yourselves for the evening."

The men came in good time as arranged. They were outwardly respectable citizens, well clad and cleanly; but a judge of faces would have read little hope for Birdy Edwards in those hard mouths and remorseless eyes. There was not a man in the room whose hands had not been reddened a dozen times before. They were as hardened to human murder as a butcher to sheep.

Foremost, of course, both in appearance and in guilt, was the formidable Boss. Harraway, the secretary, was a lean, bitter man with a long, scraggy neck and nervous, jerky limbs, a man of incorruptible fidelity where the finances of the order were concerned, and with no notion of justice or honesty to anyone beyond. The treasurer, Carter, was a middle-aged man, with an impassive, rather sulky expression, and a yellow parchment skin. He was a capable organizer, and the actual details of nearly every outrage had sprung from his plotting brain. The two Willabys were men of action, tall, lithe young fellows with determined faces, while their companion, Tiger Cormac, a heavy, dark youth, was feared even by his own comrades for the ferocity of his disposition. These were the men who assembled that night under the roof of McMurdo for the killing of the Pinkerton detective.

Their host had placed whisky upon the table, and they had hastened to prime themselves for the work before them. Baldwin and Cormac were already half-drunk, and the liquor had brought out all their ferocity. Cormac placed his hands on the stove for an instant—it had been lighted, for the nights were still cold.

"That will do," said he, with an oath.

"Ay," said Baldwin, catching his meaning. "If he is strapped to that, we will have the truth out of him."

"We'll have the truth out of him, never fear," said McMurdo. He had nerves of steel, this man; for though the whole weight of the affair was on him his manner was as cool and unconcerned as ever. The others marked it and applauded.

"You are the one to handle him," said the Boss approvingly. "Not a warning will he get till your hand is on his throat. It's pity there are no shutters to your windows."

McMurdo went from one to the other and drew the curtains tighter. "Sure no one can spy upon us now. It's close upon the hour."

"Maybe he won't come. Maybe he'll get a sniff of danger," said the secretary.

"He'll come, never fear," McMurdo answered. "He is as eager to come as you can be to see him. Hark to that!"

They all sat like wax figures, some with their glasses arrested halfway to their lips. Three loud knocks had sounded at the door.

"Hush!" McMurdo raised his hand in caution. An exulting glance went round the circle, and hands were laid upon hidden weapons.

"Not a sound, for your lives!" McMurdo whispered, as he went from the room, closing the door carefully behind him.

With strained ears the murderers waited. They counted the steps of their comrade down the passage. Then they heard him open the outer door. There were a few words as of greeting. Then they were aware of a strange step inside and of an unfamiliar voice. An instant later came the slam of the door and the turning of the key in the lock. Their prey was safe within the trap. Tiger Cormac laughed horribly, and Boss McGinty clapped his great hand across his mouth.

"Be quiet, you fool!" he whispered. "You'll be the undoing of us yet!"

There was a mutter of conversation from the next room. It seemed interminable. Then the door opened, and McMurdo appeared, his finger upon his lip.

He came to the end of the table and looked round at them. A subtle change had come over him. His manner was as of one who has great work to do. His face had set into granite firmness. His eyes shone with a fierce excitement behind his spectacles. He had become a visible leader of men. They stared at him with eager interest; but he said nothing. Still with the same singular gaze he looked from man to man.

"Well!" cried Boss McGinty at last. "Is he here? Is Birdy Edwards here?"

"Yes," McMurdo answered slowly. "Birdy Edwards is here. I am Birdy Edwards!"

There were ten seconds after that brief speech during which the room might have been empty, so profound was the silence. The hissing of a kettle upon the stove rose sharp and strident to the ear. Seven white faces, all turned upward to this man who dominated them, were set motionless with utter terror. Then, with a sudden shivering of glass, a bristle of glistening rifle barrels broke through each window, while the curtains were torn from their hangings.

At the sight Boss McGinty gave the roar of a wounded bear and plunged for the half-opened door. A levelled revolver met him there with the stern blue eyes of Captain Marvin of the Mine Police gleaming behind the sights. The Boss recoiled and fell back into his chair.

"You're safer there, Councillor," said the man whom they had known as McMurdo. "And you, Baldwin, if you don't take your hand off your pistol, you'll cheat the hangman yet. Pull it out, or by the Lord that made me——There, that will do. There are forty armed men round this house, and you can figure it out for yourself what chance you have. Take their pistols, Marvin!"

There was no possible resistance under the menace of those rifles. The men were disarmed. Sulky, sheepish, and amazed, they still sat round the table.

"I'd like to say a word to you before we separate," said the man who had trapped them. "I guess we may not meet again until you see me on the stand in the courthouse. I'll give you something to think over between now and then. You know me now for what I am. At last I can put my cards on the table. I am Birdy Edwards of Pinkerton's. I was chosen to break up your gang. I had a hard and dangerous game to play. Not a soul, not one soul, not my nearest and dearest, knew that I was playing it. Only Captain Marvin here and my employers knew that. But it's over to-night, thank God, and I am the winner!"

The seven pale, rigid faces looked up at him. There was unappeasable hatred in their eyes. He read the relentless threat.

"Maybe you think that the game is not over yet. Well, I take my chance of that. Anyhow, some of you will take no further hand, and there are sixty more besides yourselves that will see a jail this night. I'll tell you this, that when I was put upon this job I never believed there was such a society as yours. I thought it was paper talk, and that I would prove it so. They told me it was to do with the Freemen; so I went to Chicago and was made one. Then I was surer than ever that it was just paper talk; for I found no harm in the society, but a deal of good.

"Still, I had to carry out my job, and I came to the coal valleys. When I reached this place I learned that I was wrong and that it wasn't a dime novel after all. So I stayed to look after it. I never killed a man in Chicago. I never minted a dollar in my life. Those I gave you were as good as any others; but I never spent money better. But I knew the way into your good wishes, and so I pretended to you that the law was after me. It all worked just as I thought.

"So I joined your infernal lodge, and I took my share in your councils. Maybe they will say that I was as bad as you. They can say what they like, so long as I get you. But what is the truth? The night I joined you beat up old man Stanger. I could not warn him, for there was no time; but I held your hand, Baldwin, when you would have killed him. If ever I have suggested things, so as to keep my place among you, they were things which I knew I could prevent. I could not save Dunn and Menzies, for I did not know enough; but I will see that their murderers are hanged. I gave Chester Wilcox warning, so that when I blew his house in he and his folk were in hiding. There was many a crime that I could not stop; but if you look back and think how often your man came home the other road, or was down in town when you went for him, or stayed indoors when you thought he would come out, you'll see my work."

"You blasted traitor!" hissed McGinty through his closed teeth.

"Ay, John McGinty, you may call me that if it eases your smart. You and your like have been the enemy of God and man in these parts. It took a man to get between you and the poor devils of men and women that you held under your grip. There was just one way of doing it, and I did it. You call me a traitor; but I guess there's many a thousand will call me a deliverer that went down into hell to save them. I've had three months of it. I wouldn't have three such months again if they let me loose in the treasury at Washington for it. I had to stay till I had it all, every man and every secret right here in this hand. I'd have waited a little longer if it hadn't come to my knowledge that my secret was coming out. A letter had come into the town that would have set you wise to it all. Then I had to act and act quickly.

"I've nothing more to say to you, except that when my time comes I'll die the easier when I think of the work I have done in this valley. Now, Marvin, I'll keep you no more. Take them in and get it over."

There is little more to tell. Scanlan had been given a sealed note to be left at the address of Miss Ettie Shafter, a mission which he had accepted with a wink and a knowing smile. In the early hours of the morning a beautiful woman and a much muffled man boarded a special train which had been sent by the railroad company, and made a swift, unbroken journey out of the land of danger. It was the last time that ever either Ettie or her lover set foot in the Valley of Fear. Ten days later they were married in Chicago, with old Jacob Shafter as witness of the wedding.

The trial of the Scowrers was held far from the place where their adherents might have terrified the guardians of the law. In vain they struggled. In vain the money of the lodge—money squeezed by blackmail out of the whole countryside—was spent like water in the attempt to save them. That cold, clear, unimpassioned statement from one who knew every detail of their lives, their organization, and their crimes was unshaken by all the wiles of their defenders. At last after so many years they were broken and scattered. The cloud was lifted forever from the valley.

McGinty met his fate upon the scaffold, cringing and whining when the last hour came. Eight of his chief followers shared his fate. Fifty-odd had various degrees of imprisonment. The work of Birdy Edwards was complete.

And yet, as he had guessed, the game was not over yet. There was another hand to be played, and yet another and another. Ted Baldwin, for one, had escaped the scaffold; so had the Willabys; so had several others of the fiercest spirits of the gang. For ten years they were out of the world, and then came a day when they were free once more—a day which Edwards, who knew his men, was very sure would be an end of his life of peace. They had sworn an oath on all that they thought holy to have his blood as a vengeance for their comrades. And well they strove to keep vow!

From Chicago he was chased, after two attempts so near success that it was sure that the third would get him. From Chicago he went under a changed name to California, and it was there that the light went for a time out of his life when Ettie Edwards died. Once again he was nearly killed, and once again under the name of Douglas he worked in a lonely cañon, where with an English partner named Barker he amassed a fortune. At last there came a warning to him that the bloodhounds were on his track once more, and he cleared—only just in time—for England. And thence came the John Douglas who for a second time married a worthy mate, and lived for five years as a Sussex country gentleman, a life which ended with the strange happenings of which we have heard.

EPILOGUE

The Police trial had passed, in which the case of John Douglas was referred to a higher court. So had the Quarter Sessions, at which he was acquitted as having acted in self-defense.

"Get him out of England at any cost," wrote Holmes to the wife. "There are forces here which may be more dangerous than those he has escaped. There is no safety for your husband in England."

Two months had gone by, and the case had to some extent passed from our minds. Then one morning there came an enigmatic note slipped into our letter box. "Dear me, Mr. Holmes. Dear me!" said this singular epistle. There was neither superscription nor signature. I laughed at the quaint message; but Holmes showed unwonted seriousness.

"Deviltry, Watson!" he remarked, and sat long with a clouded brow.

Late last night Mrs. Hudson, our landlady, brought up a message, that a gentleman wished to see Holmes, and that the matter was of the utmost importance. Close at the heels of his messenger came Cecil Barker, our friend of the moated Manor House. His face was drawn and haggard.

"I've had bad news—terrible news, Mr. Holmes," said he.

"I feared as much," said Holmes.

"You have not had a cable, have you?"

"I have had a note from someone who has."

"It's poor Douglas. They tell me his name is Edwards; but he will always be Jack Douglas of Benito Cañon to me. I told you that they started together for South Africa in the *Palmyra* three weeks ago."

"Exactly."

"The ship reached Cape Town last night. I received this cable from Mrs. Douglas this morning:

Jack has been lost overboard in gale off St. Helena. No one knows how accident occurred.

IVY DOUGLAS.

"Ha! It came like that, did it?" said Holmes thoughtfully. "Well, I've no doubt it was well stage-managed."

"You mean that you think there was no accident?"

"None in the world."

"He was murdered?"

"Surely!"

"So I think also. These infernal Scowrers, this cursed vindictive nest of criminals——"

"No, no, my good sir," said Holmes. "There is a master hand here. It is no case of sawed-off shotguns and clumsy six-shooters. You can tell an old master by the sweep of his brush. I can tell a Moriarty when I see one. This crime is from London, not from America."

"But for what motive?"

"Because it is done by a man who cannot afford to fail, one whose whole unique position depends upon the fact that all he does must succeed. A great brain and a huge organization have been turned to the extinction of one man. It is crushing the nut with the triphammer,* an absurd extravagance of energy—but the nut is very effectually crushed all the same."

"How came this man to have anything to do with it?"

"I can only say that the first word that ever came to us of the business was from one of his lieutenants. These Americans were well advised. Having an English job to do, they took into partnership, as any foreign criminal could do, this great consultant in crime. From that moment their man was doomed. At first he would content himself by using his machinery in order to find their victim. Then he would indicate how the matter might be treated. Finally, when he read in the reports of the failure of this agent, he would step in himself with a master touch. You heard me warn this man at Birlstone Manor House that the coming danger was greater than the past. Was I right?"

Barker beat his head with his clenched fist in his impotent anger. "Do not tell me that we have to sit down under this? Do you say that no one can ever get level with this king devil?"

"No, I don't say that," said Holmes, and his eyes seemed to be looking far into the future. "I don't say that he can't be beat. But you must give me time—you must give me time!"

We all sat in silence for some minutes while those fateful eyes still strained to pierce the veil.

---

*Power-operated hammer lifted by a lever and then dropped.

HIS LAST BOW

PREFACE

His Last Bow

The friends of Mr. Sherlock Holmes will be glad to learn that he is still alive and well, though somewhat crippled by occasional attacks of rheumatism. He has, for many years, lived in a small farm upon the downs five miles from Eastbourne, where his time is divided between philosophy and agriculture. During this period of rest he has refused the most princely offers to take up various cases, having determined that his retirement was a permanent one. The approach of the German war caused him, however, to lay his remarkable combination of intellectual and practical activity at the disposal of the government, with historical results which are recounted in His Last Bow. Several previous experiences which have lain long in my portfolio have been added to His Last Bow so as to complete the volume.

JOHN H. WATSON, M. D.

THE ADVENTURE OF WISTERIA LODGE

1. The Singular Experience of Mr. John Scott Eccles

I find it recorded in my notebook that it was a bleak and windy day towards the end of March in the year 1892. Holmes had received a telegram while we sat at our lunch, and he had scribbled a reply. He made no remark, but the matter remained in his thoughts, for he stood in front of the fire afterwards with a thoughtful face, smoking his pipe, and casting an occasional glance at the message. Suddenly he turned upon me with a mischievous twinkle in his eyes.

"I suppose, Watson, we must look upon you as a man of letters," said he. "How do you define the word 'grotesque'?"

"Strange—remarkable," I suggested.

He shook his head at my definition.

"There is surely something more than that," said he; "some underlying suggestion of the tragic and the terrible. If you cast your mind back to some of those narratives with which you have afflicted a long-suffering public, you will recognize how often the grotesque has deepened into the criminal. Think of that little affair of the red-headed men.* That was grotesque enough in the outset, and yet it ended in a desperate attempt at robbery. Or, again, there was that most grotesque affair of the five orange pips,† which led straight to a murderous conspiracy. The word puts me on the alert."

"Have you it there?" I asked.

He read the telegram aloud.

"Have just had most incredible and grotesque experience. May I consult you?

SCOTT ECCLES,
Post-Office, Charing Cross."

"Man or woman?" I asked.

"Oh, man, of course. No woman would ever send a reply-paid telegram. She would have come."

"Will you see him?"

"My dear Watson, you know how bored I have been since we locked

---

*Reference to the early Holmes story "The Red-Headed League."
†Reference to another early story, "The Five Orange Pips."

up Colonel Carruthers. My mind is like a racing engine, tearing itself to pieces because it is not connected up with the work for which it was built. Life is commonplace; the papers are sterile; audacity and romance seem to have passed forever from the criminal world. Can you ask me, then, whether I am ready to look into any new problem, however trivial it may prove? But here, unless I am mistaken, is our client."

A measured step was heard upon the stairs, and a moment later a stout, tall, gray-whiskered and solemnly respectable person was ushered into the room. His life history was written in his heavy features and pompous manner. From his spats to his gold-rimmed spectacles he was a Conservative, a churchman, a good citizen, orthodox and conventional to the last degree. But some amazing experience had disturbed his native composure and left its traces in his bristling hair, his flushed, angry cheeks, and his flurried, excited manner. He plunged instantly into his business.

"I have had a most singular and unpleasant experience, Mr. Holmes," said he. "Never in my life have I been placed in such a situation. It is most improper—most outrageous. I must insist upon some explanation." He swelled and puffed in his anger.

"Pray sit down, Mr. Scott Eccles," said Holmes in a soothing voice. "May I ask, in the first place, why you came to me at all?"

"Well, sir, it did not appear to be a matter which concerned the police, and yet, when you have heard the facts, you must admit that I could not leave it where it was. Private detectives are a class with whom I have absolutely no sympathy, but none the less, having heard your name——"

"Quite so. But, in the second place, why did you not come at once?"

"What do you mean?"

Holmes glanced at his watch.

"It is a quarter-past two," he said. "Your telegram was dispatched about one. But no one can glance at your toilet and attire without seeing that your disturbance dates from the moment of your waking."

Our client smoothed down his unbrushed hair and felt his unshaven chin.

"You are right, Mr. Holmes. I never gave a thought to my toilet. I was only too glad to get out of such a house. But I have been running round making inquiries before I came to you. I went to the house agents, you know, and they said that Mr. Garcia's rent was paid up all right and that everything was in order at Wisteria Lodge."

"Come, come, sir," said Holmes, laughing. "You are like my friend, Dr. Watson, who has a bad habit of telling his stories wrong end foremost. Please arrange your thoughts and let me know, in their due sequence, exactly what those events are which have sent you out unbrushed and unkempt, with dress boots and waistcoat buttoned awry, in search of advice and assistance."

Our client looked down with a rueful face at his own unconventional appearance.

"I'm sure it must look very bad, Mr. Holmes, and I am not aware that in my whole life such a thing has ever happened before. But I will tell you the whole queer business, and when I have done so you will admit, I am sure, that there has been enough to excuse me."

But his narrative was nipped in the bud. There was a bustle outside, and Mrs. Hudson opened the door to usher in two robust and official-looking individuals, one of whom was well known to us as Inspector Gregson of Scotland Yard, an energetic, gallant, and, within his limitations, a capable officer. He shook hands with Holmes and introduced his comrade as Inspector Baynes, of the Surrey Constabulary.

"We are hunting together, Mr. Holmes, and our trail lay in this direction." He turned his bulldog eyes upon our visitor. "Are you Mr. John Scott Eccles, of Popham House, Lee?"

"I am."

"We have been following you about all the morning."

"You traced him through the telegram, no doubt," said Holmes.

"Exactly, Mr. Holmes. We picked up the scent at Charing Cross Post-Office and came on here."

"But why do you follow me? What do you want?"

"We wish a statement, Mr. Scott Eccles, as to the events which led up to the death last night of Mr. Aloysius Garcia, of Wisteria Lodge, near Esher."

Our client had sat up with staring eyes and every tinge of colour struck from his astonished face.

"Dead? Did you say he was dead?"

"Yes, sir, he is dead."

"But how? An accident?"

"Murder, if ever there was one upon earth."

"Good God! This is awful! You don't mean—you don't mean that I am suspected?"

"A letter of yours was found in the dead man's pocket, and we know by it that you had planned to pass last night at his house."

"So I did."

"Oh, you did, did you?"

Out came the official notebook.

"Wait a bit, Gregson," said Sherlock Holmes. "All you desire is a plain statement, is it not?"

"And it is my duty to warn Mr. Scott Eccles that it may be used against him."

"Mr. Eccles was going to tell us about it when you entered the room. I think, Watson, a brandy and soda would do him no harm. Now, sir, I suggest that you take no notice of this addition to your audience, and that you proceed with your narrative exactly as you would have done had you never been interrupted."

Our visitor had gulped off the brandy and the colour had returned to his face. With a dubious glance at the inspector's notebook, he plunged at once into his extraordinary statement.

"I am a bachelor," said he, "and being of a sociable turn I cultivate a large number of friends. Among these are the family of a retired brewer called Melville, living at Albemarle Mansion, Kensington. It was at his table that I met some weeks ago a young fellow named Garcia. He was, I understood, of Spanish descent and connected in some way with the embassy. He spoke perfect English, was pleasing in his manners, and as good-looking a man as ever I saw in my life.

"In some way we struck up quite a friendship, this young fellow and I. He seemed to take a fancy to me from the first, and within two days of our meeting he came to see me at Lee. One thing led to another, and it ended in his inviting me out to spend a few days at his house, Wisteria Lodge. between Esher and Oxshott. Yesterday evening I went to Esher to fulfil this engagement.

"He had described his household to me before I went there. He lived with a faithful servant, a countryman of his own, who looked after all his needs. This fellow could speak English and did his housekeeping for him. Then there was a wonderful cook, he said, a half-breed whom he had picked up in his travels, who could serve an excellent dinner. I remember that he remarked what a queer household it was to find in the heart of Surrey, and that I agreed with him, though it has proved a good deal queerer than I thought.

"I drove to the place—about two miles on the south side of Esher. The house was a fair-sized one, standing back from the road, with a curving drive which was banked with high ever-green shrubs. It was an old, tumble-down building in a crazy state of disrepair. When the trap pulled up on the grass-grown drive in front of the blotched and weather-stained door, I had doubts as to my wisdom in visiting a man whom I knew so slightly. He opened the door himself, however, and greeted me with a great show of cordiality. I was handed over to the manservant, a melancholy, swarthy individual, who led the way, my bag in his hand, to my bedroom. The whole place was depressing. Our dinner was tête-à-tête, and though my host did his best to be entertaining, his thoughts seemed to continually wander, and he talked so vaguely and wildly that I could hardly understand him. He continually drummed his fingers on the table, gnawed his nails, and gave other signs of nervous impatience. The dinner itself was neither well served nor well cooked, and the gloomy presence of the taciturn servant did not help to enliven us. I can assure you that many times in the course of the evening I wished that I could invent some excuse which would take me back to Lee.

"One thing comes back to my memory which may have a bearing upon the business that you two gentlemen are investigating. I thought nothing of it at the time. Near the end of dinner a note was handed in by the servant. I noticed that after my host had read it he seemed even more distrait and strange than before. He gave up all pretence at conversation and sat, smoking endless cigarettes, lost in his own thoughts, but he made no remark as to the contents. About eleven I was glad to go to bed. Some time later Garcia looked in at my door—the room was dark at the time—and asked me if I had rung. I said that I had not. He apologized for having disturbed me so late, saying that it was nearly one o'clock. I dropped off after this and slept soundly all night.

"And now I come to the amazing part of my tale. When I woke it was broad daylight. I glanced at my watch, and the time was nearly nine. I had particularly asked to be called at eight, so I was very much astonished at this forgetfulness. I sprang up and rang for the servant. There was no response. I rang again and again, with the same result. Then I came to the conclusion that the bell was out of order. I huddled on my clothes and hurried downstairs in an exceedingly bad temper to order some hot water. You can imagine my surprise when I found that there was no one there. I shouted in the hall. There was no answer. Then I ran from room to room. All were deserted. My host had shown me which was his bedroom the night before, so I knocked at the door. No reply. I turned the handle and walked in. The room was empty, and the bed had never been slept in. He had gone with the rest. The foreign host, the foreign footman, the foreign cook, all had vanished in the night! That was the end of my visit to Wisteria Lodge."

Sherlock Holmes was rubbing his hands and chuckling as he added this bizarre incident to his collection of strange episodes.

"Your experience is, so far as I know, perfectly unique," said he. "May I ask, sir, what you did then?"

"I was furious. My first idea was that I had been the victim of some absurd practical joke. I packed my things, banged the hall door behind me, and set off for Esher, with my bag in my hand. I called at Allan Brothers', the chief land agents in the village, and found that it was from this firm that the villa had been rented. It struck me that the whole proceeding could hardly be for the purpose of making a fool of me, and that the main object must be to get out of the rent. It is late in March, so quarter-day* is at hand. But this theory would not work. The agent was obliged to me for my warning, but told me that the rent had been paid in advance. Then I made my way to town and called at the Spanish embassy. The man was unknown there. After this I went to see Melville, at whose house I had first met Garcia, but I found that he really knew rather less about him than I did. Finally when I got your reply to my wire I came out to you, since I gather that you are a person who gives advice in difficult cases. But now, Mr. Inspector, I understand, from what you said when you entered the room, that you can carry the story on, and that some tragedy has occurred. I can assure you that every word I have said is the truth, and that, outside of what I have told you, I know absolutely nothing about the fate of this man. My only desire is to help the law in every possible way."

"I am sure of it, Mr. Scott Eccles—I am sure of it," said Inspector Gregson in a very amiable tone. "I am bound to say that everything which you have said agrees very closely with the facts as they have come to our

---

*The beginning of a quarter of a year; some payments are made on such days.

notice. For example, there was that note which arrived during dinner. Did you chance to observe what became of it?"

"Yes, I did. Garcia rolled it up and threw it into the fire."

"What do you say to that, Mr. Baynes?"

The country detective was a stout, puffy, red man, whose face was only redeemed from grossness by two extraordinarily bright eyes, almost hidden behind the heavy creases of cheek and brow. With a slow smile he drew a folded and discoloured scrap of paper from his pocket.

"It was a dog-grate, Mr. Holmes, and he overpitched it. I picked this out unburned from the back of it."

Holmes smiled his appreciation.

"You must have examined the house very carefully to find a single pellet of paper."

"I did, Mr. Holmes. It's my way. Shall I read it, Mr. Gregson?"

The Londoner nodded.

"The note is written upon ordinary cream-laid paper without watermark. It is a quarter-sheet. The paper is cut off in two snips with a short-bladed scissors. It has been folded over three times and sealed with purple wax, put on hurriedly and pressed down with some flat oval object. It is addressed to Mr. Garcia, Wisteria Lodge. It says:

Our own colours, green and white. Green open, white shut. Main stair, first corridor, seventh right, green baize. Godspeed. D.

"It is a woman's writing, done with a sharp-pointed pen, but the address is either done with another pen or by someone else. It is thicker and bolder, as you see."

"A very remarkable note," said Holmes, glancing it over. "I must compliment you, Mr. Baynes, upon your attention to detail in your examination of it. A few trifling points might perhaps be added. The oval seal is undoubtedly a plain sleeve-link—what else is of such a shape? The scissors were bent nail scissors. Short as the two snips are, you can distinctly see the same slight curve in each."

The country detective chuckled.

"I thought I had squeezed all the juice out of it, but I see there was a little over," he said. "I'm bound to say that I make nothing of the note except that there was something on hand, and that a woman, as usual, was at the bottom of it."

Mr. Scott Eccles had fidgeted in his seat during this conversation.

"I am glad you found the note, since it corroborates my story," said he. "But I beg to point out that I have not yet heard what has happened to Mr. Garcia, nor what has become of his household."

"As to Garcia," said Gregson, "that is easily answered. He was found dead this morning upon Oxshott Common, nearly a mile from his home. His head had been smashed to pulp by heavy blows of a sandbag or some such instrument, which had crushed rather than wounded. It is a lonely corner, and there is no house within a quarter of a mile of the spot. He had apparently been struck down first from behind, but his assailant had gone on beating him long after he was dead. It was a most furious assault. There are no footsteps nor any clue to the criminals."

"Robbed?"

"No, there was no attempt at robbery."

"This is very painful—very painful and terrible," said Mr. Scott Eccles in a querulous voice, "but it is really uncommonly hard upon me. I had nothing to do with my host going off upon a nocturnal excursion and meeting so sad an end. How do I come to be mixed up with the case?"

"Very simply, sir," Inspector Baynes answered. "The only document found in the pocket of the deceased was a letter from you saying that you would be with him on the night of his death. It was the envelope of this letter which gave us the dead man's name and address. It was after nine this morning when we reached his house and found neither you nor anyone else inside it. I wired to Mr. Gregson to run you down in London while I examined Wisteria Lodge. Then I came into town, joined Mr. Gregson, and here we are."

"I think now," said Gregson, rising, "we had best put this matter into an official shape. You will come round with us to the station, Mr. Scott Eccles, and let us have your statement in writing."

"Certainly, I will come at once. But I retain your services, Mr. Holmes. I desire you to spare no expense and no pains to get at the truth."

My friend turned to the country inspector.

"I suppose that you have no objection to my collaborating with you, Mr. Baynes?"

"Highly honoured, sir, I am sure."

"You appear to have been very prompt and business-like in all that you have done. Was there any clue, may I ask, as to the exact hour that the man met his death?"

"He had been there since one o'clock. There was rain about that time, and his death had certainly been before the rain."

"But that is perfectly impossible, Mr. Baynes," cried our client. "His voice is unmistakable. I could swear to it that it was he who addressed me in my bedroom at that very hour."

"Remarkable, but by no means impossible," said Holmes, smiling.

"You have a clue?" asked Gregson.

"On the face of it the case is not a very complex one, though it certainly presents some novel and interesting features. A further knowledge of facts is necessary before I would venture to give a final and definite opinion. By the way, Mr. Baynes, did you find anything remarkable besides this note in your examination of the house?"

The detective looked at my friend in a singular way.

"There were," said he, "one or two *very* remarkable things. Perhaps when I have finished at the police-station you would care to come out and give me your opinion of them."

"I am entirely at your service," said Sherlock Holmes, ringing the bell.

"You will show these gentlemen out, Mrs. Hudson, and kindly send the boy with this telegram. He is to pay a five-shilling reply."

We sat for some time in silence after our visitors had left. Holmes smoked hard, with his brows drawn down over his keen eyes, and his head thrust forward in the eager way characteristic of the man.

"Well, Watson," he asked, turning suddenly upon me, "what do you make of it?"

"I can make nothing of this mystification of Scott Eccles."

"But the crime?"

"Well, taken with the disappearance of the man's companions, I should say that they were in some way concerned in the murder and had fled from justice."

"That is certainly a possible point of view. On the face of it you must admit, however, that it is very strange that his two servants should have been in a conspiracy against him and should have attacked him on the one night when he had a guest. They had him alone at their mercy every other night in the week."

"Then why did they fly?"

"Quite so. Why did they fly? There is a big fact. Another big fact is the remarkable experience of our client, Scott Eccles. Now, my dear Watson, is it beyond the limits of human ingenuity to furnish an explanation which would cover both these big facts? If it were one which would also admit of the mysterious note with its very curious phraseology, why, then it would be worth accepting as a temporary hypothesis. If the fresh facts which come to our knowledge all fit themselves into the scheme, then our hypothesis may gradually become a solution."

"But what is our hypothesis?"

Holmes leaned back in his chair with half-closed eyes.

"You must admit, my dear Watson, that the idea of a joke is impossible. There were grave events afoot, as the sequel showed, and the coaxing of Scott Eccles to Wisteria Lodge had some connection with them."

"But what possible connection?"

"Let us take it link by link. There is, on the face of it, something unnatural about this strange and sudden friendship between the young Spaniard and Scott Eccles. It was the former who forced the pace. He called upon Eccles at the other end of London on the very day after he first met him, and he kept in close touch with him until he got him down to Esher. Now, what did he want with Eccles? What could Eccles supply? I see no charm in the man. He is not particularly intelligent—not a man likely to be congenial to a quick-witted Latin. Why, then, was he picked out from all the other people whom Garcia met as particularly suited to his purpose? Has he any one outstanding quality? I say that he has. He is the very type of conventional British respectability, and the very man as a witness to impress another Briton. You saw yourself how neither of the inspectors dreamed of questioning his statement, extraordinary as it was."

"But what was he to witness?"

"Nothing, as things turned out, but everything had they gone another way. That is how I read the matter."

"I see, he might have proved an alibi."

"Exactly, my dear Watson; he might have proved an alibi. We will suppose, for argument's sake, that the household of Wisteria Lodge are confederates in some design. The attempt, whatever it may be, is to come off, we will say, before one o'clock. By some juggling of the clocks it is quite possible that they may have got Scott Eccles to bed earlier than he thought, but in any case it is likely that when Garcia went out of his way to tell him that it was one it was really not more than twelve. If Garcia could do whatever he had to do and be back by the hour mentioned he had evidently a powerful reply to any accusation. Here was this irreproachable Englishman ready to swear in any court of law that the accused was in his house all the time. It was an insurance against the worst."

"Yes; yes, I see that. But how about the disappearance of the others?"

"I have not all my facts yet, but I do not think there are any insuperable difficulties. Still, it is an error to argue in front of your data. You find yourself insensibly twisting them round to fit your theories."

"And the message?"

"How did it run? 'Our own colours, green and white.' Sounds like racing. 'Green open, white shut.' That is clearly a signal. 'Main stair, first corridor, seventh right, green baize.' This is an assignation. We may find a jealous husband at the bottom of it all. It was clearly a dangerous quest. She would not have said 'Godspeed' had it not been so. 'D'—that should be a guide."

"The man was a Spaniard. I suggest that 'D' stands for Dolores, a common female name in Spain."

"Good, Watson, very good—but quite inadmissible. A Spaniard would write to a Spaniard in Spanish. The writer of this note is certainly English. Well, we can only possess our souls in patience until this excellent inspector comes back for us. Meanwhile we can thank our lucky fate which has rescued us for a few short hours from the insufferable fatigues of idleness."

An answer had arrived to Holmes's telegram before our Surrey officer had returned. Holmes read it and was about to place it in his notebook when he caught a glimpse of my expectant face. He tossed it across with a laugh.

"We are moving in exalted circles," said he.

The telegram was a list of names and addresses:

Lord Harringby, The Dingle; Sir George Ffolliott, Oxshott Towers; Mr. Hynes Hynes, J.P., Purdey Place; Mr. James Baker Williams, Forton Old Hall; Mr. Henderson, High Gable; Rev. Joshua Stone, Nether Walsling.

"This is a very obvious way of limiting our field of operations," said Holmes. "No doubt Baynes, with his methodical mind, has already adopted some similar plan."

"I don't quite understand."

"Well, my dear fellow, we have already arrived at the conclusion that the message received by Garcia at dinner was an appointment or an assignation. Now, if the obvious reading of it is correct, and in order to keep this tryst one has to ascend a main stair and seek the seventh door in a corridor, it is perfectly clear that the house is a very large one. It is equally certain that this house cannot be more than a mile or two from Oxshott, since Garcia was walking in that direction and hoped, according to my reading of the facts, to be back in Wisteria Lodge in time to avail himself of an alibi, which would only be valid up to one o'clock. As the number of large houses close to Oxshott must be limited, I adopted the obvious method of sending to the agents mentioned by Scott Eccles and obtaining a list of them. Here they are in this telegram, and the other end of our tangled skein must lie among them."

It was nearly six o'clock before we found ourselves in the pretty Surrey village of Esher, with Inspector Baynes as our companion.

Holmes and I had taken things for the night, and found comfortable quarters at the Bull. Finally we set out in the company of the detective on our visit to Wisteria Lodge. It was a cold, dark March evening, with a sharp wind and a fine rain beating upon our faces, a fit setting for the wild common over which our road passed and the tragic goal to which it led us.

2. The Tiger of San Pedro

A cold and melancholy walk of a couple of miles brought us to a high wooden gate, which opened into a gloomy avenue of chestnuts. The curved and shadowed drive led us to a low, dark house, pitch-black against a slate-coloured sky. From the front window upon the left of the door there peeped a glimmer of a feeble light.

"There's a constable in possession," said Baynes. "I'll knock at the window." He stepped across the grass plot and tapped with his hand on the pane. Through the fogged glass I dimly saw a man spring up from a chair beside the fire, and heard a sharp cry from within the room. An instant later a white-faced, hard-breathing policeman had opened the door, the candle wavering in his trembling hand.

"What's the matter, Walters?" asked Baynes sharply.

The man mopped his forehead with his handkerchief and gave a long sigh of relief.

"I am glad you have come, sir. It has been a long evening, and I don't think my nerve is as good as it was."

"Your nerve, Walters? I should not have thought you had a nerve in your body."

"Well, sir, it's this lonely, silent house and the queer thing in the kitchen. Then when you tapped at the window I thought it had come again."

"That what had come again?"

"The devil, sir, for all I know. It was at the window."

"What was at the window, and when?"

"It was just about two hours ago. The light was just fading. I was sitting reading in the chair. I don't know what made me look up, but there was a face looking in at me through the lower pane. Lord, sir, what a face it was! I'll see it in my dreams."

"Tut, tut, Walters. This is not talk for a police-constable."

"I know, sir, I know; but it shook me, sir, and there's no use to deny it. It wasn't black, sir, nor was it white, nor any colour that I know, but a kind of queer shade like clay with a splash of milk in it. Then there was the size of it—it was twice yours, sir. And the look of it—the great staring goggle eyes, and the line of white teeth like a hungry beast. I tell you, sir. I couldn't move a finger, nor get my breath, till it whisked away and was gone. Out I ran and through the shrubbery, but thank God there was no one there."

"If I didn't know you were a good man, Walters, I should put a black mark against you for this. If it were the devil himself a constable on duty should never thank God that he could not lay his hands upon him. I suppose the whole thing is not a vision and a touch of nerves?"

"That, at least, is very easily settled," said Holmes, lighting his little pocket lantern. "Yes," he reported, after a short examination of the grass bed, "a number twelve shoe, I should say. If he was all on the same scale as his foot he must certainly have been a giant."

"What became of him?"

"He seems to have broken through the shrubbery and made for the road."

"Well," said the inspector with a grave and thoughtful face, "whoever he may have been, and whatever he may have wanted, he's gone for the present, and we have more immediate things to attend to. Now, Mr. Holmes, with your permission, I will show you round the house."

The various bedrooms and sitting-rooms had yielded nothing to a careful search. Apparently the tenants had brought little or nothing with them, and all the furniture down to the smallest details had been taken over with the house. A good deal of clothing with the stamp of Marx and Co., High Holborn, had been left behind. Telegraphic inquiries had been already made which showed that Marx knew nothing of his customer save that he was a good payer. Odds and ends, some pipes, a few novels, two of them in Spanish, an old-fashioned pinfire revolver, and a guitar were among the personal property.

"Nothing in all this," said Baynes, stalking, candle in hand, from room to room. "But now, Mr. Holmes, I invite your attention to the kitchen."

It was a gloomy, high-ceilinged room at the back of the house, with a straw litter in one corner, which served apparently as a bed for the cook. The table was piled with half-eaten dishes and dirty plates, the debris of last night's dinner.

"Look at this," said Baynes. "What do you make of it?"

He held up his candle before an extraordinary object which stood at the back of the dresser. It was so wrinkled and shrunken and withered that it was difficult to say what it might have been. One could but say that it was black and leathery and that it bore some resemblance to a dwarfish, human figure. At first, as I examined it, I thought that it was a mummified negro baby, and then it seemed a very twisted and ancient monkey. Finally I was left in doubt as to whether it was animal or human. A double band of white shells was strung round the centre of it.

"Very interesting—very interesting, indeed!" said Holmes, peering at this sinister relic. "Anything more?"

In silence Baynes led the way to the sink and held forward his candle. The limbs and body of some large, white bird, torn savagely to pieces with the feathers still on, were littered all over it. Holmes pointed to the wattles on the severed head.

"A white cock," said he. "Most interesting! It is really a very curious case."

But Mr. Baynes had kept his most sinister exhibit to the last. From under the sink he drew a zinc pail which contained a quantity of blood. Then from the table he took a platter heaped with small pieces of charred bone.

"Something has been killed and something has been burned. We raked all these out of the fire. We had a doctor in this morning. He says that they are not human."

Holmes smiled and rubbed his hands.

"I must congratulate you, Inspector, on handling so distinctive and instructive a case. Your powers, if I may say so without offence, seem superior to your opportunities."

Inspector Baynes's small eyes twinkled with pleasure.

"You're right, Mr. Holmes. We stagnate in the provinces. A case of this sort gives a man a chance, and I hope that I shall take it. What do you make of these bones?"

"A lamb, I should say, or a kid."

"And the white cock?"

"Curious, Mr. Baynes, very curious. I should say almost unique."

"Yes, sir, there must have been some very strange people with some very strange ways in this house. One of them is dead. Did his companions follow him and kill him? If they did we should have them, for every port is watched. But my own views are different. Yes, sir, my own views are very different."

"You have a theory then?"

"And I'll work it myself, Mr. Holmes. It's only due to my own credit to do so. Your name is made, but I have still to make mine. I should be glad to be able to say afterwards that I had solved it without your help."

Holmes laughed good-humouredly.

"Well, well, Inspector," said he. "Do you follow your path and I will follow mine. My results are always very much at your service if you care to apply to me for them. I think that I have seen all that I wish in this house, and that my time may be more profitably employed elsewhere. *Au revoir* and good luck!"

I could tell by numerous subtle signs, which might have been lost upon anyone but myself, that Holmes was on a hot scent. As impassive as ever to the casual observer, there were none the less a subdued eagerness and suggestion of tension in his brightened eyes and brisker manner which assured me that the game was afoot.* After his habit he said nothing, and after mine I asked no questions. Sufficient for me to share the sport and lend my humble help to the capture without distracting that intent brain with needless interruption. All would come round to me in due time.

I waited, therefore—but to my ever-deepening disappointment I waited in vain. Day succeeded day, and my friend took no step forward. One morning he spent in town, and I learned from a casual reference that he had visited the British Museum. Save for this one excursion, he spent his days in long and often solitary walks, or in chatting with a number of village gossips whose acquaintance he had cultivated.

"I'm sure, Watson, a week in the country will be invaluable to you," he remarked. "It is very pleasant to see the first green shoots upon the hedges and the catkins on the hazels once again. With a spud, a tin box, and an elementary book on botany, there are instructive days to be spent." He prowled about with this equipment himself, but it was a poor show of plants which he would bring back of an evening.

Occasionally in our rambles we came across Inspector Baynes. His fat, red face wreathed itself in smiles and his small eyes glittered as he greeted my companion. He said little about the case, but from that little we gathered that he also was not dissatisfied at the course of events. I must admit, however, that I was somewhat surprised when, some five days after the crime, I opened my morning paper to find in large letters:

THE OXSHOTT MYSTERY

A SOLUTION

ARREST OF SUPPOSED ASSASSIN

Holmes sprang in his chair as if he had been stung when I read the headlines.

"By Jove!" he cried. "You don't mean that Baynes has got him?"

"Apparently," said I as I read the following report:

---

*Reference to Shakespeare's *Henry V* (act 3, scene 1): "The game's afoot!"

"Great excitement was caused in Esher and the neighbouring district when it was learned late last night that an arrest had been effected in connection with the Oxshott murder. It will be remembered that Mr. Garcia, of Wisteria Lodge, was found dead on Oxshott Common, his body showing signs of extreme violence, and that on the same night his servant and his cook fled, which appeared to show their participation in the crime. It was suggested, but never proved, that the deceased gentleman may have had valuables in the house, and that their abstraction was the motive of the crime. Every effort was made by Inspector Baynes, who has the case in hand, to ascertain the hiding place of the fugitives, and he had good reason to believe that they had not gone far but were lurking in some retreat which had been already prepared. It was certain from the first, however, that they would eventually be detected, as the cook, from the evidence of one or two tradespeople who have caught a glimpse of him through the window, was a man of most remarkable appearance—being a huge and hideous mulatto, with yellowish features of a pronounced negroid type. This man has been seen since the crime, for he was detected and pursued by Constable Walters on the same evening, when he had the audacity to revisit Wisteria Lodge. Inspector Baynes, considering that such a visit must have some purpose in view and was likely, therefore, to be repeated, abandoned the house but left an ambuscade in the shrubbery. The man walked into the trap and was captured last night after a struggle in which Constable Downing was badly bitten by the savage. We understand that when the prisoner is brought before the magistrates a remand will be applied for by the police, and that great developments are hoped from his capture."

"Really we must see Baynes at once," cried Holmes, picking up his hat. "We will just catch him before he starts." We hurried down the village street and found, as we had expected, that the inspector was just leaving his lodgings.

"You've seen the paper, Mr. Holmes?" he asked, holding one out to us.

"Yes, Baynes, I've seen it. Pray don't think it a liberty if I give you a word of friendly warning."

"Of warning, Mr. Holmes?"

"I have looked into this case with some care, and I am not convinced that you are on the right lines. I don't want you to commit yourself too far unless you are sure."

"You're very kind, Mr. Holmes."

"I assure you I speak for your good."

It seemed to me that something like a wink quivered for an instant over one of Mr. Baynes's tiny eyes.

"We agreed to work on our own lines, Mr. Holmes. That's what I am doing."

"Oh, very good," said Holmes. "Don't blame me."

"No, sir; I believe you mean well by me. But we all have our own systems, Mr. Holmes. You have yours, and maybe I have mine."

"Let us say no more about it."

"You're welcome always to my news. This fellow is a perfect savage, as strong as a cart-horse and as fierce as the devil. He chewed Downing's thumb nearly off before they could master him. He hardly speaks a word of English, and we can get nothing out of him but grunts."

"And you think you have evidence that he murdered his late master?"

"I didn't say so, Mr. Holmes; I didn't say so. We all have our little ways. You try yours and I will try mine. That's the agreement."

Holmes shrugged his shoulders as we walked away together. "I can't make the man out. He seems to be riding for a fall. Well, as he says, we must each try our own way and see what comes of it. But there's something in Inspector Baynes which I can't quite understand."

"Just sit down in that chair, Watson," said Sherlock Holmes when we had returned to our apartment at the Bull. "I want to put you in touch with the situation, as I may need your help to-night. Let me show you the evolution of this case so far as I have been able to follow it. Simple as it has been in its leading features, it has none the less presented surprising difficulties in the way of an arrest. There are gaps in that direction which we have still to fill.

"We will go back to the note which was handed in to Garcia upon the evening of his death. We may put aside this idea of Baynes's that Garcia's servants were concerned in the matter. The proof of this lies in the fact that it was *he* who had arranged for the presence of Scott Eccles, which could only have been done for the purpose of an alibi. It was Garcia, then, who had an enterprise, and apparently a criminal enterprise, in hand that night in the course of which he met his death. I say 'criminal' because only a man with a criminal enterprise desires to establish an alibi. Who, then, is most likely to have taken his life? Surely the person against whom the criminal enterprise was directed. So far it seems to me that we are on safe ground.

"We can now see a reason for the disappearance of Garcia's household. They were *all* confederates in the same unknown crime. If it came off when Garcia returned, any possible suspicion would be warded off by the Englishman's evidence, and all would be well. But the attempt was a dangerous one, and if Garcia did *not* return by a certain hour it was probable that his own life had been sacrificed. It had been arranged, therefore, that in such a case his two subordinates were to make for some prearranged spot where they could escape investigation and be in a position afterwards to renew their attempt. That would fully explain the facts, would it not?"

The whole inexplicable tangle seemed to straighten out before me. I wondered, as I always did, how it had not been obvious to me before.

"But why should one servant return?"

"We can imagine that in the confusion of flight something precious, something which he could not bear to part with, had been left behind. That would explain his persistence, would it not?"

"Well, what is the next step?"

"The next step is the note received by Garcia at the dinner. It indicates a confederate at the other end. Now, where was the other end? I have already shown you that it could only lie in some large house, and that the number of large houses is limited. My first days in this village were devoted to a series of walks in which in the intervals of my botanical researches I made a reconnaissance of all the large houses and an examination of the family history of the occupants. One house, and only one, riveted my attention. It is the famous old Jacobean grange of High Gable, one mile on the farther side of Oxshott, and less than half a mile from the scene of the tragedy. The other mansions belonged to prosaic and respectable people who live far aloof from romance. But Mr. Henderson, of High Gable, was by all accounts a curious man to whom curious adventures might befall. I concentrated my attention, therefore, upon him and his household.

"A singular set of people, Watson—the man himself the most singular of them all. I managed to see him on a plausible pretext, but I seemed to read in his dark, deep-set, brooding eyes that he was perfectly aware of my true business. He is a man of fifty, strong, active, with iron-gray hair, great bunched black eyebrows, the step of a deer, and the air of an emperor—a fierce, masterful man, with a red-hot spirit behind his parchment face. He is either a foreigner or has lived long in the tropics, for he is yellow and sapless, but tough as whipcord. His friend and secretary, Mr. Lucas, is undoubtedly a foreigner, chocolate brown, wily, suave, and cat-like, with a poisonous gentleness of speech. You see, Watson, we have come already upon two sets of foreigners—one at Wisteria Lodge and one at High Gable—so our gaps are beginning to close.

"These two men, close and confidential friends, are the centre of the household; but there is one other person who for our immediate purpose may be even more important. Henderson has two children—girls of eleven and thirteen. Their governess is a Miss Burnet, an Englishwoman of forty or thereabouts. There is also one confidential manservant. This little group forms the real family, for they travel about together, and Henderson is a great traveller, always on the move. It is only within the last few weeks that he has returned, after a year's absence, to High Gable. I may add that he is enormously rich, and whatever his whims may be he can very easily satisfy them. For the rest, his house is full of butlers, footmen, maidservants, and the usual overfed, underworked staff of a large English country-house.

"So much I learned partly from village gossip and partly from my own observation. There are no better instruments than discharged servants with a grievance, and I was lucky enough to find one. I call it luck, but it would not have come my way had I not been looking out for it. As Baynes remarks, we all have our systems. It was my system which enabled me to find John Warner, late gardener of High Gable, sacked in a moment of temper by his imperious employer. He in turn had friends among the indoor servants who unite in their fear and dislike of their master. So I had my key to the secrets of the establishment.

"Curious people, Watson! I don't pretend to understand it all yet, but very curious people anyway. It's a double-winged house, and the servants live on one side, the family on the other. There's no link between the two save for Henderson's own servant, who serves the family's meals. Everything is carried to a certain door, which forms the one connection. Governess and children hardly go out at all, except into the garden. Henderson never by any chance walks alone. His dark secretary is like his shadow. The gossip among the servants is that their master is terribly afraid of something. 'Sold his soul to the devil in exchange for money,' says Warner, 'and expects his creditor to come up and claim his own.' Where they came from, or who they are, nobody has an idea. They are very violent. Twice Henderson has lashed at folk with his dog-whip, and only his long purse and heavy compensation have kept him out of the courts.

"Well, now, Watson, let us judge the situation by this new information. We may take it that the letter came out of this strange household and was an invitation to Garcia to carry out some attempt which had already been planned. Who wrote the note? It was someone within the citadel, and it was a woman. Who then but Miss Burnet, the governess? All our reasoning seems to point that way. At any rate, we may take it as a hypothesis and see what consequences it would entail. I may add that Miss Burnet's age and character make it certain that my first idea that there might be a love interest in our story is out of the question.

"If she wrote the note she was presumably the friend and confederate of Garcia. What, then, might she be expected to do if she heard of his death? If he met it in some nefarious enterprise her lips might be sealed. Still, in her heart, she must retain bitterness and hatred against those who had killed him and would presumably help so far as she could to have revenge upon them. Could we see her, then, and try to use her? That was my first thought. But now we come to a sinister fact. Miss Burnet has not been seen by any human eye since the night of the murder. From that evening she has utterly vanished. Is she alive? Has she perhaps met her end on the same night as the friend whom she had summoned? Or is she merely a prisoner? There is the point which we still have to decide.

"You will appreciate the difficulty of the situation, Watson. There is nothing upon which we can apply for a warrant. Our whole scheme might seem fantastic if laid before a magistrate. The woman's disappearance counts for nothing, since in that extraordinary household any member of it might be invisible for a week. And yet she may at the present moment be in danger of her life. All I can do is to watch the house and leave my agent, Warner, on guard at the gates. We can't let such a situation continue. If the law can do nothing we must take the risk ourselves."

"What do you suggest?"

"I know which is her room. It is accessible from the top of an outhouse.* My suggestion is that you and I go to-night and see if we can strike at the very heart of the mystery."

---

*One of the outer buildings of the main house (not a toilet).

It was not, I must confess, a very alluring prospect. The old house with its atmosphere of murder, the singular and formidable inhabitants, the unknown dangers of the approach, and the fact that we were putting ourselves legally in a false position all combined to damp my ardour. But there was something in the ice-cold reasoning of Holmes which made it impossible to shrink from any adventure which he might recommend. One knew that thus, and only thus, could a solution be found. I clasped his hand in silence, and the die was cast.[11]

But it was not destined that our investigation should have so adventurous an ending. It was about five o'clock, and the shadows of the March evening were beginning to fall, when an excited rustic rushed into our room.

"They've gone, Mr. Holmes. They went by the last train. The lady broke away, and I've got her in a cab downstairs."

"Excellent, Warner!" cried Holmes, springing to his feet. "Watson, the gaps are closing rapidly."

In the cab was a woman, half-collapsed from nervous exhaustion. She bore upon her aquiline and emaciated face the traces of some recent tragedy. Her head hung listlessly upon her breast, but as she raised it and turned her dull eyes upon us I saw that her pupils were dark dots in the centre of the broad gray iris. She was drugged with opium.

"I watched at the gate, same as you advised, Mr. Holmes," said our emissary, the discharged gardener. "When the carriage came out I followed it to the station. She was like one walking in her sleep, but when they tried to get her into the train she came to life and struggled. They pushed her into the carriage. She fought her way out again. I took her part, got her into a cab, and here we are. I shan't forget the face at the carriage window as I led her away. I'd have a short life if he had his way— the black-eyed, scowling, yellow devil."

We carried her upstairs, laid her on the sofa, and a couple of cups of the strongest coffee soon cleared her brain from the mists of the drug. Baynes had been summoned by Holmes, and the situation rapidly explained to him.

"Why, sir, you've got me the very evidence I want," said the inspector warmly, shaking my friend by the hand. "I was on the same scent as you from the first."

"What! You were after Henderson?"

"Why, Mr. Holmes, when you were crawling in the shrubbery at High Gable I was up one of the trees in the plantation and saw you down below. It was just who would get his evidence first."

"Then why did you arrest the mulatto?"

Baynes chuckled.

"I was sure Henderson, as he calls himself, felt that he was suspected, and that he would lie low and make no move so long as he thought he was in any danger. I arrested the wrong man to make him believe that our eyes were off him. I knew he would be likely to clear off then and give us a chance of getting at Miss Burnet."

Holmes laid his hand upon the inspector's shoulder.

"You will rise high in your profession. You have instinct and intuition," said he.

Baynes flushed with pleasure.

"I've had a plain-clothes man waiting at the station all the week. Wherever the High Gable folk go he will keep them in sight. But he must have been hard put to it when Miss Burnet broke away. However, your man picked her up, and it all ends well. We can't arrest without her evidence, that is clear, so the sooner we get a statement the better."

"Every minute she gets stronger," said Holmes, glancing at the governess. "But tell me, Baynes, who is this man Henderson?"

"Henderson," the inspector answered, "is Don Murillo, once called the Tiger of San Pedro."

The Tiger of San Pedro! The whole history of the man came back to me in a flash. He had made his name as the most lewd and bloodthirsty tyrant that had ever governed any country with a pretence to civilization. Strong, fearless, and energetic, he had sufficient virtue to enable him to impose his odious vices upon a cowering people for ten or twelve years. His name was a terror through all Central America. At the end of that time there was a universal rising against him. But he was as cunning as he was cruel, and at the first whisper of coming trouble he had secretly conveyed his treasures aboard a ship which was manned by devoted adherents. It was an empty palace which was stormed by the insurgents next day. The dictator, his two children, his secretary, and his wealth had all escaped them. From that moment he had vanished from the world, and his identity had been a frequent subject for comment in the European press.

"Yes, sir, Don Murillo, the Tiger of San Pedro," said Baynes. "If you look it up you will find that the San Pedro colours are green and white, same as in the note, Mr. Holmes. Henderson he called himself, but I traced him back, Paris and Rome and Madrid to Barcelona, where his ship came in in '86. They've been looking for him all the time for their revenge, but it is only now that they have begun to find him out."

"They discovered him a year ago," said Miss Burnet, who had sat up and was now intently following the conversation. "Once already his life has been attempted, but some evil spirit shielded him. Now, again, it is the noble, chivalrous Garcia who has fallen, while the monster goes safe. But another will come, and yet another, until some day justice will be done; that is as certain as the rise of to-morrow's sun." Her thin hands clenched, and her worn face blanched with the passion of her hatred.

"But how come you into this matter, Miss Burnet?" asked Holmes. "How can an English lady join in such a murderous affair?"

"I join in it because there is no other way in the world by which justice can be gained. What does the law of England care for the rivers of blood shed years ago in San Pedro, or for the shipload of treasure which this man has stolen? To you they are like crimes committed in some other planet. But *we* know. We have learned the truth in sorrow and in suffering. To us there is no fiend in hell like Juan Murillo, and no peace in life while his victims still cry for vengeance."

"No doubt," said Holmes, "he was as you say. I have heard that he was atrocious. But how are you affected?"

"I will tell you it all. This villain's policy was to murder, on one pretext or another, every man who showed such promise that he might in time come to be a dangerous rival. My husband—yes, my real name is Signora Victor Durando—was the San Pedro minister in London. He met me and married me there. A nobler man never lived upon earth. Unhappily, Murillo heard of his excellence, recalled him on some pretext, and had him shot. With a premonition of his fate he had refused to take me with him. His estates were confiscated, and I was left with a pittance and a broken heart.

"Then came the downfall of the tyrant. He escaped as you have just described. But the many whose lives he had ruined, whose nearest and dearest had suffered torture and death at his hands, would not let the matter rest. They banded themselves into a society which should never be dissolved until the work was done. It was my part after we had discovered in the transformed Henderson the fallen despot, to attach myself to his household and keep the others in touch with his movements. This I was able to do by securing the position of governess in his family. He little knew that the woman who faced him at every meal was the woman whose husband he had hurried at an hour's notice into eternity. I smiled on him, did my duty to his children, and bided my time. An attempt was made in Paris and failed. We zig-zagged swiftly here and there over Europe to throw off the pursuers and finally returned to this house, which he had taken upon his first arrival in England.

"But here also the ministers of justice were waiting. Knowing that he would return there, Garcia, who is the son of the former highest dignitary in San Pedro, was waiting with two trusty companions of humble station, all three fired with the same reasons for revenge. He could do little during the day, for Murillo took every precaution and never went out save with his satellite Lucas, or Lopez as he was known in the days of his greatness. At night, however, he slept alone, and the avenger might find him. On a certain evening, which had been prearranged, I sent my friend final instructions, for the man was forever on the alert and continually changed his room. I was to see that the doors were open and the signal of a green or white light in a window which faced the drive was to give notice if all was safe or if the attempt had better be postponed.

"But everything went wrong with us. In some way I had excited the suspicion of Lopez, the secretary. He crept up behind me and sprang upon me just as I had finished the note. He and his master dragged me to my room and held judgment upon me as a convicted traitress. Then and there they would have plunged their knives into me could they have seen how to escape the consequences of the deed. Finally, after much debate, they concluded that my murder was too dangerous. But they determined to get rid forever of Garcia. They had gagged me, and Murillo twisted my arm round until I gave him the address. I swear that he might have twisted it off had I understood what it would mean to Garcia. Lopez addressed the note which I had written, sealed it with his sleeve-link, and sent it by the hand of the servant, José. How they murdered him I do not know, save that it was Murillo's hand who struck him down, for Lopez had remained to guard me. I believe he must have waited among the gorse bushes through which the path winds and struck him down as he passed. At first they were of a mind to let him enter the house and to kill him as a detected burglar; but they argued that if they were mixed up in an inquiry their own identity would at once be publicly disclosed and they would be open to further attacks. With the death of Garcia, the pursuit might cease, since such a death might frighten others from the task.

"All would now have been well for them had it not been for my knowledge of what they had done. I have no doubt that there were times when my life hung in the balance. I was confined to my room, terrorized by the most horrible threats, cruelly ill-used to break my spirit—see this stab on my shoulder and the bruises from end to end of my arms—and a gag was thrust into my mouth on the one occasion when I tried to call from the window. For five days this cruel imprisonment continued, with hardly enough food to hold body and soul together. This afternoon a good lunch was brought me, but the moment after I took it I knew that I had been drugged. In a sort of dream I remember being half-led, half-carried to the carriage; in the same state I was conveyed to the train. Only then, when the wheels were almost moving, did I suddenly realize that my liberty lay in my own hands. I sprang out, they tried to drag me back, and had it not been for the help of this good man, who led me to the cab, I should never have broken away. Now, thank God, I am beyond their power forever."

We had all listened intently to this remarkable statement. It was Holmes who broke the silence.

"Our difficulties are not over," he remarked, shaking his head. "Our police work ends, but our legal work begins."

"Exactly," said I. "A plausible lawyer could make it out as an act of self-defence. There may be a hundred crimes in the background, but it is only on this one that they can be tried."

"Come, come," said Baynes cheerily, "I think better of the law than that. Self-defence is one thing. To entice a man in cold blood with the object of murdering him is another, whatever danger you may fear from him. No, no, we shall all be justified when we see the tenants of High Gable at the next Guildford Assizes."

It is a matter of history, however, that a little time was still to elapse before the Tiger of San Pedro should meet with his deserts. Wily and bold, he and his companion threw their pursuer off their track by entering a lodging-house in Edmonton Street and leaving by the back-gate into Curzon Square. From that day they were seen no more in England. Some six months afterwards the Marquess of Montalva and Signor Rulli, his secretary, were both murdered in their rooms at the Hotel Escurial at Madrid. The crime was ascribed to Nihilism, and the murderers were never arrested. Inspector Baynes visited us at Baker Street with a printed description of the dark face of the secretary, and of the masterful features, the magnetic black eyes, and the tufted brows of his master. We could not doubt that justice, if belated, had come at last.

"A chaotic case, my dear Watson," said Holmes over an evening pipe. "It will not be possible for you to present it in that compact form which is dear to your heart. It covers two continents, concerns two groups of mysterious persons, and is further complicated by the highly respectable presence of our friend, Scott Eccles, whose inclusion shows me that the deceased Garcia had a scheming mind and a well-developed instinct of self-preservation. It is remarkable only for the fact that amid a perfect jungle of possibilities we, with our worthy collaborator, the inspector, have kept our close hold on the essentials and so been guided along the crooked and winding path. Is there any point which is not quite clear to you?"

"The object of the mulatto cook's return?"

"I think that the strange creature in the kitchen may account for it. The man was a primitive savage from the backwoods of San Pedro, and this was his fetish. When his companion and he had fled to some prearranged retreat—already occupied, no doubt by a confederate—the companion had persuaded him to leave so compromising an article of furniture. But the mulatto's heart was with it, and he was driven back to it next day, when, on reconnoitering through the window, he found policeman Walters in possession. He waited three days longer, and then his piety or his superstition drove him to try once more. Inspector Baynes, who, with his usual astuteness, had minimized the incident before me, had really recognized its importance and had left a trap into which the creature walked. Any other point, Watson?"

"The torn bird, the pail of blood, the charred bones, all the mystery of that weird kitchen?"

Holmes smiled as he turned up an entry in his notebook.

"I spent a morning in the British Museum reading up on that and other points. Here is a quotation from Eckermann's *Voodooism and the Negroid Religions:*

> The true voodoo-worshipper attempts nothing of importance without certain sacrifices which are intended to propitiate his unclean gods. In extreme cases these rites take the form of human sacrifices followed by cannibalism. The more usual victims are a white cock, which is plucked in pieces alive, or a black goat, whose throat is cut and body burned.

"So you see our savage friend was very orthodox in his ritual. It is grotesque, Watson," Holmes added, as he slowly fastened his notebook, "but, as I have had occasion to remark, there is but one step from the grotesque to the horrible."

THE ADVENTURE OF THE
CARDBOARD BOX

In choosing a few typical cases which illustrate the remarkable mental qualities of my friend, Sherlock Holmes, I have endeavoured, as far as possible, to select those which presented the minimum of sensationalism, while offering a fair field for his talents. It is, however, unfortunately impossible entirely to separate the sensational from the criminal, and a chronicler is left in the dilemma that he must either sacrifice details which are essential to his statement and so give a false impression of the problem, or he must use matter which chance, and not choice, has provided him with. With this short preface I shall turn to my notes of what proved to be a strange, though a peculiarly terrible, chain of events.

It was a blazing hot day in August. Baker Street was like an oven, and the glare of the sunlight upon the yellow brickwork of the house across the road was painful to the eye. It was hard to believe that these were the same walls which loomed so gloomily through the fogs of winter. Our blinds were half-drawn, and Holmes lay curled upon the sofa, reading and re-reading a letter which he had received by the morning post. For myself, my term of service in India had trained me to stand heat better than cold, and a thermometer at ninety was no hardship. But the morning paper was uninteresting. Parliament had risen. Everybody was out of town, and I yearned for the glades of the New Forest or the shingle of Southsea. A depleted bank account had caused me to postpone my holiday, and as to my companion, neither the country nor the sea presented the slightest attraction to him. He loved to lie in the very centre of five millions of people, with his filaments stretching out and running through them, responsive to every little rumour or suspicion of unsolved crime. Appreciation of nature found no place among his many gifts, and his only change was when he turned his mind from the evil-doer of the town to track down his brother of the country.

Finding that Holmes was too absorbed for conversation I had tossed aside the barren paper, and leaning back in my chair I fell into a brown study.* Suddenly my companion's voice broke in upon my thoughts:

"You are right, Watson," said he. "It does seem a most preposterous way of settling a dispute."

"Most preposterous!" I exclaimed, and then suddenly realizing how he had echoed the inmost thought of my soul, I sat up in my chair and stared at him in blank amazement.

"What is this, Holmes?" I cried. "This is beyond anything which I could have imagined."

He laughed heartily at my perplexity.

---

*State of deep thought or reverie.

"You remember," said he, "that some little time ago when I read you the passage in one of Poe's sketches in which a close reasoner follows the unspoken thoughts of his companion, you were inclined to treat the matter as a mere *tour-de-force* of the author. On my remarking that I was constantly in the habit of doing the same thing you expressed incredulity."*

"Oh, no!"

"Perhaps not with your tongue, my dear Watson, but certainly with your eyebrows. So when I saw you throw down your paper and enter upon a train of thought, I was very happy to have the opportunity of reading it off, and eventually of breaking into it, as a proof that I had been in rapport with you."

But I was still far from satisfied. "In the example which you read to me," said I, "the reasoner drew his conclusions from the actions of the man whom he observed. If I remember right, he stumbled over a heap of stones, looked up at the stars, and so on. But I have been seated quietly in my chair, and what clues can I have given you?"

"You do yourself an injustice. The features are given to man as the means by which he shall express his emotions, and yours are faithful servants."

"Do you mean to say that you read my train of thoughts from my features?"

"Your features and especially your eyes. Perhaps you cannot yourself recall how your reverie commenced?"

"No, I cannot."

"Then I will tell you. After throwing down your paper, which was the action which drew my attention to you, you sat for half a minute with a vacant expression. Then your eyes fixed themselves upon your newly framed picture of General Gordon,[12] and I saw by the alteration in your face that a train of thought had been started. But it did not lead very far. Your eyes flashed across to the unframed portrait of Henry Ward Beecher[13] which stands upon the top of your books. Then you glanced up at the wall, and of course your meaning was obvious. You were thinking that if the portrait were framed it would just cover that bare space and correspond with Gordon's picture over there."

"You have followed me wonderfully!" I exclaimed.

"So far I could hardly have gone astray. But now your thoughts went back to Beecher, and you looked hard across as if you were studying the character in his features. Then your eyes ceased to pucker, but you continued to look across, and your face was thoughtful. You were recalling the incidents of Beecher's career. I was well aware that you could not do this without thinking of the mission which he undertook on behalf of the North at the time of the Civil War, for I remember your expressing your passionate indignation at the way in which he was received by the more turbulent of our people. You felt so strongly about it that I knew you

*In *A Study in Scarlet* Holmes expresses a decidedly different opinion.

could not think of Beecher without thinking of that also. When a moment later I saw your eyes wander away from the picture, I suspected that your mind had now turned to the Civil War, and when I observed that your lips set, your eyes sparkled, and your hands clenched I was positive that you were indeed thinking of the gallantry which was shown by both sides in that desperate struggle. But then, again, your face grew sadder; you shook your head. You were dwelling upon the sadness and horror and useless waste of life. Your hand stole towards your own old wound and a smile quivered on your lips, which showed me that the ridiculous side of this method of settling international questions had forced itself upon your mind. At this point I agreed with you that it was preposterous and was glad to find that all my deductions had been correct."

"Absolutely!" said I. "And now that you have explained it, I confess that I am as amazed as before."

"It was very superficial, my dear Watson, I assure you. I should not have intruded it upon your attention had you not shown some incredulity the other day. But I have in my hands here a little problem which may prove to be more difficult of solution than my small essay in thought reading. Have you observed in the paper a short paragraph referring to the remarkable contents of a packet sent through the post to Miss Cushing, of Cross Street, Croydon?'

"No. I saw nothing."

"Ah! then you must have overlooked it. Just toss it over to me. Here it is, under the financial column. Perhaps you would be good enough to read it aloud."

I picked up the paper which he had thrown back to me and read the paragraph indicated. It was headed "A Gruesome Packet."

"Miss Susan Cushing, living at Cross Street, Croydon, has been made the victim of what must be regarded as a peculiarly revolting practical joke unless some more sinister meaning should prove to be attached to the incident. At two o'clock yesterday afternoon a small packet, wrapped in brown paper, was handed in by the postman. A cardboard box was inside, which was filled with coarse salt. On emptying this, Miss Cushing was horrified to find two human ears, apparently quite freshly severed. The box had been sent by parcel post from Belfast upon the morning before. There is no indication as to the sender, and the matter is the more mysterious as Miss Cushing, who is a maiden lady of fifty, has led a most retired life, and has so few acquaintances or correspondents that it is a rare event for her to receive anything through the post. Some years ago, however, when she resided at Penge, she let apartments in her house to three young medical students, whom she was obliged to get rid of on account of their noisy and irregular habits. The police are of opinion that this outrage may have been perpetrated upon Miss Cushing by these youths, who owed her a grudge and who hoped to frighten her by sending her these relics of the dissecting-rooms. Some probability is lent to the theory by the fact that one of these students came from the north of Ireland, and, to the best of Miss Cushing's belief, from Belfast. In the meantime, the matter is being actively investigated, Mr. Lestrade, one of the very smartest of our detective officers, being in charge of the case."

"So much for the *Daily Chronicle*," said Holmes as I finished reading. "Now for our friend Lestrade. I had a note from him this morning, in which he says:

"I think that this case is very much in your line. We have every hope of clearing the matter up, but we find a little difficulty in getting anything to work upon. We have, of course, wired to the Belfast post-office, but a large number of parcels were handed in upon that day, and they have no means of identifying this particular one, or of remembering the sender. The box is a half-pound box of honeydew tobacco and does not help us in any way. The medical student theory still appears to me to be the most feasible, but if you should have a few hours to spare I should be very happy to see you out here. I shall be either at the house or in the police-station all day.

"What say you, Watson? Can you rise superior to the heat and run down to Croydon with me on the off chance of a case for your annals?"

"I was longing for something to do."

"You shall have it then. Ring for our boots and tell them to order a cab. I'll be back in a moment when I have changed my dressing-gown and filled my cigar-case."

A shower of rain fell while we were in the train, and the heat was far less oppressive in Croydon than in town. Holmes had sent on a wire, so that Lestrade, as wiry, as dapper, and as ferret-like as ever, was waiting for us at the station. A walk of five minutes took us to Cross Street, where Miss Cushing resided.

It was a very long street of two-story brick houses, neat and prim, with whitened stone steps and little groups of aproned women gossiping at the doors. Halfway down, Lestrade stopped and tapped at a door, which was opened by a small servant girl. Miss Cushing was sitting in the front room, into which we were ushered. She was a placid-faced woman, with large, gentle eyes, and grizzled hair curving down over her temples on each side. A worked antimacassar lay upon her lap and a basket of coloured silks stood upon a stool beside her.

"They are in the outhouse, those dreadful things," said she as Lestrade entered. "I wish that you would take them away altogether."

"So I shall, Miss Cushing. I only kept them here until my friend, Mr. Holmes, should have seen them in your presence."

"Why in my presence, sir?"

"In case he wished to ask any questions."

"What is the use of asking me questions when I tell you I know nothing whatever about it?"

"Quite so, madam," said Holmes in his soothing way. "I have no doubt that you have been annoyed more than enough already over this business."

"Indeed, I have, sir. I am a quiet woman and live a retired life. It is something new for me to see my name in the papers and to find the police in my house. I won't have those things in here, Mr. Lestrade. If you wish to see them you must go to the outhouse."

It was a small shed in the narrow garden which ran behind the house. Lestrade went in and brought out a yellow cardboard box, with a piece of brown paper and some string. There was a bench at the end of the path, and we all sat down while Holmes examined, one by one, the articles which Lestrade had handed to him.

"The string is exceedingly interesting," he remarked, holding it up to the light and sniffing at it. "What do you make of this string, Lestrade?"

"It has been tarred."

"Precisely. It is a piece of tarred twine. You have also, no doubt, remarked that Miss Cushing has cut the cord with a scissors, as can be seen by the double fray on each side. This is of importance."

"I cannot see the importance," said Lestrade.

"The importance lies in the fact that the knot is left intact, and that this knot is of a peculiar character."

"It is very neatly tied. I had already made a note to that effect," said Lestrade complacently.

"So much for the string, then," said Holmes, smiling, "now for the box wrapper. Brown paper, with a distinct smell of coffee. What, did you not observe it? I think there can be no doubt of it. Address printed in rather straggling characters: 'Miss S. Cushing, Cross Street, Croydon.' Done with a broad-pointed pen, probably a J, and with very inferior ink. The word 'Croydon' has been originally spelled with an 'i,' which has been changed to 'y.' The parcel was directed, then, by a man—the printing is distinctly masculine—of limited education and unacquainted with the town of Croydon. So far, so good! The box is a yellow, half-pound honeydew box, with nothing distinctive save two thumb marks at the left bottom corner. It is filled with rough salt of the quality used for preserving hides and other of the coarser commercial purposes. And embedded in it are these very singular enclosures."

He took out the two ears as he spoke, and laying a board across his knee he examined them minutely, while Lestrade and I, bending forward on each side of him, glanced alternately at these dreadful relics and at the thoughtful, eager face of our companion. Finally he returned them to the box once more and sat for a while in deep meditation.

"You have observed, of course," said he at last, "that the ears are not a pair.

"Yes, I have noticed that. But if this were the practical joke of some students from the dissecting-rooms, it would be as easy for them to send two odd ears as a pair."

"Precisely. But this is not a practical joke."

"You are sure of it?"

"The presumption is strongly against it. Bodies in the dissecting-rooms are injected with preservative fluid. These ears bear no signs of this. They are fresh, too. They have been cut off with a blunt instrument, which would hardly happen if a student had done it. Again, carbolic or rectified spirits would be the preservatives which would suggest themselves to the medical mind, certainly not rough salt. I repeat that there is no practical joke here, but that we are investigating a serious crime."

A vague thrill ran through me as I listened to my companion's words and saw the stern gravity which had hardened his features. This brutal preliminary seemed to shadow forth some strange and inexplicable horror in the background. Lestrade, however, shook his head like a man who is only half convinced.

"There are objections to the joke theory, no doubt," said he, "but there are much stronger reasons against the other. We know that this woman has led a most quiet and respectable life at Penge and here for the last twenty years. She has hardly been away from her home for a day during that time. Why on earth, then, should any criminal send her the proofs of his guilt, especially as, unless she is a most consummate actress, she understands quite as little of the matter as we do?"

"That is the problem which we have to solve," Holmes answered, "and for my part I shall set about it by presuming that my reasoning is correct, and that a double murder has been committed. One of these ears is a woman's, small, finely formed, and pierced for an earring. The other is a man's, sun-burned discoloured, and also pierced for an earring. These two people are presumably dead, or we should have heard their story before now. To-day is Friday. The packet was posted on Thursday morning. The tragedy, then, occurred on Wednesday or Tuesday, or earlier. If the two people were murdered, who but their murderer would have sent this sign of his work to Miss Cushing? We may take it that the sender of the packet is the man whom we want. But he must have some strong reason for sending Miss Cushing this packet. What reason then? It must have been to tell her that the deed was done! or to pain her, perhaps. But in that case she knows who it is. Does she know? I doubt it. If she knew, why should she call the police in? She might have buried the ears, and no one would have been the wiser. That is what she would have done if she had wished to shield the criminal. But if she does not wish to shield him she would give his name. There is a tangle here which needs straightening out." He had been talking in a high, quick voice, staring blankly up over the garden fence, but now he sprang briskly to his feet and walked towards the house.

"I have a few questions to ask Miss Cushing," said he.

"In that case I may leave you here," said Lestrade, "for I have another small business on hand. I think that I have nothing further to learn from Miss Cushing. You will find me at the police-station."

"We shall look in on our way to the train," answered Holmes. A moment later he and I were back in the front room, where the impassive lady was still quietly working away at her antimacassar. She put it down on her lap as we entered and looked at us with her frank, searching blue eyes.

"I am convinced, sir," she said, "that this matter is a mistake, and that the parcel was never meant for me at all. I have said this several times to the gentleman from Scotland Yard, but he simply laughs at me. I have not an enemy in the world, as far as I know, so why should anyone play me such a trick?"

"I am coming to be of the same opinion, Miss Cushing," said Holmes, taking a seat beside her. "I think that it is more than probable——" he paused, and I was surprised, on glancing round to see that he was staring with singular intentness at the lady's profile. Surprise and satisfaction were both for an instant to be read upon his eager face, though when she glanced round to find out the cause of his silence he had become as demure as ever. I stared hard myself at her flat, grizzled hair, her trim cap, her little gilt earrings, her placid features; but I could see nothing which could account for my companion's evident excitement.

"There were one or two questions——"

"Oh, I am weary of questions!" cried Miss Cushing impatiently.

"You have two sisters, I believe."

"How could you know that?"

"I observed the very instant that I entered the room that you have a portrait group of three ladies upon the mantelpiece, one of whom is undoubtedly yourself, while the others are so exceedingly like you that there could be no doubt of the relationship."

"Yes, you are quite right. Those are my sisters, Sarah and Mary."

"And here at my elbow is another portrait, taken at Liverpool, of your younger sister, in the company of a man who appears to be a steward by his uniform. I observe that she was unmarried at the time."

"You are very quick at observing."

"That is my trade."

"Well, you are quite right. But she was married to Mr. Browner a few days afterwards. He was on the South American line when that was taken, but he was so fond of her that he couldn't abide to leave her for so long, and he got into the Liverpool and London boats."

"Ah, the *Conqueror*, perhaps?"

"No, the *May Day*, when last I heard. Jim came down here to see me once. That was before he broke the pledge; but afterwards he would always take drink when he was ashore, and a little drink would send him stark, staring mad. Ah! it was a bad day that ever he took a glass in his hand again. First he dropped me, then he quarrelled with Sarah, and now that Mary has stopped writing we don't know how things are going with them."

It was evident that Miss Cushing had come upon a subject on which she felt very deeply. Like most people who lead a lonely life, she was shy at first, but ended by becoming extremely communicative. She told us many details about her brother-in-law the steward, and then wandering off on the subject of her former lodgers, the medical students, she gave us a long account of their delinquencies, with their names and those of their hospitals. Holmes listened attentively to everything, throwing in a question from time to time.

"About your second sister, Sarah," said he. "I wonder, since you are both maiden ladies, that you do not keep house together."

"Ah! you don't know Sarah's temper or you would wonder no more. I tried it when I came to Croydon, and we kept on until about two months ago, when we had to part. I don't want to say a word against my own sister, but she was always meddlesome and hard to please, was Sarah."

"You say that she quarrelled with your Liverpool relations."

"Yes, and they were the best of friends at one time. Why, she went up there in order to be near them. And now she has no word hard enough for Jim Browner. The last six months that she was here she would speak of nothing but his drinking and his ways. He had caught her meddling, I suspect, and given her a bit of his mind, and that was the start of it."

"Thank you, Miss Cushing," said Holmes, rising and bowing. "Your sister Sarah lives, I think you said, at New Street, Wallington? Good-bye, and I am very sorry that you should have been troubled over a case with which, as you say, you have nothing whatever to do."

There was a cab passing as we came out, and Holmes hailed it.

"How far to Wallington?" he asked.

"Only about a mile, sir."

"Very good. Jump in, Watson. We must strike while the iron is hot. Simple as the case is, there have been one or two very instructive details in connection with it. Just pull up at a telegraph office as you pass, cabby."

Holmes sent off a short wire and for the rest of the drive lay back in the cab, with his hat tilted over his nose to keep the sun from his face. Our driver pulled up at a house which was not unlike the one which we had just quitted. My companion ordered him to wait, and had his hand upon the knocker, when the door opened and a grave young gentleman in black, with a very shiny hat, appeared on the step.

"Is Miss Cushing at home?" asked Holmes.

"Miss Sarah Cushing is extremely ill," said he. "She has been suffering since yesterday from brain symptoms of great severity. As her medical adviser, I cannot possibly take the responsibility of allowing anyone to see her. I should recommend you to call again in ten days." He drew on his gloves, closed the door, and marched off down the street.

"Well, if we can't we can't," said Holmes, cheerfully.

"Perhaps she could not or would not have told you much."

"I did not wish her to tell me anything. I only wanted to look at her. However, I think that I have got all that I want. Drive us to some decent hotel, cabby, where we may have some lunch, and afterwards we shall drop down upon friend Lestrade at the police-station."

We had a pleasant little meal together, during which Holmes would talk about nothing but violins, narrating with great exultation how he had purchased his own Stradivarius, which was worth at least five hundred guineas, at a Jew broker's in Tottenham Court Road for fifty-five shillings.[14] This led him to Paganini,* and we sat for an hour over a bottle of claret while he told me anecdote after anecdote of that extraordinary man. The afternoon was far advanced and the hot glare had softened into a mellow glow before we found ourselves at the police-station. Lestrade was waiting for us at the door.

"A telegram for you, Mr. Holmes," said he.

"Ha! It is the answer!" He tore it open, glanced his eyes over it, and crumpled it into his pocket. "That's all right," said he.

"Have you found out anything?"

"I have found out everything!"

"What!" Lestrade stared at him in amazement. "You are joking."

"I was never more serious in my life. A shocking crime has been committed, and I think I have now laid bare every detail of it."

"And the criminal?"

Holmes scribbled a few words upon the back of one of his visiting cards and threw it over to Lestrade.

"That is the name," he said. "You cannot effect an arrest until tomorrow night at the earliest. I should prefer that you do not mention my name at all in connection with the case, as I choose to be only associated with those crimes which present some difficulty in their solution. Come on, Watson." We strode off together to the station, leaving Lestrade still staring with a delighted face at the card which Holmes had thrown him.

"The case," said Sherlock Holmes as we chatted over our cigars that night in our rooms at Baker Street. "is one where, as in the investigations which you have chronicled under the names of 'A Study in Scarlet' and of 'The Sign of Four,' we have been compelled to reason backward from effects to causes. I have written to Lestrade asking him to supply us with the details which are now wanting, and which he will only get after he has secured his man. That he may be safely trusted to do, for although he is absolutely devoid of reason, he is as tenacious as a bulldog when he once understands what he has to do, and, indeed, it is just this tenacity which has brought him to the top at Scotland Yard."

"Your case is not complete, then?" I asked.

"It is fairly complete in essentials. We know who the author of the revolting business is, although one of the victims still escapes us. Of course, you have formed your own conclusions."

"I presume that this Jim Browner, the steward of a Liverpool boat, is the man whom you suspect?"

"Oh! it is more than a suspicion."

"And yet I cannot see anything save very vague indications."

"On the contrary, to my mind nothing could be more clear. Let me run

---

*Niccolò Paganini (1782–1840), Italian composer and virtuoso violinist.

over the principal steps. We approached the case, you remember, with an absolutely blank mind, which is always an advantage. We had formed no theories. We were simply there to observe and to draw inferences from our observations. What did we see first? A very placid and respectable lady, who seemed quite innocent of any secret, and a portrait which showed me that she had two younger sisters. It instantly flashed across my mind that the box might have been meant for one of these. I set the idea aside as one which could be disproved or confirmed at our leisure. Then we went to the garden, as you remember, and we saw the very singular contents of the little yellow box.

"The string was of the quality which is used by sailmakers aboard ship, and at once a whiff of the sea was perceptible in our investigation. When I observed that the knot was one which is popular with sailors, that the parcel had been posted at a port, and that the male ear was pierced for an earring which is so much more common among sailors than landsmen, I was quite certain that all the actors in the tragedy were to be found among our seafaring classes.

"When I came to examine the address of the packet I observed that it was to Miss S. Cushing. Now, the oldest sister would, of course, be Miss Cushing, and although her initial was 'S' it might belong to one of the others as well. In that case we should have to commence our investigation from a fresh basis altogether. I therefore went into the house with the intention of clearing up this point. I was about to assure Miss Cushing that I was convinced that a mistake had been made when you may remember that I came suddenly to a stop. The fact was that I had just seen something which filled me with surprise and at the same time narrowed the field of our inquiry immensely.

"As a medical man, you are aware, Watson, that there is no part of the body which varies so much as the human ear. Each ear is as a rule quite distinctive and differs from all other ones. In last year's *Anthropological Journal* you will find two short monographs from my pen upon the subject. I had, therefore, examined the ears in the box with the eyes of an expert and had carefully noted their anatomical peculiarities. Imagine my surprise, then, when on looking at Miss Cushing I perceived that her ear corresponded exactly with the female ear which I had just inspected. The matter was entirely beyond coincidence. There was the same shortening of the pinna, the same broad curve of the upper lobe, the same convolution of the inner cartilage. In all essentials it was the same ear.

"Of course I at once saw the enormous importance of the observation. It was evident that the victim was a blood relation, and probably a very close one. I began to talk to her about her family, and you remember that she at once gave us some exceedingly valuable details.

"In the first place, her sister's name was Sarah, and her address had until recently been the same, so that it was quite obvious how the mistake had occurred and for whom the packet was meant. Then we heard of this steward, married to the third sister, and learned that he had at one time been so intimate with Miss Sarah that she had actually gone up to Liverpool to be near the Browners, but a quarrel had afterwards divided them. This quarrel had put a stop to all communications for some months, so that if Browner had occasion to address a packet to Miss Sarah, he would undoubtedly have done so to her old address.

"And now the matter had begun to straighten itself out wonderfully. We had learned of the existence of this steward, an impulsive man, of strong passions—you remember that he threw up what must have been a very superior berth in order to be nearer to his wife—subject, too, to occasional fits of hard drinking. We had reason to believe that his wife had been murdered, and that a man—presumably a seafaring man—had been murdered at the same time. Jealousy, of course, at once suggests itself as the motive for the crime. And why should these proofs of the deed be sent to Miss Sarah Cushing? Probably because during her residence in Liverpool she had some hand in bringing about the events which led to the tragedy. You will observe that this line of boats calls at Belfast. Dublin, and Waterford; so that, presuming that Browner had committed the deed and had embarked at once upon his steamer, the *May Day*, Belfast would be the first place at which he could post his terrible packet.

"A second solution was at this stage obviously possible, and although I thought it exceedingly unlikely, I was determined to elucidate it before going further. An unsuccessful lover might have killed Mr. and Mrs. Browner, and the male ear might have belonged to the husband. There were many grave objections to this theory, but it was conceivable. I therefore sent off a telegram to my friend Algar, of the Liverpool force, and asked him to find out if Mrs. Browner were at home, and if Browner had departed in the *May Day*. Then we went on to Wallington to visit Miss Sarah.

"I was curious, in the first place, to see how far the family ear had been reproduced in her. Then, of course, she might give us very important information, but I was not sanguine that she would. She must have heard of the business the day before, since all Croydon was ringing with it, and she alone could have understood for whom the packet was meant. If she had been willing to help justice she would probably have communicated with the police already. However, it was clearly our duty to see her, so we went. We found that the news of the arrival of the packet—for her illness dated from that time—had such an effect upon her as to bring on brain fever. It was clearer than ever that she understood its full significance, but equally clear that we should have to wait some time for any assistance from her.

"However, we were really independent of her help. Our answers were waiting for us at the police-station, where I had directed Algar to send them. Nothing could be more conclusive. Mrs. Browner's house had been closed for more than three days, and the neighbours were of opinion that she had gone south to see her relatives. It had been ascertained at the shipping offices that Browner had left aboard of the *May Day*, and I calculate that she is due in the Thames to-morrow night. When he arrives he will be met by the obtuse but resolute Lestrade, and I have no doubt that we shall have all our details filled in."

Sherlock Holmes was not disappointed in his expectations. Two days later he received a bulky envelope, which contained a short note from the detective, and a typewritten document, which covered several pages of foolscap.

"Lestrade has got him all right," said Holmes, glancing up at me. "Perhaps it would interest you to hear what he says."

"MY DEAR MR. HOLMES:

"In accordance with the scheme which we had formed in order to test our theories" ["the 'we' is rather fine, Watson, is it not?"] "I went down to the Albert Dock yesterday at 6 P. M., and boarded the S. S. *May Day*, belonging to the Liverpool, Dublin, and London Steam Packet Company. On inquiry, I found that there was a steward on board of the name of James Browner and that he had acted during the voyage in such an extraordinary manner that the captain had been compelled to relieve him of his duties. On descending to his berth, I found him seated upon a chest with his head sunk upon his hands, rocking himself to and fro. He is a big, powerful chap, clean-shaven, and very swarthy—something like Aldridge, who helped us in the bogus laundry affair. He jumped up when he heard my business, and I had my whistle to my lips to call a couple of river police, who were round the corner, but he seemed to have no heart in him, and he held out his hands quietly enough for the darbies.* We brought him along to the cells, and his box as well, for we thought there might be something incriminating; but, bar a big sharp knife such as most sailors have, we got nothing for our trouble. However, we find that we shall want no more evidence, for on being brought before the inspector at the station he asked leave to make a statement, which was, of course, taken down, just as he made it, by our shorthand man. We had three copies typewritten, one of which I enclose. The affair proves, as I always thought it would, to be an extremely simple one, but I am obliged to you for assisting me in my investigation. With kind regards,
                                                        "Yours very truly,
                                                        "G. LESTRADE.

"Hum! The investigation really was a very simple one," remarked Holmes, "but I don't think it struck him in that light when he first called us in. However, let us see what Jim Browner has to say for himself. This is his statement as made before Inspector Montgomery at the Shadwell Police Station, and it has the advantage of being verbatim."

                            *   *   *

" 'Have I anything to say? Yes, I have a deal to say. I have to make a clean breast of it all. You can hang me, or you can leave me alone. I don't

---

*Handcuffs.

care a plug which you do. I tell you I've not shut an eye in sleep since I did it, and I don't believe I ever will again until I get past all waking. Sometimes it's his face, but most generally it's hers. I'm never without one or the other before me. He looks frowning and black-like, but she has a kind o' surprise upon her face. Ay, the white lamb, she might well be surprised when she read death on a face that had seldom looked anything but love upon her before.

" 'But it was Sarah's fault, and may the curse of a broken man put a blight on her and set the blood rotting in her veins! It's not that I want to clear myself. I know that I went back to drink, like the beast that I was. But she would have forgiven me; she would have stuck as close to me as a rope to a block if that woman had never darkened our door. For Sarah Cushing loved me—that's the root of the business—she loved me until all her love turned to poisonous hate when she knew that I thought more of my wife's footmark in the mud than I did of her whole body and soul.

" 'There were three sisters altogether. The old one was just a good woman, the second was a devil, and the third was an angel. Sarah was thirty-three, and Mary was twenty-nine when I married. We were just as happy as the day was long when we set up house together, and in all Liverpool there was no better woman than my Mary. And then we asked Sarah up for a week, and the week grew into a month, and one thing led to another, until she was just one of ourselves.

" 'I was blue ribbon* at that time, and we were putting a little money by, and all was as bright as a new dollar. My God, whoever would have thought that it could have come to this? Whoever would have dreamed it?

" 'I used to be home for the week-ends very often, and sometimes if the ship were held back for cargo I would have a whole week at a time, and in this way I saw a deal of my sister-in-law, Sarah. She was a fine tall woman, black and quick and fierce, with a proud way of carrying her head, and a glint from her eye like a spark from a flint. But when little Mary was there I had never a thought of her, and that I swear as I hope for God's mercy.

" 'It had seemed to me sometimes that she liked to be alone with me, or to coax me out for a walk with her, but I had never thought anything of that. But one evening my eyes were opened. I had come up from the ship and found my wife out, but Sarah at home. "Where's Mary?" I asked. "Oh, she has gone to pay some accounts." I was impatient and paced up and down the room. "Can't you be happy for five minutes without Mary, Jim?" says she. "It's a bad compliment to me that you can't be contented with my society for so short a time." "That's all right, my lass," said I, putting out my hand towards her in a kindly way, but she had it in both hers in an instant, and they burned as if they were in a fever. I looked into her eyes and I read it all there. There was no need for her to speak, nor for me either. I frowned and drew my hand away. Then she stood by my side

---

*Not drinking alcohol.

in silence for a bit, and then put up her hand and patted me on the shoulder. "Steady old Jim!" said she, and with a kind o' mocking laugh, she ran out of the room.

" 'Well, from that time Sarah hated me with her whole heart and soul, and she is a woman who can hate, too. I was a fool to let her go on biding with us—a besotted fool—but I never said a word to Mary, for I knew it would grieve her. Things went on much as before, but after a time I began to find that there was a bit of a change in Mary herself. She had always been so trusting and so innocent, but now she became queer and suspicious, wanting to know where I had been and what I had been doing, and whom my letters were from, and what I had in my pockets, and a thousand such follies. Day by day she grew queerer and more irritable, and we had ceaseless rows about nothing. I was fairly puzzled by it all. Sarah avoided me now, but she and Mary were just inseparable. I can see now how she was plotting and scheming and poisoning my wife's mind against me, but I was such a blind beetle that I could not understand it at the time. Then I broke my blue ribbon and began to drink again, but I think I should not have done it if Mary had been the same as ever. She had some reason to be disgusted with me now, and the gap between us began to be wider and wider. And then this Alec Fairbairn chipped in, and things became a thousand times blacker.

" 'It was to see Sarah that he came to my house first, but soon it was to see us, for he was a man with winning ways, and he made friends wherever he went. He was a dashing, swaggering chap, smart and curled, who had seen half the world and could talk of what he had seen. He was good company, I won't deny it, and he had wonderful polite ways with him for a sailor man, so that I think there must have been a time when he knew more of the poop than the forecastle.* For a month he was in and out of my house, and never once did it cross my mind that harm might come of his soft, tricky ways. And then at last something made me suspect, and from that day my peace was gone forever.

" 'It was only a little thing, too. I had come into the parlour unexpected, and as I walked in at the door I saw a light of welcome on my wife's face. But as she saw who it was it faded again, and she turned away with a look of disappointment. That was enough for me. There was no one but Alec Fairbairn whose step she could have mistaken for mine. If I could have seen him then I should have killed him, for I have always been like a madman when my temper gets loose. Mary saw the devil's light in my eyes, and she ran forward with her hands on my sleeve. "Don't, Jim, don't!" says she. "Where's Sarah?" I asked. "In the kitchen," says she. "Sarah," says I as I went in, "this man Fairbairn is never to darken my door again." "Why not?" says she. "Because I order it." "Oh!" says she, "if my friends are not good enough for this house, then I am not good enough for it either." "You can do what you like," says I, "but if Fairbairn

---

*Enlisted men lived in the forecastle; officers, in the poop deck.

shows his face here again I'll send you one of his ears for a keepsake."
She was frightened by my face, I think, for she never answered a word,
and the same evening she left my house.

"'Well, I don't know now whether it was pure devilry on the part of
this woman, or whether she thought that she could turn me against my
wife by encouraging her to misbehave. Anyway, she took a house just two
streets off and let lodgings to sailors. Fairbairn used to stay there, and
Mary would go round to have tea with her sister and him. How often she
went I don't know, but I followed her one day, and as I broke in at the
door Fairbairn got away over the back garden wall, like the cowardly
skunk that he was. I swore to my wife that I would kill her if I found her
in his company again, and I led her back with me, sobbing and trembling,
and as white as a piece of paper. There was no trace of love between us
any longer. I could see that she hated me and feared me, and when the
thought of it drove me to drink, then she despised me as well.

"'Well, Sarah found that she could not make a living in Liverpool, so
she went back, as I understand, to live with her sister in Croydon, and
things jogged on much the same as ever at home. And then came this last
week and all the misery and ruin.

"'It was in this way. We had gone on the *May Day* for a round voyage
of seven days, but a hogshead* got loose and started one of our plates, so
that we had to put back into port for twelve hours. I left the ship and
came home, thinking what a surprise it would be for my wife, and hoping
that maybe she would be glad to see me so soon. The thought was in my
head as I turned into my own street, and at that moment a cab passed me,
and there she was, sitting by the side of Fairbairn, the two chatting and
laughing, with never a thought for me as I stood watching them from the
footpath.

"'I tell you, and I give you my word for it, that from that moment I was
not my own master, and it is all like a dim dream when I look back on it.
I had been drinking hard of late, and the two things together fairly turned
my brain. There's something throbbing in my head now, like a docker's
hammer, but that morning I seemed to have all Niagara whizzing and
buzzing in my ears.

"'Well, I took to my heels, and I ran after the cab. I had a heavy oak
stick in my hand, and I tell you I saw red from the first; but as I ran I got
cunning, too, and hung back a little to see them without being seen. They
pulled up soon at the railway station. There was a good crowd round the
booking-office, so I got quite close to them without being seen. They took
tickets for New Brighton. So did I, but I got in three carriages behind
them. When we reached it they walked along the Parade, and I was never
more than a hundred yards from them. At last I saw them hire a boat and
start for a row, for it was a very hot day, and they thought, no doubt, that
it would be cooler on the water.

---

*Large barrel.

" 'It was just as if they had been given into my hands. There was a bit of a haze, and you could not see more than a few hundred yards. I hired a boat for myself; and I pulled after them. I could see the blur of their craft, but they were going nearly as fast as I, and they must have been a long mile from the shore before I caught them up. The haze was like a curtain all round us, and there were we three in the middle of it. My God, shall I ever forget their faces when they saw who was in the boat that was closing in upon them? She screamed out. He swore like a madman and jabbed at me with an oar, for he must have seen death in my eyes. I got past it and got one in with my stick that crushed his head like an egg. I would have spared her, perhaps, for all my madness, but she threw her arms round him, crying out to him, and calling him "Alec." I struck again, and she lay stretched beside him. I was like a wild beast then that had tasted blood. If Sarah had been there, by the Lord, she should have joined them. I pulled out my knife, and—well, there! I've said enough. It gave me a kind of savage joy when I thought how Sarah would feel when she had such signs as these of what her meddling had brought about. Then I tied the bodies into the boat, stove a plank, and stood by until they had sunk. I knew very well that the owner would think that they had lost their bearings in the haze, and had drifted off out to sea. I cleaned myself up, got back to land, and joined my ship without a soul having a suspicion of what had passed. That night I made up the packet for Sarah Cushing, and next day I sent it from Belfast.

" 'There you have the whole truth of it. You can hang me, or do what you like with me, but you cannot punish me as I have been punished already. I cannot shut my eyes but I see those two faces staring at me—staring at me as they stared when my boat broke through the haze. I killed them quick, but they are killing me slow; and if I have another night of it I shall be either mad or dead before morning. You won't put me alone into a cell, sir? For pity's sake don't, and may you be treated in your day of agony as you treat me now.'

"What is the meaning of it, Watson?" said Holmes solemnly as he laid down the paper. "What object is served by this circle of misery and violence and fear? It must tend to some end, or else our universe is ruled by chance, which is unthinkable. But what end? There is the great standing perennial problem to which human reason is as far from an answer as ever."

THE ADVENTURE OF THE RED CIRCLE

1

"**W**ell, Mrs. Warren, I cannot see that you have any particular cause for uneasiness, nor do I understand why I, whose time is of some value, should interfere in the matter. I really have other things to engage me." So spoke Sherlock Holmes and turned back to the great scrapbook in which he was arranging and indexing some of his recent material.

But the landlady had the pertinacity and also the cunning of her sex. She held her ground firmly.

"You arranged an affair for a lodger of mine last year," she said—"Mr. Fairdale Hobbs."

"Ah, yes—a simple matter."

"But he would never cease talking of it—your kindness, sir, and the way in which you brought light into the darkness. I remembered his words when I was in doubt and darkness myself. I know you could if you only would."

Holmes was accessible upon the side of flattery, and also, to do him justice, upon the side of kindliness. The two forces made him lay down his gum-brush with a sigh of resignation and push back his chair.

"Well, well, Mrs. Warren, let us hear about it, then. You don't object to tobacco, I take it? Thank you, Watson—the matches! You are uneasy, as I understand, because your new lodger remains in his rooms and you cannot see him. Why, bless you, Mrs. Warren, if I were your lodger you often would not see me for weeks on end."

"No doubt, sir; but this is different. It frightens me, Mr. Holmes. I can't sleep for fright. To hear his quick step moving here and moving there from early morning to late at night, and yet never to catch so much as a glimpse of him—it's more than I can stand. My husband is as nervous over it as I am, but he is out at his work all day, while I get no rest from it. What is he hiding for? What has he done? Except for the girl, I am all alone in the house with him, and it's more than my nerves can stand."

Holmes leaned forward and laid his long, thin fingers upon the woman's shoulder. He had an almost hypnotic power of soothing when he wished. The scared look faded from her eyes, and her agitated features smoothed into their usual commonplace. She sat down in the chair which he had indicated.

"If I take it up I must understand every detail," said he. "Take time to consider. The smallest point may be the most essential. You say that the man came ten days ago and paid you for a fortnight's board and lodging?"

"He asked my terms, sir. I said fifty shillings a week. There is a small sitting-room and bedroom, and all complete, at the top of the house."

"Well?"

"He said, 'I'll pay you five pounds a week if I can have it on my own terms.' I'm a poor woman, sir, and Mr. Warren earns little, and the money meant much to me. He took out a ten-pound note, and he held it out to me then and there. 'You can have the same every fortnight for a long time to come if you keep the terms,' he said. 'If not, I'll have no more to do with you.'"

"What were the terms?"

"Well, sir, they were that he was to have a key of the house. That was all right. Lodgers often have them. Also, that he was to be left entirely to himself and never, upon any excuse, to be disturbed."

"Nothing wonderful in that, surely?"

"Not in reason, sir. But this is out of all reason. He has been there for ten days, and neither Mr. Warren, nor I, nor the girl has once set eyes upon him. We can hear that quick step of his pacing up and down, up and down, night, morning, and noon; but except on that first night he has never once gone out of the house."

"Oh, he went out the first night, did he?"

"Yes, sir, and returned very late—after we were all in bed. He told me after he had taken the rooms that he would do so and asked me not to bar the door. I heard him come up the stair after midnight."

"But his meals?"

"It was his particular direction that we should always, when he rang, leave his meal upon a chair, outside his door. Then he rings again when he has finished, and we take it down from the same chair. If he wants anything else he prints it on a slip of paper and leaves it."

"Prints it?"

"Yes, sir; prints it in pencil. Just the word, nothing more. Here's one I brought to show you—SOAP. Here's another—MATCH. This is one he left the first morning—DAILY GAZETTE. I leave that paper with his breakfast every morning."

"Dear me, Watson," said Holmes, staring with great curiosity at the slips of foolscap which the landlady had handed to him, "this is certainly a little unusual. Seclusion I can understand; but why print? Printing is a clumsy process. Why not write? What would it suggest, Watson?"

"That he desired to conceal his handwriting."

"But why? What can it matter to him that his landlady should have a word of his writing? Still, it may be as you say. Then, again, why such laconic messages?"

"I cannot imagine."

"It opens a pleasing field for intelligent speculation. The words are written with a broad-pointed, violet-tinted pencil of a not unusual pattern. You will observe that the paper is torn away at the side here after the printing was done, so that the 's' of 'SOAP' is partly gone. Suggestive, Watson, is it not?"

"Of caution?"

"Exactly. There was evidently some mark, some thumbprint, something which might give a clue to the person's identity. Now, Mrs. Warren, you say that the man was of middle size, dark, and bearded. What age would he be?"

"Youngish, sir—not over thirty."

"Well, can you give me no further indications?"

"He spoke good English, sir, and yet I thought he was a foreigner by his accent."

"And he was well dressed?"

"Very smartly dressed, sir—quite the gentleman. Dark clothes—nothing you would note."

"He gave no name?"

"No, sir."

"And has had no letters or callers?"

"None."

"But surely you or the girl enter his room of a morning?"

"No, sir; he looks after himself entirely."

"Dear me! that is certainly remarkable. What about his luggage?"

"He had one big brown bag with him—nothing else."

"Well, we don't seem to have much material to help us. Do you say nothing has come out of that room—absolutely nothing?"

The landlady drew an envelope from her bag; from it she shook out two burnt matches and a cigarette-end upon the table.

"They were on his tray this morning. I brought them because I had heard that you can read great things out of small ones."

Holmes shrugged his shoulders.

"There is nothing here," said he. "The matches have, of course, been used to light cigarettes. That is obvious from the shortness of the burnt end. Half the match is consumed in lighting a pipe or cigar. But, dear me! this cigarette stub is certainly remarkable. The gentleman was bearded and moustached, you say?"

"Yes, sir."

"I don't understand that. I should say that only a clean-shaven man could have smoked this. Why, Watson, even your modest moustache would have been singed."

"A holder?" I suggested.

"No, no; the end is matted. I suppose there could not be two people in your rooms, Mrs. Warren?"

"No, sir. He eats so little that I often wonder it can keep life in one."

"Well, I think we must wait for a little more material. After all, you have nothing to complain of. You have received your rent, and he is not a troublesome lodger, though he is certainly an unusual one. He pays you well, and if he chooses to lie concealed it is no direct business of yours. We have no excuse for an intrusion upon his privacy until we have some reason to think that there is a guilty reason for it. I've taken up the matter, and I won't lose sight of it. Report to me if anything fresh occurs, and rely upon my assistance if it should be needed.

"There are certainly some points of interest in this case, Watson," he remarked when the landlady had left us. "It may, of course, be trivial—individual eccentricity; or it may be very much deeper than appears on the surface. The first thing that strikes one is the obvious possibility that the person now in the rooms may be entirely different from the one who engaged them."

"Why should you think so?"

"Well, apart from this cigarette-end, was it not suggestive that the only time the lodger went out was immediately after his taking the rooms? He came back—or someone came back—when all witnesses were out of the way. We have no proof that the person who came back was the person who went out. Then, again, the man who took the rooms spoke English well. This other, however, prints 'match' when it should have been 'matches.' I can imagine that the word was taken out of a dictionary, which would give the noun but not the plural. The laconic style may be to conceal the absence of knowledge of English. Yes, Watson, there are good reasons to suspect that there has been a substitution of lodgers."

"But for what possible end?"

"Ah! there lies our problem. There is one rather obvious line of investigation." He took down the great book in which, day by day, he filed the agony columns of the various London journals. "Dear me!" said he, turning over the pages, "what a chorus of groans, cries, and bleatings! What a rag-bag of singular happenings! But surely the most valuable hunting-ground that ever was given to a student of the unusual! This person is alone and cannot be approached by letter without a breach of that absolute secrecy which is desired. How is any news or any message to reach him from without? Obviously by advertisement through a newspaper. There seems no other way, and fortunately we need concern ourselves with the one paper only. Here are the *Daily Gazette* extracts of the last fortnight. 'Lady with a black boa at Prince's Skating Club'—that we may pass. 'Surely Jimmy will not break his mother's heart'—that appears to be irrelevant. 'If the lady who fainted in the Brixton bus'—she does not interest me. 'Every day my heart longs——' Bleat, Watson—unmitigated bleat! Ah, this is a little more possible. Listen to this: 'Be patient. Will find some sure means of communication. Meanwhile, this column. G.' That is two days after Mrs. Warren's lodger arrived. It sounds plausible, does it not? The mysterious one could understand English, even if he could not print it. Let us see if we can pick up the trace again. Yes, here we are—three days later. 'Am making successful arrangements. Patience and prudence. The clouds will pass. G.' Nothing for a week after that. Then comes something much more definite: 'The path is clearing. If I find chance signal message remember code agreed—one A, two B, and so on. You will hear soon. G.' That was in yesterday's paper, and there is nothing in to-day's. It's all very appropriate to Mrs. Warren's lodger. If we wait a little, Watson, I don't doubt that the affair will grow more intelligible."

So it proved; for in the morning I found my friend standing on the hearthrug with his back to the fire and a smile of complete satisfaction upon his face.

"How's this, Watson?" he cried, picking up the paper from the table. "'High red house with white stone facings. Third floor. Second window left. After dusk. G.' That is definite enough. I think after breakfast we must make a little reconnaissance of Mrs. Warren's neighbourhood. Ah, Mrs. Warren! what news do you bring us this morning?"

Our client had suddenly burst into the room with an explosive energy which told of some new and momentous development.

"It's a police matter, Mr. Holmes!" she cried. "I'll have no more of it! He shall pack out of there with his baggage. I would have gone straight up and told him so, only I thought it was but fair to you to take your opinion first. But I'm at the end of my patience, and when it comes to knocking my old man about——"

"Knocking Mr. Warren about?"

"Using him roughly, anyway."

"But who used him roughly?"

"Ah! that's what we want to know! It was this morning, sir. Mr. Warren is a timekeeper at Morton and Waylight's, in Tottenham Court Road. He has to be out of the house before seven. Well, this morning he had not gone ten paces down the road when two men came up behind him, threw a coat over his head, and bundled him into a cab that was beside the curb. They drove him an hour, and then opened the door and shot him out. He lay in the roadway so shaken in his wits that he never saw what became of the cab. When he picked himself up he found he was on Hampstead Heath; so he took a bus home, and there he lies now on the sofa, while I came straight round to tell you what had happened."

"Most interesting," said Holmes. "Did he observe the appearance of these men—did he hear them talk?"

"No; he is clean dazed. He just knows that he was lifted up as if by magic and dropped as if by magic. Two at least were in it, and maybe three."

"And you connect this attack with your lodger?"

"Well, we've lived there fifteen years and no such happenings ever came before. I've had enough of him. Money's not everything. I'll have him out of my house before the day is done."

"Wait a bit, Mrs. Warren. Do nothing rash. I begin to think that this affair may be very much more important than appeared at first sight. It is clear now that some danger is threatening your lodger. It is equally clear that his enemies, lying in wait for him near your door, mistook your husband for him in the foggy morning light. On discovering their mistake they released him. What they would have done had it not been a mistake, we can only conjecture.

"Well, what am I to do, Mr. Holmes?"

"I have a great fancy to see this lodger of yours, Mrs. Warren."

"I don't see how that is to be managed, unless you break in the door. I always hear him unlock it as I go down the stair after I leave the tray."

"He has to take the tray in. Surely we could conceal ourselves and see him do it."

The landlady thought for a moment.

"Well, sir, there's the box-room opposite. I could arrange a looking-glass, maybe, and if you were behind the door——"

"Excellent!" said Holmes: "When does he lunch?"

"About one, sir."

"Then Dr. Watson and I will come round in time. For the present, Mrs. Warren, good-bye."

At half-past twelve we found ourselves upon the steps of Mrs. Warren's house—a high, thin, yellow-brick edifice in Great Orme Street, a narrow thoroughfare at the northeast side of the British Museum. Standing as it does near the corner of the street, it commands a view down Howe Street, with its more pretentious houses. Holmes pointed with a chuckle to one of these, a row of residential flats, which projected so that they could not fail to catch the eye.

"See, Watson!" said he. " 'High red house with stone facings.' There is the signal station all right. We know the place, and we know the code; so surely our task should be simple. There's a 'to let' card in that window. It is evidently an empty flat to which the confederate has access. Well, Mrs. Warren, what now?"

"I have it all ready for you. If you will both come up and leave your boots below on the landing, I'll put you there now."

It was an excellent hiding-place which she had arranged. The mirror was so placed that, seated in the dark, we could very plainly see the door opposite. We had hardly settled down in it, and Mrs. Warren left us, when a distant tinkle announced that our mysterious neighbour had rung. Presently the landlady appeared with the tray, laid it down upon a chair beside the closed door, and then, treading heavily, departed. Crouching together in the angle of the door, we kept our eyes fixed upon the mirror. Suddenly, as the landlady's footsteps died away, there was the creak of a turning key, the handle revolved, and two thin hands darted out and lifted the tray from the chair. An instant later it was hurriedly replaced, and I caught a glimpse of a dark, beautiful, horrified face glaring at the narrow opening of the box-room. Then the door crashed to, the key turned once more, and all was silence. Holmes twitched my sleeve, and together we stole down the stair.

"I will call again in the evening," said he to the expectant landlady. "I think, Watson, we can discuss this business better in our own quarters."

"My surmise, as you saw, proved to be correct," said he, speaking from the depths of his easy-chair. "There has been a substitution of lodgers. What I did not foresee is that we should find a woman, and no ordinary woman, Watson."

"She saw us."

"Well, she saw something to alarm her. That is certain. The general sequence of events is pretty clear, is it not? A couple seek refuge in London from a very terrible and instant danger. The measure of that danger is the rigour of their precautions. The man, who has some work which he must do, desires to leave the woman in absolute safety while he does it. It is not an easy problem, but he solved it in an original fashion, and so effectively that her presence was not even known to the landlady who supplies her with food. The printed messages, as is now evident, were to prevent her sex being discovered by her writing. The man cannot come near the woman, or he will guide their enemies to her. Since he cannot communicate with her direct, he has recourse to the agony column of a paper. So far all is clear."

"But what is at the root of it?"

"Ah, yes, Watson—severely practical, as usual! What is at the root of it all? Mrs. Warren's whimsical problem enlarges somewhat and assumes a more sinister aspect as we proceed. This much we can say: that it is no ordinary love escapade. You saw the woman's face at the sign of danger. We have heard, too, of the attack upon the landlord, which was undoubtedly meant for the lodger. These alarms, and the desperate need for secrecy, argue that the matter is one of life or death. The attack upon Mr. Warren further shows that the enemy, whoever they are, are themselves not aware of the substitution of the female lodger for the male. It is very curious and complex, Watson."

"Why should you go further in it? What have you to gain from it?"

"What, indeed? It is art for art's sake, Watson. I suppose when you doctored you found yourself studying cases without thought of a fee?"

"For my education, Holmes."

"Education never ends, Watson. It is a series of lessons with the greatest for the last. This is an instructive case. There is neither money nor credit in it, and yet one would wish to tidy it up. When dusk comes we should find ourselves one stage advanced in our investigation."

When we returned to Mrs. Warren's rooms, the gloom of a London winter evening had thickened into one gray curtain, a dead monotone of colour, broken only by the sharp yellow squares of the windows and the blurred haloes of the gas-lamps. As we peered from the darkened sitting-room of the lodging-house, one more dim light glimmered high up through the obscurity.

"Someone is moving in that room," said Holmes in a whisper, his gaunt and eager face thrust forward to the window-pane. "Yes, I can see his shadow. There he is again! He has a candle in his hand. Now he is peering across. He wants to be sure that she is on the lookout. Now he begins to flash. Take the message also, Watson, that we may check each other. A single flash—that is A, surely. Now, then. How many did you make it? Twenty. So did I. That should mean T. AT—that's intelligible enough! Another T. Surely this is the beginning of a second word. Now, then—TENTA. Dead stop. That can't be all, Watson? ATTENTA gives no sense. Nor is it any better as three words AT, TEN, TA, unless T. A. are a person's initials.

There it goes again! What's that? ATTE—why, it is the same message over again. Curious, Watson, very curious! Now he is off once more! AT—why, he is repeating it for the third time. ATTENTA three times! How often will he repeat it? No, that seems to be the finish. He has withdrawn from the window. What do you make of it, Watson?"

"A cipher message, Holmes."

My companion gave a sudden chuckle of comprehension. "And not a very obscure cipher, Watson," said he. "Why, of course, it is Italian! The A means that it is addressed to a woman. 'Beware! Beware! Beware!' How's that, Watson?"

"I believe you have hit it."

"Not a doubt of it. It is a very urgent message, thrice repeated to make it more so. But beware of what? Wait a bit; he is coming to the window once more."

Again we saw the dim silhouette of a crouching man and the whisk of the small flame across the window as the signals were renewed. They came more rapidly than before—so rapid that it was hard to follow them.

"PERICOLO—*pericolo*—eh, what's that, Watson? 'Danger,' isn't it? Yes, by Jove, it's a danger signal. There he goes again! PERI. Halloa, what on earth——"

The light had suddenly gone out, the glimmering square of window had disappeared, and the third floor formed a dark band round the lofty building, with its tiers of shining casements. That last warning cry had been suddenly cut short. How, and by whom? The same thought occurred on the instant to us both. Holmes sprang up from where he crouched by the window.

"This is serious, Watson," he cried. "There is some devilry going forward! Why should such a message stop in such a way? I should put Scotland Yard in touch with this business—and yet, it is too pressing for us to leave."

"Shall I go for the police?"

"We must define the situation a little more clearly. It may bear some more innocent interpretation. Come, Watson, let us go across ourselves and see what we can make of it."

2

As we walked rapidly down Howe Street I glanced back at the building which we had left. There, dimly outlined at the top window, I could see the shadow of a head, a woman's head, gazing tensely, rigidly, out into the night, waiting with breathless suspense for the renewal of that interrupted message. At the doorway of the Howe Street flats a man, muffled in a cravat and greatcoat, was leaning against the railing. He started as the hall-light fell upon our faces.

"Holmes!" he cried.

"Why, Gregson!" said my companion as he shook hands with the Scotland Yard detective. "Journeys end with lovers' meetings.* What brings you here?"

"The same reasons that bring you, I expect," said Gregson. "How you got on to it I can't imagine."

"Different threads, but leading up to the same tangle. I've been taking the signals."

"Signals?"

"Yes, from that window. They broke off in the middle. We came over to see the reason. But since it is safe in your hands I see no object in continuing the business."

"Wait a bit!" cried Gregson eagerly. "I'll do you this justice, Mr. Holmes, that I was never in a case yet that I didn't feel stronger for having you on my side. There's only the one exit to these flats, so we have him safe."

"Who is he?"

"Well, well, we score over you for once, Mr. Holmes. You must give us best this time." He struck his stick sharply upon the ground, on which a cabman, his whip in his hand, sauntered over from a four-wheeler which stood on the far side of the street. "May I introduce you to Mr. Sherlock Holmes?" he said to the cabman. "This is Mr. Leverton, of Pinkerton's American Agency."

"The hero of the Long Island cave mystery?" said Holmes. "Sir, I am pleased to meet you."

The American, a quiet, businesslike young man, with a clean-shaven, hatchet face, flushed up at the words of commendation. "I am on the trail of my life now, Mr. Holmes," said he. "If I can get Gorgiano——"

"What! Gorgiano of the Red Circle?"

"Oh, he has a European fame, has he? Well, we've learned all about him in America. We *know* he is at the bottom of fifty murders, and yet we have nothing positive we can take him on. I tracked him over from New York, and I've been close to him for a week in London, waiting some excuse to get my hand on his collar. Mr. Gregson and I ran him to ground in that big tenement house, and there's only the one door, so he can't slip us. There's three folk come out since he went in, but I'll swear he wasn't one of them."

"Mr. Holmes talks of signals," said Gregson. "I expect, as usual, he knows a good deal that we don't."

In a few clear words Holmes explained the situation as it had appeared to us.

The American struck his hands together with vexation.

"He's on to us!" he cried.

---

*Again Holmes misquotes *Twelfth Night* (scene 2, scene 3); Shakespeare wrote: "Journeys end in lovers meeting."

"Why do you think so?"

"Well, it figures out that way, does it not? Here he is, sending out messages to an accomplice—there are several of his gang in London. Then suddenly, just as by your own account he was telling them that there was danger, he broke short off. What could it mean except that from the window he had suddenly either caught sight of us in the street, or in some way come to understand how close the danger was, and that he must act right away if he was to avoid it? What do you suggest, Mr. Holmes?"

"That we go up at once and see for ourselves."

"But we have no warrant for his arrest."

"He is in unoccupied premises under suspicious circumstances," said Gregson. "That is good enough for the moment. When we have him by the heels we can see if New York can't help us to keep him. I'll take the responsibility of arresting him now."

Our official detectives may blunder in the matter of intelligence, but never in that of courage. Gregson climbed the stair to arrest this desperate murderer with the same absolutely quiet and businesslike bearing with which he would have ascended the official staircase of Scotland Yard. The Pinkerton man had tried to push past him, but Gregson had firmly elbowed him back. London dangers were the privilege of the London force.

The door of the left-hand flat upon the third landing was standing ajar. Gregson pushed it open. Within all was absolute silence and darkness. I struck a match and lit the detective's lantern. As I did so, and as the flicker steadied into a flame, we all gave a gasp of surprise. On the deal boards of the carpetless floor there was outlined a fresh track of blood. The red steps pointed towards us and led away from an inner room, the door of which was closed. Gregson flung it open and held his light full blaze in front of him, while we all peered eagerly over his shoulders.

In the middle of the floor of the empty room was huddled the figure of an enormous man, his clean-shaven, swarthy face grotesquely horrible in its contortion and his head encircled by a ghastly crimson halo of blood, lying in a broad wet circle upon the white woodwork. His knees were drawn up, his hands thrown out in agony, and from the centre of his broad, brown, upturned throat there projected the white haft of a knife driven blade-deep into his body. Giant as he was, the man must have gone down like a pole-axed ox before that terrific blow. Beside his right hand a most formidable horn-handled, two-edged dagger lay upon the floor, and near it a black kid glove.

"By George! it's Black Gorgiano himself!" cried the American detective. "Someone has got ahead of us this time."

"Here is the candle in the window, Mr. Holmes," said Gregson. "Why, whatever are you doing?"

Holmes had stepped across, had lit the candle, and was passing it backward and forward across the window-panes. Then he peered into the darkness, blew the candle out, and threw it on the floor.

"I rather think that will be helpful," said he. He came over and stood in deep thought while the two professionals were examining the body. "You say that three people came out from the flat while you were waiting downstairs," said he at last. "Did you observe them closely?"

"Yes, I did."

"Was there a fellow about thirty, black-bearded, dark, of middle size?"

"Yes; he was the last to pass me."

"That is your man, I fancy. I can give you his description, and we have a very excellent outline of his footmark. That should be enough for you."

"Not much, Mr. Holmes, among the millions of London."

"Perhaps not. That is why I thought it best to summon this lady to your aid."

We all turned round at the words. There, framed in the doorway, was a tall and beautiful woman—the mysterious lodger of Bloomsbury. Slowly she advanced, her face pale and drawn with a frightful apprehension, her eyes fixed and staring, her terrified gaze riveted upon the dark figure on the floor.

"You have killed him!" she muttered. "Oh, *Dio mio*, you have killed him!" Then I heard a sudden sharp intake of her breath, and she sprang into the air with a cry of joy. Round and round the room she danced, her hands clapping, her dark eyes gleaming with delighted wonder, and a thousand pretty Italian exclamations pouring from her lips. It was terrible and amazing to see such a woman so convulsed with joy at such a sight. Suddenly she stopped and gazed at us all with a questioning stare.

"But you! You are police, are you not? You have killed Giuseppe Gorgiano. Is it not so?"

"We are police, madam."

She looked round into the shadows of the room.

"But where, then, is Gennaro?" she asked. "He is my husband, Gennaro Lucca. I am Emilia Lucca, and we are both from New York. Where is Gennaro? He called me this moment from this window, and I ran with all my speed."

"It was I who called," said Holmes.

"You! How could you call?"

"Your cipher was not difficult, madam. Your presence here was desirable. I knew that I had only to flash '*Vieni*' and you would surely come."

The beautiful Italian looked with awe at my companion.

"I do not understand how you know these things," she said. "Giuseppe Gorgiano—how did he——" She paused, and then suddenly her face lit up with pride and delight. "Now I see it! My Gennaro! My splendid, beautiful Gennaro, who has guarded me safe from all harm, he did it, with his own strong hand he killed the monster! Oh, Gennaro, how wonderful you are! What woman could ever be worthy of such a man?"

"Well, Mrs. Lucca," said the prosaic Gregson, laying his hand upon the lady's sleeve with as little sentiment as if she were a Notting Hill hooligan, "I am not very clear yet who you are or what you are; but you've said enough to make it very clear that we shall want you at the Yard."

"One moment, Gregson," said Holmes. "I rather fancy that this lady may be as anxious to give us information as we can be to get it. You understand, madam, that your husband will be arrested and tried for the death of the man who lies before us? What you say may be used in evidence. But if you think that he has acted from motives which are not criminal, and which he would wish to have known, then you cannot serve him better than by telling us the whole story."

"Now that Gorgiano is dead we fear nothing," said the lady. "He was a devil and a monster, and there can be no judge in the world who would punish my husband for having killed him."

"In that case," said Holmes, "my suggestion is that we lock this door, leave things as we found them, go with this lady to her room, and form our opinion after we have heard what it is that she has to say to us."

Half an hour later we were seated, all four, in the small sitting-room of Signora Lucca, listening to her remarkable narrative of those sinister events, the ending of which we had chanced to witness. She spoke in rapid and fluent but very unconventional English, which, for the sake of clearness, I will make grammatical.

"I was born in Posilippo, near Naples," said she, "and was the daughter of Augusto Barelli, who was the chief lawyer and once the deputy of that part. Gennaro was in my father's employment, and I came to love him, as any woman must. He had neither money nor position—nothing but his beauty and strength and energy—so my father forbade the match. We fled together, were married at Bari, and sold my jewels to gain the money which would take us to America. This was four years ago, and we have been in New York ever since.

"Fortune was very good to us at first. Gennaro was able to do a service to an Italian gentleman—he saved him from some ruffians in the place called the Bowery, and so made a powerful friend. His name was Tito Castalotte, and he was the senior partner of the great firm of Castalotte and Zamba, who are the chief fruit importers of New York. Signor Zamba is an invalid, and our new friend Castalotte has all power within the firm, which employs more than three hundred men. He took my husband into his employment, made him head of a department, and showed his goodwill towards him in every way. Signor Castalotte was a bachelor, and I believe that he felt as if Gennaro was his son, and both my husband and I loved him as if he were our father. We had taken and furnished a little house in Brooklyn, and our whole future seemed assured when that black cloud appeared which was soon to overspread our sky.

"One night, when Gennaro returned from his work, he brought a fellow-countryman back with him. His name was Gorgiano, and he had come also from Posilippo. He was a huge man, as you can testify, for you have looked upon his corpse. Not only was his body that of a giant but everything about him was grotesque, gigantic, and terrifying. His voice was like thunder in our little house. There was scarce room for the whirl of his great arms as he talked. His thoughts, his emotions, his passions, all were exaggerated and monstrous. He talked, or rather roared, with such energy that others could but sit and listen, cowed with the mighty stream of words. His eyes blazed at you and held you at his mercy. He was a terrible and wonderful man. I thank God that he is dead!

"He came again and again. Yet I was aware that Gennaro was no more happy than I was in his presence. My poor husband would sit pale and listless, listening to the endless raving upon politics and upon social questions which made up our visitor's conversation. Gennaro said nothing, but I, who knew him so well, could read in his face some emotion which I had never seen there before. At first I thought that it was dislike. And then, gradually, I understood that it was more than dislike. It was fear—a deep, secret, shrinking fear. That night—the night that I read his terror—I put my arms round him and I implored him by his love for me and by all that he held dear to hold nothing from me, and to tell me why this huge man overshadowed him so.

"He told me, and my own heart grew cold as ice as I listened. My poor Gennaro, in his wild and fiery days, when all the world seemed against him and his mind was driven half mad by the injustices of life, had joined a Neapolitan society, the Red Circle, which was allied to the old Carbonari.* The oaths and secrets of this brotherhood were frightful, but once within its rule no escape was possible. When we had fled to America Gennaro thought that he had cast it all off forever. What was his horror one evening to meet in the streets the very man who had initiated him in Naples, the giant Gorgiano, a man who had earned the name of 'Death' in the south of Italy, for he was red to the elbow in murder! He had come to New York to avoid the Italian police, and he had already planted a branch of this dreadful society in his new home. All this Gennaro told me and showed me a summons which he had received that very day, a Red Circle drawn upon the head of it telling him that a lodge would be held upon a certain date, and that his presence at it was required and ordered.

"That was bad enough, but worse was to come. I had noticed for some time that when Gorgiano came to us, as he constantly did, in the evening, he spoke much to me; and even when his words were to my husband those terrible, glaring, wild-beast eyes of his were always turned upon me. One night his secret came out. I had awakened what he called 'love' within him—the love of a brute—a savage. Gennaro had not yet returned when he came. He pushed his way in, seized me in his mighty arms, hugged me in his bear's embrace, covered me with kisses, and implored me to come away with him. I was struggling and screaming when Gennaro entered and attacked him. He struck Gennaro senseless and fled from the house which he was never more to enter. It was a deadly enemy that we made that night.

"A few days later came the meeting. Gennaro returned from it with a face which told me that something dreadful had occurred. It was worse than we could have imagined possible. The funds of the society were raised by blackmailing rich Italians and threatening them with violence

---

*Secret political society in France and Italy in the early nineteenth century.

should they refuse the money. It seems that Castalotte, our dear friend and benefactor, had been approached. He had refused to yield to threats, and he had handed the notices to the police. It was resolved now that such an example should be made of him as would prevent any other victim from rebelling. At the meeting it was arranged that he and his house should be blown up with dynamite. There was a drawing of lots as to who should carry out the deed. Gennaro saw our enemy's cruel face smiling at him as he dipped his hand in the bag. No doubt it had been prearranged in some fashion, for it was the fatal disc with the Red Circle upon it, the mandate for murder, which lay upon his palm. He was to kill his best friend, or he was to expose himself and me to the vengeance of his comrades. It was part of their fiendish system to punish those whom they feared or hated by injuring not only their own persons but those whom they loved, and it was the knowledge of this which hung as a terror over my poor Gennaro's head and drove him nearly crazy with apprehension.

"All that night we sat together, our arms round each other, each strengthening each for the troubles that lay before us. The very next evening had been fixed for the attempt. By midday my husband and I were on our way to London, but not before he had given our benefactor full warning of his danger, and had also left such information for the police as would safeguard his life for the future.

"The rest, gentlemen, you know for yourselves. We were sure that our enemies would be behind us like our own shadows. Gorgiano had his private reasons for vengeance, but in any case we knew how ruthless, cunning, and untiring he could be. Both Italy and America are full of stories of his dreadful powers. If ever they were exerted it would be now. My darling made use of the few clear days which our start had given us in arranging for a refuge for me in such a fashion that no possible danger could reach me. For his own part, he wished to be free that he might communicate both with the American and with the Italian police. I do not myself know where he lived, or how. All that I learned was through the columns of a newspaper. But once as I looked through my window, I saw two Italians watching the house, and I understood that in some way Gorgiano had found out our retreat. Finally Gennaro told me, through the paper, that he would signal to me from a certain window, but when the signals came they were nothing but warnings, which were suddenly interrupted. It is very clear to me now that he knew Gorgiano to be close upon him, and that, thank God! he was ready for him when he came. And now, gentlemen, I would ask you whether we have anything to fear from the law, or whether any judge upon earth would condemn my Gennaro for what he has done?"

"Well, Mr. Gregson," said the American, looking across at the official, "I don't know what your British point of view may be, but I guess that in New York this lady's husband will receive a pretty general vote of thanks."

"She will have to come with me and see the chief," Gregson answered. "If what she says is corroborated, I do not think she or her husband has much to fear. But what I can't make head or tail of, Mr. Holmes, is how on earth *you* got yourself mixed up in the matter."

"Education, Gregson, education. Still seeking knowledge at the old university. Well, Watson, you have one more specimen of the tragic and grotesque to add to your collection. By the way, it is not eight o'clock, and a Wagner night at Covent Garden!* If we hurry, we might be in time for the second act."

---

*Covent Garden Theatre is London's world-renowned opera house.

THE ADVENTURE OF THE
BRUCE-PARTINGTON PLANS

In the third week of November, in the year 1895, a dense yellow fog settled down upon London. From the Monday to the Thursday I doubt whether it was ever possible from our windows in Baker Street to see the loom of the opposite houses. The first day Holmes had spent in cross-indexing his huge book of references. The second and third had been patiently occupied upon a subject which he had recently made his hobby—the music of the Middle Ages. But when, for the fourth time, after pushing back our chairs from breakfast we saw the greasy, heavy brown swirl still drifting past us and condensing in oily drops upon the window-panes, my comrade's impatient and active nature could endure this drab existence no longer. He paced restlessly about our sitting-room in a fever of suppressed energy, biting his nails, tapping the furniture, and chafing against inaction.

"Nothing of interest in the paper, Watson?" he said.

I was aware that by anything of interest, Holmes meant anything of criminal interest. There was the news of a revolution, of a possible war, and of an impending change of government; but these did not come within the horizon of my companion. I could see nothing recorded in the shape of crime which was not commonplace and futile. Holmes groaned and resumed his restless meanderings.

"The London criminal is certainly a dull fellow," said he in the querulous voice of the sportsman whose game has failed him. "Look out of this window, Watson. See how the figures loom up, are dimly seen, and then blend once more into the cloud-bank. The thief or the murderer could roam London on such a day as the tiger does the jungle, unseen until he pounces, and then evident only to his victim."

"There have," said I, "been numerous petty thefts."

Holmes snorted his contempt.

"This great and sombre stage is set for something more worthy than that," said he. "It is fortunate for this community that I am not a criminal."

"It is, indeed!" said I heartily.

"Suppose that I were Brooks or Woodhouse, or any of the fifty men who have good reason for taking my life, how long could I survive against my own pursuit? A summons, a bogus appointment, and all would be over. It is well they don't have days of fog in the Latin countries—the countries of assassination. By Jove! here comes something at last to break our dead monotony."

It was the maid with a telegram. Holmes tore it open and burst out laughing.

"Well, well! What next?" said he. "Brother Mycroft is coming round."

"Why not?" I asked.

"Why not? It is as if you met a tram-car coming down a country lane. Mycroft has his rails and he runs on them. His Pall Mall lodgings, the Diogenes Club, Whitehall—that is his cycle. Once, and only once, he has been here. What upheaval can possibly have derailed him?"

"Does he not explain?"

Holmes handed me his brother's telegram.

Must see you over Cadogan West. Coming at once.

MYCROFT.

"Cadogan West? I have heard the name."

"It recalls nothing to my mind. But that Mycroft should break out in this erratic fashion! A planet might as well leave its orbit. By the way, do you know what Mycroft is?"

I had some vague recollection of an explanation at the time of the Adventure of the Greek Interpreter.

"You told me that he had some small office under the British government."

Holmes chuckled.

"I did not know you quite so well in those days. One has to be discreet when one talks of high matters of state. You are right in thinking that he is under the British government. You would also be right in a sense if you said that occasionally he *is* the British government."

"My dear Holmes!"

"I thought I might surprise you. Mycroft draws four hundred and fifty pounds a year, remains a subordinate, has no ambitions of any kind, will receive neither honour nor title, but remains the most indispensable man in the country."

"But how?"

"Well, his position is unique. He has made it for himself. There has never been anything like it before, nor will be again. He has the tidiest and most orderly brain, with the greatest capacity for storing facts, of any man living. The same great powers which I have turned to the detection of crime he has used for this particular business. The conclusions of every department are passed to him, and he is the central exchange, the clearing-house, which makes out the balance. All other men are specialists, but his specialism is omniscience. We will suppose that a minister needs information as to a point which involves the Navy, India, Canada and the bimetallic question; he could get his separate advices from various departments upon each, but only Mycroft can focus them all, and say offhand how each factor would affect the other. They began by using him as a short-cut, a convenience; now he has made himself an essential. In that great brain of his everything is pigeon-holed and can be handed out in an instant.* Again and again his word has decided the national policy.

---

*Mycroft functions as what we call today a relational database.

He lives in it. He thinks of nothing else save when, as an intellectual exercise, he unbends if I call upon him and ask him to advise me on one of my little problems. But Jupiter is descending to-day. What on earth can it mean? Who is Cadogan West, and what is he to Mycroft?"

"I have it," I cried, and plunged among the litter of papers upon the sofa. "Yes, yes, here he is, sure enough! Cadogan West was the young man who was found dead on the Underground on Tuesday morning."

Holmes sat up at attention, his pipe halfway to his lips.

"This must be serious, Watson. A death which has caused my brother to alter his habits can be no ordinary one. What in the world can he have to do with it? The case was featureless as I remember it. The young man had apparently fallen out of the train and killed himself. He had not been robbed, and there was no particular reason to suspect violence. Is that not so?"

"There has been an inquest," said I, "and a good many fresh facts have come out. Looked at more closely, I should certainly say that it was a curious case."

"Judging by its effect upon my brother, I should think it must be a most extraordinary one." He snuggled down in his armchair. "Now, Watson, let us have the facts."

"The man's name was Arthur Cadogan West. He was twenty-seven years of age, unmarried, and a clerk at Woolwich Arsenal."

"Government employ. Behold the link with Brother Mycroft!"

"He left Woolwich suddenly on Monday night. Was last seen by his fiancée, Miss Violet Westbury, whom he left abruptly in the fog about 7:30 that evening. There was no quarrel between them and she can give no motive for his action. The next thing heard of him was when his dead body was discovered by a plate-layer named Mason, just outside Aldgate Station on the Underground system in London."

"When?"

"The body was found at six on the Tuesday morning. It was lying wide of the metals* upon the left hand of the track as one goes eastward, at a point close to the station, where the line emerges from the tunnel in which it runs. The head was badly crushed—an injury which might well have been caused by a fall from the train. The body could only have come on the line in that way. Had it been carried down from any neighbouring street, it must have passed the station barriers, where a collector is always standing. This point seems absolutely certain."

"Very good. The case is definite enough. The man, dead or alive, either fell or was precipitated from a train. So much is clear to me. Continue."

"The trains which traverse the lines of rail beside which the body was found are those which run from west to east, some being purely Metropolitan, and some from Willesden and outlying junctions. It can be stated

---

*Train-track rails.

for certain that this young man, when he met his death, was travelling in this direction at some late hour of the night, but at what point he entered the train it is impossible to state."

"His ticket, of course, would show that."

"There was no ticket in his pockets."

"No ticket! Dear me, Watson, this is really very singular. According to my experience it is not possible to reach the platform of a Metropolitan train without exhibiting one's ticket. Presumably, then, the young man had one. Was it taken from him in order to conceal the station from which he came? It is possible. Or did he drop it in the carriage? That also is possible. But the point is of curious interest. I understand that there was no sign of robbery?"

"Apparently not. There is a list here of his possessions. His purse contained two pounds fifteen. He had also a check-book on the Woolwich branch of the Capital and Counties Bank. Through this his identity was established. There were also two dress-circle tickets for the Woolwich Theatre, dated for that very evening. Also a small packet of technical papers."

Holmes gave an exclamation of satisfaction.

"There we have it at last, Watson! British government—Woolwich. Arsenal—technical papers—Brother Mycroft, the chain is complete. But here he comes, if I am not mistaken, to speak for himself."

A moment later the tall and portly form of Mycroft Holmes was ushered into the room. Heavily built and massive, there was a suggestion of uncouth physical inertia in the figure, but above this unwieldy frame there was perched a head so masterful in its brow, so alert in its steel-gray, deep-set eyes, so firm in its lips, and so subtle in its play of expression, that after the first glance one forgot the gross body and remembered only the dominant mind.

At his heels came our old friend Lestrade, of Scotland Yard—thin and austere. The gravity of both their faces foretold some weighty quest. The detective shook hands without a word. Mycroft Holmes struggled out of his overcoat and subsided into an armchair.

"A most annoying business, Sherlock," said he. "I extremely dislike altering my habits, but the powers that be would take no denial. In the present state of Siam it is most awkward that I should be away from the office. But it is a real crisis. I have never seen the Prime Minister so upset. As to the Admiralty—it is buzzing like an overturned bee-hive. Have you read up the case?"

"We have just done so. What were the technical papers?"

"Ah, there's the point! Fortunately, it has not come out. The press would be furious if it did. The papers which this wretched youth had in his pocket were the plans of the Bruce-Partington submarine."

Mycroft Holmes spoke with a solemnity which showed his sense of the importance of the subject. His brother and I sat expectant.

"Surely you have heard of it? I thought everyone had heard of it."

"Only as a name."

"Its importance can hardly be exaggerated. It has been the most jealously guarded of all government secrets.[15] You may take it from me that naval warfare becomes impossible within the radius of a Bruce-Partington's operation. Two years ago a very large sum was smuggled through the Estimates and was expended in acquiring a monopoly of the invention. Every effort has been made to keep the secret. The plans, which are exceedingly intricate, comprising some thirty separate patents, each essential to the working of the whole, are kept in an elaborate safe in a confidential office adjoining the arsenal, with burglar-proof doors and windows. Under no conceivable circumstances were the plans to be taken from the office. If the chief constructor of the Navy desired to consult them, even he was forced to go to the Woolwich office for the purpose. And yet here we find them in the pocket of a dead junior clerk in the heart of London. From an official point of view it's simply awful."

"But you have recovered them?"

"No, Sherlock, no! That's the pinch. We have not. Ten papers were taken from Woolwich. There were seven in the pocket of Cadogan West. The three most essential are gone—stolen, vanished. You must drop everything, Sherlock. Never mind your usual petty puzzles of the police-court. It's a vital international problem that you have to solve. Why did Cadogan West take the papers, where are the missing ones, how did he die, how came his body where it was found, how can the evil be set right? Find an answer to all these questions, and you will have done good service for your country."

"Why do you not solve it yourself, Mycroft? You can see as far as I."

"Possibly, Sherlock. But it is a question of getting details. Give me your details, and from an armchair I will return you an excellent expert opinion. But to run here and run there, to cross-question railway guards, and lie on my face with a lens to my eye—it is not my *métier*. No, you are the one man who can clear the matter up. If you have a fancy to see your name in the next honours list——"

My friend smiled and shook his head.

"I play the game for the game's own sake," said he. "But the problem certainly presents some points of interest, and I shall be very pleased to look into it. Some more facts, please."

"I have jotted down the more essential ones upon this sheet of paper, together with a few addresses which you will find of service. The actual official guardian of the papers is the famous government expert, Sir James Walter, whose decorations and sub-titles fill two lines of a book of reference. He has grown gray in the service, is a gentleman, a favoured guest in the most exalted houses, and, above all, a man whose patriotism is beyond suspicion. He is one of two who have a key of the safe. I may add that the papers were undoubtedly in the office during working hours on Monday, and that Sir James left for London about three o'clock taking his key with him. He was at the house of Admiral Sinclair at Barclay Square during the whole of the evening when this incident occurred."

"Has the fact been verified?"

"Yes; his brother, Colonel Valentine Walter, has testified to his departure from Woolwich, and Admiral Sinclair to his arrival in London; so Sir James is no longer a direct factor in the problem."

"Who was the other man with a key?"

"The senior clerk and draughtsman, Mr. Sidney Johnson. He is a man of forty, married, with five children. He is a silent, morose man, but he has, on the whole, an excellent record in the public service. He is unpopular with his colleagues, but a hard worker. According to his own account, corroborated only by the word of his wife, he was at home the whole of Monday evening after office hours, and his key has never left the watchchain upon which it hangs."

"Tell us about Cadogan West."

"He has been ten years in the service and has done good work. He has the reputation of being hot-headed and impetuous, but a straight, honest man. We have nothing against him. He was next to Sidney Johnson in the office. His duties brought him into daily, personal contact with the plans. No one else had the handling of them."

"Who locked the plans up that night?"

"Mr. Sidney Johnson, the senior clerk."

"Well, it is surely perfectly clear who took them away. They are actually found upon the person of this junior clerk, Cadogan West. That seems final, does it not?"

"It does, Sherlock, and yet it leaves so much unexplained. In the first place, why did he take them?"

"I presume they were of value?"

"He could have got several thousands for them very easily."

"Can you suggest any possible motive for taking the papers to London except to sell them?"

"No, I cannot."

"Then we must take that as our working hypothesis. Young West took the papers. Now this could only be done by having a false key——"

"Several false keys. He had to open the building and the room."

"He had, then, several false keys. He took the papers to London to sell the secret, intending, no doubt, to have the plans themselves back in the safe next morning before they were missed. While in London on this treasonable mission he met his end."

"How?"

"We will suppose that he was travelling back to Woolwich when he was killed and thrown out of the compartment."

"Aldgate, where the body was found, is considerably past the station for London Bridge, which would be his route to Woolwich."

"Many circumstances could be imagined under which he would pass London Bridge. There was someone in the carriage, for example, with whom he was having an absorbing interview. This interview led to a violent scene in which he lost his life. Possibly he tried to leave the carriage, fell out on the line, and so met his end. The other closed the door. There was a thick fog, and nothing could be seen."

"No better explanation can be given with our present knowledge; and yet consider, Sherlock, how much you leave untouched. We will suppose, for argument's sake, that young Cadogan West *had* determined to convey these papers to London. He would naturally have made an appointment with the foreign agent and kept his evening clear. Instead of that he took two tickets for the theatre, escorted his fiancée halfway there, and then suddenly disappeared."

"A blind," said Lestrade, who had sat listening with some impatience to the conversation.

"A very singular one. That is objection No. 1. Objection No. 2: We will suppose that he reaches London and sees the foreign agent. He must bring back the papers before morning or the toss will be discovered. He took away ten. Only seven were in his pocket. What had become of the other three? He certainly would not leave them of his own free will. Then, again, where is the price of his treason? One would have expected to find a large sum of money in his pocket."

"It seems to me perfectly clear," said Lestrade. "I have no doubt at all as to what occurred. He took the papers to sell them. He saw the agent. They could not agree as to price. He started home again, but the agent went with him. In the train the agent murdered him, took the more essential papers, and threw his body from the carriage. That would account for everything, would it not?"

"Why had he no ticket?"

"The ticket would have shown which station was nearest the agent's house. Therefore he took it from the murdered man's pocket."

"Good, Lestrade, very good," said Holmes. "Your theory holds together. But if this is true, then the case is at an end. On the one hand, the traitor is dead. On the other, the plans of the Bruce-Partington submarine are presumably already on the Continent. What is there for us to do?"

"To act, Sherlock—to act!" cried Mycroft, springing to his feet. "All my instincts are against this explanation. Use your powers! Go to the scene of the crime! See the people concerned! Leave no stone unturned! In all your career you have never had so great a chance of serving your country."

"Well, well!" said Holmes, shrugging his shoulders. "Come, Watson! And you, Lestrade, could you favour us with your company for an hour or two? We will begin our investigation by a visit to Aldgate Station. Good-bye, Mycroft. I shall let you have a report before evening, but I warn you in advance that you have little to expect."

An hour later Holmes, Lestrade and I stood upon the Underground railroad at the point where it emerges from the tunnel immediately before Aldgate Station. A courteous red-faced old gentleman represented the railway company.

"This is where the young man's body lay," said he, indicating a spot about three feet from the metals. "It could not have fallen from above, for these, as you see, are all blank walls. Therefore, it could only have come from a train, and that train, so far as we can trace it, must have passed about midnight on Monday."

"Have the carriages been examined for any sign of violence?"

"There are no such signs, and no ticket has been found."

"No record of a door being found open?"

"None."

"We have had some fresh evidence this morning," said Lestrade. "A passenger who passed Aldgate in an ordinary Metropolitan train about 11:40 on Monday night declares that he heard a heavy thud, as of a body striking the line, just before the train reached the station. There was dense fog, however, and nothing could be seen. He made no report of it at the time. Why, whatever is the matter with Mr. Holmes?"

My friend was standing with an expression of strained intensity upon his face, staring at the railway metals where they curved out of the tunnel. Aldgate is a junction, and there was a network of points. On these his eager, questioning eyes were fixed, and I saw on his keen, alert face that tightening of the lips, that quiver of the nostrils, and concentration of the heavy, tufted brows which I knew so well.

"Points," he muttered; "the points."

"What of it? What do you mean?"

"I suppose there are no great number of points on a system such as this?"

"No; there are very few."

"And a curve, too. Points, and a curve. By Jove! if it were only so."

"What is it, Mr. Holmes? Have you a clue?"

"An idea—an indication, no more. But the case certainly grows in interest. Unique, perfectly unique, and yet why not? I do not see any indications of bleeding on the line."

"There were hardly any."

"But I understand that there was a considerable wound."

"The bone was crushed, but there was no great external injury."

"And yet one would have expected some bleeding. Would it be possible for me to inspect the train which contained the passenger who heard the thud of a fall in the fog?"

"I fear not, Mr. Holmes. The train has been broken up before now, and the carriages redistributed."

"I can assure you, Mr. Holmes," said Lestrade, "that every carriage has been carefully examined. I saw to it myself."

It was one of my friend's most obvious weaknesses that he was impatient with less alert intelligences than his own.

"Very likely," said he, turning away. "As it happens, it was not the carriages which I desired to examine. Watson, we have done all we can here. We need not trouble you any further, Mr. Lestrade. I think our investigations must now carry us to Woolwich."

At London Bridge, Holmes wrote a telegram to his brother, which he handed to me before dispatching it. It ran thus:

See some light in the darkness, but it may possibly flicker out. Meanwhile, please send by messenger, to await return at Baker Street, a complete list of all foreign spies or international agents known to be in England, with full address.

SHERLOCK.

"That should be helpful, Watson," he remarked as we took our seats in the Woolwich train. "We certainly owe Brother Mycroft a debt for having introduced us to what promises to be a really very remarkable case."

His eager face still wore that expression of intense and high-strung energy, which showed me that some novel and suggestive circumstance had opened up a stimulating line of thought. See the foxhound with hanging ears and drooping tail as it lolls about the kennels, and compare it with the same hound as, with gleaming eyes and straining muscles, it runs upon a breast-high scent—such was the change in Holmes since the morning. He was a different man from the limp and lounging figure in the mouse-coloured dressing-gown who had prowled so restlessly only a few hours before round the fog-girt room.

"There is material here. There is scope," said he. "I am dull indeed not to have understood its possibilities."

"Even now they are dark to me."

"The end is dark to me also, but I have hold of one idea which may lead us far. The man met his death elsewhere, and his body was on the *roof* of a carriage."

"On the roof!"

"Remarkable, is it not? But consider the facts. Is it a coincidence that it is found at the very point where the train pitches and sways as it comes round on the points? Is not that the place where an object upon the roof might be expected to fall off? The points would affect no object inside the train. Either the body fell from the roof, or a very curious coincidence has occurred. But now consider the question of the blood. Of course, there was no bleeding on the line if the body had bled elsewhere. Each fact is suggestive in itself. Together they have a cumulative force."

"And the ticket, too!" I cried.

"Exactly. We could not explain the absence of a ticket. This would explain it. Everything fits together."

"But suppose it were so, we are still as far as ever from unravelling the mystery of his death. Indeed, it becomes not simpler but stranger."

"Perhaps," said Holmes thoughtfully, "perhaps." He relapsed into a silent reverie, which lasted until the slow train drew up at last in Woolwich Station. There he called a cab and drew Mycroft's paper from his pocket.

"We have quite a little round of afternoon calls to make," said he. "I think that Sir James Walter claims our first attention."

The house of the famous official was a fine villa with green lawns stretching down to the Thames. As we reached it the fog was lifting, and a thin, watery sunshine was breaking through. A butler answered our ring.

"Sir James, sir!" said he with solemn face. "Sir James died this morning."

"Good heavens!" cried Holmes in amazement. "How did he die?"

"Perhaps you would care to step in, sir, and see his brother, Colonel Valentine?"

"Yes, we had best do so."

We were ushered into a dim-lit drawing-room, where an instant later we were joined by a very tall, handsome, light-bearded man of fifty, the younger brother of the dead scientist. His wild eyes, stained cheeks, and unkempt hair all spoke of the sudden blow which had fallen upon the household. He was hardly articulate as he spoke of it.

"It was this horrible scandal," said he. "My brother, Sir James, was a man of very sensitive honour, and he could not survive such an affair. It broke his heart. He was always so proud of the efficiency of his department, and this was a crushing blow."

"We had hoped that he might have given us some indications which would have helped us to clear the matter up."

"I assure you that it was all a mystery to him as it is to you and to all of us. He had already put all his knowledge at the disposal of the police. Naturally he had no doubt that Cadogan West was guilty. But all the rest was inconceivable."

"You cannot throw any new light upon the affair?"

"I know nothing myself save what I have read or heard. I have no desire to be discourteous, but you can understand, Mr. Holmes, that we are much disturbed at present, and I must ask you to hasten this interview to an end."

"This is indeed an unexpected development," said my friend when we had regained the cab. "I wonder if the death was natural, or whether the poor old fellow killed himself! If the latter, may it be taken as some sign of self-reproach for duty neglected? We must leave that question to the future. Now we shall turn to the Cadogan Wests."

A small but well-kept house in the outskirts of the town sheltered the bereaved mother. The old lady was too dazed with grief to be of any use to us, but at her side was a white-faced young lady, who introduced herself as Miss Violet Westbury, the fiancée of the dead man, and the last to see him upon that fatal night.

"I cannot explain it, Mr. Holmes," she said. "I have not shut an eye since the tragedy, thinking, thinking, thinking, night and day, what the true meaning of it can be. Arthur was the most single-minded, chivalrous, patriotic man upon earth. He would have cut his right hand off before he would sell a State secret confided to his keeping. It is absurd, impossible, preposterous to anyone who knew him."

"But the facts, Miss Westbury?"

"Yes, yes; I admit I cannot explain them."

"Was he in any want of money?"

"No; his needs were very simple and his salary ample. He had saved a few hundreds, and we were to marry at the New Year."

"No signs of any mental excitement? Come, Miss Westbury, be absolutely frank with us."

The quick eye of my companion had noted some change in her manner. She coloured and hesitated.

"Yes," she said at last, "I had a feeling that there was something on his mind."

"For long?"

"Only for the last week or so. He was thoughtful and worried. Once I pressed him about it. He admitted that there was something, and that it was concerned with his official life. 'It is too serious for me to speak about, even to you,' said he. I could get nothing more."

Holmes looked grave.

"Go on, Miss Westbury. Even if it seems to tell against him, go on. We cannot say what it may lead to."

"Indeed, I have nothing more to tell. Once or twice it seemed to me that he was on the point of telling me something. He spoke one evening of the importance of the secret, and I have some recollection that he said that no doubt foreign spies would pay a great deal to have it."

My friend's face grew graver still.

"Anything else?"

"He said that we were slack about such matters—that it would be easy for a traitor to get the plans."

"Was it only recently that he made such remarks?"

"Yes, quite recently."

"Now tell us of that last evening."

"We were to go to the theatre. The fog was so thick that a cab was useless. We walked, and our way took us close to the office. Suddenly he darted away into the fog."

"Without a word?"

"He gave an exclamation; that was all. I waited but he never returned. Then I walked home. Next morning, after the office opened, they came to inquire. About twelve o'clock we heard the terrible news. Oh, Mr. Holmes, if you could only, only save his honour! It was so much to him."

Holmes shook his head sadly.

"Come, Watson," said he, "our ways lie elsewhere. Our next station must be the office from which the papers were taken.

"It was black enough before against this young man, but our inquiries make it blacker," he remarked as the cab lumbered off. "His coming marriage gives a motive for the crime. He naturally wanted money. The idea was in his head, since he spoke about it. He nearly made the girl an accomplice in the treason by telling her his plans. It is all very bad."

"But surely, Holmes, character goes for something? Then, again, why should he leave the girl in the street and dart away to commit a felony?"

"Exactly! There are certainly objections. But it is a formidable case which they have to meet."

Mr. Sidney Johnson, the senior clerk, met us at the office and received us with that respect which my companion's card always commanded. He was a thin, gruff, bespectacled man of middle age, his cheeks haggard, and his hands twitching from the nervous strain to which he had been subjected.

"It is bad, Mr. Holmes, very bad! Have you heard of the death of the chief?"

"We have just come from his house."

"The place is disorganized. The chief dead, Cadogan West dead, our papers stolen. And yet, when we closed our door on Monday evening, we were as efficient an office as any in the government service. Good God, it's dreadful to think of! That West, of all men, should have done such a thing!"

"You are sure of his guilt, then?"

"I can see no other way out of it. And yet I would have trusted him as I trust myself."

"At what hour was the office closed on Monday?"

"At five."

"Did you close it?"

"I am always the last man out."

"Where were the plans?"

"In that safe. I put them there myself."

"Is there no watchman to the building?"

"There is, but he has other departments to look after as well. He is an old soldier and a most trustworthy man. He saw nothing that evening. Of course the fog was very thick."

"Suppose that Cadogan West wished to make his way into the building after hours; he would need three keys, would he not, before he could reach the papers?"

"Yes, he would. The key of the outer door, the key of the office, and the key of the safe."

"Only Sir James Walter and you had those keys?"

"I had no keys of the doors—only of the safe."

"Was Sir James a man who was orderly in his habits?"

"Yes, I think he was. I know that so far as those three keys are concerned he kept them on the same ring. I have often seen them there."

"And that ring went with him to London?"

"He said so."

"And your key never left your possession?"

"Never."

"Then West, if he is the culprit, must have had a duplicate. And yet none was found upon his body. One other point: if a clerk in this office desired to sell the plans, would it not be simpler to copy the plans for himself than to take the originals, as was actually done?"

"It would take considerable technical knowledge to copy the plans in an effective way."

"But I suppose either Sir James, or you, or West, had that technical knowledge?"

"No doubt we had, but I beg you won't try to drag me into the matter, Mr. Holmes. What is the use of our speculating in this way when the original plans were actually found on West?"

"Well, it is certainly singular that he should run the risk of taking originals if he could safely have taken copies, which would have equally served his turn."

"Singular, no doubt—and yet he did so."

"Every inquiry in this case reveals something inexplicable. Now there are three papers still missing. They are, as I understand, the vital ones."

"Yes, that is so."

"Do you mean to say that anyone holding these three papers, and without the seven others, could construct a Bruce-Partington submarine?"

"I reported to that effect to the Admiralty. But to-day I have been over the drawings again, and I am not so sure of it. The double valves with the automatic self-adjusting slots are drawn in one of the papers which have been returned. Until the foreigners had invented that for themselves they could not make the boat. Of course they might soon get over the difficulty."

"But the three missing drawings are the most important?"

"Undoubtedly."

"I think, with your permission, I will now take a stroll round the premises. I do not recall any other question which I desired to ask."

He examined the lock of the safe, the door of the room, and finally the iron shutters of the window. It was only when we were on the lawn outside that his interest was strongly excited. There was a laurel bush outside the window, and several of the branches bore signs of having been twisted or snapped. He examined them carefully with his lens, and then some dim and vague marks upon the earth beneath. Finally he asked the chief clerk to close the iron shutters, and he pointed out to me that they hardly met in the centre, and that it would be possible for anyone outside to see what was going on within the room.

"The indications are ruined by the three days' delay. They may mean something or nothing. Well, Watson, I do not think that Woolwich can help us further. It is a small crop which we have gathered. Let us see if we can do better in London."

Yet we added one more sheaf to our harvest before we left Woolwich Station. The clerk in the ticket office was able to say with confidence that he saw Cadogan West—whom he knew well by sight—upon the Monday night, and that he went to London by the 8:15 to London Bridge. He was alone and took a single third-class ticket. The clerk was struck at the time by his excited and nervous manner. So shaky was he that he could hardly pick up his change, and the clerk had helped him with it. A reference to the timetable showed that the 8:15 was the first train which it was possible for West to take after he had left the lady about 7:30.

"Let us reconstruct, Watson," said Holmes after half an hour of silence. "I am not aware that in all our joint researches we have ever had a case which was more difficult to get at. Every fresh advance which we make only reveals a fresh ridge beyond. And yet we have surely made some appreciable progress.

"The effect of our inquiries at Woolwich has in the main been against young Cadogan West; but the indications at the window would lend themselves to a more favourable hypothesis. Let us suppose, for example, that he had been approached by some foreign agent. It might have been done under such pledges as would have prevented him from speaking of it, and yet would have affected his thoughts in the direction indicated by his remarks to his fiancée. Very good. We will now suppose that as he went to the theatre with the young lady he suddenly, in the fog, caught a glimpse of this same agent going in the direction of the office. He was an impetuous man, quick in his decisions. Everything gave way to his duty. He followed the man, reached the window, saw the abstraction of the documents, and pursued the thief. In this way we get over the objection that no one would take originals when he could make copies. This outsider had to take originals. So far it holds together."

"What is the next step?"

"Then we come into difficulties. One would imagine that under such circumstances the first act of young Cadogan West would be to seize the villain and raise the alarm. Why did he not do so? Could it have been an official superior who took the papers? That would explain West's conduct. Or could the chief have given West the slip in the fog, and West started at once to London to head him off from his own rooms, presuming that he knew where the rooms were? The call must have been very pressing, since he left his girl standing in the fog and made no effort to communicate with her. Our scent runs cold here, and there is a vast gap between either hypothesis and the laying of West's body, with seven papers in his pocket, on the roof of a Metropolitan train. My instinct now is to work from the other end. If Mycroft has given us the list of addresses we may be able to pick our man and follow two tracks instead of one."

Surely enough, a note awaited us at Baker Street. A government messenger had brought it post-haste. Holmes glanced at it and threw it over to me.

There are numerous small fry, but few who would handle so big an affair. The only men worth considering are Adolph Meyer, of 13 Great George Street, Westminster; Louis La Rothière, of Campden Mansions, Notting Hill; and Hugo Oberstein, 13 Caulfield Gardens, Kensington. The latter was known to be in town on Monday and is now reported as having left. Glad to hear you have seen some light. The Cabinet awaits your final report with the utmost anxiety. Urgent representations have arrived from the very highest quarter. The whole force of the State is at your back if you should need it.

MYCROFT.

"I'm afraid," said Holmes smiling, "that all the queen's horses and all the queen's men* cannot avail in this matter." He had spread out his big map of London and leaned eagerly over it. "Well, well," said he presently with an exclamation of satisfaction, "things are turning a little in our direction at last. Why, Watson, I do honestly believe that we are going to pull it off, after all." He slapped me on the shoulder with a sudden burst of hilarity. "I am going out now. It is only a reconnaissance. I will do nothing serious without my trusted comrade and biographer at my elbow. Do you stay here, and the odds are that you will see me again in an hour or two. If time hangs heavy get foolscap and a pen, and begin your narrative of how we saved the State."

I felt some reflection of his elation in my own mind, for I knew well that he would not depart so far from his usual austerity of demeanour unless there was good cause for exultation. All the long November evening I waited, filled with impatience for his return. At last, shortly after nine o'clock, there arrived a messenger with a note:

> Am dining at Goldini's Restaurant, Gloucester Road, Kensington. Please come at once and join me there. Bring with you a jemmy, a dark lantern,† a chisel, and a revolver.
>
>   S. H.

It was a nice equipment for a respectable citizen to carry through the dim, fog-draped streets. I stowed them all discreetly away in my overcoat and drove straight to the address given. There sat my friend at a little round table near the door of the garish Italian restaurant.

"Have you had something to eat? Then join me in a coffee and curaçao. Try one of the proprietor's cigars. They are less poisonous than one would expect. Have you the tools?"

"They are here, in my overcoat."

"Excellent. Let me give you a short sketch of what I have done, with some indication of what we are about to do. Now it must be evident to you, Watson, that this young man's body was *placed* on the roof of the train. That was clear from the instant that I determined the fact that it was from the roof, and not from a carriage, that he had fallen."

"Could it not have been dropped from a bridge?"

"I should say it was impossible. If you examine the roofs you will find that they are slightly rounded, and there is no railing round them. Therefore, we can say for certain that young Cadogan West was placed on it."

"How could he be placed there?"

"That was the question which we had to answer. There is only one possible way. You are aware that the Underground runs clear of tunnels at some points in the West End. I had a vague memory that as I have trav-

---

*Yes, Holmes quotes "Humpty Dumpty."

†Lantern with a panel for blocking the light.

elled by it I have occasionally seen windows just above my head. Now, suppose that a train halted under such a window, would there be any difficulty in laying a body upon the roof?"

"It seems most improbable."

"We must fall back upon the old axiom that when all other contingencies fail, whatever remains, however improbable, must be the truth. Here all other contingencies *have* failed. When I found that the leading international agent, who had just left London, lived in a row of houses which abutted upon the Underground, I was so pleased that you were a little astonished at my sudden frivolity."

"Oh, that was it, was it?"

"Yes, that was it. Mr. Hugo Oberstein, of 13 Caulfield Gardens, had become my objective. I began my operations at Gloucester Road Station, where a very helpful official walked with me along the track and allowed me to satisfy myself not only that the back-stair windows of Caulfield Gardens open on the line but the even more essential fact that, owing to the intersection of one of the larger railways, the Underground trains are frequently held motionless for some minutes at that very spot."

"Splendid, Holmes! You have got it!"

"So far—so far, Watson. We advance, but the goal is afar. Well, having seen the back of Caulfield Gardens, I visited the front and satisfied myself that the bird was indeed flown. It is a considerable house, unfurnished, so far as I could judge, in the upper rooms. Oberstein lived there with a single valet, who was probably a confederate entirely in his confidence. We must bear in mind that Oberstein has gone to the Continent to dispose of his booty, but not with any idea of flight; for he had no reason to fear a warrant, and the idea of an amateur domiciliary visit would certainly never occur to him. Yet that is precisely what we are about to make."

"Could we not get a warrant and legalize it?"

"Hardly on the evidence."

"What can we hope to do?"

"We cannot tell what correspondence may be there."

"I don't like it, Holmes."

"My dear fellow, you shall keep watch in the street. I'll do the criminal part. It's not a time to stick at trifles. Think of Mycroft's note, of the Admiralty, the Cabinet, the exalted person who waits for news. We are bound to go."

My answer was to rise from the table.

"You are right, Holmes. We are bound to go."

He sprang up and shook me by the hand.

"I knew you would not shrink at the last," said he, and for a moment I saw something in his eyes which was nearer to tenderness than I had ever seen. The next instant he was his masterful, practical self once more.

"It is nearly half a mile, but there is no hurry. Let us walk," said he. "Don't drop the instruments, I beg. Your arrest as a suspicious character would be a most unfortunate complication."

Caulfield Gardens was one of those lines of flat-faced, pillared, and porticoed houses which are so prominent a product of the middle Victorian epoch in the West End of London. Next door there appeared to be a children's party, for the merry buzz of young voices and the clatter of a piano resounded through the night. The fog still hung about and screened us with its friendly shade. Holmes had lit his lantern and flashed it upon the massive door.

"This is a serious proposition," said he. "It is certainly bolted as well as locked. We would do better in the area. There is an excellent archway down yonder in case a too zealous policeman should intrude. Give me a hand, Watson, and I'll do the same for you."

A minute later we were both in the area. Hardly had we reached the dark shadows before the step of the policeman was heard in the fog above. As its soft rhythm died away, Holmes set to work upon the lower door. I saw him stoop and strain until with a sharp crash it flew open. We sprang through into the dark passage, closing the area door behind us. Holmes led the way up the curving, uncarpeted stair. His little fan of yellow light shone upon a low window.

"Here we are, Watson—this must be the one." He threw it open, and as he did so there was a low, harsh murmur, growing steadily into a loud roar as a train dashed past us in the darkness. Holmes swept his light along the window-sill. It was thickly coated with soot from the passing engines, but the black surface was blurred and rubbed in places.

"You can see where they rested the body. Halloa, Watson! what is this? There can be no doubt that it is a blood mark." He was pointing to faint discolourations along the woodwork of the window. "Here it is on the stone of the stair also. The demonstration is complete. Let us stay here until a train stops."

We had not long to wait. The very next train roared from the tunnel as before, but slowed in the open, and then, with a creaking of brakes, pulled up immediately beneath us. It was not four feet from the window-ledge to the roof of the carriages. Holmes softly closed the window.

"So far we are justified," said he. "What do you think of it, Watson?"

"A masterpiece. You have never risen to a greater height."

"I cannot agree with you there. From the moment that I conceived the idea of the body being upon the roof, which surely was not a very abstruse one, all the rest was inevitable. If it were not for the grave interests involved the affair up to this point would be insignificant. Our difficulties are still before us. But perhaps we may find something here which may help us."

We had ascended the kitchen stair and entered the suite of rooms upon the first floor. One was a dining-room, severely furnished and containing nothing of interest. A second was a bedroom, which also drew blank. The remaining room appeared more promising, and my companion settled down to a systematic examination. It was littered with books and papers, and was evidently used as a study. Swiftly and methodically Holmes turned over the contents of drawer after drawer and cupboard after cupboard, but no gleam of success came to brighten his austere face. At the end of an hour he was no further than when he started.

"The cunning dog has covered his tracks," said he. "He has left nothing to incriminate him. His dangerous correspondence has been destroyed or removed. This is our last chance."

It was a small tin cash-box which stood upon the writing-desk. Holmes pried it open with his chisel. Several rolls of paper were within, covered with figures and calculations, without any note to show to what they referred. The recurring words "water pressure" and "pressure to the square inch" suggested some possible relation to a submarine. Holmes tossed them all impatiently aside. There only remained an envelope with some small newspaper slips inside it. He shook them out on the table, and at once I saw by his eager face that his hopes had been raised.

"What's this, Watson? Eh? What's this? Record of a series of messages in the advertisements of a paper. *Daily Telegraph* agony column by the print and paper. Right-hand top corner of a page. No dates—but messages arrange themselves. This must be the first:

"Hoped to hear sooner. Terms agreed to. Write fully to address given on card.

PIERROT.

"Next comes:

"Too complex for description. Must have full report. Stuff awaits you when goods delivered.

PIERROT.

"Then comes:

"Matter presses. Must withdraw offer unless contract completed. Make appointment by letter. Will confirm by advertisement.

PIERROT.

"Finally:

"Monday night after nine. Two taps. Only ourselves. Do not be so suspicious. Payment in hard cash when goods delivered.

PIERROT.

"A fairly complete record, Watson! If we could only get at the man at the other end!" He sat lost in thought, tapping his fingers on the table. Finally he sprang to his feet.

"Well, perhaps it won't be so difficult, after all. There is nothing more to be done here, Watson. I think we might drive round to the offices of the *Daily Telegraph*, and so bring a good day's work to a conclusion."

Mycroft Holmes and Lestrade had come round by appointment after breakfast next day and Sherlock Holmes had recounted to them our proceedings of the day before. The professional shook his head over our confessed burglary.

"We can't do these things in the force, Mr. Holmes," said he. "No wonder you get results that are beyond us. But some of these days you'll go too far, and you'll find yourself and your friend in trouble."

"For England, home and beauty—eh, Watson? Martyrs on the altar of our country. But what do you think of it, Mycroft?"

"Excellent, Sherlock! Admirable! But what use will you make of it?"

Holmes picked up the *Daily Telegraph* which lay upon the table.

"Have you seen Pierrot's advertisement to-day?"

"What? Another one?"

"Yes, here it is:

"To-night. Same hour. Same place. Two taps. Most vitally important. Your own safety at stake.

PIERROT."

"By George!" cried Lestrade. "If he answers that we've got him!"

"That was my idea when I put it in. I think if you could both make it convenient to come with us about eight o'clock to Caulfield Gardens we might possibly get a little nearer to a solution."

One of the most remarkable characteristics of Sherlock Holmes was his power of throwing his brain out of action and switching all his thoughts on to lighter things whenever he had convinced himself that he could no longer work to advantage. I remember that during the whole of that memorable day he lost himself in a monograph which he had undertaken upon the Polyphonic Motets of Lassus.[16] For my own part I had none of this power of detachment, and the day, in consequence, appeared to be interminable. The great national importance of the issue, the suspense in high quarters, the direct nature of the experiment which we were trying—all combined to work upon my nerve. It was a relief to me when at last, after a light dinner, we set out upon our expedition. Lestrade and Mycroft met us by appointment at the outside of Gloucester Road Station. The area door of Oberstein's house had been left open the night before, and it was necessary for me, as Mycroft Holmes absolutely and indignantly declined to climb the railings, to pass in and open the hall door. By nine o'clock we were all seated in the study, waiting patiently for our man.

An hour passed and yet another. When eleven struck, the measured beat of the great church clock seemed to sound the dirge of our hopes. Lestrade and Mycroft were fidgeting in their seats and looking twice a minute at their watches. Holmes sat silent and composed, his eyelids half shut, but every sense on the alert. He raised his head with a sudden jerk.

"He is coming," said he.

There had been a furtive step past the door. Now it returned. We heard a shuffling sound outside, and then two sharp taps with the knocker. Holmes rose, motioning to us to remain seated. The gas in the hall was a mere point of light. He opened the outer door, and then as a dark figure slipped past him he closed and fastened it. "This way!" we heard him say, and a moment later our man stood before us. Holmes had followed him closely, and as the man turned with a cry of surprise and alarm he caught him by the collar and threw him back into the room. Before our prisoner had recovered his balance the door was shut and Holmes standing with his back against it. The man glared round him, staggered, and fell senseless upon the floor. With the shock, his broad-brimmed hat flew from his head, his cravat slipped down from his lips, and there were the long light beard and the soft, handsome delicate features of Colonel Valentine Walter.

Holmes gave a whistle of surprise.

"You can write me down an ass this time, Watson," said he. "This was not the bird that I was looking for."

"Who is he?" asked Mycroft eagerly.

"The younger brother of the late Sir James Walter, the head of the Submarine Department. Yes, yes; I see the fall of the cards. He is coming to. I think that you had best leave his examination to me."

We had carried the prostrate body to the sofa. Now our prisoner sat up, looked round him with a horror-stricken face, and passed his hand over his forehead, like one who cannot believe his own senses.

"What is this?" he asked. "I came here to visit Mr. Oberstein."

"Everything is known, Colonel Walter," said Holmes. "How an English gentleman could behave in such a manner is beyond my comprehension. But your whole correspondence and relations with Oberstein are within our knowledge. So also are the circumstances connected with the death of young Cadogan West. Let me advise you to gain at least the small credit for repentance and confession, since there are still some details which we can only learn from your lips."

The man groaned and sank his face in his hands. We waited, but he was silent.

"I can assure you," said Holmes, "that every essential is already known. We know that you were pressed for money; that you took an impress of the keys which your brother held; and that you entered into a correspondence with Oberstein, who answered your letters through the advertisement columns of the *Daily Telegraph*. We are aware that you went down to the office in the fog on Monday night, but that you were seen and followed by young Cadogan West, who had probably some previous reason to suspect you. He saw your theft, but could not give the alarm, as it was just possible that you were taking the papers to your brother in London. Leaving all his private concerns, like the good citizen that he was, he followed you closely in the fog and kept at your heels until you reached this very house. There he intervened, and then it was, Colonel Walter, that to treason you added the more terrible crime of murder."

"I did not! I did not! Before God I swear that I did not!" cried our wretched prisoner.

"Tell us, then, how Cadogan West met his end before you laid him upon the roof of a railway carriage."

"I will. I swear to you that I will. I did the rest. I confess it. It was just as you say. A Stock Exchange debt had to be paid. I needed the money badly. Oberstein offered me five thousand. It was to save myself from ruin. But as to murder, I am as innocent as you."

"What happened, then?"

"He had his suspicions before, and he followed me as you describe. I never knew it until I was at the very door. It was thick fog, and one could not see three yards. I had given two taps and Oberstein had come to the door. The young man rushed up and demanded to know what we were about to do with the papers. Oberstein had a short life-preserver. He always carried it with him. As West forced his way after us into the house Oberstein struck him on the head. The blow was a fatal one. He was dead within five minutes. There he lay in the hall, and we were at our wit's end what to do. Then Oberstein had this idea about the trains which halted under his back window. But first he examined the papers which I had brought. He said that three of them were essential, and that he must keep them. 'You cannot keep them,' said I. 'There will be a dreadful row at Woolwich if they are not returned.' 'I must keep them,' said he, 'for they are so technical that it is impossible in the time to make copies.' 'Then they must all go back together tonight,' said I. He thought for a little, and then he cried out that he had it. 'Three I will keep,' said he. 'The others we will stuff into the pocket of this young man. When he is found the whole business will assuredly be put to his account.' I could see no other way out of it, so we did as he suggested. We waited half an hour at the window before a train stopped. It was so thick that nothing could be seen, and we had no difficulty in lowering West's body on to the train. That was the end of the matter so far as I was concerned."

"And your brother?"

"He said nothing, but he had caught me once with his keys, and I think that he suspected. I read in his eyes that he suspected. As you know, he never held up his head again."

There was silence in the room. It was broken by Mycroft Holmes.

"Can you not make reparation? It would ease your conscience, and possibly your punishment."

"What reparation can I make?"

"Where is Oberstein with the papers?"

"I do not know."

"Did he give you no address?"

"He said that letters to the Hôtel du Louvre, Paris, would eventually reach him."

"Then reparation is still within your power," said Sherlock Holmes.

"I will do anything I can. I owe this fellow no particular good-will. He has been my ruin and my downfall."

"Here are paper and pen. Sit at this desk and write to my dictation. Direct the envelope to the address given. That is right. Now the letter:

"DEAR SIR:
    With regard to our transaction, you will no doubt have observed by now that one essential detail is missing. I have a tracing which will make it complete. This has involved me in extra trouble, however, and I must ask you for a further advance of five hundred pounds. I will not trust it to the post, nor will I take anything but gold or notes. I would come to you abroad, but it would excite remark if I left the country at present. Therefore I shall expect to meet you in the smoking-room of the Charing Cross Hotel at noon on Saturday. Remember that only English notes, or gold, will be taken.

That will do very well. I shall be very much surprised if it does not fetch our man."

And it did! It is a matter of history—that secret history of a nation which is often so much more intimate and interesting than its public chronicles—that Oberstein, eager to complete the coup of his lifetime, came to the lure and was safely engulfed for fifteen years in a British prison. In his trunk were found the invaluable Bruce-Partington plans, which he had put up for auction in all the naval centres of Europe.

Colonel Walter died in prison towards the end of the second year of his sentence. As to Holmes, he returned refreshed to his monograph upon the Polyphonic Motets of Lassus, which has since been printed for private circulation, and is said by experts to be the last word upon the subject. Some weeks afterwards I learned incidentally that my friend spent a day at Windsor, whence he returned with a remarkably fine emerald tie-pin. When I asked him if he had bought it, he answered that it was a present from a certain gracious lady in whose interests he had once been fortunate enough to carry out a small commission. He said no more; but I fancy that I could guess at that lady's august name, and I have little doubt that the emerald pin will forever recall to my friend's memory the adventure of the Bruce-Partington plans.

THE ADVENTURE OF THE
DYING DETECTIVE

Mrs. Hudson, the landlady of Sherlock Holmes, was a long-suffering woman. Not only was her first-floor flat* invaded at all hours by throngs of singular and often undesirable characters but her remarkable lodger showed an eccentricity and irregularity in his life which must have sorely tried her patience. His incredible untidiness, his addiction to music at strange hours, his occasional revolver practice within doors, his weird and often malodorous scientific experiments, and the atmosphere of violence and danger which hung around him made him the very worst tenant in London. On the other hand, his payments were princely. I have no doubt that the house might have been purchased at the price which Holmes paid for his rooms during the years that I was with him.

The landlady stood in the deepest awe of him and never dared to interfere with him, however outrageous his proceedings might seem. She was fond of him, too, for he had a remarkable gentleness and courtesy in his dealings with women. He disliked and distrusted the sex, but he was always a chivalrous opponent. Knowing how genuine was her regard for him, I listened earnestly to her story when she came to my rooms in the second year of my married life and told me of the sad condition to which my poor friend was reduced.

"He's dying, Dr. Watson," said she. "For three days he has been sinking, and I doubt if he will last the day. He would not let me get a doctor. This morning when I saw his bones sticking out of his face and his great bright eyes looking at me I could stand no more of it. 'With your leave or without it, Mr. Holmes, I am going for a doctor this very hour,' said I. 'Let it be Watson, then,' said he. I wouldn't waste an hour in coming to him, sir, or you may not see him alive."

I was horrified for I had heard nothing of his illness. I need not say that I rushed for my coat and my hat. As we drove back I asked for the details.

"There is little I can tell you, sir. He has been working at a case down at Rotherhithe, in an alley near the river, and he has brought this illness back with him. He took to his bed on Wednesday afternoon and has never moved since. For these three days neither food nor drink has passed his lips."

"Good God! Why did you not call in a doctor?"

"He wouldn't have it, sir. You know how masterful he is. I didn't dare to disobey him. But he's not long for this world, as you'll see for yourself the moment that you set eyes on him."

He was indeed a deplorable spectacle. In the dim light of a foggy No-

---

*European term for what Americans call the second floor.

vember day the sick room was a gloomy spot, but it was that gaunt, wasted face staring at me from the bed which sent a chill to my heart. His eyes had the brightness of fever, there was a hectic flush upon either cheek, and dark crusts clung to his lips; the thin hands upon the coverlet twitched incessantly, his voice was croaking and spasmodic. He lay listlessly as I entered the room, but the sight of me brought a gleam of recognition to his eyes.

"Well, Watson, we seem to have fallen upon evil days," said he in a feeble voice, but with something of his old carelessness of manner.

"My dear fellow!" I cried, approaching him.

"Stand back! Stand right back!" said he with the sharp imperiousness which I had associated only with moments of crisis. "If you approach me, Watson, I shall order you out of the house."

"But why?"

"Because it is my desire. Is that not enough?"

Yes, Mrs. Hudson was right. He was more masterful than ever. It was pitiful, however, to see his exhaustion.

"I only wished to help," I explained.

"Exactly! You will help best by doing what you are told."

"Certainly, Holmes."

He relaxed the austerity of his manner.

"You are not angry?" he asked, gasping for breath.

Poor devil, how could I be angry when I saw him lying in such a plight before me?

"It's for your own sake, Watson," he croaked.

"For *my* sake?"

"I know what is the matter with me. It is a coolie disease from Sumatra—a thing that the Dutch know more about than we, though they have made little of it up to date. One thing only is certain. It is infallibly deadly, and it is horribly contagious."

He spoke now with a feverish energy, the long hands twitching and jerking as he motioned me away.

"Contagious by touch, Watson—that's it, by touch. Keep your distance and all is well."

"Good heavens, Holmes! Do you suppose that such a consideration weighs with me for an instant? It would not affect me in the case of a stranger. Do you imagine it would prevent me from doing my duty to so old a friend?"

Again I advanced, but he repulsed me with a look of furious anger.

"If you will stand there I will talk. If you do not you must leave the room."

I have so deep a respect for the extraordinary qualities of Holmes that I have always deferred to his wishes, even when I least understood them. But now all my professional instincts were aroused. Let him be my master elsewhere, I at least was his in a sick room.

"Holmes," said I, "you are not yourself. A sick man is but a child, and so I will treat you. Whether you like it or not, I will examine your symptoms and treat you for them."

He looked at me with venomous eyes.

"If I am to have a doctor whether I will or not, let me at least have someone in whom I have confidence," said he.

"Then you have none in me?"

"In your friendship, certainly. But facts are facts, Watson, and, after all, you are only a general practitioner with very limited experience and mediocre qualifications. It is painful to have to say these things, but you leave me no choice."

I was bitterly hurt.

"Such a remark is unworthy of you, Holmes. It shows me very clearly the state of your own nerves. But if you have no confidence in me I would not intrude my services. Let me bring Sir Jasper Meek or Penrose Fisher, or any of the best men in London. But someone you *must* have, and that is final. If you think that I am going to stand here and see you die without either helping you myself or bringing anyone else to help you, then you have mistaken your man."

"You mean well, Watson," said the sick man with something between a sob and a groan. "Shall I demonstrate your own ignorance? What do you know, pray, of Tapanuli fever? What do you know of the black Formosa corruption?"

"I have never heard of either."

"There are many problems of disease, many strange pathological possibilities, in the East, Watson." He paused after each sentence to collect his failing strength. "I have learned so much during some recent researches which have a medico-criminal aspect. It was in the course of them that I contracted this complaint. You can do nothing."

"Possibly not. But I happen to know that Dr. Ainstree, the greatest living authority upon tropical disease, is now in London. All remonstrance is useless, Holmes, I am going this instant to fetch him." I turned resolutely to the door.

Never have I had such a shock! In an instant, with a tiger-spring, the dying man had intercepted me. I heard the sharp snap of a twisted key. The next moment he had staggered back to his bed, exhausted and panting after his one tremendous outflame of energy.

"You won't take the key from me by force, Watson. I've got you, my friend. Here you are, and here you will stay until I will otherwise. But I'll humour you." (All this in little gasps, with terrible struggles for breath between.) "You've only my own good at heart. Of course I know that very well. You shall have your way, but give me time to get my strength. Not now, Watson, not now. It's four o'clock. At six you can go."

"This is insanity, Holmes."

"Only two hours, Watson. I promise you will go at six. Are you content to wait?"

"I seem to have no choice."

"None in the world, Watson. Thank you, I need no help in arranging the clothes. You will please keep your distance. Now, Watson, there is one other condition that I would make. You will seek help, not from the man you mention, but from the one that I choose."

"By all means."

"The first three sensible words that you have uttered since you entered this room, Watson. You will find some books over there. I am somewhat exhausted; I wonder how a battery feels when it pours electricity into a non-conductor? At six, Watson, we resume our conversation."

But it was destined to be resumed long before that hour, and in circumstances which gave me a shock hardly second to that caused by his spring to the door. I had stood for some minutes looking at the silent figure in the bed. His face was almost covered by the clothes and he appeared to be asleep. Then, unable to settle down to reading, I walked slowly round the room, examining the pictures of celebrated criminals with which every wall was adorned. Finally, in my aimless perambulation, I came to the mantelpiece. A litter of pipes, tobacco-pouches, syringes, penknives, revolver-cartridges, and other débris was scattered over it. In the midst of these was a small black and white ivory box with a sliding lid. It was a neat little thing, and I had stretched out my hand to examine it more closely when—— It was a dreadful cry that he gave—a yell which might have been heard down the street. My skin went cold and my hair bristled at that horrible scream. As I turned I caught a glimpse of a convulsed face and frantic eyes. I stood paralyzed, with the little box in my hand.

"Put it down! Down, this instant, Watson—this instant, I say!" His head sank back upon the pillow and he gave a deep sigh of relief as I replaced the box upon the mantelpiece. "I hate to have my things touched, Watson. You know that I hate it. You fidget me beyond endurance. You, a doctor—you are enough to drive a patient into an asylum. Sit down, man, and let me have my rest!"

The incident left a most unpleasant impression upon my mind. The violent and causeless excitement, followed by this brutality of speech, so far removed from his usual suavity, showed me how deep was the disorganization of his mind. Of all ruins, that of a noble mind is the most deplorable. I sat in silent dejection until the stipulated time had passed. He seemed to have been watching the clock as well as I, for it was hardly six before he began to talk with the same feverish animation as before.

"Now, Watson," said he. "Have you any change in your pocket?"

"Yes."

"Any silver?"

"A good deal."

"How many half-crowns?"

"I have five."

"Ah, too few! Too few! How very unfortunate, Watson! However, such as they are you can put them in your watchpocket. And all the rest of your money in your left trouserpocket. Thank you. It will balance you so much better like that."

This was raving insanity. He shuddered, and again made a sound between a cough and a sob.

"You will now light the gas, Watson, but you will be very careful that not for one instant shall it be more than half on. I implore you to be careful, Watson. Thank you, that is excellent. No, you need not draw the blind. Now you will have the kindness to place some letters and papers upon this table within my reach. Thank you. Now some of that litter from the mantelpiece. Excellent, Watson! There is a sugar-tongs there. Kindly raise that small ivory box with its assistance. Place it here among the papers. Good! You can now go and fetch Mr. Culverton Smith, of 13 Lower Burke Street."

To tell the truth, my desire to fetch a doctor had somewhat weakened, for poor Holmes was so obviously delirious that it seemed dangerous to leave him. However, he was as eager now to consult the person named as he had been obstinate in refusing.

"I never heard the name," said I.

"Possibly not, my good Watson. It may surprise you to know that the man upon earth who is best versed in this disease is not a medical man, but a planter. Mr. Culverton Smith is a well-known resident of Sumatra, now visiting London. An outbreak of the disease upon his plantation, which was distant from medical aid, caused him to study it himself, with some rather far-reaching consequences. He is a very methodical person, and I did not desire you to start before six, because I was well aware that you would not find him in his study. If you could persuade him to come here and give us the benefit of his unique experience of this disease, the investigation of which has been his dearest hobby, I cannot doubt that he could help me."

I give Holmes's remarks as a consecutive whole and will not attempt to indicate how they were interrupted by gaspings for breath and those clutchings of his hands which indicated the pain from which he was suffering. His appearance had changed for the worse during the few hours that I had been with him. Those hectic spots were more pronounced, the eyes shone more brightly out of darker hollows, and a cold sweat glimmered upon his brow. He still retained, however, the jaunty gallantry of his speech. To the last gasp he would always be the master.

"You will tell him exactly how you have left me," said he. "You will convey the very impression which is in your own mind—a dying man—a dying and delirious man. Indeed, I cannot think why the whole bed of the ocean is not one solid mass of oysters, so prolific the creatures seem. Ah, I am wandering! Strange how the brain controls the brain! What was I saying, Watson?"

"My directions for Mr. Culverton Smith."

"Ah, yes, I remember. My life depends upon it. Plead with him, Watson. There is no good feeling between us. His nephew, Watson—I had suspicions of foul play and I allowed him to see it. The boy died horribly. He has a grudge against me. You will soften him, Watson. Beg him, pray him, get him here by any means. He can save me—only he!"

"I will bring him in a cab, if I have to carry him down to it."

"You will do nothing of the sort. You will persuade him to come. And then you will return in front of him. Make any excuse so as not to come with him. Don't forget, Watson. You won't fail me. You never did fail me. No doubt there are natural enemies which limit the increase of the creatures. You and I, Watson, we have done our part. Shall the world, then, be overrun by oysters? No, no; horrible! You'll convey all that is in your mind."

I left him full of the image of this magnificent intellect babbling like a foolish child. He had handed me the key, and with a happy thought I took it with me lest he should lock himself in. Mrs. Hudson was waiting, trembling and weeping, in the passage. Behind me as I passed from the flat I heard Holmes's high, thin voice in some delirious chant. Below, as I stood whistling for a cab, a man came on me through the fog.

"How is Mr. Holmes, sir?" he asked.

It was an old acquaintance, Inspector Morton, of Scotland Yard, dressed in unofficial tweeds.

"He is very ill," I answered.

He looked at me in a most singular fashion. Had it not been too fiendish, I could have imagined that the gleam of the fanlight showed exultation in his face.

"I heard some rumour of it," said he.

The cab had driven up, and I left him.

Lower Burke Street proved to be a line of fine houses lying in the vague borderland between Notting Hill and Kensington. The particular one at which my cabman pulled up had an air of smug and demure respectability in its old-fashioned iron railings, its massive folding-door, and its shining brasswork. All was in keeping with a solemn butler who appeared framed in the pink radiance of a tinted electric light behind him.

"Yes, Mr. Culverton Smith is in. Dr. Watson! Very good, sir, I will take up your card."

My humble name and title did not appear to impress Mr. Culverton Smith. Through the half-open door I heard a high, petulant, penetrating voice.

"Who is this person? What does he want? Dear me, Staples, how often have I said that I am not to be disturbed in my hours of study?"

There came a gentle flow of soothing explanation from the butler.

"Well, I won't see him, Staples. I can't have my work interrupted like this. I am not at home. Say so. Tell him to come in the morning if he really must see me."

Again the gentle murmur.

"Well, well, give him that message. He can come in the morning, or he can stay away. My work must not be hindered."

I thought of Holmes tossing upon his bed of sickness and counting the minutes, perhaps, until I could bring help to him. It was not a time to stand upon ceremony. His life depended upon my promptness. Before the apologetic butler had delivered his message I had pushed past him and was in the room.

With a shrill cry of anger a man rose from a reclining chair beside the fire. I saw a great yellow face, coarse-grained and greasy, with heavy, double-chin, and two sullen, menacing gray eyes which glared at me from under tufted and sandy brows. A high bald head had a small velvet smoking-cap poised coquettishly upon one side of its pink curve. The skull was of enormous capacity, and yet as I looked down I saw to my amazement that the figure of the man was small and frail, twisted in the shoulders and back like one who has suffered from rickets in his childhood.

"What's this?" he cried in a high, screaming voice. "What is the meaning of this intrusion? Didn't I send you word that I would see you to-morrow morning?"

"I am sorry," said I, "but the matter cannot be delayed. Mr. Sherlock Holmes——"

The mention of my friend's name had an extraordinary effect upon the little man. The look of anger passed in an instant from his face. His features became tense and alert.

"Have you come from Holmes?" he asked.

"I have just left him."

"What about Holmes? How is he?"

"He is desperately ill. That is why I have come."

The man motioned me to a chair, and turned to resume his own. As he did so I caught a glimpse of his face in the mirror over the mantelpiece. I could have sworn that it was set in a malicious and abominable smile. Yet I persuaded myself that it must have been some nervous contraction which I had surprised, for he turned to me an instant later with genuine concern upon his features.

"I am sorry to hear this," said he. "I only know Mr. Holmes through some business dealings which we have had, but I have every respect for his talents and his character. He is an amateur of crime, as I am of disease. For him the villain, for me the microbe. There are my prisons," he continued, pointing to a row of bottles and jars which stood upon a side table. "Among those gelatine cultivations some of the very worst offenders in the world are now doing time."

"It was on account of your special knowledge that Mr. Holmes desired to see you. He has a high opinion of you and thought that you were the one man in London who could help him."

The little man started, and the jaunty smoking-cap slid to the floor.

"Why?" he asked. "Why should Mr. Holmes think that I could help him in his trouble?"

"Because of your knowledge of Eastern diseases."

"But why should he think that this disease which he has contracted is Eastern?"

"Because, in some professional inquiry, he has been working among Chinese sailors down in the docks."

Mr. Culverton Smith smiled pleasantly and picked up his smoking-cap.

"Oh, that's it—is it?" said he. "I trust the matter is not so grave as you suppose. How long has he been ill?"

"About three days."

"Is he delirious?"

"Occasionally."

"Tut, tut! This sounds serious. It would be inhuman not to answer his call. I very much resent any interruption to my work, Dr. Watson, but this case is certainly exceptional. I will come with you at once."

I remembered Holmes's injunction.

"I have another appointment," said I.

"Very good. I will go alone. I have a note of Mr. Holmes's address. You can rely upon my being there within half an hour at most."

It was with a sinking heart that I reëntered Holmes's bedroom. For all that I knew the worst might have happened in my absence. To my enormous relief, he had improved greatly in the interval. His appearance was as ghastly as ever, but all trace of delirium had left him and he spoke in a feeble voice, it is true, but with even more than his usual crispness and lucidity.

"Well, did you see him, Watson?"

"Yes; he is coming."

"Admirable, Watson! Admirable! You are the best of messengers."

"He wished to return with me."

"That would never do, Watson. That would be obviously impossible. Did he ask what ailed me?"

"I told him about the Chinese in the East End."

"Exactly! Well, Watson, you have done all that a good friend could. You can now disappear from the scene."

"I must wait and hear his opinion, Holmes."

"Of course you must. But I have reasons to suppose that this opinion would be very much more frank and valuable if he imagines that we are alone. There is just room behind the head of my bed, Watson."

"My dear Holmes!"

"I fear there is no alternative, Watson. The room does not lend itself to concealment, which is as well, as it is the less likely to arouse suspicion. But just there, Watson, I fancy that it could be done." Suddenly he sat up with a rigid intentness upon his haggard face. "There are the wheels, Watson. Quick, man, if you love me! And don't budge, whatever happens— whatever happens, do you hear? Don't speak! Don't move! Just listen with all your ears." Then in an instant his sudden access of strength departed, and his masterful, purposeful talk droned away into the low, vague murmurings of a semi-delirious man.

From the hiding-place into which I had been so swiftly hustled I heard the footfalls upon the stair, with the opening and the closing of the bedroom door. Then, to my surprise, there came a long silence, broken only by the heavy breathings and gaspings of the sick man. I could imagine that our visitor was standing by the bedside and looking down at the sufferer. At last that strange hush was broken.

"Holmes!" he cried. "Holmes!" in the insistent tone of one who awakens a sleeper. "Can't you hear me, Holmes?" There was a rustling, as if he had shaken the sick man roughly by the shoulder.

"Is that you, Mr. Smith?" Holmes whispered. "I hardly dared hope that you would come."

The other laughed.

"I should imagine not," he said. "And yet, you see, I am here. Coals of fire, Holmes—coals of fire!"

"It is very good of you—very noble of you. I appreciate your special knowledge."

Our visitor sniggered.

"You do. You are, fortunately, the only man in London who does. Do you know what is the matter with you?"

"The same," said Holmes.

"Ah! You recognize the symptoms?"

"Only too well."

"Well, I shouldn't be surprised, Holmes. I shouldn't be surprised if it *were* the same. A bad lookout for you if it is. Poor Victor was a dead man on the fourth day—a strong, hearty young fellow. It was certainly, as you said, very surprising that he should have contracted an out-of-the-way Asiatic disease in the heart of London—a disease, too, of which I had made such a very special study. Singular coincidence, Holmes. Very smart of you to notice it, but rather uncharitable to suggest that it was cause and effect."

"I knew that you did it."

"Oh, you did, did you? Well, you couldn't prove it, anyhow. But what do you think of yourself spreading reports about me like that, and then crawling to me for help the moment you are in trouble? What sort of a game is that—eh?"

I heard the rasping, laboured breathing of the sick man. "Give me the water!" he gasped.

"You're precious near your end, my friend, but I don't want you to go till I have had a word with you. That's why I give you water. There, don't slop it about! That's right. Can you understand what I say?"

Holmes groaned.

"Do what you can for me. Let bygones be bygones," he whispered. "I'll put the words out of my head—I swear I will. Only cure me, and I'll forget it."

"Forget what?"

"Well, about Victor Savage's death. You as good as admitted just now that you had done it. I'll forget it."

"You can forget it or remember it, just as you like. I don't see you in the witness-box. Quite another shaped box, my good Holmes, I assure you. It matters nothing to me that you should know how my nephew died. It's not him we are talking about. It's you."

"Yes, yes."

"The fellow who came for me—I've forgotten his name—said that you contracted it down in the East End among the sailors."

"I could only account for it so."

"You are proud of your brains, Holmes, are you not? Think yourself smart, don't you? You came across someone who was smarter this time. Now cast your mind back, Holmes. Can you think of no other way you could have got this thing?"

"I can't think. My mind is gone. For heaven's sake help me!"

"Yes, I will help you. I'll help you to understand just where you are and how you got there. I'd like you to know before you die."

"Give me something to ease my pain."

"Painful, is it? Yes, the coolies used to do some squealing towards the end. Takes you as cramp, I fancy."

"Yes, yes; it is cramp."

"Well, you can hear what I say, anyhow. Listen now! Can you remember any unusual incident in your life just about the time your symptoms began?"

"No, no; nothing."

"Think again."

"I'm too ill to think."

"Well, then, I'll help you. Did anything come by post?"

"By post?"

"A box by chance?"

"I'm fainting—I'm gone!"

"Listen, Holmes!" There was a sound as if he was shaking the dying man, and it was all that I could do to hold myself quiet in my hiding-place. "You must hear me. You *shall* hear me. Do you remember a box—an ivory box? It came on Wednesday. You opened it—do you remember?"

"Yes, yes, I opened it. There was a sharp spring inside it. Some joke——"

"It was no joke, as you will find to your cost. You fool, you would have it and you have got it. Who asked you to cross my path? If you had left me alone I would not have hurt you."

"I remember," Holmes gasped. "The spring! It drew blood. This box—this on the table."

"The very one, by George! And it may as well leave the room in my pocket. There goes your last shred of evidence. But you have the truth now, Holmes, and you can die with the knowledge that I killed you. You knew too much of the fate of Victor Savage, so I have sent you to share it. You are very near your end, Holmes. I will sit here and I will watch you die."

Holmes's voice had sunk to an almost inaudible whisper.

"What is that?" said Smith. "Turn up the gas? Ah, the shadows begin to fall, do they? Yes, I will turn it up, that I may see you the better." He crossed the room and the light suddenly brightened. "Is there any other little service that I can do you, my friend?"

"A match and a cigarette."

I nearly called out in my joy and my amazement. He was speaking in his natural voice—a little weak, perhaps, but the very voice I knew. There was a long pause, and I felt that Culverton Smith was standing in silent amazement looking down at his companion.

"What's the meaning of this?" I heard him say at last in a dry, rasping tone.

"The best way of successfully acting a part is to be it," said Holmes. "I give you my word that for three days I have tasted neither food nor drink until you were good enough to pour me out that glass of water. But it is the tobacco which I find most irksome. Ah, here *are* some cigarettes." I heard the striking of a match. "That is very much better. Halloa! halloa! Do I hear the step of a friend?"

There were footfalls outside, the door opened, and Inspector Morton appeared.

"All is in order and this is your man," said Holmes.

The officer gave the usual cautions.

"I arrest you on the charge of the murder of one Victor Savage," he concluded.

"And you might add of the attempted murder of one Sherlock Holmes," remarked my friend with a chuckle. "To save an invalid trouble, Inspector, Mr. Culverton Smith was good enough to give our signal by turning up the gas. By the way, the prisoner has a small box in the right-hand pocket of his coat which it would be as well to remove. Thank you. I would handle it gingerly if I were you. Put it down here. It may play its part in the trial."

There was a sudden rush and a scuffle, followed by the clash of iron and a cry of pain.

"You'll only get yourself hurt," said the inspector. "Stand still, will you?" There was the click of the closing handcuffs.

"A nice trap!" cried the high, snarling voice. "It will bring *you* into the dock, Holmes, not me. He asked me to come here to cure him. I was sorry for him and I came. Now he will pretend, no doubt, that I have said anything which he may invent which will corroborate his insane suspicions. You can lie as you like, Holmes. My word is always as good as yours."

"Good heavens!" cried Holmes. "I had totally forgotten him. My dear Watson, I owe you a thousand apologies. To think that I should have overlooked you! I need not introduce you to Mr. Culverton Smith, since I understand that you met somewhat earlier in the evening. Have you the cab below? I will follow you when I am dressed, for I may be of some use at the station.

"I never needed it more," said Holmes as he refreshed himself with a glass of claret and some biscuits in the intervals of his toilet. "However, as you know, my habits are irregular, and such a feat means less to me than to most men. It was very essential that I should impress Mrs. Hudson with the reality of my condition, since she was to convey it to you, and you in turn to him. You won't be offended, Watson? You will realize that among your many talents dissimulation finds no place, and that if you had shared my secret you would never have been able to impress Smith with the urgent necessity of his presence, which was the vital point of the whole scheme. Knowing his vindictive nature, I was perfectly certain that he would come to look upon his handiwork."

"But your appearance, Holmes—your ghastly face?"

"Three days of absolute fast does not improve one's beauty, Watson. For the rest, there is nothing which a sponge may not cure. With vaseline upon one's forehead, belladonna in one's eyes, rouge over the cheek-bones, and crusts of beeswax round one's lips, a very satisfying effect can be produced. Malingering is a subject upon which I have sometimes thought of writing a monograph. A little occasional talk about half-crowns, oysters, or any other extraneous subject produces a pleasing effect of delirium."

"But why would you not let me near you, since there was in truth no infection?"

"Can you ask, my dear Watson? Do you imagine that I have no respect for your medical talents? Could I fancy that your astute judgment would pass a dying man who, however weak, had no rise of pulse or temperature? At four yards, I could deceive you. If I failed to do so, who would bring my Smith within my grasp? No, Watson, I would not touch that box. You can just see if you look at it sideways where the sharp spring like a viper's tooth emerges as you open it. I dare say it was by some such device that poor Savage, who stood between this monster and a reversion,* was done to death. My correspondence, however, is, as you know, a varied one, and I am somewhat upon my guard against any packages which reach me. It was clear to me, however, that by pretending that he had really succeeded in his design I might surprise a confession. That pretence I have carried out with the thoroughness of the true artist. Thank you, Watson, you must help me on with my coat. When we have finished at the police-station I think that something nutritious at Simpson's would not be out of place."

---

*Legal term for the return of an estate to its grantor after the grant has terminated.

THE DISAPPEARANCE OF LADY
FRANCES CARFAX*

B ut why Turkish?" asked Mr. Sherlock Holmes, gazing fixedly at
my boots. I was reclining in a cane-backed chair at the moment,
and my protruded feet had attracted his ever-active attention.

"English," I answered in some surprise. "I got them at Latimer's, in
Oxford Street."

Holmes smiled with an expression of weary patience.

"The bath!" he said; "the bath! Why the relaxing and expensive Turkish rather than the invigorating home-made article?"

"Because for the last few days I have been feeling rheumatic and old.
A Turkish bath is what we call an alternative in medicine—a fresh starting-
point, a cleanser of the system.

"By the way, Holmes," I added, "I have no doubt the connection between my boots and a Turkish bath is a perfectly self-evident one to a logical mind, and yet I should be obliged to you if you would indicate it."

"The train of reasoning is not very obscure, Watson," said Holmes
with a mischievous twinkle. "It belongs to the same elementary class of
deduction which I should illustrate if I were to ask you who shared your
cab in your drive this morning."

"I don't admit that a fresh illustration is an explanation," said I with
some asperity.

"Bravo, Watson! A very dignified and logical remonstrance. Let me see,
what were the points? Take the last one first—the cab. You observe that
you have some splashes on the left sleeve and shoulder of your coat. Had
you sat in the centre of a hansom you would probably have had no splashes,
and if you had they would certainly have been symmetrical. Therefore it is
clear that you sat at the side. Therefore it is equally clear that you had a
companion."

"That is very evident."

"Absurdly commonplace, is it not?"

"But the boots and the bath?"

"Equally childish. You are in the habit of doing up your boots in a certain way. I see them on this occasion fastened with an elaborate double
bow, which is not your usual method of tying them. You have, therefore,
had them off. Who has tied them? A bootmaker—or the boy at the bath.
It is unlikely that it is the bootmaker, since your boots are nearly new.
Well, what remains? The bath. Absurd, is it not? But, for all that, the
Turkish bath has served a purpose."

"What is that?"

"You say that you have had it because you need a change. Let me sug-

---

*The name may ring a bell: Count Dracula rented Carfax Abbey.

gest that you take one. How would Lausanne do, my dear Watson—first-class tickets and all expenses paid on a princely scale?"

"Splendid! But why?"

Holmes leaned back in his armchair and took his notebook from his pocket.

"One of the most dangerous classes in the world," said he, "is the drifting and friendless woman. She is the most harmless and often the most useful of mortals, but she is the inevitable inciter of crime in others. She is helpless. She is migratory. She has sufficient means to take her from country to country and from hotel to hotel. She is lost, as often as not, in a maze of obscure *pensions* and boarding-houses. She is a stray chicken in a world of foxes. When she is gobbled up she is hardly missed. I much fear that some evil has come to the Lady Frances Carfax."

I was relieved at this sudden descent from the general to the particular. Holmes consulted his notes.

"Lady Frances," he continued, "is the sole survivor of the direct family of the late Earl of Rufton. The estates went, as you may remember, in the male line. She was left with limited means, but with some very remarkable old Spanish jewellery of silver and curiously cut diamonds to which she was fondly attached—too attached, for she refused to leave them with her banker and always carried them about with her. A rather pathetic figure, the Lady Frances, a beautiful woman, still in fresh middle age, and yet, by a strange chance, the last derelict of what only twenty years ago was a goodly fleet."

"What has happened to her, then?"

"Ah, what has happened to the Lady Frances? Is she alive or dead? There is our problem. She is a lady of precise habits, and for four years it has been her invariable custom to write every second week to Miss Dobney, her old governess, who has long retired and lives in Camberwell. It is this Miss Dobney who has consulted me. Nearly five weeks have passed without a word. The last letter was from the Hôtel National at Lausanne. Lady Frances seems to have left there and given no address. The family are anxious, and as they are exceedingly wealthy no sum will be spared if we can clear the matter up."

"Is Miss Dobney the only source of information? Surely she had other correspondents?"

"There is one correspondent who is a sure draw, Watson. That is the bank. Single ladies must live, and their passbooks are compressed diaries. She banks at Silvester's. I have glanced over her account. The last check but one paid her bill at Lausanne, but it was a large one and probably left her with cash in hand. Only one check has been drawn since."

"To whom, and where?"

"To Miss Marie Devine. There is nothing to show where the check was drawn. It was cashed at the Crédit Lyonnais at Montpellier less than three weeks ago. The sum was fifty pounds."

"And who is Miss Marie Devine?"

"That also I have been able to discover. Miss Marie Devine was the maid of Lady Frances Carfax. Why she should have paid her this check we have not yet determined. I have no doubt, however, that your researches will soon clear the matter up."

"*My* researches!"

"Hence the health-giving expedition to Lausanne. You know that I cannot possibly leave London while old Abrahams is in such mortal terror of his life. Besides, on general principles it is best that I should not leave the country. Scotland Yard feels lonely without me, and it causes an unhealthy excitement among the criminal classes. Go, then, my dear Watson, and if my humble counsel can ever be valued at so extravagant a rate as two pence a word, it waits your disposal night and day at the end of the Continental wire."

Two days later found me at the Hôtel National at Lausanne, where I received every courtesy at the hands of M. Moser, the well-known manager. Lady Frances, as he informed me, had stayed there for several weeks. She had been much liked by all who met her. Her age was not more than forty. She was still handsome and bore every sign of having in her youth been a very lovely woman. M. Moser knew nothing of any valuable jewellery, but it had been remarked by the servants that the heavy trunk in the lady's bedroom was always scrupulously locked. Marie Devine, the maid, was as popular as her mistress. She was actually engaged to one of the head waiters in the hotel, and there was no difficulty in getting her address. It was 11 Rue de Trajan, Montpellier. All this I jotted down and felt that Holmes himself could not have been more adroit in collecting his facts.

Only one corner still remained in the shadow. No light which I possessed could clear up the cause for the lady's sudden departure. She was very happy at Lausanne. There was every reason to believe that she intended to remain for the season in her luxurious rooms overlooking the lake. And yet she had left at a single day's notice, which involved her in the useless payment of a week's rent. Only Jules Vibart, the lover of the maid, had any suggestion to offer. He connected the sudden departure with the visit to the hotel a day or two before of a tall, dark, bearded man. "*Un sauvage—un véritable sauvage!*"* cried Jules Vibart. The man had rooms somewhere in the town. He had been seen talking earnestly to Madame on the promenade by the lake. Then he had called. She had refused to see him. He was English, but of his name there was no record. Madame had left the place immediately afterwards. Jules Vibart, and, what was of more importance, Jules Vibart's sweetheart, thought that this call and this departure were cause and effect. Only one thing Jules would not discuss. That was the reason why Marie had left her mistress. Of that he could or would say nothing. If I wished to know, I must go to Montpellier and ask her.

So ended the first chapter of my inquiry. The second was devoted to

---

*A savage—a veritable savage! (French).

the place which Lady Frances Carfax had sought when she left Lausanne. Concerning this there had been some secrecy, which confirmed the idea that she had gone with the intention of throwing someone off her track. Otherwise why should not her luggage have been openly labelled for Baden? Both she and it reached the Rhenish spa by some circuitous route. This much I gathered from the manager of Cook's local office. So to Baden I went, after dispatching to Holmes an account of all my proceedings and receiving in reply a telegram of half-humorous commendation.

At Baden the track was not difficult to follow. Lady Frances had stayed at the Englischer Hof for a fortnight. While there she had made the acquaintance of a Dr. Shlessinger and his wife, a missionary from South America. Like most lonely ladies, Lady Frances found her comfort and occupation in religion. Dr. Shlessinger's remarkable personality, his whole-hearted devotion, and the fact that he was recovering from a disease contracted in the exercise of his apostolic duties affected her deeply. She had helped Mrs. Shlessinger in the nursing of the convalescent saint. He spent his day, as the manager described it to me, upon a lounge-chair on the veranda, with an attendant lady upon either side of him. He was preparing a map of the Holy Land, with special reference to the kingdom of the Midianites, upon which he was writing a monograph. Finally, having improved much in health, he and his wife had returned to London, and Lady Frances had started thither in their company. This was just three weeks before, and the manager had heard nothing since. As to the maid, Marie, she had gone off some days beforehand in floods of tears, after informing the other maids that she was leaving service forever. Dr. Shlessinger had paid the bill of the whole party before his departure.

"By the way," said the landlord in conclusion, "you are not the only friend of Lady Frances Carfax who is inquiring after her just now. Only a week or so ago we had a man here upon the same errand."

"Did he give a name?" I asked.

"None; but he was an Englishman, though of an unusual type."

"A savage?" said I, linking my facts after the fashion of my illustrious friend.

"Exactly. That describes him very well. He is a bulky, bearded, sunburned fellow, who looks as if he would be more at home in a farmers' inn than in a fashionable hotel. A hard, fierce man, I should think, and one whom I should be sorry to offend."

Already the mystery began to define itself, as figures grow clearer with the lifting of a fog. Here was this good and pious lady pursued from place to place by a sinister and unrelenting figure. She feared him, or she would not have fled from Lausanne. He had still followed. Sooner or later he would overtake her. Had he already overtaken her? Was *that* the secret of her continued silence? Could the good people who were her companions not screen her from his violence or his blackmail? What horrible purpose, what deep design, lay behind this long pursuit? There was the problem which I had to solve.

To Holmes I wrote showing how rapidly and surely I had got down to the roots of the matter. In reply I had a telegram asking for a description of Dr. Shlessinger's left ear. Holmes's ideas of humour are strange and occasionally offensive, so I took no notice of his ill-timed jest—indeed, I had already reached Montpellier in my pursuit of the maid, Marie, before his message came.

I had no difficulty in finding the ex-servant and in learning all that she could tell me. She was a devoted creature, who had only left her mistress because she was sure that she was in good hands, and because her own approaching marriage made a separation inevitable in any case. Her mistress had, as she confessed with distress, shown some irritability of temper towards her during their stay in Baden, and had even questioned her once as if she had suspicions of her honesty, and this had made the parting easier than it would otherwise have been. Lady Frances had given her fifty pounds as a wedding-present. Like me, Marie viewed with deep distrust the stranger who had driven her mistress from Lausanne. With her own eyes she had seen him seize the lady's wrist with great violence on the public promenade by the lake. He was a fierce and terrible man. She believed that it was out of dread of him that Lady Frances had accepted the escort of the Shlessingers to London. She had never spoken to Marie about it, but many little signs had convinced the maid that her mistress lived in a state of continual nervous apprehension. So far she had got in her narrative, when suddenly she sprang from her chair and her face was convulsed with surprise and fear. "See!" she cried. "The miscreant follows still! There is the very man of whom I speak."

Through the open sitting-room window I saw a huge, swarthy man with a bristling black beard walking slowly down the centre of the street and staring eagerly at the numbers of the houses. It was clear that, like myself, he was on the track of the maid. Acting upon the impulse of the moment, I rushed out and accosted him.

"You are an Englishman," I said.

"What if I am?" he asked with a most villainous scowl.

"May I ask what your name is?"

"No, you may not," said he with decision.

The situation was awkward, but the most direct way is often the best.

"Where is the Lady Frances Carfax?" I asked.

He stared at me in amazement.

"What have you done with her? Why have you pursued her? I insist upon an answer!" said I.

The fellow gave a bellow of anger and sprang upon me like a tiger. I have held my own in many a struggle, but the man had a grip of iron and the fury of a fiend. His hand was on my throat and my senses were nearly gone before an unshaven French *ouvrier** in a blue blouse darted out from a *cabaret* opposite, with a cudgel in his hand, and struck my assailant

---

*Workman (French).

a sharp crack over the forearm, which made him leave go his hold. He stood for an instant fuming with rage and uncertain whether he should not renew his attack. Then, with a snarl of anger, he left me and entered the cottage from which I had just come. I turned to thank my preserver, who stood beside me in the roadway.

"Well, Watson," said he, "a very pretty hash you have made of it! I rather think you had better come back with me to London by the night express."

An hour afterwards, Sherlock Holmes, in his usual garb and style, was seated in my private room at the hotel. His explanation of his sudden and opportune appearance was simplicity itself, for, finding that he could get away from London, he determined to head me off at the next obvious point of my travels. In the disguise of a workingman he had sat in the *cabaret* waiting for my appearance.

"And a singularly consistent investigation you have made, my dear Watson," said he. "I cannot at the moment recall any possible blunder which you have omitted. The total effect of your proceeding has been to give the alarm everywhere and yet to discover nothing."

"Perhaps you would have done no better," I answered bitterly.

"There is no 'perhaps' about it. I *have* done better. Here is the Hon. Philip Green, who is a fellow-lodger with you in this hotel, and we may find him the starting-point for a more successful investigation."

A card had come up on a salver, and it was followed by the same bearded ruffian who had attacked me in the street. He started when he saw me.

"What is this, Mr. Holmes?" he asked. "I had your note and I have come. But what has this man to do with the matter?"

"This is my old friend and associate, Dr. Watson, who is helping us in this affair."

The stranger held out a huge, sunburned hand, with a few words of apology.

"I hope I didn't harm you. When you accused me of hurting her I lost my grip of myself. Indeed, I'm not responsible in these days. My nerves are like live wires. But this situation is beyond me. What I want to know, in the first place, Mr. Holmes, is, how in the world you came to hear of my existence at all."

"I am in touch with Miss Dobney, Lady Frances's governess."

"Old Susan Dobney with the mob cap!* I remember her well."

"And she remembers you. It was in the days before—before you found it better to go to South Africa."

"Ah, I see you know my whole story. I need hide nothing from you. I swear to you, Mr. Holmes, that there never was in this world a man who loved a woman with a more wholehearted love than I had for Frances. I was a wild youngster, I know—not worse than others of my class. But her

---

*Big, high cap trimmed with frills and ribbons.

mind was pure as snow. She could not bear a shadow of coarseness. So, when she came to hear of things that I had done, she would have no more to say to me. And yet she loved me—that is the wonder of it!—loved me well enough to remain single all her sainted days just for my sake alone. When the years had passed and I had made my money at Barberton* I thought perhaps I could seek her out and soften her. I had heard that she was still unmarried. I found her at Lausanne and tried all I knew. She weakened, I think, but her will was strong, and when next I called she had left the town. I traced her to Baden, and then after a time heard that her maid was here. I'm a rough fellow, fresh from a rough life, and when Dr. Watson spoke to me as he did I lost hold of myself for a moment. But for God's sake tell me what has become of the Lady Frances."

"That is for us to find out," said Sherlock Holmes with peculiar gravity. "What is your London address, Mr. Green?"

"The Langham Hotel will find me."

"Then may I recommend that you return there and be on hand in case I should want you? I have no desire to encourage false hopes, but you may rest assured that all that can be done will be done for the safety of Lady Frances. I can say no more for the instant. I will leave you this card so that you may be able to keep in touch with us. Now, Watson, if you will pack your bag I will cable to Mrs. Hudson to make one of her best efforts for two hungry travellers at 7:30 to-morrow."

A telegram was awaiting us when we reached our Baker Street rooms, which Holmes read with an exclamation of interest and threw across to me. "Jagged or torn," was the message, and the place of origin, Baden.

"What is this?" I asked.

"It is everything," Holmes answered. "You may remember my seemingly irrelevant question as to this clerical gentleman's left ear. You did not answer it."

"I had left Baden and could not inquire."

"Exactly. For this reason I sent a duplicate to the manager of the Englischer Hof, whose answer lies here."

"What does it show?"

"It shows, my dear Watson, that we are dealing with an exceptionally astute and dangerous man. The Rev. Dr. Shlessinger, missionary from South America, is none other than Holy Peters, one of the most unscrupulous rascals that Australia has ever evolved—and for a young country it has turned out some very finished types. His particular specialty is the beguiling of lonely ladies by playing upon their religious feelings, and his so-called wife, an Englishwoman named Fraser, is a worthy helpmate. The nature of his tactics suggested his identity to me, and this physical peculiarity—he was badly bitten in a saloon-fight at Adelaide in '89—confirmed my suspicion. This poor lady is in the hands of a most in-

---

*South African gold mining town.

fernal couple, who will stick at nothing, Watson. That she is already dead is a very likely supposition. If not, she is undoubtedly in some sort of confinement and unable to write to Miss Dobney or her other friends. It is always possible that she never reached London, or that she has passed through it, but the former is improbable, as, with their system of registration, it is not easy for foreigners to play tricks with the Continental police; and the latter is also unlikely, as these rogues could not hope to find any other place where it would be as easy to keep a person under restraint. All my instincts tell me that she is in London, but as we have at present no possible means of telling where, we can only take the obvious steps, eat our dinner, and possess our souls in patience. Later in the evening I will stroll down and have a word with friend Lestrade at Scotland Yard."

But neither the official police nor Holmes's own small but very efficient organization sufficed to clear away the mystery. Amid the crowded millions of London the three persons we sought were as completely obliterated as if they had never lived. Advertisements were tried, and failed. Clues were followed, and led to nothing. Every criminal resort which Shlessinger might frequent was drawn in vain. His old associates were watched, but they kept clear of him. And then suddenly, after a week of helpless suspense, there came a flash of light. A silver-and-brilliant pendant of old Spanish design had been pawned at Bovington's, in Westminster Road. The pawner was a large, clean-shaven man of clerical appearance. His name and address were demonstrably false. The ear had escaped notice, but the description was surely that of Shlessinger.

Three times had our bearded friend from the Langham called for news—the third time within an hour of this fresh development. His clothes were getting looser on his great body. He seemed to be wilting away in his anxiety. "If you will only give me something to do!" was his constant wail. At last Holmes could oblige him.

"He has begun to pawn the jewels. We should get him now."

"But does this mean that any harm has befallen the Lady Frances?"

Holmes shook his head very gravely.

"Supposing that they have held her prisoner up to now, it is clear that they cannot let her loose without their own destruction. We must prepare for the worst."

"What can I do?"

"These people do not know you by sight?"

"No."

"It is possible that he will go to some other pawnbroker in the future. In that case, we must begin again. On the other hand, he has had a fair price and no questions asked, so if he is in need of ready-money he will probably come back to Bovington's. I will give you a note to them, and they will let you wait in the shop. If the fellow comes you will follow him home. But no indiscretion, and, above all, no violence. I put you on your honour that you will take no step without my knowledge and consent."

For two days the Hon. Philip Green (he was, I may mention, the son of the famous admiral of that name who commanded the Sea of Azof fleet in the Crimean War) brought us no news. On the evening of the third he rushed into our sitting-room, pale, trembling, with every muscle of his powerful frame quivering with excitement.

"We have him! We have him!" he cried.

He was incoherent in his agitation. Holmes soothed him with a few words and thrust him into an armchair.

"Come, now, give us the order of events," said he.

"She came only an hour ago. It was the wife, this time, but the pendant she brought was the fellow of the other. She is a tall, pale woman, with ferret eyes."

"That is the lady," said Holmes.

"She left the office and I followed her. She walked up the Kennington Road, and I kept behind her. Presently she went into a shop. Mr. Holmes, it was an undertaker's."

My companion started. "Well?" he asked in that vibrant voice which told of the fiery soul behind the cold gray face.

"She was talking to the woman behind the counter. I entered as well. 'It is late,' I heard her say, or words to that effect. The woman was excusing herself. 'It should be there before now,' she answered. 'It took longer, being out of the ordinary.' They both stopped and looked at me, so I asked some question and then left the shop."

"You did excellently well. What happened next?"

"The woman came out, but I had hid myself in a doorway. Her suspicions had been aroused, I think, for she looked round her. Then she called a cab and got in. I was lucky enough to get another and so to follow her. She got down at last at No. 36, Poultney Square, Brixton. I drove past, left my cab at the corner of the square, and watched the house."

"Did you see anyone?"

"The windows were all in darkness save one on the lower floor. The blind was down, and I could not see in. I was standing there, wondering what I should do next, when a covered van drove up with two men in it. They descended, took something out of the van, and carried it up the steps to the hall door. Mr. Holmes, it was a coffin."

"Ah!"

"For an instant I was on the point of rushing in. The door had been opened to admit the men and their burden. It was the woman who had opened it. But as I stood there she caught a glimpse of me, and I think that she recognized me. I saw her start, and she hastily closed the door. I remembered my promise to you, and here I am."

"You have done excellent work," said Holmes, scribbling a few words upon a half-sheet of paper. "We can do nothing legal without a warrant, and you can serve the cause best by taking this note down to the authorities and getting one. There may be some difficulty, but I should think that the sale of the jewellery should be sufficient. Lestrade will see to all details."

"But they may murder her in the meanwhile. What could the coffin mean, and for whom could it be but for her?"

"We will do all that can be done, Mr. Green. Not a moment will be lost.

Leave it in our hands. Now, Watson," he added as our client hurried away, "he will set the regular forces on the move. We are, as usual, the irregulars, and we must take our own line of action. The situation strikes me as so desperate that the most extreme measures are justified. Not a moment is to be lost in getting to Poultney Square.

"Let us try to reconstruct the situation," said he as we drove swiftly past the Houses of Parliament and over Westminster Bridge. "These villains have coaxed this unhappy lady to London, after first alienating her from her faithful maid. If she has written any letters they have been intercepted. Through some confederate they have engaged a furnished house. Once inside it, they have made her a prisoner, and they have become possessed of the valuable jewellery which has been their object from the first. Already they have begun to sell part of it, which seems safe enough to them, since they have no reason to think that anyone is interested in the lady's fate. When she is released she will, of course, denounce them. Therefore, she must not be released. But they cannot keep her under lock and key forever. So murder is their only solution."

"That seems very clear."

"Now we will take another line of reasoning. When you follow two separate chains of thought, Watson, you will find some point of intersection which should approximate to the truth. We will start now, not from the lady but from the coffin and argue backward. That incident proves, I fear, beyond all doubt that the lady is dead. It points also to an orthodox burial with proper accompaniment of medical certificate and official sanction. Had the lady been obviously murdered, they would have buried her in a hole in the back garden. But here all is open and regular. What does that mean? Surely that they have done her to death in some way which has deceived the doctor and simulated a natural end—poisoning, perhaps. And yet how strange that they should ever let a doctor approach her unless he were a confederate, which is hardly a credible proposition."

"Could they have forged a medical certificate?"

"Dangerous, Watson, very dangerous. No, I hardly see them doing that. Pull up, cabby! This is evidently the undertaker's, for we have just passed the pawnbroker's. Would you go in, Watson? Your appearance inspires confidence. Ask what hour the Poultney Square funeral takes place to-morrow."

The woman in the shop answered me without hesitation that it was to be at eight o'clock in the morning. "You see, Watson, no mystery; everything aboveboard! In some way the legal forms have undoubtedly been complied with, and they think that they have little to fear. Well, there's nothing for it now but a direct frontal attack. Are you armed?"

"My stick!"

"Well, well, we shall be strong enough. 'Thrice is he armed who hath his quarrel just.'* We simply can't afford to wait for the police or to keep

---

*Reference to Shakespeare's *Henry VI, Part II* (act 3, scene 2): "Thrice is he armed who hath his quarrel just."

within the four corners of the law. You can drive off, cabby. Now, Watson, we'll just take our luck together, as we have occasionally done in the past."

He had rung loudly at the door of a great dark house in the centre of Poultney Square. It was opened immediately, and the figure of a tall woman was outlined against the dim-lit hall.

"Well, what do you want?" she asked sharply, peering at us through the darkness.

"I want to speak to Dr. Shlessinger," said Holmes.

"There is no such person here," she answered, and tried to close the door, but Holmes had jammed it with his foot.

"Well, I want to see the man who lives here, whatever he may call himself," said Holmes firmly.

She hesitated. Then she threw open the door. "Well, come in!" said she. "My husband is not afraid to face any man in the world." She closed the door behind us and showed us into a sitting-room on the right side of the hall, turning up the gas as she left us. "Mr. Peters will be with you in an instant," she said.

Her words were literally true, for we had hardly time to look around the dusty and moth-eaten apartment in which we found ourselves before the door opened and a big, clean-shaven bald-headed man stepped lightly into the room. He had a large red face, with pendulous cheeks, and a general air of superficial benevolence which was marred by a cruel, vicious mouth.

"There is surely some mistake here, gentlemen," he said in an unctuous, make-everything-easy voice. "I fancy that you have been misdirected. Possibly if you tried farther down the street——"

"That will do; we have no time to waste," said my companion firmly. "You are Henry Peters, of Adelaide, late the Rev. Dr. Shlessinger, of Baden and South America. I am as sure of that as that my own name is Sherlock Holmes."

Peters, as I will now call him, started and stared hard at his formidable pursuer. "I guess your name does not frighten me, Mr. Holmes," said he coolly. "When a man's conscience is easy you can't rattle him. What is your business in my house?"

"I want to know what you have done with the Lady Frances Carfax, whom you brought away with you from Baden."

"I'd be very glad if you could tell me where that lady may be," Peters answered coolly. "I've a bill against her for nearly a hundred pounds, and nothing to show for it but a couple of trumpery pendants that the dealer would hardly look at. She attached herself to Mrs. Peters and me at Baden—it is a fact that I was using another name at the time—and she stuck on to us until we came to London. I paid her bill and her ticket. Once in London, she gave us the slip, and, as I say, left these out-of-date jewels to pay her bills. You find her, Mr. Holmes, and I'm your debtor."

"I *mean* to find her," said Sherlock Holmes. "I'm going through this house till I do find her."

"Where is your warrant?"

Holmes half drew a revolver from his pocket. "This will have to serve till a better one comes."

"Why, you are a common burglar."

"So you might describe me," said Holmes cheerfully. "My companion is also a dangerous ruffian. And together we are going through your house."

Our opponent opened the door.

"Fetch a policeman, Annie!" said he. There was a whisk of feminine skirts down the passage, and the hall door was opened and shut.

"Our time is limited, Watson," said Holmes. "If you try to stop us, Peters, you will most certainly get hurt. Where is that coffin which was brought into your house?"

"What do you want with the coffin? It is in use. There is a body in it."

"I must see that body."

"Never with my consent."

"Then without it." With a quick movement Holmes pushed the fellow to one side and passed into the hall. A door half opened stood immediately before us. We entered. It was the dining-room. On the table, under a half-lit chandelier, the coffin was lying. Holmes turned up the gas and raised the lid. Deep down in the recesses of the coffin lay an emaciated figure. The glare from the lights above beat down upon an aged and withered face. By no possible process of cruelty, starvation, or disease could this worn-out wreck be the still beautiful Lady Frances. Holmes's face showed his amazement, and also his relief.

"Thank God!" he muttered. "It's someone else."

"Ah, you've blundered badly for once, Mr. Sherlock Holmes," said Peters, who had followed us into the room.

"Who is this dead woman?"

"Well, if you really must know, she is an old nurse of my wife's, Rose Spender by name, whom we found in the Brixton Workhouse Infirmary. We brought her round here, called in Dr. Horsom, of 13 Firbank Villas—mind you take the address, Mr. Holmes—and had her carefully tended, as Christian folk should. On the third day she died—certificate says senile decay—but that's only the doctor's opinion, and of course you know better. We ordered her funeral to be carried out by Stimson and Co., of the Kennington Road, who will bury her at eight o'clock to-morrow morning. Can you pick any hole in that, Mr. Holmes? You've made a silly blunder, and you may as well own up to it. I'd give something for a photograph of your gaping, staring face when you pulled aside that lid expecting to see the Lady Frances Carfax and only found a poor old woman of ninety."

Holmes's expression was as impassive as ever under the jeers of his antagonist, but his clenched hands betrayed his acute annoyance.

"I am going through your house," said he.

"Are you, though!" cried Peters as a woman's voice and heavy steps sounded in the passage. "We'll soon see about that. This way, officers, if you please. These men have forced their way into my house, and I cannot get rid of them. Help me to put them out."

A sergeant and a constable stood in the doorway. Holmes drew his card from his case.

"This is my name and address. This is my friend, Dr. Watson."

"Bless you, sir, we know you very well," said the sergeant, "but you can't stay here without a warrant."

"Of course not. I quite understand that."

"Arrest him!" cried Peters.

"We know where to lay our hands on this gentleman if he is wanted," said the sergeant majestically, "but you'll have to go, Mr. Holmes."

"Yes, Watson, we shall have to go."

A minute later we were in the street once more. Holmes was as cool as ever, but I was hot with anger and humiliation. The sergeant had followed us.

"Sorry, Mr. Holmes, but that's the law."

"Exactly, Sergeant, you could not do otherwise."

"I expect there was good reason for your presence there. If there is anything I can do——"

"It's a missing lady, Sergeant, and we think she is in that house. I expect a warrant presently."

"Then I'll keep my eye on the parties, Mr. Holmes. If anything comes along, I will surely let you know."

It was only nine o'clock, and we were off full cry upon the trail at once. First we drove to Brixton Workhouse Infirmary, where we found that it was indeed the truth that a charitable couple had called some days before, that they had claimed an imbecile old woman as a former servant, and that they had obtained permission to take her away with them. No surprise was expressed at the news that she had since died.

The doctor was our next goal. He had been called in, had found the woman dying of pure senility, had actually seen her pass away, and had signed the certificate in due form. "I assure you that everything was perfectly normal and there was no room for foul play in the matter," said he. Nothing in the house had struck him as suspicious save that for people of their class it was remarkable that they should have no servant. So far and no farther went the doctor.

Finally we found our way to Scotland Yard. There had been difficulties of procedure in regard to the warrant. Some delay was inevitable. The magistrate's signature might not be obtained until next morning. If Holmes would call about nine he could go down with Lestrade and see it acted upon. So ended the day, save that near midnight our friend, the sergeant, called to say that he had seen flickering lights here and there in the windows of the great dark house, but that no one had left it and none had entered. We could but pray for patience and wait for the morrow.

Sherlock Holmes was too irritable for conversation and too restless for sleep. I left him smoking hard, with his heavy, dark brows knotted together, and his long, nervous fingers tapping upon the arms of his chair, as he turned over in his mind every possible solution of the mystery. Several times in the course of the night I heard him prowling about the house. Finally, just after I had been called in the morning, he rushed into my room. He was in his dressing-gown, but his pale, hollow-eyed face told me that his night had been a sleepless one.

"What time was the funeral? Eight, was it not?" he asked eagerly. "Well, it is 7:20 now. Good heavens, Watson, what has become of any brains that God has given me? Quick, man, quick! It's life or death—a hundred chances on death to one on life. I'll never forgive myself, never, if we are too late!"

Five minutes had not passed before we were flying in a hansom down Baker Street. But even so it was twenty-five to eight as we passed Big Ben, and eight struck as we tore down the Brixton Road. But others were late as well as we. Ten minutes after the hour the hearse was still standing at the door of the house, and even as our foaming horse came to a halt the coffin, supported by three men, appeared on the threshold. Holmes darted forward and barred their way.

"Take it back!" he cried, laying his hand on the breast of the foremost. "Take it back this instant!"

"What the devil do you mean? Once again I ask you, where is your warrant?" shouted the furious Peters, his big red face glaring over the farther end of the coffin.

"The warrant is on its way. This coffin shall remain in the house until it comes."

The authority in Holmes's voice had its effect upon the bearers. Peters had suddenly vanished into the house, and they obeyed these new orders. "Quick, Watson, quick! Here is a screw-driver!" he shouted as the coffin was replaced upon the table. "Here's one for you, my man! A sovereign if the lid comes off in a minute! Ask no questions—work away! That's good! Another! And another! Now pull all together! It's giving! It's giving! Ah, that does it at last."

With a united effort we tore off the coffin-lid. As we did so there came from the inside a stupefying and overpowering smell of chloroform. A body lay within, its head all wreathed in cotton-wool, which had been soaked in the narcotic. Holmes plucked it off and disclosed the statuesque face of a handsome and spiritual woman of middle age. In an instant he had passed his arm round the figure and raised her to a sitting position.

"Is she gone, Watson? Is there a spark left? Surely we are not too late!"

For half an hour it seemed that we were. What with actual suffocation, and what with the poisonous fumes of the chloroform, the Lady Frances seemed to have passed the last point of recall. And then, at last, with artificial respiration, with injected ether, with every device that science could suggest, some flutter of life, some quiver of the eyelids, some dimming of a mirror, spoke of the slowly returning life. A cab had driven up, and Holmes, parting the blind, looked out at it. "Here is Lestrade with his warrant," said he. "He will find that his birds have flown. And here," he added as a heavy step hurried along the passage, "is someone who has a better right to nurse this lady than we have. Good morning, Mr. Green; I think that the sooner we can move the Lady Frances the better. Meanwhile, the funeral may proceed, and the poor old woman who still lies in that coffin may go to her last resting-place alone."

"Should you care to add the case to your annals, my dear Watson," said Holmes that evening, "it can only be as an example of that temporary eclipse to which even the best-balanced mind may be exposed. Such slips are common to all mortals, and the greatest is he who can recognize and repair them. To this modified credit I may, perhaps, make some claim. My night was haunted by the thought that somewhere a clue, a strange sentence, a curious observation, had come under my notice and had been too easily dismissed. Then, suddenly, in the gray of the morning, the words came back to me. It was the remark of the undertaker's wife, as reported by Philip Green. She had said, 'It should be there before now. It took longer, being out of the ordinary.' It was the coffin of which she spoke. It had been out of the ordinary. That could only mean that it had been made to some special measurement. But why? Why? Then in an instant I remembered the deep sides, and the little wasted figure at the bottom. Why so large a coffin for so small a body? To leave room for another body. Both would be buried under the one certificate. It had all been so clear, if only my own sight had not been dimmed. At eight the Lady Frances would be buried. Our one chance was to stop the coffin before it left the house.

"It was a desperate chance that we might find her alive, but it *was* a chance, as the result showed. These people had never, to my knowledge, done a murder. They might shrink from actual violence at the last. They could bury her with no sign of how she met her end, and even if she were exhumed there was a chance for them. I hoped that such considerations might prevail with them. You can reconstruct the scene well enough. You saw the horrible den upstairs, where the poor lady had been kept so long. They rushed in and overpowered her with their chloroform, carried her down, poured more into the coffin to insure against her waking, and then screwed down the lid. A clever device, Watson. It is new to me in the annals of crime. If our ex-missionary friends escape the clutches of Lestrade, I shall expect to hear of some brilliant incidents in their future career."

THE ADVENTURE OF THE
DEVIL'S FOOT

In recording from time to time some of the curious experiences and interesting recollections which I associate with my long and intimate friendship with Mr. Sherlock Holmes, I have continually been faced by difficulties caused by his own aversion to publicity. To his sombre and cynical spirit all popular applause was always abhorrent, and nothing amused him more at the end of a successful case than to hand over the actual exposure to some orthodox official, and to listen with a mocking smile to the general chorus of misplaced congratulation. It was indeed this attitude upon the part of my friend and certainly not any lack of interesting material which has caused me of late years to lay very few of my records before the public. My participation in some of his adventures was always a privilege which entailed discretion and reticence upon me.

It was, then, with considerable surprise that I received a telegram from Holmes last Tuesday—he has never been known to write where a telegram would serve—in the following terms:

> Why not tell them of the Cornish horror—strangest case I have handled.

I have no idea what backward sweep of memory had brought the matter fresh to his mind, or what freak had caused him to desire that I should recount it; but I hasten, before another cancelling telegram may arrive, to hunt out the notes which give me the exact details of the case and to lay the narrative before my readers.

It was, then, in the spring of the year 1897 that Holmes's iron constitution showed some symptoms of giving way in the face of constant hard work of a most exacting kind, aggravated, perhaps, by occasional indiscretions of his own. In March of that year Dr. Moore Agar, of Harley Street, whose dramatic introduction to Holmes I may some day recount, gave positive injunctions that the famous private agent lay aside all his cases and surrender himself to complete rest if he wished to avert an absolute breakdown. The state of his health was not a matter in which he himself took the faintest interest, for his mental detachment was absolute, but he was induced at last, on the threat of being permanently disqualified from work, to give himself a complete change of scene and air. Thus it was that in the early spring of that year we found ourselves together in a small cottage near Poldhu Bay, at the further extremity of the Cornish peninsula.

It was a singular spot, and one peculiarly well suited to the grim humour of my patient. From the windows of our little whitewashed house, which stood high upon a grassy headland, we looked down upon the whole sinister semicircle of Mounts Bay, that old death trap of sailing vessels, with its fringe of black cliffs and surge-swept reefs on which innumerable seamen have met their end. With a northerly breeze it lies placid and sheltered, inviting the storm-tossed craft to tack into it for rest and protection.

Then come the sudden swirl round of the wind, the blustering gale from the south-west, the dragging anchor, the lee shore, and the last battle in the creaming breakers. The wise mariner stands far out from that evil place.

On the land side our surroundings were as sombre as on the sea. It was a country of rolling moors, lonely and dun-coloured, with an occasional church tower to mark the site of some old-world village. In every direction upon these moors there were traces of some vanished race which had passed utterly away, and left as its sole record strange monuments of stone, irregular mounds which contained the burned ashes of the dead, and curious earthworks which hinted at prehistoric strife. The glamour and mystery of the place, with its sinister atmosphere of forgotten nations, appealed to the imagination of my friend, and he spent much of his time in long walks and solitary meditations upon the moor. The ancient Cornish language had also arrested his attention, and he had, I remember, conceived the idea that it was akin to the Chaldean, and had been largely derived from the Phœnician traders in tin. He had received a consignment of books upon philology and was settling down to develop this thesis when suddenly, to my sorrow and to his unfeigned delight, we found ourselves, even in that land of dreams, plunged into a problem at our very doors which was more intense, more engrossing, and infinitely more mysterious than any of those which had driven us from London. Our simple life and peaceful, healthy routine were violently interrupted, and we were precipitated into the midst of a series of events which caused the utmost excitement not only in Cornwall but throughout the whole west of England. Many of my readers may retain some recollection of what was called at the time "The Cornish Horror," though a most imperfect account of the matter reached the London press. Now, after thirteen years, I will give the true details of this inconceivable affair to the public.

I have said that scattered towers marked the villages which dotted this part of Cornwall. The nearest of these was the hamlet of Tredannick Wollas, where the cottages of a couple of hundred inhabitants clustered round an ancient, moss-grown church. The vicar of the parish, Mr. Roundhay, was something of an archæologist, and as such Holmes had made his acquaintance. He was a middle-aged man, portly and affable, with a considerable fund of local lore. At his invitation we had taken tea at the vicarage and had come to know, also, Mr. Mortimer Tregennis, an independent gentleman, who increased the clergyman's scanty resources by taking rooms in his large, straggling house. The vicar, being a bachelor, was glad to come to such an arrangement, though he had little in common with his lodger, who was a thin, dark, spectacled man, with a stoop which gave the impression of actual, physical deformity. I remember that during our short visit we found the vicar garrulous, but his lodger strangely reticent, a sad-faced, introspective man, sitting with averted eyes, brooding apparently upon his own affairs.

These were the two men who entered abruptly into our little sitting-room on Tuesday, March the 16th, shortly after our breakfast hour, as we were smoking together, preparatory to our daily excursion upon the moors.

"Mr. Holmes," said the vicar in an agitated voice, "the most extraordinary and tragic affair has occurred during the night. It is the most unheard-of business. We can only regard it as a special Providence that you should chance to be here at the time, for in all England you are the one man we need."

I glared at the intrusive vicar with no very friendly eyes; but Holmes took his pipe from his lips and sat up in his chair like an old hound who hears the view-halloa.* He waved his hand to the sofa, and our palpitating visitor with his agitated companion sat side by side upon it. Mr. Mortimer Tregennis was more self-contained than the clergyman, but the twitching of his thin hands and the brightness of his dark eyes showed that they shared a common emotion.

"Shall I speak or you?" he asked of the vicar.

"Well, as you seem to have made the discovery, whatever it may be, and the vicar to have had it second-hand, perhaps you had better do the speaking," said Holmes.

I glanced at the hastily clad clergyman, with the formally dressed lodger seated beside him, and was amused at the surprise which Holmes's simple deduction had brought to their faces.

"Perhaps I had best say a few words first," said the vicar, "and then you can judge if you will listen to the details from Mr. Tregennis, or whether we should not hasten at once to the scene of this mysterious affair. I may explain, then, that our friend here spent last evening in the company of his two brothers, Owen and George, and of his sister Brenda, at their house of Tredannick Wartha, which is near the old stone cross upon the moor. He left them shortly after ten o'clock, playing cards round the dining-room table, in excellent health and spirits. This morning, being an early riser, he walked in that direction before breakfast and was overtaken by the carriage of Dr. Richards, who explained that he had just been sent for on a most urgent call to Tredannick Wartha. Mr. Mortimer Tregennis naturally went with him. When he arrived at Tredannick Wartha he found an extraordinary state of things. His two brothers and his sister were seated round the table exactly as he had left them, the cards still spread in front of them and the candles burned down to their sockets. The sister lay back stone-dead in her chair, while the two brothers sat on each side of her laughing, shouting, and singing, the senses stricken clean out of them. All three of them, the dead woman and the two demented men, retained upon their faces an expression of the utmost

---

*Call sounded during a fox hunt to let the riders know a fox has been sighted.

horror—a convulsion of terror which was dreadful to look upon. There was no sign of the presence of anyone in the house, except Mrs. Porter, the old cook and housekeeper, who declared that she had slept deeply and heard no sound during the night. Nothing had been stolen or disarranged, and there is absolutely no explanation of what the horror can be which has frightened a woman to death and two strong men out of their senses. There is the situation, Mr. Holmes, in a nutshell, and if you can help us to clear it up you will have done a great work."

I had hoped that in some way I could coax my companion back into the quiet which had been the object of our journey; but one glance at his intense face and contracted eyebrows told me how vain was now the expectation. He sat for some little time in silence, absorbed in the strange drama which had broken in upon our peace.

"I will look into this matter," he said at last. "On the face of it, it would appear to be a case of a very exceptional nature. Have you been there yourself, Mr. Roundhay?"

"No, Mr. Holmes. Mr. Tregennis brought back the account to the vicarage, and I at once hurried over with him to consult you."

"How far is it to the house where this singular tragedy occurred?"

"About a mile inland."

"Then we shall walk over together. But before we start I must ask you a few questions, Mr. Mortimer Tregennis."

The other had been silent all this time, but I had observed that his more controlled excitement was even greater than the obtrusive emotion of the clergyman. He sat with a pale, drawn face, his anxious gaze fixed upon Holmes, and his thin hands clasped convulsively together. His pale lips quivered as he listened to the dreadful experience which had befallen his family, and his dark eyes seemed to reflect something of the horror of the scene.

"Ask what you like, Mr. Holmes," said he eagerly. "It is a bad thing to speak of, but I will answer you the truth."

"Tell me about last night."

"Well, Mr. Holmes, I supped there, as the vicar has said, and my elder brother George proposed a game of whist afterwards. We sat down about nine o'clock. It was a quarter-past ten when I moved to go. I left them all round the table, as merry as could be."

"Who let you out?"

"Mrs. Porter had gone to bed, so I let myself out. I shut the hall door behind me. The window of the room in which they sat was closed, but the blind was not drawn down. There was no change in door or window this morning, nor any reason to think that any stranger had been to the house. Yet there they sat, driven clean mad with terror, and Brenda lying dead of fright, with her head hanging over the arm of the chair. I'll never get the sight of that room out of my mind so long as I live."

"The facts, as you state them, are certainly most remarkable," said Holmes. "I take it that you have no theory yourself which can in any way account for them?"

"It's devilish, Mr. Holmes, devilish!" cried Mortimer Tregennis. "It is not of this world. Something has come into that room which has dashed the light of reason from their minds. What human contrivance could do that?"

"I fear," said Holmes, "that if the matter is beyond humanity it is certainly beyond me. Yet we must exhaust all natural explanations before we fall back upon such a theory as this. As to yourself, Mr. Tregennis, I take it you were divided in some way from your family, since they lived together and you had rooms apart?"

"That is so, Mr. Holmes, though the matter is past and done with. We were a family of tin-miners at Redruth, but we sold out our venture to a company, and so retired with enough to keep us. I won't deny that there was some feeling about the division of the money and it stood between us for a time, but it was all forgiven and forgotten, and we were the best of friends together."

"Looking back at the evening which you spent together, does anything stand out in your memory as throwing any possible light upon the tragedy? Think carefully, Mr. Tregennis, for any clue which can help me."

"There is nothing at all, sir."

"Your people were in their usual spirits?"

"Never better."

"Were they nervous people? Did they ever show any apprehension of coming danger?"

"Nothing of the kind."

"You have nothing to add then, which could assist me?"

Mortimer Tregennis considered earnestly for a moment.

"There is one thing occurs to me," said he at last. "As we sat at the table my back was to the window, and my brother George, he being my partner at cards, was facing it. I saw him once look hard over my shoulder, so I turned round and looked also. The blind was up and the window shut, but I could just make out the bushes on the lawn, and it seemed to me for a moment that I saw something moving among them. I couldn't even say if it was man or animal, but I just thought there was something there. When I asked him what he was looking at, he told me that he had the same feeling. That is all that I can say."

"Did you not investigate?"

"No; the matter passed as unimportant."

"You left them, then, without any premonition of evil?"

"None at all."

"I am not clear how you came to hear the news so early this morning."

"I am an early riser and generally take a walk before breakfast. This morning I had hardly started when the doctor in his carriage overtook me. He told me that old Mrs. Porter had sent a boy down with an urgent message. I sprang in beside him and we drove on. When we got there we looked into that dreadful room. The candles and the fire must have burned out hours before, and they had been sitting there in the dark until dawn had broken. The doctor said Brenda must have been dead at least six hours. There were no signs of violence. She just lay across the arm of the chair with that look on her face. George and Owen were singing snatches of songs and gibbering like two great apes. Oh, it was awful to see! I couldn't stand it, and the doctor was as white as a sheet. Indeed, he fell into a chair in a sort of faint, and we nearly had him on our hands as well."

"Remarkable—most remarkable!" said Holmes, rising and taking his hat. "I think, perhaps, we had better go down to Tredannick Wartha without further delay. I confess that I have seldom known a case which at first sight presented a more singular problem."

Our proceedings of that first morning did little to advance the investigation. It was marked, however, at the outset by an incident which left the most sinister impression upon my mind. The approach to the spot at which the tragedy occurred is down a narrow, winding, country lane. While we made our way along it we heard the rattle of a carriage coming towards us and stood aside to let it pass. As it drove by us I caught a glimpse through the closed window of a horribly contorted, grinning face glaring out at us. Those staring eyes and gnashing teeth flashed past us like a dreadful vision.

"My brothers!" cried Mortimer Tregennis, white to his lips. "They are taking them to Helston."

We looked with horror after the black carriage, lumbering upon its way. Then we turned our steps towards this ill-omened house in which they had met their strange fate.

It was a large and bright dwelling, rather a villa than a cottage, with a considerable garden which was already, in that Cornish air, well filled with spring flowers. Towards this garden the window of the sitting-room fronted, and from it, according to Mortimer Tregennis, must have come that thing of evil which had by sheer horror in a single instant blasted their minds. Holmes walked slowly and thoughtfully among the flower-plots and along the path before we entered the porch. So absorbed was he in his thoughts, I remember, that he stumbled over the watering-pot, upset its contents, and deluged both our feet and the garden path. Inside the house we were met by the elderly Cornish housekeeper, Mrs. Porter, who, with the aid of a young girl, looked after the wants of the family. She readily answered all Holmes's questions. She had heard nothing in the night. Her employers had all been in excellent spirits lately, and she had never known them more cheerful and prosperous. She had fainted with horror upon entering the room in the morning and seeing that dreadful company round the table. She had, when she recovered, thrown open the window to let the morning air in, and had run down to the lane, whence she sent a farm-lad for the doctor. The lady was on her bed upstairs if we cared to see her. It took four strong men to get the brothers into the asylum carriage. She would not herself stay in the house another day and was starting that very afternoon to rejoin her family at St. Ives.

We ascended the stairs and viewed the body. Miss Brenda Tregennis had been a very beautiful girl, though now verging upon middle age. Her dark, clear-cut face was handsome, even in death, but there still lingered upon it something of that convulsion of horror which had been her last human emotion. From her bedroom we descended to the sitting-room, where this strange tragedy had actually occurred. The charred ashes of the overnight fire lay in the grate. On the table were the four guttered and burned-out candles, with the cards scattered over its surface. The chairs had been moved back against the walls, but all else was as it had been the night before. Holmes paced with light, swift steps about the room; he sat in the various chairs, drawing them up and reconstructing their positions. He tested how much of the garden was visible; he examined the floor, the ceiling, and the fireplace; but never once did I see that sudden brightening of his eyes and tightening of his lips which would have told me that he saw some gleam of light in this utter darkness.

"Why a fire?" he asked once. "Had they always a fire in this small room on a spring evening?"

Mortimer Tregennis explained that the night was cold and damp. For that reason, after his arrival, the fire was lit. "What are you going to do now, Mr. Holmes?" he asked.

My friend smiled and laid his hand upon my arm. "I think, Watson, that I shall resume that course of tobacco-poisoning which you have so often and so justly condemned," said he. "With your permission, gentlemen, we will now return to our cottage, for I am not aware that any new factor is likely to come to our notice here. I will turn the facts over in my mind, Mr. Tregennis, and should anything occur to me I will certainly communicate with you and the vicar. In the meantime I wish you both good-morning."

It was not until long after we were back in Poldhu Cottage that Holmes broke his complete and absorbed silence. He sat coiled in his armchair, his haggard and ascetic face hardly visible amid the blue swirl of his tobacco smoke, his black brows drawn down, his forehead contracted, his eyes vacant and far away. Finally he laid down his pipe and sprang to his feet.

"It won't do, Watson!" said he with a laugh. "Let us walk along the cliffs together and search for flint arrows. We are more likely to find them than clues to this problem. To let the brain work without sufficient material is like racing an engine. It racks itself to pieces. The sea air, sunshine, and patience, Watson—all else will come.

"Now, let us calmly define our position, Watson," he continued as we skirted the cliffs together. "Let us get a firm grip of the very little which we *do* know, so that when fresh facts arise we may be ready to fit them into their places. I take it, in the first place, that neither of us is prepared to admit diabolical intrusions into the affairs of men. Let us begin by ruling that entirely out of our minds. Very good. There remain three persons who have been grievously stricken by some conscious or unconscious human agency. That is firm ground. Now, when did this occur? Evidently, assuming his narrative to be true, it was immediately after Mr. Mortimer

Tregennis had left the room. That is a very important point. The presumption is that it was within a few minutes afterwards. The cards still lay upon the table. It was already past their usual hour for bed. Yet they had not changed their position or pushed back their chairs. I repeat, then, that the occurrence was immediately after his departure, and not later than eleven o'clock last night.

"Our next obvious step is to check, so far as we can, the movements of Mortimer Tregennis after he left the room. In this there is no difficulty, and they seem to be above suspicion. Knowing my methods as you do, you were, of course, conscious of the somewhat clumsy water-pot expedient by which I obtained a clearer impress of his foot than might otherwise have been possible. The wet, sandy path took it admirably. Last night was also wet, you will remember, and it was not difficult—having obtained a sample print—to pick out his track among others and to follow his movements. He appears to have walked away swiftly in the direction of the vicarage.

"If, then, Mortimer Tregennis disappeared from the scene, and yet some outside person affected the cardplayers, how can we reconstruct that person, and how was such an impression of horror conveyed? Mrs. Porter may be eliminated. She is evidently harmless. Is there any evidence that someone crept up to the garden window and in some manner produced so terrific an effect that he drove those who saw it out of their senses? The only suggestion in this direction comes from Mortimer Tregennis himself, who says that his brother spoke about some movement in the garden. That is certainly remarkable, as the night was rainy, cloudy, and dark. Anyone who had the design to alarm these people would be compelled to place his very face against the glass before he could be seen. There is a three-foot flower-border outside this window, but no indication of a footmark. It is difficult to imagine, then, how an outsider could have made so terrible an impression upon the company, nor have we found any possible motive for so strange and elaborate an attempt. You perceive our difficulties, Watson?"

"They are only too clear," I answered with conviction.

"And yet, with a little more material, we may prove that they are not insurmountable," said Holmes. "I fancy that among your extensive archives, Watson, you may find some which were nearly as obscure. Meanwhile, we shall put the case aside until more accurate data are available, and devote the rest of our morning to the pursuit of neolithic man."

I may have commented upon my friend's power of mental detachment, but never have I wondered at it more than upon that spring morning in Cornwall when for two hours he discoursed upon Celts, arrowheads, and shards, as lightly as if no sinister mystery were waiting for his solution. It was not until we had returned in the afternoon to our cottage that we found a visitor awaiting us, who soon brought our minds back to the matter in hand. Neither of us needed to be told who that visitor was. The huge body, the craggy and deeply seamed face with the fierce eyes and hawk-like nose, the grizzled hair which nearly brushed our cottage ceiling, the beard—golden at the fringes and white near the lips, save for the nicotine stain from his perpetual cigar—all these were as well known in London as in Africa, and could only be associated with the tremendous personality of Dr. Leon Sterndale, the great lion-hunter and explorer.

We had heard of his presence in the district and had once or twice caught sight of his tall figure upon the moorland paths. He made no advances to us, however, nor would we have dreamed of doing so to him, as it was well known that it was his love of seclusion which caused him to spend the greater part of the intervals between his journeys in a small bungalow buried in the lonely wood of Beauchamp Arriance. Here, amid his books and his maps, he lived an absolutely lonely life, attending to his own simple wants and paying little apparent heed to the affairs of his neighbours. It was a surprise to me, therefore, to hear him asking Holmes in an eager voice whether he had made any advance in his reconstruction of this mysterious episode. "The county police are utterly at fault," said he, "but perhaps your wider experience has suggested some conceivable explanation. My only claim to being taken into your confidence is that during my many residences here I have come to know this family of Tregennis very well—indeed, upon my Cornish mother's side I could call them cousins—and their strange fate has naturally been a great shock to me. I may tell you that I had got as far as Plymouth upon my way to Africa, but the news reached me this morning, and I came straight back again to help in the inquiry."

Holmes raised his eyebrows.

"Did you lose your boat through it?"

"I will take the next."

"Dear me! that is friendship indeed."

"I tell you they were relatives."

"Quite so—cousins of your mother. Was your baggage aboard the ship?"

"Some of it, but the main part at the hotel."

"I see. But surely this event could not have found its way into the Plymouth morning papers."

"No, sir; I had a telegram."

"Might I ask from whom?"

A shadow passed over the gaunt face of the explorer.

"You are very inquisitive, Mr. Holmes."

"It is my business."

With an effort Dr. Sterndale recovered his ruffled composure.

"I have no objection to telling you," he said. "It was Mr. Roundhay, the vicar, who sent me the telegram which recalled me."

"Thank you," said Holmes. "I may say in answer to your original question that I have not cleared my mind entirely on the subject of this case, but that I have every hope of reaching some conclusion. It would be premature to say more."

"Perhaps you would not mind telling me if your suspicions point in any particular direction?"

"No, I can hardly answer that."

"Then I have wasted my time and need not prolong my visit." The famous doctor strode out of our cottage in considerable ill-humour, and within five minutes Holmes had followed him. I saw him no more until the evening, when he returned with a slow step and haggard face which assured me that he had made no great progress with his investigation. He glanced at a telegram which awaited him and threw it into the grate.

"From the Plymouth hotel, Watson," he said. "I learned the name of it from the vicar, and I wired to make certain that Dr. Leon Sterndale's account was true. It appears that he did indeed spend last night there, and that he has actually allowed some of his baggage to go on to Africa, while he returned to be present at this investigation. What do you make of that, Watson?"

"He is deeply interested."

"Deeply interested—yes. There is a thread here which we have not yet grasped and which might lead us through the tangle. Cheer up, Watson, for I am very sure that our material has not yet all come to hand. When it does we may soon leave our difficulties behind us."

Little did I think how soon the words of Holmes would be realized, or how strange and sinister would be that new development which opened up an entirely fresh line of investigation. I was shaving at my window in the morning when I heard the rattle of hoofs and, looking up, saw a dog-cart coming at a gallop down the road. It pulled up at our door, and our friend, the vicar, sprang from it and rushed up our garden path. Holmes was already dressed, and we hastened down to meet him.

Our visitor was so excited that he could hardly articulate, but at last in gasps and bursts his tragic story came out of him.

"We are devil-ridden, Mr. Holmes! My poor parish is devil-ridden!" he cried. "Satan himself is loose in it! We are given over into his hands!" He danced about in his agitation, a ludicrous object if it were not for his ashy face and startled eyes. Finally he shot out his terrible news.

"Mr. Mortimer Tregennis died during the night, and with exactly the same symptoms as the rest of his family."

Holmes sprang to his feet, all energy in an instant.

"Can you fit us both into your dog-cart?"

"Yes, I can."

"Then, Watson, we will postpone our breakfast. Mr. Roundhay, we are entirely at your disposal. Hurry—hurry, before things get disarranged."

The lodger occupied two rooms at the vicarage, which were in an angle by themselves, the one above the other. Below was a large sitting-room; above, his bedroom. They looked out upon a croquet lawn which came up to the windows. We had arrived before the doctor or the police, so that everything was absolutely undisturbed. Let me describe exactly the scene as we saw it upon that misty March morning. It has left an impression which can never be effaced from my mind.

The atmosphere of the room was of a horrible and depressing stuffiness. The servant who had first entered had thrown up the window, or it would have been even more intolerable. This might partly be due to the fact that a lamp stood flaring and smoking on the centre table. Beside it sat the dead man, leaning back in his chair, his thin beard projecting, his spectacles pushed up on to his forehead, and his lean dark face turned towards the window and twisted into the same distortion of terror which had marked the features of his dead sister. His limbs were convulsed and his fingers contorted as though he had died in a very paroxysm of fear. He was fully clothed, though there were signs that his dressing had been done in a hurry. We had already learned that his bed had been slept in, and that the tragic end had come to him in the early morning.

One realized the red-hot energy which underlay Holmes's phlegmatic exterior when one saw the sudden change which came over him from the moment that he entered the fatal apartment. In an instant he was tense and alert, his eyes shining, his face set, his limbs quivering with eager activity. He was out on the lawn, in through the window, round the room, and up into the bedroom, for all the world like a dashing foxhound drawing a cover. In the bedroom he made a rapid cast around and ended by throwing open the window, which appeared to give him some fresh cause for excitement, for he leaned out of it with loud ejaculations of interest and delight. Then he rushed down the stair, out through the open window, threw himself upon his face on the lawn, sprang up and into the room once more, all with the energy of the hunter who is at the very heels of his quarry. The lamp, which was an ordinary standard, he examined with minute care, making certain measurements upon its bowl. He carefully scrutinized with his lens the talc shield which covered the top of the chimney and scraped off some ashes which adhered to its upper surface, putting some of them into an envelope, which he placed in his pocketbook. Finally, just as the doctor and the official police put in an appearance, he beckoned to the vicar and we all three went out upon the lawn.

"I am glad to say that my investigation has not been entirely barren," he remarked. "I cannot remain to discuss the matter with the police, but I should be exceedingly obliged, Mr. Roundhay, if you would give the inspector my compliments and direct his attention to the bedroom window and to the sitting-room lamp. Each is suggestive, and together they are almost conclusive. If the police would desire further information I shall be happy to see any of them at the cottage. And now, Watson, I think that, perhaps, we shall be better employed elsewhere."

It may be that the police resented the intrusion of an amateur, or that they imagined themselves to be upon some hopeful line of investigation; but it is certain that we heard nothing from them for the next two days. During this time Holmes spent some of his time smoking and dreaming in the cottage; but a greater portion in country walks which he undertook alone, returning after many hours without remark as to where he had been. One experiment served to show me the line of his investigation. He had bought a lamp which was the duplicate of the one which had burned in the room of Mortimer Tregennis on the morning of the tragedy. This he filled with the same oil as that used at the vicarage, and he carefully timed the period which it would take to be exhausted. Another experiment which he made was of a more unpleasant nature, and one which I am not likely ever to forget.

"You will remember, Watson," he remarked one afternoon, "that there is a single common point of resemblance in the varying reports which have reached us. This concerns the effect of the atmosphere of the room in each case upon those who had first entered it. You will recollect that Mortimer Tregennis, in describing the episode of his last visit to his brother's house, remarked that the doctor on entering the room fell into a chair? You had forgotten? Well, I can answer for it that it was so. Now, you will remember also that Mrs. Porter, the housekeeper, told us that she herself fainted upon entering the room and had afterwards opened the window. In the second case—that of Mortimer Tregennis himself—you cannot have forgotten the horrible stuffiness of the room when we arrived, though the servant had thrown open the window. That servant, I found upon inquiry, was so ill that she had gone to her bed. You will admit, Watson, that these facts are very suggestive. In each case there is evidence of a poisonous atmosphere. In each case, also, there is combustion going on in the room—in the one case a fire, in the other a lamp. The fire was needed, but the lamp was lit—as a comparison of the oil consumed will show—long after it was broad daylight. Why? Surely because there is some connection between three things—the burning, the stuffy atmosphere, and, finally, the madness or death of those unfortunate people. That is clear, is it not?"

"It would appear so."

"At least we may accept it as a working hypothesis. We will suppose, then, that something was burned in each case which produced an atmosphere causing strange toxic effects. Very good. In the first instance—that of the Tregennis family—this substance was placed in the fire. Now the window was shut, but the fire would naturally carry fumes to some extent up the chimney. Hence one would expect the effects of the poison to be less than in the second case, where there was less escape for the vapour. The result seems to indicate that it was so, since in the first case only the woman, who had presumably the more sensitive organism, was killed, the others exhibiting that temporary or permanent lunacy which is evidently the first effect of the drug. In the second case the result was complete. The facts, therefore, seem to bear out the theory of a poison which worked by combustion.

"With this train of reasoning in my head I naturally looked about in Mortimer Tregennis's room to find some remains of this substance. The obvious place to look was the talc shield or smoke-guard of the lamp. There, sure enough, I perceived a number of flaky ashes, and round the edges a fringe of brownish powder, which had not yet been consumed. Half of this I took, as you saw, and I placed it in an envelope."

"Why half, Holmes?"

"It is not for me, my dear Watson, to stand in the way of the official police force. I leave them all the evidence which I found. The poison still remained upon the talc had they the wit to find it. Now, Watson, we will light our lamp; we will, however, take the precaution to open our window to avoid the premature decease of two deserving members of society, and you will seat yourself near that open window in an armchair unless, like a sensible man, you determine to have nothing to do with the affair. Oh, you will see it out, will you? I thought I knew my Watson. This chair I will place opposite yours, so that we may be the same distance from the poison and face to face. The door we will leave ajar. Each is now in a position to watch the other and to bring the experiment to an end should the symptoms seem alarming. Is that all clear? Well, then, I take our powder—or what remains of it—from the envelope, and I lay it above the burning lamp. So! Now, Watson, let us sit down and await developments."

They were not long in coming. I had hardly settled in my chair before I was conscious of a thick, musky odour, subtle and nauseous. At the very first whiff of it my brain and my imagination were beyond all control. A thick, black cloud swirled before my eyes, and my mind told me that in this cloud, unseen as yet, but about to spring out upon my appalled senses, lurked all that was vaguely horrible, all that was monstrous and inconceivably wicked in the universe. Vague shapes swirled and swam amid the dark cloud-bank, each a menace and a warning of something coming, the advent of some unspeakable dweller upon the threshold, whose very shadow would blast my soul. A freezing horror took possession of me. I felt that my hair was rising, that my eyes were protruding, that my mouth was opened, and my tongue like leather. The turmoil within my brain was such that something must surely snap. I tried to scream and was vaguely aware of some hoarse croak which was my own voice, but distant and detached from myself. At the same moment, in some effort of escape, I broke through that cloud of despair and had a glimpse of Holmes's face, white, rigid, and drawn with horror—the very look which I had seen upon the features of the dead. It was that vision which gave me an instant of sanity and of strength. I dashed from my chair, threw my arms round Holmes, and together we lurched through the door, and an instant afterwards had thrown ourselves down upon the grass plot and were lying side by side, conscious only of the glorious sunshine which was bursting its way through the hellish cloud of terror which had girt us in. Slowly it rose from our souls like the mists from a landscape until peace and reason had returned, and we were sitting upon the grass, wiping our clammy foreheads, and looking with apprehension at each other to mark the last traces of that terrific experience which we had undergone.

"Upon my word, Watson!" said Holmes at last with an unsteady voice, "I owe you both my thanks and an apology. It was an unjustifiable experiment even for one's self, and doubly so for a friend. I am really very sorry."

"You know," I answered with some emotion, for I had never seen so much of Holmes's heart before, "that it is my greatest joy and privilege to help you."

He relapsed at once into the half-humorous, half-cynical vein which was his habitual attitude to those about him. "It would be superfluous to drive us mad, my dear Watson," said he. "A candid observer would certainly declare that we were so already before we embarked upon so wild an experiment. I confess that I never imagined that the effect could be so sudden and so severe." He dashed into the cottage, and, reappearing with the burning lamp held at full arm's length, he threw it among a bank of brambles. "We must give the room a little time to clear. I take it, Watson, that you have no longer a shadow of a doubt as to how these tragedies were produced?"

"None whatever."

"But the cause remains as obscure as before. Come into the arbour here and let us discuss it together. That villainous stuff seems still to linger round my throat. I think we must admit that all the evidence points to this man, Mortimer Tregennis, having been the criminal in the first tragedy, though he was the victim in the second one. We must remember, in the first place, that there is some story of a family quarrel, followed by a reconciliation. How bitter that quarrel may have been, or how hollow the reconciliation, we cannot tell. When I think of Mortimer Tregennis, with the foxy face and the small shrewd, beady eyes behind the spectacles, he is not a man whom I should judge to be of a particularly forgiving disposition. Well, in the next place, you will remember that this idea of someone moving in the garden, which took our attention for a moment from the real cause of the tragedy, emanated from him. He had a motive in misleading us. Finally, if he did not throw this substance into the fire at the moment of leaving the room, who did do so? The affair happened immediately after his departure. Had anyone else come in, the family would certainly have risen from the table. Besides, in peaceful Cornwall, visitors do not arrive after ten o'clock at night. We may take it, then, that all the evidence points to Mortimer Tregennis as the culprit."

"Then his own death was suicide!"

"Well, Watson, it is on the face of it a not impossible supposition. The man who had the guilt upon his soul of having brought such a fate upon his own family might well be driven by remorse to inflict it upon himself. There are, however, some cogent reasons against it. Fortunately, there is one man in England who knows all about it, and I have made arrangements by which we shall hear the facts this afternoon from his own lips. Ah! he is a little before his time. Perhaps you would kindly step this way, Dr. Leon Sterndale. We have been conducting a chemical experiment indoors which has left our little room hardly fit for the reception of so distinguished a visitor."

I had heard the click of the garden gate, and now the majestic figure of the great African explorer appeared upon the path. He turned in some surprise towards the rustic arbour in which we sat.

"You sent for me, Mr. Holmes. I had your note about an hour ago, and I have come, though I really do not know why I should obey your summons."

"Perhaps we can clear the point up before we separate," said Holmes.

"Meanwhile, I am much obliged to you for your courteous acquiescence. You will excuse this informal reception in the open air, but my friend Watson and I have nearly furnished an additional chapter to what the papers call the Cornish Horror, and we prefer a clear atmosphere for the present. Perhaps, since the matters which we have to discuss will affect you personally in a very intimate fashion, it is as well that we should talk where there can be no eavesdropping."

The explorer took his cigar from his lips and gazed sternly at my companion.

"I am at a loss to know, sir," he said, "what you can have to speak about which affects me personally in a very intimate fashion."

"The killing of Mortimer Tregennis," said Holmes.

For a moment I wished that I were armed. Sterndale's fierce face turned to a dusky red, his eyes glared, and the knotted, passionate veins started out in his forehead, while he sprang forward with clenched hands towards my companion. Then he stopped, and with a violent effort he resumed a cold, rigid calmness, which was, perhaps, more suggestive of danger than his hot-headed outburst.

"I have lived so long among savages and beyond the law," said he, "that I have got into the way of being a law to myself. You would do well, Mr. Holmes, not to forget it, for I have no desire to do you an injury."

"Nor have I any desire to do you an injury, Dr. Sterndale. Surely the clearest proof of it is that, knowing what I know, I have sent for you and not for the police."

Sterndale sat down with a gasp, overawed for, perhaps, the first time in his adventurous life. There was a calm assurance of power in Holmes's manner which could not be withstood. Our visitor stammered for a moment, his great hands opening and shutting in his agitation.

"What do you mean?" he asked at last. "If this is bluff upon your part, Mr. Holmes, you have chosen a bad man for your experiment. Let us have no more beating about the bush. What *do* you mean?"

"I will tell you," said Holmes, "and the reason why I tell you is that I hope frankness may beget frankness. What my next step may be will depend entirely upon the nature of your own defence."

"My defence?"

"Yes, sir."

"My defence against what?"

"Against the charge of killing Mortimer Tregennis."

Sterndale mopped his forehead with his handkerchief. "Upon my word, you are getting on," said he. "Do all your successes depend upon this prodigious power of bluff?"

"The bluff," said Holmes sternly, "is upon your side, Dr. Leon Sterndale, and not upon mine. As a proof I will tell you some of the facts upon which my conclusions are based. Of your return from Plymouth, allowing much of your property to go on to Africa, I will say nothing save that it first informed me that you were one of the factors which had to be taken into account in reconstructing this drama——"

"I came back——"

"I have heard your reasons and regard them as unconvincing and inadequate. We will pass that. You came down here to ask me whom I suspected. I refused to answer you. You then went to the vicarage, waited outside it for some time, and finally returned to your cottage."

"How do you know that?"

"I followed you."

"I saw no one."

"That is what you may expect to see when I follow you. You spent a restless night at your cottage, and you formed certain plans, which in the early morning you proceeded to put into execution. Leaving your door just as day was breaking, you filled your pocket with some reddish gravel that was lying heaped beside your gate."

Sterndale gave a violent start and looked at Holmes in amazement.

"You then walked swiftly for the mile which separated you from the vicarage. You were wearing, I may remark, the same pair of ribbed tennis shoes which are at the present moment upon your feet. At the vicarage you passed through the orchard and the side hedge, coming out under the window of the lodger Tregennis. It was now daylight, but the household was not yet stirring. You drew some of the gravel from your pocket, and you threw it up at the window above you."

Sterndale sprang to his feet.

"I believe that you are the devil himself!" he cried.

Holmes smiled at the compliment. "It took two, or possibly three, handfuls before the lodger came to the window. You beckoned him to come down. He dressed hurriedly and descended to his sitting-room. You entered by the window. There was an interview—a short one—during which you walked up and down the room. Then you passed out and closed the window, standing on the lawn outside smoking a cigar and watching what occurred. Finally, after the death of Tregennis, you withdrew as you had come. Now, Dr. Sterndale, how do you justify such conduct, and what were the motives for your actions? If you prevaricate or trifle with me, I give you my assurance that the matter will pass out of my hands forever."

Our visitor's face had turned ashen gray as he listened to the words of his accuser. Now he sat for some time in thought with his face sunk in his hands. Then with a sudden impulsive gesture he plucked a photograph from his breast-pocket and threw it on the rustic table before us.

"That is why I have done it," said he.

It showed the bust and face of a very beautiful woman. Holmes stooped over it.

"Brenda Tregennis," said he.

"Yes, Brenda Tregennis," repeated our visitor. "For years I have loved her. For years she has loved me. There is the secret of that Cornish seclusion which people have marvelled at. It has brought me close to the one thing on earth that was dear to me. I could not marry her, for I have a wife who has left me for years and yet whom, by the deplorable laws of England, I could not divorce. For years Brenda waited. For years I waited. And this is what we have waited for." A terrible sob shook his great frame, and he clutched his throat under his brindled beard. Then with an effort he mastered himself and spoke on:

"The vicar knew. He was in our confidence. He would tell you that she was an angel upon earth. That was why he telegraphed to me and I returned. What was my baggage or Africa to me when I learned that such a fate had come upon my darling? There you have the missing clue to my action, Mr. Holmes."

"Proceed," said my friend.

Dr. Sterndale drew from his pocket a paper packet and laid it upon the table. On the outside was written "*Radix pedis diaboli*" with a red poison label beneath it. He pushed it towards me. "I understand that you are a doctor, sir. Have you ever heard of this preparation?"

"Devil's-foot root! No, I have never heard of it."

"It is no reflection upon your professional knowledge," said he, "for I believe that, save for one sample in a laboratory at Buda, there is no other specimen in Europe. It has not yet found its way either into the pharmacopœia or into the literature of toxicology. The root is shaped like a foot, half human, half goatlike; hence the fanciful name given by a botanical missionary. It is used as an ordeal poison by the medicine-men in certain districts of West Africa and is kept as a secret among them. This particular specimen I obtained under very extraordinary circumstances in the Ubangi country." He opened the paper as he spoke and disclosed a heap of reddish-brown, snuff-like powder.

"Well, sir?" asked Holmes sternly.

"I am about to tell you, Mr. Holmes, all that actually occurred, for you already know so much that it is clearly to my interest that you should know all. I have already explained the relationship in which I stood to the Tregennis family. For the sake of the sister I was friendly with the brothers. There was a family quarrel about money which estranged this man Mortimer, but it was supposed to be made up, and I afterwards met him as I did the others. He was a sly, subtle, scheming man, and several things arose which gave me a suspicion of him, but I had no cause for any positive quarrel.

"One day, only a couple of weeks ago, he came down to my cottage and I showed him some of my African curiosities. Among other things I exhibited this powder, and I told him of its strange properties, how it stimulates those brain centres which control the emotion of fear, and how either madness or death is the fate of the unhappy native who is subjected to the ordeal by the priest of his tribe. I told him also how powerless European science would be to detect it. How he took it I cannot say, for I never left the room, but there is no doubt that it was then, while I was opening cabinets and stooping to boxes, that he managed to abstract some of the devil's-foot root. I well remember how he plied me with questions as to the amount and the time that was needed for its effect, but I little dreamed that he could have a personal reason for asking.

"I thought no more of the matter until the vicar's telegram reached me at Plymouth. This villain had thought that I would be at sea before the news could reach me, and that I should be lost for years in Africa. But I returned at once. Of course, I could not listen to the details without feeling assured that my poison had been used. I came round to see you on the chance that some other explanation had suggested itself to you. But there could be none. I was convinced that Mortimer Tregennis was the murderer; that for the sake of money, and with the idea, perhaps, that if the other members of his family were all insane he would be the sole guardian of their joint property, he had used the devil's-foot powder upon them, driven two of them out of their senses, and killed his sister Brenda, the one human being whom I have ever loved or who has ever loved me. There was his crime; what was to be his punishment?

"Should I appeal to the law? Where were my proofs? I knew that the facts were true, but could I help to make a jury of countrymen believe so fantastic a story? I might or I might not. But I could not afford to fail. My soul cried out for revenge. I have said to you once before, Mr. Holmes, that I have spent much of my life outside the law, and that I have come at last to be a law to myself. So it was now. I determined that the fate which he had given to others should be shared by himself. Either that or I would do justice upon him with my own hand. In all England there can be no man who sets less value upon his own life than I do at the present moment.

"Now I have told you all. You have yourself supplied the rest. I did, as you say, after a restless night, set off early from my cottage. I foresaw the difficulty of arousing him, so I gathered some gravel from the pile which you have mentioned, and I used it to throw up to his window. He came down and admitted me through the window of the sitting-room. I laid his offence before him. I told him that I had come both as judge and executioner. The wretch sank into a chair, paralyzed at the sight of my revolver. I lit the lamp, put the powder above it, and stood outside the window, ready to carry out my threat to shoot him should he try to leave the room. In five minutes he died. My God! how he died! But my heart was flint, for he endured nothing which my innocent darling had not felt before him. There is my story, Mr. Holmes. Perhaps, if you loved a woman, you would have done as much yourself. At any rate, I am in your hands. You can take what steps you like. As I have already said, there is no man living who can fear death less than I do."

Holmes sat for some little time in silence.

"What were your plans?" he asked at last.

"I had intended to bury myself in central Africa. My work there is but half finished."

"Go and do the other half," said Holmes. "I, at least, am not prepared to prevent you."

Dr. Sterndale raised his giant figure, bowed gravely, and walked from the arbour. Holmes lit his pipe and handed me his pouch.

"Some fumes which are not poisonous would be a welcome change," said he. "I think you must agree, Watson, that it is not a case in which we are called upon to interfere. Our investigation has been independent, and our action shall be so also. You would not denounce the man?"

"Certainly not," I answered.

"I have never loved, Watson, but if I did and if the woman I loved had met such an end, I might act even as our lawless lion-hunter has done. Who knows? Well, Watson, I will not offend your intelligence by explaining what is obvious. The gravel upon the window-sill was, of course, the starting-point of my research. It was unlike anything in the vicarage garden. Only when my attention had been drawn to Dr. Sterndale and his cottage did I find its counterpart. The lamp shining in broad daylight and the remains of powder upon the shield were successive links in a fairly obvious chain. And now, my dear Watson, I think we may dismiss the matter from our mind and go back with a clear conscience to the study of those Chaldean* roots which are surely to be traced in the Cornish branch of the great Celtic speech."

---

*Relating to the Chaldeans, an ancient Semitic people who once ruled Babylonia.

HIS LAST BOW

An Epilogue of Sherlock Holmes

It was nine o'clock at night upon the second of August—the most terrible August in the history of the world.* One might have thought already that God's curse hung heavy over a degenerate world, for there was an awesome hush and a feeling of vague expectancy in the sultry and stagnant air. The sun had long set, but one blood-red gash like an open wound lay low in the distant west. Above, the stars were shining brightly, and below, the lights of the shipping glimmered in the bay. The two famous Germans stood beside the stone parapet of the garden walk, with the long, low, heavily gabled house behind them, and they looked down upon the broad sweep of the beach at the foot of the great chalk cliff on which Von Bork, like some wandering eagle, had perched himself four years before. They stood with their heads close together, talking in low, confidential tones. From below the two glowing ends of their cigars might have been the smouldering eyes of some malignant fiend looking down in the darkness.

A remarkable man this Von Bork—a man who could hardly be matched among all the devoted agents of the Kaiser. It was his talents which had first recommended him for the English mission, the most important mission of all, but since he had taken it over those talents had become more and more manifest to the half-dozen people in the world who were really in touch with the truth. One of these was his present companion, Baron Von Herling, the chief secretary of the legation, whose huge 100-horse-power Benz car was blocking the country lane as it waited to waft its owner back to London.

"So far as I can judge the trend of events, you will probably be back in Berlin within the week," the secretary was saying. "When you get there, my dear Von Bork, I think you will be surprised at the welcome you will receive. I happen to know what is thought in the highest quarters of your work in this country." He was a huge man, the secretary, deep, broad, and tall, with a slow, heavy fashion of speech which had been his main asset in his political career.

Von Bork laughed.

"They are not very hard to deceive," he remarked. "A more docile, simple folk could not be imagined."

"I don't know about that," said the other thoughtfully. "They have strange limits and one must learn to observe them. It is that surface simplicity of theirs which makes a trap for the stranger. One's first impression

---

*Germany declared war on Russia to start World War I on that day.

is that they are entirely soft. Then one comes suddenly upon something very hard, and you know that you have reached the limit and must adapt yourself to the fact. They have, for example, their insular conventions which simply *must* be observed."

"Meaning, 'good form' and that sort of thing?" Von Bork sighed as one who had suffered much.

"Meaning British prejudice in all its queer manifestations. As an example I may quote one of my own worst blunders—I can afford to talk of my blunders, for you know my work well enough to be aware of my successes. It was on my first arrival. I was invited to a week-end gathering at the country house of a cabinet minister. The conversation was amazingly indiscreet."

Von Bork nodded. "I've been there," said he dryly.

"Exactly. Well, I naturally sent a résumé of the information to Berlin. Unfortunately our good chancellor is a little heavy-handed in these matters, and he transmitted a remark which showed that he was aware of what had been said. This, of course, took the trail straight up to me. You've no idea the harm that it did me. There was nothing soft about our British hosts on that occasion, I can assure you. I was two years living it down. Now you, with this sporting pose of yours——"

"No, no, don't call it a pose. A pose is an artificial thing. This is quite natural. I am a born sportsman. I enjoy it."

"Well, that makes it the more effective. You yacht against them, you hunt with them, you play polo, you match them in every game, your four-in-hand* takes the prize at Olympia. I have even heard that you go the length of boxing with the young officers. What is the result? Nobody takes you seriously. You are a 'good old sport,' 'quite a decent fellow for a German,' a hard-drinking, night-club, knock-about-town, devil-may-care young fellow. And all the time this quiet country house of yours is the centre of half the mischief in England, and the sporting squire the most astute secret-service man in Europe. Genius, my dear Von Bork—genius!"

"You flatter me, Baron. But certainly I may claim that my four years in this country have not been unproductive. I've never shown you my little store. Would you mind stepping in for a moment?"

The door of the study opened straight on to the terrace. Von Bork pushed it back, and, leading the way, he clicked the switch of the electric light. He then closed the door behind the bulky form which followed him and carefully adjusted the heavy curtain over the latticed window. Only when all these precautions had been taken and tested did he turn his sunburned aquiline face to his guest.

"Some of my papers have gone," said he. "When my wife and the household left yesterday for Flushing they took the less important with them. I must, of course, claim the protection of the embassy for the others."

"Your name has already been filed as one of the personal suite. There

---

*Four-horse team controlled by a single driver.

will be no difficulties for you or your baggage. Of course, it is just possible that we may not have to go. England may leave France to her fate. We are sure that there is no binding treaty between them."

"And Belgium?"

"Yes, and Belgium, too."

Von Bork shook his head. "I don't see how that could be. There is a definite treaty there. She could never recover from such a humiliation."

"She would at least have peace for the moment."

"But her honour?"

"Tut, my dear sir, we live in a utilitarian age. Honour is a mediæval conception. Besides England is not ready. It is an inconceivable thing, but even our special war tax of fifty million, which one would think made our purpose as clear as if we had advertised it on the front page of the *Times*, has not roused these people from their slumbers. Here and there one hears a question. It is my business to find an answer. Here and there also there is an irritation. It is my business to soothe it. But I can assure you that so far as the essentials go—the storage of munitions, the preparation for submarine attack, the arrangements for making high explosives—nothing is prepared. How, then, can England come in, especially when we have stirred her up such a devil's brew of Irish civil war, window-breaking Furies, and God knows what to keep her thoughts at home."

"She must think of her future."

"Ah, that is another matter. I fancy that in the future we have our own very definite plans about England, and that your information will be very vital to us. It is to-day or to-morrow with Mr. John Bull. If he prefers to-day we are perfectly ready. If it is to-morrow we shall be more ready still. I should think they would be wiser to fight with allies than without them, but that is their own affair. This week is their week of destiny. But you were speaking of your papers." He sat in the armchair with the light shining upon his broad bald head, while he puffed sedately at his cigar.

The large oak-panelled, book-lined room had a curtain hung in the further corner. When this was drawn it disclosed a large, brass-bound safe. Von Bork detached a small key from his watch chain, and after some considerable manipulation of the lock he swung open the heavy door.

"Look!" said he, standing clear, with a wave of his hand.

The light shone vividly into the opened safe, and the secretary of the embassy gazed with an absorbed interest at the rows of stuffed pigeon-holes with which it was furnished. Each pigeon-hole had its label, and his eyes as he glanced along them read a long series of such titles as "Fords," "Harbour-defences," "Aeroplanes," "Ireland," "Egypt," "Portsmouth forts," "The Channel," "Rosythe," and a score of others. Each compartment was bristling with papers and plans.

"Colossal!" said the secretary. Putting down his cigar he softly clapped his fat hands.

"And all in four years, Baron. Not such a bad show for the hard-drinking, hard-riding country squire. But the gem of my collection is coming and there is the setting all ready for it." He pointed to a space over which "Naval Signals" was printed.

"But you have a good dossier there already."

"Out of date and waste paper. The Admiralty in some way got the alarm and every code has been changed. It was a blow, Baron—the worst setback in my whole campaign. But thanks to my check-book and the good Altamont all will be well to-night."

The Baron looked at his watch and gave a guttural exclamation of disappointment.

"Well, I really can wait no longer. You can imagine that things are moving at present in Canton Terrace and that we have all to be at our posts. I had hoped to be able to bring news of your great coup. Did Altamont name no hour?"

Von Bork pushed over a telegram.

Will come without fail to-night and bring new sparking plugs.

ALTAMONT.

"Sparking plugs, eh?"

"You see he poses as a motor expert and I keep a full garage. In our code everything likely to come up is named after some spare part. If he talks of a radiator it is a battleship, of an oil pump a cruiser, and so on. Sparking plugs are naval signals."

"From Portsmouth at midday," said the secretary, examining the superscription. "By the way, what do you give him?"

"Five hundred pounds for this particular job. Of course he has a salary as well."

"The greedy rogue. They are useful, these traitors, but I grudge them their blood money."

"I grudge Altamont nothing. He is a wonderful worker. If I pay him well, at least he delivers the goods, to use his own phrase. Besides he is not a traitor. I assure you that our most pan-Germanic Junker is a sucking dove in his feelings towards England as compared with a real bitter Irish-American."

"Oh, an Irish-American?"

"If you heard him talk you would not doubt it. Sometimes I assure you I can hardly understand him. He seems to have declared war on the King's English as well as on the English king. Must you really go? He may be here any moment."

"No. I'm sorry, but I have already overstayed my time. We shall expect you early to-morrow, and when you get that signal book through the little door on the Duke of York's steps[17] you can put a triumphant finis to your record in England. What! Tokay!" He indicated a heavily sealed dust-covered bottle which stood with two high glasses upon a salver.

"May I offer you a glass before your journey?"

"No, thanks. But it looks like revelry."

"Altamont has a nice taste in wines, and he took a fancy to my Tokay.

He is a touchy fellow and needs humouring in small things. I have to study him, I assure you." They had strolled out on to the terrace again, and along it to the further end where at a touch from the Baron's chauffeur the great car shivered and chuckled. "Those are the lights of Harwich, I suppose," said the secretary, pulling on his dust coat. "How still and peaceful it all seems. There may be other lights within the week, and the English coast a less tranquil place! The heavens, too, may not be quite so peaceful if all that the good Zeppelin promises us comes true. By the way, who is that?"

Only one window showed a light behind them; in it there stood a lamp, and beside it, seated at a table, was a dear old ruddy-faced woman in a country cap. She was bending over her knitting and stopping occasionally to stroke a large black cat upon a stool beside her.

"That is Martha, the only servant I have left."

The secretary chuckled.

"She might almost personify Britannia," said he, "with her complete self-absorption and general air of comfortable somnolence. Well, *au revoir*, Von Bork!" With a final wave of his hand he sprang into the car, and a moment later the two golden cones from the headlights shot forward through the darkness. The secretary lay back in the cushions of the luxurious limousine, with his thoughts so full of the impending European tragedy that he hardly observed that as his car swung round the village street it nearly passed over a little Ford coming in the opposite direction.

Von Bork walked slowly back to the study when the last gleams of the motor lamps had faded into the distance. As he passed he observed that his old housekeeper had put out her lamp and retired. It was a new experience to him, the silence and dankness of his widespread house, for his family and household had been a large one. It was a relief to him, however, to think that they were all in safety and that, but for that one old woman who had lingered in the kitchen, he had the whole place to himself. There was a good deal of tidying up to do inside his study and he set himself to do it until his keen, handsome face was flushed with the heat of the burning papers. A leather valise stood beside his table, and into this he began to pack very neatly and systematically the precious contents of his safe. He had hardly got started with the work, however, when his quick ears caught the sound of a distant car. Instantly he gave an exclamation of satisfaction, strapped up the valise, shut the safe, locked it, and hurried out on to the terrace. He was just in time to see the lights of a small car come to a halt at the gate. A passenger sprang out of it and advanced swiftly towards him, while the chauffeur, a heavily built, elderly man with a gray moustache, settled down like one who resigns himself to a long vigil.

"Well?" asked Von Bork eagerly, running forward to meet his visitor.

For answer the man waved a small brown-paper parcel triumphantly above his head.

"You can give me the glad hand to-night, mister," he cried. "I'm bringing home the bacon at last."

"The signals?"

"Same as I said in my cable. Every last one of them, semaphore, lamp code, Marconi—a copy, mind you, not the original. That was too danger-ous. But it's the real goods, and you can lay to that." He slapped the Ger-man upon the shoulder with a rough familiarity from which the other winced.

"Come in," he said. "I'm all alone in the house. I was only waiting for this. Of course a copy is better than the original. If an original were miss-ing they would change the whole thing. You think it's all safe about the copy?"

The Irish-American had entered the study and stretched his long limbs from the armchair. He was a tall, gaunt man of sixty, with clear-cut features and a small goatee beard which gave him a general resemblance to the car-icatures of Uncle Sam. A half-smoked, sodden cigar hung from the corner of his mouth, and as he sat down he struck a match and relit it. "Making ready for a move?" he remarked as he looked round him. "Say, mister," he added, as his eyes fell upon the safe from which the curtain was now re-moved, "you don't tell me you keep your papers in that?"

"Why not?"

"Gosh, in a wide-open contraption like that! And they reckon you to be some spy. Why, a Yankee crook would be into that with a can-opener. If I'd known that any letter of mine was goin' to lie loose in a thing like that I'd have been a mug to write to you at all."

"It would puzzle any crook to force that safe," Von Bork answered. "You won't cut that metal with any tool."

"But the lock?"

"No, it's a double combination lock. You know what that is?"

"Search me," said the American.

"Well, you need a word as well as a set of figures before you can get the lock to work." He rose and showed a double-radiating disc round the key-hole. "This outer one is for the letters, the inner one for the figures."

"Well, well, that's fine."

"So it's not quite as simple as you thought. It was four years ago that I had it made, and what do you think I chose for the word and figures?"

"It's beyond me."

"Well, I chose August for the word, and 1914 for the figures, and here we are."

The American's face showed his surprise and admiration.

"My, but that was smart! You had it down to a fine thing."

"Yes, a few of us even then could have guessed the date. Here it is, and I'm shutting down to-morrow morning."

"Well, I guess you'll have to fix me up also. I'm not staying in this gol-darned country all on my lonesome. In a week or less, from what I see, John Bull will be on his hind legs and fair ramping. I'd rather watch him from over the water."

"But you're an American citizen?"

"Well, so was Jack James an American citizen, but he's doing time in Portland all the same. It cuts no ice with a British copper to tell him you're an American citizen. 'It's British law and order over here,' says he. By the way, mister, talking of Jack James, it seems to me you don't do much to cover your men."

"What do you mean?" Von Bork asked sharply.

"Well, you are their employer, ain't you? It's up to you to see that they don't fall down. But they do fall down, and when did you ever pick them up? There's James——"

"It was James's own fault. You know that yourself. He was too self-willed for the job."

"James was a bonehead—I give you that. Then there was Hollis."

"The man was mad."

"Well, he went a bit woozy towards the end. It's enough to make a man bughouse when he has to play a part from morning to night with a hundred guys all ready to set the coppers wise to him. But now there is Steiner——"

Von Bork started violently, and his ruddy face turned a shade paler.

"What about Steiner?"

"Well, they've got him, that's all. They raided his store last night, and he and his papers are all in Portsmouth jail. You'll go off and he, poor devil, will have to stand the racket, and lucky if he gets off with his life. That's why I want to get over the water as soon as you do."

Von Bork was a strong, self-contained man, but it was easy to see that the news had shaken him.

"How could they have got on to Steiner?" he muttered. "That's the worst blow yet."

"Well, you nearly had a worse one, for I believe they are not far off me."

"You don't mean that!"

"Sure thing. My landlady down Fratton way had some inquiries, and when I heard of it I guessed it was time for me to hustle. But what I want to know, mister, is how the coppers know these things? Steiner is the fifth man you've lost since I signed on with you, and I know the name of the sixth if I don't get a move on. How do you explain it, and ain't you ashamed to see your men go down like this?"

Von Bork flushed crimson.

"How dare you speak in such a way!"

"If I didn't dare things, mister, I wouldn't be in your service. But I'll tell you straight what is in my mind. I've heard that with you German politicians when an agent has done his work you are not sorry to see him put away."

Von Bork sprang to his feet.

"Do you dare to suggest that I have given away my own agents!"

"I don't stand for that, mister, but there's a stool pigeon or a cross somewhere, and it's up to you to find out where it is. Anyhow I am taking no more chances. It's me for little Holland, and the sooner the better."

Von Bork had mastered his anger.

"We have been allies too long to quarrel now at the very hour of victory," he said. "You've done splendid work and taken risks, and I can't forget it. By all means go to Holland, and you can get a boat from Rotterdam to New York. No other line will be safe a week from now. I'll take that book and pack it with the rest."

The American held the small parcel in his hand, but made no motion to give it up.

"What about the dough?" he asked.

"The what?"

"The boodle. The reward. The £500. The gunner turned damned nasty at the last, and I had to square him with an extra hundred dollars or it would have been nitsky for you and me. 'Nothin' doin'!' says he, and he meant it, too, but the last hundred did it. It's cost me two hundred pound from first to last, so it isn't likely I'd give it up without gettin' my wad."

Von Bork smiled with some bitterness. "You don't seem to have a very high opinion of my honour," said he, "you want the money before you give up the book."

"Well, mister, it is a business proposition."

"All right. Have your way." He sat down at the table and scribbled a check, which he tore from the book, but he refrained from handing it to his companion. "After all, since we are to be on such terms, Mr. Altamont," said he, "I don't see why I should trust you any more than you trust me. Do you understand?" he added, looking back over his shoulder at the American. "There's the check upon the table. I claim the right to examine that parcel before you pick the money up."

The American passed it over without a word. Von Bork undid a winding of string and two wrappers of paper. Then he sat gazing for a moment in silent amazement at a small blue book which lay before him. Across the cover was printed in golden letters *Practical Handbook of Bee Culture*. Only for one instant did the master spy glare at this strangely irrelevant inscription. The next he was gripped at the back of his neck by a grasp of iron, and a chloroformed sponge was held in front of his writhing face.

"Another glass, Watson!" said Mr. Sherlock Holmes as he extended the bottle of Imperial Tokay.*

The thickset chauffeur, who had seated himself by the table, pushed forward his glass with some eagerness.

"It is a good wine, Holmes."

"A remarkable wine, Watson. Our friend upon the sofa has assured me that it is from Franz Josef's† special cellar at the Schoenbrunn Palace. Might I trouble you to open the window, for chloroform vapour does not help the palate."

The safe was ajar, and Holmes standing in front of it was removing dossier after dossier, swiftly examining each, and then packing it neatly in

---

*Usually sweet, white wine from the Tokay district of Hungary.

†Franz Josef (1830–1916) was emperor of Austria and king of Hungary.

Von Bork's valise. The German lay upon the sofa sleeping stertorously
with a strap round his upper arms and another round his legs.

"We need not hurry ourselves, Watson. We are safe from interruption.
Would you mind touching the bell? There is no one in the house except
old Martha, who has played her part to admiration. I got her the situation
here when first I took the matter up. Ah, Martha, you will be glad to hear
that all is well."

The pleasant old lady had appeared in the doorway. She curtseyed with
a smile to Mr. Holmes, but glanced with some apprehension at the figure
upon the sofa.

"It is all right, Martha. He has not been hurt at all."

"I am glad of that, Mr. Holmes. According to his lights he has been a
kind master. He wanted me to go with his wife to Germany yesterday, but
that would hardly have suited your plans, would it, sir?"

"No, indeed, Martha. So long as you were here I was easy in my mind.
We waited some time for your signal to-night."

"It was the secretary, sir."

"I know. His car passed ours."

"I thought he would never go. I knew that it would not suit your plans,
sir, to find him here."

"No, indeed. Well, it only meant that we waited half an hour or so until
I saw your lamp go out and knew that the coast was clear. You can report
to me to-morrow in London, Martha, at Claridge's Hotel."

"Very good, sir."

"I suppose you have everything ready to leave."

"Yes, sir. He posted seven letters to-day. I have the addresses as usual."

"Very good, Martha. I will look into them to-morrow. Good-night.
These papers," he continued as the old lady vanished, "are not of very
great importance, for, of course, the information which they represent has
been sent off long ago to the German government. These are the originals
which could not safely be got out of the country."

"Then they are of no use."

"I should not go so far as to say that, Watson. They will at least show
our people what is known and what is not. I may say that a good many of
these papers have come through me, and I need not add are thoroughly
untrustworthy. It would brighten my declining years to see a German
cruiser navigating the Solent* according to the mine-field plans which I
have furnished. But you, Watson"—he stopped his work and took his old
friend by the shoulders—"I've hardly seen you in the light yet. How have
the years used you? You look the same blithe boy as ever."

"I feel twenty years younger, Holmes. I have seldom felt so happy as
when I got your wire asking me to meet you at Harwich with the car. But
you, Holmes—you have changed very little—save for that horrible
goatee."

---

*Strait 15 miles long between Hampshire and the Isle of Wight.

"These are the sacrifices one makes for one's country, Watson," said Holmes, pulling at his little tuft. "To-morrow it will be but a dreadful memory. With my hair cut and a few other superficial changes I shall no doubt reappear at Claridge's to-morrow as I was before this American stunt—I beg your pardon, Watson, my well of English seems to be permanently defiled—before this American job came my way."

"But you have retired, Holmes. We heard of you as living the life of a hermit among your bees and your books in a small farm upon the South Downs."

"Exactly, Watson. Here is the fruit of my leisured ease, the *magnum opus* of my latter years!" He picked up the volume from the table and read out the whole title, *Practical Handbook of Bee Culture, with Some Observations upon the Segregation of the Queen.* "Alone I did it. Behold the fruit of pensive nights and laborious days when I watched the little working gangs as once I watched the criminal world of London."

"But how did you get to work again?"

"Ah, I have often marvelled at it myself. The Foreign Minister alone I could have withstood, but when the Premier also deigned to visit my humble roof——! The fact is, Watson, that this gentleman upon the sofa was a bit too good for our people. He was in a class by himself. Things were going wrong, and no one could understand why they were going wrong. Agents were suspected or even caught, but there was evidence of some strong and secret central force. It was absolutely necessary to expose it. Strong pressure was brought upon me to look into the matter. It has cost me two years, Watson, but they have not been devoid of excitement. When I say that I started my pilgrimage at Chicago, graduated in an Irish secret society at Buffalo, gave serious trouble to the constabulary at Skibbareen, and so eventually caught the eye of a subordinate agent of Von Bork, who recommended me as a likely man, you will realize that the matter was complex. Since then I have been honoured by his confidence, which has not prevented most of his plans going subtly wrong and five of his best agents being in prison. I watched them, Watson, and I picked them as they ripened. Well, sir, I hope that you are none the worse!"

The last remark was addressed to Von Bork himself, who after much gasping and blinking had lain quietly listening to Holmes's statement. He broke out now into a furious stream of German invective, his face convulsed with passion. Holmes continued his swift investigation of documents while his prisoner cursed and swore.

"Though unmusical, German is the most expressive of all languages," he observed when Von Bork had stopped from pure exhaustion. "Hullo! Hullo!" he added as he looked hard at the corner of a tracing before putting it in the box. "This should put another bird in the cage. I had no idea that the paymaster was such a rascal, though I have long had an eye upon him. Mister Von Bork, you have a great deal to answer for."

The prisoner had raised himself with some difficulty upon the sofa and was staring with a strange mixture of amazement and hatred at his captor.

"I shall get level with you, Altamont," he said, speaking with slow deliberation. "If it takes me all my life I shall get level with you!"

"The old sweet song," said Holmes. "How often have I heard it in days gone by. It was a favourite ditty of the late lamented Professor Moriarty. Colonel Sebastian Moran has also been known to warble it. And yet I live and keep bees upon the South Downs."

"Curse you, you double traitor!" cried the German, straining against his bonds and glaring murder from his furious eyes.

"No, no, it is not so bad as that," said Holmes, smiling. "As my speech surely shows you, Mr. Altamont of Chicago had no existence in fact. I used him and he is gone."

"Then who are you?"

"It is really immaterial who I am, but since the matter seems to interest you, Mr. Von Bork, I may say that this is not my first acquaintance with the members of your family. I have done a good deal of business in Germany in the past and my name is probably familiar to you."

"I would wish to know it," said the Prussian grimly.

"It was I who brought about the separation between Irene Adler and the late King of Bohemia when your cousin Heinrich was the Imperial Envoy. It was I also who saved from murder, by the Nihilist Klopman, Count Von und Zu Grafenstein, who was your mother's elder brother. It was I——"

Von Bork sat up in amazement.

"There is only one man," he cried.

"Exactly," said Holmes.

Von Bork groaned and sank back on the sofa. "And most of that information came through you," he cried. "What is it worth? What have I done? It is my ruin forever!"

"It is certainly a little untrustworthy," said Holmes. "It will require some checking and you have little time to check it. Your admiral may find the new guns rather larger than he expects, and the cruisers perhaps a trifle faster."

Von Bork clutched at his own throat in despair.

"There are a good many other points of detail which will, no doubt, come to light in good time. But you have one quality which is very rare in a German, Mr. Von Bork: you are a sportsman and you will bear me no ill-will when you realize that you, who have outwitted so many other people, have at last been outwitted yourself. After all, you have done your best for your country, and I have done my best for mine, and what could be more natural? Besides," he added, not unkindly, as he laid his hand upon the shoulder of the prostrate man, "it is better than to fall before some more ignoble foe. These papers are now ready, Watson. If you will help me with our prisoner, I think that we may get started for London at once."

It was no easy task to move Von Bork, for he was a strong and a desperate man. Finally, holding either arm, the two friends walked him very slowly down the garden walk which he had trod with such proud confidence when he received the congratulations of the famous diplomatist only a few hours before. After a short, final struggle he was hoisted, still bound hand and foot, into the spare seat of the little car. His precious valise was wedged in beside him.

"I trust that you are as comfortable as circumstances permit," said Holmes when the final arrangements were made. "Should I be guilty of a liberty if I lit a cigar and placed it between your lips?"

But all amenities were wasted upon the angry German.

"I suppose you realize, Mr. Sherlock Holmes," said he, "that if your government bears you out in this treatment it becomes an act of war."

"What about your government and all this treatment?" said Holmes, tapping the valise.

"You are a private individual. You have no warrant for my arrest. The whole proceeding is absolutely illegal and outrageous."

"Absolutely," said Holmes.

"Kidnapping a German subject."

"And stealing his private papers."

"Well, you realize your position, you and your accomplice here. If I were to shout for help as we pass through the village——"

"My dear sir, if you did anything so foolish you would probably enlarge the two limited titles of our village inns by giving us 'The Dangling Prussian' as a signpost. The Englishman is a patient creature, but at present his temper is a little inflamed, and it would be as well not to try him too far. No, Mr. Von Bork, you will go with us in a quiet, sensible fashion to Scotland Yard, whence you can send for your friend, Baron Von Herling, and see if even now you may not fill that place which he has reserved for you in the ambassadorial suite. As to you, Watson, you are joining us with your old service, as I understand, so London won't be out of your way. Stand with me here upon the terrace, for it may be the last quiet talk that we shall ever have."

The two friends chatted in intimate converse for a few minutes, recalling once again the days of the past, while their prisoner vainly wriggled to undo the bonds that held him. As they turned to the car Holmes pointed back to the moonlit sea and shook a thoughtful head.

"There's an east wind coming, Watson."

"I think not, Holmes. It is very warm."

"Good old Watson! You are the one fixed point in a changing age. There's an east wind coming all the same, such a wind as never blew on England yet. It will be cold and bitter, Watson, and a good many of us may wither before its blast. But it's God's own wind none the less, and a cleaner, better, stronger land will lie in the sunshine when the storm has cleared. Start her up, Watson, for it's time that we were on our way. I have a check for five hundred pounds which should be cashed early, for the drawer is quite capable of stopping it if he can."

THE CASE BOOK OF
SHERLOCK HOLMES

PREFACE

The Case Book of Sherlock Holmes

I fear that Mr. Sherlock Holmes may become like one of those popular tenors who, having outlived their time, are still tempted to make repeated farewell bows to their indulgent audiences. This must cease and he must go the way of all flesh, material or imaginary. One likes to think that there is some fantastic limbo for the children of imagination, some strange, impossible place where the beaux of Fielding may still make love to the belles of Richardson, where Scott's heroes still may strut, Dickens's delightful Cockneys still raise a laugh, and Thackeray's worldlings continue to carry on their reprehensible careers. Perhaps in some humble corner of such a Valhalla, Sherlock and his Watson may for a time find a place, while some more astute sleuth with some even less astute comrade may fill the stage which they have vacated.

His career has been a long one—though it is possible to exaggerate it; decrepit gentlemen who approach me and declare that his adventures formed the reading of their boyhood do not meet the response from me which they seem to expect. One is not anxious to have one's personal dates handled so unkindly. As a matter of cold fact, Holmes made his début in A Study in Scarlet *and in* The Sign of Four, *two small booklets which appeared between 1887 and 1889. It was in 1891 that "A Scandal in Bohemia," the first of the long series of short stories, appeared in* The Strand Magazine. *The public seemed appreciative and desirous of more, so that from that date, thirty-nine years ago, they have been produced in a broken series which now contains no fewer than fifty-six stories, republished in* The Adventures, The Memoirs, The Return, *and* His Last Bow, *and there remain these twelve published during the last few years which are here produced under the title of* The Case Book of Sherlock Holmes. *He began his adventures in the very heart of the later Victorian era, carried it through the all-too-short reign of Edward, and has managed to hold his own little niche even in these feverish days. Thus it would be true to say that those who first read of him, as young men, have lived to see their own grown-up children following the same adventures in the same magazine. It is a striking example of the patience and loyalty of the British public.*

I had fully determined at the conclusion of The Memoirs *to bring Holmes to an end, as I felt that my literary energies should not be directed too much into one channel. That pale, clear-cut face and loose-limbed figure were taking up an undue share of my imagination. I did the deed, but fortunately no coroner had pronounced upon the remains, and so, after a long interval, it was not difficult for me to respond to the flattering demand and to explain my rash act away. I have never regretted it, for I have not in actual practice found that these lighter sketches have prevented me from exploring and finding my limitations in such varied branches of literature as history, poetry, historical novels, psychic research, and the drama. Had Holmes never existed I could not have done more, though he may perhaps have stood a little in the way of the recognition of my more serious literary work.*

And so, reader, farewell to Sherlock Holmes! I thank you for your past constancy, and can but hope that some return has been made in the shape of that distraction from the worries of life and stimulating change of thought which can only be found in the fairy kingdom of romance.

ARTHUR CONAN DOYLE.

THE ADVENTURE OF THE
ILLUSTRIOUS CLIENT

I t can't hurt now," was Mr. Sherlock Holmes's comment when, for the tenth time in as many years, I asked his leave to reveal the following narrative. So it was that at last I obtained permission to put on record what was, in some ways, the supreme moment of my friend's career.

Both Holmes and I had a weakness for the Turkish bath. It was over a smoke in the pleasant lassitude of the drying-room that I have found him less reticent and more human than anywhere else. On the upper floor of the Northumberland Avenue establishment there is an isolated corner where two couches lie side by side, and it was on these that we lay upon September 3, 1902, the day when my narrative begins. I had asked him whether anything was stirring, and for answer he had shot his long, thin, nervous arm out of the sheets which enveloped him and had drawn an envelope from the inside pocket of the coat which hung beside him.

"It may be some fussy, self-important fool; it may be a matter of life or death," said he as he handed me the note. "I know no more than this message tells me."

It was from the Carlton Club and dated the evening before. This is what I read:

Sir James Damery presents his compliments to Mr. Sherlock Holmes and will call upon him at 4:30 to-morrow. Sir James begs to say that the matter upon which he desires to consult Mr. Holmes is very delicate and also very important. He trusts, therefore, that Mr. Holmes will make every effort to grant this interview, and that he will confirm it over the telephone to the Carlton Club.

"I need not say that I have confirmed it, Watson," said Holmes as I returned the paper. "Do you know anything of this man Damery?"

"Only that this name is a household word in society."

"Well, I can tell you a little more than that. He has rather a reputation for arranging delicate matters which are to be kept out of the papers. You may remember his negotiations with Sir George Lewis* over the Hammerford Will case. He is a man of the world with a natural turn for diplomacy. I am bound, therefore, to hope that it is not a false scent and that he has some real need for our assistance."

"Our?"

"Well, if you will be so good, Watson."

---

*George Lewis (1833–1911), the most prestigious solicitor (lawyer) of the age.

"I shall be honoured."

"Then you have the hour—4:30. Until then we can put the matter out of our heads."

I was living in my own rooms in Queen Anne Street at the time, but I was round at Baker Street before the time named. Sharp to the half-hour, Colonel Sir James Damery was announced. It is hardly necessary to describe him, for many will remember that large, bluff, honest personality, that broad, clean-shaven face, and, above all, that pleasant, mellow voice. Frankness shone from his gray Irish eyes, and good humour played round his mobile, smiling lips. His lucent top-hat, his dark frock-coat, indeed, every detail, from the pearl pin in the black satin cravat to the lavender spats over the varnished shoes, spoke of the meticulous care in dress for which he was famous. The big, masterful aristocrat dominated the little room.

"Of course, I was prepared to find Dr. Watson," he remarked with a courteous bow. "His collaboration may be very necessary, for we are dealing on this occasion, Mr. Holmes, with a man to whom violence is familiar and who will, literally, stick at nothing. I should say that there is no more dangerous man in Europe."

"I have had several opponents to whom that flattering term has been applied," said Holmes with a smile. "Don't you smoke? Then you will excuse me if I light my pipe. If your man is more dangerous than the late Professor Moriarty, or than the living Colonel Sebastian Moran, then he is indeed worth meeting. May I ask his name?"

"Have you ever heard of Baron Gruner?"

"You mean the Austrian murderer?"

Colonel Damery threw up his kid-gloved hands with a laugh. "There is no getting past you, Mr. Holmes! Wonderful! So you have already sized him up as a murderer?"

"It is my business to follow the details of Continental crime. Who could possibly have read what happened at Prague and have any doubts as to the man's guilt! It was a purely technical legal point and the suspicious death of a witness that saved him! I am as sure that he killed his wife when the so-called 'accident' happened in the Splugen Pass as if I had seen him do it. I knew, also, that he had come to England and had a presentiment that sooner or later he would find me some work to do. Well, what has Baron Gruner been up to? I presume it is not this old tragedy which has come up again?"

"No, it is more serious than that. To revenge crime is important, but to prevent it is more so. It is a terrible thing, Mr. Holmes, to see a dreadful event, an atrocious situation, preparing itself before your eyes, to clearly understand whither it will lead and yet to be utterly unable to avert it. Can a human being be placed in a more trying position?"

"Perhaps not."

"Then you will sympathize with the client in whose interests I am acting."

"I did not understand that you were merely an intermediary. Who is the principal?"

"Mr. Holmes, I must beg you not to press that question. It is important that I should be able to assure him that his honoured name has been in no way dragged into the matter. His motives are, to the last degree, honourable and chivalrous, but he prefers to remain unknown. I need not say that your fees will be assured and that you will be given a perfectly free hand. Surely the actual name of your client is immaterial?"

"I am sorry," said Holmes. "I am accustomed to have mystery at one end of my cases, but to have it at both ends is too confusing. I fear, Sir James, that I must decline to act."

Our visitor was greatly disturbed. His large, sensitive face was darkened with emotion and disappointment.

"You hardly realize the effect of your own action, Mr. Holmes," said he. "You place me in a most serious dilemma, for I am perfectly certain that you would be proud to take over the case if I could give you the facts, and yet a promise forbids me from revealing them all. May I, at least, lay all that I can before you?"

"By all means, so long as it is understood that I commit myself to nothing."

"That is understood. In the first place, you have no doubt heard of General de Merville?"

"De Merville of Khyber fame? Yes, I have heard of him."

"He has a daughter, Violet de Merville, young, rich, beautiful, accomplished, a wonder-woman in every way. It is this daughter, this lovely, innocent girl, whom we are endeavouring to save from the clutches of a fiend."

"Baron Gruner has some hold over her, then?"

"The strongest of all holds where a woman is concerned—the hold of love. The fellow is, as you may have heard, extraordinarily handsome, with a most fascinating manner, a gentle voice, and that air of romance and mystery which means so much to a woman. He is said to have the whole sex at his mercy and to have made ample use of the fact."

"But how came such a man to meet a lady of the standing of Miss Violet de Merville?"

"It was on a Mediterranean yachting voyage. The company, though select, paid their own passages. No doubt the promoters hardly realized the Baron's true character until it was too late. The villain attached himself to the lady, and with such effect that he has completely and absolutely won her heart. To say that she loves him hardly expresses it. She dotes upon him; she is obsessed by him. Outside of him there is nothing on earth. She will not hear one word against him. Everything has been done to cure her of her madness, but in vain. To sum up, she proposes to marry him next month. As she is of age and has a will of iron, it is hard to know how to prevent her."

"Does she know about the Austrian episode?"

"The cunning devil has told her every unsavoury public scandal of his past life, but always in such a way as to make himself out to be an innocent martyr. She absolutely accepts his version and will listen to no other."

"Dear me! But surely you have inadvertently let out the name of your client? It is no doubt General de Merville."

Our visitor fidgeted in his chair.

"I could deceive you by saying so, Mr. Holmes, but it would not be true. De Merville is a broken man. The strong soldier has been utterly demoralized by this incident. He has lost the nerve which never failed him on the battlefield and has become a weak, doddering old man, utterly incapable of contending with a brilliant, forceful rascal like this Austrian. My client, however, is an old friend, one who has known the General intimately for many years and taken a paternal interest in this young girl since she wore short frocks. He cannot see this tragedy consummated without some attempt to stop it. There is nothing in which Scotland Yard can act. It was his own suggestion that you should be called in, but it was, as I have said, on the express stipulation that he should not be personally involved in the matter. I have no doubt, Mr. Holmes, with your great powers you could easily trace my client back through me, but I must ask you, as a point of honour, to refrain from doing so, and not to break in upon his incognito."

Holmes gave a whimsical smile.

"I think I may safely promise that," said he. "I may add that your problem interests me, and that I shall be prepared to look into it. How shall I keep in touch with you?"

"The Carlton Club will find me. But in case of emergency, there is a private telephone call, 'XX.31.'"

Holmes noted it down and sat, still smiling, with the open memorandum-book upon his knee.

"The Baron's present address, please?"

"Vernon Lodge, near Kingston. It is a large house. He has been fortunate in some rather shady speculations and is a rich man, which naturally makes him a more dangerous antagonist."

"Is he at home at present?"

"Yes."

"Apart from what you have told me, can you give me any further information about the man?"

"He has expensive tastes. He is a horse fancier. For a short time he played polo at Hurlingham, but then this Prague affair got noised about and he had to leave. He collects books and pictures. He is a man with a considerable artistic side to his nature. He is, I believe, a recognized authority upon Chinese pottery and has written a book upon the subject."

"A complex mind," said Holmes. "All great criminals have that. My old friend Charlie Peace* was a violin virtuoso. Wainwright† was no mean

---

*Charlie Peace (1832–1879), a violinist and burglar who was hanged for several murders.

†Thomas Griffiths Wainwright (1794–1852), painter and poisoner.

artist. I could quote many more. Well, Sir James, you will inform your client that I am turning my mind upon Baron Gruner. I can say no more. I have some sources of information of my own, and I dare say we may find some means of opening the matter up."

When our visitor had left us Holmes sat so long in deep thought that it seemed to me that he had forgotten my presence. At last, however, he came briskly back to earth.

"Well, Watson, any views?" he asked.

"I should think you had better see the young lady herself."

"My dear Watson, if her poor old broken father cannot move her, how shall I, a stranger, prevail? And yet there is something in the suggestion if all else fails. But I think we must begin from a different angle. I rather fancy that Shinwell Johnson might be a help."

I have not had occasion to mention Shinwell Johnson in these memoirs because I have seldom drawn my cases from the latter phases of my friend's career. During the first years of the century he became a valuable assistant. Johnson, I grieve to say, made his name first as a very dangerous villain and served two terms at Parkhurst.* Finally he repented and allied himself to Holmes, acting as his agent in the huge criminal underworld of London and obtaining information which often proved to be of vital importance. Had Johnson been a "nark" of the police he would soon have been exposed, but as he dealt with cases which never came directly into the courts, his activities were never realized by his companions. With the glamour of his two convictions upon him, he had the entrée of every night-club, doss house, and gambling-den in the town, and his quick observation and active brain made him an ideal agent for gaining information. It was to him that Sherlock Holmes now proposed to turn.

It was not possible for me to follow the immediate steps taken by my friend, for I had some pressing professional business of my own, but I met him by appointment that evening at Simpson's, where, sitting at a small table in the front window and looking down at the rushing stream of life in the Strand, he told me something of what had passed.

"Johnson is on the prowl," said he. "He may pick up some garbage in the darker recesses of the underworld, for it is down there, amid the black roots of crime, that we must hunt for this man's secrets."

"But if the lady will not accept what is already known, why should any fresh discovery of yours turn her from her purpose?"

"Who knows, Watson? Woman's heart and mind are insoluble puzzles to the male. Murder might be condoned or explained, and yet some smaller offence might rankle. Baron Gruner remarked to me——"

"He remarked to you!"

"Oh, to be sure, I had not told you of my plans. Well, Watson, I love to come to close grips with my man. I like to meet him eye to eye and read for myself the stuff that he is made of. When I had given Johnson his in-

---

*Prison on the Isle of Wight.

structions I took a cab out to Kingston and found the Baron in a most affable mood."

"Did he recognize you?"

"There was no difficulty about that, for I simply sent in my card. He is
an excellent antagonist, cool as ice, silky voiced and soothing as one of
your fashionable consultants, and poisonous as a cobra. He has breeding
in him—a real aristocrat of crime, with a superficial suggestion of afternoon tea and all the cruelty of the grave behind it. Yes, I am glad to have
had my attention called to Baron Adelbert Gruner."

"You say he was affable?"

"A purring cat who thinks he sees prospective mice. Some people's af-
fability is more deadly than the violence of coarser souls. His greeting was
characteristic. 'I rather thought I should see you sooner or later, Mr.
Holmes,' said he. 'You have been engaged, no doubt by General de
Merville, to endeavour to stop my marriage with his daughter, Violet.
That is so, is it not?'

"I acquiesced.

" 'My dear man,' said he, 'you will only ruin your own well-deserved
reputation. It is not a case in which you can possibly succeed. You will
have barren work, to say nothing of incurring some danger. Let me very
strongly advise you to draw off at once.'

" 'It is curious,' I answered, 'but that was the very advice which I had
intended to give you. I have a respect for your brains, Baron, and the little which I have seen of your personality has not lessened it. Let me put
it to you as man to man. No one wants to rake up your past and make you
unduly uncomfortable. It is over, and you are now in smooth waters, but
if you persist in this marriage you will raise up a swarm of powerful enemies who will never leave you alone until they have made England too
hot to hold you. Is the game worth it? Surely you would be wiser if you
left the lady alone. It would not be pleasant for you if these facts of your
past were brought to her notice.'

"The Baron has little waxed tips of hair under his nose, like the short
antennæ of an insect. These quivered with amusement as he listened, and
he finally broke into a gentle chuckle.

" 'Excuse my amusement, Mr. Holmes,' said he, 'but it is really funny
to see you trying to play a hand with no cards in it. I don't think anyone
could do it better, but it is rather pathetic, all the same. Not a colour card*
there. Mr. Holmes, nothing but the smallest of the small.'

" 'So you think.'

" 'So I know. Let me make the thing clear to you, for my own hand is
so strong that I can afford to show it. I have been fortunate enough to win
the entire affection of this lady. This was given to me in spite of the fact
that I told her very clearly of all the unhappy incidents in my past life. I
also told her that certain wicked and designing persons—I hope you rec-

---

*A king, queen, jack, or ace.

ognize yourself—would come to her and tell her these things, and I warned her how to treat them. You have heard of post-hypnotic suggestion, Mr. Holmes? Well, you will see how it works, for a man of personality can use hypnotism without any vulgar passes or tomfoolery. So she is ready for you and, I have no doubt, would give you an appointment, for she is quite amenable to her father's will—save only in the one little matter.'

"Well, Watson, there seemed to be no more to say, so I took my leave with as much cold dignity as I could summon, but, as I had my hand on the door-handle, he stopped me.

"'By the way, Mr. Holmes,' said he, 'did you know Le Brun, the French agent?'

"'Yes,' said I.

"'Do you know what befell him?'

"'I heard that he was beaten by some Apaches* in the Montmartre district and crippled for life.'

"'Quite true, Mr. Holmes. By a curious coincidence he had been inquiring into my affairs only a week before. Don't do it, Mr. Holmes; it's not a lucky thing to do. Several have found that out. My last word to you is, go your own way and let me go mine. Good-bye!'

"So there you are, Watson. You are up to date now."

"The fellow seems dangerous."

"Mighty dangerous. I disregard the blusterer, but this is the sort of man who says rather less than he means."

"Must you interfere? Does it really matter if he marries the girl?"

"Considering that he undoubtedly murdered his last wife, I should say it mattered very much. Besides, the client! Well, well, we need not discuss that. When you have finished your coffee you had best come home with me, for the blithe Shinwell will be there with his report."

We found him sure enough, a huge, coarse, red-faced, scorbutic man, with a pair of vivid black eyes which were the only external sign of the very cunning mind within. It seems that he had dived down into what was peculiarly his kingdom, and beside him on the settee was a brand which he had brought up in the shape of a slim, flame-like young woman with a pale, intense face, youthful, and yet so worn with sin and sorrow that one read the terrible years which had left their leprous mark upon her.

"This is Miss Kitty Winter," said Shinwell Johnson, waving his fat hand as an introduction. "What she don't know—well, there, she'll speak for herself. Put my hand right on her, Mr. Holmes, within an hour of your message."

"I'm easy to find," said the young woman. "Hell, London gets me every time. Same address for Porky Shinwell. We're old mates, Porky, you and I. But, by cripes! there is another who ought to be down in a

---

*Street thugs.

lower hell than we if there was any justice in the world! That is the man
you are after, Mr. Holmes."

Holmes smiled. "I gather we have your good wishes, Miss Winter,"

"If I can help to put him where he belongs, I'm yours to the rattle."
said our visitor with fierce energy. There was an intensity of hatred in her
white, set face and her blazing eyes such as woman seldom and man never
can attain. "You needn't go into my past, Mr. Holmes. That's neither here
nor there. But what I am Adelbert Gruner made me. If I could pull him
down!" She clutched frantically with her hands into the air. "Oh, if I could
only pull him into the pit where he has pushed so many!"

"You know how the matter stands?"

"Porky Shinwell has been telling me. He's after some other poor fool
and wants to marry her this time. You want to stop it. Well, you surely
know enough about this devil to prevent any decent girl in her senses
wanting to be in the same parish with him."

"She is not in her senses. She is madly in love. She has been told all
about him. She cares nothing."

"Told about the murder?"

"Yes."

"My Lord, she must have a nerve!"

"She puts them all down as slanders."

"Couldn't you lay proofs before her silly eyes?"

"Well, can you help us do so?"

"Ain't I a proof myself? If I stood before her and told her how he used
me——"

"Would you do this?"

"Would I? Would I not!"

"Well, it might be worth trying. But he has told her most of his sins and
had pardon from her, and I understand she will not reopen the question."

"I'll lay he didn't tell her all," said Miss Winter. "I caught a glimpse of
one or two murders besides the one that made such a fuss. He would
speak of someone in his velvet way and then look at me with a steady eye
and say: 'He died within a month.' It wasn't hot air, either. But I took little notice—you see, I loved him myself at that time. Whatever he did
went with me, same as with this poor fool! There was just one thing that
shook me. Yes, by cripes! if it had not been for his poisonous, lying tongue
that explains and soothes, I'd have left him that very night. It's a book he
has—a brown leather book with a lock, and his arms in gold on the outside. I think he was a bit drunk that night, or he would not have shown it
to me."

"What was it, then?"

"I tell you, Mr. Holmes, this man collects women, and takes a pride in
his collection, as some men collect moths or butterflies. He had it all in
that book. Snapshot photographs, names, details, everything about them.
It was a beastly book—a book no man, even if he had come from the gut-
ter, could have put together. But it was Adelbert Gruner's book all the
same. 'Souls I have ruined.' He could have put that on the outside if he

had been so minded. However, that's neither here nor there, for the book would not serve you, and, if it would, you can't get it."

"Where is it?"

"How can I tell you where it is now? It's more than a year since I left him. I know where he kept it then. He's a precise, tidy cat of a man in many of his ways, so maybe it is still in the pigeon-hole of the old bureau in the inner study. Do you know his house?"

"I've been in the study," said Holmes.

"Have you, though? You haven't been slow on the job if you only started this morning. Maybe dear Adelbert has met his match this time. The outer study is the one with the Chinese crockery in it—big glass cupboard between the windows. Then behind his desk is the door that leads to the inner study—a small room where he keeps papers and things."

"Is he not afraid of burglars?"

"Adelbert is no coward. His worst enemy couldn't say that of him. He can look after himself. There's a burglar alarm at night. Besides, what is there for a burglar—unless they got away with all this fancy crockery?"

"No good," said Shinwell Johnson with the decided voice of the expert. "No fence wants stuff of that sort that you can neither melt nor sell."

"Quite so," said Holmes. "Well, now, Miss Winter, if you would call here to-morrow evening at five, I would consider in the meanwhile whether your suggestion of seeing this lady personally may not be arranged. I am exceedingly obliged to you for your coöperation. I need not say that my clients will consider liberally——"

"None of that, Mr. Holmes," cried the young woman. "I am not out for money. Let me see this man in the mud, and I've got all I've worked for— in the mud with my foot on his cursed face. That's my price. I'm with you to-morrow or any other day so long as you are on his track. Porky here can tell you always where to find me."

I did not see Holmes again until the following evening when we dined once more at our Strand restaurant. He shrugged his shoulders when I asked him what luck he had had in his interview. Then he told the story, which I would repeat in this way. His hard, dry statement needs some little editing to soften it into the terms of real life.

"There was no difficulty at all about the appointment." said Holmes, "for the girl glories in showing abject filial obedience in all secondary things in an attempt to atone for her flagrant breach of it in her engagement. The General 'phoned that all was ready, and the fiery Miss W. turned up according to schedule, so that at half-past five a cab deposited us outside 104 Berkeley Square, where the old soldier resides—one of those awful gray London castles which would make a church seem frivolous. A footman showed us into a great yellow-curtained drawing-room, and there was the lady awaiting us, demure, pale, self-contained, as inflexible and remote as a snow image on a mountain.

"I don't quite know how to make her clear to you, Watson. Perhaps you may meet her before we are through, and you can use your own gift of words. She is beautiful, but with the ethereal other-world beauty of some fanatic whose thoughts are set on high. I have seen such faces in the pictures of the old masters of the Middle Ages. How a beastman could have laid his vile paws upon such a being of the beyond I cannot imagine. You may have noticed how extremes call to each other, the spiritual to the animal, the cave-man to the angel. You never saw a worse case than this.

"She knew what we had come for, of course—that villain had lost no time in poisoning her mind against us. Miss Winter's advent rather amazed her, I think, but she waved us into our respective chairs like a reverend abbess receiving two rather leprous mendicants. If your head is inclined to swell, my dear Watson, take a course of Miss Violet de Merville.

"'Well, sir,' said she in a voice like the wind from an iceberg, 'your name is familiar to me. You have called, as I understand, to malign my fiancé, Baron Gruner. It is only by my father's request that I see you at all, and I warn you in advance that anything you can say could not possibly have the slightest effect upon my mind.'

"I was sorry for her, Watson. I thought of her for the moment as I would have thought of a daughter of my own. I am not often eloquent. I use my head, not my heart. But I really did plead with her with all the warmth of words that I could find in my nature. I pictured to her the awful position of the woman who only wakes to a man's character after she is his wife—a woman who has to submit to be caressed by bloody hands and lecherous lips. I spared her nothing—the shame, the fear, the agony, the hopelessness of it all. All my hot words could not bring one tinge of colour to those ivory cheeks or one gleam of emotion to those abstracted eyes. I thought of what the rascal had said about a post-hypnotic influence. One could really believe that she was living above the earth in some ecstatic dream. Yet there was nothing indefinite in her replies.

"'I have listened to you with patience, Mr. Holmes,' said she. 'The effect upon my mind is exactly as predicted. I am aware that Adelbert, that my fiancé, has had a stormy life in which he has incurred bitter hatreds and most unjust aspersions. You are only the last of a series who have brought their slanders before me. Possibly you mean well, though I learn that you are a paid agent who would have been equally willing to act for the Baron as against him. But in any case I wish you to understand once for all that I love him and that he loves me, and that the opinion of all the world is no more to me than the twitter of those birds outside the window. If his noble nature has ever for an instant fallen, it may be that I have been specially sent to raise it to its true and lofty level. I am not clear'—here she turned eyes upon my companion—'who this young lady may be.'

"I was about to answer when the girl broke in like a whirlwind. If ever you saw flame and ice face to face, it was those two women.

"'I'll tell you who I am,' she cried, springing out of her chair, her mouth all twisted with passion—'I am his last mistress. I am one of a hundred that he has tempted and used and ruined and thrown into the refuse heap, as he will you also. *Your* refuse heap is more likely to be a grave, and maybe that's the best. I tell you, you foolish woman, if you marry this man he'll be the death of you. It may be a broken heart or it may be a broken neck, but he'll have you one way or the other. It's not out of love for you I'm speaking. I don't care a tinker's curse whether you live or die. It's out of hate for him and to spite him and to get back on him for what he did to me. But it's all the same, and you needn't look at me like that, my fine lady, for you may be lower than I am before you are through with it.'

" 'I should prefer not to discuss such matters,' said Miss de Merville coldly. 'Let me say once for all that I am aware of three passages in my fiancé's life in which he became entangled with designing women, and that I am assured of his hearty repentance for any evil that he may have done.'

" 'Three passages!' screamed my companion. 'You fool! You unutterable fool!'

" 'Mr. Holmes, I beg that you will bring this interview to an end,' said the icy voice. 'I have obeyed my father's wish in seeing you, but I am not compelled to listen to the ravings of this person.'

"With an oath Miss Winter darted forward, and if I had not caught her wrist she would have clutched this maddening woman by the hair. I dragged her towards the door and was lucky to get her back into the cab without a public scene, for she was beside herself with rage. In a cold way I felt pretty furious myself, Watson, for there was something indescribably annoying in the calm aloofness and supreme self-complaisance of the woman whom we were trying to save. So now once again you know exactly how we stand, and it is clear that I must plan some fresh opening move, for this gambit won't work. I'll keep in touch with you, Watson, for it is more than likely that you will have your part to play, though it is just possible that the next move may lie with them rather than with us."

And it did. Their blow fell—or his blow rather, for never could I believe that the lady was privy to it. I think I could show you the very paving-stone upon which I stood when my eyes fell upon the placard, and a pang of horror passed through my very soul. It was between the Grand Hotel and Charing Cross Station, where a one-legged news-vender displayed his evening papers. The date was just two days after the last conversation. There, black upon yellow, was the terrible news-sheet:

MURDEROUS ATTACK UPON
SHERLOCK HOLMES

I think I stood stunned for some moments. Then I have a confused recollection of snatching at a paper, of the remonstrance of the man, whom I had not paid, and, finally, of standing in the doorway of a chemist's shop while I turned up the fateful paragraph. This was how it ran:

We learn with regret that Mr. Sherlock Holmes, the well-known private detective, was the victim this morning of a murderous assault which has left him in a precarious position. There are no exact details to hand, but the event seems to have occurred about twelve o'clock in Regent Street, outside the Café Royal. The attack was made by two men armed with sticks, and Mr. Holmes was beaten about the head and body, receiving injuries which the doctors describe as most serious. He was carried to Charing Cross Hospital and afterwards insisted upon being taken to his rooms in Baker Street. The miscreants who attacked him appear to have been respectably dressed men, who escaped from the bystanders by passing through the Café Royal and out into Glasshouse Street behind it. No doubt they belonged to that criminal fraternity which has so often had occasion to bewail the activity and ingenuity of the injured man.

I need not say that my eyes had hardly glanced over the paragraph before I had sprung into a hansom and was on my way to Baker Street. I found Sir Leslie Oakshott, the famous surgeon, in the hall and his brougham waiting at the curb.

"No immediate danger," was his report. "Two lacerated scalp wounds and some considerable bruises. Several stitches have been necessary. Morphine has been injected and quiet is essential, but an interview of a few minutes would not be absolutely forbidden."

With this permission I stole into the darkened room. The sufferer was wide awake, and I heard my name in a hoarse whisper. The blind was three-quarters down, but one ray of sunlight slanted through and struck the bandaged head of the injured man. A crimson patch had soaked through the white linen compress. I sat beside him and bent my head.

"All right, Watson. Don't look so scared," he muttered in a very weak voice. "It's not as bad as it seems."

"Thank God for that!"

"I'm a bit of a single-stick* expert, as you know. I took most of them on my guard. It was the second man that was too much for me."

"What can I do, Holmes? Of course, it was that damned fellow who set them on. I'll go and thrash the hide off him if you give the word."

"Good old Watson! No, we can do nothing there unless the police lay their hands on the men. But their get-away had been well prepared. We may be sure of that. Wait a little. I have my plans. The first thing is to exaggerate my injuries. They'll come to you for news. Put it on thick, Watson. Lucky if I live the week out—concussion—delirium—what you like! You can't overdo it."

"But Sir Leslie Oakshott?"

"Oh, he's all right. He shall see the worst side of me. I'll look after that."

"Anything else?"

"Yes. Tell Shinwell Johnson to get that girl out of the way. Those beauties will be after her now. They know, of course, that she was with me in the case. If they dared to do me in it is not likely they will neglect her. That is urgent. Do it to-night."

---

*One-handed fencing stick fitted with a hand guard.

"I'll go now. Anything more?"

"Put my pipe on the table—and the tobacco-slipper. Right! Come in each morning and we will plan our campaign."

I arranged with Johnson that evening to take Miss Winter to a quiet suburb and see that she lay low until the danger was past.

For six days the public were under the impression that Holmes was at the door of death. The bulletins were very grave and there were sinister paragraphs in the papers. My continual visits assured me that it was not so bad as that. His wiry constitution and his determined will were working wonders. He was recovering fast, and I had suspicions at times that he was really finding himself faster than he pretended even to me. There was a curious secretive streak in the man which led to many dramatic effects, but left even his closest friend guessing as to what his exact plans might be. He pushed to an extreme the axiom that the only safe plotter was he who plotted alone. I was nearer him than anyone else, and yet I was always conscious of the gap between.

On the seventh day the stitches were taken out, in spite of which there was a report of erysipelas* in the evening papers. The same evening papers had an announcement which I was bound, sick or well, to carry to my friend. It was simply that among the passengers on the Cunard boat *Ruritania*, starting from Liverpool on Friday, was the Baron Adelbert Gruner, who had some important financial business to settle in the States before his impending wedding to Miss Violet de Merville, only daughter of, etc., etc. Holmes listened to the news with a cold, concentrated look upon his pale face, which told me that it hit him hard.

"Friday!" he cried. "Only three clear days. I believe the rascal wants to put himself out of danger's way. But he won't, Watson! By the Lord Harry, he won't! Now, Watson, I want you to do something for me."

"I am here to be used, Holmes."

"Well, then, spend the next twenty-four hours in an intensive study of Chinese pottery."

He gave no explanations and I asked for none. By long experience I had learned the wisdom of obedience. But when I had left his room I walked down Baker Street, revolving in my head how on earth I was to carry out so strange an order. Finally I drove to the London Library in St. James's Square, put the matter to my friend Lomax, the sublibrarian, and departed to my rooms with a goodly volume under my arm.

It is said that the barrister who crams up a case with such care that he can examine an expert witness upon the Monday has forgotten all his forced knowledge before the Saturday. Certainly I should not like now to pose as an authority upon ceramics. And yet all that evening, and all that night with a short interval for rest, and all next morning, I was sucking in knowledge and committing names to memory. There I learned of the hallmarks of the great artist-decorators, of the mystery of cyclical dates, the

---

*Inflammatory skin disease.

marks of the Hung-wu and the beauties of the Yung-lo, the writings of Tang-ying, and the glories of the primitive period of the Sung and the Yuan. I was charged with all this information when I called upon Holmes next evening. He was out of bed now, though you would not have guessed it from the published reports, and he sat with his much-bandaged head resting upon his hand in the depth of his favourite armchair.

"Why, Holmes," I said, "if one believed the papers, you are dying."

"That," said he, "is the very impression which I intended to convey. And now, Watson, have you learned your lessons?"

"At least I have tried to."

"Good. You could keep up an intelligent conversation on the subject?"

"I believe I could."

"Then hand me that little box from the mantelpiece."

He opened the lid and took out a small object most carefully wrapped in some fine Eastern silk. This he unfolded, and disclosed a delicate little saucer of the most beautiful deep-blue colour.

"It needs careful handling, Watson. This is the real egg-shell pottery of the Ming dynasty. No finer piece ever passed through Christie's.* A complete set of this would be worth a king's ransom—in fact, it is doubtful if there is a complete set outside the imperial palace of Peking. The sight of this would drive a real connoisseur wild."

"What am I to do with it?"

Holmes handed me a card upon which was printed: "Dr. Hill Barton, 369 Half Moon Street."

"That is your name for the evening, Watson. You will call upon Baron Gruner. I know something of his habits, and at half-past eight he would probably be disengaged. A note will tell him in advance that you are about to call, and you will say that you are bringing him a specimen of an absolutely unique set of Ming china. You may as well be a medical man, since that is a part which you can play without duplicity. You are a collector, this set has come your way, you have heard of the Baron's interest in the subject, and you are not averse to selling at a price."

"What price?"

"Well asked, Watson. You would certainly fall down badly if you did not know the value of your own wares. This saucer was got for me by Sir James, and comes, I understand, from the collection of his client. You will not exaggerate if you say that it could hardly be matched in the world."

"I could perhaps suggest that the set should be valued by an expert."

"Excellent, Watson! You scintillate to-day. Suggest Christie or Sotheby. Your delicacy prevents your putting a price for yourself."

"But if he won't see me?"

"Oh, yes, he will see you. He has the collection mania in its most acute form—and especially on this subject, on which he is an acknowledged au-

---

*Well-known auction house, like Sotheby, mentioned below.

thority. Sit down, Watson. and I will dictate the letter. No answer needed. You will merely say that you are coming, and why."

It was an admirable document, short, courteous, and stimulating to the curiosity of the connoisseur. A district messenger was duly dispatched with it. On the same evening, with the precious saucer in my hand and the card of Dr. Hill Barton in my pocket, I set off on my own adventure.

The beautiful house and grounds indicated that Baron Gruner was, as Sir James had said, a man of considerable wealth. A long winding drive, with banks of rare shrubs on either side, opened out into a great gravelled square adorned with statues. The place had been built by a South African gold king in the days of the great boom, and the long, low house with the turrets at the corners, though an architectural nightmare, was imposing in its size and solidity. A butler, who would have adorned a bench of bishops, showed me in and handed me over to a plush-clad footman, who ushered me into the Baron's presence.

He was standing at the open front of a great case which stood between the windows and which contained part of his Chinese collection. He turned as I entered with a small brown vase in his hand.

"Pray sit down, Doctor," said he. "I was looking over my own treasures and wondering whether I could really afford to add to them. This little Tang specimen, which dates from the seventh century, would probably interest you. I am sure you never saw finer workmanship or a richer glaze. Have you the Ming saucer with you of which you spoke?"

I carefully unpacked it and handed it to him. He seated himself at his desk, pulled over the lamp, for it was growing dark, and set himself to examine it. As he did so the yellow light beat upon his own features, and I was able to study them at my ease.

He was certainly a remarkably handsome man. His European reputation for beauty was fully deserved. In figure he was not more than of middle size, but was built upon graceful and active lines. His face was swarthy, almost Oriental, with large, dark, languorous eyes which might easily hold an irresistible fascination for women. His hair and moustache were raven black, the latter short, pointed, and carefully waxed. His features were regular and pleasing, save only his straight, thin-lipped mouth. If ever I saw a murderer's mouth it was there—a cruel, hard gash in the face, compressed, inexorable, and terrible. He was ill-advised to train his moustache away from it, for it was Nature's danger-signal, set as a warning to his victims. His voice was engaging and his manners perfect. In age I should have put him at little over thirty, though his record afterwards showed that he was forty-two.

"Very fine—very fine indeed!" he said at last. "And you say you have a set of six to correspond. What puzzles me is that I should not have heard of such magnificent specimens. I only know of one in England to match this, and it is certainly not likely to be in the market. Would it be indiscreet if I were to ask you, Dr. Hill Barton, how you obtained this?"

"Does it really matter?" I asked with as careless an air as I could muster. "You can see that the piece is genuine, and, as to the value, I am content to take an expert's valuation."

"Very mysterious," said he with a quick, suspicious flash of his dark eyes. "In dealing with objects of such value, one naturally wishes to know all about the transaction. That the piece is genuine is certain. I have no doubts at all about that. But suppose—I am bound to take every possibility into account—that it should prove afterwards that you had no right to sell?"

"I would guarantee you against any claim of the sort."

"That, of course, would open up the question as to what your guarantee was worth."

"My bankers would answer that."

"Quite so. And yet the whole transaction strikes me as rather unusual."

"You can do business or not," said I with indifference. "I have given you the first offer as I understood that you were a connoisseur, but I shall have no difficulty in other quarters."

"Who told you I was a connoisseur?"

"I was aware that you had written a book upon the subject."

"Have you read the book?"

"No."

"Dear me, this becomes more and more difficult for me to understand! You are a connoisseur and collector with a very valuable piece in your collection, and yet you have never troubled to consult the one book which would have told you of the real meaning and value of what you held. How do you explain that?"

"I am a very busy man. I am a doctor in practice."

"That is no answer. If a man has a hobby he follows it up, whatever his other pursuits may be. You said in your note that you were a connoisseur."

"So I am."

"Might I ask you a few questions to test you? I am obliged to tell you, Doctor—if you are indeed a doctor—that the incident becomes more and more suspicious. I would ask you what do you know of the Emperor Shomu and how do you associate him with the Shoso-in near Nara? Dear me, does that puzzle you? Tell me a little about the Northern Wei dynasty and its place in the history of ceramics."

I sprang from my chair in simulated anger.

"This is intolerable, sir," said I. "I came here to do you a favour, and not to be examined as if I were a schoolboy. My knowledge on these subjects may be second only to your own, but I certainly shall not answer questions which have been put in so offensive a way."

He looked at me steadily. The languor had gone from his eyes. They suddenly glared. There was a gleam of teeth from between those cruel lips.

"What is the game? You are here as a spy. You are an emissary of Holmes. This is a trick that you are playing upon me. The fellow is dying

I hear, so he sends his tools to keep watch upon me. You've made your way in here without leave, and, by God! you may find it harder to get out than to get in."

He had sprung to his feet, and I stepped back, bracing myself for an attack, for the man was beside himself with rage. He may have suspected me from the first; certainly this cross-examination had shown him the truth; but it was clear that I could not hope to deceive him. He dived his hand into a side-drawer and rummaged furiously. Then something struck upon his ear, for he stood listening intently.

"Ah!" he cried. "Ah!" and dashed into the room behind him.

Two steps took me to the open door, and my mind will ever carry a clear picture of the scene within. The window leading out to the garden was wide open. Beside it, looking like some terrible ghost, his head girt with bloody bandages, his face drawn and white, stood Sherlock Holmes. The next instant he was through the gap, and I heard the crash of his body among the laurel bushes outside. With a howl of rage the master of the house rushed after him to the open window.

And then! It was done in an instant, and yet I clearly saw it. An arm— a woman's arm—shot out from among the leaves. At the same instant the Baron uttered a horrible cry—a yell which will always ring in my memory. He clapped his two hands to his face and rushed round the room, beating his head horribly against the walls. Then he fell upon the carpet, rolling and writhing, while scream after scream resounded through the house.

"Water! For God's sake, water!" was his cry.

I seized a carafe from a side-table and rushed to his aid. At the same moment the butler and several footmen ran in from the hall. I remember that one of them fainted as I knelt by the injured man and turned that awful face to the light of the lamp. The vitriol* was eating into it everywhere and dripping from the ears and the chin. One eye was already white and glazed. The other was red and inflamed. The features which I had admired a few minutes before were now like some beautiful painting over which the artist has passed a wet and foul sponge. They were blurred, discoloured, inhuman, terrible.

In a few words I explained exactly what had occurred, so far as the vitriol attack was concerned. Some had climbed through the window and others had rushed out on to the lawn, but it was dark and it had begun to rain. Between his screams the victim raged and raved against the avenger. "It was that hell-cat, Kitty Winter!" he cried. "Oh, the she-devil! She shall pay for it! She shall pay! Oh, God in heaven, this pain is more than I can bear!"

I bathed his face in oil, put cotton wadding on the raw surfaces, and administered a hypodermic of morphia. All suspicion of me had passed from his mind in the presence of this shock, and he clung to my hands as if I might have the power even yet to clear those dead-fish eyes which

---

*Sulfuric acid.

gazed up at me. I could have wept over the ruin had I not remembered very clearly the vile life which had led up to so hideous a change. It was loathsome to feel the pawing of his burning hands, and I was relieved when his family surgeon, closely followed by a specialist, came to relieve me of my charge. An inspector of police had also arrived, and to him I handed my real card. It would have been useless as well as foolish to do otherwise, for I was nearly as well known by sight at the Yard as Holmes himself. Then I left that house of gloom and terror. Within an hour I was at Baker Street.

Holmes was seated in his familiar chair, looking very pale and exhausted. Apart from his injuries, even his iron nerves had been shocked by the events of the evening, and he listened with horror to my account of the Baron's transformation.

"The wages of sin,* Watson—the wages of sin!" said he. "Sooner or later it will always come. God knows, there was sin enough," he added, taking up a brown volume from the table. "Here is the book the woman talked of. If this will not break off the marriage, nothing ever could. But it will, Watson. It must. No self-respecting woman could stand it."

"It is his love diary?"

"Or his lust diary. Call it what you will. The moment the woman told us of it I realized what a tremendous weapon was there if we could but lay our hands on it. I said nothing at the time to indicate my thoughts, for this woman might have given it away. But I brooded over it. Then this assault upon me gave me the chance of letting the Baron think that no precautions need be taken against me. That was all to the good. I would have waited a little longer, but his visit to America forced my hand. He would never have left so compromising a document behind him. Therefore we had to act at once. Burglary at night is impossible. He takes precautions. But there was a chance in the evening if I could only be sure that his attention was engaged. That was where you and your blue saucer came in. But I had to be sure of the position of the book, and I knew I had only a few minutes in which to act, for my time was limited by your knowledge of Chinese pottery. Therefore I gathered the girl up at the last moment. How could I guess what the little packet was that she carried so carefully under her cloak? I thought she had come altogether on my business, but it seems she had some of her own."

"He guessed I came from you."

"I feared he would. But you held him in play just long enough for me to get the book, though not long enough for an unobserved escape. Ah, Sir James, I am very glad you have come!"

Our courtly friend had appeared in answer to a previous summons. He listened with the deepest attention to Holmes's account of what had occurred.

"You have done wonders—wonders!" he cried when he had heard the

---

*Reference to the Bible, Romans 6:23: "The wages of sin is death" (KJV).

narrative. "But if these injuries are as terrible as Dr. Watson describes, then surely our purpose of thwarting the marriage is sufficiently gained without the use of this horrible book."

Holmes shook his head.

"Women of the De Merville type do not act like that. She would love him the more as a disfigured martyr. No, no. It is his moral side, not his physical, which we have to destroy. That book will bring her back to earth—and I know nothing else that could. It is in his own writing. She cannot get past it."

Sir James carried away both it and the precious saucer. As I was myself overdue, I went down with him into the street. A brougham was waiting for him. He sprang in, gave a hurried order to the cockaded* coachman, and drove swiftly away. He flung his overcoat half out of the window to cover the armorial bearings† upon the panel, but I had seen them in the glare of our fanlight none the less. I gasped with surprise. Then I turned back and ascended the stair to Holmes's room.

"I have found out who our client is," I cried, bursting with my great news. "Why, Holmes, it is——"

"It is a loyal friend and a chivalrous gentleman," said Holmes, holding up a restraining hand. "Let that now and forever be enough for us."

I do not know how the incriminating book was used. Sir James may have managed it. Or it is more probable that so delicate a task was entrusted to the young lady's father. The effect, at any rate, was all that could be desired. Three days later appeared a paragraph in the *Morning Post* to say that the marriage between Baron Adelbert Gruner and Miss Violet de Merville would not take place. The same paper had the first police-court hearing of the proceedings against Miss Kitty Winter on the grave charge of vitriol-throwing. Such extenuating circumstances came out in the trial that the sentence, as will be remembered, was the lowest that was possible for such an offence. Sherlock Holmes was threatened with a prosecution for burglary, but when an object is good and a client is sufficiently illustrious, even the rigid British law becomes human and elastic. My friend has not yet stood in the dock.

---

*A cockade was an ornament worn on a coachman's hat as a livery badge.
†Family coat of arms.

THE ADVENTURE OF THE
BLANCHED SOLDIER

The ideas of my friend Watson, though limited, are exceedingly pertinacious. For a long time he has worried me to write an experience of my own. Perhaps I have rather invited this persecution, since I have often had occasion to point out to him how superficial are his own accounts and to accuse him of pandering to popular taste instead of confining himself rigidly to facts and figures. "Try it yourself, Holmes!" he has retorted, and I am compelled to admit that, having taken my pen in my hand, I do begin to realize that the matter must be presented in such a way as may interest the reader. The following case can hardly fail to do so, as it is among the strangest happenings in my collection, though it chanced that Watson had no note of it in his collection. Speaking of my old friend and biographer, I would take this opportunity to remark that if I burden myself with a companion in my various little inquiries it is not done out of sentiment or caprice, but it is that Watson has some remarkable characteristics of his own to which in his modesty he has given small attention amid his exaggerated estimates of my own performances. A confederate who foresees your conclusions and course of action is always dangerous, but one to whom each development comes as a perpetual surprise, and to whom the future is always a closed book, is indeed an ideal helpmate.

I find from my notebook that it was in January, 1903, just after the conclusion of the Boer War, that I had my visit from Mr. James M. Dodd, a big, fresh, sunburned, upstanding Briton. The good Watson had at that time deserted me for a wife, the only selfish action which I can recall in our association. I was alone.

It is my habit to sit with my back to the window and to place my visitors in the opposite chair, where the light falls full upon them. Mr. James M. Dodd seemed somewhat at a loss how to begin the interview. I did not attempt to help him, for his silence gave me more time for observation. I have found it wise to impress clients with a sense of power, and so I gave him some of my conclusions.

"From South Africa, sir, I perceive."

"Yes, sir," he answered, with some surprise.

"Imperial Yeomanry, I fancy."

"Exactly."

"Middlesex Corps, no doubt."

"That is so. Mr. Holmes, you are a wizard."

I smiled at his bewildered expression.

"When a gentleman of virile appearance enters my room with such tan upon his face as an English sun could never give, and with his handkerchief in his sleeve instead of in his pocket, it is not difficult to place him. You wear a short beard, which shows that you were not a regular. You have the cut of a riding-man. As to Middlesex, your card has already shown me that you are a stockbroker from Throgmorton Street.* What other regiment would you join?"

"You see everything."

"I see no more than you, but I have trained myself to notice what I see. However, Mr. Dodd, it was not to discuss the science of observation that you called upon me this morning. What has been happening at Tuxbury Old Park?"

"Mr. Holmes——!"

"My dear sir, there is no mystery. Your letter came with that heading, and as you fixed this appointment in very pressing terms it was clear that something sudden and important had occurred."

"Yes, indeed. But the letter was written in the afternoon, and a good deal has happened since then. If Colonel Emsworth had not kicked me out——"

"Kicked you out!"

"Well, that was what it amounted to. He is a hard nail, is Colonel Emsworth. The greatest martinet in the Army in his day, and it was a day of rough language, too. I couldn't have stuck the colonel if it had not been for Godfrey's sake."

I lit my pipe and leaned back in my chair.

"Perhaps you will explain what you are talking about."

My client grinned mischievously.

"I had got into the way of supposing that you knew everything without being told," said he. "But I will give you the facts, and I hope to God that you will be able to tell me what they mean. I've been awake all night puzzling my brain, and the more I think the more incredible does it become.

"When I joined up in January, 1901—just two years ago—young Godfrey Emsworth had joined the same squadron. He was Colonel Emsworth's only son—Emsworth the Crimean V. C.†—and he had the fighting blood in him, so it is no wonder he volunteered. There was not a finer lad in the regiment. We formed a friendship—the sort of friendship which can only be made when one lives the same life and shares the same joys and sorrows. He was my mate—and that means a good deal in the Army. We took the rough and the smooth together for a year of hard fighting. Then he was hit with a bullet from an elephant gun in the action near Diamond Hill outside Pretoria. I got one letter from the hospital at Cape Town and one from Southampton. Since then not a word—not one word, Mr. Holmes, for six months and more, and he my closest pal.

"Well, when the war was over, and we all got back, I wrote to his father and asked where Godfrey was. No answer. I waited a bit and then I wrote again. This time I had a reply, short and gruff. Godfrey had gone

---

*London's equivalent of Wall Street.

†Victoria Cross, a medal for bravery.

on a voyage round the world, and it was not likely that he would be back for a year. That was all.

"I wasn't satisfied, Mr. Holmes. The whole thing seemed to me so damned unnatural. He was a good lad, and he would not drop a pal like that. It was not like him. Then, again, I happened to know that he was heir to a lot of money, and also that his father and he did not always hit it off too well. The old man was sometimes a bully, and young Godfrey had too much spirit to stand it. No, I wasn't satisfied, and I determined that I would get to the root of the matter. It happened, however, that my own affairs needed a lot of straightening out, after two years' absence, and so it is only this week that I have been able to take up Godfrey's case again. But since I have taken it up I mean to drop everything in order to see it through."

Mr. James M. Dodd appeared to be the sort of person whom it would be better to have as a friend than as an enemy. His blue eyes were stern and his square jaw had set hard as he spoke.

"Well, what have you done?" I asked.

"My first move was to get down to his home, Tuxbury Old Park, near Bedford, and to see for myself how the ground lay. I wrote to the mother, therefore—I had had quite enough of the curmudgeon of a father—and I made a clean frontal attack: Godfrey was my chum, I had a great deal of interest which I might tell her of our common experiences, I should be in the neighbourhood, would there be any objection, et cetera? In reply I had quite an amiable answer from her and an offer to put me up for the night. That was what took me down on Monday.

"Tuxbury Old Hall is inaccessible—five miles from anywhere. There was no trap at the station, so I had to walk, carrying my suitcase, and it was nearly dark before I arrived. It is a great wandering house, standing in a considerable park. I should judge it was of all sorts of ages and styles, starting on a half-timbered Elizabethan foundation and ending in a Victorian portico. Inside it was all panelling and tapestry and half-effaced old pictures, a house of shadows and mystery. There was a butler, old Ralph, who seemed about the same age as the house, and there was his wife, who might have been older. She had been Godfrey's nurse, and I had heard him speak of her as second only to his mother in his affections, so I was drawn to her in spite of her queer appearance. The mother I liked also—a gentle little white mouse of a woman. It was only the colonel himself whom I barred.

"We had a bit of barney* right away, and I should have walked back to the station if I had not felt that it might be playing his game for me to do so. I was shown straight into his study, and there I found him, a huge, bow-backed man with a smoky skin and a straggling gray beard, seated behind his littered desk. A red-veined nose jutted out like a vulture's beak, and two fierce gray eyes glared at me from under tufted brows. I could understand now why Godfrey seldom spoke of his father.

---

*Quarrel.

" 'Well, sir,' said he in a rasping voice, 'I should be interested to know the real reasons for this visit.'

"I answered that I had explained them in my letter to his wife.

" 'Yes, yes, you said that you had known Godfrey in Africa. We have, of course, only your word for that.'

" 'I have his letters to me in my pocket.'

" 'Kindly let me see them.'

"He glanced at the two which I handed him, and then he tossed them back.

" 'Well, what then?' he asked.

" 'I was fond of your son Godfrey, sir. Many ties and memories united us. Is it not natural that I should wonder at his sudden silence and should wish to know what has become of him?'

" 'I have some recollections, sir, that I had already corresponded with you and had told you what had become of him. He has gone upon a voyage round the world. His health was in a poor way after his African experiences, and both his mother and I were of opinion that complete rest and change were needed. Kindly pass that explanation on to any other friends who may be interested in the matter.'

" 'Certainly,' I answered. 'But perhaps you would have the goodness to let me have the name of the steamer and of the line by which he sailed, together with the date. I have no doubt that I should be able to get a letter through to him.'

"My request seemed both to puzzle and to irritate my host. His great eyebrows came down over his eyes, and he tapped his fingers impatiently on the table. He looked up at last with the expression of one who has seen his adversary make a dangerous move at chess, and has decided how to meet it.

" 'Many people, Mr. Dodd,' said he, 'would take offence at your infernal pertinacity and would think that this insistence had reached the point of damned impertinence.'

" 'You must put it down, sir, to my real love for your son.'

" 'Exactly. I have already made every allowance upon that score. I must ask you, however, to drop these inquiries. Every family has its own inner knowledge and its own motives, which cannot always be made clear to outsiders, however well-intentioned. My wife is anxious to hear something of Godfrey's past which you are in a position to tell her, but I would ask you to let the present and the future alone. Such inquiries serve no useful purpose, sir, and place us in a delicate and difficult position.'

"So I came to a dead end, Mr. Holmes. There was no getting past it. I could only pretend to accept the situation and register a vow inwardly that I would never rest until my friend's fate had been cleared up. It was a dull evening. We dined quietly, the three of us, in a gloomy, faded old room. The lady questioned me eagerly about her son, but the old man seemed morose and depressed. I was so bored by the whole proceeding that I made an excuse as soon as I decently could and retired to my bedroom. It was a large, bare room on the ground floor, as gloomy as the rest of the house, but after a year of sleeping upon the veldt, Mr. Holmes, one is not too particular about one's quarters. I opened the curtains and looked out into the garden, remarking that it was a fine night with a bright half-moon. Then I sat down by the roaring fire with the lamp on a table beside me, and endeavoured to distract my mind with a novel. I was interrupted, however, by Ralph, the old butler, who came in with a fresh supply of coals.

" 'I thought you might run short in the night-time, sir. It is bitter weather and these rooms are cold.'

"He hesitated before leaving the room, and when I looked round he was standing facing me with a wistful look upon his wrinkled face.

" 'Beg your pardon, sir, but I could not help hearing what you said of young Master Godfrey at dinner. You know, sir, that my wife nursed him, and so I may say I am his foster-father. It's natural we should take an interest. And you say he carried himself well, sir?'

" 'There was no braver man in the regiment. He pulled me out once from under the rifles of the Boers, or maybe I should not be here.'

"The old butler rubbed his skinny hands.

" 'Yes, sir, yes, that is Master Godfrey all over. He was always courageous. There's not a tree in the park, sir, that he has not climbed. Nothing would stop him. He was a fine boy—and oh, sir, he was a fine man.'

"I sprang to my feet.

" 'Look here!' I cried. 'You say he *was*. You speak as if he were dead. What is all this mystery? What has become of Godfrey Emsworth?'

"I gripped the old man by the shoulder, but he shrank away.

" 'I don't know what you mean, sir. Ask the master about Master Godfrey. He knows. It is not for me to interfere.'

"He was leaving the room, but I held his arm.

" 'Listen,' I said. 'You are going to answer one question before you leave if I have to hold you all night. Is Godfrey dead?'

"He could not face my eyes. He was like a man hypnotized. The answer was dragged from his lips. It was a terrible and unexpected one.

" 'I wish to God he was!' he cried, and, tearing himself free, he dashed from the room.

"You will think, Mr. Holmes, that I returned to my chair in no very happy state of mind. The old man's words seemed to me to bear only one interpretation. Clearly my poor friend had become involved in some criminal or, at the least, disreputable transaction which touched the family honour. That stern old man had sent his son away and hidden him from the world lest some scandal should come to light. Godfrey was a reckless fellow. He was easily influenced by those around him. No doubt he had fallen into bad hands and been misled to his ruin. It was a piteous business, if it was indeed so, but even now it was my duty to hunt him out and see if I could aid him. I was anxiously pondering the matter when I looked up, and there was Godfrey Emsworth standing before me."

My client had paused as one in deep emotion.

"Pray continue," I said. "Your problem presents some very unusual features."

"He was outside the window, Mr. Holmes, with his face pressed against the glass. I have told you that I looked out at the night. When I did so I left the curtains partly open. His figure was framed in this gap. The window came down to the ground and I could see the whole length of it, but it was his face which held my gaze. He was deadly pale—never have I seen a man so white. I reckon ghosts may look like that; but his eyes met mine, and they were the eyes of a living man. He sprang back when he saw that I was looking at him, and he vanished into the darkness.

"There was something shocking about the man, Mr. Holmes. It wasn't merely that ghastly face glimmering as white as cheese in the darkness. It was more subtle than that—something slinking, something furtive, something guilty—something very unlike the frank, manly lad that I had known. It left a feeling of horror in my mind.

"But when a man has been soldiering for a year or two with brother Boer as a playmate, he keeps his nerve and acts quickly. Godfrey had hardly vanished before I was at the window. There was an awkward catch, and I was some little time before I could throw it up. Then I nipped through and ran down the garden path in the direction that I thought he might have taken.

"It was a long path and the light was not very good, but it seemed to me something was moving ahead of me. I ran on and called his name, but it was no use. When I got to the end of the path there were several others branching in different directions to various outhouses. I stood hesitating, and as I did so I heard distinctly the sound of a closing door. It was not behind me in the house, but ahead of me, somewhere in the darkness. That was enough, Mr. Holmes, to assure me that what I had seen was not a vision. Godfrey had run away from me, and he had shut a door behind him. Of that I was certain.

"There was nothing more I could do, and I spent an uneasy night turning the matter over in my mind and trying to find some theory which would cover the facts. Next day I found the colonel rather more conciliatory, and as his wife remarked that there were some places of interest in the neighbourhood, it gave me an opening to ask whether my presence for one more night would incommode them. A somewhat grudging acquiescence from the old man gave me a clear day in which to make my observations. I was already perfectly convinced that Godfrey was in hiding somewhere near, but where and why remained to be solved.

"The house was so large and so rambling that a regiment might be hid away in it and no one the wiser. If the secret lay there it was difficult for me to penetrate it. But the door which I had heard close was certainly not in the house. I must explore the garden and see what I could find. There was no difficulty in the way, for the old people were busy in their own fashion and left me to my own devices.

"There were several small outhouses, but at the end of the garden there was a detached building of some size—large enough for a gardener's or a gamekeeper's residence. Could this be the place whence the sound of that shutting door had come? I approached it in a careless fashion as though I were strolling aimlessly round the grounds. As I did so, a small, brisk, bearded man in a black coat and bowler hat—not at all the gardener type—came out of the door. To my surprise, he locked it after him and put the key in his pocket. Then he looked at me with some surprise on his face.

" 'Are you a visitor here?' he asked.

"I explained that I was and that I was a friend of Godfrey's.

" 'What a pity that he should be away on his travels, for he would have so liked to see me,' I continued.

" 'Quite so. Exactly,' said he with a rather guilty air. 'No doubt you will renew your visit at some more propitious time.' He passed on, but when I turned I observed that he was standing watching me, half-concealed by the laurels at the far end of the garden.

"I had a good look at the little house as I passed it, but the windows were heavily curtained, and, so far as one could see, it was empty. I might spoil my own game and even be ordered off the premises if I were too audacious, for I was still conscious that I was being watched. Therefore, I strolled back to the house and waited for night before I went on with my inquiry. When all was dark and quiet I slipped out of my window and made my way as silently as possible to the mysterious lodge.

"I have said that it was heavily curtained, but now I found that the windows were shuttered as well. Some light, however, was breaking through one of them, so I concentrated my attention upon this. I was in luck, for the curtain had not been quite closed, and there was a crack in the shutter, so that I could see the inside of the room. It was a cheery place enough, a bright lamp and a blazing fire. Opposite to me was seated the little man whom I had seen in the morning. He was smoking a pipe and reading a paper."

"What paper?" I asked.

My client seemed annoyed at the interruption of his narrative.

"Can it matter?" he asked.

"It is most essential."

"I really took no notice."

"Possibly you observed whether it was a broad-leafed paper or of that smaller type which one associates with weeklies."

"Now that you mention it, it was not large. It might have been the *Spectator*. However, I had little thought to spare upon such details, for a second man was seated with his back to the window, and I could swear that this second man was Godfrey. I could not see his face, but I knew the familiar slope of his shoulders. He was leaning upon his elbow in an attitude of great melancholy, his body turned towards the fire. I was hesitating as to what I should do when there was a sharp tap on my shoulder, and there was Colonel Emsworth beside me.

" 'This way, sir!' said he in a low voice. He walked in silence to the house, and I followed him into my own bedroom. He had picked up a time-table in the hall.

" 'There is a train to London at 8:30,' said he. 'The trap will be at the door at eight.'

"He was white with rage, and, indeed, I felt myself in so difficult a position that I could only stammer out a few incoherent apologies in which I tried to excuse myself by urging my anxiety for my friend.

" 'The matter will not bear discussion,' said he abruptly. 'You have made a most damnable intrusion into the privacy of our family. You were here as a guest and you have become a spy. I have nothing more to say, sir, save that I have no wish ever to see you again.'

"At this I lost my temper, Mr. Holmes, and I spoke with some warmth.

" 'I have seen your son, and I am convinced that for some reason of your own you are concealing him from the world. I have no idea what your motives are in cutting him off in this fashion, but I am sure that he is no longer a free agent. I warn you, Colonel Emsworth, that until I am assured as to the safety and well-being of my friend I shall never desist in my efforts to get to the bottom of the mystery, and I shall certainly not allow myself to be intimidated by anything which you may say or do.'

"The old fellow looked diabolical, and I really thought he was about to attack me. I have said that he was a gaunt, fierce old giant, and though I am no weakling I might have been hard put to it to hold my own against him. However, after a long glare of rage he turned upon his heel and walked out of the room. For my part, I took the appointed train in the morning, with the full intention of coming straight to you and asking for your advice and assistance at the appointment for which I had already written."

Such was the problem which my visitor laid before me. It presented, as the astute reader will have already perceived, few difficulties in its solution, for a very limited choice of alternatives must get to the root of the matter. Still, elementary as it was, there were points of interest and novelty about it which may excuse my placing it upon record. I now proceeded, using my familiar method of logical analysis, to narrow down the possible solutions.

"The servants," I asked; "how many were in the house?"

"To the best of my belief there were only the old butler and his wife. They seemed to live in the simplest fashion."

"There was no servant, then, in the detached house?"

"None, unless the little man with the beard acted as such. He seemed, however, to be quite a superior person."

"That seems very suggestive. Had you any indication that food was conveyed from the one house to the other?"

"Now that you mention it, I did see old Ralph carrying a basket down the garden walk and going in the direction of this house. The idea of food did not occur to me at the moment."

"Did you make any local inquiries?"

"Yes, I did. I spoke to the station-master and also to the innkeeper in the village. I simply asked if they knew anything of my old comrade, Godfrey Emsworth. Both of them assured me that he had gone for a voyage round the world. He had come home and then had almost at once started off again. The story was evidently universally accepted."

"You said nothing of your suspicions?"

"Nothing."

"That was very wise. The matter should certainly be inquired into. I will go back with you to Tuxbury Old Park."

"To-day?"

It happened that at the moment I was clearing up the case which my friend Watson has described as that of the Abbey School, in which the Duke of Greyminster was so deeply involved. I had also a commission from the Sultan of Turkey which called for immediate action, as political consequences of the gravest kind might arise from its neglect. Therefore it was not until the beginning of the next week, as my diary records, that I was able to start forth on my mission to Bedfordshire in company with Mr. James M. Dodd. As we drove to Euston we picked up a grave and taciturn gentleman of iron-gray aspect, with whom I had made the necessary arrangements.

"This is an old friend," said I to Dodd. "It is possible that his presence may be entirely unnecessary, and, on the other hand, it may be essential. It is not necessary at the present stage to go further into the matter."

The narratives of Watson have accustomed the reader, no doubt, to the fact that I do not waste words or disclose my thoughts while a case is actually under consideration. Dodd seemed surprised, but nothing more was said, and the three of us continued our journey together. In the train I asked Dodd one more question which I wished our companion to hear.

"You say that you saw your friend's face quite clearly at the window, so clearly that you are sure of his identity?"

"I have no doubt about it whatever. His nose was pressed against the glass. The lamplight shone full upon him."

"It could not have been someone resembling him?"

"No, no, it was he."

"But you say he was changed?"

"Only in colour. His face was—how shall I describe it?—it was of a fish-belly-whiteness. It was bleached."

"Was it equally pale all over?"

"I think not. It was his brow which I saw so clearly as it was pressed against the window."

"Did you call to him?"

"I was too startled and horrified for the moment. Then I pursued him, as I have told you, but without result."

My case was practically complete, and there was only one small incident needed to round it off. When, after a considerable drive, we arrived at the strange old rambling house which my client had described, it was Ralph, the elderly butler, who opened the door. I had requisitioned the carriage for the day and had asked my elderly friend to remain within it unless we should summon him. Ralph, a little wrinkled old fellow, was in the conventional costume of black coat and pepper-and-salt trousers, with only one curious variant. He wore brown leather gloves, which at sight of us he instantly shuffled off, laying them down on the hall-table as we passed in. I have, as my friend Watson may have remarked, an abnormally acute set of senses, and a faint but incisive scent was apparent. It seemed to centre on the hall-table. I turned, placed my hat there, knocked it off, stooped to pick it up, and contrived to bring my nose within a foot of the gloves. Yes, it was undoubtedly from them that the curious tarry odour was oozing. I passed on into the study with my case complete. Alas, that I should have to show my hand so when I tell my own story! It was by concealing such links in the chain that Watson was enabled to produce his meretricious finales.

Colonel Emsworth was not in his room, but he came quickly enough on receipt of Ralph's message. We heard his quick, heavy step in the passage. The door was flung open and he rushed in with bristling beard and twisted features, as terrible an old man as ever I have seen. He held our cards in his hand, and he tore them up and stamped on the fragments.

"Have I not told you, you infernal busybody, that you are warned off the premises? Never dare to show your damned face here again. If you enter again without my leave I shall be within my rights if I use violence. I'll shoot you, sir! By God, I will! As to you, sir," turning upon me, "I extend the same warning to you. I am familiar with your ignoble profession, but you must take your reputed talents to some other field. There is no opening for them here."

"I cannot leave here," said my client firmly, "until I hear from Godfrey's own lips that he is under no restraint."

Our involuntary host rang the bell.

"Ralph," he said, "telephone down to the county police and ask the inspector to send up two constables. Tell him there are burglars in the house."

"One moment," said I. "You must be aware, Mr. Dodd, that Colonel Emsworth is within his rights and that we have no legal status within his house. On the other hand, he should recognize that your action is prompted entirely by solicitude for his son. I venture to hope that if I were allowed to have five minutes' conversation with Colonel Emsworth I could certainly alter his view of the matter."

"I am not so easily altered," said the old soldier. "Ralph, do what I have told you. What the devil are you waiting for? Ring up the police!"

"Nothing of the sort," I said, putting my back to the door. "Any police interference would bring about the very catastrophe which you dread." I took out my notebook and scribbled one word upon a loose sheet. "That," said I as I handed it to Colonel Emsworth, "is what has brought us here."

He stared at the writing with a face from which every expression save amazement had vanished.

"How do you know?" he gasped, sitting down heavily in his chair.

"It is my business to know things. That is my trade."

He sat in deep thought, his gaunt hand tugging at his straggling beard. Then he made a gesture of resignation.

"Well, if you wish to see Godfrey, you shall. It is no doing of mine, but you have forced my hand. Ralph, tell Mr. Godfrey and Mr. Kent that in five minutes we shall be with them."

At the end of that time we passed down the garden path and found ourselves in front of the mystery house at the end. A small bearded man stood at the door with a look of considerable astonishment upon his face.

"This is very sudden, Colonel Emsworth," said he. "This will disarrange all our plans."

"I can't help it, Mr. Kent. Our hands have been forced. Can Mr. Godfrey see us?"

"Yes, he is waiting inside." He turned and led us into a large, plainly furnished front room. A man was standing with his back to the fire, and at the sight of him my client sprang forward with outstretched hand.

"Why, Godfrey, old man, this is fine!"

But the other waved him back.

"Don't touch me, Jimmie. Keep your distance. Yes, you may well stare! I don't quite look the smart Lance-Corporal Emsworth, of B Squadron, do I?"

His appearance was certainly extraordinary. One could see that he had indeed been a handsome man with clear-cut features sunburned by an African sun, but mottled in patches over this darker surface were curious whitish patches which had bleached his skin.

"That's why I don't court visitors," said he. "I don't mind you, Jimmie, but I could have done without your friend. I suppose there is some good reason for it, but you have me at a disadvantage."

"I wanted to be sure that all was well with you, Godfrey. I saw you that night when you looked into my window, and I could not let the matter rest till I had cleared things up."

"Old Ralph told me you were there, and I couldn't help taking a peep at you. I hoped you would not have seen me, and I had to run to my burrow when I heard the window go up."

"But what in heaven's name is the matter?"

"Well, it's not a long story to tell," said he, lighting a cigarette. "You remember that morning fight at Buffelsspruit, outside Pretoria, on the Eastern railway line? You heard I was hit?"

"Yes, I heard that but I never got particulars."

"Three of us got separated from the others. It was very broken country, you may remember. There was Simpson—the fellow we called Baldy Simpson—and Anderson, and I. We were clearing brother Boer, but he lay low and got the three of us. The other two were killed. I got an elephant bullet through my shoulder. I stuck on to my horse, however, and he galloped several miles before I fainted and rolled off the saddle.

"When I came to myself it was nightfall, and I raised myself up, feeling very weak and ill. To my surprise there was a house close beside me, a fairly large house with a broad *stoep** and many windows. It was deadly cold. You remember the kind of numb cold which used to come at evening, a deadly, sickening sort of cold, very different from a crisp healthy frost. Well, I was chilled to the bone, and my only hope seemed to lie in reaching that house. I staggered to my feet and dragged myself along, hardly conscious of what I did. I have a dim memory of slowly ascending the steps, entering a wide-opened door, passing into a large room which contained several beds, and throwing myself down with a gasp of satisfaction upon one of them. It was unmade, but that troubled me not at all. I drew the clothes over my shivering body and in a moment I was in a deep sleep.

"It was morning when I wakened, and it seemed to me that instead of coming out into a world of sanity I had emerged into some extraordinary nightmare. The African sun flooded through the big, curtainless windows, and every detail of the great, bare, whitewashed dormitory stood out hard and clear. In front of me was standing a small, dwarf-like man with a huge, bulbous head, who was jabbering excitedly in Dutch, waving two horrible hands which looked to me like brown sponges. Behind him stood a group of people who seemed to be intensely amused by the situation, but a chill came over me as I looked at them. Not one of them was a normal human being. Every one was twisted or swollen or disfigured in some strange way. The laughter of these strange monstrosities was a dreadful thing to hear.

"It seemed that none of them could speak English, but the situation wanted clearing up, for the creature with the big head was growing furiously angry, and, uttering wild-beast cries, he had laid his deformed hands upon me and was dragging me out of bed, regardless of the fresh flow of blood from my wound. The little monster was as strong as a bull, and I don't know what he might have done to me had not an elderly man who was clearly in authority been attracted to the room by the hubbub. He said a few stern words in Dutch, and my persecutor shrank away. Then he turned upon me, gazing at me in the utmost amazement.

" 'How in the world did you come here?' he asked in amazement. 'Wait a bit! I see that you are tired out and that wounded shoulder of yours wants looking after. I am a doctor, and I'll soon have you tied up. But, man alive! you are in far greater danger here than ever you were on the battlefield. You are in the Leper Hospital, and you have slept in a leper's bed.'

"Need I tell you more, Jimmie? It seems that in view of the approaching battle all these poor creatures had been evacuated the day before. Then, as the British advanced, they had been brought back by this, their medical superintendent, who assured me that, though he believed he was immune to the disease, he would none the less never have dared to do what I had done. He put me in a private room, treated me kindly, and within a week or so I was removed to the general hospital at Pretoria.

---

*South African Dutch for veranda.

"So there you have my tragedy. I hoped against hope, but it was not until I had reached home that the terrible signs which you see upon my face told me that I had not escaped. What was I to do? I was in this lonely house. We had two servants whom we could utterly trust. There was a house where I could live. Under pledge of secrecy, Mr. Kent, who is a surgeon, was prepared to stay with me. It seemed simple enough on those lines. The alternative was a dreadful one—segregation for life among strangers with never a hope of release. But absolute secrecy was necessary, or even in this quiet countryside there would have been an outcry, and I should have been dragged to my horrible doom. Even you, Jimmie—even you had to be kept in the dark. Why my father has relented I cannot imagine."

Colonel Emsworth pointed to me.

"This is the gentleman who forced my hand." He unfolded the scrap of paper on which I had written the word "Leprosy." "It seemed to me that if he knew so much as that it was safer that he should know all."

"And so it was," said I. "Who knows but good may come of it? I understand that only Mr. Kent has seen the patient. May I ask, sir, if you are an authority on such complaints, which are, I understand, tropical or semi-tropical in their nature?"

"I have the ordinary knowledge of the educated medical man," he observed with some stiffness.

"I have no doubt, sir, that you are fully competent, but I am sure that you will agree that in such a case a second opinion is valuable. You have avoided this, I understand, for fear that pressure should be put upon you to segregate the patient."

"That is so," said Colonel Emsworth.

"I foresaw this situation," I explained, "and I have brought with me a friend whose discretion may absolutely be trusted. I was able once to do him a professional service, and he is ready to advise as a friend rather than as a specialist. His name is Sir James Saunders."

The prospect of an interview with Lord Roberts would not have excited greater wonder and pleasure in a raw subaltern than was now reflected upon the face of Mr. Kent.

"I shall indeed be proud," he murmured.

"Then I will ask Sir James to step this way. He is at present in the carriage outside the door. Meanwhile, Colonel Emsworth, we may perhaps assemble in your study, where I could give the necessary explanations."

And here it is that I miss my Watson. By cunning questions and ejaculations of wonder he could elevate my simple art, which is but systematized common sense, into a prodigy. When I tell my own story I have no such aid. And yet I will give my process of thought even as I gave it to my small audience, which included Godfrey's mother in the study of Colonel Emsworth.

"That process," said I, "starts upon the supposition that when you have eliminated all which is impossible, then whatever remains, however improbable, must be the truth. It may well be that several explanations remain, in which case one tries test after test until one or other of them has a convincing amount of support. We will now apply this principle to the case in point. As it was first presented to me, there were three possible explanations of the seclusion or incarceration of this gentleman in an outhouse of his father's mansion. There was the explanation that he was in hiding for a crime, or that he was mad and that they wished to avoid an asylum, or that he had some disease which caused his segregation. I could think of no other adequate solutions. These, then, had to be sifted and balanced against each other.

"The criminal solution would not bear inspection. No unsolved crime had been reported from that district. I was sure of that. If it were some crime not yet discovered, then clearly it would be to the interest of the family to get rid of the delinquent and send him abroad rather than keep him concealed at home. I could see no explanation for such a line of conduct.

"Insanity was more plausible. The presence of the second person in the outhouse suggested a keeper. The fact that he locked the door when he came out strengthened the supposition and gave the idea of constraint. On the other hand, this constraint could not be severe or the young man could not have got loose and come down to have a look at his friend. You will remember, Mr. Dodd, that I felt round for points, asking you, for example, about the paper which Mr. Kent was reading. Had it been the *Lancet* or the *British Medical Journal* it would have helped me. It is not illegal, however, to keep a lunatic upon private premises so long as there is a qualified person in attendance and that the authorities have been duly notified. Why, then, all this desperate desire for secrecy? Once again I could not get the theory to fit the facts.

"There remained the third possibility, into which, rare and unlikely as it was, everything seemed to fit. Leprosy is not uncommon in South Africa. By some extraordinary chance this youth might have contracted it. His people would be placed in a very dreadful position, since they would desire to save him from segregation. Great secrecy would be needed to prevent rumours from getting about and subsequent interference by the authorities. A devoted medical man, if sufficiently paid, would easily be found to take charge of the sufferer. There would be no reason why the latter should not be allowed freedom after dark. Bleaching of the skin is a common result of the disease. The case was a strong one—so strong that I determined to act as if it were actually proved. When on arriving here I noticed that Ralph, who carries out the meals, had gloves which are impregnated with disinfectants, my last doubts were removed. A single word showed you, sir, that your secret was discovered, and if I wrote rather than said it, it was to prove to you that my discretion was to be trusted."

I was finishing this little analysis of the case when the door was opened and the austere figure of the great dermatologist was ushered in. But for once his sphinx-like features had relaxed and there was a warm humanity in his eyes. He strode up to Colonel Emsworth and shook him by the hand.

"It is often my lot to bring ill-tidings and seldom good," said he. "This occasion is the more welcome. It is not leprosy."

"What?"

"A well-marked case of pseudo-leprosy or ichthyosis, a scale-like affection of the skin, unsightly, obstinate, but possibly curable, and certainly noninfective. Yes, Mr. Holmes, the coincidence is a remarkable one. But is it coincidence? Are there not subtle forces at work of which we know little? Are we assured that the apprehension from which this young man has no doubt suffered terribly since his exposure to its contagion may not produce a physical effect which simulates that which it fears? At any rate, I pledge my professional reputation—— But the lady has fainted! I think that Mr. Kent had better be with her until she recovers from this joyous shock."

THE ADVENTURE OF THE
MAZARIN STONE

It was pleasant to Dr. Watson to find himself once more in the untidy room of the first floor in Baker Street which had been the starting-point of so many remarkable adventures. He looked round him at the scientific charts upon the wall, the acid-charred bench of chemicals, the violin-case leaning in the corner, the coal-scuttle, which contained of old the pipes and tobacco. Finally, his eyes came round to the fresh and smiling face of Billy, the young but very wise and tactful page, who had helped a little to fill up the gap of loneliness and isolation which surrounded the saturnine figure of the great detective.

"It all seems very unchanged, Billy. You don't change, either. I hope the same can be said of him?"

Billy glanced with some solicitude at the closed door of the bedroom.

"I think he's in bed and asleep," he said.

It was seven in the evening of a lovely summer's day, but Dr. Watson was sufficiently familiar with the irregularity of his old friend's hours to feel no surprise at the idea.

"That means a case, I suppose?"

"Yes, sir, he is very hard at it just now. I'm frightened for his health. He gets paler and thinner, and he eats nothing. 'When will you be pleased to dine, Mr. Holmes?' Mrs. Hudson asked. 'Seven-thirty, the day after to-morrow,' said he. You know his way when he is keen on a case."

"Yes, Billy, I know."

"He's following someone. Yesterday he was out as a workman looking for a job. To-day he was an old woman. Fairly took me in, he did, and I ought to know his ways by now." Billy pointed with a grin to a very baggy parasol which leaned against the sofa. "That's part of the old woman's outfit," he said.

"But what is it all about, Billy?"

Billy sank his voice, as one who discusses great secrets of State. "I don't mind telling you, sir, but it should go no farther. It's this case of the Crown diamond."

"What—the hundred-thousand-pound burglary?"

"Yes, sir. They must get it back, sir. Why, we had the Prime Minister and the Home Secretary both sitting on that very sofa. Mr. Holmes was very nice to them. He soon put them at their ease and promised he would do all he could. Then there is Lord Cantlemere——"

"Ah!"

"Yes, sir, you know what that means. He's a stiff'un, sir, if I may say so. I can get along with the Prime Minister, and I've nothing against the Home Secretary, who seemed a civil, obliging sort of man, but I can't stand his Lordship. Neither can Mr. Holmes, sir. You see, he don't believe in Mr. Holmes and he was against employing him. He'd *rather* he failed."

"And Mr. Holmes knows it?"

"Mr. Holmes always knows whatever there is to know."

"Well, we'll hope he won't fail and that Lord Cantlemere will be confounded. But I say, Billy, what is that curtain for across the window?"

"Mr. Holmes had it put up there three days ago. We've got something funny behind it."

Billy advanced and drew away the drapery which screened the alcove of the bow window.

Dr. Watson could not restrain a cry of amazement. There was a facsimile of his old friend, dressing-gown and all, the face turned three-quarters towards the window and downward, as though reading an invisible book, while the body was sunk deep in an armchair. Billy detached the head and held it in the air.

"We put it at different angles, so that it may seem more lifelike. I wouldn't dare touch it if the blind were not down. But when it's up you can see this from across the way."

"We used something of the sort once before."*

"Before my time," said Billy. He drew the window curtains apart and looked out into the street. "There are folk who watch us from over yonder. I can see a fellow now at the window. Have a look for yourself."

Watson had taken a step forward when the bedroom door opened, and the long, thin form of Holmes emerged, his face pale and drawn, but his step and bearing as active as ever. With a single spring he was at the window, and had drawn the blind once more.

"That will do, Billy," said he. "You were in danger of your life then, my boy, and I can't do without you just yet. Well, Watson, it is good to see you in your old quarters once again. You come at a critical moment."

"So I gather."

"You can go, Billy. That boy is a problem, Watson. How far am I justified in allowing him to be in danger?"

"Danger of what, Holmes?"

"Of sudden death. I'm expecting something this evening."

"Expecting what?"

"To be murdered, Watson."

"No, no, you are joking, Holmes!"

"Even my limited sense of humour could evolve a better joke than that. But we may be comfortable in the meantime, may we not? Is alcohol permitted? The gasogene† and cigars are in the old place. Let me see you once more in the customary armchair. You have not, I hope, learned to despise my pipe and my lamentable tobacco? It has to take the place of food these days."

"But why not eat?"

---

*See the first story in this volume, "The Adventure of the Empty House."

†Apparatus for carbonating water.

"Because the faculties become refined when you starve them. Why, surely, as a doctor, my dear Watson, you must admit that what your digestion gains in the way of blood supply is so much lost to the brain. I am a brain, Watson. The rest of me is a mere appendix. Therefore, it is the brain I must consider."

"But this danger, Holmes?"

"Ah, yes, in case it should come off, it would perhaps be as well that you should burden your memory with the name and address of the murderer. You can give it to Scotland Yard, with my love and a parting blessing. Sylvius is the name—Count Negretto Sylvius.[18] Write it down, man, write it down! 136 Moorside Gardens, N.W. Got it?"

Watson's honest face was twitching with anxiety. He knew only too well the immense risks taken by Holmes and was well aware that what he said was more likely to be under-statement than exaggeration. Watson was always the man of action, and he rose to the occasion.

"Count me in, Holmes. I have nothing to do for a day or two."

"Your morals don't improve, Watson. You have added fibbing to your other vices. You bear every sign of the busy medical man, with calls on him every hour."

"Not such important ones. But can't you have this fellow arrested?"

"Yes, Watson, I could. That's what worries him so."

"But why don't you?"

"Because I don't know where the diamond is."

"Ah! Billy told me—the missing Crown jewel!"

"Yes, the great yellow Mazarin stone.* I've cast my net and I have my fish. But I have not got the stone. What is the use of taking *them*? We can make the world a better place by laying them by the heels. But that is not what I am out for. It's the stone I want."

"And is this Count Sylvius one of your fish?"

"Yes, and he's a shark. He bites. The other is Sam Merton, the boxer. Not a bad fellow, Sam, but the Count has used him. Sam's not a shark. He is a great big silly bull-headed gudgeon. But he is flopping about in my net all the same."

"Where is this Count Sylvius?"

"I've been at his very elbow all the morning. You've seen me as an old lady, Watson. I was never more convincing. He actually picked up my parasol for me once. 'By your leave, madame,' said he—half-Italian, you know, and with the Southern graces of manner when in the mood, but a devil incarnate in the other mood. Life is full of whimsical happenings, Watson."

"It might have been tragedy."

"Well, perhaps it might. I followed him to old Straubenzee's workshop in the Minories. Straubenzee made the air-gun—a very pretty bit of work,

---

*Named for Cardinal Jules Mazarin (1602–1661), minister to Louis XIV of France.

as I understand, and I rather fancy it is in the opposite window at the present moment. Have you seen the dummy? Of course, Billy showed it to you. Well, it may get a bullet through its beautiful head at any moment. Ah, Billy, what is it?"

The boy had reappeared in the room with a card upon a tray. Holmes glanced at it with raised eyebrows and an amused smile.

"The man himself. I had hardly expected this. Grasp the nettle, Watson! A man of nerve. Possibly you have heard of his reputation as a shooter of big game. It would indeed be a triumphant ending to his excellent sporting record if he added me to his bag. This is a proof that he feels my toe very close behind his heel."

"Send for the police."

"I probably shall. But not just yet. Would you glance carefully out of the window, Watson, and see if anyone is hanging about in the street?"

Watson looked warily round the edge of the curtain.

"Yes, there is one rough fellow near the door."

"That will be Sam Merton—the faithful but rather fatuous Sam. Where is this gentleman, Billy?"

"In the waiting-room, sir."*

"Show him up when I ring."

"Yes, sir."

"If I am not in the room, show him in all the same."

"Yes, sir."

Watson waited until the door was closed, and then he turned earnestly to his companion.

"Look here, Holmes, this is simply impossible. This is a desperate man, who sticks at nothing. He may have come to murder you."

"I should not be surprised."

"I insist upon staying with you."

"You would be horribly in the way."

"In *his* way?"

"No, my dear fellow—in my way."

"Well, I can't possibly leave you."

"Yes, you can, Watson. And you will, for you have never failed to play the game. I am sure you will play it to the end. This man has come for his own purpose, but he may stay for mine." Holmes took out his notebook and scribbled a few lines. "Take a cab to Scotland Yard and give this to Youghal of the C. I. D. Come back with the police. The fellow's arrest will follow."

"I'll do that with joy."

"Before you return I may have just time enough to find out where the stone is." He touched the bell. "I think we will go out through the bedroom. This second exit is exceedingly useful. I rather want to see my

---

*This is the first time in all the stories that we hear of a waiting room at 221B Baker Street; or of the "second exit" on the this page.

shark without his seeing me, and I have, as you will remember, my own way of doing it."

It was, therefore, an empty room into which Billy, a minute later, ushered Count Sylvius. The famous game-shot, sportsman, and man-about-town was a big, swarthy fellow, with a formidable dark moustache shading a cruel, thin-lipped mouth, and surmounted by a long, curved nose like the beak of an eagle. He was well dressed, but his brilliant necktie, shining pin, and glittering rings were flamboyant in their effect. As the door closed behind him he looked round him with fierce, startled eyes, like one who suspects a trap at every turn. Then he gave a violent start as he saw the impassive head and the collar of the dressing-gown which projected above the armchair in the window. At first his expression was one of pure amazement. Then the light of a horrible hope gleamed in his dark, murderous eyes. He took one more glance round to see that there were no witnesses, and then, on tiptoe, his thick stick half raised, he approached the silent figure. He was crouching for his final spring and blow when a cool, sardonic voice greeted him from the open bedroom door:

"Don't break it, Count! Don't break it!"

The assassin staggered back, amazement in his convulsed face. For an instant he half raised his loaded cane once more, as if he would turn his violence from the effigy to the original; but there was something in that steady gray eye and mocking smile which caused his hand to sink to his side.

"It's a pretty little thing," said Holmes, advancing towards the image. "Tavernier, the French modeller, made it. He is as good at waxworks as your friend Straubenzee is at air-guns."

"Air-guns, sir! What do you mean?"

"Put your hat and stick on the side-table. Thank you! Pray take a seat. Would you care to put your revolver out also? Oh, very good, if you prefer to sit upon it. Your visit is really most opportune, for I wanted badly to have a few minutes' chat with you."

The Count scowled, with heavy, threatening eyebrows.

"I, too, wished to have some words with you, Holmes. That is why I am here. I won't deny that I intended to assault you just now."

Holmes swung his leg on the edge of the table.

"I rather gathered that you had some idea of the sort in your head," said he. "But why these personal attentions?"

"Because you have gone out of your way to annoy me. Because you have put your creatures upon my track."

"My creatures! I assure you no!"

"Nonsense! I have had them followed. Two can play at that game, Holmes."

"It is a small point, Count Sylvius, but perhaps you would kindly give me my prefix when you address me. You can understand that, with my routine of work, I should find myself on familiar terms with half the rogues' gallery, and you will agree that exceptions are invidious."

"Well, *Mr.* Holmes, then."

"Excellent! But I assure you you are mistaken about my alleged agents."

Count Sylvius laughed contemptuously.

"Other people can observe as well as you. Yesterday there was an old sporting man. To-day it was an elderly woman. They held me in view all day."

"Really, sir, you compliment me. Old Baron Dowson said the night before he was hanged that in my case what the law had gained the stage had lost. And now you give my little impersonations your kindly praise?"

"It was you—you yourself?"

Holmes shrugged his shoulders. "You can see in the corner the parasol which you so politely handed to me in the Minories before you began to suspect."

"If I had known, you might never——"

"Have seen this humble home again. I was well aware of it. We all have neglected opportunities to deplore. As it happens, you did not know, so here we are!"

The Count's knotted brows gathered more heavily over his menacing eyes. "What you say only makes the matter worse. It was not your agents but your play-acting, busybody self! You admit that you have dogged me. Why?"

"Come now, Count. You used to shoot lions in Algeria."

"Well?"

"But why?"

"Why? The sport—the excitement—the danger!"

"And, no doubt, to free the country from a pest?"

"Exactly!"

"My reasons in a nutshell!"

The Count sprang to his feet, and his hand involuntarily moved back to his hip-pocket.

"Sit down, sir, sit down! There was another, more practical, reason. I want that yellow diamond!"

Count Sylvius lay back in his chair with an evil smile.

"Upon my word!" said he.

"You knew that I was after you for that. The real reason why you are here to-night is to find out how much I know about the matter and how far my removal is absolutely essential. Well, I should say that, from your point of view, it *is* absolutely essential, for I know all about it, save only one thing, which you are about to tell me."

"Oh, indeed! And pray, what is this missing fact?"

"Where the Crown diamond now is."

The Count looked sharply at his companion. "Oh, you want to know that, do you? How the devil should I be able to tell you where it is?"

"You can, and you will."

"Indeed!"

"You can't bluff me, Count Sylvius." Holmes's eyes, as he gazed at him, contracted and lightened until they were like two menacing points of steel. "You are absolute plate-glass. I see to the very back of your mind."

"Then, of course, you see where the diamond is!"

Holmes clapped his hands with amusement, and then pointed a derisive finger. "Then you do know. You have admitted it!"

"I admit nothing."

"Now, Count, if you will be reasonable we can do business. If not, you will get hurt."

Count Sylvius threw up his eyes to the ceiling. "And you talk about bluff!" said he.

Holmes looked at him thoughtfully like a master chess-player who meditates his crowning move. Then he threw open the table drawer and drew out a squat notebook.

"Do you know what I keep in this book?"

"No, sir, I do not!"

"You!"

"Me!"

"Yes, sir, *you*! You are all here—every action of your vile and dangerous life."

"Damn you, Holmes!" cried the Count with blazing eyes. "There are limits to my patience!"

"It's all here, Count. The real facts as to the death of old Mrs. Harold, who left you the Blymer estate, which you so rapidly gambled away."

"You are dreaming!"

"And the complete life history of Miss Minnie Warrender."

"Tut! You will make nothing of that!"

"Plenty more here, Count. Here is the robbery in the train de-luxe to the Riviera on February 13, 1892. Here is the forged check in the same year on the Crédit Lyonnais."

"No; you're wrong there."

"Then I am right on the others! Now, Count, you are a card-player. When the other fellow has all the trumps, it saves time to throw down your hand."

"What has all this talk to do with the jewel of which you spoke?"

"Gently, Count. Restrain that eager mind! Let me get to the points in my own humdrum fashion. I have all this against you; but, above all, I have a clear case against both you and your fighting bully in the case of the Crown diamond."

"Indeed!"

"I have the cabman who took you to Whitehall and the cabman who brought you away. I have the commissionaire who saw you near the case. I have Ikey Sanders, who refused to cut it up for you. Ikey has peached,* and the game is up."

The veins stood out on the Count's forehead. His dark, hairy hands

---

*Squealed, ratted on.

were clenched in a convulsion of restrained emotion. He tried to speak, but the words would not shape themselves.

"That's the hand I play from," said Holmes. "I put it all upon the table. But one card is missing. It's the king of diamonds. I don't know where the stone is."

"You never shall know."

"No? Now, be reasonable, Count. Consider the situation. You are going to be locked up for twenty years. So is Sam Merton. What good are you going to get out of your diamond? None in the world. But if you hand it over—well, I'll compound a felony. We don't want you or Sam. We want the stone. Give that up, and so far as I am concerned you can go free so long as you behave yourself in the future. If you make another slip—well, it will be the last. But this time my commission is to get the stone, not you."

"But if I refuse?"

"Why, then—alas!—it must be you and not the stone."

Billy had appeared in answer to a ring.

"I think, Count, that it would be as well to have your friend Sam at this conference. After all, his interests should be represented. Billy, you will see a large and ugly gentleman outside the front door. Ask him to come up."

"If he won't come, sir?"

"No violence, Billy. Don't be rough with him. If you tell him that Count Sylvius wants him he will certainly come."

"What are you going to do now?" asked the Count as Billy disappeared.

"My friend Watson was with me just now. I told him that I had a shark and a gudgeon in my net; now I am drawing the net and up they come together."

The Count had risen from his chair, and his hand was behind his back. Holmes held something half protruding from the pocket of his dressing-gown.

"You won't die in your bed, Holmes."

"I have often had the same idea. Does it matter very much? After all, Count, your own exit is more likely to be perpendicular than horizontal. But these anticipations of the future are morbid. Why not give ourselves up to the unrestrained enjoyment of the present?"

A sudden wild-beast light sprang up in the dark, menacing eyes of the master criminal. Holmes's figure seemed to grow taller as he grew tense and ready.

"It is no use your fingering your revolver, my friend," he said in a quiet voice. "You know perfectly well that you dare not use it, even if I gave you time to draw it. Nasty, noisy things, revolvers, Count. Better stick to air-guns. Ah! I think I hear the fairy footstep of your estimable partner. Good day, Mr. Merton. Rather dull in the street, is it not?"

The prize-fighter, a heavily built young man with a stupid, obstinate, slab-sided face, stood awkwardly at the door, looking about him with a puzzled expression. Holmes's debonair manner was a new experience, and though he vaguely felt that it was hostile, he did not know how to counter it. He turned to his more astute comrade for help.

"What's the game now, Count? What's this fellow want? What's up?" His voice was deep and raucous.

The Count shrugged his shoulders, and it was Holmes who answered.

"If I may put it in a nutshell, Mr. Merton, I should say it was *all* up."

The boxer still addressed his remarks to his associate.

"Is this cove trying to be funny, or what? I'm not in the funny mood myself."

"No, I expect not," said Holmes. "I think I can promise you that you will feel even less humorous as the evening advances. Now, look here, Count Sylvius. I'm a busy man and I can't waste time. I'm going into that bedroom. Pray make yourselves quite at home in my absence. You can explain to your friend how the matter lies without the restraint of my presence. I shall try over the Hoffman 'Barcarole'* upon my violin. In five minutes I shall return for your final answer. You quite grasp the alternative, do you not? Shall we take you, or shall we have the stone?"

Holmes withdrew, picking up his violin from the corner as he passed. A few moments later the long-drawn, wailing notes of that most haunting of tunes[19] came faintly through the closed door of the bedroom.

"What is it, then?" asked Merton anxiously as his companion turned to him. "Does he know about the stone?"

"He knows a damned sight too much about it. I'm not sure that he doesn't know all about it."

"Good Lord!" The boxer's sallow face turned a shade whiter.

"Ikey Sanders has split on us."

"He has, has he? I'll do him down a thick 'un for that if I swing for it."

"That won't help us much. We've got to make up our minds what to do."

"Half a mo'," said the boxer, looking suspiciously at the bedroom door. "He's a leary cove† that wants watching. I suppose he's not listening?"

"How can he be listening with that music going?"

"That's right. Maybe somebody's behind a curtain. Too many curtains in this room." As he looked round he suddenly saw for the first time the effigy in the window, and stood staring and pointing, too amazed for words.

"Tut! it's only a dummy," said the Count.

"A fake, is it? Well, strike me! Madame Tussaud ain't in it. It's the living spit of him, gown and all. But them curtains, Count!"

"Oh, confound the curtains! We are wasting our time, and there is none too much. He can lag us over this stone."

---

*Boatman's song from *Tales of Hoffman*, by Jacques Offenbach (1819–1880).
†Sly fellow.

"The deuce he can!"

"But he'll let us slip if we only tell him where the swag is."

"What! Give it up? Give up a hundred thousand quid?"

"It's one or the other."

Merton scratched his short-cropped pate.

"He's alone in there. Let's do him in. If his light were out we should have nothing to fear."

The Count shook his head.

"He is armed and ready. If we shot him we could hardly get away in a place like this. Besides, it's likely enough that the police know whatever evidence he has got. Hallo! What was that?"

There was a vague sound which seemed to come from the window. Both men sprang round, but all was quiet. Save for the one strange figure seated in the chair, the room was certainly empty.

"Something in the street," said Merton. "Now, look here, guv'nor, you've got the brains. Surely you can think a way out of it. If slugging is no use then it's up to you."

"I've fooled better men than he," the Count answered. "The stone is here in my secret pocket. I take no chances leaving it about. It can be out of England to-night and cut into four pieces in Amsterdam before Sunday. He knows nothing of Van Seddar."

"I thought Van Seddar was going next week."

"He *was*. But now he must get off by the next boat. One or other of us must slip round with the stone to Lime Street and tell him."

"But the false bottom ain't ready."

"Well, he must take it as it is and chance it. There's not a moment to lose." Again, with the sense of danger which becomes an instinct with the sportsman, he paused and looked hard at the window. Yes, it was surely from the street that the faint sound had come.

"As to Holmes," he continued, "we can fool him easily enough. You see, the damned fool won't arrest us if he can get the stone. Well, we'll promise him the stone. We'll put him on the wrong track about it, and before he finds that it *is* the wrong track it will be in Holland and we out of the country."

"That sounds good to me!" cried Sam Merton with a grin.

"You go on and tell the Dutchman to get a move on him. I'll see this sucker and fill him up with a bogus confession. I'll tell him that the stone is in Liverpool. Confound that whining music; it gets on my nerves! By the time he finds it isn't in Liverpool it will be in quarters and we on the blue water. Come back here, out of a line with that keyhole. Here is the stone."

"I wonder you dare carry it."

"Where could I have it safer? If we could take it out of Whitehall someone else could surely take it out of my lodgings."

"Let's have a look at it."

Count Sylvius cast a somewhat unflattering glance at his associate and disregarded the unwashed hand which was extended towards him.

"What—d'ye think I'm going to snatch it off you? See here, mister, I'm getting a bit tired of your ways."

"Well, well, no offence, Sam. We can't afford to quarrel. Come over to the window if you want to see the beauty properly. Now hold it to the light! Here!"

"Thank you!"

With a single spring Holmes had leaped from the dummy's chair and had grasped the precious jewel. He held it now in one hand, while his other pointed a revolver at the Count's head. The two villains staggered back in utter amazement. Before they had recovered Holmes had pressed the electric bell.

"No violence, gentlemen—no violence, I beg of you! Consider the furniture! It must be very clear to you that your position is an impossible one. The police are waiting below."

The Count's bewilderment overmastered his rage and fear.

"But how the deuce——?" he gasped.

"Your surprise is very natural. You are not aware that a second door from my bedroom leads behind that curtain. I fancied that you must have heard me when I displaced the figure, but luck was on my side. It gave me a chance of listening to your racy conversation which would have been painfully constrained had you been aware of my presence."

The Count gave a gesture of resignation.

"We give you best, Holmes. I believe you are the devil himself."

"Not far from him, at any rate," Holmes answered with a polite smile.

Sam Merton's slow intellect had only gradually appreciated the situation. Now, as the sound of heavy steps came from the stairs outside, he broke silence at last.

"A fair cop!" said he. "But, I say, what about that bloomin' fiddle! I hear it yet."

"Tut, tut!" Holmes answered. "You are perfectly right. Let it play! These modern gramophones are a remarkable invention."

There was an inrush of police, the handcuffs clicked and the criminals were led to the waiting cab. Watson lingered with Holmes, congratulating him upon this fresh leaf added to his laurels. Once more their conversation was interrupted by the imperturbable Billy with his card-tray.

"Lord Cantlemere, sir."

"Show him up, Billy. This is the eminent peer who represents the very highest interests," said Holmes. "He is an excellent and loyal person, but rather of the old régime. Shall we make him unbend? Dare we venture upon a slight liberty? He knows, we may conjecture, nothing of what has occurred."

The door opened to admit a thin, austere figure with a hatchet face and drooping mid-Victorian whiskers of a glossy blackness which hardly corresponded with the rounded shoulders and feeble gait. Holmes advanced affably, and shook an unresponsive hand.

"How do you do, Lord Cantlemere? It is chilly for the time of year, but rather warm indoors. May I take your overcoat?"

"No, I thank you; I will not take it off."

Holmes laid his hand insistently upon the sleeve.

"Pray allow me! My friend Dr. Watson would assure you that these changes of temperature are most insidious."

His Lordship shook himself free with some impatience.

"I am quite comfortable, sir. I have no need to stay. I have simply looked in to know how your self-appointed task was progressing."

"It is difficult—very difficult."

"I feared that you would find it so."

There was a distinct sneer in the old courtier's words and manner.

"Every man finds his limitations, Mr. Holmes, but at least it cures us of the weakness of self-satisfaction."

"Yes, sir, I have been much perplexed."

"No doubt."

"Especially upon one point. Possibly you could help me upon it?"

"You apply for my advice rather late in the day. I thought that you had your own all-sufficient methods. Still, I am ready to help you."

"You see, Lord Cantlemere, we can no doubt frame a case against the actual thieves."

"When you have caught them."

"Exactly. But the question is—how shall we proceed against the receiver?"

"Is this not rather premature?"

"It is as well to have our plans ready. Now, what would you regard as final evidence against the receiver?"

"The actual possession of the stone."

"You would arrest him upon that?"

"Most undoubtedly."

Holmes seldom laughed, but he got as near it as his old friend Watson could remember.

"In that case, my dear sir, I shall be under the painful necessity of advising your arrest."

Lord Cantlemere was very angry. Some of the ancient fires flickered up into his sallow cheeks.

"You take a great liberty, Mr. Holmes. In fifty years of official life I cannot recall such a case. I am a busy man, sir, engaged upon important affairs, and I have no time or taste for foolish jokes. I may tell you frankly, sir, that I have never been a believer in your powers, and that I have always been of the opinion that the matter was far safer in the hands of the regular police force. Your conduct confirms all my conclusions. I have the honour, sir, to wish you good-evening."

Holmes had swiftly changed his position and was between the peer and the door.

"One moment, sir," said he. "To actually go off with the Mazarin stone would be a more serious offence than to be found in temporary possession of it."

"Sir, this is intolerable! Let me pass."

"Put your hand in the right-hand pocket of your overcoat."

"What do you mean, sir?"

"Come—come, do what I ask."

An instant later the amazed peer was standing, blinking and stammering, with the great yellow stone on his shaking palm.

"What! What! How is this, Mr. Holmes?"

"Too bad, Lord Cantlemere, too bad!" cried Holmes. "My old friend here will tell you that I have an impish habit of practical joking. Also that I can never resist a dramatic situation. I took the liberty—the very great liberty, I admit—of putting the stone into your pocket at the beginning of our interview."

The old peer stared from the stone to the smiling face before him.

"Sir, I am bewildered. But—yes—it is indeed the Mazarin stone. We are greatly your debtors, Mr. Holmes. Your sense of humour may, as you admit, be somewhat perverted, and its exhibition remarkably untimely, but at least I withdraw any reflection I have made upon your amazing professional powers. But how——"

"The case is but half finished; the details can wait. No doubt, Lord Cantlemere, your pleasure in telling of this successful result in the exalted circle to which you return will be some small atonement for my practical joke. Billy, you will show his Lordship out, and tell Mrs. Hudson that I should be glad if she would send up dinner for two as soon as possible."

THE ADVENTURE OF THE
THREE GABLES

I don't think that any of my adventures with Mr. Sherlock Holmes opened quite so abruptly, or so dramatically, as that which I associate with The Three Gables. I had not seen Holmes for some days and had no idea of the new channel into which his activities had been directed. He was in a chatty mood that morning, however, and had just settled me into the well-worn low armchair on one side of the fire, while he had curled down with his pipe in his mouth upon the opposite chair, when our visitor arrived. If I had said that a mad bull had arrived it would give a clearer impression of what occurred.

The door had flown open and a huge negro had burst into the room. He would have been a comic figure if he had not been terrific, for he was dressed in a very loud gray check suit with a flowing salmon-coloured tie. His broad face and flattened nose were thrust forward, as his sullen dark eyes, with a smouldering gleam of malice in them, turned from one of us to the other.

"Which of you gen'l'men is Masser Holmes?" he asked.

Holmes raised his pipe with a languid smile.

"Oh! it's you, is it?" said our visitor, coming with an unpleasant, stealthy step round the angle of the table. "See here, Masser Holmes, you keep your hands out of other folks' business. Leave folks to manage their own affairs. Got that, Masser Holmes?"

"Keep on talking," said Holmes. "It's fine."

"Oh! it's fine, is it?" growled the savage. "It won't be so damn fine if I have to trim you up a bit. I've handled your kind before now, and they didn't look fine when I was through with them. Look at that, Masser Holmes!"

He swung a huge knotted lump of a fist under my friend's nose. Holmes examined it closely with an air of great interest. "Were you born so?" he asked. "Or did it come by degrees?"

It may have been the icy coolness of my friend, or it may have been the slight clatter which I made as I picked up the poker. In any case, our visitor's manner became less flamboyant.

"Well, I've given you fair warnin'," said he. "I've a friend that's interested out Harrow way—you know what I'm meaning—and he don't intend to have no buttin' in by you. Got that? You ain't the law, and I ain't the law either, and if you come in I'll be on hand also. Don't you forget it."

"I've wanted to meet you for some time," said Holmes. "I won't ask you to sit down, for I don't like the smell of you, but aren't you Steve Dixie, the bruiser?"

"That's my name, Masser Holmes, and you'll get put through it for sure if you give me any lip."

"It is certainly the last thing you need," said Holmes, staring at our visitor's hideous mouth. "But it was the killing of young Perkins outside the Holborn Bar——What! you're not going?"

The negro had sprung back, and his face was leaden. "I won't listen to no such talk," said he. "What have I to do with this 'ere Perkins, Masser Holmes? I was trainin' at the Bull Ring in Birmingham when this boy done gone get into trouble."

"Yes, you'll tell the magistrate about it, Steve,"* said Holmes. "I've been watching you and Barney Stockdale——"

"So help me the Lord! Masser Holmes——"

"That's enough. Get out of it. I'll pick you up when I want you."

"Good-mornin', Masser Holmes. I hope there ain't no hard feelin's about this 'ere visit?"

"There will be unless you tell me who sent you."

"Why, there ain't no secret about that, Masser Holmes. It was that same gen'l'man that you have just done gone mention."

"And who set him on to it?"

"S'elp me. I don't know, Masser Holmes. He just say, 'Steve, you go see Mr. Holmes, and tell him his life ain't safe if he go down Harrow way.' That's the whole truth." Without waiting for any further questioning, our visitor bolted out of the room almost as precipitately as he had entered. Holmes knocked out the ashes of his pipe with a quiet chuckle.

"I am glad you were not forced to break his woolly head, Watson. I observed your manœuvres with the poker. But he is really rather a harmless fellow, a great muscular, foolish, blustering baby, and easily cowed, as you have seen. He is one of the Spencer John gang and has taken part in some dirty work of late which I may clear up when I have time. His immediate principal, Barney, is a more astute person. They specialize in assaults, intimidation, and the like. What I want to know is, who is at the back of them on this particular occasion?"

"But why do they want to intimidate you?"

"It is this Harrow Weald case. It decides me to look into the matter, for if it is worth anyone's while to take so much trouble, there must be something in it."

"But what is it?"

"I was going to tell you when we had this comic interlude. Here is Mrs. Maberley's note. If you care to come with me we will wire her and go out at once."

DEAR MR. SHERLOCK HOLMES [I read]:

I have had a succession of strange incidents occur to me in connection with this house, and I should much value your advice. You would find me at home any time to-morrow. The house is within a

---

*This first-name address is very un-Holmesian, raising deep suspicions about the authorship of the story.

short walk of the Weald Station. I believe that my late husband, Mortimer Maberley, was one of your early clients.

> Yours faithfully,
> MARY MABERLEY.

The address was "The Three Gables, Harrow Weald."

"So that's that!" said Holmes. "And now, if you can spare the time, Watson, we will get upon our way."

A short railway journey, and a shorter drive, brought us to the house, a brick and timber villa, standing in its own acre of undeveloped grassland. Three small projections above the upper windows made a feeble attempt to justify its name. Behind was a grove of melancholy, half-grown pines, and the whole aspect of the place was poor and depressing. None the less, we found the house to be well furnished, and the lady who received us was a most engaging elderly person, who bore every mark of refinement and culture.

"I remember your husband well, madam," said Holmes, "though it is some years since he used my services in some trifling matter."

"Probably you would be more familiar with the name of my son Douglas."

Holmes looked at her with great interest.

"Dear me! Are you the mother of Douglas Maberley? I knew him slightly. But of course all London knew him. What a magnificent creature he was! Where is he now?"

"Dead, Mr. Holmes, dead! He was attaché at Rome, and he died there of pneumonia last month."

"I am sorry. One could not connect death with such a man. I have never known anyone so vitally alive. He lived intensely—every fibre of him!"

"Too intensely, Mr. Holmes. That was the ruin of him. You remember him as he was—debonair and splendid. You did not see the moody, morose, brooding creature into which he developed. His heart was broken. In a single month I seemed to see my gallant boy turn into a worn-out cynical man."

"A love affair—a woman?"

"Or a fiend. Well, it was not to talk of my poor lad that I asked you to come, Mr. Holmes."

"Dr. Watson and I are at your service."

"There have been some very strange happenings. I have been in this house more than a year now, and as I wished to lead a retired life I have seen little of my neighbours. Three days ago I had a call from a man who said that he was a house agent. He said that this house would exactly suit a client of his, and that if I would part with it money would be no object. It seemed to me very strange as there are several empty houses on the market which appear to be equally eligible, but naturally I was interested in what he said. I therefore named a price which was five hundred pounds more than I gave. He at once closed with the offer, but added that his client desired to buy the furniture as well and would I put a price upon it.

Some of this furniture is from my old home, and it is, as you see, very good, so that I named a good round sum. To this also he at once agreed. I had always wanted to travel, and the bargain was so good a one that it really seemed that I should be my own mistress for the rest of my life.

"Yesterday the man arrived with the agreement all drawn out. Luckily I showed it to Mr. Sutro, my lawyer, who lives in Harrow. He said to me, 'This is a very strange document. Are you aware that if you sign it you could not legally take *anything* out of the house—not even your own private possessions?' When the man came again in the evening I pointed this out, and I said that I meant only to sell the furniture.

" 'No, no, everything,' said he.

" 'But my clothes? My jewels?'

" 'Well, well, some concession might be made for your personal effects. But nothing shall go out of the house unchecked. My client is a very liberal man, but he has his fads and his own way of doing things. It is everything or nothing with him.'

" 'Then it must be nothing,' said I. And there the matter was left, but the whole thing seemed to me to be so unusual that I thought——"

Here we had a very extraordinary interruption.

Holmes raised his hand for silence. Then he strode across the room, flung open the door, and dragged in a great gaunt woman whom he had seized by the shoulder. She entered with ungainly struggle like some huge awkward chicken, torn, squawking, out of its coop.

"Leave me alone! What are you a-doin' of?" she screeched.

"Why, Susan, what is this?"

"Well, ma'am, I was comin' in to ask if the visitors was stayin' for lunch when this man jumped out at me."

"I have been listening to her for the last five minutes, but did not wish to interrupt your most interesting narrative. Just a little wheezy, Susan, are you not? You breathe too heavily for that kind of work."

Susan turned a sulky but amazed face upon her captor. "Who be you, anyhow, and what right have you a-pullin' me about like this?"

"It was merely that I wished to ask a question in your presence. Did you, Mrs. Maberley, mention to anyone that you were going to write to me and consult me?"

"No, Mr. Holmes, I did not."

"Who posted your letter?"

"Susan did."

"Exactly. Now, Susan, to whom was it that you wrote or sent a message to say that your mistress was asking advice from me?"

"It's a lie. I sent no message."

"Now, Susan, wheezy people may not live long, you know. It's a wicked thing to tell fibs. Whom did you tell?"

"Susan!" cried her mistress, "I believe you are a bad, treacherous woman. I remember now that I saw you speaking to someone over the hedge."

"That was my own business," said the woman sullenly.

"Suppose I tell you that it was Barney Stockdale to whom you spoke?" said Holmes.

"Well, if you know, what do you want to ask for?"

"I was not sure, but I know now. Well now, Susan, it will be worth ten pounds to you if you will tell me who is at the back of Barney."

"Someone that could lay down a thousand pounds for every ten you have in the world."

"So, a rich man? No; you smiled—a rich woman. Now we have got so far, you may as well give the name and earn the tenner."

"I'll see you in hell first."

"Oh, Susan! Language!"

"I am clearing out of here. I've had enough of you all. I'll send for my box to-morrow." She flounced for the door.

"Good-bye, Susan. Paregoric is the stuff.* ... Now," he continued, turning suddenly from lively to severe when the door had closed behind the flushed and angry woman, "this gang means business. Look how close they play the game. Your letter to me had the 10 P.M. postmark. And yet Susan passes the word to Barney. Barney has time to go to his employer and get instructions; he or she—I incline to the latter from Susan's grin when she thought I had blundered—forms a plan. Black Steve is called in, and I am warned off by eleven o'clock next morning. That's quick work, you know."

"But what do they want?"

"Yes, that's the question. Who had the house before you?"

"A retired sea captain called Ferguson."

"Anything remarkable about him?"

"Not that ever I heard of."

"I was wondering whether he could have buried something. Of course, when people bury treasure nowadays they do it in the Post-Office bank. But there are always some lunatics about. It would be a dull world without them. At first I thought of some buried valuable. But why, in that case, should they want your furniture? You don't happen to have a Raphael† or a first folio Shakespeare‡ without knowing it?"

"No, I don't think I have anything rarer than a Crown Derby tea-set."

"That would hardly justify all this mystery. Besides, why should they not openly state what they want? If they covet your tea-set, they can surely offer a price for it without buying you out, lock, stock, and barrel. No, as I read it, there is something which you do not know that you have, and which you would not give up if you did know."

---

*This snide comment to a social inferior is behavior inconceivable for a gentleman.

†Raphael Sanzio (1483–1520) was one of the great painters of the Italian High Renaissance.

‡The First Folio, the first collected edition of Shakespeare's works, was printed in 1623. It is extremely valuable.

"That is how I read it," said I.

"Dr. Watson agrees, so that settles it."*

"Well, Mr. Holmes, what can it be?"

"Let us see whether by this purely mental analysis we can get it to a finer point. You have been in this house a year."

"Nearly two."

"All the better. During this long period no one wants anything from you. Now suddenly within three or four days you have urgent demands. What would you gather from that?"

"It can only mean," said I, "that the object, whatever it may be, has only just come into the house."

"Settled once again," said Holmes. "Now, Mrs. Maberley, has any object just arrived?"

"No, I have bought nothing new this year."

"Indeed! That is very remarkable. Well, I think we had best let matters develop a little further until we have clearer data. Is that lawyer of yours a capable man?"

"Mr. Sutro is most capable."

"Have you another maid, or was the fair Susan, who has just banged your front door, alone?"

"I have a young girl."

"Try and get Sutro to spend a night or two in the house. You might possibly want protection."

"Against whom?"

"Who knows? The matter is certainly obscure. If I can't find what they are after, I must approach the matter from the other end and try to get at the principal. Did this house-agent man give any address?"

"Simply his card and occupation. Haines-Johnson, Auctioneer and Valuer."

"I don't think we shall find him in the directory. Honest business men don't conceal their place of business. Well, you will let me know any fresh development. I have taken up your case, and you may rely upon it that I shall see it through."

As we passed through the hall Holmes's eyes, which missed nothing, lighted upon several trunks and cases which were piled in a corner. The labels shone out upon them.

" 'Milano.' 'Lucerne.' These are from Italy."

"They are poor Douglas's things."

"You have not unpacked them? How long have you had them?"

"They arrived last week."

"But you said—why, surely this might be the missing link. How do we know that there is not something of value there?"

"There could not possibly be, Mr. Holmes. Poor Douglas had only his pay and a small annuity. What could he have of value?"

---

*Since when did Holmes ever need anyone else's opinion to settle a matter?

Holmes was lost in thought.

"Delay no longer, Mrs. Maberley," he said at last. "Have these things taken upstairs to your bedroom. Examine them as soon as possible and see what they contain. I will come to-morrow and hear your report."

It was quite evident that The Three Gables was under very close surveillance, for as we came round the high hedge at the end of the lane there was the negro prize-fighter standing in the shadow. We came on him quite suddenly, and a grim and menacing figure he looked in that lonely place. Holmes clapped his hand to his pocket.

"Lookin' for your gun, Masser Holmes?"

"No, for my scent-bottle, Steve."

"You are funny, Masser Holmes, ain't you?"

"It won't be funny for you, Steve, if I get after you. I gave you fair warning this morning."

"Well, Masser Holmes, I done gone think over what you said, and I don't want no more talk about that affair of Masser Perkins. S'pose I can help you, Masser Holmes, I will."

"Well, then, tell me who is behind you on this job."

"So help me the Lord! Masser Holmes, I told you the truth before. I don't know. My boss Barney gives me orders and that's all."

"Well, just bear in mind, Steve, that the lady in that house, and everything under that roof, is under my protection. Don't forget it."

"All right, Masser Holmes. I'll remember."

"I've got him thoroughly frightened for his own skin, Watson," Holmes remarked as we walked on. "I think he would double-cross his employer if he knew who he was. It was lucky I had some knowledge of the Spencer John crowd, and that Steve was one of them. Now, Watson, this is a case for Langdale Pike, and I am going to see him now. When I get back I may be clearer in the matter."

I saw no more of Holmes during the day, but I could well imagine how he spent it, for Langdale Pike was his human book of reference upon all matters of social scandal. This strange, languid creature spent his waking hours in the bow window of a St. James's Street club and was the receiving-station as well as the transmitter for all the gossip of the metropolis. He made, it was said, a four-figure income by the paragraphs which he contributed every week to the garbage papers which cater to an inquisitive public. If ever, far down in the turbid depths of London life, there was some strange swirl or eddy, it was marked with automatic exactness by this human dial upon the surface. Holmes discreetly helped Langdale to knowledge, and on occasion was helped in turn.

When I met my friend in his room early next morning, I was conscious from his bearing that all was well, but none the less a most unpleasant surprise was awaiting us. It took the shape of the following telegram:

Please come out at once. Client's house burgled in the night. Police in possession.

                                                                    SUTRO.

Holmes whistled. "The drama has come to a crisis, and quicker than I had expected. There is a great driving-power at the back of this business, Watson, which does not surprise me after what I have heard. This Sutro, of course, is her lawyer. I made a mistake, I fear, in not asking you to spend the night on guard. This fellow has clearly proved a broken reed.* Well, there is nothing for it but another journey to Harrow Weald."

We found The Three Gables a very different establishment to the orderly household of the previous day. A small group of idlers had assembled at the garden gate, while a couple of constables were examining the windows and the geranium beds. Within we met a gray old gentleman, who introduced himself as the lawyer, together with a bustling, rubicund inspector, who greeted Holmes as an old friend.

"Well, Mr. Holmes, no chance for you in this case, I'm afraid. Just a common, ordinary burglary, and well within the capacity of the poor old police. No experts need apply."

"I am sure the case is in very good hands," said Holmes. "Merely a common burglary, you say?"

"Quite so. We know pretty well who the men are and where to find them. It is that gang of Barney Stockdale, with the big nigger in it— they've been seen about here."

"Excellent! What did they get?"

"Well, they don't seem to have got much. Mrs. Maberley was chloroformed and the house was——Ah! here is the lady herself."

Our friend of yesterday, looking very pale and ill, had entered the room, leaning upon a little maidservant.

"You gave me good advice, Mr. Holmes," said she, smiling ruefully. "Alas, I did not take it! I did not wish to trouble Mr. Sutro, and so I was unprotected."

"I only heard of it this morning," the lawyer explained.

"Mr. Holmes advised me to have some friend in the house. I neglected his advice, and I have paid for it."

"You look wretchedly ill," said Holmes. "Perhaps you are hardly equal to telling me what occurred."

"It is all here," said the inspector, tapping a bulky notebook.

"Still, if the lady is not too exhausted——"

"There is really so little to tell. I have no doubt that wicked Susan had planned an entrance for them. They must have known the house to an inch. I was conscious for a moment of the chloroform rag which was thrust over my mouth, but I have no notion how long I may have been senseless. When I woke, one man was at the bedside and another was rising with a bundle in his hand from among my son's baggage, which was partially opened and littered over the floor. Before he could get away I sprang up and seized him."

---

*Reference to the Bible, Isaiah 36:6: "Thou trustest in the staff of this broken reed" (KJV).

"You took a big risk," said the inspector.

"I clung to him, but he shook me off, and the other may have struck me, for I can remember no more. Mary the maid heard the noise and began screaming out of the window. That brought the police, but the rascals had got away."

"What did they take?"

"Well, I don't think there is anything of value missing. I am sure there was nothing in my son's trunks."

"Did the men leave no clue?"

"There was one sheet of paper which I may have torn from the man that I grasped. It was lying all crumpled on the floor. It is in my son's handwriting."

"Which means that it is not of much use," said the inspector. "Now if it had been in the burglar's——"

"Exactly," said Holmes. "What rugged common sense! None the less, I should be curious to see it."

The inspector drew a folded sheet of foolscap from his pocketbook.

"I never pass anything, however trifling," said he with some pomposity. "That is my advice to you, Mr. Holmes. In twenty-five years' experience I have learned my lesson. There is always the chance of finger-marks or something."

Holmes inspected the sheet of paper.

"What do you make of it, Inspector?"

"Seems to be the end of some queer novel, so far as I can see."

"It may certainly prove to be the end of a queer tale," said Holmes. "You have noticed the number on the top of the page. It is two hundred and forty-five. Where are the odd two hundred and forty-four pages?"

"Well, I suppose the burglars got those. Much good may it do them!"

"It seems a queer thing to break into a house in order to steal such papers as that. Does it suggest anything to you, Inspector?"

"Yes, sir, it suggests that in their hurry the rascals just grabbed at what came first to hand. I wish them joy of what they got."

"Why should they go to my son's things?" asked Mrs. Maberley.

"Well, they found nothing valuable downstairs, so they tried their luck upstairs. That is how I read it. What do you make of it, Mr. Holmes?"

"I must think it over, Inspector. Come to the window, Watson." Then, as we stood together, he read over the fragment of paper. It began in the middle of a sentence and ran like this:

"... face bled considerably from the cuts and blows, but it was nothing to the bleeding of his heart as he saw that lovely face, the face for which he had been prepared to sacrifice his very life, looking out at his agony and humiliation. She smiled—yes, by Heaven! she smiled, like the heartless fiend she was, as he looked up at her. It was at that moment that love died and hate was born. Man must live for something. If it is not for your embrace, my lady, then it shall surely be for your undoing and my complete revenge."

"Queer grammar!" said Holmes with a smile as he handed the paper back to the inspector. "Did you notice how the 'he' suddenly changed to 'my'? The writer was so carried away by his own story that he imagined himself at the supreme moment to be the hero."

"It seemed mighty poor stuff," said the inspector as he replaced it in his book. "What! are you off, Mr. Holmes?"

"I don't think there is anything more for me to do now that the case is in such capable hands. By the way, Mrs. Maberley, did you say you wished to travel?"

"It has always been my dream, Mr. Holmes."

"Where would you like to go—Cairo, Madeira, the Riviera?"

"Oh, if I had the money I would go round the world."

"Quite so. Round the world. Well, good-morning. I may drop you a line in the evening." As we passed the window I caught a glimpse of the inspector's smile and shake of the head. "These clever fellows have always a touch of madness." That was what I read in the inspector's smile.

"Now, Watson, we are at the last lap of our little journey," said Holmes when we were back in the roar of central London once more. "I think we had best clear the matter up at once, and it would be well that you should come with me, for it is safer to have a witness when you are dealing with such a lady as Isadora Klein."

We had taken a cab and were speeding to some address in Grosvenor Square. Holmes had been sunk in thought, but he roused himself suddenly.

"By the way, Watson, I suppose you see it all clearly?"

"No, I can't say that I do. I only gather that we are going to see the lady who is behind all this mischief."

"Exactly! But does the name Isadora Klein convey nothing to you? She was, of course, *the* celebrated beauty. There was never a woman to touch her. She is pure Spanish, the real blood of the masterful Conquistadors, and her people have been leaders in Pernambuco for generations. She married the aged German sugar king, Klein, and presently found herself the richest as well as the most lovely widow upon earth. Then there was an interval of adventure when she pleased her own tastes. She had several lovers, and Douglas Maberley, one of the most striking men in London, was one of them. It was by all accounts more than an adventure with him. He was not a society butterfly but a strong, proud man who gave and expected all. But she is the '*belle dame sans merci*'[20] of fiction. When her caprice is satisfied the matter is ended, and if the other party in the matter can't take her word for it she knows how to bring it home to him."

"Then that was his own story——"

"Ah! you are piecing it together now. I hear that she is about to marry the young Duke of Lomond, who might almost be her son. His Grace's ma might overlook the age, but a big scandal would be a different matter, so it is imperative——Ah! here we are."

It was one of the finest corner-houses of the West End. A machine-like footman took up our cards and returned with word that the lady was not at home. "Then we shall wait until she is," said Holmes cheerfully.

The machine broke down.

"Not at home means not at home to *you*," said the footman.

"Good," Holmes answered. "That means that we shall not have to wait. Kindly give this note to your mistress."

He scribbled three or four words upon a sheet of his notebook, folded it, and handed it to the man.

"What did you say, Holmes?" I asked.

"I simply wrote: 'Shall it be the police, then?' I think that should pass us in."

It did—with amazing celerity. A minute later we were in an Arabian Nights drawing-room, vast and wonderful, in a half gloom, picked out with an occasional pink electric light. The lady had come, I felt, to that time of life when even the proudest beauty finds the half light more welcome. She rose from a settee as we entered: tall, queenly, a perfect figure, a lovely mask-like face, with two wonderful Spanish eyes which looked murder at us both.

"What is this intrusion—and this insulting message?" she asked, holding up the slip of paper.

"I need not explain, madame. I have too much respect for your intelligence to do so—though I confess that intelligence has been surprisingly at fault of late."

"How so, sir?"

"By supposing that your hired bullies could frighten me from my work. Surely no man would take up my profession if it were not that danger attracts him. It was you, then, who forced me to examine the case of young Maberley."

"I have no idea what you are talking about. What have I to do with hired bullies?"

Holmes turned away wearily.

"Yes, I have underrated your intelligence. Well, good-afternoon!"

"Stop! Where are you going?"

"To Scotland Yard."

We had not got halfway to the door before she had overtaken us and was holding his arm. She had turned in a moment from steel to velvet.

"Come and sit down, gentlemen. Let us talk this matter over. I feel that I may be frank with you, Mr. Holmes. You have the feelings of a gentleman. How quick a woman's instinct is to find it out. I will treat you as a friend."

"I cannot promise to reciprocate, madame. I am not the law, but I represent justice so far as my feeble powers* go. I am ready to listen, and then I will tell you how I will act."

"No doubt it was foolish of me to threaten a brave man like yourself."

---

*Not the sort of self-assessment we've ever heard from Holmes before.

"What was really foolish, madame, is that you have placed yourself in the power of a band of rascals who may blackmail or give you away."

"No, no! I am not so simple. Since I have promised to be frank, I may say that no one, save Barney Stockdale and Susan, his wife, have the least idea who their employer is. As to them, well, it is not the first——" She smiled and nodded with a charming coquettish intimacy.

"I see. You've tested them before."

"They are good hounds who run silent."

"Such hounds have a way sooner or later of biting the hand that feeds them. They will be arrested for this burglary. The police are already after them."

"They will take what comes to them. That is what they are paid for. I shall not appear in the matter."

"Unless I bring you into it."

"No, no, you would not. You are a gentleman. It is a woman's secret."

"In the first place, you must give back this manuscript."

She broke into a ripple of laughter and walked to the fireplace. There was a calcined mass which she broke up with the poker. "Shall I give this back?" she asked. So roguish and exquisite did she look as she stood before us with a challenging smile that I felt of all Holmes's criminals this was the one whom he would find it hardest to face. However, he was immune from sentiment.

"That seals your fate," he said coldly. "You are very prompt in your actions, madame, but you have overdone it on this occasion."

She threw the poker down with a clatter.

"How hard you are!" she cried. "May I tell you the whole story?"

"I fancy I could tell it to you."

"But you must look at it with my eyes, Mr. Holmes. You must realize it from the point of view of a woman who sees all her life's ambition about to be ruined at the last moment. Is such a woman to be blamed if she protects herself?"

"The original sin was yours."

"Yes, yes! I admit it. He was a dear boy, Douglas, but it so chanced that he could not fit into my plans. He wanted marriage—marriage, Mr. Holmes—with a penniless commoner. Nothing less would serve him. Then he became pertinacious. Because I had given he seemed to think that I still must give, and to him only. It was intolerable. At last I had to make him realize it."

"By hiring ruffians to beat him under your own window."

"You do indeed seem to know everything. Well, it is true. Barney and the boys drove him away, and were, I admit, a little rough in doing so. But what did he do then? Could I have believed that a gentleman would do such an act? He wrote a book in which he described his own story. I, of course, was the wolf; he the lamb. It was all there, under different names, of course; but who in all London would have failed to recognize it? What do you say to that, Mr. Holmes?"

"Well, he was within his rights."

"It was as if the air of Italy had got into his blood and brought with it the old cruel Italian spirit. He wrote to me and sent me a copy of his book that I might have the torture of anticipation. There were two copies, he said—one for me, one for his publisher."

"How did you know the publisher's had not reached him?"

"I knew who his publisher was. It is not his only novel, you know. I found out that he had not heard from Italy. Then came Douglas's sudden death. So long as that other manuscript was in the world there was no safety for me. Of course, it must be among his effects, and these would be returned to his mother. I set the gang at work. One of them got into the house as servant. I wanted to do the thing honestly. I really and truly did. I was ready to buy the house and everything in it. I offered any price she cared to ask. I only tried the other way when everything else had failed. Now, Mr. Holmes, granting that I was too hard on Douglas—and, God knows, I am sorry for it!—what else could I do with my whole future at stake?"

Sherlock Holmes shrugged his shoulders.

"Well, well," said he, "I suppose I shall have to compound a felony as usual. How much does it cost to go round the world in first-class style?"

The lady stared in amazement.

"Could it be done on five thousand pounds?"

"Well, I should think so, indeed!"

"Very good. I think you will sign me a check for that, and I will see that it comes to Mrs. Maberley. You owe her a little change of air. Meantime, lady"—he wagged a cautionary forefinger—"have a care! Have a care! You can't play with edged tools forever without cutting those dainty hands."

THE ADVENTURE OF THE
SUSSEX VAMPIRE

Holmes had read carefully a note which the last post had brought him. Then, with the dry chuckle which was his nearest approach to a laugh, he tossed it over to me.

"For a mixture of the modern and the mediæval, of the practical and of the wildly fanciful, I think this is surely the limit," said he. "What do you make of it, Watson?"

I read as follows:

46, OLD JEWRY,
Nov. 19th.

Re Vampires

SIR:

Our client, Mr. Robert Ferguson, of Ferguson and Muirhead, tea brokers, of Mincing Lane, has made some inquiry from us in a communication of even date concerning vampires. As our firm specializes entirely upon the assessment of machinery the matter hardly comes within our purview, and we have therefore recommended Mr. Ferguson to call upon you and lay the matter before you. We have not forgotten your successful action in the case of Matilda Briggs.

We are, sir,

Faithfully yours,
MORRISON, MORRISON, AND DODD.
per E. J. C.

"Matilda Briggs was not the name of a young woman, Watson," said Holmes in a reminiscent voice. "It was a ship which is associated with the giant rat of Sumatra, a story for which the world is not yet prepared. But what do we know about vampires? Does it come within our purview either? Anything is better than stagnation, but really we seem to have been switched on to a Grimms' fairy tale. Make a long arm, Watson, and see what V has to say."

I leaned back and took down the great index volume to which he referred. Holmes balanced it on his knee, and his eyes moved slowly and lovingly over the record of old cases, mixed with the accumulated information of a lifetime.

"Voyage of the *Gloria Scott*," he read. "That was a bad business. I have some recollection that you made a record of it, Watson, though I was unable to congratulate you upon the result. Victor Lynch, the forger. Venomous lizard or gila. Remarkable case, that! Vittoria, the circus belle. Vanderbilt and the Yeggman. Vipers. Vigor, the Hammersmith wonder.

Hullo! Hullo! Good old index. You can't beat it. Listen to this, Watson. Vampirism in Hungary. And again, Vampires in Transylvania." He turned over the pages with eagerness, but after a short intent perusal he threw down the great book with a snarl of disappointment.

"Rubbish, Watson, rubbish! What have we to do with walking corpses who can only be held in their grave by stakes driven through their hearts? It's pure lunacy."

"But surely," said I, "the vampire was not necessarily a dead man? A living person might have the habit. I have read, for example, of the old sucking the blood of the young in order to retain their youth."

"You are right, Watson. It mentions the legend in one of these references. But are we to give serious attention to such things? This agency* stands flat-footed upon the ground, and there it must remain. The world is big enough for us. No ghosts need apply. I fear that we cannot take Mr. Robert Ferguson very seriously. Possibly this note may be from him and may throw some light upon what is worrying him."

He took up a second letter which had lain unnoticed upon the table while he had been absorbed with the first. This he began to read with a smile of amusement upon his face which gradually faded away into an expression of intense interest and concentration. When he had finished he sat for some little time lost in thought with the letter dangling from his fingers. Finally, with a start, he aroused himself from his reverie.

"Cheeseman's, Lamberley. Where is Lamberley, Watson?"

"It is in Sussex, South of Horsham."

"Not very far, eh? And Cheeseman's?"

"I know that country, Holmes. It is full of old houses which are named after the men who built them centuries ago. You get Odley's and Harvey's and Carriton's—the folk are forgotten but their names live in their houses."

"Precisely," said Holmes coldly. It was one of the peculiarities of his proud, self-contained nature that though he docketed any fresh information very quietly and accurately in his brain, he seldom made any acknowledgment to the giver. "I rather fancy we shall know a good deal more about Cheeseman's, Lamberley, before we are through. The letter is, as I had hoped, from Robert Ferguson. By the way, he claims acquaintance with you."

"With me!"

"You had better read it."

He handed the letter across. It was headed with the address quoted.

DEAR MR. HOLMES [it said]:

I have been recommended to you by my lawyers, but indeed the matter is so extraordinarily delicate that it is most difficult to discuss. It concerns a friend for whom I am acting. This gentleman married

---

*Mentioned here and on p. 560 but nowhere else in the stories.

some five years ago a Peruvian lady, the daughter of a Peruvian merchant, whom he had met in connection with the importation of nitrates. The lady was very beautiful, but the fact of her foreign birth and of her alien religion always caused a separation of interests and of feelings between husband and wife, so that after a time his love may have cooled towards her and he may have come to regard their union as a mistake. He felt there were sides of her character which he could never explore or understand. This was the more painful as she was as loving a wife as a man could have—to all appearance absolutely devoted.

Now for the point which I will make more plain when we meet. Indeed, this note is merely to give you a general idea of the situation and to ascertain whether you would care to interest yourself in the matter. The lady began to show some curious traits quite alien to her ordinarily sweet and gentle disposition. The gentleman had been married twice and he had one son by the first wife. This boy was now fifteen, a very charming and affectionate youth, though unhappily injured through an accident in childhood. Twice the wife was caught in the act of assaulting this poor lad in the most unprovoked way. Once she struck him with a stick and left a great weal on his arm.

This was a small matter, however, compared with her conduct to her own child, a dear boy just under one year of age. On one occasion about a month ago this child had been left by its nurse for a few minutes. A loud cry from the baby, as of pain, called the nurse back. As she ran into the room she saw her employer, the lady, leaning over the baby and apparently biting his neck. There was a small wound in the neck from which a stream of blood had escaped. The nurse was so horrified that she wished to call the husband, but the lady implored her not to do so and actually gave her five pounds as a price for her silence. No explanation was ever given, and for the moment the matter was passed over.

It left, however, a terrible impression upon the nurse's mind, and from that time she began to watch her mistress closely and to keep a closer guard upon the baby, whom she tenderly loved. It seemed to her that even as she watched the mother, so the mother watched her, and that every time she was compelled to leave the baby alone the mother was waiting to get at it. Day and night the nurse covered the child, and day and night the silent, watchful mother seemed to be lying in wait as a wolf waits for a lamb. It must read most incredible to you, and yet I beg you to take it seriously, for a child's life and a man's sanity may depend upon it.

At last there came one dreadful day when the facts could no longer be concealed from the husband. The nurse's nerve had given way; she could stand the strain no longer, and she made a clean breast of it all to the man. To him it seemed as wild a tale as it may now seem to you. He knew his wife to be a loving wife, and, save for the assaults upon her stepson, a loving mother. Why, then, should she wound her own dear little baby? He told the nurse that she was dreaming, that her suspicions were those of a lunatic, and that such libels upon her mistress were not to be tolerated. While they were talking a sudden cry of pain was heard. Nurse and master rushed together to the nursery. Imagine his feelings, Mr. Holmes, as he saw his wife rise from a kneeling position beside the cot and saw blood upon the child's exposed neck and upon the sheet. With a cry of horror, he turned his wife's face to the light and saw blood all round her lips. It was she—she beyond all question—who had drunk the poor baby's blood.

So the matter stands. She is now confined to her room. There has been no explanation. The husband is half demented. He knows, and I know, little of vampirism beyond the name. We had thought it was some wild tale of foreign parts. And yet here in the very heart of the English Sussex—well, all this can be discussed with you in the morning. Will you see me? Will you use your great powers in aiding a distracted man? If so, kindly wire to Ferguson, Cheeseman's, Lamberley, and I will be at your rooms by ten o'clock.

Yours faithfully,
ROBERT FERGUSON.

P. S. I believe your friend Watson played Rugby for Blackheath when I was three-quarter for Richmond. It is the only personal introduction which I can give.

"Of course I remembered him," said I as I laid down the letter. "Big Bob Ferguson, the finest three-quarter Richmond ever had. He was always a good-natured chap. It's like him to be so concerned over a friend's case."

Holmes looked at me thoughtfully and shook his head.

"I never get your limits, Watson," said he. "There are unexplored possibilities about you. Take a wire down, like a good fellow. 'Will examine your case with pleasure.'"

"*Your* case!"

"We must not let him think that this agency is a home for the weak-minded. Of course it is his case. Send him that wire and let the matter rest till morning."

Promptly at ten o'clock next morning Ferguson strode into our room. I had remembered him as a long, slab-sided man with loose limbs and a fine turn of speed which had carried him round many an opposing back. There is surely nothing in life more painful than to meet the wreck of a fine athlete whom one has known in his prime. His great frame had fallen in, his flaxen hair was scanty, and his shoulders were bowed. I fear that I roused corresponding emotions in him.

"Hullo, Watson," said he, and his voice was still deep and hearty. "You don't look quite the man you did when I threw you over the ropes into the crowd at the Old Deer Park. I expect I have changed a bit also. But it's this last day or two that has aged me. I see by your telegram, Mr. Holmes, that it is no use my pretending to be anyone's deputy."

"It is simpler to deal direct," said Holmes.

"Of course it is. But you can imagine how difficult it is when you are speaking of the one woman whom you are bound to protect and help. What can I do? How am I to go to the police with such a story? And yet the kiddies have got to be protected. Is it madness, Mr. Holmes? Is it something in the blood? Have you any similar case in your experience? For God's sake, give me some advice, for I am at my wit's end."

"Very naturally, Mr. Ferguson. Now sit here and pull yourself together and give me a few clear answers. I can assure you that I am very far from being at my wit's end, and that I am confident we shall find some solution. First of all, tell me what steps you have taken. Is your wife still near the children?"

"We had a dreadful scene. She is a most loving woman, Mr. Holmes. If ever a woman loved a man with all her heart and soul, she loves me. She was cut to the heart that I should have discovered this horrible, this incredible, secret. She would not even speak. She gave no answer to my reproaches, save to gaze at me with a sort of wild, despairing look in her eyes. Then she rushed to her room and locked herself in. Since then she has refused to see me. She has a maid who was with her before her marriage, Dolores by name—a friend rather than a servant. She takes her food to her."

"Then the child is in no immediate danger?"

"Mrs. Mason, the nurse, has sworn that she will not leave it night or day. I can absolutely trust her. I am more uneasy about poor little Jack, for, as I told you in my note, he has twice been assaulted by her."

"But never wounded?"

"No, she struck him savagely. It is the more terrible as he is a poor little inoffensive cripple." Ferguson's gaunt features softened as he spoke of his boy. "You would think that the dear lad's condition would soften anyone's heart. A fall in childhood and a twisted spine, Mr. Holmes. But the dearest, most loving heart within."

Holmes had picked up the letter of yesterday and was reading it over. "What other inmates are there in your house, Mr. Ferguson?"

"Two servants who have not been long with us. One stablehand, Michael, who sleeps in the house. My wife, myself, my boy Jack, baby, Dolores, and Mrs. Mason. That is all."

"I gather that you did not know your wife well at the time of your marriage?"

"I had only known her a few weeks."

"How long had this maid Dolores been with her?"

"Some years."

"Then your wife's character would really be better known by Dolores than by you?"

"Yes, you may say so."

Holmes made a note.

"I fancy," said he, "that I may be of more use at Lamberley than here. It is eminently a case for personal investigation. If the lady remains in her room, our presence could not annoy or inconvenience her. Of course, we would stay at the inn."

Ferguson gave a gesture of relief.

"It is what I hoped, Mr. Holmes. There is an excellent train at two from Victoria if you could come."

"Of course we could come. There is a lull at present. I can give you my undivided energies. Watson, of course, comes with us. But there are one or two points upon which I wish to be very sure before I start. This unhappy lady, as I understand it, has appeared to assault both the children, her own baby and your little son?"

"That is so."

"But the assaults take different forms, do they not? She has beaten your son."

"Once with a stick and once very savagely with her hands."

"Did she give no explanation why she struck him?"

"None save that she hated him. Again and again she said so."

"Well, that is not unknown among stepmothers. A posthumous jealousy, we will say. Is the lady jealous by nature?"

"Yes, she is very jealous—jealous with all the strength of her fiery tropical love."

"But the boy—he is fifteen, I understand, and probably very developed in mind, since his body has been circumscribed in action. Did he give you no explanation of these assaults?"

"No, he declared there was no reason."

"Were they good friends at other times?"

"No, there was never any love between them."

"Yet you say he is affectionate?"

"Never in the world could there be so devoted a son. My life is his life. He is absorbed in what I say or do."

Once again Holmes made a note. For some time he sat lost in thought.

"No doubt you and the boy were great comrades before this second marriage. You were thrown very close together, were you not?"

"Very much so."

"And the boy, having so affectionate a nature, was devoted, no doubt, to the memory of his mother?"

"Most devoted."

"He would certainly seem to be a most interesting lad. There is one other point about these assaults. Were the strange attacks upon the baby and the assaults upon your son at the same period?"

"In the first case it was so. It was as if some frenzy had seized her, and she had vented her rage upon both. In the second case it was only Jack who suffered. Mrs. Mason had no complaint to make about the baby."

"That certainly complicates matters."

"I don't quite follow you, Mr. Holmes."

"Possibly not. One forms provisional theories and waits for time or fuller knowledge to explode them. A bad habit, Mr. Ferguson, but human nature is weak. I fear that your old friend here has given an exaggerated view of my scientific methods. However, I will only say at the present stage that your problem does not appear to me to be insoluble, and that you may expect to find us at Victoria at two o'clock."

It was evening of a dull, foggy November day when, having left our bags at the Chequers, Lamberley, we drove through the Sussex clay of a long winding lane and finally reached the isolated and ancient farmhouse in which Ferguson dwelt. It was a large, straggling building, very old in the centre, very new at the wings with towering Tudor chimneys and a lichen-spotted, high-pitched roof of Horsham slabs. The doorsteps were worn into curves, and the ancient tiles which lined the porch were marked with the rebus* of a cheese and a man after the original builder. Within, the ceilings were corrugated with heavy oaken beams, and the uneven floors sagged into sharp curves. An odour of age and decay pervaded the whole crumbling building.

There was one very large central room into which Ferguson led us. Here, in a huge old-fashioned fireplace with an iron screen behind it dated 1670, there blazed and spluttered a splendid log fire.

The room, as I gazed round, was a most singular mixture of dates and of places. The half-panelled walls may well have belonged to the original yeoman farmer of the seventeenth century. They were ornamented, however, on the lower part by a line of well-chosen modern water-colours; while above, where yellow plaster took the place of oak, there was hung a fine collection of South American utensils and weapons, which had been brought, no doubt, by the Peruvian lady upstairs. Holmes rose, with that quick curiosity which sprang from his eager mind, and examined them with some care. He returned with his eyes full of thought.

"Hullo!" he cried. "Hullo!"

A spaniel had lain in a basket in the corner. It came slowly forward towards its master, walking with difficulty. Its hind legs moved irregularly and its tail was on the ground. It licked Ferguson's hand.

"What is it, Mr. Holmes?"

"The dog. What's the matter with it?"

"That's what puzzled the vet. A sort of paralysis. Spinal meningitis, he thought. But it is passing. He'll be all right soon—won't you, Carlo?"

A shiver of assent passed through the drooping tail. The dog's mournful eyes passed from one of us to the other. He knew that we were discussing his case.

"Did it come on suddenly?"

"In a single night."

"How long ago?"

"It may have been four months ago."

"Very remarkable. Very suggestive."

"What do you see in it, Mr. Holmes?"

---

*Puzzle that represents a word or phrase by a picture or symbol that sound like parts of the words in question.

"A confirmation of what I had already thought."

"For God's sake, what do you think, Mr. Holmes? It may be a mere intellectual puzzle to you, but it is life and death to me! My wife a would-be murderer—my child in constant danger! Don't play with me, Mr. Holmes. It is too terribly serious."

The big Rugby three-quarter was trembling all over. Holmes put his hand soothingly upon his arm.

"I fear that there is pain for you, Mr. Ferguson, whatever the solution may be," said he. "I would spare you all I can. I cannot say more for the instant, but before I leave this house I hope I may have something definite."

"Please God you may! If you will excuse me, gentlemen, I will go up to my wife's room and see if there has been any change."

He was away some minutes, during which Holmes resumed his examination of the curiosities upon the wall. When our host returned it was clear from his downcast face that he had made no progress. He brought with him a tall, slim, brown-faced girl.

"The tea is ready, Dolores," said Ferguson. "See that your mistress has everything she can wish."

"She verra ill," cried the girl, looking with indignant eyes at her master. "She no ask for food. She verra ill. She need doctor. I frightened stay alone with her without doctor."

Ferguson looked at me with a question in his eyes.

"I should be so glad if I could be of use."

"Would your mistress see Dr. Watson?"

"I take him. I no ask leave. She needs doctor."

"Then I'll come with you at once."

I followed the girl, who was quivering with strong emotion, up the staircase and down an ancient corridor. At the end was an iron-clamped and massive door. It struck me as I looked at it that if Ferguson tried to force his way to his wife he would find it no easy matter. The girl drew a key from her pocket, and the heavy oaken planks creaked upon their old hinges. I passed in and she swiftly followed, fastening the door behind her.

On the bed a woman was lying who was clearly in a high fever. She was only half conscious, but as I entered she raised a pair of frightened but beautiful eyes and glared at me in apprehension. Seeing a stranger, she appeared to be relieved and sank back with a sigh upon the pillow. I stepped up to her with a few reassuring words, and she lay still while I took her pulse and temperature. Both were high, and yet my impression was that the condition was rather that of mental and nervous excitement than of any actual seizure.

"She lie like that one day, two day. I 'fraid she die," said the girl.

The woman turned her flushed and handsome face towards me.

"Where is my husband?"

"He is below and would wish to see you."

"I will not see him. I will not see him." Then she seemed to wander off into delirium. "A fiend! A fiend! Oh, what shall I do with this devil?"

"Can I help you in any way?"

"No. No one can help. It is finished. All is destroyed. Do what I will, all is destroyed."

The woman must have some strange delusion. I could not see honest Bob Ferguson in the character of fiend or devil.

"Madame," I said, "your husband loves you dearly. He is deeply grieved at this happening."

Again she turned on me those glorious eyes.

"He loves me. Yes. But do I not love him? Do I not love him even to sacrifice myself rather than break his dear heart? That is how I love him. And yet he could think of me—he could speak of me so."

"He is full of grief, but he cannot understand."

"No, he cannot understand. But he should trust."

"Will you not see him?" I suggested.

"No, no, I cannot forget those terrible words nor the look upon his face. I will not see him. Go now. You can do nothing for me. Tell him only one thing. I want my child. I have a right to my child. That is the only message I can send him." She turned her face to the wall and would say no more.

I returned to the room downstairs, where Ferguson and Holmes still sat by the fire. Ferguson listened moodily to my account of the interview.

"How can I send her the child?" he said. "How do I know what strange impulse might come upon her? How can I ever forget how she rose from beside it with its blood upon her lips?" He shuddered at the recollection. "The child is safe with Mrs. Mason, and there he must remain."

A smart maid, the only modern thing which we had seen in the house, had brought in some tea. As she was serving it the door opened and a youth entered the room. He was a remarkable lad, pale-faced and fair-haired, with excitable light blue eyes which blazed into a sudden flame of emotion and joy as they rested upon his father. He rushed forward and threw his arms round his neck with the abandon of a loving girl.

"Oh, daddy," he cried, "I did not know that you were due yet. I should have been here to meet you. Oh, I am so glad to see you!"

Ferguson gently disengaged himself from the embrace with some little show of embarrassment.

"Dear old chap," said he, patting the flaxen head with a very tender hand. "I came early because my friends, Mr. Holmes and Dr. Watson, have been persuaded to come down and spend an evening with us."

"Is that Mr. Holmes, the detective?"

"Yes."

The youth looked at us with a very penetrating and, as it seemed to me, unfriendly gaze.

"What about your other child, Mr. Ferguson?" asked Holmes. "Might we make the acquaintance of the baby?"

"Ask Mrs. Mason to bring baby down," said Ferguson. The boy went off with a curious, shambling gait which told my surgical eyes that he was suffering from a weak spine. Presently he returned, and behind him came a tall, gaunt woman bearing in her arms a very beautiful child, dark-eyed, golden-haired, a wonderful mixture of the Saxon and the Latin. Ferguson was evidently devoted to it, for he took it into his arms and fondled it most tenderly.

"Fancy anyone having the heart to hurt him," he muttered as he glanced down at the small, angry red pucker upon the cherub throat.

It was at this moment that I chanced to glance at Holmes and saw a most singular intentness in his expression. His face was as set as if it had been carved out of old ivory, and his eyes, which had glanced for a moment at father and child, were now fixed with eager curiosity upon something at the other side of the room. Following his gaze I could only guess that he was looking out through the window at the melancholy, dripping garden. It is true that a shutter had half closed outside and obstructed the view, but none the less it was certainly at the window that Holmes was fixing his concentrated attention. Then he smiled, and his eyes came back to the baby. On its chubby neck there was this small puckered mark. Without speaking, Holmes examined it with care. Finally he shook one of the dimpled fists which waved in front of him.

"Good-bye, little man. You have made a strange start in life. Nurse, I should wish to have a word with you in private."

He took her aside and spoke earnestly for a few minutes. I only heard the last words, which were: "Your anxiety will soon, I hope, be set at rest." The woman, who seemed to be a sour, silent kind of creature, withdrew with the child.

"What is Mrs. Mason like?" asked Holmes.

"Not very prepossessing externally, as you can see, but a heart of gold, and devoted to the child."

"Do you like her, Jack?" Holmes turned suddenly upon the boy. His expressive mobile face shadowed over, and he shook his head.

"Jacky has very strong likes and dislikes," said Ferguson, putting his arm round the boy. "Luckily I am one of his likes."

The boy cooed and nestled his head upon his father's breast. Ferguson gently disengaged him.

"Run away, little Jacky," said he, and he watched his son with loving eyes until he disappeared. "Now, Mr. Holmes," he continued when the boy was gone, "I really feel that I have brought you on a fool's errand, for what can you possibly do save give me your sympathy? It must be an exceedingly delicate and complex affair from your point of view."

"It is certainly delicate," said my friend with an amused smile, "but I have not been struck up to now with its complexity. It has been a case for intellectual deduction, but when this original intellectual deduction is confirmed point by point by quite a number of independent incidents, then the subjective becomes objective and we can say confidently that we have reached our goal. I had, in fact, reached it before we left Baker Street, and the rest has merely been observation and confirmation."

Ferguson put his big hand to his furrowed forehead.

"For heaven's sake, Holmes," he said hoarsely; "if you can see the truth in this matter, do not keep me in suspense. How do I stand? What shall I do? I care nothing as to how you have found your facts so long as you have really got them."

"Certainly I owe you an explanation, and you shall have it. But you will permit me to handle the matter in my own way? Is the lady capable of seeing us, Watson?"

"She is ill, but she is quite rational."

"Very good. It is only in her presence that we can clear the matter up. Let us go up to her."

"She will not see me," cried Ferguson.

"Oh, yes, she will," said Holmes. He scribbled a few lines upon a sheet of paper. "You at least have the entrée, Watson. Will you have the goodness to give the lady this note?"

I ascended again and handed the note to Dolores, who cautiously opened the door. A minute later I heard a cry from within, a cry in which joy and surprise seemed to be blended. Dolores looked out.

"She will see them. She will leesten," said she.

At my summons Ferguson and Holmes came up. As we entered the room Ferguson took a step or two towards his wife, who had raised herself in the bed, but she held out her hand to repulse him. He sank into an armchair, while Holmes seated himself beside him, after bowing to the lady, who looked at him with wide-eyed amazement.

"I think we can dispense with Dolores," said Holmes. "Oh, very well, madame, if you would rather she stayed I can see no objection. Now, Mr. Ferguson, I am a busy man with many calls, and my methods have to be short and direct. The swiftest surgery is the least painful. Let me first say what will ease your mind. Your wife is a very good, a very loving, and a very ill-used woman."

Ferguson sat up with a cry of joy.

"Prove that, Mr. Holmes, and I am your debtor forever."

"I will do so, but in doing so I must wound you deeply in another direction."

"I care nothing so long as you clear my wife. Everything on earth is insignificant compared to that."

"Let me tell you, then, the train of reasoning which passed through my mind in Baker Street. The idea of a vampire was to me absurd. Such things do not happen in criminal practice in England. And yet your observation was precise. You had seen the lady rise from beside the child's cot with the blood upon her lips."

"I did."

"Did it not occur to you that a bleeding wound may be sucked for some other purpose than to draw the blood from it? Was there not a queen in English history[21] who sucked such a wound to draw poison from it?"

"Poison!"

"A South American household. My instinct felt the presence of those weapons upon the wall before my eyes ever saw them. It might have been other poison, but that was what occurred to me. When I saw that little empty quiver beside the small bird-bow, it was just what I expected to see. If the child were pricked with one of those arrows dipped in curare or some other devilish drug, it would mean death if the venom were not sucked out.

"And the dog! If one were to use such a poison, would one not try it first in order to see that it had not lost its power? I did not foresee the dog, but at least I understand him and he fitted into my reconstruction.

"Now do you understand? Your wife feared such an attack. She saw it made and saved the child's life, and yet she shrank from telling you all the truth, for she knew how you loved the boy and feared lest it break your heart."

"Jacky!"

"I watched him as you fondled the child just now. His face was clearly reflected in the glass of the window where the shutter formed a background. I saw such jealousy, such cruel hatred, as I have seldom seen in a human face."

"My Jacky!"

"You have to face it, Mr. Ferguson. It is the more painful because it is a distorted love, a maniacal exaggerated love for you, and possibly for his dead mother, which has prompted his action. His very soul is consumed with hatred for this splendid child, whose health and beauty are a contrast to his own weakness."

"Good God! It is incredible!"

"Have I spoken the truth, madame?"

The lady was sobbing, with her face buried in the pillows. Now she turned to her husband.

"How could I tell you, Bob? I felt the blow it would be to you. It was better that I should wait and that it should come from some other lips than mine. When this gentleman, who seems to have powers of magic, wrote that he knew all, I was glad."

"I think a year at sea would be my prescription for Master Jacky," said Holmes, rising from his chair. "Only one thing is still clouded, madame. We can quite understand your attacks upon Master Jacky. There is a limit to a mother's patience. But how did you dare to leave the child these last two days?"

"I had told Mrs. Mason. She knew."

"Exactly. So I imagined."

Ferguson was standing by the bed, choking, his hands outstretched and quivering.

"This, I fancy, is the time for our exit, Watson," said Holmes in a whisper. "If you will take one elbow of the too faithful Dolores, I will take the other. There, now," he added as he closed the door behind him, "I think we may leave them to settle the rest among themselves."

I have only one further note of this case. It is the letter which Holmes wrote in final answer to that with which the narrative begins. It ran thus:

> BAKER STREET,
> *Nov. 21st.*

Re Vampires

SIR:

Referring to your letter of the 19th, I beg to state that I have looked into the inquiry of your client, Mr. Robert Ferguson, of Ferguson and Muirhead, tea brokers, of Mincing Lane, and that the matter has been brought to a satisfactory conclusion. With thanks for your recommendation, I am, sir,

> Faithfully yours,
> SHERLOCK HOLMES.

THE ADVENTURE OF THE
THREE GARRIDEBS

It may have been a comedy, or it may have been a tragedy. It cost one man his reason, it cost me a blood-letting, and it cost yet another man the penalties of the law. Yet there was certainly an element of comedy. Well, you shall judge for yourselves.

I remember the date very well, for it was in the same month that Holmes refused a knighthood for services which may perhaps some day be described. I only refer to the matter in passing, for in my position of partner and confidant I am obliged to be particularly careful to avoid any indiscretion. I repeat, however, that this enables me to fix the date, which was the latter end of June, 1902, shortly after the conclusion of the South African War. Holmes had spent several days in bed, as was his habit from time to time, but he emerged that morning with a long foolscap document in his hand and a twinkle of amusement in his austere gray eyes.

"There is a chance for you to make some money, friend Watson," said he. "Have you ever heard the name of Garrideb?"

I admitted that I had not.

"Well, if you can lay your hand upon a Garrideb, there's money in it."

"Why?"

"Ah, that's a long story—rather a whimsical one, too. I don't think in all our explorations of human complexities we have ever come upon anything more singular. The fellow will be here presently for cross-examination, so I won't open the matter up till he comes. But, meanwhile, that's the name we want."

The telephone directory lay on the table beside me, and I turned over the pages in a rather hopeless quest. But to my amazement there was this strange name in its due place. I gave a cry of triumph.

"Here you are, Holmes! Here it is!"

Holmes took the book from my hand.

" 'Garrideb, N.,' " he read, " '136 Little Ryder Street, W.' Sorry to disappoint you, my dear Watson, but this is the man himself. That is the address upon his letter. We want another to match him."

Mrs. Hudson had come in with a card upon a tray. I took it up and glanced at it.

"Why, here it is!" I cried in amazement. "This is a different initial. John Garrideb, Counsellor at Law, Moorville, Kansas, U. S. A."

Holmes smiled as he looked at the card. "I am afraid you must make yet another effort, Watson," said he. "This gentleman is also in the plot already, though I certainly did not expect to see him this morning. However, he is in a position to tell us a good deal which I want to know."

A moment later he was in the room. Mr. John Garrideb, Counsellor at Law, was a short, powerful man with the round, fresh, clean-shaven face characteristic of so many American men of affairs. The general effect was chubby and rather childlike, so that one received the impression of quite a young man with a broad set smile upon his face. His eyes, however, were arresting. Seldom in any human head have I seen a pair which bespoke a more intense inward life, so bright were they, so alert, so responsive to every change of thought. His accent was American, but was not accompanied by any eccentricity of speech.

"Mr. Holmes?" he asked, glancing from one to the other. "Ah, yes! Your pictures are not unlike you, sir, if I may say so. I believe you have had a letter from my namesake, Mr. Nathan Garrideb, have you not?"

"Pray sit down," said Sherlock Holmes. "We shall, I fancy, have a good deal to discuss." He took up his sheets of foolscap. "You are, of course, the Mr. John Garrideb mentioned in this document. But surely you have been in England some time?"

"Why do you say that, Mr. Holmes?" I seemed to read sudden suspicion in those expressive eyes.

"Your whole outfit is English."

Mr. Garrideb forced a laugh. "I've read of your tricks, Mr. Holmes, but I never thought I would be the subject of them. Where do you read that?"

"The shoulder cut of your coat, the toes of your boots—could anyone doubt it?"

"Well, well, I had no idea I was so obvious a Britisher. But business brought me over here some time ago, and so, as you say, my outfit is nearly all London. However, I guess your time is of value, and we did not meet to talk about the cut of my socks. What about getting down to that paper you hold in your hand?"

Holmes had in some way ruffled our visitor, whose chubby face had assumed a far less amiable expression.

"Patience! Patience, Mr. Garrideb!" said my friend in a soothing voice. "Dr. Watson would tell you that these little digressions of mine sometimes prove in the end to have some bearing on the matter. But why did Mr. Nathan Garrideb not come with you?"

"Why did he ever drag you into it at all?" asked our visitor with a sudden outflame of anger. "What in thunder had you to do with it? Here was a bit of professional business between two gentlemen, and one of them must needs call in a detective! I saw him this morning, and he told me this fool-trick he had played me, and that's why I am here. But I feel bad about it, all the same."

"There was no reflection upon you, Mr. Garrideb. It was simply zeal upon his part to gain your end—an end which is, I understand, equally vital for both of you. He knew that I had means of getting information, and, therefore, it was very natural that he should apply to me."

Our visitor's angry face gradually cleared.

"Well, that puts it different," said he. "When I went to see him this morning and he told me he had sent to a detective, I just asked for your address and came right away. I don't want police butting into a private matter. But if you are content just to help us find the man, there can be no harm in that."

"Well, that is just how it stands," said Holmes. "And now, sir, since you are here, we had best have a clear account from your own lips. My friend here knows nothing of the details."

Mr. Garrideb surveyed me with not too friendly a gaze.

"Need he know?" he asked.

"We usually work together."

"Well, there's no reason it should be kept a secret. I'll give you the facts as short as I can make them. If you came from Kansas I would not need to explain to you who Alexander Hamilton Garrideb was. He made his money in real estate, and afterwards in the wheat pit* at Chicago, but he spent it in buying up as much land as would make one of your counties, lying along the Arkansas River, west of Fort Dodge. It's grazing-land and lumber-land and arable-land and mineralized-land, and just every sort of land that brings dollars to the man that owns it.

"He had no kith nor kin—or, if he had, I never heard of it. But he took a kind of pride in the queerness of his name. That was what brought us together. I was in the law at Topeka, and one day I had a visit from the old man, and he was tickled to death to meet another man with his own name. It was his pet fad, and he was dead set to find out if there were any more Garridebs in the world. 'Find me another!' said he. I told him I was a busy man and could not spend my life hiking round the world in search of Garridebs. 'None the less,' said he, 'that is just what you will do if things pan out as I planned them.' I thought he was joking, but there was a powerful lot of meaning in the words, as I was soon to discover.

"For he died within a year of saying them, and he left a will behind him. It was the queerest will that has ever been filed in the State of Kansas. His property was divided into three parts, and I was to have one on condition that I found two Garridebs who would share the remainder. It's five million dollars for each if it is a cent, but we can't lay a finger on it until we all three stand in a row.

"It was so big a chance that I just let my legal practice slide and I set forth looking for Garridebs. There is not one in the United States. I went through it, sir, with a fine-toothed comb and never a Garrideb could I catch. Then I tried the old country. Sure enough there was the name in the London telephone directory. I went after him two days ago and explained the whole matter to him. But he is a lone man, like myself, with some women relations, but no men. It says three adult men in the will. So you see we still have a vacancy, and if you can help to fill it we will be very ready to pay your charges."

"Well, Watson," said Holmes with a smile, "I said it was rather whimsical, did I not? I should have thought, sir, that your obvious way was to advertise in the agony columns of the papers."

"I have done that, Mr. Holmes. No replies."

"Dear me! Well, it is certainly a most curious little problem. I may take a glance at it in my leisure. By the way, it is curious that you should have

---

*Commodities market, where wheat and other grains are traded.

come from Topeka. I used to have a correspondent—he is dead now—old Dr. Lysander Starr, who was mayor in 1890."

"Good old Dr. Starr!" said our visitor. "His name is still honoured. Well, Mr. Holmes, I suppose all we can do is to report to you and let you know how we progress. I reckon you will hear within a day or two." With this assurance our American bowed and departed.

Holmes had lit his pipe, and he sat for some time with a curious smile upon his face.

"Well?" I asked at last.

"I am wondering, Watson—just wondering!"

"At what?"

Holmes took his pipe from his lips.

"I was wondering, Watson, what on earth could be the object of this man in telling us such a rigmarole of lies. I nearly asked him so—for there are times when a brutal frontal attack is the best policy—but I judged it better to let him think he had fooled us. Here is a man with an English coat frayed at the elbow and trousers bagged at the knee with a year's wear, and yet by this document and by his own account he is a provincial American lately landed in London. There have been no advertisements in the agony columns. You know that I miss nothing there. They are my favourite covert for putting up a bird, and I would never have overlooked such a cock pheasant as that. I never knew a Dr. Lysander Starr, of Topeka. Touch him where you would he was false. I think the fellow is really an American, but he has worn his accent smooth with years of London. What is his game, then, and what motive lies behind this preposterous search for Garridebs? It's worth our attention, for, granting that the man is a rascal, he is certainly a complex and ingenious one. We must now find out if our other correspondent is a fraud also. Just ring him up, Watson."

I did so, and heard a thin, quavering voice at the other end of the line.

"Yes, yes, I am Mr. Nathan Garrideb. Is Mr. Holmes there? I should very much like to have a word with Mr. Holmes."

My friend took the instrument and I heard the usual syncopated dialogue.

"Yes, he has been here. I understand that you don't know him. . . . How long? . . . Only two days! . . . Yes, yes, of course, it is a most captivating prospect. Will you be at home this evening? I suppose your namesake will not be there? Very good, we will come then, for I would rather have a chat without him. . . . Dr. Watson will come with me. . . . I understand from your note that you did not go out often. . . . Well, we shall be round about six. You need not mention it to the American lawyer. . . . Very good. Good-bye!"

It was twilight of a lovely spring evening, and even Little Ryder Street, one of the smaller offshoots from the Edgware Road, within a stone-cast of old Tyburn Tree of evil memory,* looked golden and wonderful in the

---

*Hanging tree where public executions took place until 1783; stood near Speakers' Corner in Hyde Park, London.

slanting rays of the setting sun. The particular house to which we were directed was a large, old-fashioned, Early Georgian* edifice, with a flat brick face broken only by two deep bay windows on the ground floor. It was on this ground floor that our client lived, and, indeed, the low windows proved to be the front of the huge room in which he spent his waking hours. Holmes pointed as we passed to the small brass plate which bore the curious name.

"Up some years, Watson," he remarked, indicating its discoloured surface. "It's *his* real name, anyhow, and that is something to note."

The house had a common stair, and there were a number of names painted in the hall, some indicating offices and some private chambers. It was not a collection of residential flats, but rather the abode of Bohemian bachelors. Our client opened the door for us himself and apologized by saying that the woman in charge left at four o'clock. Mr. Nathan Garrideb proved to be a very tall, loose-jointed, round-backed person, gaunt and bald, some sixty-odd years of age. He had a cadaverous face, with the dull dead skin of a man to whom exercise was unknown. Large round spectacles and a small projecting goat's beard combined with his stooping attitude to give him an expression of peering curiosity. The general effect, however, was amiable, though eccentric.

The room was as curious as its occupant. It looked like a small museum. It was both broad and deep, with cupboards and cabinets all round, crowded with specimens, geological and anatomical. Cases of butterflies and moths flanked each side of the entrance. A large table in the centre was littered with all sorts of debris, while the tall brass tube of a powerful microscope bristled up among them. As I glanced round I was surprised at the universality of the man's interests. Here was a case of ancient coins. There was a cabinet of flint instruments. Behind his central table was a large cupboard of fossil bones. Above was a line of plaster skulls with such names as "Neanderthal," "Heidelberg," "Cro-Magnon" printed beneath them. It was clear that he was a student of many subjects. As he stood in front of us now, he held a piece of chamois leather in his right hand with which he was polishing a coin.

"Syracusan†——of the best period," he explained, holding it up. "They degenerated greatly towards the end. At their best I hold them supreme, though some prefer the Alexandrian school. You will find a chair here, Mr. Holmes. Pray allow me to clear these bones. And you, sir—ah, yes, Dr. Watson—if you would have the goodness to put the Japanese vase to one side. You see round me my little interests in life. My doctor lectures me about never going out, but why should I go out when I have so much to hold me here? I can assure you that the adequate cataloguing of one of those cabinets would take me three good months."

---

*The early Georges (I–IV) ruled between 1714 and 1830; George V ruled from 1910 to 1936.

†From the ancient Greek city of Syracuse in Sicily.

Holmes looked round him with curiosity.

"But do you tell me that you *never* go out?" he said.

"Now and again I drive down to Sotheby's or Christie's. Otherwise I very seldom leave my room. I am not too strong, and my researches are very absorbing. But you can imagine, Mr. Holmes, what a terrific shock—pleasant but terrific—it was for me when I heard of this unparalleled good fortune. It only needs one more Garrideb to complete the matter, and surely we can find one. I had a brother, but he is dead, and female relatives are disqualified. But there must surely be others in the world. I had heard that you handled strange cases, and that was why I sent to you. Of course, this American gentleman is quite right, and I should have taken his advice first, but I acted for the best."

"I think you acted very wisely indeed," said Holmes. "But are you really anxious to acquire an estate in America?"

"Certainly not, sir. Nothing would induce me to leave my collection. But this gentleman has assured me that he will buy me out as soon as we have established our claim. Five million dollars was the sum named. There are a dozen specimens in the market at the present moment which fill gaps in my collection, and which I am unable to purchase for want of a few hundred pounds. Just think what I could do with five million dollars. Why, I have the nucleus of a national collection. I shall be the Hans Sloane* of my age."

His eyes gleamed behind his great spectacles. It was very clear that no pains would be spared by Mr. Nathan Garrideb in finding a namesake.

"I merely called to make your acquaintance, and there is no reason why I should interrupt your studies," said Holmes. "I prefer to establish personal touch with those with whom I do business. There are few questions I need ask, for I have your very clear narrative in my pocket, and I filled up the blanks when this American gentleman called. I understand that up to this week you were unaware of his existence."

"That is so. He called last Tuesday."

"Did he tell you of our interview to-day?"

"Yes, he came straight back to me. He had been very angry."

"Why should he be angry?"

"He seemed to think it was some reflection on his honour. But he was quite cheerful again when he returned."

"Did he suggest any course of action?"

"No, sir, he did not."

"Has he had, or asked for, any money from you?"

"No, sir, never!"

"You see no possible object he has in view?"

"None, except what he states."

---

*Sloane (1660–1753) was a naturalist, physician, and collector; his library and collection of curiosities were important contributions to the British Museum when it was founded in 1753.

"Did you tell him of our telephone appointment?"

"Yes, sir, I did."

Holmes was lost in thought. I could see that he was puzzled.

"Have you any articles of great value in your collection?"

"No, sir. I am not a rich man. It is a good collection, but not a very valuable one."

"You have no fear of burglars?"

"Not the least."

"How long have you been in these rooms?"

"Nearly five years."

Holmes's cross-examination was interrupted by an imperative knocking at the door. No sooner had our client unlatched it than the American lawyer burst excitedly into the room.

"Here you are!" he cried, waving a paper over his head. "I thought I should be in time to get you. Mr. Nathan Garrideb, my congratulations! You are a rich man, sir. Our business is happily finished and all is well. As to you, Mr. Holmes, we can only say we are sorry if we have given you any useless trouble."

He handed over the paper to our client, who stood staring at a marked advertisement. Holmes and I leaned forward and read it over his shoulder. This is how it ran:

HOWARD GARRIDEB
CONSTRUCTOR OF AGRICULTURAL MACHINERY
Binders, reapers, steam and hand plows, drills, harrows,
farmer's carts, buckboards, and all other appliances.
Estimates for Artesian Wells
Apply Grosvenor Buildings, Aston

"Glorious!" gasped our host. "That makes our third man."

"I had opened up inquiries in Birmingham," said the American, "and my agent there has sent me this advertisement from a local paper. We must hustle and put the thing through. I have written to this man and told him that you will see him in his office to-morrow afternoon at four o'clock."

"You want *me* to see him?"

"What do you say, Mr. Holmes? Don't you think it would be wiser? Here am I, a wandering American with a wonderful tale. Why should he believe what I tell him? But you are a Britisher with solid references, and he is bound to take notice of what you say. I would go with you if you wished, but I have a very busy day to-morrow, and I could always follow you if you are in any trouble."

"Well, I have not made such a journey for years."

"It is nothing, Mr. Garrideb. I have figured out our connections. You leave at twelve and should be there soon after two. Then you can be back the same night. All you have to do is to see this man, explain the matter, and get an affidavit of his existence. By the Lord!" he added hotly, "considering I've come all the way from the centre of America, it is surely little enough if you go a hundred miles in order to put this matter through."

"Quite so," said Holmes. "I think what this gentleman says is very true."

Mr. Nathan Garrideb shrugged his shoulders with a disconsolate air. "Well, if you insist I shall go," said he. "It is certainly hard for me to refuse you anything, considering the glory of hope that you have brought into my life."

"Then that is agreed," said Holmes, "and no doubt you will let me have a report as soon as you can."

"I'll see to that," said the American. "Well," he added, looking at his watch, "I'll have to get on. I'll call to-morrow, Mr. Nathan, and see you off to Birmingham. Coming my way, Mr. Holmes? Well, then, good-bye, and we may have good news for you to-morrow night."

I noticed that my friend's face cleared when the American left the room, and the look of thoughtful perplexity had vanished.

"I wish I could look over your collection, Mr. Garrideb," said he. "In my profession all sorts of odd knowledge comes useful, and this room of yours is a storehouse of it."

Our client shone with pleasure and his eyes gleamed from behind his big glasses.

"I had always heard, sir, that you were a very intelligent man," said he. "I could take you round now if you have the time."

"Unfortunately, I have not. But these specimens are so well labelled and classified that they hardly need your personal explanation. If I should be able to look in to-morrow, I presume that there would be no objection to my glancing over them?"

"None at all. You are most welcome. The place will, of course, be shut up, but Mrs. Saunders is in the basement up to four o'clock and would let you in with her key."

"Well, I happen to be clear to-morrow afternoon. If you would say a word to Mrs. Saunders it would be quite in order. By the way, who is your house-agent?"

Our client was amazed at the sudden question.

"Holloway and Steele, in the Edgware Road. But why?"

"I am a bit of an archæologist myself when it comes to houses," said Holmes, laughing. "I was wondering if this was Queen Anne or Georgian."

"Georgian, beyond doubt."

"Really. I should have thought a little earlier. However, it is easily ascertained. Well, good-bye, Mr. Garrideb, and may you have every success in your Birmingham journey."

The house-agent's was close by, but we found that it was closed for the day, so we made our way back to Baker Street. It was not till after dinner that Holmes reverted to the subject.

"Our little problem draws to a close," said he. "No doubt you have outlined the solution in your own mind."

"I can make neither head nor tail of it."

"The head is surely clear enough and the tail we should see to-morrow. Did you notice nothing curious about that advertisement?"

"I saw that the word 'plough' was misspelt."

"Oh, you did notice that, did you? Come, Watson, you improve all the time. Yes, it was bad English but good American. The printer had set it up as received. Then the buckboards. That is American also. And artesian wells are commoner with them than with us. It was a typical American advertisement, but purporting to be from an English firm. What do you make of that?"

"I can only suppose that this American lawyer put it in himself. What his object was I fail to understand."

"Well, there are alternative explanations. Anyhow, he wanted to get this good old fossil up to Birmingham. That is very clear. I might have told him that he was clearly going on a wild-goose chase, but, on second thoughts, it seemed better to clear the stage by letting him go. To-morrow, Watson—well, to-morrow will speak for itself."

Holmes was up and out early. When he returned at lunchtime I noticed that his face was very grave.

"This is a more serious matter than I had expected, Watson," said he. "It is fair to tell you so, though I know it will only be an additional reason to you for running your head into danger. I should know my Watson by now. But there is danger, and you should know it."

"Well, it is not the first we have shared, Holmes. I hope it may not be the last. What is the particular danger this time?"

"We are up against a very hard case. I have identified Mr. John Garrideb, Counsellor at Law. He is none other than 'Killer' Evans, of sinister and murderous reputation."

"I fear I am none the wiser."

"Ah, it is not part of your profession to carry about a portable Newgate Calendar* in your memory. I have been down to see friend Lestrade at the Yard. There may be an occasional want of imaginative intuition down there, but they lead the world for thoroughness and method. I had an idea that we might get on the track of our American friend in their records. Sure enough, I found his chubby face smiling up at me from the rogues' portrait gallery. 'James Winter, alias Morecroft, alias Killer Evans,' was the inscription below." Holmes drew an envelope from his pocket. "I scribbled down a few points from his dossier: Aged forty-four. Native of Chicago. Known to have shot three men in the States. Escaped from penitentiary through political influence. Came to London in 1893. Shot a man over cards in a night-club in the Waterloo Road in January, 1895. Man died, but he was shown to have been the aggressor in the row. Dead man was identified as Rodger Prescott, famous as forger and coiner in Chicago. Killer Evans released in 1901. Has been under police supervision since, but so far as known has led an honest life. Very dangerous

---

*Catalog of the crimes of the inmates of London's Newgate Prison.

man, usually carries arms and is prepared to use them. That is our bird,
Watson—a sporting bird, as you must admit."

"But what is his game?"

"Well, it begins to define itself. I have been to the houseagent's. Our
client, as he told us, has been there five years. It was unlet for a year before then. The previous tenant was a gentleman at large named Waldron.
Waldron's appearance was well remembered at the office. He had suddenly vanished and nothing more been heard of him. He was a tall,
bearded man with very dark features. Now, Prescott, the man whom
Killer Evans had shot, was, according to Scotland Yard, a tall, dark man
with a beard. As a working hypothesis, I think we may take it that
Prescott, the American criminal, used to live in the very room which
our innocent friend now devotes to his museum. So at last we get a link,
you see."

"And the next link?"

"Well, we must go now and look for that."

He took a revolver from the drawer and handed it to me.

"I have my old favourite with me. If our Wild West friend tries to live
up to his nickname, we must be ready for him. I'll give you an hour for a
siesta, Watson, and then I think it will be time for our Ryder Street adventure."

It was just four o'clock when we reached the curious apartment of
Nathan Garrideb. Mrs. Saunders, the caretaker, was about to leave, but
she had no hesitation in admitting us, for the door shut with a spring lock,
and Holmes promised to see that all was safe before we left. Shortly afterwards the outer door closed, her bonnet passed the bow window, and
we knew that we were alone in the lower floor of the house. Holmes made
a rapid examination of the premises. There was one cupboard in a dark
corner which stood out a little from the wall. It was behind this that we
eventually crouched while Holmes in a whisper outlined his intentions.

"He wanted to get our amiable friend out of his room—that is very
clear, and, as the collector never went out, it took some planning to do it.
The whole of this Garrideb invention was apparently for no other end. I
must say, Watson, that there is a certain devilish ingenuity about it, even
if the queer name of the tenant did give him an opening which he could
hardly have expected. He wove his plot with remarkable cunning."

"But what did he want?"

"Well, that is what we are here to find out. It has nothing whatever to
do with our client, so far as I can read the situation. It is something connected with the man he murdered—the man who may have been his confederate in crime. There is some guilty secret in the room. That is how I
read it. At first I thought our friend might have something in his collection more valuable than he knew—something worth the attention of a big
criminal. But the fact that Rodger Prescott of evil memory inhabited
these rooms points to some deeper reason. Well, Watson, we can but possess our souls in patience and see what the hour may bring."

That hour was not long in striking. We crouched closer in the shadow as we heard the outer door open and shut. Then came the sharp, metallic snap of a key, and the American was in the room. He closed the door softly behind him, took a sharp glance around him to see that all was safe, threw off his overcoat, and walked up to the central table with the brisk manner of one who knows exactly what he has to do and how to do it. He pushed the table to one side, tore up the square of carpet on which it rested, rolled it completely back, and then, drawing a jemmy* from his inside pocket, he knelt down and worked vigorously upon the floor. Presently we heard the sound of sliding boards, and an instant later a square had opened in the planks. Killer Evans struck a match, lit a stump of candle, and vanished from our view.

Clearly our moment had come. Holmes touched my wrist as a signal, and together we stole across to the open trap-door. Gently as we moved, however, the old floor must have creaked under our feet, for the head of our American, peering anxiously round, emerged suddenly from the open space. His face turned upon us with a glare of baffled rage, which gradually softened into a rather shamefaced grin as he realized that two pistols were pointed at his head.

"Well, well!" said he coolly as he scrambled to the surface. "I guess you have been one too many for me, Mr. Holmes. Saw through my game, I suppose, and played me for a sucker from the first. Well, sir, I hand it to you; you have me beat and——"

In an instant he had whisked out a revolver from his breast and had fired two shots. I felt a sudden hot sear as if a red-hot iron had been pressed to my thigh. There was a crash as Holmes's pistol came down on the man's head. I had a vision of him sprawling upon the floor with blood running down his face while Holmes rummaged him for weapons. Then my friend's wiry arms were round me, and he was leading me to a chair.

"You're not hurt, Watson? For God's sake, say that you are not hurt!"

It was worth a wound—it was worth many wounds—to know the depth of loyalty and love which lay behind that cold mask. The clear, hard eyes were dimmed for a moment, and the firm lips were shaking. For the one and only time I caught a glimpse of a great heart as well as of a great brain. All my years of humble but single-minded service culminated in that moment of revelation.

"It's nothing, Holmes. It's a mere scratch."

He had ripped up my trousers with his pocket-knife.

"You are right," he cried with an immense sigh of relief. "It is quite superficial." His face set like flint as he glared at our prisoner, who was sitting up with a dazed face. "By the Lord, it is as well for you. If you had killed Watson, you would not have got out of this room alive. Now, sir, what have you to say for yourself?"

He had nothing to say for himself. He only sat and scowled. I leaned on Holmes's arm, and together we looked down into the small cellar

---

*Short crowbar used in burglaries.

which had been disclosed by the secret flap. It was still illuminated by the candle which Evans had taken down with him. Our eyes fell upon a mass of rusted machinery, great rolls of paper, a litter of bottles, and, neatly arranged upon a small table, a number of neat little bundles.

"A printing press—a counterfeiter's outfit," said Holmes.

"Yes, sir," said our prisoner, staggering slowly to his feet and then sinking into the chair. "The greatest counterfeiter London ever saw. That's Prescott's machine, and those bundles on the table are two thousand of Prescott's notes worth a hundred each and fit to pass anywhere. Help yourselves, gentlemen. Call it a deal and let me beat it."

Holmes laughed.

"We don't do things like that, Mr. Evans. There is no bolt-hole for you in this country. You shot this man Prescott, did you not?"

"Yes, sir, and got five years for it, though it was he who pulled on me. Five years—when I should have had a medal the size of a soup plate. No living man could tell a Prescott from a Bank of England, and if I hadn't put him out he would have flooded London with them. I was the only one in the world who knew where he made them. Can you wonder that I wanted to get to the place? And can you wonder that when I found this crazy boob of a bug-hunter with the queer name squatting right on the top of it, and never quitting his room, I had to do the best I could to shift him? Maybe I would have been wiser if I had put him away. It would have been easy enough, but I'm a soft-hearted guy that can't begin shooting unless the other man has a gun also. But say, Mr. Holmes, what have I done wrong, anyhow? I've not used this plant. I've not hurt this old stiff. Where do you get me?"

"Only attempted murder, so far as I can see," said Holmes. "But that's not our job. They take that at the next stage. What we wanted at present was just your sweet self. Please give the Yard a call, Watson. It won't be entirely unexpected."

So those were the facts about Killer Evans and his remarkable invention of the three Garridebs. We heard later that our poor old friend never got over the shock of his dissipated dreams. When his castle in the air fell down, it buried him beneath the ruins. He was last heard of at a nursing-home in Brixton. It was a glad day at the Yard when the Prescott outfit was discovered, for, though they knew that it existed, they had never been able, after the death of the man, to find out where it was. Evans had indeed done great service and caused several worthy C. I. D. men to sleep the sounder, for the counterfeiter stands in a class by himself as a public danger. They would willingly have subscribed to that soup-plate medal of which the criminal had spoken, but an unappreciative bench took a less favourable view, and the Killer returned to those shades from which he had just emerged.

THE PROBLEM OF THOR BRIDGE

Somewhere in the vaults of the bank of Cox and Co., at Charing Cross, there is a travel-worn and battered tin dispatch-box with my name, John H. Watson, M. D., Late Indian Army, painted upon the lid. It is crammed with papers, nearly all of which are records of cases to illustrate the curious problems which Mr. Sherlock Holmes had at various times to examine. Some, and not the least interesting, were complete failures, and as such will hardly bear narrating, since no final explanation is forthcoming. A problem without a solution may interest the student, but can hardly fail to annoy the casual reader. Among these unfinished tales is that of Mr. James Phillimore, who, stepping back into his own house to get his umbrella, was never more seen in this world. No less remarkable is that of the cutter *Alicia*, which sailed one spring morning into a small patch of mist from where she never again emerged, nor was anything further ever heard of herself and her crew. A third case worthy of note is that of Isadora Persano, the well-known journalist and duellist, who was found stark staring mad with a match box in front of him which contained a remarkable worm said to be unknown to science. Apart from these unfathomed cases, there are some which involve the secrets of private families to an extent which would mean consternation in many exalted quarters if it were thought possible that they might find their way into print. I need not say that such a breach of confidence is unthinkable, and that these records will be separated and destroyed now that my friend has time to turn his energies to the matter. There remain a considerable residue of cases of greater or less interest which I might have edited before had I not feared to give the public a surfeit which might react upon the reputation of the man whom above all others I revere. In some I was myself concerned and can speak as an eye-witness, while in others I was either not present or played so small a part that they could only be told as by a third person. The following narrative is drawn from my own experience.

It was a wild morning in October, and I observed as I was dressing how the last remaining leaves were being whirled from the solitary plane tree* which graces the yard behind our house. I descended to breakfast prepared to find my companion in depressed spirits, for, like all great artists, he was easily impressed by his surroundings. On the contrary, I found that he had nearly finished his meal, and that his mood was particularly bright and joyous, with that somewhat sinister cheerfulness which was characteristic of his lighter moments.

"You have a case, Holmes?" I remarked.

"The faculty of deduction is certainly contagious, Watson," he answered.

---

*Sycamore tree.

"It has enabled you to probe my secret. Yes, I have a case. After a month of trivialities and stagnation the wheels move once more."

"Might I share it?"

"There is little to share, but we may discuss it when you have consumed the two hard-boiled eggs with which our new cook has favoured us. Their condition may not be unconnected with the copy of the *Family Herald** which I observed yesterday upon the hall-table. Even so trivial a matter as cooking an egg demands an attention which is conscious of the passage of time and incompatible with the love romance in that excellent periodical."

A quarter of an hour later the table had been cleared and we were face to face. He had drawn a letter from his pocket.

"You have heard of Neil Gibson, the Gold King?" he said.

"You mean the American Senator?"

"Well, he was once Senator for some Western state, but is better known as the greatest gold-mining magnate in the world."

"Yes, I know of him. He has surely lived in England for some time. His name is very familiar."

"Yes, he bought a considerable estate in Hampshire some five years ago. Possibly you have already heard of the tragic end of his wife?"

"Of course. I remember it now. That is why the name is familiar. But I really know nothing of the details."

Holmes waved his hand towards some papers on a chair. "I had no idea that the case was coming my way or I should have had my extracts ready," said he. "The fact is that the problem, though exceedingly sensational, appeared to present no difficulty. The interesting personality of the accused does not obscure the clearness of the evidence. That was the view taken by the coroner's jury and also in the police-court proceedings. It is now referred to the Assizes at Winchester. I fear it is a thankless business. I can discover facts, Watson, but I cannot change them. Unless some entirely new and unexpected ones come to light I do not see what my client can hope for."

"Your client?"

"Ah, I forgot I had not told you. I am getting into your involved habit, Watson, of telling a story backward. You had best read this first."

The letter which he handed to me, written in a bold, masterful hand, ran as follows:

CLARIDGE'S HOTEL,
October 3rd.

DEAR MR. SHERLOCK HOLMES:

I can't see the best woman God ever made go to her death without doing all that is possible to save her. I can't explain things—I can't even try to explain them, but I know beyond all doubt that Miss Dun-

---

*Popular women's magazine specializing in romances.

bar is innocent. You know the facts—who doesn't? It has been the gossip of the country. And never a voice raised for her! It's the damned injustice of it all that, makes me crazy. That woman has a heart that wouldn't let her kill a fly. Well, I'll come at eleven to-morrow and see if you can get some ray of light in the dark. Maybe I have a clue and don't know it. Anyhow, all I know and all I have and all I am are for your use if only you can save her. If ever in your life you showed your powers, put them now into this case.

> Yours faithfully,
> J. NEIL GIBSON.

"There you have it," said Sherlock Holmes, knocking out the ashes of his after-breakfast pipe and slowly refilling it. "That is the gentleman I await. As to the story, you have hardly time to master all these papers, so I must give it to you in a nutshell if you are to take an intelligent interest in the proceedings. This man is the greatest financial power in the world, and a man, as I understand, of most violent and formidable character. He married a wife, the victim of this tragedy, of whom I know nothing save that she was past her prime, which was the more unfortunate as a very attractive governess superintended the education of two young children. These are the three people concerned, and the scene is a grand old manor house, the centre of a historical English state. Then as to the tragedy. The wife was found in the grounds nearly half a mile from the house, late at night, clad in her dinner dress, with a shawl over her shoulders and a revolver bullet through her brain. No weapon was found near her and there was no local clue as to the murder. No weapon near her. Watson—mark that! The crime seems to have been committed late in the evening, and the body was found by a gamekeeper about eleven o'clock, when it was examined by the police and by a doctor before being carried up to the house. Is this too condensed, or can you follow it clearly?"

"It is all very clear. But why suspect the governess?"

"Well, in the first place there is some very direct evidence. A revolver with one discharged chamber and a calibre which corresponded with the bullet was found on the floor of her wardrobe." His eyes fixed and he repeated in broken words, "On—the—floor—of—her—wardrobe." Then he sank into silence, and I saw that some train of thought had been set moving which I should be foolish to interrupt. Suddenly with a start he emerged into brisk life once more. "Yes, Watson, it was found. Pretty damning, eh? So the two juries thought. Then the dead woman had a note upon her making an appointment at that very place and signed by the governess. How's that? Finally there is the motive. Senator Gibson is an attractive person. If his wife dies, who more likely to succeed her than the young lady who had already by all accounts received pressing attentions from her employer? Love, fortune, power, all depending upon one middle-aged life. Ugly, Watson—very ugly!"

"Yes, indeed, Holmes."

"Nor could she prove an alibi. On the contrary, she had to admit that she was down near Thor Bridge—that was the scene of the tragedy—about that hour. She couldn't deny it, for some passing villager had seen her there."

"That really seems final."

"And yet, Watson—and yet! This bridge—a single broad span of stone with balustraded sides—carries the drive over the narrowest part of a long, deep, reed-girt sheet of water. Thor Mere it is called. In the mouth of the bridge lay the dead woman. Such are the main facts. But here, if I mistake not, is our client, considerably before his time."

Billy had opened the door, but the name which he announced was an unexpected one. Mr. Marlow Bates was a stranger to both of us. He was a thin, nervous wisp of a man with frightened eyes and a twitching, hesitating manner—a man whom my own professional eye would judge to be on the brink of an absolute nervous breakdown.

"You seem agitated, Mr. Bates," said Holmes. "Pray sit down. I fear I can only give you a short time, for I have an appointment at eleven."

"I know you have," our visitor gasped, shooting out short sentences like a man who is out of breath. "Mr. Gibson is coming. Mr. Gibson is my employer. I am manager of his estate. Mr. Holmes, he is a villain—an infernal villain."

"Strong language, Mr. Bates."

"I have to be emphatic, Mr. Holmes, for the time is so limited. I would not have him find me here for the world. He is almost due now. But I was so situated that I could not come earlier. His secretary, Mr. Ferguson, only told me this morning of his appointment with you."

"And you are his manager?"

"I have given him notice. In a couple of weeks I shall have shaken off his accursed slavery. A hard man, Mr. Holmes, hard to all about him. Those public charities are a screen to cover his private iniquities. But his wife was his chief victim. He was brutal to her—yes, sir, brutal! How she came by her death I do not know, but I am sure that he had made her life a misery to her. She was a creature of the tropics, a Brazilian by birth, as no doubt you know."

"No, it had escaped me."

"Tropical by birth and tropical by nature. A child of the sun and of passion. She had loved him as such women can love, but when her own physical charms had faded—I am told that they once were great—there was nothing to hold him. We all liked her and felt for her and hated him for the way that he treated her. But he is plausible and cunning. That is all I have to say to you. Don't take him at his face value. There is more behind. Now I'll go. No, no, don't detain me! He is almost due."

With a frightened look at the clock our strange visitor literally ran to the door and disappeared.

"Well! Well!" said Holmes after an interval of silence. "Mr. Gibson seems to have a nice loyal household. But the warning is a useful one, and now we can only wait till the man himself appears."

Sharp at the hour we heard a heavy step upon the stairs, and the famous millionaire was shown into the room. As I looked upon him I understood not only the fears and dislike of his manager but also the execrations which so many business rivals have heaped upon his head. If I were a sculptor and desired to idealize the successful man of affairs, iron of nerve and leathery of conscience, I should choose Mr. Neil Gibson as my model. His tall, gaunt, craggy figure had a suggestion of hunger and rapacity. An Abraham Lincoln keyed to base uses instead of high ones would give some idea of the man. His face might have been chiselled in granite, hard-set, craggy, remorseless, with deep lines upon it, the scars of many a crisis. Cold gray eyes, looking shrewdly out from under bristling brows, surveyed us each in turn. He bowed in perfunctory fashion as Holmes mentioned my name, and then with a masterful air of possession he drew a chair up to my companion and seated himself with his bony knees almost touching him.

"Let me say right here, Mr. Holmes," he began, "that money is nothing to me in this case. You can burn it if it's any use in lighting you to the truth. This woman is innocent and this woman has to be cleared, and it's up to you to do it. Name your figure!"

"My professional charges are upon a fixed scale," said Holmes coldly. "I do not vary them, save when I remit them altogether."

"Well, if dollars make no difference to you, think of the reputation. If you pull this off every paper in England and America will be booming* you. You'll be the talk of two continents."

"Thank you, Mr. Gibson, I do not think that I am in need of booming. It may surprise you to know that I prefer to work anonymously, and that it is the problem itself which attracts me. But we are wasting time. Let us get down to the facts."

"I think that you will find all the main ones in the press reports. I don't know that I can add anything which will help you. But if there is anything you would wish more light upon—well, I am here to give it."

"Well, there is just one point."

"What is it?"

"What were the exact relations between you and Miss Dunbar?"

The Gold King gave a violent start and half rose from his chair. Then his massive calm came back to him.

"I suppose you are within your rights—and maybe doing your duty—in asking such a question, Mr. Holmes."

"We will agree to suppose so," said Holmes.

"Then I can assure you that our relations were entirely and always those of an employer towards a young lady whom he never conversed with, or ever saw, save when she was in the company of his children."

Holmes rose from his chair.

"I am a rather busy man, Mr. Gibson," said he, "and I have no time or taste for aimless conversations. I wish you good-morning."

---

*Boosting your reputation.

Our visitor had risen also, and his great loose figure towered above Holmes. There was an angry gleam from under those bristling brows and a tinge of colour in the sallow cheeks.

"What the devil do you mean by this, Mr. Holmes? Do you dismiss my case?"

"Well, Mr. Gibson, at least I dismiss you. I should have thought my words were plain."

"Plain enough, but what's at the back of it? Raising the price on me, or afraid to tackle it, or what? I've a right to a plain answer."

"Well, perhaps you have," said Holmes. "I'll give you one. This case is quite sufficiently complicated to start with without the further difficulty of false information."

"Meaning that I lie."

"Well, I was trying to express it as delicately as I could, but if you insist upon the word I will not contradict you."

I sprang to my feet, for the expression upon the millionaire's face was fiendish in its intensity, and he had raised his great knotted fist. Holmes smiled languidly and reached his hand out for his pipe.

"Don't be noisy, Mr. Gibson. I find that after breakfast even the smallest argument is unsettling. I suggest that a stroll in the morning air and a little quiet thought will be greatly to your advantage."

With an effort the Gold King mastered his fury. I could not but admire him, for by a supreme self-command he had turned in a minute from a hot flame of anger to a frigid and contemptuous indifference.

"Well, it's your choice. I guess you know how to run your own business. I can't make you touch the case against your will. You've done yourself no good this morning, Mr. Holmes, for I have broken stronger men than you. No man ever crossed me and was the better for it."

"So many have said so, and yet here I am," said Holmes, smiling. "Well, good-morning, Mr. Gibson. You have a good deal yet to learn."

Our visitor made a noisy exit, but Holmes smoked in imperturbable silence with dreamy eyes fixed upon the ceiling.

"Any views, Watson?" he asked at last.

"Well, Holmes, I must confess that when I consider that this is a man who would certainly brush any obstacle from his path, and when I remember that his wife may have been an obstacle and an object of dislike, as that man Bates plainly told us, it seems to me——"

"Exactly. And to me also."

"But what were his relations with the governess, and how did you discover them?"

"Bluff, Watson, bluff! When I considered the passionate, unconventional, unbusinesslike tone of his letter and contrasted it with his self-contained manner and appearance, it was pretty clear that there was some deep emotion which centred upon the accused woman rather than upon the victim. We've got to understand the exact relations of those three people if we are to reach the truth. You saw the frontal attack which I made upon him, and how imperturbably he received it. Then I bluffed him by giving him the impression that I was absolutely certain, when in reality I was only extremely suspicious."

"Perhaps he will come back?"

"He is sure to come back. He *must* come back. He can't leave it where it is. Ha! isn't that a ring? Yes, there is his footstep. Well, Mr. Gibson, I was just saying to Dr. Watson that you were somewhat overdue."

The Gold King had reëntered the room in a more chastened mood than he had left it. His wounded pride still showed in his resentful eyes, but his common sense had shown him that he must yield if he would attain his end.

"I've been thinking it over, Mr. Holmes, and I feel that I have been hasty in taking your remarks amiss. You are justified in getting down to the facts, whatever they may be, and I think the more of you for it. I can assure you, however, that the relations between Miss Dunbar and me don't really touch this case."

"That is for me to decide, is it not?"

"Yes, I guess that is so. You're like a surgeon who wants every symptom before he can give his diagnosis."

"Exactly. That expresses it. And it is only a patient who has an object in deceiving his surgeon who would conceal the facts of his case."

"That may be so, but you will admit, Mr. Holmes, that most men would shy off a bit when they are asked point-blank what their relations with a woman may be—if there is really some serious feeling in the case. I guess most men have a little private reserve of their own in some corner of their souls where they don't welcome intruders. And you burst suddenly into it. But the object excuses you, since it was to try and save her. Well, the stakes are down and the reserve open, and you can explore where you will. What is it you want?"

"The truth."

The Gold King paused for a moment as one who marshals his thoughts. His grim, deep-lined face had become even sadder and more grave.

"I can give it to you in a very few words, Mr. Holmes," said he at last. "There are some things that are painful as well as difficult to say, so I won't go deeper than is needful. I met my wife when I was gold-hunting in Brazil. Maria Pinto was the daughter of a government official at Manaos, and she was very beautiful. I was young and ardent in those days, but even now, as I look back with colder blood and a more critical eye, I can see that she was rare and wonderful in her beauty. It was a deep rich nature, too, passionate, whole-hearted, tropical, ill-balanced, very different from the American women whom I had known. Well, to make a long story short, I loved her and I married her. It was only when the romance had passed—and it lingered for years—that I realized that we had nothing—absolutely nothing—in common. My love faded. If hers had faded also it might have been easier. But you know the wonderful way of women! Do what I might, nothing could turn her from me. If I have been harsh to her, even brutal as some have said, it has been because I knew that if I could kill her love, or if it turned to hate, it would be easier for both of us. But nothing changed her. She adored me in those English woods as she had adored me twenty years ago on the banks of the Amazon. Do what I might, she was as devoted as ever.

"Then came Miss Grace Dunbar. She answered our advertisement and became governess to our two children. Perhaps you have seen her portrait in the papers. The whole world has proclaimed that she also is a very beautiful woman. Now, I make no pretence to be more moral than my neighbours, and I will admit to you that I could not live under the same roof with such a woman and in daily contact with her without feeling a passionate regard for her. Do you blame me, Mr. Holmes?"

"I do not blame you for feeling it. I should blame you if you expressed it, since this young lady was in a sense under your protection."

"Well, maybe so," said the millionaire, though for a moment the reproof had brought the old angry gleam into his eyes. "I'm not pretending to be any better than I am. I guess all my life I've been a man that reached out his hand for what he wanted, and I never wanted anything more than the love and possession of that woman. I told her so."

"Oh, you did, did you?"

Holmes could look very formidable when he was moved.

"I said to her that if I could marry her I would, but that it was out of my power. I said that money was no object and that all I could do to make her happy and comfortable would be done."

"Very generous, I am sure," said Holmes with a sneer.

"See here, Mr. Holmes. I came to you on a question of evidence, not on a question of morals. I'm not asking for your criticism."

"It is only for the young lady's sake that I touch your case at all," said Holmes sternly. "I don't know that anything she is accused of is really worse than what you have yourself admitted, that you have tried to ruin a defenceless girl who was under your roof. Some of you rich men have to be taught that all the world cannot be bribed into condoning your offences."

To my surprise the Gold King took the reproof with equanimity.

"That's how I feel myself about it now. I thank God that my plans did not work out as I intended. She would have none of it, and she wanted to leave the house instantly."

"Why did she not?"

"Well, in the first place, others were dependent upon her, and it was no light matter for her to let them all down by sacrificing her living. When I had sworn—as I did—that she should never be mole͏ ͏ again, she consented to remain. But there was another reason. She knew the influence she had over me, and that it was stronger than any other influence in the world. She wanted to use it for good."

"How?"

"Well, she knew something of my affairs. They are large, Mr. Holmes—large beyond the belief of an ordinary man. I can make or break—and it is usually break. It wasn't individuals only. It was communities, cities, even nations. Business is a hard game, and the weak go to the wall. I played the game for all it was worth. I never squealed myself, and I never cared if the other fellow squealed. But she saw it different. I guess she was right. She believed and said that a fortune for one man that was more than he needed should not be built on ten thousand ruined men who were left without the means of life. That was how she saw it, and I guess she could see past the dollars to something that was more lasting. She found that I listened to what she said, and she believed she was serving the world by influencing my actions. So she stayed—and then this came along."

"Can you throw any light upon that?"

The Gold King paused for a minute or more, his head sunk in his hands, lost in deep thought.

"It's very black against her. I can't deny that. And women lead an inward life and may do things beyond the judgment of a man. At first I was so rattled and taken aback that I was ready to think she had been led away in some extraordinary fashion that was clean against her usual nature. One explanation came into my head. I give it to you, Mr. Holmes, for what it is worth. There is no doubt that my wife was bitterly jealous. There is a soul-jealousy that can be as frantic as any body-jealousy, and though my wife had no cause—and I think she understood this—for the latter, she was aware that this English girl exerted an influence upon my mind and my acts that she herself never had. It was an influence for good, but that did not mend the matter. She was crazy with hatred, and the heat of the Amazon was always in her blood. She might have planned to murder Miss Dunbar—or we will say to threaten her with a gun and so frighten her into leaving us. Then there might have been a scuffle and the gun gone off and shot the woman who held it."

"That possibility had already occurred to me," said Holmes. "Indeed, it is the only obvious alternative to deliberate murder."

"But she utterly denies it."

"Well, that is not final—is it? One can understand that a woman placed in so awful a position might hurry home still in her bewilderment holding the revolver. She might even throw it down among her clothes, hardly knowing what she was doing, and when it was found she might try to lie her way out by a total denial, since all explanation was impossible. What is against such a supposition?"

"Miss Dunbar herself."

"Well, perhaps."

Holmes looked at his watch. "I have no doubt we can get the necessary permits this morning and reach Winchester by the evening train. When I have seen this young lady it is very possible that I may be of more use to you in the matter, though I cannot promise that my conclusions will necessarily be such as you desire."

There was some delay in the official pass, and instead of reaching Winchester that day we went down to Thor Place, the Hampshire estate of Mr. Neil Gibson. He did not accompany us himself, but we had the address of Sergeant Coventry, of the local police, who had first examined into the affair. He was a tall, thin, cadaverous man, with a secretive and mysterious manner which conveyed the idea that he knew or suspected a very great deal more than he dared say. He had a trick, too, of suddenly sinking his voice to a whisper as if he had come upon something of vital importance, though the information was usually commonplace enough. Behind these tricks of manner he soon showed himself to be a decent, honest fellow who was not too proud to admit that he was out of his depth and would welcome any help.

"Anyhow, I'd rather have you than Scotland Yard, Mr. Holmes," said he. "If the Yard gets called into a case, then the local loses all credit for success and may be blamed for failure. Now, you play straight, so I've heard."

"I need not appear in the matter at all," said Holmes to the evident relief of our melancholy acquaintance. "If I can clear it up I don't ask to have my name mentioned."

"Well, it's very handsome of you, I am sure. And your friend, Dr. Watson, can be trusted, I know. Now, Mr. Holmes, as we walk down to the place there is one question I should like to ask you. I'd breathe it to no soul but you." He looked round as though he hardly dare utter the words. "Don't you think there might be a case against Mr. Neil Gibson himself?"

"I have been considering that."

"You've not seen Miss Dunbar. She is a wonderful fine woman in every way. He may well have wished his wife out of the road.* And these Americans are readier with pistols than our folk are. It was *his* pistol, you know."

"Was that clearly made out?"

"Yes, sir. It was one of a pair that he had."

"One of a pair? Where is the other?"

"Well, the gentleman has a lot of firearms of one sort and another. We never quite matched that particular pistol—but the box was made for two."

"If it was one of a pair you should surely be able to match it."

"Well, we have them all laid out at the house if you would care to look them over."

"Later, perhaps. I think we will walk down together and have a look at the scene of the tragedy."

This conversation had taken place in the little front room of Sergeant Coventry's humble cottage which served as the local police-station. A walk of half a mile or so across a wind-swept heath, all gold and bronze with the fading ferns, brought us to a side-gate opening into the grounds of the Thor Place estate. A path led us through the pheasant preserves, and then from a clearing we saw the widespread, half-timbered house, half Tudor and half Georgian, upon the crest of the hill. Beside us there

---

*Scottish expression meaning "out of the way."

was a long, reedy pool, constricted in the centre where the main carriage drive passed over a stone bridge, but swelling into small lakes on either side. Our guide paused at the mouth of this bridge, and he pointed to the ground.

"That was where Mrs. Gibson's body lay. I marked it by that stone."

"I understand that you were there before it was moved?"

"Yes, they sent for me at once."

"Who did?"

"Mr. Gibson himself. The moment the alarm was given and he had rushed down with others from the house, he insisted that nothing should be moved until the police should arrive."

"That was sensible. I gathered from the newspaper report that the shot was fired from close quarters."

"Yes, sir, very close."

"Near the right temple?"

"Just behind it, sir."

"How did the body lie?"

"On the back, sir. No trace of a struggle. No marks. No weapon. The short note from Miss Dunbar was clutched in her left hand."

"Clutched, you say?"

"Yes, sir, we could hardly open the fingers."

"That is of great importance. It excludes the idea that anyone could have placed the note there after death in order to furnish a false clue. Dear me! The note, as I remember, was quite short:

> I will be at Thor Bridge at nine o'clock.
>
> G. Dunbar.

Was that not so?"

"Yes, sir."

"Did Miss Dunbar admit writing it?"

"Yes, sir."

"What was her explanation?"

"Her defence was reserved for the Assizes. She would say nothing."

"The problem is certainly a very interesting one. The point of the letter is very obscure, is it not?"

"Well, sir," said the guide, "it seemed, if I may be so bold as to say so, the only really clear point in the whole case."

Holmes shook his head.

"Granting that the letter is genuine and was really written, it was certainly received some time before—say one hour or two. Why, then, was this lady still clasping it in her left hand? Why should she carry it so carefully? She did not need to refer to it in the interview. Does it not seem remarkable?"

"Well, sir, as you put it, perhaps it does."

"I think I should like to sit quietly for a few minutes and think it out." He seated himself upon the stone ledge of the bridge, and I could see his quick gray eyes darting their questioning glances in every direction. Suddenly he sprang up again and ran across to the opposite parapet, whipped his lens from his pocket, and began to examine the stonework.

"This is curious," said he.

"Yes, sir, we saw the chip on the ledge. I expect it's been done by some passer-by."

The stonework was gray, but at this one point it showed white for a space not larger than a sixpence. When examined closely one could see that the surface was chipped as by a sharp blow.

"It took some violence to do that," said Holmes thoughtfully. With his cane he struck the ledge several times without leaving a mark. "Yes, it was a hard knock. In a curious place, too. It was not from above but from below, for you see that it is on the *lower* edge of the parapet."

"But it is at least fifteen feet from the body."

"Yes, it is fifteen feet from the body. It may have nothing to do with the matter, but it is a point worth noting. I do not think that we have anything more to learn here. There were no footsteps, you say?"

"The ground was iron hard, sir. There were no traces at all."

"Then we can go. We will go up to the house first and look over these weapons of which you speak. Then we shall get on to Winchester, for I should desire to see Miss Dunbar before we go farther."

Mr. Neil Gibson had not returned from town, but we saw in the house the neurotic Mr. Bates who had called upon us in the morning. He showed us with a sinister relish the formidable array of firearms of various shapes and sizes which his employer had accumulated in the course of an adventurous life.

"Mr. Gibson has his enemies, as anyone would expect who knew him and his methods," said he. "He sleeps with a loaded revolver in the drawer beside his bed. He is a man of violence, sir, and there are times when all of us are afraid of him. I am sure that the poor lady who has passed was often terrified."

"Did you ever witness physical violence towards her?"

"No, I cannot say that. But I have heard words which were nearly as bad—words of cold, cutting contempt, even before the servants."

"Our millionaire does not seem to shine in private life," remarked Holmes as we made our way to the station. "Well, Watson, we have come on a good many facts, some of them new ones, and yet I seem some way from my conclusion. In spite of the very evident dislike which Mr. Bates has to his employer, I gather from him that when the alarm came he was undoubtedly in his library. Dinner was over at 8:30 and all was normal up to then. It is true that the alarm was somewhat late in the evening, but the tragedy certainly occurred about the hour named in the note. There is no evidence at all that Mr. Gibson had been out of doors since his return from town at five o'clock. On the other hand, Miss Dunbar, as I understand it, admits that she had made an appointment to meet Mrs. Gibson at the bridge. Beyond this she would say nothing, as her lawyer had advised her to reserve her defence. We have several very vital questions to ask that young lady, and my mind will not be easy until we have seen her. I must confess that the case would seem to me to be very black against her if it were not for one thing."

"And what is that, Holmes?"

"The finding of the pistol in her wardrobe."

"Dear me, Holmes!" I cried, "that seemed to me to be the most damning incident of all."

"Not so, Watson. It had struck me even at my first perfunctory reading as very strange, and now that I am in closer touch with the case it is my only firm ground for hope. We must look for consistency. Where there is a want of it we must suspect deception."

"I hardly follow you."

"Well now, Watson, suppose for a moment that we visualize you in the character of a woman who, in a cold, premeditated fashion, is about to get rid of a rival. You have planned it. A note has been written. The victim has come. You have your weapon. The crime is done. It has been workmanlike and complete. Do you tell me that after carrying out so crafty a crime you would now ruin your reputation as a criminal by forgetting to fling your weapon into those adjacent reed-beds which would forever cover it, but you must needs carry it carefully home and put it in your own wardrobe, the very first place that would be searched? Your best friends would hardly call you a schemer, Watson, and yet I could not picture you doing anything so crude as that."

"In the excitement of the moment——"

"No, no, Watson, I will not admit that it is possible. Where a crime is coolly premeditated, then the means of covering it are coolly premeditated also. I hope, therefore, that we are in the presence of a serious misconception."

"But there is so much to explain."

"Well, we shall set about explaining it. When once your point of view is changed, the very thing which was so damning becomes a clue to the truth. For example, there is this revolver. Miss Dunbar disclaims all knowledge of it. On our new theory she is speaking truth when she says so. Therefore, it was placed in her wardrobe. Who placed it there? Someone who wished to incriminate her. Was not that person the actual criminal? You see how we come at once upon a most fruitful line of inquiry."

We were compelled to spend the night at Winchester, as the formalities had not yet been completed, but next morning, in the company of Mr. Joyce Cummings, the rising barrister who was entrusted with the defence, we were allowed to see the young lady in her cell. I had expected from all that we had heard to see a beautiful woman, but I can never forget the effect which Miss Dunbar produced upon me. It was no wonder that even the masterful millionaire had found in her something more powerful than himself—something which could control and guide him. One felt, too, as one looked at the strong, clear-cut, and yet sensitive face, that even should she be capable of some impetuous deed, none the less there was an innate nobility of character which would make her influence always for the good. She was a brunette, tall, with a noble figure and command-ing presence, but her dark eyes had in them the appealing, helpless ex-pression of the hunted creature who feels the nets around it, but can see no way out from the toils. Now, as she realized the presence and the help of my famous friend, there came a touch of colour in her wan cheeks and a light of hope began to glimmer in the glance which she turned upon us.

"Perhaps Mr. Neil Gibson has told you something of what occurred between us?" she asked in a low, agitated voice.

"Yes," Holmes answered, "you need not pain yourself by entering into that part of the story. After seeing you, I am prepared to accept Mr. Gib-son's statement both as to the influence which you had over him and as to the innocence of your relations with him. But why was the whole situa-tion not brought out in court?"

"It seemed to me incredible that such a charge could be sustained. I thought that if we waited the whole thing must clear itself up without our being compelled to enter into painful details of the inner life of the fam-ily. But I understand that far from clearing it has become even more seri-ous."

"My dear young lady," cried Holmes earnestly, "I beg you to have no illusions upon the point. Mr. Cummings here would assure you that all the cards are at present against us, and that we must do everything that is pos-sible if we are to win clear. It would be a cruel deception to pretend that you are not in very great danger. Give me all the help you can, then, to get at the truth."

"I will conceal nothing."

"Tell us, then, of your true relations with Mr. Gibson's wife."

"She hated me, Mr. Holmes. She hated me with all the fervour of her tropical nature. She was a woman who would do nothing by halves, and the measure of her love for her husband was the measure also of her hatred for me. It is probable that she misunderstood our relations. I would not wish to wrong her, but she loved so vividly in a physical sense that she could hardly understand the mental, and even spiritual, tie which held her husband to me, or imagine that it was only my desire to influence his power to good ends which kept me under his roof. I can see now that I was wrong. Nothing could justify me in remaining where I was a cause of unhappiness, and yet it is certain that the unhappiness would have re-mained even if I had left the house."

"Now, Miss Dunbar," said Holmes, "I beg you to tell us exactly what occurred that evening."

"I can tell you the truth so far as I know it, Mr. Holmes, but I am in a position to prove nothing, and there are points—the most vital points—which I can neither explain nor can I imagine any explanation."

"If you will find the facts, perhaps others may find the explanation."

"With regard, then, to my presence at Thor Bridge that night, I re-ceived a note from Mrs. Gibson in the morning. It lay on the table of the schoolroom, and it may have been left there by her own hand. It implored me to see her there after dinner, said she had something important to say to me, and asked me to leave an answer on the sundial in the garden, as she desired no one to be in our confidence. I saw no reason for such secrecy, but I did as she asked, accepting the appointment. She asked me to destroy her note and I burned it in the schoolroom grate. She was very much afraid of her husband, who treated her with a harshness for which I frequently reproached him, and I could only imagine that she acted in this way because she did not wish him to know of our interview."

"Yet she kept your reply very carefully?"

"Yes. I was surprised to hear that she had it in her hand when she died."

"Well, what happened then?"

"I went down as I had promised. When I reached the bridge she was waiting for me. Never did I realize till that moment how this poor creature hated me. She was like a mad woman—indeed, I think she *was* a mad woman, subtly mad with the deep power of deception which insane people may have. How else could she have met me with unconcern every day and yet had so raging a hatred of me in her heart? I will not say what she said. She poured her whole wild fury out in burning and horrible words. I did not even answer—I could not. It was dreadful to see her. I put my hands to my ears and rushed away. When I left her she was standing, still shrieking out her curses at me, in the mouth of the bridge."

"Where she was afterwards found?"

"Within a few yards from the spot."

"And yet, presuming that she met her death shortly after you left her, you heard no shot?"

"No, I heard nothing. But, indeed, Mr. Holmes, I was so agitated and horrified by this terrible outbreak that I rushed to get back to the peace of my own room, and I was incapable of noticing anything which happened."

"You say that you returned to your room. Did you leave it again before next morning?"

"Yes, when the alarm came that the poor creature had met her death I ran out with the others."

"Did you see Mr. Gibson?"

"Yes, he had just returned from the bridge when I saw him. He had sent for the doctor and the police."

"Did he seem to you much perturbed?"

"Mr. Gibson is a very strong, self-contained man. I do not think that he would ever show his emotions on the surface. But I, who knew him so well, could see that he was deeply concerned."

"Then we come to the all-important point. This pistol that was found in your room. Had you ever seen it before?"

"Never, I swear it."

"When was it found?"

"Next morning, when the police made their search."

"Among your clothes?"

"Yes, on the floor of my wardrobe under my dresses."

"You could not guess how long it had been there?"

"It had not been there the morning before."

"How do you know?"

"Because I tidied out the wardrobe."

"That is final. Then someone came into your room and placed the pistol there in order to inculpate you."

"It must have been so."

"And when?"

"It could only have been at meal-time, or else at the hours when I would be in the schoolroom with the children."

"As you were when you got the note?"

"Yes, from that time onward for the whole morning."

"Thank you, Miss Dunbar. Is there any other point which could help me in the investigation?"

"I can think of none."

"There was some sign of violence on the stonework of the bridge—a perfectly fresh chip just opposite the body. Could you suggest any possible explanation of that?"

"Surely it must be a mere coincidence."

"Curious, Miss Dunbar, very curious. Why should it appear at the very time of the tragedy, and why at the very place?"

"But what could have caused it? Only great violence could have such an effect."

Holmes did not answer. His pale, eager face had suddenly assumed that tense, far-away expression which I had learned to associate with the supreme manifestations of his genius. So evident was the crisis in his mind that none of us dared to speak, and we sat, barrister, prisoner, and myself, watching him in a concentrated and absorbed silence. Suddenly he sprang from his chair, vibrating with nervous energy and the pressing need for action.

"Come, Watson, come!" he cried.

"What is it, Mr. Holmes?"

"Never mind, my dear lady. You will hear from me, Mr. Cummings. With the help of the god of justice I will give you a case which will make England ring. You will get news by to-morrow, Miss Dunbar, and meanwhile take my assurance that the clouds are lifting and that I have every hope that the light of truth is breaking through."

It was not a long journey from Winchester to Thor Place, but it was long to me in my impatience, while for Holmes it was evident that it seemed endless; for, in his nervous restlessness, he could not sit still, but paced the carriage or drummed with his long, sensitive fingers upon the cushions beside him. Suddenly, however, as we neared our destination he seated himself opposite to me—we had a first-class carriage to ourselves—and laying a hand upon each of my knees he looked into my eyes with the peculiarly mischievous gaze which was characteristic of his more imp-like moods.

"Watson," said he, "I have some recollection that you go armed upon these excursions of ours."

It was as well for him that I did so, for he took little care for his own safety when his mind was once absorbed by a problem, so that more than once my revolver had been a good friend in need. I reminded him of the fact.

"Yes, yes, I am a little absent-minded in such matters. But have you your revolver on you?"

I produced it from my hip-pocket, a short, handy, but very serviceable little weapon. He undid the catch, shook out the cartridges, and examined it with care.

"It's heavy—remarkably heavy," said he.

"Yes, it is a solid bit of work."

He mused over it for a minute.

"Do you know, Watson," said he, "I believe your revolver is going to have a very intimate connection with the mystery which we are investigating."

"My dear Holmes, you are joking."

"No, Watson, I am very serious. There is a test before us. If the test comes off, all will be clear. And the test will depend upon the conduct of this little weapon. One cartridge out. Now we will replace the other five and put on the safety-catch. So! That increases the weight and makes it a better reproduction."

I had no glimmer of what was in his mind, nor did he enlighten me, but sat lost in thought until we pulled up in the little Hampshire station. We secured a ramshackle trap, and in a quarter of an hour were at the house of our confidential friend, the sergeant.

"A clue, Mr. Holmes? What is it?"

"It all depends upon the behaviour of Dr. Watson's revolver," said my friend. "Here it is. Now, officer, can you give me ten yards of string?"

The village shop provided a ball of stout twine.

"I think that this is all we will need," said Holmes. "Now, if you please, we will get off on what I hope is the last stage of our journey."

The sun was setting and turning the rolling Hampshire moor into a wonderful autumnal panorama. The sergeant, with many critical and incredulous glances, which showed his deep doubts of the sanity of my companion, lurched along beside us. As we approached the scene of the crime I could see that my friend under all his habitual coolness was in truth deeply agitated.

"Yes," he said in answer to my remark, "you have seen me miss my mark before, Watson. I have an instinct for such things, and yet it has sometimes played me false. It seemed a certainty when first it flashed across my mind in the cell at Winchester, but one drawback of an active mind is that one can always conceive alternative explanations which would make our scent a false one. And yet—and yet—Well, Watson, we can but try."

As he walked he had firmly tied one end of the string to the handle of the revolver. We had now reached the scene of the tragedy. With great care he marked out under the guidance of the policeman the exact spot where the body had been stretched. He then hunted among the heather and the ferns until he found a considerable stone. This he secured to the other end of his line of string, and he hung it over the parapet of the bridge so that it swung clear above the water. He then stood on the fatal spot, some distance from the edge of the bridge, with my revolver in his hand, the string being taut between the weapon and the heavy stone on the farther side.

"Now for it!" he cried.

At the words he raised the pistol to his head, and then let go his grip. In an instant it had been whisked away by the weight of the stone, had struck with a sharp crack against the parapet, and had vanished over the side into the water. It had hardly gone before Holmes was kneeling beside the stonework, and a joyous cry showed that he had found what he expected.

"Was there ever a more exact demonstration?" he cried. "See, Watson, your revolver has solved the problem!" As he spoke he pointed to a second chip of the exact size and shape of the first which had appeared on the under edge of the stone balustrade.

"We'll stay at the inn to-night," he continued as he rose and faced the astonished sergeant. "You will, of course, get a grappling-hook and you will easily restore my friend's revolver. You will also find beside it the revolver, string and weight with which this vindictive woman attempted to disguise her own crime and to fasten a charge of murder upon an innocent victim. You can let Mr. Gibson know that I will see him in the morning, when steps can be taken for Miss Dunbar's vindication."

Late that evening, as we sat together smoking our pipes in the village inn, Holmes gave me a brief review of what had passed.

"I fear, Watson," said he, "that you will not improve any reputation which I may have acquired by adding the case of the Thor Bridge mystery to your annals. I have been sluggish in mind and wanting in that mixture of imagination and reality which is the basis of my art. I confess that the chip in the stonework was a sufficient clue to suggest the true solution, and that I blame myself for not having attained it sooner.

"It must be admitted that the workings of this unhappy woman's mind were deep and subtle, so that it was no very simple matter to unravel her plot. I do not think that in our adventures we have ever come across a stranger example of what perverted love can bring about. Whether Miss Dunbar was her rival in a physical or in a merely mental sense seems to have been equally unforgivable in her eyes. No doubt she blamed this innocent lady for all those harsh dealings and unkind words with which her husband tried to repel her too demonstrative affection. Her first resolution was to end her own life. Her second was to do it in such a way as to involve her victim in a fate which was worse far than any sudden death could be.

"We can follow the various steps quite clearly, and they show a remarkable subtlety of mind. A note was extracted very cleverly from Miss Dunbar which would make it appear that she had chosen the scene of the crime. In her anxiety that it should be discovered she somewhat overdid it by holding it in her hand to the last. This alone should have excited my suspicions earlier than it did.

"Then she took one of her husband's revolvers—there was, as you saw, an arsenal in the house—and kept it for her own use. A similar one she concealed that morning in Miss Dunbar's wardrobe after discharging one barrel, which she could easily do in the woods without attracting attention. She then went down to the bridge where she had contrived this exceedingly ingenious method for getting rid of her weapon. When Miss Dunbar appeared she used her last breath in pouring out her hatred, and then, when she was out of hearing, carried out her terrible purpose. Every link is now in its place and the chain is complete. The papers may ask why the mere was not dragged in the first instance, but it is easy to be wise after the event, and in any case the expanse of a reed-filled lake is no easy matter to drag unless you have a clear perception of what you are looking for and where. Well, Watson, we have helped a remarkable woman, and also a formidable man. Should they in the future join their forces, as seems not unlikely, the financial world may find that Mr. Neil Gibson has learned something in that schoolroom of sorrow where our earthly lessons are taught."

THE ADVENTURE OF THE
CREEPING MAN

Mr. Sherlock Holmes was always of opinion that I should publish the singular facts connected with Professor Presbury, if only to dispel once for all the ugly rumours which some twenty years ago agitated the university and were echoed in the learned societies of London. There were, however, certain obstacles in the way, and the true history of this curious case remained entombed in the tin box which contains so many records of my friend's adventures. Now we have at last obtained permission to ventilate the facts which formed one of the very last cases handled by Holmes before his retirement from practice. Even now a certain reticence and discretion have to be observed in laying the matter before the public.

It was one Sunday evening early in September of the year 1903 that I received one of Holmes's laconic messages:

Come at once if convenient—if inconvenient come all the same.
                                                              S. H.

The relations between us in those latter days were peculiar. He was a man of habits, narrow and concentrated habits, and I had become one of them. As an institution I was like the violin, the shag tobacco, the old black pipe, the index books, and others perhaps less excusable. When it was a case of active work and a comrade was needed upon whose nerve he could place some reliance, my rôle was obvious. But apart from this I had uses. I was a whetstone for his mind. I stimulated him. He liked to think aloud in my presence. His remarks could hardly be said to be made to me—many of them would have been as appropriately addressed to his bedstead—but none the less, having formed the habit, it had become in some way helpful that I should register and interject. If I irritated him by a certain methodical slowness in my mentality, that irritation served only to make his own flame-like intuitions and impressions flash up the more vividly and swiftly. Such was my humble rôle in our alliance.

When I arrived at Baker Street I found him huddled up in his armchair with updrawn knees, his pipe in his mouth and his brow furrowed with thought. It was clear that he was in the throes of some vexatious problem. With a wave of his hand he indicated my old armchair, but otherwise for half an hour he gave no sign that he was aware of my presence. Then with a start he seemed to come from his reverie, and with his usual whimsical smile he greeted me back to what had once been my home.

"You will excuse a certain abstraction of mind, my dear Watson," said he. "Some curious facts have been submitted to me within the last twenty-four hours, and they in turn have given rise to some speculations of a more general character. I have serious thoughts of writing a small monograph upon the uses of dogs in the work of the detective."

"But surely, Holmes, this has been explored," said I. "Bloodhounds—sleuth-hounds——"

"No, no, Watson, that side of the matter is, of course, obvious. But there is another which is far more subtle. You may recollect that in the case which you, in your sensational way, coupled with the Copper Beeches, I was able, by watching the mind of the child, to form a deduction as to the criminal habits of the very smug and respectable father."

"Yes, I remember it well."

"My line of thoughts, about dogs is analogous. A dog reflects the family life. Whoever saw a frisky dog in a gloomy family, or a sad dog in a happy one? Snarling people have snarling dogs, dangerous people have dangerous ones. And their passing moods may reflect the passing moods of others."

I shook my head. "Surely, Holmes, this is a little far-fetched," said I.

He had refilled his pipe and resumed his seat, taking no notice of my comment.

"The practical application of what I have said is very close to the problem which I am investigating. It is a tangled skein, you understand, and I am looking for a loose end. One possible loose end lies in the question: Why does Professor Presbury's wolfhound, Roy, endeavour to bite him?"

I sank back in my chair in some disappointment. Was it for so trivial a question as this that I had been summoned from my work? Holmes glanced across at me.

"The same old Watson!" said he. "You never learn that the gravest issues may depend upon the smallest things. But is it not on the face of it strange that a staid, elderly philosopher—you've heard of Presbury, of course, the famous Camford* physiologist?—that such a man, whose friend has been his devoted wolfhound, should now have been twice attacked by his own dog? What do you make of it?"

"The dog is ill."

"Well, that has to be considered. But he attacks no one else, nor does he apparently molest his master, save on very special occasions. Curious, Watson—very curious. But young Mr. Bennett is before his time if that is his ring. I had hoped to have a longer chat with you before he came."

There was a quick step on the stairs, a sharp tap at the door, and a moment later the new client presented himself. He was a tall, handsome youth about thirty, well dressed and elegant, but with something in his bearing which suggested the shyness of the student rather than the self-possession of the man of the world. He shook hands with Holmes, and then looked with some surprise at me.

"This matter is very delicate, Mr. Holmes," he said. "Consider the re-

---

*Fictitious place; combination of Cambridge and Oxford.

lation in which I stand to Professor Presbury both privately and publicly.
I really can hardly justify myself if I speak before any third person."

"Have no fear, Mr. Bennett. Dr. Watson is the very soul of discretion,
and I can assure you that this is a matter in which I am very likely to need
an assistant."

"As you like, Mr. Holmes. You will, I am sure, understand my having
some reserves in the matter."

"You will appreciate it, Watson, when I tell you that this gentleman,
Mr. Trevor Bennett, is professional assistant to the great scientist, lives
under his roof, and is engaged to his only daughter. Certainly we must
agree that the professor has every claim upon his loyalty and devotion.
But it may best be shown by taking the necessary steps to clear up this
strange mystery."

"I hope so, Mr. Holmes. That is my one object. Does Dr. Watson know
the situation?"

"I have not had time to explain it."

"Then perhaps I had better go over the ground again explaining some
fresh developments."

"I will do so myself," said Holmes, "in order to show that I have the
events in their due order. The professor, Watson, is a man of European
reputation. His life has been academic. There has never been a breath of
scandal. He is a widower with one daughter, Edith. He is, I gather, a man
of very virile and positive, one might almost say combative, character. So
the matter stood until a very few months ago.

"Then the current of his life was broken. He is sixty-one years of age,
but he became engaged to the daughter of Professor Morphy, his colleague in the chair of comparative anatomy. It was not, as I understand,
the reasoned courting of an elderly man but rather the passionate frenzy
of youth, for no one could have shown himself a more devoted lover. The
lady, Alice Morphy, was a very perfect girl both in mind and body, so that
there was every excuse for the professor's infatuation. None the less, it
did not meet with full approval in his own family."

"We thought it rather excessive," said our visitor.

"Exactly. Excessive and a little violent and unnatural. Professor Presbury was rich, however, and there was no objection upon the part of the
father. The daughter, however, had other views, and there were already
several candidates for her hand, who, if they were less eligible from a
worldly point of view, were at least more of an age. The girl seemed to
like the professor in spite of his eccentricities. It was only age which stood
in the way.

"About this time a little mystery suddenly clouded the normal routine
of the professor's life. He did what he had never done before. He left
home and gave no indication where he was going. He was away a fortnight and returned looking rather travel-worn. He made no allusion to
where he had been, although he was usually the frankest of men. It
chanced, however, that our client here, Mr. Bennett, received a letter
from a fellow-student in Prague, who said that he was glad to have seen

Professor Presbury there, although he had not been able to talk to him. Only in this way did his own household learn where he had been.

"Now comes the point. From that time onward a curious change came over the professor. He became furtive and sly. Those around him had always the feeling that he was not the man that they had known, but that he was under some shadow which had darkened his higher qualities. His intellect was not affected. His lectures were as brilliant as ever. But always there was something new, something sinister and unexpected. His daughter, who was devoted to him, tried again and again to resume the old relations and to penetrate this mask which her father seemed to have put on. You, sir, as I understand, did the same—but all was in vain. And now, Mr. Bennett, tell in your own words the incident of the letters."

"You must understand, Dr. Watson, that the professor had no secrets from me. If I were his son or his younger brother I could not have more completely enjoyed his confidence. As his secretary I handled every paper which came to him, and I opened and subdivided his letters. Shortly after his return all this was changed. He told me that certain letters might come to him from London which would be marked by a cross under the stamp. These were to be set aside for his own eyes only. I may say that several of these did pass through my hands, that they had the E. C. mark,* and were in an illiterate handwriting. If he answered them at all the answers did not pass through my hands nor into the letter-basket in which our correspondence was collected."

"And the box," said Holmes.

"Ah, yes, the box. The professor brought back a little wooden box from his travels. It was the one thing which suggested a Continental tour, for it was one of those quaint carved things which one associates with Germany. This he placed in his instrument cupboard. One day, in looking for a canula,† I took up the box. To my surprise he was very angry, and reproved me in words which were quite savage for my curiosity. It was the first time such a thing had happened, and I was deeply hurt. I endeavoured to explain that it was a mere accident that I had touched the box, but all the evening I was conscious that he looked at me harshly and that the incident was rankling in his mind." Mr. Bennett drew a little diary book from his pocket. "That was on July 2d," said he.

"You are certainly an admirable witness," said Holmes. "I may need some of these dates which you have noted."

"I learned method among other things from my great teacher. From the time that I observed abnormality in his behaviour I felt that it was my duty to study his case. Thus I have it here that it was on that very day, July 2d, that Roy attacked the professor as he came from his study into the hall. Again, on July 11th, there was a scene of the same sort, and then I have a

---

*London Post Office abbreviation for "Eastern Central."
†Tube inserted into a body cavity to drain fluid or give medicine.

note of yet another upon July 20th. After that we had to banish Roy to the stables. He was a dear, affectionate animal—but I fear I weary you."

Mr. Bennett spoke in a tone of reproach, for it was very clear that Holmes was not listening. His face was rigid and his eyes gazed abstractedly at the ceiling. With an effort he recovered himself.

"Singular! Most singular!" he murmured. "These details were new to me, Mr. Bennett. I think we have now fairly gone over the old ground, have we not? But you spoke of some fresh developments."

The pleasant, open face of our visitor clouded over, shadowed by some grim remembrance. "What I speak of occurred the night before last," said he. "I was lying awake about two in the morning, when I was aware of a dull muffled sound coming from the passage. I opened my door and peeped out. I should explain that the professor sleeps at the end of the passage——"

"The date being——?" asked Holmes.

Our visitor was clearly annoyed at so irrelevant an interruption.

"I have said, sir, that it was the night before last—that is, September 4th."

Holmes nodded and smiled.

"Pray continue," said he.

"He sleeps at the end of the passage and would have to pass my door in order to reach the staircase. It was a really terrifying experience, Mr. Holmes. I think that I am as strong-nerved as my neighbours, but I was shaken by what I saw. The passage was dark save that one window halfway along it threw a patch of light. I could see that something was coming along the passage, something dark and crouching. Then suddenly it emerged into the light, and I saw that it was he. He was crawling, Mr. Holmes—crawling! He was not quite on his hands and knees. I should rather say on his hands and feet, with his face sunk between his hands. Yet he seemed to move with ease. I was so paralyzed by the sight that it was not until he had reached my door that I was able to step forward and ask if I could assist him. His answer was extraordinary. He sprang up, spat out some atrocious word at me, and hurried on past me, and down the staircase. I waited about for an hour, but he did not come back. It must have been daylight before he regained his room."

"Well, Watson, what make you of that?" asked Holmes with the air of the pathologist who presents a rare specimen.

"Lumbago, possibly. I have known a severe attack make a man walk in just such a way, and nothing would be more trying to the temper."

"Good, Watson! You always keep us flat-footed on the ground. But we can hardly accept lumbago, since he was able to stand erect in a moment."

"He was never better in health," said Bennett. "In fact, he is stronger than I have known him for years. But there are the facts, Mr. Holmes. It is not a case in which we can consult the police, and yet we are utterly at our wit's end as to what to do, and we feel in some strange way that we are drifting towards disaster. Edith—Miss Presbury—feels as I do, that we cannot wait passively any longer."

"It is certainly a very curious and suggestive case. What do you think, Watson?"

"Speaking as a medical man," said I, "it appears to be a case for an alienist.* The old gentleman's cerebral processes were disturbed by the love affair. He made a journey abroad in the hope of breaking himself of the passion. His letters and the box may be connected with some other private transaction—a loan, perhaps, or share certificates, which are in the box."

"And the wolfhound no doubt disapproved of the financial bargain. No, no, Watson, there is more in it than this. Now, I can only suggest——"

What Sherlock Holmes was about to suggest will never be known, for at this moment the door opened and a young lady was shown into the room. As she appeared Mr. Bennett sprang up with a cry and ran forward with his hands out to meet those which she had herself outstretched.

"Edith, dear! Nothing the matter, I hope?"

"I felt I must follow you. Oh, Jack, I have been so dreadfully frightened! It is awful to be there alone."

"Mr. Holmes, this is the young lady I spoke of. This is my fiancée."

"We were gradually coming to that conclusion, were we not, Watson?" Holmes answered with a smile. "I take it, Miss Presbury, that there is some fresh development in the case, and that you thought we should know?"

Our new visitor, a bright, handsome girl of a conventional English type, smiled back at Holmes as she seated herself beside Mr. Bennett.

"When I found Mr. Bennett had left his hotel I thought I should probably find him here. Of course, he had told me that he would consult you. But, oh, Mr. Holmes, can you do nothing for my poor father?"

"I have hopes, Miss Presbury, but the case is still obscure. Perhaps what you have to say may throw some fresh light upon it."

"It was last night, Mr. Holmes. He had been very strange all day. I am sure that there are times when he has no recollection of what he does. He lives as in a strange dream. Yesterday was such a day. It was not my father with whom I lived. His outward shell was there, but it was not really he."

"Tell me what happened."

"I was awakened in the night by the dog barking most furiously. Poor Roy, he is chained now near the stable. I may say that I always sleep with my door locked; for, as Jack—as Mr. Bennett—will tell you, we all have a feeling of impending danger. My room is on the second floor. It happened that the blind was up in my window, and there was bright moonlight outside. As I lay with my eyes fixed upon the square of light, listening to the frenzied barkings of the dog, I was amazed to my father's face looking in at me. Mr. Holmes, I nearly died of surprise and horror. There it was pressed against the windowpane, and one hand seemed to be raised as if to push up the window. If that window had opened, I think I should have gone mad. It was no delusion, Mr. Holmes. Don't deceive yourself by

---

*Old word for psychiatrist.

thinking so. I dare say it was twenty seconds or so that I lay paralyzed and watched the face. Then it vanished, but I could not—I could not spring out of bed and look out after it. I lay cold and shivering till morning. At breakfast he was sharp and fierce in manner, and made no allusion to the adventure of the night. Neither did I, but I gave an excuse for coming to town—and here I am."

Holmes looked thoroughly surprised at Miss Presbury's narrative.

"My dear young lady, you say that your room is on second floor. Is there a long ladder in the garden?"

"No, Mr. Holmes, that is the amazing part of it. There is no possible way of reaching the window—and yet he was there."

"The date being September 5th," said Holmes. "That certainly complicates matters."

It was the young lady's turn to look surprised. "This is the second time that you have alluded to the date, Mr. Holmes," said Bennett. "Is it possible that it has any bearing upon the case?"

"It is possible—very possible—and yet I have not my full material at present."

"Possibly you are thinking of the connection between insanity and phases of the moon?"

"No, I assure you. It was quite a different line of thought. Possibly you can leave your notebook with me, and I will check the dates. Now I think, Watson, that our line of action is perfectly clear. This young lady has informed us—and I have the greatest confidence in her intuition—that her father remembers little or nothing which occurs upon certain dates. We will therefore call upon him as if he had given us an appointment upon such a date. He will put it down to his own lack of memory. Thus we will open our campaign by having a good close view of him."

"That is excellent," said Mr. Bennett. "I warn you, however, that the professor is irascible and violent at times."

Holmes smiled. "There are reasons why we should come at once—very cogent reasons if my theories hold good. To-morrow, Mr. Bennett, will certainly see us in Camford. There is, if I remember right, an inn called the Chequers where the port used to be above mediocrity and the linen was above reproach. I think, Watson, that our lot for the next few days might lie in less pleasant places."

Monday morning found us on our way to the famous university town—an easy effort on the part of Holmes, who had no roots to pull up, but one which involved frantic planning and hurrying on my part, as my practice was by this time not inconsiderable. Holmes made no allusion to the case until after we had deposited our suitcases at the ancient hostel of which he had spoken.

"I think, Watson, that we can catch the professor just before lunch. He lectures at eleven and should have an interval at home."

"What possible excuse have we for calling?"

Holmes glanced at his notebook.

"There was a period of excitement upon August 26th. We will assume that he is a little hazy as to what he does at such times. If we insist that we are there by appointment I think he will hardly venture to contradict us. Have you the effrontery necessary to put it through?"

"We can but try."

"Excellent, Watson! Compound of the Busy Bee and Excelsior. We can but try—the motto of the firm. A friendly native will surely guide us."

Such a one on the back of a smart hansom swept us past a row of ancient colleges and, finally turning into a tree-lined drive, pulled up at the door of a charming house, girt round with lawns and covered with purple wisteria. Professor Presbury was certainly surrounded with every sign not only of comfort but of luxury. Even as we pulled up, a grizzled head appeared at the front window, and we were aware of a pair of keen eyes from under shaggy brows which surveyed us through large horn glasses. A moment later we were actually in his sanctum, and the mysterious scientist, whose vagaries had brought us from London, was standing before us. There was certainly no sign of eccentricity either in his manner or appearance, for he was a portly, large-featured man, grave, tall, and frock-coated, with the dignity of bearing which a lecturer needs. His eyes were his most remarkable feature, keen, observant, and clever to the verge of cunning.

He looked at our cards. "Pray sit down gentlemen. What can I do for you?"

Mr. Holmes smiled amiably.

"It was the question which I was about to put to you, Professor."

"To me, sir!"

"Possibly there is some mistake. I heard through a second person that Professor Presbury of Camford had need of my services."

"Oh, indeed!" It seemed to me that there was a malicious sparkle in the intense gray eyes. "You heard that, did you? May I ask the name of your informant?"

"I am sorry, Professor, but the matter was rather confidential. If I have made a mistake there is no harm done. I can only express my regret."

"Not at all. I should wish to go further into this matter. It interests me. Have you any scrap of writing, any letter or telegram, to bear out your assertion?"

"No, I have not."

"I presume that you do not go so far as to assert that I summoned you?"

"I would rather answer no questions," said Holmes.

"No, I dare say not," said the professor with asperity. "However, that particular one can be answered very easily without your aid."

He walked across the room to the bell. Our London friend, Mr. Bennett, answered the call.

"Come in, Mr. Bennett. These two gentlemen have come from London under the impression that they have been summoned. You handle all my correspondence. Have you a note of anything going to a person named Holmes?"

"No, sir," Bennett answered with a flush.

"That is conclusive," said the professor, glaring angrily at my compan-

ion. "Now, sir"—he leaned forward with his two hands upon the table—
"it seems to me that your position is a very questionable one."

Holmes shrugged his shoulders.

"I can only repeat that I am sorry that we have made a needless intrusion."

"Hardly enough, Mr. Holmes!" the old man cried in a high screaming
voice, with extraordinary malignancy upon his face. He got between us
and the door as he spoke, and he shook his two hands at us with furious
passion. "You can hardly get out of it so easily as that." His face was convulsed, and he grinned and gibbered at us in his senseless rage. I am convinced that we should have had to fight our way out of the room if Mr.
Bennett had not intervened.

"My dear Professor," he cried, "consider your position! Consider the
scandal at the university! Mr. Holmes is a well-known man. You cannot
possibly treat him with such discourtesy."

Sulkily our host—if I may call him so—cleared the path to the door.
We were glad to find ourselves outside the house and in the quiet of the
tree-lined drive. Holmes seemed greatly amused by the episode.

"Our learned friend's nerves are somewhat out of order," said he.
"Perhaps our intrusion was a little crude, and yet we have gained that personal contact which I desired. But, dear me, Watson, he is surely at our
heels. The villain still pursues us."

There were the sounds of running feet behind, but it was, to my relief,
not the formidable professor but his assistant who appeared round the
curve of the drive. He came panting up to us.

"I am so sorry, Mr. Holmes. I wished to apologize."

"My dear sir, there is no need. It is all in the way of professional experience."

"I have never seen him in a more dangerous mood. But he grows more
sinister. You can understand now why his daughter and I are alarmed.
And yet his mind is perfectly clear."

"Too clear!" said Holmes. "That was my miscalculation. It is evident
that his memory is much more reliable than I had thought. By the way,
can we, before we go, see the window of Miss Presbury's room?"

Mr. Bennett pushed his way through some shrubs, and we had a view
of the side of the house.

"It is there. The second on the left."

"Dear me, it seems hardly accessible. And yet you will observe that
there is a creeper below and a water-pipe above which give some
foothold."

"I could not climb it myself," said Mr. Bennett.

"Very likely. It would certainly be a dangerous exploit for any normal
man."

"There was one other thing I wish to tell you, Mr. Holmes. I have the
address of the man in London to whom the professor writes. He seems to
have written this morning, and I got it from his blotting-paper. It is an ignoble position for a trusted secretary, but what else can I do?"

Holmes glanced at the paper and put it into his pocket.

"Dorak—a curious name. Slavonic, I imagine. Well, it is an important link in the chain. We return to London this afternoon, Mr. Bennett. I see no good purpose to be served by our remaining. We cannot arrest the professor because he has done no crime, nor can we place him under constraint, for he cannot be proved to be mad. No action is as yet possible."

"Then what on earth are we to do?"

"A little patience, Mr. Bennett. Things will soon develop. Unless I am mistaken, next Tuesday may mark a crisis. Certainly we shall be in Camford on that day. Meanwhile, the general position is undeniably unpleasant, and if Miss Presbury can prolong her visit—"

"That is easy."

"Then let her stay till we can assure her that all danger is past. Meanwhile, let him have his way and do not cross him. So long as he is in a good humour all is well."

"There he is!" said Bennett in a startled whisper. Looking between the branches we saw the tall, erect figure emerge from the hall door and look around him. He stood leaning forward, his hands swinging straight before him, his head turning from side to side. The secretary with a last wave slipped off among the trees, and we saw him presently rejoin his employer, the two entering the house together in what seemed to be animated and even excited conversation.

"I expect the old gentleman has been putting two and two together," said Holmes as we walked hotelward. "He struck me as having a particularly clear and logical brain from the little I saw of him. Explosive, no doubt, but then from his point of view he has something to explode about if detectives are put on his track and he suspects his own household of doing it. I rather fancy that friend Bennett is in for an uncomfortable time."

Holmes stopped at a post-office and sent off a telegram on our way. The answer reached us in the evening, and he tossed it across to me.

Have visited the Commercial Road and seen Dorak. Suave person, Bohemian, elderly. Keeps large general store.

MERCER.

"Mercer is since your time," said Holmes. "He is my general utility man who looks up routine business. It was important to know something of the man with whom our professor was so secretly corresponding. His nationality connects up with the Prague visit."

"Thank goodness that something connects with something," said I. "At present we seem to be faced by a long series of inexplicable incidents with no bearing upon each other. For example, what possible connection can there be between an angry wolfhound and a visit to Bohemia, or either of them with a man crawling down a passage at night? As to your dates, that is the biggest mystification of all."

Holmes smiled and rubbed his hands. We were, I may say, seated in the old sitting-room of the ancient hotel, with a bottle of the famous vintage of which Holmes had spoken on the table between us.

"Well, now, let us take the dates first," said he, his fingertips together and his manner as if he were addressing a class. "This excellent young man's diary shows that there was trouble upon July 2d, and from then onward it seems to have been at nine-day intervals, with, so far as I remember, only one exception. Thus the last outbreak upon Friday was on September 3d, which also falls into the series, as did August 26th, which preceded it. The thing is beyond coincidence."

I was forced to agree.

"Let us, then, form the provisional theory that every nine days the professor takes some strong drug which has a passing but highly poisonous effect. His naturally violent nature is intensified by it. He learned to take this drug while he was in Prague, and is now supplied with it by a Bohemian intermediary in London. This all hangs together, Watson!"

"But the dog, the face at the window, the creeping man in the passage?"

"Well, well, we have made a beginning. I should not expect any fresh developments until next Tuesday. In the meantime we can only keep in touch with friend Bennett and enjoy the amenities of this charming town."

In the morning Mr. Bennett slipped round to bring us the latest report. As Holmes had imagined, times had not been easy with him. Without exactly accusing him of being responsible for our presence, the professor had been very rough and rude in his speech, and evidently felt some strong grievance. This morning he was quite himself again, however, and had delivered his usual brilliant lecture to a crowded class. "Apart from his queer fits," said Bennett, "he has actually more energy and vitality than I can ever remember, nor was his brain ever clearer. But it's not he— it's never the man whom we have known."

"I don't think you have anything to fear now for a week a least," Holmes answered. "I am a busy man, and Dr. Watson has his patients to attend to. Let us agree that we meet here at this hour next Tuesday, and I shall be surprised if before we leave you again we are not able to explain, even if we cannot perhaps put an end to, your troubles. Meanwhile, keep us posted in what occurs."

I saw nothing of my friend for the next few days, but on the following Monday evening I had a short note asking me to meet him next day at the train. From what he told me as we travelled up to Camford all was well, the peace of the professor's house had been unruffled, and his own conduct perfectly normal. This also was the report which was given us by Mr. Bennett himself when he called upon us that evening at our old quarters in the Chequers. "He heard from his London correspondent to-day. There was a letter and there was a small packet, each with the cross under the stamp which warned me not to touch them. There has been nothing else."

"That may prove quite enough," said Holmes grimly. "Now, Mr. Bennett, we shall, I think, come to some conclusion to-night. If my deductions are correct we should have an opportunity of bringing matters to a head.

In order to do so it is necessary to hold the professor under observation. I would suggest, therefore, that you remain awake and on the lookout. Should you hear him pass your door, do not interrupt him, but follow him as discreetly as you can. Dr. Watson and I will not be far off. By the way, where is the key of that little box of which you spoke?"

"Upon his watch-chain."

"I fancy our researches must lie in that direction. At the worst the lock should not be very formidable. Have you any other able-bodied man on the premises?"

"There is the coachman, Macphail."

"Where does he sleep?"

"Over the stables."

"We might possibly want him. Well, we can do no more until we see how things develop, Good-bye—but I expect that we shall see you before morning."

It was nearly midnight before we took our station among some bushes immediately opposite the hall door of the professor. It was a fine night, but chilly, and we were glad of our warm overcoats. There was a breeze, and clouds were scudding across the sky, obscuring from time to time the half-moon. It would have been a dismal vigil were it not for the expectation and excitement which carried us along, and the assurance of my comrade that we had probably reached the end of the strange sequence of events which had engaged our attention.

"If the cycle of nine days holds good then we shall have the professor at his worst to-night," said Holmes. "The fact that these strange symptoms began after his visit to Prague, that he is in secret correspondence with a Bohemian dealer in London, who presumably represents someone in Prague, and that he received a packet from him this very day, all point in one direction. What he takes and why he takes it are still beyond our ken, but that it emanates in some way from Prague is clear enough. He takes it under definite directions which regulate this ninth-day system, which was the first point which attracted my attention. But his symptoms are most remarkable. Did you observe his knuckles?"

I had to confess that I did not.

"Thick and horny in a way which is quite new in my experience. Always look at the hands first, Watson. Then cuffs, trouser-knees, and boots. Very curious knuckles which can only be explained by the mode of progression observed by——" Holmes paused and suddenly clapped his hand to his forehead. "Oh, Watson, Watson, what a fool I have been! It seems incredible, and yet it must be true. All points in one direction. How could I miss seeing the connection of ideas? Those knuckles—how could I have passed those knuckles? And the dog! And the ivy! It's surely time that I disappeared into that little farm of my dreams. Look out, Watson! Here he is! We shall have the chance of seeing for ourselves."

The hall door had slowly opened, and against the lamplit background we saw the tall figure of Professor Presbury. He was clad in his dressing gown. As he stood outlined in the doorway he was erect but leaning forward with dangling arms, as when we saw him last.

Now he stepped forward into the drive, and an extraordinary change came over him. He sank down into a crouching position and moved along upon his hands and feet, skipping every now and then as if he were overflowing with energy and vitality. He moved along the face of the house and then round the corner. As he disappeared Bennett slipped through the hall door and softly followed him.

"Come, Watson, come!" cried Holmes, and we stole as softly as we could through the bushes until we had gained a spot whence we could see the other side of the house, which was bathed in the light of the half-moon. The professor was clearly visible crouching at the foot of the ivy-covered wall. As we watched him he suddenly began with incredible agility to ascend it. From branch to branch he sprang, sure of foot and firm of grasp, climbing apparently in mere joy at his own powers, with no definite object in view. With his dressing-gown flapping on each side of him, he looked like some huge bat glued against the side of his own house, a great square dark patch upon the moonlit wall. Presently he tired of this amusement, and, dropping from branch to branch, he squatted down into the old attitude and moved towards the stables, creeping along in the same strange way as before. The wolfhound was out now, barking furiously, and more excited than ever when it actually caught sight of its master. It was straining on its chain and quivering with eagerness and rage. The professor squatted down very deliberately just out of reach of the hound and began to provoke it in every possible way. He took handfuls of pebbles from the drive and threw them in the dog's face, prodded him with a stick which he had picked up, flicked his hands about only a few inches from the gaping mouth, and endeavoured in every way to increase the animal's fury, which was already beyond all control. In all our adventures I do not know that I have ever seen a more strange sight than this impassive and still dignified figure crouching frog-like upon the ground and goading to a wilder exhibition of passion the maddened hound, which ramped* and raged in front of him, by all manner of ingenious and calculated cruelty.

And then in a moment it happened! It was not the chain that broke, but it was the collar that slipped, for it had been made for a thick-necked Newfoundland. We heard the rattle of falling metal, and the next instant dog and man were rolling on the ground together, the one roaring in rage, the other screaming in a strange shrill falsetto of terror. It was a very narrow thing for the professor's life. The savage creature had him fairly by the throat, its fangs had bitten deep, and he was senseless before we could reach them and drag the two apart. It might have been a dangerous task for us, but Bennett's voice and presence brought the great wolfhound instantly to reason. The uproar had brought the sleepy and astonished coachman from his room

---

*Reared up.

above the stables. "I'm not surprised," said he, shaking his head. "I've seen him at it before. I knew the dog would get him sooner or later."

The hound was secured, and together we carried the professor up to his room, where Bennett, who had a medical degree, helped me to dress his torn throat. The sharp teeth had passed dangerously near the carotid artery, and the hæmorrhage was serious. In half an hour the danger was past, I had given the patient an injection of morphia, and he had sunk into deep sleep. Then, and only then, were we able to look at each other and to take stock of the situation.

"I think a first-class surgeon should see him," said I.

"For God's sake, no!" cried Bennett. "At present the scandal is confined to our own household. It is safe with us. If it gets beyond these walls it will never stop. Consider his position at the university, his European reputation, the feelings of his daughter."

"Quite so," said Holmes. "I think it may be quite possible to keep the matter to ourselves, and also to prevent its recurrence now that we have a free hand. The key from the watch-chain, Mr. Bennett. Macphail will guard the patient and let us know if there is any change. Let us see what we can find in the professor's mysterious box."

There was not much, but there was enough—an empty phial, another nearly full, a hypodermic syringe, several letters in a crabbed, foreign hand. The marks on the envelopes showed that they were those which had disturbed the routine of the secretary, and each was dated from the Commercial Road and signed "A. Dorak." They were mere invoices to say that a fresh bottle was being sent to Professor Presbury, or receipt to acknowledge money. There was one other envelope, however, in a more educated hand and bearing the Austrian stamp with the postmark of Prague. "Here we have our material!" cried Holmes as he tore out the enclosure.

HONOURED COLLEAGUE [it ran]:

Since your esteemed visit I have thought much of your case, and though in your circumstances there are some special reasons for the treatment, I would none the less enjoin caution, as my results have shown that it is not without danger of a kind.

It is possible that the serum of anthropoid would have been better. I have, as I explained to you, used black-faced langur because a specimen was accessible. Langur is, of course, a crawler and climber, while anthropoid walks erect and is in all ways nearer.

I beg you to take every possible precaution that there be no premature revelation of the process. I have one other client in England, and Dorak is my agent for both.

Weekly reports will oblige.

Yours with high esteem,
H. LOWENSTEIN.

Lowenstein! The name brought back to me the memory of some snippet from a newspaper which spoke of an obscure scientist who was striving in some unknown way for the secret of rejuvenescence and the elixir of life. Lowenstein of Prague! Lowenstein with the wondrous strength-giving serum, tabooed by the profession because he refused to reveal its source. In a few words I said what I remembered. Bennett had taken a manual of zoölogy from the shelves. "'Langur,'" he read, "'the great black-faced monkey of the Himalayan slopes, biggest and most human of climbing monkeys.' Many details are added. Well, thanks to you, Mr. Holmes, it is very clear that we have traced the evil to its source."

"The real source," said Holmes, "lies, of course, in that untimely love affair which gave our impetuous professor the idea that he could only gain his wish by turning himself into a younger man. When one tries to rise above Nature one is liable to fall below it. The highest type of man may revert to the animal if he leaves the straight road of destiny." He sat musing for a little with the phial in his hand, looking at the clear liquid within. "When I have written to this man and told him that I hold him criminally responsible for the poisons which he circulates, we will have no more trouble. But it may recur. Others may find a better way. There is danger there—a very real danger to humanity. Consider, Watson, that the material, the sensual, the worldly would all prolong their worthless lives. The spiritual would not avoid the call to something higher. It would be the survival of the least fit. What sort of cesspool may not our poor world become?" Suddenly the dreamer disappeared, and Holmes, the man of action, sprang from his chair. "I think there is nothing more to be said, Mr. Bennett. The various incidents will now fit themselves easily into the general scheme. The dog, of course, was aware of the change far more quickly than you. His smell would insure that. It was the monkey, not the professor, whom Roy attacked, just as it was the monkey who teased Roy. Climbing was a joy to the creature, and it was a mere chance, I take it, that the pastime brought him to the young lady's window. There is an early train to town, Watson, but I think we shall just have time for a cup of tea at the Chequers before we catch it."

THE ADVENTURE OF THE
LION'S MANE

It is a most singular thing that a problem which was certainly as abstruse and unusual as any which I have faced in my long professional career should have come to me after my retirement, and be brought, as it were, to my very door. It occurred after my withdrawal to my little Sussex home, when I had given myself up entirely to that soothing life of Nature for which I had so often yearned during the long years spent amid the gloom of London. At this period of my life the good Watson had passed almost beyond my ken. An occasional week-end visit was the most that I ever saw of him. Thus I must act as my own chronicler. Ah! had he but been with me, how much he might have made of so wonderful a happening and of my eventual triumph against every difficulty! As it is, however, I must needs tell my tale in my own plain way, showing by my words each step upon the difficult road which lay before me as I searched for the mystery of the Lion's Mane.

My villa is situated upon the southern slope of the Downs,* commanding a great view of the Channel. At this point the coast-line is entirely of chalk cliffs, which can only be descended by a single, long, tortuous path, which is steep and slippery. At the bottom of the path lie a hundred yards of pebbles and shingle, even when the tide is at full. Here and there, however, there are curves and hollows which make splendid swimming-pools filled afresh with each flow. This admirable beach extends for some miles in each direction, save only at one point where the little cove and village of Fulworth break the line.

My house is lonely. I, my old housekeeper, and my bees have the estate all to ourselves. Half a mile off, however, is Harold Stackhurst's well-known coaching establishment, The Gables, quite a large place, which contains some score of young fellows preparing for various professions, with a staff of several masters. Stackhurst himself was a well-known rowing Blue† in his day, and an excellent all-round scholar. He and I were always friendly from the day I came to the coast, and he was the one man who was on such terms with me that we could drop in on each other in the evenings without an invitation.

Towards the end of July 1907, there was a severe gale, the wind blowing up-channel, heaping the seas to the base of the cliffs and leaving a lagoon at the turn of the tide. On the morning of which I speak the wind had abated, and all Nature was newly washed and fresh. It was impossible to work upon so delightful a day, and I strolled out before breakfast

---

*Sussex Downs, a chalky, treeless expanse on the southern coast of England.
†Student at Oxford or Cambridge who represents the university in a sport.

to enjoy the exquisite air. I walked along the cliff path which led to the steep descent to the beach. As I walked I heard a shout behind me, and there was Harold Stackhurst waving his hand in cheery greeting.

"What a morning, Mr. Holmes! I thought I should see you out."

"Going for a swim, I see."

"At your old tricks again," he laughed, patting his bulging pocket. "Yes. McPherson started early, and I expect I may find him there."

Fitzroy McPherson was the science master, a fine upstanding young fellow whose life had been crippled by heart trouble following rheumatic fever. He was a natural athlete, however, and excelled in every game which did not throw too great a strain upon him. Summer and winter he went for his swim, and, as I am a swimmer myself, I have often joined him.

At this moment we saw the man himself. His head showed above the edge of the cliff where the path ends. Then his whole figure appeared at the top, staggering like a drunken man. The next instant he threw up his hands and, with a terrible cry, fell upon his face. Stackhurst and I rushed forward—it may have been fifty yards—and turned him on his back. He was obviously dying. Those glazed sunken eyes and dreadful livid cheeks could mean nothing else. One glimmer of life came into his face for an instant, and he uttered two or three words with an eager air of warning. They were slurred and indistinct, but to my ear the last of them, which burst in a shriek from his lips, were "the Lion's Mane." It was utterly irrelevant and unintelligible, and yet I could twist the sound into no other sense. Then he half raised himself from the ground, threw his arms into the air, and fell forward on his side. He was dead.

My companion was paralyzed by the sudden horror of it, but I, as may well be imagined, had every sense on the alert. And I had need, for it was speedily evident that we were in the presence of an extraordinary case. The man was dressed only in his Burberry overcoat, his trousers, and an unlaced pair of canvas shoes. As he fell over, his Burberry, which had been simply thrown round his shoulders, slipped off, exposing his trunk. We stared at it in amazement. His back was covered with dark red lines as though he had been terribly flogged by a thin wire scourge. The instrument with which this punishment had been inflicted was clearly flexible, for the long, angry weals curved round his shoulders and ribs. There was blood dripping down his chin, for he had bitten through his lower lip in the paroxysm of his agony. His drawn and distorted face told how terrible that agony had been.

I was kneeling and Stackhurst standing by the body when a shadow fell across us, and we found that Ian Murdoch was by our side. Murdoch was the mathematical coach at the establishment, a tall, dark, thin man, so taciturn and aloof that none can be said to have been his friend. He seemed to live in some high, abstract region of surds and conic sections,[22] with little to connect him with ordinary life. He was looked upon as an oddity by the students, and would have been their butt, but there was some strange outlandish blood in the man, which showed itself not only in his coal-black eyes and swarthy face but also in occasional outbreaks of temper, which could only be described as ferocious. On one occasion, being plagued by a little dog belonging to McPherson, he had caught the creature up and hurled it through the plate-glass window, an action for which Stackhurst would certainly have given him his dismissal had he not been a very valuable teacher. Such was the strange complex man who now appeared beside us. He seemed to be honestly shocked at the sight before him, though the incident of the dog may show that there was no great sympathy between the dead man and himself.

"Poor fellow! Poor fellow! What can I do? How can I help?"

"Were you with him? Can you tell us what has happened?"

"No, no, I was late this morning. I was not on the beach at all. I have come straight from The Gables. What can I do?"

"You can hurry to the police-station at Fulworth. Report the matter at once."

Without a word he made off at top speed, and I proceeded to take the matter in hand, while Stackhurst, dazed at this tragedy, remained by the body. My first task naturally was to note who was on the beach. From the top of the path I could see the whole sweep of it, and it was absolutely deserted save that two or three dark figures could be seen far away moving towards the village of Fulworth. Having satisfied myself upon this point, I walked slowly down the path. There was clay or soft marl* mixed with the chalk, and every here and there I saw the same footstep, both ascending and descending. No one else had gone down to the beach by this track that morning. At one place I observed the print of an open hand with the fingers towards the incline. This could only mean that poor McPherson had fallen as he ascended. There were rounded depressions, too, which suggested that he had come down upon his knees more than once. At the bottom of the path was the considerable lagoon left by the retreating tide. At the side of it McPherson had undressed, for there lay his towel on a rock. It was folded and dry, so that it would seem that, after all, he had never entered the water. Once or twice as I hunted round amid the hard shingle I came on little patches of sand where the print of his canvas shoe, and also of his naked foot, could be seen. The latter fact proved that he had made all ready to bathe, though the towel indicated that he had not actually done so.

And here was the problem clearly defined—as strange a one as had ever confronted me. The man had not been on the beach more than a quarter of an hour at the most. Stackhurst had followed him from The Gables, so there could be no doubt about that. He had gone to bathe and had stripped, as the naked footsteps showed. Then he had suddenly huddled on his clothes again—they were all dishevelled and unfastened—and he had returned without bathing, or at any rate without drying himself. And the reason for his change of purpose had been that he had been

---

*Loose or crumbly earthy deposit containing calcium carbonate; can be used as a fertilizer.

scourged in some savage, inhuman fashion, tortured until he bit his lip through in his agony, and was left with only strength enough to crawl away and to die. Who had done this barbarous deed? There were, it is true, small grottos and caves in the base of the cliffs, but the low sun shone directly into them, and there was no place for concealment. Then, again, there were those distant figures on the beach. They seemed too far away to have been connected with the crime, and the broad lagoon in which McPherson had intended to bathe lay between him and them, lapping up to the rocks. On the sea two or three fishing-boats were at no great distance. Their occupants might be examined at our leisure. There were several roads for inquiry, but none which led to any very obvious goal.

When I at last returned to the body I found that a little group of wondering folk had gathered round it. Stackhurst was, of course, still there, and Ian Murdoch had just arrived with Anderson, the village constable, a big, ginger-moustached man of the slow, solid Sussex breed—a breed which covers much good sense under a heavy, silent exterior. He listened to everything, took note of all we said, and finally drew me aside.

"I'd be glad of your advice, Mr. Holmes. This is a big thing for me to handle, and I'll hear of it from Lewes if I go wrong."

I advised him to send for his immediate superior, and for a doctor; also to allow nothing to be moved, and as few fresh footmarks as possible to be made, until they came. In the meantime I searched the dead man's pockets. There were his handkerchief, a large knife, and a small folding card-case. From this projected a slip of paper, which I unfolded and handed to the constable. There was written on it in a scrawling, feminine hand:

I will be there, you may be sure.

MAUDIE.

It read like a love affair, an assignation, though when and where were a blank. The constable replaced it in the card-ease and returned it with the other things to the pockets of the Burberry. Then, as nothing more suggested itself, I walked back to my house for breakfast, having first arranged that the base of the cliffs should be thoroughly searched.

Stackhurst was round in an hour or two to tell me that the body had been removed to The Gables, where the inquest would be held. He brought with him some serious and definite news. As I expected, nothing had been found in the small caves below the cliff, but he had examined the papers in McPherson's desk, and there were several which showed an intimate correspondence with a certain Miss Maud Bellamy, of Fulworth. We had then established the identity of the writer of the note.

"The police have the letters," he explained. "I could not bring them. But there is no doubt that it was a serious love affair. I see no reason, however, to connect it with that horrible happening save, indeed, that the lady had made an appointment with him."

"But hardly at a bathing-pool which all of you were in the habit of using," I remarked.

"It is mere chance," said he, "that several of the students were not with McPherson."

"*Was* it mere chance?"

Stackhurst knit his brows in thought.

"Ian Murdoch held them back," said he. "He would insist upon some algebraic demonstration before breakfast. Poor chap, he is dreadfully cut up about it all."

"And yet I gather that they were not friends."

"At one time they were not. But for a year or more Murdoch has been as near to McPherson as he ever could be to anyone. He is not of a very sympathetic disposition by nature."

"So I understand. I seem to remember your telling me once about a quarrel over the ill-usage of a dog."

"That blew over all right."

"But left some vindictive feeling, perhaps."

"No, no, I am sure they were real friends."

"Well, then, we must explore the matter of the girl. Do you know her?"

"Everyone knows her. She is the beauty of the neighbourhood—a real beauty, Holmes, who would draw attention everywhere. I knew that McPherson was attracted by her, but I had no notion that it had gone so far as these letters would seem to indicate."

"But who is she?"

"She is the daughter of old Tom Bellamy who owns all the boats and bathing-cots at Fulworth. He was a fisherman to start with, but is now a man of some substance. He and his son William run the business."

"Shall we walk into Fulworth and see them?"

"On what pretext?"

"Oh, we can easily find a pretext. After all, this poor man did not ill-use himself in this outrageous way. Some human hand was on the handle of that scourge, if indeed it was a scourge which inflicted the injuries. His circle of acquaintances in this lonely place was surely limited. Let us follow it up in every direction and we can hardly fail to come upon the motive, which in turn should lead us to the criminal."

It would have been a pleasant walk across the thyme-scented downs had our minds not been poisoned by the tragedy we had witnessed. The village of Fulworth lies in a hollow curving in a semicircle round the bay. Behind the old-fashioned hamlet several modern houses have been built upon the rising ground. It was to one of these that Stackhurst guided me.

"That's The Haven, as Bellamy called it. The one with the corner tower and slate roof. Not bad for a man who started with nothing but—— By Jove, look at that!"

The garden gate of The Haven had opened and a man had emerged. There was no mistaking that tall, angular, straggling figure. It was Ian Murdoch, the mathematician. A moment later we confronted him upon the road.

"Hullo!" said Stackhurst. The man nodded, gave us a sideways glance from his curious dark eyes, and would have passed us, but his principal pulled him up.

"What were you doing there?" he asked.

Murdoch's face flushed with anger. "I am your subordinate, sir, under your roof. I am not aware that I owe you any account of my private actions."

Stackhurst's nerves were near the surface after all he had endured. Otherwise, perhaps, he would have waited. Now he lost his temper completely.

"In the circumstances your answer is pure impertinence, Mr. Murdoch."

"Your own question might perhaps come under the same heading."

"This is not the first time that I have had to overlook your insubordinate ways. It will certainly be the last. You will kindly make fresh arrangements for your future as speedily as you can."

"I had intended to do so. I have lost to-day the only person who made The Gables habitable."

He strode off upon his way, while Stackhurst, with angry eyes, stood glaring after him. "Is he not an impossible, intolerable man?" he cried.

The one thing that impressed itself forcibly upon my mind was that Mr. Ian Murdoch was taking the first chance to open a path of escape from the scene of the crime. Suspicion, vague and nebulous, was now beginning to take outline in my mind. Perhaps the visit to the Bellamys might throw some further light upon the matter. Stackhurst pulled himself together, and we went forward to the house.

Mr. Bellamy proved to be a middle-aged man with a flaming red beard. He seemed to be in a very angry mood, and his face was soon as florid as his hair.

"No, sir, I do not desire any particulars. My son here"—indicating a powerful young man, with a heavy, sullen face, in the corner of the sitting-room—"is of one mind with me that Mr. McPherson's attentions to Maud were insulting. Yes, sir, the word 'marriage' was never mentioned, and yet there were letters and meetings, and a great deal more of which neither of us could approve. She has no mother, and we are her only guardians. We are determined——"

But the words were taken from his mouth by the appearance of the lady herself. There was no gainsaying that she would have graced any assembly in the world. Who could have imagined that so rare a flower would grow from such a root and in such an atmosphere? Women have seldom been an attraction to me, for my brain has always governed my heart, but I could not look upon her perfect clear-cut face, with all the soft freshness of the downlands in her delicate colouring, without realizing that no young man would cross her path unscathed. Such was the girl who had pushed open the door and stood now, wide-eyed and intense, in front of Harold Stackhurst.

"I know already that Fitzroy is dead," she said. "Do not be afraid to tell me the particulars."

"This other gentleman of yours let us know the news," explained the father.

"There is no reason why my sister should be brought into the matter," growled the younger man.

The sister turned a sharp, fierce look upon him. "This is my business, William. Kindly leave me to manage it in my own way. By all accounts there has been a crime committed. If I can help to show who did it, it is the least I can do for him who is gone."

She listened to a short account from my companion, with a composed concentration which showed me that she possessed strong character as well as great beauty. Maud Bellamy will always remain in my memory as a most complete and remarkable woman. It seems that she already knew me by sight, for she turned to me at the end.

"Bring them to justice, Mr. Holmes. You have my sympathy and my help, whoever they may be." It seemed to me that she glanced defiantly at her father and brother as she spoke.

"Thank you," said I. "I value a woman's instinct in such matters. You use the word 'they.' You think that more than one was concerned?"

"I knew Mr. McPherson well enough to be aware that he was a brave and a strong man. No single person could ever have inflicted such an outrage upon him."

"Might I have one word with you alone?"

"I tell you, Maud, not to mix yourself up in the matter," cried her father angrily.

She looked at me helplessly. "What can I do?"

"The whole world will know the facts presently, so there can be no harm if I discuss them here," said I. "I should have preferred privacy, but if your father will not allow it he must share the deliberations." Then I spoke of the note which had been found in the dead man's pocket. "It is sure to be produced at the inquest. May I ask you to throw any light upon it that you can?"

"I see no reason for mystery," she answered. "We were engaged to be married, and we only kept it secret because Fitzroy's uncle, who is very old and said to be dying, might have disinherited him if he had married against his wish. There was no other reason."

"You could have told us," growled Mr. Bellamy.

"So I would, father, if you had ever shown sympathy."

"I object to my girl picking up with men outside her own station."

"It was your prejudice against him which prevented us from telling you. As to this appointment"—she fumbled in her dress and produced a crumpled note— "it was in answer to this."

DEAREST [ran the message]:
    The old place on the beach just after sunset on Tuesday. It is the only time I can get away.

                                     F. M.

"Tuesday was to-day, and I had meant to meet him to-night."

I turned over the paper. "This never came by post. How did you get it?"

"I would rather not answer that question. It has really nothing to do with the matter which you are investigating. But anything which bears upon that I will most freely answer."

She was as good as her word, but there was nothing which was helpful in our investigation. She had no reason to think that her fiancé had any hidden enemy, but she admitted that she had had several warm admirers.

"May I ask if Mr. Ian Murdoch was one of them?"

She blushed and seemed confused.

"There was a time when I thought he was. But that was all changed when he understood the relations between Fitzroy and myself."

Again the shadow round this strange man seemed to me to be taking more definite shape. His record must be examined. His rooms must be privately searched. Stackhurst was a willing collaborator, for in his mind also suspicions were forming. We returned from our visit to The Haven with the hope that one free end of this tangled skein was already in our hands.

A week passed. The inquest had thrown no light upon the matter and had been adjourned for further evidence. Stackhurst had made discreet inquiry about his subordinate, and there had been a superficial search of his room, but without result. Personally, I had gone over the whole ground again, both physically and mentally, but with no new conclusions. In all my chronicles the reader will find no case which brought me so completely to the limit of my powers. Even my imagination could conceive no solution to the mystery. And then there came the incident of the dog.

It was my old housekeeper who heard of it first by that strange wireless by which such people collect the news of the countryside.

"Sad story this, sir, about Mr. McPherson's dog," said she one evening.

I do not encourage such conversations, but the words arrested my attention.

"What of Mr. McPherson's dog?"

"Dead, sir. Died of grief for its master."

"Who told you this?"

"Why, sir, everyone is talking of it. It took on terrible, and has eaten nothing for a week. Then to-day two of the young gentlemen from The Gables found it dead—down on the beach, sir, at the very place where its master met his end."

"At the very place." The words stood out clear in my memory. Some dim perception that the matter was vital rose in my mind. That the dog should die was after the beautiful, faithful nature of dogs. But "at the very place"! Why should this lonely beach be fatal to it? Was it possible that it also had been sacrificed to some revengeful feud? Was it possible——? Yes, the perception was dim, but already something was building up in my mind. In a few minutes I was on my way to The Gables, where I found Stackhurst in his study. At my request he sent for Sudbury and Blount, the two students who had found the dog.

"Yes, it lay on the very edge of the pool," said one of them. "It must have followed the trail of its dead master."

I saw the faithful little creature, an Airedale terrier, laid out upon the mat in the hall. The body was stiff and rigid, the eyes projecting, and the limbs contorted. There was agony in every line of it.

From The Gables I walked down to the bathing-pool. The sun had sunk and the shadow of the great cliff lay black across the water, which glimmered dully like a sheet of lead. The place was deserted and there was no sign of life save for two sea-birds circling and screaming overhead. In the fading light I could dimly make out the little dog's spoor upon the sand round the very rock on which his master's towel had been laid. For a long time I stood in deep meditation while the shadows grew darker around me. My mind was filled with racing thoughts. You have known what it was to be in a nightmare in which you feel there is some all-important thing for which you search and which you know is there, though it remains forever just beyond your reach. That was how I felt that evening as I stood alone by that place of death. Then at last I turned and walked slowly homeward.

I had just reached the top of the path when it came to me. Like a flash, I remembered the thing for which I had so eagerly and vainly grasped. You will know, or Watson has written in vain, that I hold a vast store of out-of-the-way knowledge without scientific system, but very available for the needs of my work. My mind is like a crowded box-room with packets of all sorts stowed away therein—so many that I may well have but a vague perception of what was there. I had known that there was something which might bear upon this matter. It was still vague, but at least I knew how I could make it clear. It was monstrous, incredible, and yet it was always a possibility. I would test it to the full.

There is a great garret in my little house which is stuffed with books. It was into this that I plunged and rummaged for an hour. At the end of that time I emerged with a little chocolate and silver volume. Eagerly I turned up the chapter of which I had a dim remembrance. Yes, it was indeed a far-fetched and unlikely proposition, and yet I could not be at rest until I had made sure if it might, indeed, be so. It was late when I retired, with my mind eagerly awaiting the work of the morrow.

But that work met with an annoying interruption. I had hardly swallowed my early cup of tea and was starting for the beach when I had a call from Inspector Bardle of the Sussex Constabulary—a steady, solid, bovine man with thoughtful eyes, which looked at me now with a very troubled expression.

"I know your immense experience, sir," said he. "This is quite unofficial, of course, and need go no farther. But I am fairly up against it in this McPherson case. The question is, shall I make an arrest, or shall I not?"

"Meaning Mr. Ian Murdoch?"

"Yes, sir. There is really no one else when you come to think of it. That's the advantage of this solitude. We narrow it down to a very small compass. If he did not do it, then who did?"

"What have you against him?"

He had gleaned along the same furrows as I had. There was Murdoch's character and the mystery which seemed to hang round the man. His furious bursts of temper, as shown in the incident of the dog. The fact that he had quarrelled with McPherson in the past, and that there was some reason to think that he might have resented his attentions to Miss Bellamy. He had all my points, but no fresh ones, save that Murdoch seemed to be making every preparation for departure.

"What would my position be if I let him slip away with all this evidence against him?" The burly, phlegmatic man was sorely troubled in his mind.

"Consider," I said, "all the essential gaps in your case. On the morning of the crime he can surely prove an alibi. He had been with his scholars till the last moment, and within a few minutes of McPherson's appearance he came upon us from behind. Then bear in mind the absolute impossibility that he could single-handed have inflicted this outrage upon a man quite as strong as himself. Finally, there is this question of the instrument with which these injuries were inflicted."

"What could it be but a scourge or flexible whip of some sort?"

"Have you examined the marks?" I asked.

"I have seen them. So has the doctor."

"But I have examined them very carefully with a lens. They have peculiarities."

"What are they, Mr. Holmes?"

I stepped to my bureau and brought out an enlarged photograph. "This is my method in such cases," I explained.

"You certainly do things thoroughly, Mr. Holmes."

"I should hardly be what I am if I did not. Now let us consider this weal which extends round the right shoulder. Do you observe nothing remarkable?"

"I can't say I do."

"Surely it is evident that it is unequal in its intensity. There is a dot of extravasated* blood here, and another there. There are similar indications in this other weal down here. What can that mean?"

"I have no idea. Have you?"

"Perhaps I have. Perhaps I haven't. I may be able to say more soon. Anything which will define what made that mark will bring us a long way towards the criminal."

"It is, of course, an absurd idea," said the policeman, "but if a red-hot net of wire had been laid across the back, then these better marked points would represent where the meshes crossed each other."

"A most ingenious comparison. Or shall we say a very stiff cat-o'-nine-tails with small hard knots upon it?"

"By Jove, Mr. Holmes, I think you have hit it."

"Or there may be some very different cause, Mr. Bardle. But your case

---

*Forced out of its normal vessels into surrounding tissue.

is far too weak for an arrest. Besides, we have those last words—the 'Lion's Mane.'"

"I have wondered whether Ian——"

"Yes, I have considered that. If the second word had borne any resemblance to Murdoch—but it did not. He gave it almost in a shriek. I am sure that it was 'Mane.'"

"Have you no alternative, Mr. Holmes?"

"Perhaps I have. But I do not care to discuss it until there is something more solid to discuss."

"And when will that be?"

"In an hour—possibly less."

The inspector rubbed his chin and looked at me with dubious eyes.

"I wish I could see what was in your mind, Mr. Holmes. Perhaps it's those fishing-boats."

"No, no, they were too far out."

"Well, then, is it Bellamy and that big son of his? They were not too sweet upon Mr. McPherson. Could they have done him a mischief?"

"No, no, you won't draw me until I am ready," said I with a smile. "Now, Inspector, we each have our own work to do. Perhaps if you were to meet me here at midday——"

So far we had got when there came the tremendous interruption which was the beginning of the end.

My outer door was flung open, there were blundering footsteps in the passage, and Ian Murdoch staggered into the room, pallid, dishevelled, his clothes in wild disorder, clawing with his bony hands at the furniture to hold himself erect. "Brandy! Brandy!" he gasped, and fell groaning upon the sofa.

He was not alone. Behind him came Stackhurst, hatless and panting, almost as distrait as his companion.

"Yes, yes, brandy!" he cried. "The man is at his last gasp. It was all I could do to bring him here. He fainted twice upon the way."

Half a tumbler of the raw spirit brought about a wondrous change. He pushed himself up on one arm and swung his coat from his shoulders. "For God's sake, oil, opium, morphia!" he cried. "Anything to ease this infernal agony!"

The inspector and I cried out at the sight. There, crisscrossed upon the man's naked shoulder, was the same strange reticulated pattern of red, inflamed lines which had been the death-mark of Fitzroy McPherson.

The pain was evidently terrible and was more than local, for the sufferer's breathing would stop for a time, his face would turn black, and then with loud gasps he would clap his hand to his heart, while his brow dropped beads of sweat. At any moment he might die. More and more brandy was poured down his throat, each fresh dose bringing him back to life. Pads of cotton-wool soaked in salad-oil seemed to take the agony from the strange wounds. At last his head fell heavily upon the cushion. Exhausted Nature had taken refuge in its last storehouse of vitality. It was half a sleep and half a faint, but at least it was ease from pain.

To question him had been impossible, but the moment we were assured of his condition Stackhurst turned upon me.

"My God!" he cried, "what is it, Holmes? What is it?"

"Where did you find him?"

"Down on the beach. Exactly where poor McPherson met his end. If this man's heart had been weak as McPherson's was, he would not be here now. More than once I thought he was gone as I brought him up. It was too far to The Gables, so I made for you."

"Did you see him on the beach?"

"I was walking on the cliff when I heard his cry. He was at the edge of the water, reeling about like a drunken man. I ran down, threw some clothes about him, and brought him up. For heaven's sake, Holmes, use all the powers you have and spare no pains to lift the curse from this place, for life is becoming unendurable. Can you, with all your worldwide reputation, do nothing for us?"

"I think I can, Stackhurst. Come with me now! And you, Inspector, come along! We will see if we cannot deliver this murderer into your hands."

Leaving the unconscious man in the charge of my housekeeper, we all three went down to the deadly lagoon. On the shingle there was piled a little heap of towels and clothes left by the stricken man. Slowly I walked round the edge of the water, my comrades in Indian file behind me. Most of the pool was quite shallow, but under the cliff where the beach was hollowed out it was four or five feet deep. It was to this part that a swimmer would naturally go, for it formed a beautiful pellucid green pool as clear as crystal. A line of rocks lay above it at the base of the cliff, and along this I led the way, peering eagerly into the depths beneath me. I had reached the deepest and stillest pool when my eyes caught that for which they were searching, and I burst into a shout of triumph.

"Cyanea!"* I cried. "Cyanea! Behold the Lion's Mane!"

The strange object at which I pointed did indeed look like a tangled mass torn from the mane of a lion. It lay upon a rocky shelf some three feet under the water, a curious waving, vibrating, hairy creature with streaks of silver among its yellow tresses. It pulsated with a slow, heavy dilation and contraction.

"It has done mischief enough. Its day is over!" I cried. "Help me, Stackhurst! Let us end the murderer forever."

There was a big boulder just above the ledge, and we pushed it until it fell with a tremendous splash into the water. When the ripples had cleared we saw that it had settled upon the ledge below. One flapping edge of yellow membrane showed that our victim was beneath it. A thick oily scum oozed out from below the stone and stained the water round, rising slowly to the surface.

"Well, this gets me!" cried the inspector. "What was it, Mr. Holmes?

---

*The text never makes quite clear that *Cyanea capillata*, also known as the Lion's Mane, is a type of jellyfish.

I'm born and bred in these parts, but I never saw such thing. It don't belong to Sussex."

"Just as well for Sussex," I remarked. "It may have been the southwest gale that brought it up. Come back to my house, both of you, and I will give you the terrible experience of one who has good reason to remember his own meeting with the same peril of the seas."

When we reached my study we found that Murdoch was so far recovered that he could sit up. He was dazed in mind, and every now and then was shaken by a paroxysm of pain. In broken words he explained that he had no notion what had occurred to him, save that terrific pangs had suddenly shot through him, and that it had taken all his fortitude to reach the bank.

"Here is a book," I said, taking up the little volume, "which first brought light into what might have been forever dark. It is *Out of Doors*, by the famous observer, J. G. Wood. Wood himself very nearly perished from contact with this vile creature, so he wrote with a very full knowledge. *Cyanea capillata* is the miscreant's full name, and he can be as dangerous to life as, and far more painful than, the bite of the cobra. Let me briefly give this extract.

> If the bather should see a loose roundish mass of tawny membranes and fibres, something like very large handfuls of lion's mane and silver paper, let him beware, for this is the fearful stinger, *Cyanea capillata*.

Could our sinister acquaintance be more clearly described?

"He goes on to tell of his own encounter with one when swimming off the coast of Kent. He found that the creature radiated almost invisible filaments to the distance of fifty feet, and that anyone within that circumference from the deadly centre was in danger of death. Even at a distance the effect upon Wood was almost fatal.

> The multitudinous threads caused light scarlet lines upon the skin which on closer examination resolved into minute dots or pustules, each dot charged as it were with a red-hot needle making its way through the nerves.

"The local pain was, as he explains, the least part of the exquisite torment.

> Pangs shot through the chest, causing me to fall as if struck by a bullet. The pulsation would cease, and then the heart would give six or seven leaps as if it would force its way through the chest.

"It nearly killed him, although he had only been exposed to it in the disturbed ocean and not in the narrow calm waters of a bathing-pool. He says that he could hardly recognize himself afterwards, so white, wrinkled and shrivelled was his face. He gulped down brandy, a whole bottleful, and it seems to have saved his life. There is the book, Inspector. I leave it with you, and you cannot doubt that it contains a full explanation of the tragedy of poor McPherson."

"And incidentally exonerates me," remarked Ian Murdoch with a wry smile. "I do not blame you, Inspector, nor you, Mr. Holmes, for your suspicions were natural. I feel that on the very eve of my arrest I have only cleared myself by sharing the fate of my poor friend."

"No, Mr. Murdoch. I was already upon the track, and had I been out as early as I intended I might well have saved you from this terrific experience."

"But how did you know, Mr. Holmes?"

"I am an omnivorous reader with a strangely retentive memory for trifles. That phrase 'the Lion's Mane' haunted my mind. I knew that I had seen it somewhere in an unexpected context. You have seen that it does describe the creature. I have no doubt that it was floating on the water when McPherson saw it, and that this phrase was the only one by which he could convey to us a warning as to the creature which had been his death."

"Then I, at least, am cleared," said Murdoch, rising slowly to his feet. "There are one or two words of explanation which I should give, for I know the direction in which your inquiries have run. It is true that I loved this lady, but from the day when she chose my friend McPherson my one desire was to help her to happiness. I was well content to stand aside and act as their go-between. Often I carried their messages, and it was because I was in their confidence and because she was so dear to me that I hastened to tell her of my friend's death, lest someone should forestall me in a more sudden and heartless manner. She would not tell you, sir, of our relations lest you should disapprove and I might suffer. But with your leave I must try to get back to The Gables, for my bed will be very welcome."

Stackhurst held out his hand. "Our nerves have all been at concert-pitch," said he. "Forgive what is past, Murdoch. We shall understand each other better in the future." They passed out together with their arms linked in friendly fashion. The inspector remained, staring at me in silence with his ox-like eyes.

"Well, you've done it!" he cried at last. "I had read of you, but I never believed it. It's wonderful!"

I was forced to shake my head. To accept such praise was to lower one's own standards.

"I was slow at the outset—culpably slow. Had the body been found in the water I could hardly have missed it. It was the towel which misled me. The poor fellow had never thought to dry himself, and so I in turn was led to believe that he had never been in the water. Why, then, should the attack of any water creature suggest itself to me? That was where I went astray. Well, well, Inspector, I often ventured to chaff you gentlemen of the police force, but *Cyanea capillata* very nearly avenged Scotland Yard."

THE ADVENTURE OF THE
VEILED LODGER

When one considers that Mr. Sherlock Holmes was in active practice for twenty-three years, and that during seventeen of these I was allowed to coöperate with him and to keep notes of his doings, it will be clear that I have a mass of material at my command. The problem has always been not to find but to choose. There is the long row of year-books which fill a shelf, and there are the dispatch-cases filled with documents, a perfect quarry for the student not only of crime but of the social and official scandals of the late Victorian era. Concerning these latter, I may say that the writers of agonized letters, who beg that the honour of their families or the reputation of famous forebears may not be touched, have nothing to fear. The discretion and high sense of professional honour which have always distinguished my friend are still at work in the choice of these memoirs, and no confidence will be abused. I deprecate, however, in the strongest way the attempts which have been made lately to get at and to destroy these papers. The source of these outrages is known, and if they are repeated I have Mr. Holmes's authority for saying that the whole story concerning the politician, the lighthouse, and the trained cormorant will be given to the public. There is at least one reader who will understand.

It is not reasonable to suppose that every one of these cases gave Holmes the opportunity of showing those curious gifts of instinct and observation which I have endeavoured to set forth in these memoirs. Sometimes he had with much effort to pick the fruit, sometimes it fell easily into his lap. But the most terrible human tragedies were often involved in those cases which brought him the fewest personal opportunities, and it is one of these which I now desire to record. In telling it, I have made a slight change of name and place, but otherwise the facts are as stated.

One forenoon—it was late in 1896—I received a hurried note from Holmes asking for my attendance. When I arrived I found him seated in a smoke-laden atmosphere, with an elderly, motherly woman of the buxom landlady type in the corresponding chair in front of him.

"This is Mrs. Merrilow, of South Brixton," said my friend with a wave of the hand. "Mrs. Merrilow does not object to tobacco, Watson, if you wish to indulge your filthy habits. Mrs. Merrilow has an interesting story to tell which may well lead to further developments in which your presence may be useful."

"Anything I can do——"

"You will understand, Mrs. Merrilow, that if I come to Mrs. Ronder I should prefer to have a witness. You will make her understand that before we arrive."

"Lord bless you, Mr. Holmes," said our visitor, "she is that anxious to see you that you might bring the whole parish at your heels!"

"Then we shall come early in the afternoon. Let us see that we have our facts correct before we start. If we go over them it will help Dr. Watson to understand the situation. You say that Mrs. Ronder has been your lodger for seven years and that you have only once seen her face."

"And I wish to God I had not!" said Mrs. Merrilow.

"It was, I understand, terribly mutilated."

"Well, Mr. Holmes, you would hardly say it was a face at all. That's how it looked. Our milkman got a glimpse of her once peeping out of the upper window, and he dropped his tin and the milk all over the front garden. That is the kind of face it is. When I saw her—I happened on her unawares—she covered up quick, and then she said, 'Now, Mrs. Merrilow, you know at last why it is that I never raise my veil.'"

"Do you know anything about her history?"

"Nothing at all."

"Did she give references when she came?"

"No, sir, but she gave hard cash, and plenty of it. A quarter's rent right down on the table in advance and no arguing about terms. In these times a poor woman like me can't afford to turn down a chance like that."

"Did she give any reason for choosing your house?"

"Mine stands well back from the road and is more private than most. Then, again, I only take the one, and I have no family of my own. I reckon she had tried others and found that mine suited her best. It's privacy she is after, and she is ready to pay for it."

"You say that she never showed her face from first to last save on the one accidental occasion. Well, it is a very remarkable story, most remarkable, and I don't wonder that you want it examined."

"I don't, Mr. Holmes. I am quite satisfied so long as I get my rent. You could not have a quieter lodger, or one who gives less trouble."

"Then what has brought matters to a head?"

"Her health, Mr. Holmes. She seems to be wasting away. And there's something terrible on her mind. 'Murder!' she cries. 'Murder!' And once I heard her: 'You cruel beast! You monster!' she cried. It was in the night, and it fair rang through the house and sent the shivers through me. So I went to her in the morning. 'Mrs. Ronder,' I says, 'if you have anything that is troubling your soul, there's the clergy,' I says, 'and there's the police. Between them you should get some help.' 'For God's sake, not the police!' says she, 'and the clergy can't change what is past. And yet,' she says, 'it would ease my mind if someone knew the truth before I died.' 'Well,' says I, 'if you won't have the regulars, there is this detective man what we read about'—beggin' your pardon, Mr. Holmes. And she, she fair jumped at it. 'That's the man,' says she. 'I wonder I never thought of it before. Bring him here, Mrs. Merrilow, and if he won't come, tell him I am the wife of Ronder's wild beast show. Say that, and give him the name Abbas Parva. Here it is as she wrote it, Abbas Parva. 'That will bring him if he's the man I think he is.'"

"And it will, too," remarked Holmes. "Very good, Mrs. Merrilow. I should like to have a little chat with Dr. Watson. That will carry us till lunch-time. About three o'clock you may expect to see us at your house in Brixton."

Our visitor had no sooner waddled out of the room—no other verb can describe Mrs. Merrilow's method of progression—than Sherlock Holmes threw himself with fierce energy upon the pile of commonplace books in the corner. For a few minutes there was a constant swish of the leaves, and then with a grunt of satisfaction he came upon what he sought. So excited was he that he did not rise, but sat upon the floor like some strange Buddha, with crossed legs, the huge books all round him, and one open upon his knees.

"The case worried me at the time, Watson. Here are my marginal notes to prove it. I confess that I could make nothing of it. And yet I was convinced that the coroner was wrong. Have you no recollection of the Abbas Parva tragedy?"

"None, Holmes."

"And yet you were with me then. But certainly my own impression was very superficial. For there was nothing to go by, and none of the parties had engaged my services. Perhaps you would care to read the papers?"

"Could you not give me the points?"

"That is very easily done. It will probably come back to your memory as I talk. Ronder, of course, was a household word. He was the rival of Wombwell, and of Sanger,* one of the greatest showmen of his day. There is evidence, however, that he took to drink, and that both he and his show were on the down grade at the time of the great tragedy. The caravan had halted for the night at Abbas Parva, which is a small village in Berkshire, when this horror occurred. They were on their way to Wimbledon, travelling by road, and they were simply camping and not exhibiting, as the place is so small a one that it would not have paid them to open.

"They had among their exhibits a very fine North African lion. Sahara King was its name, and it was the habit, both of Ronder and his wife, to give exhibitions inside its cage. Here, you see, is a photograph of the performance by which you will perceive that Ronder was a huge porcine person and that his wife was a very magnificent woman. It was deposed at the inquest that there had been some signs that the lion was dangerous, but, as usual, familiarity begat contempt, and no notice was taken of the fact.

"It was usual for either Ronder or his wife to feed the lion at night. Sometimes one went, sometimes both, but they never allowed anyone else to do it, for they believed that so long as they were the food-carriers he would regard them as benefactors and would never molest them. On this particular night, seven years ago, they both went, and a very terrible happening followed, the details of which have never been made clear.

"It seems that the whole camp was roused near midnight by the roars of the animal and the screams of the woman. The different grooms and

---

*Wombwell and Sanger were proprietors of well-known traveling circuses.

employees rushed from their tents, carrying lanterns, and by their light an awful sight was revealed. Ronder lay, with the back of his head crushed in and deep claw-marks across his scalp, some ten yards from the cage, which was open. Close to the door of the cage lay Mrs. Ronder upon her back, with the creature squatting and snarling above her. It had torn her face in such a fashion that it was never thought that she could live. Several of the circus men, headed by Leonardo, the strong man, and Griggs, the clown, drove the creature off with poles, upon which it sprang back into the cage and was at once locked in. How it had got loose was a mystery. It was conjectured that the pair intended to enter the cage, but that when the door was loosed the creature bounded out upon them. There was no other point of interest in the evidence save that the woman in a delirium of agony kept screaming, 'Coward! Coward!' as she was carried back to the van in which they lived. It was six months before she was fit to give evidence, but the inquest was duly held, with the obvious verdict of death from misadventure."

"What alternative could be conceived?" said I.

"You may well say so. And yet there were one or two points which worried young Edmunds, of the Berkshire Constabulary. A smart lad that! He was sent later to Allahabad. That was how I came into the matter, for he dropped in and smoked a pipe or two over it."

"A thin, yellow-haired man?"

"Exactly. I was sure you would pick up the trail presently."

"But what worried him?"

"Well, we were both worried. It was so deucedly difficult to reconstruct the affair. Look at it from the lion's point of view. He is liberated. What does he do? He takes half a dozen bounds forward, which brings him to Ronder. Ronder turns to fly—the claw-marks were on the back of his head—but the lion strikes him down. Then, instead of bounding on and escaping, he returns to the woman, who was close to the cage, and he knocks her over and chews her face up. Then, again, those cries of hers would seem to imply that her husband had in some way failed her. What could the poor devil have done to help her? You see the difficulty?"

"Quite."

"And then there was another thing. It comes back to me now as I think it over. There was some evidence that just at the time the lion roared and the woman screamed, a man began shouting in terror."

"This man Ronder, no doubt."

"Well, if his skull was smashed in you would hardly expect to hear from him again. There were at least two witnesses who spoke of the cries of a man being mingled with those of a woman."

"I should think the whole camp was crying out by then. As to the other points, I think I could suggest a solution."

"I should be glad to consider it."

"The two were together, ten yards from the cage, when the lion got loose. The man turned and was struck down. The woman conceived the idea of getting into the cage and shutting the door. It was her only refuge.

She made for it, and just as she reached it the beast bounded after her and knocked her over. She was angry with her husband for having encouraged the beast's rage by turning. If they had faced it they might have cowed it. Hence her cries of 'Coward!'"

"Brilliant, Watson! Only one flaw in your diamond."

"What is the flaw, Holmes?"

"If they were both ten paces from the cage, how came the beast to get loose?"

"Is it possible that they had some enemy who loosed it?"

"And why should it attack them savagely when it was in the habit of playing with them, and doing tricks with them inside the cage?"

"Possibly the same enemy had done something to enrage it."

Holmes looked thoughtful and remained in silence for some moments.

"Well, Watson, there is this to be said for your theory. Ronder was a man of many enemies. Edmunds told me that in his cups he was horrible. A huge bully of a man, he cursed and slashed at everyone who came in his way. I expect those cries about a monster, of which our visitor has spoken, were nocturnal reminiscences of the dear departed. However, our speculations are futile until we have all the facts. There is a cold partridge on the sideboard, Watson, and a bottle of Montrachet.* Let us renew our energies before we make a fresh call upon them."

When our hansom deposited us at the house of Mrs. Merrilow, we found that plump lady blocking up the open door of her humble but retired abode. It was very clear that her chief preoccupation was lest she should lose a valuable lodger, and she implored, us, before showing us up, to say and do nothing which could lead to so undesirable an end. Then, having reassured her, we followed her up the straight, badly carpeted staircase and were shown into the room of the mysterious lodger.

It was a close, musty, ill-ventilated place, as might be expected, since its inmate seldom left it. From keeping beasts in a cage, the woman seemed, by some retribution of fate, to have become herself a beast in a cage. She sat now in a broken armchair in the shadowy corner of the room. Long years of inaction had coarsened the lines of her figure, but at some period it must have been beautiful, and was still full and voluptuous. A thick dark veil covered her face, but it was cut off close at her upper lip and disclosed a perfectly shaped mouth and a delicately rounded chin. I could well conceive that she had indeed been a very remarkable woman. Her voice, too, was well modulated and pleasing.

"My name is not unfamiliar to you, Mr. Holmes," said she. "I thought that it would bring you."

"That is so, madam, though I do not know how you are aware that I was interested in your case."

"I learned it when I had recovered my health and was examined by Mr.

---

*A white wine from Burgundy.

Edmunds, the county detective. I fear I lied to him. Perhaps it would have been wiser had I told the truth."

"It is usually wiser to tell the truth. But why did you lie to him?"

"Because the fate of someone else depended upon it. I know that he was a very worthless being, and yet I would not have his destruction upon my conscience. We had been so close—so close!"

"But has this impediment been removed?"

"Yes, sir. The person that I allude to is dead."

"Then why should you not now tell the police anything you know?"

"Because there is another person to be considered. That other person is myself. I could not stand the scandal and publicity which would come from a police examination. I have not long to live, but I wish to die undisturbed. And yet I wanted to find one man of judgment to whom I could tell my terrible story, so that when I am gone all might be understood."

"You compliment me, madam. At the same time, I am a responsible person. I do not promise you that when you have spoken I may not myself think it my duty to refer the case to the police."

"I think not, Mr. Holmes. I know your character and methods too well, for I have followed your work for some years. Reading is the only pleasure which fate has left me, and I miss little which passes in the world. But in any case, I will take my chance of the use which you may make of my tragedy. It will ease my mind to tell it."

"My friend and I would be glad to hear it."

The woman rose and took from a drawer the photograph of a man. He was clearly a professional acrobat, a man of magnificent physique, taken with his huge arms folded across his swollen chest and a smile breaking from under his heavy moustache—the self-satisfied smile of the man of many conquests.

"That is Leonardo," she said.

"Leonardo, the strong man, who gave evidence?"

"The same. And this—this is my husband."

It was a dreadful face—a human pig, or rather a human wild boar, for it was formidable in its bestiality. One could imagine that vile mouth champing and foaming in its rage, and one could conceive those small, vicious eyes darting pure malignancy as they looked forth upon the world. Ruffian, bully, beast—it was all written on that heavy-jowled face.

"Those two pictures will help you, gentlemen, to understand the story. I was a poor circus girl brought up on the sawdust, and doing springs through the hoop before I was ten. When I became a woman this man loved me, if such lust as his can be called love, and in an evil moment I became his wife. From that day I was in hell, and he the devil who tormented me. There was no one in the show who did not know of his treatment. He deserted me for others. He tied me down and lashed me with his riding-whip when I complained. They all pitied me and they all loathed him, but what could they do? They feared him, one and all. For he was terrible at all times, and murderous when he was drunk. Again and again he was had up for assault, and for cruelty to the beasts, but he had plenty of money and the fines were nothing to him. The best men all left us, and the show began to go downhill. It was only Leonardo and I who kept it up—with little Jimmy Griggs, the clown. Poor devil, he had not much to be funny about, but he did what he could to hold things together.

"Then Leonardo came more and more into my life. You see what he was like. I know now the poor spirit that was hidden in that splendid body, but compared to my husband he seemed like the angel Gabriel. He pitied me and helped me, till at last our intimacy turned to love— deep, deep, passionate love, such love as I had dreamed of but never hoped to feel. My husband suspected it, but I think that he was a coward as well as a bully, and that Leonardo was the one man that he was afraid of. He took revenge in his own way by torturing me more than ever. One night my cries brought Leonardo to the door of our van. We were near tragedy that night, and soon my lover and I understood that it could not be avoided. My husband was not fit to live. We planned that he should die.

"Leonardo had a clever, scheming brain. It was he who planned it. I do not say that to blame him, for I was ready to go with him every inch of the way. But I should never have had the wit to think of such a plan. We made a club—Leonardo made it—and in the leaden head he fastened five long steel nails, the points outward, with just such a spread as the lion's paw. This was to give my husband his death-blow, and yet to leave the evidence that it was the lion which we would loose who had done the deed.

"It was a pitch-dark night when my husband and I went down, as was our custom, to feed the beast. We carried with us the raw meat in a zinc pail. Leonardo was waiting at the corner of the big van which we should have to pass before we reached the cage. He was too slow, and we walked past him before he could strike, but he followed us on tiptoe and I heard the crash as the club smashed my husband's skull. My heart leaped with joy at the sound. I sprang forward, and I undid the catch which held the door of the great lion's cage.

"And then the terrible thing happened. You may have heard how quick these creatures are to scent human blood, and how it excites them. Some strange instinct had told the creature in one instant that a human being had been slain. As I slipped the bars it bounded out and was on me in an instant. Leonardo could have saved me. If he had rushed forward and struck the beast with his club he might have cowed it. But the man lost his nerve. I heard him shout in his terror, and then I saw him turn and fly. At the same instant the teeth of the lion met in my face. Its hot, filthy breath had already poisoned me and I was hardly conscious of pain. With the palms of my hands I tried to push the great steaming, blood-stained jaws away from me, and I screamed for help. I was conscious that the camp was stirring, and then dimly I remembered a group of men. Leonardo, Griggs, and others, dragging me from under the creature's paws. That was my last memory, Mr. Holmes, for many a weary month. When I came to myself and saw myself in the mirror, I cursed that lion—oh, how I cursed him!—not because he had torn away my beauty but because he had not torn away my life. I had but one desire, Mr. Holmes, and I had enough money to gratify it. It was that I should cover myself so that my poor face should be seen by none, and that I should dwell where none whom I had ever known should find me. That was all that was left to me to do—and that is what I have done. A poor wounded beast that has crawled into its hole to die—that is the end of Eugenia Ronder."

We sat in silence for some time after the unhappy woman had told her story. Then Holmes stretched out his long arm and patted her hand with such a show of sympathy as I had seldom known him to exhibit.

"Poor girl!" he said. "Poor girl! The ways of fate are indeed hard to understand. If there is not some compensation hereafter, then the world is a cruel jest. But what of this man Leonardo?"

"I never saw him or heard from him again. Perhaps I have been wrong to feel so bitterly against him. He might as soon have loved one of the freaks whom we carried round the county as the thing which the lion had left. But a woman's love is not so easily set aside. He had left me under the beast's claws, he had deserted me in my need, and yet I could not bring myself to give him to the gallows. For myself, I cared nothing what became of me. What could be more dreadful than my actual life? But I stood between Leonardo and his fate."

"And he is dead?"

"He was drowned last month when bathing near Margate. I saw his death in the paper."

"And what did he do with this five-clawed club, which is the most singular and ingenious part of all your story?"

"I cannot tell, Mr. Holmes. There is a chalk-pit by the camp, with a deep green pool at the base of it. Perhaps in the depths of that pool——"

"Well, well, it is of little consequence now. The case is closed."

"Yes," said the woman, "the case is closed."

We had risen to go, but there was something in the woman's voice which arrested Holmes's attention. He turned swiftly upon her.

"Your life is not your own," he said. "Keep your hands off it."

"What use is it to anyone?"

"How can you tell? The example of patient suffering is in itself the most precious of all lessons to an impatient world."

The woman's answer was a terrible one. She raised her veil and stepped forward into the light.

"I wonder if you would bear it," she said.

It was horrible. No words can describe the framework of a face when the face itself is gone. Two living and beautiful brown eyes looking sadly out from that grisly ruin did but make the view more awful. Holmes held up his hand in a gesture of pity and protest, and together we left the room.

Two days later, when I called upon my friend, he pointed with some pride to a small blue bottle upon his mantelpiece. I picked it up. There was a red poison label. A pleasant almondy odour rose when I opened it.

"Prussic acid?" said I.

"Exactly. It came by post. 'I send you my temptation. I will follow your advice.' That was the message. I think, Watson, we can guess the name of the brave woman who sent it."

THE ADVENTURE OF
SHOSCOMBE OLD PLACE

Sherlock Holmes had been bending for a long time over a low-power microscope. Now he straightened himself up and looked round at me in triumph.

"It is glue, Watson," said he. "Unquestionably it is glue. Have a look at these scattered objects in the field!"

I stooped to the eyepiece and focussed for my vision.

"Those hairs are threads from a tweed coat. The irregular gray masses are dust. There are epithelial scales on the left. Those brown blobs in the centre are undoubtedly glue."

"Well," I said, laughing, "I am prepared to take your word for it. Does anything depend upon it?"

"It is a very fine demonstration," he answered. "In the St. Pancras case you may remember that a cap was found beside the dead policeman. The accused man denies that it is his. But he is a picture-frame maker who habitually handles glue."

"Is it one of your cases?"

"No; my friend, Merivale, of the Yard, asked me to look into the case. Since I ran down that coiner* by the zinc and copper filings in the seam of his cuff they have begun to realize the importance of the microscope." He looked impatiently at his watch. "I had a new client calling, but he is overdue. By the way, Watson, you know something of racing?"

"I ought to. I pay for it with about half my wound pension."

"Then I'll make you my 'Handy Guide to the Turf.' What about Sir Robert Norberton? Does the name recall anything?"

"Well, I should say so. He lives at Shoscombe Old Place, and I know it well, for my summer quarters were down there once. Norberton nearly came within your province once."

"How was that?"

"It was when he horsewhipped Sam Brewer, the well-known Curzon Street money-lender, on Newmarket Heath. He nearly killed the man."

"Ah, he sounds interesting! Does he often indulge in that way?"

"Well, he has the name of being a dangerous man. He is about the most daredevil rider in England—second in the Grand National a few years back. He is one of those men who have overshot their true generation. He should have been a buck in the days of the Regency[23]—a boxer, an athlete, a plunger on the turf,† a lover of fair ladies, and, by all

---

*Counterfeiter.
†Reckless gambler on horse races.

account, so far down Queer Street* that he may never find his way back again."

"Capital, Watson! A thumb-nail sketch. I seem to know the man. Now, can you give me some idea of Shoscombe Old Place?"

"Only that it is in the centre of Shoscombe Park, and that the famous Shoscombe stud and training quarters are to be found there."

"And the head trainer," said Holmes, "is John Mason. You need not look surprised at my knowledge, Watson, for this is a letter from him which I am unfolding. But let us have some more about Shoscombe. I seem to have struck a rich vein."

"There are the Shoscombe spaniels," said I. "You hear of them at every dog show. The most exclusive breed in England. They are the special pride of the lady of Shoscombe Old Place."

"Sir Robert Norberton's wife, I presume!"

"Sir Robert has never married. Just as well, I think, considering his prospects. He lives with his widowed sister, Lady Beatrice Falder."

"You mean that she lives with him?"

"No, no. The place belonged to her late husband, Sir James. Norberton has no claim on it at all. It is only a life interest and reverts to her husband's brother. Meantime, she draws the rents every year."

"And brother Robert, I suppose, spends the said rents?"

"That is about the size of it. He is a devil of a fellow and must lead her a most uneasy life. Yet I have heard that she is devoted to him. But, what is amiss at Shoscombe?"

"Ah, that is just what I want to know. And here, I expect, is the man who can tell us."

The door had opened and the page had shown in a tall, clean-shaven man with the firm, austere expression which is only seen upon those who have to control horses or boys. Mr. John Mason had many of both under his sway, and he looked equal to the task. He bowed with cold self-possession and seated himself upon the chair to which Holmes had waved him.

"You had my note, Mr. Holmes?"

"Yes, but it explained nothing."

"It was too delicate a thing for me to put the details on paper. And too complicated. It was only face to face I could do it."

"Well, we are at your disposal."

"First of all, Mr. Holmes, I think that my employer, Sir Robert, has gone mad."

Holmes raised his eyebrows. "This is Baker Street, not Harley Street,"† said he. "But why do you say so?"

"Well, sir, when a man does one queer thing, or two queer things, there may be a meaning to it, but when everything he does is queer, then you

---

*Uncomfortable circumstances, especially financial trouble.
†Fashionable street known for its many doctors.

begin to wonder. I believe Shoscombe Prince and the Derby have turned his brain."

"That is a colt you are running?"

"The best in England, Mr. Holmes. I should know, if anyone does. Now, I'll be plain with you, for I know you are gentlemen of honour and that it won't go beyond the room. Sir Robert has got to win this Derby. He's up to the neck, and it's his last chance. Everything he could raise or borrow is on the horse—and at fine odds, too! You can get forties now, but it was nearer the hundred when he began to back him."

"But how is that if the horse is so good?"

"The public don't know how good he is. Sir Robert has been too clever for the touts.* He has the Prince's half-brother out for spins. You can't tell 'em apart. But there are two lengths in a furlong between them when it comes to a gallop. He thinks of nothing but the horse and the race. His whole life is on it. He's holding off the Jews till then. If the Prince fails him he is done."

"It seems a rather desperate gamble, but where does the madness come in?"

"Well, first of all, you have only to look at him. I don't believe he sleeps at night. He is down at the stables at all hours. His eyes are wild. It has all been too much for his nerves. Then there is his conduct to Lady Beatrice!"

"Ah! What is that?"

"They have always been the best of friends. They had the same tastes, the two of them, and she loved the horses as much as he did. Every day at the same hour she would drive down to see them—and, above all, she loved the Prince. He would prick up his ears when he heard the wheels on the gravel, and he would trot out each morning to the carriage to get his lump of sugar. But that's all over now."

"Why?"

"Well, she seems to have lost all interest in the horses. For a week now she has driven past the stables with never so much as 'Good-morning'!"

"You think there has been a quarrel?"

"And a bitter, savage, spiteful quarrel at that. Why else would he give away her pet spaniel that she loved as if he were her child? He gave it a few days ago to old Barnes, what keeps the Green Dragon, three miles off, at Crendall."

"That certainly did seem strange."

"Of course, with her weak heart and dropsy one couldn't expect that she could get about with him, but he spent two hours every evening in her room. He might well do what he could, for she has been a rare good friend to him. But that's all over, too. He never goes near her. And she takes it to heart. She is brooding and sulky and drinking, Mr. Holmes— drinking like a fish."

---

*People who hang around racetracks looking for tips about horses.

"Did she drink before this estrangement?"

"Well, she took her glass, but now it is often a whole bottle of an evening. So Stephens, the butler, told me. It's all changed, Mr. Holmes, and there is something damned rotten about it. But then, again, what is master doing down at the old church crypt at night? And who is the man that meets him there?"

Holmes rubbed his hands.

"Go on, Mr. Mason. You get more and more interesting."

"It was the butler who saw him go. Twelve o'clock at night and raining hard. So next night I was up at the house and, sure enough, master was off again. Stephens and I went after him, but it was jumpy work, for it would have been a bad job if he had seen us. He's a terrible man with his fists if he gets started, and no respecter of persons. So we were shy of getting too near, but we marked him down all right. It was the haunted crypt that he was making for, and there was a man waiting for him there."

"What is this haunted crypt?"

"Well, sir, there is an old ruined chapel in the park. It is so old that nobody could fix its date. And under it there's a crypt which has a bad name among us. It's a dark, damp, lonely place by day, but there are few in that county that would have the nerve to go near it at night. But master's not afraid. He never feared anything in his life. But what is he doing there in the night-time?"

"Wait a bit!" said Holmes. "You say there is another man there. It must be one of your own stablemen, or someone from the house! Surely you have only to spot who it is and question him?"

"It's no one I know."

"How can you say that?"

"Because I have seen him, Mr. Holmes. It was on that second night. Sir Robert turned and passed us—me and Stephens, quaking in the bushes like two bunny-rabbits, for there was a bit of moon that night. But we could hear the other moving about behind. We were not afraid of him. So we up when Sir Robert was gone and pretended we were just having a walk like in the moonlight, and so we came right on him as casual and innocent as you please. 'Hullo, mate! who may you be?' says I. I guess he had not heard us coming, so he looked over his shoulder with a face as if he had seen the devil coming out of hell. He let out a yell, and away he went as hard as he could lick it in the darkness. He could run!—I'll give him that. In a minute he was out of sight and hearing, and who he was, or what he was, we never found."

"But you saw him clearly in the moonlight?"

"Yes, I would swear to his yellow face—a mean dog, I should say. What could he have in common with Sir Robert?"

Holmes sat for some time lost in thought.

"Who keeps Lady Beatrice Falder company?" he asked at last.

"There is her maid, Carrie Evans. She has been with her this five years."

"And is, no doubt, devoted?"

Mr. Mason shuffled uncomfortably.

"She's devoted enough," he answered at last. "But I won't say to whom."

"Ah!" said Holmes.

"I can't tell tales out of school."

"I quite understand, Mr. Mason. Of course, the situation is clear enough. From Dr. Watson's description of Sir Robert I can realize that no woman is safe from him. Don't you think the quarrel between brother and sister may lie there?"

"Well, the scandal has been pretty clear for a long time."

"But she may not have seen it before. Let us suppose that she has suddenly found it out. She wants to get rid of the woman. Her brother will not permit it. The invalid, with her weak heart and inability to get about, has no means of enforcing her will. The hated maid is still tied to her. The lady refuses to speak, sulks, takes to drink. Sir Robert in his anger takes her pet spaniel away from her. Does not all this hang together?"

"Well, it might do—so far as it goes."

"Exactly! As far as it goes. How would all that bear upon the visits by night to the old crypt? We can't fit that into our plot."

"No, sir, and there is something more that I can't fit in. Why should Sir Robert want to dig up a dead body?"

Holmes sat up abruptly.

"We only found it out yesterday—after I had written to you. Yesterday Sir Robert had gone to London, so Stephens and I went down to the crypt. It was all in order, sir, except that in one corner was a bit of a human body."

"You informed the police, I suppose?"

Our visitor smiled grimly.

"Well, sir, I think it would hardly interest them. It was just the head and a few bones of a mummy. It may have been a thousand years old. But it wasn't there before. That I'll swear, and so will Stephens. It had been stowed away in a corner and covered over with a board, but that corner had always been empty before."

"What did you do with it?"

"Well, we just left it there."

"That was wise. You say Sir Robert was away yesterday. Has he returned?"

"We expect him back to-day."

"When did Sir Robert give away his sister's dog?"

"It was just a week ago to-day. The creature was howling outside the old wellhouse, and Sir Robert was in one of his tantrums that morning. He caught it up, and I thought he would have killed it. Then he gave it to Sandy Bain, the jockey, and told him to take the dog to old Barnes at the Green Dragon, for he never wished to see it again."

Holmes sat for some time in silent thought. He had lit the oldest and foulest of his pipes.

"I am not clear yet what you want me to do in this matter, Mr. Mason," he said at last. "Can't you make it more definite?"

"Perhaps this will make it more definite, Mr. Holmes," said our visitor.

He took a paper from his pocket, and, unwrapping it carefully, he exposed a charred fragment of bone.

Holmes examined it with interest.

"Where did you get it?"

"There is a central heating furnace in the cellar under Lady Beatrice's room. It's been off for some time, but Sir Robert complained of cold and had it on again.

"Harvey runs it—he's one of my lads. This very morning he came to me with this which he found raking out the cinders. He didn't like the look of it."

"Nor do I," said Holmes. "What do you make of it, Watson?"

It was burned to a black cinder, but there could be no question as to its anatomical significance.

"It's the upper condyle of a human femur,"* said I.

"Exactly!" Holmes had become very serious. "When does this lad tend to the furnace?"

"He makes it up every evening and then leaves it."

"Then anyone could visit it during the night?"

"Yes, sir."

"Can you enter it from outside?"

"There is one door from outside. There is another which leads up by a stair to the passage in which Lady Beatrice's room is situated."

"These are deep waters, Mr. Mason; deep and rather dirty. You say that Sir Robert was not at home last night?"

"No, sir."

"Then, whoever was burning bones, it was not he."

"That's true, sir."

"What is the name of that inn you spoke of?"

"The Green Dragon."

"Is there good fishing in that part of Berkshire?" The honest trainer showed very clearly upon his face that he was convinced that yet another lunatic had come into his harassed life.

"Well, sir, I've heard there are trout in the mill-stream and pike in the Hall lake."

"That's good enough. Watson and I are famous fishermen—are we not, Watson? You may address us in future at the Green Dragon. We should reach it to-night. I need not say that we don't want to see you, Mr. Mason, but a note will reach us, and no doubt I could find you if I want you. When we have gone a little farther into the matter I will let you have a considered opinion."

Thus it was that on a bright May evening Holmes and I found ourselves

---

*Actually, the femur doesn't have an upper condyle (protuberance).

alone in a first-class carriage and bound for the little "halt-on-demand" station of Shoscombe. The rack above us was covered with a formidable litter of rods, reels, and baskets. On reaching our destination a short drive took us to an old-fashioned tavern, where a sporting host, Josiah Barnes, entered eagerly into our plans for the extirpation of the fish of the neighbourhood.

"What about the Hall lake and the chance of a pike?" said Holmes.

The face of the innkeeper clouded.

"That wouldn't do, sir. You might chance to find yourself in the lake before you were through."

"How's that, then?"

"It's Sir Robert, sir. He's terrible jealous of touts. If you two strangers were as near his training quarters as that he'd be after you as sure as fate. He ain't taking no chances, Sir Robert ain't."

"I've heard he has a horse entered for the Derby."

"Yes, and a good colt, too. He carries all our money for the race, and all Sir Robert's into the bargain. By the way"—he looked at us with thoughtful eyes—"I suppose you ain't on the turf yourselves?"

"No, indeed. Just two weary Londoners who badly need some good Berkshire air."

"Well, you are in the right place for that. There is a deal of it lying about. But mind what I have told you about Sir Robert. He's the sort that strikes first and speaks afterwards. Keep clear of the park."

"Surely, Mr. Barnes! We certainly shall. By the way, that was a most beautiful spaniel that was whining in the hall."

"I should say it was. That was the real Shoscombe breed. There ain't a better in England."

"I am a dog-fancier myself," said Holmes. "Now, if it is a fair question, what would a prize dog like that cost?"

"More than I could pay, sir. It was Sir Robert himself who gave me this one. That's why I have to keep it on a lead. It would be off to the Hall in a jiffy if I gave it its head."

"We are getting some cards in our hand, Watson," said Holmes when the landlord had left us. "It's not an easy one to play, but we may see our way in a day or two. By the way, Sir Robert is still in London, I hear. We might, perhaps, enter the sacred domain to-night without fear of bodily assault. There are one or two points on which I should like reassurance."

"Have you any theory, Holmes?"

"Only this, Watson, that something happened a week or so ago which has cut deep into the life of the Shoscombe household. What is that something? We can only guess at it from its effects. They seem to be of a curiously mixed character. But that should surely help us. It is only the colourless, uneventful case which is hopeless.

"Let us consider our data. The brother no longer visits the beloved invalid sister. He gives away her favourite dog. Her dog, Watson! Does that suggest nothing to you?"

"Nothing but the brother's spite."

"Well, it might be so. Or—well, there is an alternative. Now to continue our review of the situation from the time that the quarrel, if there is a quarrel, began. The lady keeps her room, alters her habits, is not seen save when she drives out with her maid, refuses to stop at the stables to greet her favourite horse, and apparently takes to drink. That covers the case, does it not?"

"Save for the business in the crypt."

"That is another line of thought. There are two, and I beg you will not tangle them. Line A, which concerns Lady Beatrice, has a vaguely sinister flavour, has it not?"

"I can make nothing of it."

"Well, now, let us take up line B, which concerns Sir Robert. He is mad keen upon winning the Derby. He is in the hands of the Jews, and may at any moment be sold up and his racing stables seized by his creditors. He is a daring and desperate man. He derives his income from his sister. His sister's maid is his willing tool. So far we seem to be on fairly safe ground, do we not?"

"But the crypt?"

"Ah, yes, the crypt! Let us suppose, Watson—it is merely a scandalous supposition, a hypothesis put forward for argument's sake—that Sir Robert has done away with his sister."

"My dear Holmes, it is out of the question."

"Very possibly, Watson. Sir Robert is a man of an honourable stock. But you do occasionally find a carrion crow among the eagles. Let us for a moment argue upon this supposition. He could not fly the country until he had realized his fortune, and that fortune could only be realized by bringing off this coup with Shoscombe Prince. Therefore, he has still to stand his ground. To do this he would have to dispose of the body of his victim, and he would also have to find a substitute who would impersonate her. With the maid as his confidante that would not be impossible. The woman's body might be conveyed to the crypt, which is a place so seldom visited, and it might be secretly destroyed at night in the furnace, leaving behind it such evidence as we have already seen. What say you to that, Watson?"

"Well, it is all possible if you grant the original monstrous supposition."

"I think that there is a small experiment which we may try to-morrow, Watson, in order to throw some light on the matter. Meanwhile, if we mean to keep up our characters, I suggest that we have our host in for a glass of his own wine and hold some high converse upon eels and dace, which seems to be the straight road to his affections. We may chance to come upon some useful local gossip in the process."

In the morning Holmes discovered that we had come without our spoon-bait for jack, which absolved us from fishing for the day. About eleven o'clock we started for a walk, and he obtained leave to take the black spaniel with us.

"This is the place," said he as we came to two high park gates with heraldic griffins towering above them. "About midday, Mr. Barnes informs me, the old lady takes a drive, and the carriage must slow down while the gates are opened. When it comes through, and before it gathers speed, I want you, Watson, to stop the coachman with some question. Never mind me. I shall stand behind this holly-bush and see what I can see."

It was not a long vigil. Within a quarter of an hour we saw the big open yellow barouche* coming down the long avenue, with two splendid, high-stepping gray carriage horses in the shafts. Holmes crouched behind his bush with the dog. I stood unconcernedly swinging a cane in the roadway. A keeper ran out and the gates swung open.

The carriage had slowed to a walk, and I was able to get a good look at the occupants. A highly coloured young woman with flaxen hair and impudent eyes sat on the left. At her right was an elderly person with rounded back and a huddle of shawls about her face and shoulders which proclaimed the invalid. When the horses reached the highroad I held up my hand with an authoritative gesture, and as the coachman pulled up I inquired if Sir Robert was at Shoscombe Old Place.

At the same moment Holmes stepped out and released the spaniel. With a joyous cry it dashed forward to the carriage and sprang upon the step. Then in a moment its eager greeting changed to furious rage, and it snapped at the black skirt above it.

"Drive on! Drive on!" shrieked a harsh voice. The coachman lashed the horses, and we were left standing in the roadway.

"Well, Watson, that's done it," said Holmes as he fastened the lead to the neck of the excited spaniel. "He thought it was his mistress, and he found it was a stranger. Dogs don't make mistakes."

"But it was the voice of a man!" I cried.

"Exactly! We have added one card to our hand, Watson, but it needs careful playing, all the same."

My companion seemed to have no further plans for the day, and we did actually use our fishing tackle in the mill-stream, with the result that we had a dish of trout for our supper. It was only after that meal that Holmes showed signs of renewed activity. Once more we found ourselves upon the same road as in the morning, which led us to the park gates. A tall, dark figure was awaiting us there, who proved to be our London acquaintance, Mr. John Mason, the trainer.

"Good-evening, gentlemen," said he. "I got your note, Mr. Holmes. Sir Robert has not returned yet, but I hear that he is expected to-night."

"How far is this crypt from the house?" asked Holmes.

"A good quarter of a mile."

"Then I think we can disregard him altogether."

"I can't afford to do that, Mr. Holmes. The moment he arrives he will want to see me to get the last news of Shoscombe Prince."

---

*Four-wheeled carriage that has an elevated seat in front for the driver; inside, two facing double seats; and, over the back seats, a folding top.

"I see! In that case we must work without you, Mr. Mason. You can show us the crypt and then leave us."

It was pitch-dark and without a moon, but Mason led us over the grasslands until a dark mass loomed up in front of us which proved to be the ancient chapel. We entered the broken gap which was once the porch, and our guide, stumbling among heaps of loose masonry, picked his way to the corner of the building, where a steep stair led down into the crypt. Striking a match, he illuminated the melancholy place—dismal and evil-smelling, with ancient crumbling walls of rough-hewn stone, and piles of coffins, some of lead and some of stone, extending upon one side right up to the arched and groined roof which lost itself in the shadows above our heads. Holmes had lit his lantern, which shot a tiny tunnel of vivid yellow light upon the mournful scene. Its rays were reflected back from the coffin-plates, many of them adorned with the griffin and coronet of this old family which carried its honours even to the gate of Death.

"You spoke of some bones, Mr. Mason. Could you show them before you go?"

"They are here in this corner." The trainer strode across and then stood in silent surprise as our light was turned upon the place. "They are gone," said he.

"So I expected," said Holmes, chuckling. "I fancy the ashes of them might even now be found in that oven which had already consumed a part."

"But why in the world would anyone want to burn the bones of a man who has been dead a thousand years?" asked John Mason.

"That is what we are here to find out," said Holmes. "It may mean a long search, and we need not detain you. I fancy that we shall get our solution before morning."

When John Mason had left us, Holmes set to work making a very careful examination of the graves, ranging from a very ancient one, which appeared to be Saxon, in the centre, through a long line of Norman Hugos and Odos, until we reached the Sir William and Sir Denis Falder of the eighteenth century. It was an hour or more before Holmes came to a leaden coffin standing on end before the entrance to the vault. I heard his little cry of satisfaction and was aware from his hurried but purposeful movements that he had reached a goal. With his lens he was eagerly examining the edges of the heavy lid. Then he drew from his pocket a short jemmy, a box-opener, which he thrust into a chink, levering back the whole front, which seemed to be secured by only a couple of clamps. There was a rending, tearing sound as it gave way, but it had hardly hinged back and partly revealed the contents before we had an unforeseen interruption.

Someone was walking in the chapel above. It was the firm, rapid step of one who came with a definite purpose and knew well the ground upon which he walked. A light streamed down the stairs, and an instant later the man who bore it was framed in the Gothic archway. He was a terrible figure, huge in stature and fierce in manner. A large stable-lantern which he held in front of him shone upward upon a strong, heavily moustached face and angry eyes, which glared round him into every recess of the vault, finally fixing themselves with a deadly stare upon my companion and myself.

"Who the devil are you?" he thundered. "And what are you doing upon my property?" Then, as Holmes returned no answer, he took a couple of steps forward and raised a heavy stick which he carried. "Do you hear me?" he cried. "Who are you? What are you doing here?" His cudgel quivered in the air.

But instead of shrinking Holmes advanced to meet him.

"I also have a question to ask you, Sir Robert," he said in his sternest tone. "Who is this? And what is it doing here?"

He turned and tore open the coffin-lid behind him. In the glare of the lantern I saw a body swathed in a sheet from head to foot, with dreadful, witch-like features, all nose and chin, projecting at one end, the dim, glazed eyes staring from a discoloured and crumbling face.

The baronet had staggered back with a cry and supported himself against a stone sarcophagus.

"How came you to know of this?" he cried. And then, with some return of his truculent manner: "What business is it of yours?"

"My name is Sherlock Holmes," said my companion. "Possibly it is familiar to you. In any case, my business is that of every other good citizen—to uphold the law. It seems to me that you have much to answer for."

Sir Robert glared for a moment, but Holmes's quiet voice and cool, assured manner had their effect.

"'Fore God, Mr. Holmes, it's all right," said he. "Appearances are against me, I'll admit, but I could act no otherwise."

"I should be happy to think so, but I fear your explanations must be before the police."

Sir Robert shrugged his broad shoulders.

"Well, if it must be, it must. Come up to the house and you can judge for yourself how the matter stands."

A quarter of an hour later we found ourselves in what I judge, from the lines of polished barrels behind glass covers, to be the gun-room of the old house. It was comfortably furnished, and here Sir Robert left us for a few moments. When he returned he had two companions with him; the one, the florid young woman whom we had seen in the carriage; the other, a small rat-faced man with a disagreeably furtive manner. These two wore an appearance of utter bewilderment, which showed that the baronet had not yet had time to explain to them the turn events had taken.

"There," said Sir Robert with a wave of his hand, "are Mr. and Mrs. Norlett. Mrs. Norlett, under her maiden name of Evans, has for some years been my sister's confidential maid. I have brought them here because I feel that my best course is to explain the true position to you, and they are the two people upon earth who can substantiate what I say."

"Is this necessary, Sir Robert? Have you thought what you are doing?" cried the woman.

"As to me, I entirely disclaim all responsibility," said her husband.

Sir Robert gave him a glance of contempt. "I will take all responsibility," said he. "Now, Mr. Holmes, listen to a plain statement of the facts.

"You have clearly gone pretty deeply into my affairs or I should not have found you where I did. Therefore, you know already, in all probability, that I am running a dark horse for the Derby and that everything depends upon my success. If I win, all is easy. If I lose—well, I dare not think of that!"

"I understand the position," said Holmes.

"I am dependent upon my sister, Lady Beatrice, for everything. But it is well known that her interest in the estate is for her own life only. For myself, I am deeply in the hands of the Jews. I have always known that if my sister were to die my creditors would be on to my estate like a flock of vultures. Everything would be seized—my stables, my horses—everything. Well, Mr. Holmes; my sister *did* die just a week ago."

"And you told no one!"

"What could I do? Absolute ruin faced me. If I could stave things off for three weeks all would be well. Her maid's husband—this man here—is an actor. It came into our heads—it came into my head—that he could for that short period personate my sister. It was but a case of appearing daily in the carriage, for no one need enter her room save the maid. It was not difficult to arrange. My sister died of the dropsy which had long afflicted her."

"That will be for a coroner to decide."

"Her doctor would certify that for months her symptoms have threatened such an end."

"Well, what did you do?"

"The body could not remain there. On the first night Norlett and I carried it out to the old well-house, which is now never used. We were followed, however, by her pet spaniel, which yapped continually at the door, so I felt some safer place was needed. I got rid of the spaniel, and we carried the body to the crypt of the church. There was no indignity or irreverence, Mr. Holmes. I do not feel that I have wronged the dead."

"Your conduct seems to me inexcusable, Sir Robert."

The baronet shook his head impatiently. "It is easy to preach," said he. "Perhaps you would have felt differently if you had been in my position. One cannot see all one's hopes and all one's plans shattered at the last moment and make no effort to save them. It seemed to me that it would be no unworthy resting-place if we put her for the time in one of the coffins of her husband's ancestors lying in what is still consecrated ground. We opened such a coffin, removed the contents, and placed her as you have seen her. As to the old relics which we took out, we could not leave them on the floor of the Crypt. Norlett and I removed them, and he descended at night and burned them in the central furnace. There is my story, Mr. Holmes, though how you forced my hand so that I have to tell it is more than I can say."

Holmes sat for some time lost in thought.

"There is one flaw in your narrative, Sir Robert," he said at last. "Your bets on the race, and therefore your hopes for the future, would hold good even if your creditors seized your estate."

"The horse would be part of the estate. What do they care for my bets? As likely as not they would not run him at all. My chief creditor is, unhappily, my most bitter enemy—a rascally fellow, Sam Brewer, whom I was once compelled to horsewhip on Newmarket Heath. Do you suppose that he would try to save me?"

"Well, Sir Robert," said Holmes, rising, "this matter must, of course, be referred to the police. It was my duty to bring the facts to light, and there I must leave it. As to the morality or decency of your conduct, it is not for me to express an opinion. It is nearly midnight, Watson, and I think we may make our way back to our humble abode."

It is generally known now that this singular episode ended upon a happier note than Sir Robert's actions deserved. Shoscombe Prince did win the Derby, the sporting owner did net eighty thousand pounds in bets, and the creditors did hold their hand until the race was over, when they were paid in full, and enough was left to reëstablish Sir Robert in a fair position in life. Both police and coroner took a lenient view of the transaction, and beyond a mild censure for the delay in registering the lady's decease, the lucky owner got away scatheless from this strange incident in a career which has now outlived its shadows and promises to end in an honoured old age.

THE ADVENTURE OF THE
RETIRED COLOURMAN

Sherlock Holmes was in a melancholy and philosophic mood that morning. His alert practical nature was subject to such reactions.

"Did you see him?" he asked.

"You mean the old fellow, who has just gone out?"

"Precisely."

"Yes, I met him at the door."

"What did you think of him?"

"A pathetic, futile, broken creature."

"Exactly, Watson. Pathetic and futile. But is not all life pathetic and futile? Is not his story a microcosm of the whole? We reach. We grasp. And what is left in our hands at the end? A shadow. Or worse than a shadow—misery."

"Is he one of your clients?"

"Well, I suppose I may call him so. He has been sent on by the Yard. Just as medical men occasionally send their incurables to a quack. They argue that they can do nothing more, and that whatever happens the patient can be no worse than he is."

"What is the matter?"

Holmes took a rather soiled card from the table. "Josiah Amberley. He says he was junior partner of Brickfall and Amberley, who are manufacturers of artistic materials. You will see their names upon paint-boxes. He made his little pile, retired from business at the age of sixty-one, bought a house at Lewisham, and settled down to rest after a life of ceaseless grind. One would think his future was tolerably assured."

"Yes, indeed."

Holmes glanced over some notes which he had scribbled upon the back of an envelope.

"Retired in 1896, Watson. Early in 1897 he married a woman twenty years younger than himself—a good-looking woman, too, if the photograph does not flatter. A competence,* a wife, leisure—it seemed a straight road which lay before him. And yet within two years he is, as you have seen, as broken and miserable a creature as crawls beneath the sun."

"But what has happened?"

"The old story, Watson. A treacherous friend and a fickle wife. It would appear that Amberley has one hobby in life, and it is chess. Not far from him at Lewisham there lives a young doctor who is also a chess-player. I have noted his name as Dr. Ray Ernest. Ernest was frequently in the house, and an intimacy between him and Mrs. Amberley was a natural sequence, for you must admit that our unfortunate client has few out-

---

*Sufficient retirement income to meet one's needs.

ward graces, whatever his inner virtues may be. The couple went off together last week—destination untraced. What is more, the faithless
spouse carried off the old man's deed-box as her personal luggage with a
good part of his life's savings within. Can we find the lady? Can we save
the money? A commonplace problem so far as it has developed, and yet
a vital one for Josiah Amberley."

"What will you do about it?"

"Well, the immediate question, my dear Watson, happens to be, What
will *you* do?—if you will be good enough to understudy me. You know
that I am preoccupied with this case of the two Coptic Patriarchs,* which
should come to a head to-day. I really have not time to go out to
Lewisham, and yet evidence taken on the spot has a special value. The
old fellow was quite insistent that I should go, but I explained my difficulty. He is prepared to meet a representative."

"By all means," I answered. "I confess I don't see that I can be of much
service, but I am willing to do my best." And so it was that on a summer
afternoon I set forth to Lewisham, little dreaming that within a week the
affair in which I was engaging would be the eager debate of all England.

It was late that evening before I returned to Baker Street and gave an
account of my mission. Holmes lay with his gaunt figure stretched in his
deep chair, his pipe curling forth slow wreaths of acrid tobacco, while his
eyelids drooped over his eyes so lazily that he might almost have been
asleep were it not that at any halt or questionable passage of my narrative they half lifted, and two gray eyes, as bright and keen as rapiers,
transfixed me with their searching glance.

"The Haven is the name of Mr. Josiah Amberley's house," I explained.
"I think it would interest you, Holmes. It is like some penurious patrician
who has sunk into the company of his inferiors. You know that particular
quarter, the monotonous brick streets, the weary suburban highways.
Right in the middle of them, a little island of ancient culture and comfort,
lies this old home, surrounded by a high sun-baked wall mottled with
lichens and topped with moss, the sort of wall——"

"Cut out the poetry, Watson," said Holmes severely. "I note that it was
a high brick wall."

"Exactly. I should not have known which was The Haven had I not
asked a lounger who was smoking in the street. I have a reason for men-
tioning him. He was a tall, dark, heavily moustached, rather military-
looking man. He nodded in answer to my inquiry and gave me a curiously
questioning glance, which came back to my memory a little later.

"I had hardly entered the gateway before I saw Mr. Amberley coming
down the drive. I only had a glimpse of him this morning, and he certainly
gave me the impression of a strange creature, but when I saw him in full
light his appearance was even more abnormal."

---

*Principal bishops in the Coptic Church, an Egyptian branch of Christianity.

"I have, of course, studied it, and yet I should be interested to have your impression," said Holmes.

"He seemed to me like a man who was literally bowed down by care. His back was curved as though he carried a heavy burden. Yet he was not the weakling that I had at first imagined, for his shoulders and chest have the framework of a giant, though his figure tapers away into a pair of spindled legs."

"Left shoe wrinkled, right one smooth."

"I did not observe that."

"No, you wouldn't. I spotted his artificial limb. But proceed."

"I was struck by the snaky locks of grizzled hair which curled from under his old straw hat, and his face with its fierce, eager expression and the deeply lined features."

"Very good, Watson. What did he say?"

"He began pouring out the story of his grievances. We walked down the drive together, and of course I took a good look round. I have never seen a worse-kept place. The garden was all running to seed, giving me an impression of wild neglect in which the plants had been allowed to find the way of Nature rather than of art. How any decent woman could have tolerated such a state of things, I don't know. The house, too, was slatternly to the last degree, but the poor man seemed himself to be aware of it and to be trying to remedy it, for a great pot of green paint stood in the centre of the hall, and he was carrying a thick brush in his left hand. He had been working on the woodwork.

"He took me into his dingy sanctum, and we had a long chat. Of course, he was disappointed that you had not come yourself. 'I hardly expected,' he said, 'that so humble an individual as myself, especially after my heavy financial loss, could obtain the complete attention of so famous a man as Mr. Sherlock Holmes.'

"I assured him that the financial question did not arise. 'No, of course, it is art for art's sake with him,' said he, 'but even on the artistic side of crime he might have found something here to study. And human nature, Dr. Watson—the black ingratitude of it all! When did I ever refuse one of her requests? Was ever a woman so pampered? And that young man—he might have been my own son. He had the run of my house. And yet see how they have treated me! Oh, Dr. Watson, it is a dreadful, dreadful world!'

"That was the burden of his song for an hour or more. He had, it seems, no suspicion of an intrigue. They lived alone save for a woman who comes in by the day and leaves every evening at six. On that particular evening old Amberley, wishing to give his wife a treat, had taken two upper circle seats at the Haymarket Theatre. At the last moment she had complained of a headache and had refused to go. He had gone alone. There seemed to be no doubt about the fact, for he produced the unused ticket which he had taken for his wife."

"That is remarkable—most remarkable," said Holmes, whose interest in the case seemed to be rising. "Pray continue, Watson. I find your narrative most arresting. Did you personally examine this ticket? You did not, perchance, take the number?"

"It so happens that I did," I answered with some pride. "It chanced to be my old school number, thirty-one, and so is stuck in my head."

"Excellent, Watson! His seat, then, was either thirty or thirty-two."

"Quite so," I answered with some mystification. "And on B row."

"That is most satisfactory. What else did he tell you?"

"He showed me his strong-room, as he called it. It really is a strong-room—like a bank—with iron door and shutter—burglarproof, as he claimed. However, the woman seems to have had a duplicate key, and between them they had carried off some seven thousand pounds' worth of cash and securities."

"Securities! How could they dispose of those?"

"He said that he had given the police a list and that he hoped they would be unsaleable. He had got back from the theatre about midnight and found the place plundered, the door and window open, and the fugitives gone. There was no letter or message, nor has he heard a word since. He at once gave the alarm to the police."

Holmes brooded for some minutes.

"You say he was painting. What was he painting?"

"Well, he was painting the passage. But he had already painted the door and woodwork of this room I spoke of."

"Does it not strike you as a strange occupation in the circumstances?"

" 'One must do something to ease an aching heart.' That was his own explanation. It was eccentric, no doubt, but he is clearly an eccentric man. He tore up one of his wife's photographs in my presence—tore it up furiously in a tempest of passion. 'I never wish to see her damned face again,' he shrieked."

"Anything more, Watson?"

"Yes, one thing which struck me more than anything else. I had driven to the Blackheath Station and had caught my train there when, just as it was starting, I saw a man dart into the carriage next to my own. You know that I have a quick eye for faces, Holmes. It was undoubtedly the tall, dark man whom I had addressed in the street. I saw him once more at London Bridge, and then I lost him in the crowd. But I am convinced that he was following me."

"No doubt! No doubt!" said Holmes. "A tall, dark, heavily moustached man, you say, with gray-tinted sun-glasses?"

"Holmes, you are a wizard. I did not say so, but he *had* gray-tinted sun-glasses."

"And a Masonic tie-pin?"

"Holmes!"

"Quite simple, my dear Watson. But let us get down to what is practical. I must admit to you that the case, which seemed to me to be so absurdly simple as to be hardly worth my notice, is rapidly assuming a very different aspect. It is true that though in your mission you have missed everything of importance, yet even those things which have obtruded themselves upon your notice give rise to serious thought."

"What have I missed?"

"Don't be hurt, my dear fellow. You know that I am quite impersonal. No one else would have done better. Some possibly not so well. But clearly you have missed some vital points. What is the opinion of the neighbours about this man Amberley and his wife? That surely is of importance. What of Dr. Ernest? Was he the gay Lothario one would expect? With your natural advantages, Watson, every lady is your helper and accomplice. What about the girl at the post-office, or the wife of the greengrocer? I can picture you whispering soft nothings with the young lady at the Blue Anchor, and receiving hard somethings in exchange. All this you have left undone."

"It can still be done."

"It has been done. Thanks to the telephone and the help of the Yard, I can usually get my essentials without leaving this room. As a matter of fact, my information confirms the man's story. He has the local repute of being a miser as well as a harsh and exacting husband. That he had a large sum of money in that strong-room of his is certain. So also is it that young Dr. Ernest, an unmarried man, played chess with Amberley, and probably played the fool with his wife. All this seems plain sailing, one would think that there was no more to be said—and yet!—and yet!"

"Where lies the difficulty?"

"In my imagination, perhaps. Well, leave it there, Watson. Let us escape from this weary workaday world by the side door of music. Carina sings to-night at the Albert Hall,* and we have time to dress, dine, and enjoy."

In the morning I was up betimes, but some toast crumbs and two empty eggshells told me that my companion was earlier still. I found a scribbled note upon the table.

DEAR WATSON:

There are one or two points of contact which I should wish to establish with Mr. Josiah Amberley. When I have done so we can dismiss the case—or not. I would only ask you to be on hand about three o'clock, as I conceive it possible that I may want you.

                                                                    S. H.

I saw nothing of Holmes all day, but at the hour named he returned, grave, preoccupied, and aloof. At such times it was wiser to leave him to himself.

"Has Amberley been here yet?"

"No."

---

*Royal Albert Hall is a huge concert building in London; no singer named Carina has been identified.

"Ah! I am expecting him."

He was not disappointed, for presently the old fellow arrived with a very worried and puzzled expression upon his austere face.

"I've had a telegram, Mr. Holmes. I can make nothing of it." He handed it over, and Holmes read it aloud.

"Come at once without fail. Can give you information as to your recent loss.

ELMAN.
The Vicarage."

"Dispatched at 2:10 from Little Purlington," said Holmes. "Little Purlington is in Essex, I believe, not far from Frinton. Well, of course you will start at once. This is evidently from a responsible person, the vicar of the place. Where is my Crockford?* Yes, here we have him: 'J. C. Elman, M. A., Living of Moosmoor cum Little Purlington.' Look up the trains, Watson."

"There is one at 5:20 from Liverpool Street."

"Excellent. You had best go with him, Watson. He may need help or advice. Clearly we have come to a crisis in this affair."

But our client seemed by no means eager to start.

"It's perfectly absurd, Mr. Holmes," he said. "What can this man possibly know of what has occurred? It is waste of time and money."

"He would not have telegraphed to you if he did not know something. Wire at once that you are coming."

"I don't think I shall go."

Holmes assumed his sternest aspect.

"It would make the worst possible impression both on the police and upon myself, Mr. Amberley, if when so obvious a clue arose you should refuse to follow it up. We should feel that you were not really in earnest in this investigation."

Our client seemed horrified at the suggestion.

"Why, of course I shall go if you look at it in that way," said he. "On the face of it, it seems absurd to suppose that this parson knows anything; but if you think——"

"I *do* think," said Holmes with emphasis, and so we were launched upon our journey. Holmes took me aside before we left the room and gave me one word of counsel, which showed that he considered the matter to be of importance. "Whatever you do, see that he really *does* go," said he. "Should he break away or return, get to the nearest telephone exchange and send the single word 'Bolted.' I will arrange here that it shall reach me wherever I am."

Little Purlington is not an easy place to reach, for it is on a branch line. My remembrance of the journey is not a pleasant one, for the weather

---

*Crockford's *Clerical Directory* lists all the clergy of the Church of England.

was hot, the train slow, and my companion sullen and silent, hardly talking at all save to make an occasional sardonic remark as to the futility of our proceedings. When we at last reached the little station it was a two-mile drive before we came to the Vicarage, where a big, solemn, rather pompous clergyman received us in his study. Our telegram lay before him.

"Well, gentlemen," he asked, "what can I do for you?"

"We came," I explained, "in answer to your wire."

"My wire! I sent no wire."

"I mean the wire which you sent to Mr. Josiah Amberley about his wife and his money."

"If this is a joke, sir, it is a very questionable one," said the vicar angrily. "I have never heard of the gentleman you name, and I have not sent a wire to anyone."

Our client and I looked at each other in amazement.

"Perhaps there is some mistake," said I; "are there perhaps two vicarages? Here is the wire itself, signed Elman and dated from the Vicarage."

"There is only one vicarage, sir, and only one vicar, and this wire is a scandalous forgery, the origin of which shall certainly be investigated by the police. Meanwhile, I can see no possible object in prolonging this interview."

So Mr. Amberley and I found ourselves on the roadside in what seemed to me to be the most primitive village in England. We made for the telegraph office, but it was already closed. There was a telephone, however, at the little Railway Arms, and by it I got into touch with Holmes, who shared in our amazement at the result of our journey.

"Most singular!" said the distant voice. "Most remarkable! I much fear, my dear Watson, that there is no return train to-night. I have unwittingly condemned you to the horrors of a country inn. However, there is always Nature, Watson—Nature and Josiah Amberley—you can be in close commune with both." I heard his dry chuckle as he turned away.

It was soon apparent to me that my companion's reputation as a miser was not undeserved. He had grumbled at the expense of the journey, had insisted upon travelling third-class, and was now clamorous in his objections to the hotel bill. Next morning, when we did at last arrive in London, it was hard to say which of us was in the worse humour.

"You had best take Baker Street as we pass," said I. "Mr. Holmes may have some fresh instructions."

"If they are not worth more than the last ones they are not of much use," said Amberley with a malevolent scowl. None the less, he kept me company. I had already warned Holmes by telegram of the hour of our arrival, but we found a message waiting that he was at Lewisham and would expect us there. That was a surprise, but an even greater one was to find that he was not alone in the sitting-room of our client. A stern-looking, impassive man sat beside him, a dark man with gray-tinted glasses and a large Masonic pin projecting from his tie.

"This is my friend Mr. Barker," said Holmes. "He has been interesting himself also in your business, Mr. Josiah Amberley, though we have been working independently. But we both have the same question to ask you!"

Mr. Amberley sat down heavily. He sensed impending danger. I read it in his straining eyes and his twitching features.

"What is the question, Mr. Holmes?"

"Only this: What did you do with the bodies?"

The man sprang to his feet with a hoarse scream. He clawed into the air with his bony hands. His mouth was open, and for the instant he looked like some horrible bird of prey. In a flash we got a glimpse of the real Josiah Amberley, a misshapen demon with a soul as distorted as his body. As he fell back into his chair he clapped his hand to his lips as if to stifle a cough. Holmes sprang at his throat like a tiger and twisted his face towards the ground. A white pellet fell from between his gasping lips.

"No short cuts, Josiah Amberley. Things must be done decently and in order.* What about it, Barker?"

"I have a cab at the door," said our taciturn companion.

"It is only a few hundred yards to the station. We will go together. You can stay here, Watson. I shall be back within half an hour."

The old colourman had the strength of a lion in that great trunk of his, but he was helpless in the hands of the two experienced man-handlers. Wriggling and twisting he was dragged to the waiting cab, and I was left to my solitary vigil in the ill-omened house. In less time than he had named, however, Holmes was back, in company with a smart young police inspector.

"I've left Barker to look after the formalities," said Holmes. "You had not met Barker, Watson. He is my hated rival upon the Surrey shore. When you said a tall dark man it was not difficult for me to complete the picture. He has several good cases to his credit, has he not, Inspector?"

"He has certainly interfered several times," the inspector answered with reserve.

"His methods are irregular, no doubt, like my own. The irregulars are useful sometimes, you know. You, for example, with your compulsory warning about whatever he said being used against him, could never have bluffed this rascal into what is virtually a confession."

"Perhaps not. But we get there all the same, Mr. Holmes. Don't imagine that we had not formed our own views of this case, and that we would not have laid our hands on our man. You will excuse us for feeling sore when you jump in with methods which we cannot use, and so rob us of the credit."

"There shall be no such robbery, MacKinnon. I assure you that I efface myself from now onward, and as to Barker, he has done nothing save what I told him."

---

*Reference to the Bible, I Corinthians 14:40: "Let all things be done decently and in order" (KJV).

The inspector seemed considerably relieved.

"That is very handsome of you, Mr. Holmes. Praise or blame can matter little to you, but it is very different to us when the newspapers begin to ask questions."

"Quite so. But they are pretty sure to ask questions anyhow, so it would be as well to have answers. What will you say, for example, when the intelligent and enterprising reporter asks you what the exact points were which aroused your suspicion, and finally gave you a certain conviction as to the real facts?"

The inspector looked puzzled.

"We don't seem to have got any real facts yet, Mr. Holmes. You say that the prisoner, in the presence of three witnesses, practically confessed by trying to commit suicide, that he had murdered his wife and her lover. What other facts have you?"

"Have you arranged for a search?"

"There are three constables on their way."

"Then you will soon get the clearest fact of all. The bodies cannot be far away. Try the cellars and the garden. It should not take long to dig up the likely places. This house is older than the water-pipes. There must be a disused well somewhere. Try your luck there."

"But how did you know of it, and how was it done?"

"I'll show you first how it was done, and then I will give the explanation which is due to you, and even more to my long-suffering friend here, who has been invaluable throughout. But, first, I would give you an insight into this man's mentality. It is a very unusual one—so much so that I think his destination is more likely to be Broadmoor* than the scaffold. He has, to a high degree, the sort of mind which one associates with the mediæval Italian nature rather than with the modern Briton. He was a miserable miser who made his wife so wretched by his niggardly ways that she was a ready prey for any adventurer. Such a one came upon the scene in the person of this chess-playing doctor. Amberley excelled at chess—one mark, Watson, of a scheming mind. Like all misers, he was a jealous man, and his jealousy became a frantic mania. Rightly or wrongly, he suspected an intrigue. He determined to have his revenge, and he planned it with diabolical cleverness. Come here!"

Holmes led us along the passage with as much certainty as if he had lived in the house and halted at the open door of the strong-room.

"Pooh! What an awful smell of paint!" cried the inspector.

"That was our first clue," said Holmes. "You can thank Dr. Watson's observation for that, though he failed to draw the inference. It set my foot upon the trail. Why should this man at such a time be filling his house with strong odours? Obviously, to cover some other smell which he wished to conceal—some guilty smell which would suggest suspicions. Then came the idea of a room such as you see here with iron door and

---

*Institution in Berkshire for the criminally insane.

shutter—a hermetically sealed room. Put those two facts together, and whither do they lead? I could only determine that by examining the house myself. I was already certain that the case was serious, for I had examined the box-office chart at the Haymarket Theatre—another of Dr. Watson's bull's-eyes—and ascertained that neither B thirty nor thirty-two of the upper circle had been occupied that night. Therefore, Amberley had not been to the theatre, and his alibi fell to the ground. He made a bad slip when he allowed my astute friend to notice the number of the seat taken for his wife. The question now arose how I might be able to examine the house. I sent an agent to the most impossible village I could think of, and summoned my man to it at such an hour that he could not possibly get back. To prevent any miscarriage, Dr. Watson accompanied him. The good vicar's name I took, of course, out of my Crockford. Do I make it all clear to you?"

"It is masterly," said the inspector in an awed voice.

"There being no fear of interruption I proceeded to burgle the house. Burglary has always been an alternative profession had I cared to adopt it, and I have little doubt that I should have come to the front. Observe what I found. You see the gas-pipe along the skirting here. Very good. It rises in the angle of the wall, and there is a tap here in the corner. The pipe runs out into the strong-room, as you can see, and ends in that plaster rose in the centre of the ceiling, where it is concealed by the ornamentation. That end is wide open. At any moment by turning the outside tap the room could be flooded with gas. With door and shutter closed and the tap full on I would not give two minutes of conscious sensation to anyone shut up in that little chamber. By what devilish device he decoyed them there I do not know, but once inside the door they were at his mercy."

The inspector examined the pipe with interest. "One of our officers mentioned the smell of gas," said he, "but of course the window and door were open then, and the paint—or some of it—was already about. He had begun the work of painting the day before, according to his story. But what next, Mr. Holmes?"

"Well, then came an incident which was rather unexpected to myself. I was slipping through the pantry window in the early dawn when I felt a hand inside my collar, and a voice said: 'Now, you rascal, what are you doing in there?' When I could twist my head round I looked into the tinted spectacles of my friend and rival, Mr. Barker. It was a curious foregathering and set us both smiling. It seems that he had been engaged by Dr. Ray Ernest's family to make some investigations and had come to the same conclusion as to foul play. He had watched the house for some days and had spotted Dr. Watson as one of the obviously suspicious characters who had called there. He could hardly arrest Watson, but when he saw a man actually climbing out of the pantry window there came a limit to his restraint. Of course, I told him how matters stood and we continued the case together."

"Why him? Why not us?"

"Because it was in my mind to put that little test which answered so admirably. I fear you would not have gone so far."

The inspector smiled.

"Well, maybe not. I understand that I have your word, Mr. Holmes, that you step right out of the case now and that you turn all your results over to us."

"Certainly, that is always my custom."

"Well, in the name of the force I thank you. It seems a clear case, as you put it, and there can't be much difficulty over the bodies."

"I'll show you a grim little bit of evidence," said Holmes, "and I am sure Amberley himself never observed it. You'll get results, Inspector, by always putting yourself in the other fellow's place, and thinking what you would do yourself. It takes some imagination, but it pays. Now, we will suppose that you were shut up in this little room, had not two minutes to live, but wanted to get even with the fiend who was probably mocking at you from the other side of the door. What would you do?"

"Write a message."

"Exactly. You would like to tell people how you died. No use writing on paper. That would be seen. If you wrote on the wall someone might rest upon it. Now, look here! Just above the skirting is scribbled with a purple indelible pencil: 'We we——' That's all."

"What do you make of that?"

"Well, it's only a foot above the ground. The poor devil was on the floor dying when he wrote it. He lost his senses before he could finish."

"He was writing, 'We were murdered.' "

"That's how I read it. If you find an indelible pencil on the body——"

"We'll look out for it, you may be sure. But those securities? Clearly there was no robbery at all. And yet he *did* possess those bonds. We verified that."

"You may be sure he has them hidden in a safe place. When the whole elopement had passed into history, he would suddenly discover them and announce that the guilty couple had relented and sent back the plunder or had dropped it on the way."

"You certainly seem to have met every difficulty," said the inspector. "Of course, he was bound to call us in, but why he should have gone to you I can't understand."

"Pure swank!" Holmes answered. "He felt so clever and so sure of himself that he imagined no one could touch him. He could say to any suspicious neighbour, 'Look at the steps I have taken. I have consulted not only the police but even Sherlock Holmes.' "

The inspector laughed.

"We must forgive you your 'even,' Mr. Holmes," said he, "it's as workmanlike a job as I can remember."

A couple of days later my friend tossed across to me a copy of the bi-weekly *North Surrey Observer*. Under a series of flaming headlines, which began with "The Haven Horror" and ended with "Brilliant Police Investigation," there was a packed column of print which gave the first consecutive account of the affair. The concluding paragraph is typical of the whole. It ran thus:

> The remarkable acumen by which Inspector MacKinnon deduced from the smell of paint that some other smell, that of gas, for example, might be concealed; the bold deduction that the strong-room might also be the death-chamber, and the subsequent inquiry which led to the discovery of the bodies in a disused well, cleverly concealed by a dog-kennel, should live in the history of crime as a standing example of the intelligence of our professional detectives.

"Well, well, MacKinnon is a good fellow," said Holmes with a tolerant smile. "You can file it in our archives, Watson. Some day the true story may be told."

TWO PARODIES BY
SIR ARTHUR CONAN DOYLE

AN INTRODUCTION TO DOYLE'S PARODIES

From nearly the very beginning of his existence, Sherlock Holmes has been the subject of parodies and spoofs. Arthur Conan Doyle himself took comic aim at his best-known creation in two of the better mock adventures. He contributed the first, "The Field Bazaar: A Short Travesty," in 1896 to *The Student*, a publication at his alma mater, the University of Edinburgh, as a good-humored gift from a famed alumnus. The story was written between the time Holmes apparently had met his end in "The Final Problem" in 1893 and his "resurrection" in "The Empty House" in 1903. Can you detect any clue to the author's feelings about reviving Holmes in this delightful little mind-reading caper?

The second, "How Watson Learned the Trick," was published in 1924, near the end of the Holmes cycle. It seems to counter an implied belief that the methods Holmes used to solve his crimes were not so hard to fathom, once you saw the predictable pattern at work in most of the stories: "Oh, yeah? Let's see if you can do it!"

TWO PARODIES BY
SIR ARTHUR CONAN DOYLE

THE FIELD BAZAAR

"I should certainly do it," said Sherlock Holmes.

I started at the interruption, for my companion had been eating his breakfast with his attention entirely centred upon the paper which was propped up by the coffee pot. Now I looked across at him to find his eyes fastened upon me with the half-amused, half-questioning expression which he usually assumed when he felt that he had made an intellectual point.

"Do what?" I asked.

He smiled as he took his slipper from the mantelpiece and drew from it enough shag tobacco to fill the old clay pipe with which he invariably rounded off his breakfast.

"A most characteristic question of yours, Watson," said he. "You will not, I am sure, be offended if I say that any reputation for sharpness which I may possess has been entirely gained by the admirable foil which you have made for me. Have I not heard of debutantes who have insisted upon plainness in their chaperones? There is a certain analogy."

Our long companionship in the Baker Street rooms had left us on those easy terms of intimacy when much may be said without offence. And yet I acknowledge that I was nettled at his remark.

"I may be very obtuse," said I, "but I confess that I am unable to see how you have managed to know that I was . . . I was . . ."

"Asked to help in the Edinburgh University Bazaar."

"Precisely. The letter has only just come to hand, and I have not spoken to you since."

"In spite of that," said Holmes, leaning back in his chair and putting his finger tips together, "I would even venture to suggest that the object of the bazaar is to enlarge the University cricket field."

I looked at him in such bewilderment that he vibrated with silent laughter.

"The fact is, my dear Watson, that you are an excellent subject," said he. "You are never *blasé*. You respond instantly to any external stimulus. Your mental processes may be slow but they are never obscure, and I found during breakfast that you were easier reading than the leader in the *Times* in front of me."

"I should be glad to know how you arrived at your conclusions," said I.

"I fear that my good nature in giving explanations has seriously compromised my reputation," said Holmes. "But in this case the train of reasoning is based upon such obvious facts that no credit can be claimed for it. You entered the room with a thoughtful expression, the expression of a man who is debating some point in his mind. In your hand you held a solitary letter. Now last night you retired in the best of spirits, so it was clear that it was this letter in your hand which had caused the change in you."

671

"This is obvious."

"It is all obvious when it is explained to you. I naturally asked myself what the letter could contain which might have this effect upon you. As you walked you held the flap side of the envelope towards me, and I saw upon it the same shield-shaped device which I have observed upon your old college cricket cap. It was clear, then, that the request came from Edinburgh University—or from some club connected with the University. When you reached the table you laid down the letter beside your plate with the address uppermost, and you walked over to look at the framed photograph upon the left of the mantelpiece."

It amazed me to see the accuracy with which he had observed my movements. "What next?" I asked.

"I began by glancing at the address, and I could tell, even at the distance of six feet, that it was an unofficial communication. This I gathered from the use of the word "Doctor" upon the address, to which, as a Bachelor of Medicine, you have no legal claim. I knew that University officials are pedantic in their correct use of titles, and I was thus enabled to say with certainty that your letter was unofficial. When on your return to the table you turned over your letter and allowed me to perceive that the enclosure was a printed one, the idea of a bazaar first occurred to me. I had already weighed the possibility of its being a political communication, but this seemed improbable in the present stagnant conditions of politics.

"When you returned to the table your face still retained its expression and it was evident that your examination of the photograph had not changed the current of your thoughts. In that case it must itself bear upon the subject in question. I turned my attention to the photograph, therefore, and saw at once that it consisted of yourself as a member of the Edinburgh University Eleven,* with the pavilion and cricket-field in the background. My small experience of cricket clubs has taught me that next to churches and cavalry ensigns they are the most debt-laden things upon earth. When upon your return to the table I saw you take out your pencil and draw lines upon the envelope, I was convinced that you were endeavouring to realize some projected improvement which was to be brought about by a bazaar. Your face still showed some indecision, so that I was able to break in upon you with my advice that you should assist in so good an object."

I could not help smiling at the extreme simplicity of his explanation.

"Of course, it was as easy as possible," said I.

My remark appeared to nettle him.

"I may add," said he, "that the particular help which you have been asked to give was that you should write in their album, and that you have already made up your mind that the present incident will be the subject of your article."

"But how—!" I cried.

---

*So called because cricket features eleven players on each side.

"It is as easy as possible," said he, "and I leave its solution to your own ingenuity. In the meantime," he added, raising his paper, "you will excuse me if I return to this very interesting article upon the trees of Cremona,* and the exact reasons for their pre-eminence in the manufacture of violins. It is one of those small outlying problems to which I am sometimes tempted to direct my attention."

---

*Home of great violin makers from the Amati family, as well as Antonio Stradivari.

HOW WATSON LEARNED THE TRICK

Watson had been watching his companion intently ever since he had sat down to the breakfast table. Holmes happened to look up and catch his eye.

"Well, Watson, what are you thinking about?" he asked.

"About you."

"Me?"

"Yes, Holmes, I was thinking how superficial are these tricks of yours, and how wonderful it is that the public should continue to show interest in them."

"I quite agree," said Holmes. "In fact, I have a recollection that I have myself made a similar remark."

"Your methods," said Watson severely, "are really easily acquired."

"No doubt," Holmes answered with a smile. "Perhaps you will yourself give an example of this method of reasoning."

"With pleasure," said Watson. "I am able to say that you were greatly preoccupied when you got up this morning."

"Excellent!" said Holmes. "How could you possibly know that?"

"Because you are usually a very tidy man and yet you have forgotten to shave."

"Dear me! How very clever!" said Holmes, "I had no idea, Watson, that you were so apt a pupil. Has your eagle eye detected anything more?"

"Yes, Holmes. You have a client named Barlow, and you have not been successful in his case."

"Dear me, how could you know that?"

"I saw the name outside his envelope. When you opened it you gave a groan and thrust it into your pocket with a frown on your face."

"Admirable! You are indeed observant. Any other points?"

"I fear, Holmes, that you have taken to financial speculation."

"How *could* you tell that, Watson?"

"You opened the paper, turned to the financial page, and gave a loud exclamation of interest."

"Well, that is very clever of you Watson. Any more?"

"Yes, Holmes, you have put on your black coat, instead of your dressing gown, which proves that you are expecting some important visitor at once."

"Anything more?"

"I have no doubt that I could find other points, Holmes, but I only give you these few, in order to show you that there are other people in the world who can be as clever as you."

"And some not so clever," said Holmes. "I admit that they are few, but I am afraid, my dear Watson, that I must count you among them."

"What do you mean, Holmes?"

"Well, my dear fellow, I fear your deductions have not been so happy as I should have wished."

"You mean that I was mistaken."

"Just a little that way, I fear. Let us take the points in their order: I did not shave because I sent my razor to be sharpened. I put on my coat because I have, worse luck, an early meeting with my dentist. His name is Barlow, and the letter was to confirm the appointment. The cricket page is beside the financial one, and I turned to it to find if Surrey was holding its own against Kent. But go on, Watson, go on! It's a very superficial trick, and no doubt you will soon acquire it."

TWO ESSAYS BY
SIR ARTHUR CONAN DOYLE

THE TRUTH ABOUT
SHERLOCK HOLMES

When Sir Arthur Conan Doyle deliberately killed Sherlock Holmes the vehement protests which came from all quarters made him realise, to his amazement, how completely the great detective had captured the world's imagination. In this essay Sir Arthur answers all our questions about Holmes—how he was born and developed and why it became necessary to kill him. It is amusing to read here that Dr. Bell, Holmes's prototype, was never able to help Doyle in contriving the stories. And he tells the story of that disastrous flyer in comic opera with Sir James Barrie, out of which came one good thing—Barrie's delightful parody on Sherlock Holmes which he wrote to console Doyle and which is also included here.

COLLIER'S *The National Weekly*
29 DECEMBER 1923

It was in October, 1876 that I began my medical course at the University of Edinburgh. The most notable of the characters whom I met was one Joseph Bell, surgeon at the Edinburgh Infirmary. Bell was a very remarkable man in body and mind. He was thin, wiry, dark with a high-nosed, acute face, penetrating grey eyes, angular shoulders, and a jerky way of walking. His voice was high and discordant. He was a very skilful surgeon, but his strong point was diagnosis, not only of disease, but of occupation and character. For some reason which I have never understood he singled me out from the drove of students who frequented his wards and made me his out-patient clerk, which meant that I had to array his out-patients, make simple notes of their cases, and then show them in, one by one, to the large room in which Bell sat in state surrounded by his dressers* and students. Then I had ample chance of studying his methods and in noticing that he often learned more of the patient by a few quick glances than I had done by my questions. Occasionally the results were very dramatic, though there were times when he blundered. In one of his best cases he said to a civilian patient:

"Well, my man, you've served in the army?"

"Aye, sir."

"Not long discharged?"

"No sir."

"A Highland regiment?"

"Aye, sir."

"A noncom officer?"

"Aye, sir."

---

*Medical personnel who bandage wounds and surgical incisions.

"Stationed at Barbados?"

"Aye, sir."

"You see, gentlemen," he would explain, "the man was a respectful man, but did not remove his hat. They do not in the army, but he would have learned civilian ways had he been long discharged. He has an air of authority and he is obviously Scottish. As to Barbados, his complaint is elephantiasis, which is West Indian and not British." To his audience of Watsons it all seemed most miraculous until it was explained, and then it became simple enough. It is no wonder that after the study of such a character I used and amplified his methods when in later life I tried to build up a scientific detective who solved cases on his own merits and not through the folly of the criminal. Bell took a keen interest in these detective tales and made suggestions, which were not, I am bound to say, very practical.

The Twopenny Box

I endeavoured almost from the first to compress the classes for a year into half a year, so as to have some months in which to earn a little money. It was at this time that I first learned that shillings might be earned in other ways than by filling phials. Some friend remarked to me that my letters were very vivid, and surely I could write some things to sell. I may say that the general aspiration toward literature was tremendously strong upon me, and that my mind was reaching out in what seemed an aimless way in all sorts of directions. I used to be allowed twopence for my lunch, that being the price of a mutton pie, but near the pie shop was a second-hand bookshop with a barrel full of old books and the legend, "Your choice for 2d,"* stuck above it. Often the price of my luncheon used to be spent on some sample out of this barrel, and I have within reach of my arm, as I write these lines, copies of Gordon's *Tacitus*, Temple's works, Pope's *Homer*, Addison's *Spectator* and Swift's works,† which all came out of the twopenny box.

Anyone observing my actions and tastes would have said that so strong a spring would certainly overflow, but for my own part I never dreamed I could myself produce decent prose, and the remark of my friend, who was by no means given to flattery, took me greatly by sur-

---

*Abbreviation for two pence, or 1/6 of a shilling.

†Scottish writer Thomas Gordon translated the works of the Roman historian Tacitus into English in 1728. Sir William Temple (1628–1699) was an English essayist. Alexander Pope wrote acclaimed translations of Homer's *Iliad* (1720) and *Odyssey* (1725–1726). The *Spectator* was a popular and influential daily paper published from 1711 to 1712 by Joseph Addison and Richard Steele. Jonathan Swift (1667–1745) was a poet, essayist, novelist, and dean of St. Patrick's Cathedral in Dublin.

prise. I sat down, however, and I wrote a little adventure story which I called "The Mystery of the Sasassa Valley." To my great joy and surprise, it was accepted by *Chambers's Journal*, and I received three guineas. It mattered not that other attempts failed. I had done it once and I cheered myself by the thought that I could do it again.

Upon emerging from Edinburgh as a bachelor of medicine in 1881, my plans were all exceedingly fluid and I was ready to join army, navy, Indian service,* or anything which offered an opening. But after taking a trip in a cargo vessel along the west coast of Africa, I finally settled down to practice in Plymouth.

I had at this time contributed several stories to *London Society*, a magazine now defunct, but then flourishing under the editorship of a Mr. Hogg. It had never entered my head yet that literature might give me a career, or anything beyond a little casual pocket money, but already it was a deciding factor in my life, for I could not have held on, and must have either starved or given in but for the few pounds which Mr. Hogg sent me.

During the years before my marriage I had from time to time written short stories which were good enough to be marketable at very small prices—five pounds on average—but not good enough to reproduce. They are scattered about amid the pages of *London Society*, of *All the Year Round*, of *Temple Bar*, the *Boys' Own Paper* and other journals. There let them lie. They served their purpose in relieving me of a little of that financial burden which always pressed upon me. I can hardly have earned more than ten or fifteen pounds a year from this source, so that the idea of making a living by it never occurred to me. But though I was not putting out, I was taking in. I still have notebooks full of all sorts of knowledge which I acquired during that time. It is a great mistake to start putting out cargo when you have hardly stowed any on board.

Enter Holmes and Watson

I had for some time from 1884 onward been engaged upon a sensational book of adventure which I had called *The Firm of Girdlestone*, which represented my first attempt at a connected narrative. Save for occasional patches, it is a worthless book. I felt now that I was capable of something cleaner and crisper and more workmanlike. Gaboriau had rather attracted me by the neat dovetailing of his plots, and Poe's masterful detective, M. Dupin, had from boyhood been one of my heroes. But could I bring an addition of my own? I thought of my old teacher Joe Bell, of his eagle face, of his curious ways, of his eerie trick of spotting details. If he were a detective he would surely reduce this fascinating but unorganized business to something nearer to an exact science. I would try if I could get this effect. It was surely possible in real life, so why should I not

---

*The huge bureaucracy that administered British rule in India.

make it plausible in fiction? It is all very well to say that a man is clever, but the reader wants to see examples of it—such examples as Bell gave us every day in the wards.

The idea amused me. What should I call the fellow? I still possess the leaf of a notebook with various alternative names. One rebelled against the elementary art which gives some inkling of character in the name, and creates Mr. Sharps or Mr. Ferrets. First it was Sherringford Holmes; then it was Sherlock Holmes. He could not tell his own exploits, so he must have a commonplace comrade as a foil—an educated man of action who could both join in the exploits and narrate them. A drab, quiet name for this unostentatious man. Watson would do. And so I had my purpose and wrote my *Study in Scarlet*.

I knew that the book was as good as I could make it and I had high hopes. When *Girdlestone* used to come circling back* with the precision of a homing pigeon I was grieved but not surprised, for I acquiesced in the decision. But when my little Holmes book began also to do the circular tour I was hurt, for I knew that it deserved a better fate. James Payn applauded, but found it both too short and too long, which was true enough. Arrowsmith received it in May 1886, and returned it unread in July. Two or three others sniffed and turned away. Finally, as Ward, Lock & Co. made a specialty of cheap and often sensational literature, I sent it to them. They said:

> DEAR SIR—*We have read your story and are pleased with it. We could not publish it this year, as the market is flooded at present with cheap fiction, but if you do not object to its being held over till next year, we will give you twenty-five pounds for the copyright.*
>
> *Yours faithfully,*
> WARD, LOCK & CO.
> Oct. 30, 1886.

It was not a very tempting offer, and even I, poor as I was, hesitated to accept it. It was not merely the small sum offered, but it was the long delay, for this book might open a road for me. I was heartsick, however, at repeated disappointments, and I felt that perhaps it was true wisdom to make sure of publicity, however late. Therefore I accepted, and the book became Beeton's Christmas Annual of 1887.

It was in consequence of a publishers' dinner, at which I was a guest, that I wrote *The Sign of the Four*, in which Holmes made his second appearance. But thereafter for a time he was laid on the shelf, for, encouraged by the kind reception which "Micah Clarke" had received from the critics, I now determined upon an even bolder and more ambitious flight.

Hence came my two books. *The White Company*, written in 1889, and *Sir Nigel*, written fourteen years later. Of the two I consider the latter the

---

*Returning by the post office after rejection by a publisher.

better book, but I have no hesitation in saying that the two of them taken together did thoroughly achieve my purpose, that they made an accurate picture of that great age, and that, as a single piece of work, they form the most complete, satisfying, and ambitious thing that I have ever done. All things find their level, but I believe that if I had never touched Holmes, who has tended to obscure my higher work, my position in literature would at the present moment be a more commanding one.* The work needed much research and I have still got my notebooks full of all sorts of lore. I cultivate a simple style and avoid long words so far as possible, and it may be that this surface of ease has sometimes caused the reader to underrate the amount of real research which lies in all my historical novels. It is not a matter which troubles me, however, for I have always felt that justice is done in the end, and that the real merit of any work is never permanently lost.

I remember that as I wrote the last words of *The White Company* I felt a wave of exultation and, with a cry of "That's done it!" I hurled my inky pen across the room, where it left a black smudge upon the duck's-egg wall paper. I knew in my heart that the book would live and that it would illuminate our national traditions. Now that it has passed through fifty editions I suppose I may say with all modesty that my forecast has proved to be correct. This was the last book which I wrote in my days of doctoring at Southsea, and marks an epoch in my life, so I can now hark back to some other phases of my last years at Bush Villa† before I broke away into a new existence.

A number of monthly magazines were coming out at that time, notable among which was the *Strand* then, as now, under the very able editorship of Greenhough Smith. Considering these various journals with their disconnected stories, it had struck me that a single character running through a series, if only it engaged the attention of the reader, would bind that reader to that particular magazine.

Looking round for my central character, I felt that Sherlock Holmes, whom I had already handled in two little books, would easily lend himself to a succession of short stories. These I began in the long hours of waiting in my consulting room. Smith liked them from the first, and encouraged me to go ahead with them.

It was at this time that I definitely saw how foolish I was to waste my literary earnings in keeping up an oculist's room in Wimpole Street, and I determined with a wild rush of joy to cut the painter‡ and to trust forever to my power of writing. So I settled down with a stout heart to do some literary work worthy of the name. The difficulty of the Holmes work was that every story really needed as clear-cut and original a plot as

---

*Just the opposite judgment has been true: Without Holmes, his name would be known only to scholars and his descendants.

†Name of the home in which Arthur Conan Doyle lived.

‡The painter is the rope that attaches the bow of a boat to its mooring.

a longish book would do. One cannot without effort spin plots at such a rate. They are apt to become thin or to break. I was determined, now that I had no longer the excuse of absolute pecuniary pressure, never again to write anything which was not as good as I could possibly make it, and therefore I would not write a Holmes story without a worthy plot and without a problem which interested my own mind, for that is the first requisite before you can interest anyone else. If I have been able to sustain this character for a long time, and if the public find, as they will find, that the last story is as good as the first, it is entirely due to the fact that I never, or hardly ever, forced a story. Some have thought there was a falling off in the stories, and the criticism was neatly expressed by a Cornish boatman who said to me, "I think, sir, when Holmes fell over that cliff, he may not have killed himself, but all the same he was never quite the same man afterwards."

I was weary, however, of inventing plots and I set myself now to do some work which would certainly be less renumerative but would be more ambitious from a literary point of view. I had long been attracted by the epoch of Louis XIV and by those Huguenots who were the French equivalents of our Puritans. I had a good knowledge of the memoirs of that date, and many notes already prepared, so that it did not take me long to write *The Refugees*.

Yet it was still the Sherlock Holmes stories for which the public clamoured, and these from time to time I endeavoured to supply. At last, after I had done two series of them, I saw that I was in danger of having my hand forced, and of being entirely identified with what I regarded as a lower stratum of literary achievement. Therefore, as a sign of my resolution, I determined to end the life of my hero. The idea was in my mind when I went with my wife for a short holiday in Switzerland, in the course of which we walked down the Lauterbrunnen Valley. I saw there the wonderful falls of Reichenbach, a terrible place, and that, I thought, would make a worthy tomb for poor Sherlock, even if I buried my banking account along with him. So there I laid him, fully determined that he should stay there—as indeed for some twenty years he did.

I was amazed at the concern expressed by the public. They say that a man is never properly appreciated until he is dead, and the general protest against my summary execution of Holmes taught me how many and how numerous were his friends. "You brute" was the beginning of the letter of remonstrance which one lady sent me, and I expect she spoke for others beside herself. I heard of many who wept. I fear I was utterly callous myself.

James Barrie is one of my oldest literary friends, and I knew him within a year or two of the time when we both came to London. He and I had one most unfortunate venture together. The facts were that he had promised Mr D'Oyly Carte that he would provide the libretto of a light opera for the Savoy. I was brought into the matter because Barrie's health failed on account of some family bereavement. I had an urgent telegram from him. I found him worried because he had bound himself by contract, and he felt in his present state unable to go forward with it. There were to be two acts, and he had written the first one, and had the rough scenario of the second. Would I come in with him and help him to complete it as part author? I did my best and wrote the lyrics for the second act, and much of the dialogue, but it had to take the predestined shape. The result was not good, and on the first night I felt inclined, like Charles Lamb, to hiss it from my box. The opera, *Jane Annie*, was one of the few failures in Barrie's brilliant career. We were well abused by the critics, but Barrie took it all in the bravest spirit, and I still retain the comic verses of consolation which I received from him next morning.

There followed a parody on Holmes, written on the flyleaves of one one of his books. It ran thus:

The Adventure of the Two Collaborators

In bringing to a close the adventures of my friend Sherlock Holmes I am perforce reminded that he never, save on the occasion which, as you will now hear, brought his singular career to an end, consented to act in any mystery which was concerned with persons who made a livelihood by their pen. "I am not particular about the people I mix among for business purposes," he would say, "but at literary characters I draw the line."

We were in our rooms in Baker Street one evening. I was (I remember) by the centre table writing out "The Adventure of the Man Without a Cork Leg" (which had so puzzled the Royal Society and all the other scientific bodies of Europe), and Holmes was amusing himself with a little revolver practice.

It was his custom of a summer evening to fire round my head, just shaving my face, until he had made a photograph of me on the opposite wall, and it is a slight proof of his skill that many of these portraits in pistol shots are considered admirable likenesses.

I happened to look out of the window, and, perceiving two gentlemen advancing rapidly along Baker Street, asked him who they were. He immediately lit his pipe, and, twisting himself on a chair into a figure 8, replied:

"They are two collaborators in comic opera, and their play has not been a triumph."

I sprang from my chair to the ceiling in amazement, and he then explained:

"My dear Watson, they are obviously men who follow some low calling. That much even you should be able to read in their faces. Those little pieces of blue paper which they fling angrily from them are Durrant's Press Notices. Of these they have obviously hundreds about their person (see how their pockets bulge). They would not dance on them if they were pleasant reading."

I again sprang to the ceiling (which is much dented) and shouted: "Amazing! But they may be mere authors."

"No," said Holmes, "for mere authors only get one press notice a week. Only criminals, dramatists, and actors get them by the hundred."

"Then they may be actors."

"No, actors would come in a carriage."

"Can you tell me anything else about them?"

"A great deal. From the mud on the boots of the tall one I perceive that he comes from South Norwood. The other is obviously a Scotch author."

"How can you tell that?"

"He is carrying in his pocket a book called (I clearly see) 'Auld Licht Something.' Would anyone but the author be likely to carry about a book with such a title?"

I had to confess that this was improbable.

It was now evident that the two men (if such they can be called) were seeking our lodgings. I have said (often) that Holmes seldom gave way to emotion of any kind, but he now turned livid with passion. Presently this gave place to a strange look of triumph.

"Watson," he said, "that big fellow has for years taken the credit for my most remarkable doings, but at last I have him—at last!"

Up I went to the ceiling, and when I returned the strangers were in the room.

"I perceive, gentlemen," said Mr. Sherlock Holmes, "that you are at present afflicted by an extraordinary novelty."

The handsomer of our visitors asked in amazement how he knew this, but the big one only scowled.

"You forget that you wear a ring on your fourth finger," replied Mr. Holmes calmly.

I was about to jump to the ceiling when the big brute interposed.

"That tommyrot is all very well for the public, Holmes," said he, "but you can drop it before me. And, Watson, if you go up to the ceiling again I shall make you stay there."

Here I observed a curious phenomenon. My friend Sherlock Holmes *shrank*. He became small before my eyes. I looked longingly at the ceiling, but dared not.

"Let us cut out the first four pages," said the big man, "and proceed to business. I want to know why—"

"Allow me," said Mr. Holmes, with some of his old courage. "You want to know why the public does not go to your opera."

"Exactly," said the other ironically, "as you perceive by my shirt stud." He added more gravely: "And as you can only find out in one way I must insist on your witnessing an entire performance of the piece."

It was an anxious moment for me. I shuddered, for I knew that if Holmes went I should have to go with him. But my friend had a heart of gold. "Never!" he cried fiercely. "I will do anything for you save that."

"Your continued existence depends on it," said the big man menacingly.

"I would rather melt into air," replied Holmes proudly, taking another chair. "But I can tell you why the public don't go to your piece without sitting the thing out myself."

"Why?"

"Because," replied Holmes calmly, "they prefer to stay away."

A dead silence followed that extraordinary remark. For a moment the two intruders gazed with awe upon the man who had unravelled their mystery so wonderfully. Then, drawing their knives—

Holmes grew less and less, until nothing was left save a ring of smoke which slowly circled to the ceiling.

The last words of great men are often noteworthy. These were the last words of Sherlock Holmes: "Fool, fool! I have kept you in luxury for years. By my help you have ridden extensively in cabs where no author was ever seen before. *Henceforth you will ride in buses!*"

The brute sank into a chair aghast. The other author did not turn a hair.

To A. Conan Doyle,
From his friend, J. M. BARRIE.

Dangerous Ground

This parody, the best of all the numerous parodies, may be taken as an example, not only of the author's wit, but of his debonair courage, for it was written immediately after our joint failure, which at the moment was a bitter thought for both of us. There is, indeed, nothing more miserable than a theatrical failure, for you feel how many others who have backed you have been affected. It was, I am glad to say, my only experience of it, and I have no doubt that Barrie could say the same.

Before I leave the subject of the many impersonations of Holmes, I may say that all of them, and all the drawings, are very unlike my own original idea of the man. I saw him as very tall—"over six feet, but so excessively lean that he seemed considerably taller," said *A Study in Scarlet.* He had, as I imagined him, a thin razorlike face, with a great hawk's-bill of a nose, and two small eyes, set close together on either side of it. Such was my conception. It chanced, however, that poor Arthur Paget, who, before his premature death, drew all the original pictures, had a younger brother whose name, I think, was Harold, who served him as a model. The handsome Harold took the place of the more powerful but uglier Sherlock, and, perhaps from the point of view of my lady readers, it was as well. The stage has followed the type set up by the pictures.

People have often asked me whether I knew the end of a Holmes story before I started it. Of course I did. One could not possibly steer a course if one did not know one's destination. The first thing is to get your idea. We will suppose that this idea is that a woman, as in the last story, is suspected of biting a wound in her child, when she was really sucking that wound for fear of poison injected by some one else. Having got that key idea, one's next task is to conceal it and lay emphasis upon everything which can make for a different explanation. Holmes, however, can see all the fallacies of the alternatives, and arrives more or less dramatically at the true solution by steps which he can describe and justify.

He shows his powers by what the South Americans now call "Sherlocholmitos," which means clever little deductions, which often have nothing to do with the matter in hand, but impress the reader with a general sense of power. The same effect is gained by his offhand allusion to other cases. Heaven knows how many titles I have thrown about in a casual way, and how many readers have begged me to satisfy their curiosity as to "Rigoletto and His Abominable Wife," "The Adventure of the Tired Captain," or "The Curious Experience of the Patterson Family in the Island of Uffa." Once or twice, as in "The Adventure of the Second Stain," which in my judgment is one of the neatest of the stories, I did actually use the title years before I wrote a story to correspond.

There are some questions concerned with particular stories which turn up periodically from every quarter of the globe. In "The Adventure of the Priory School," Holmes remarks in his offhand way that by looking at a bicycle track on a damp moor one can say which way it is heading. I had so many remonstrances upon this point, varying from pity to anger, that I took out my bicycle and tried. I had imagined that the observations of the way in which the track of the hind wheel overlaid the track of the front one when the machine was not running dead straight would show the direction. I found that my correspondents were right and I was wrong, for this would be the same whichever way the cycle was moving. On the other hand, the real solution was much simpler, for on an undulating moor the wheels make a deeper impression uphill and a more shallow one downhill, so Holmes was justified of his wisdom after all.

Sometimes I have got upon dangerous ground, where I have taken risks through my own want of knowledge of the correct atmosphere. I have, for example, never been a racing man, and yet I ventured to write "Silver Blaze," where the mystery depends upon the laws of training and racing. The story is all right, and Holmes may have been at the top of his form, but my ignorance cries aloud to Heaven. I read an excellent and very damaging criticism of the story in some sporting paper, written clearly by a man who *did* know, in which he explained the exact penalties which would have come upon all concerned if they had acted as I described. Half would have been in jail and the other half warned off the turf forever. However, I have never been nervous about details, and one must be masterful sometimes. When an alarmed editor wrote to me once: "There is no second line of rails at this point," I answered: "I make one." On the other hand, there are cases where accuracy is essential.

I do not wish to be ungrateful to Holmes, who has been a good friend to me in many ways. If I have sometimes been inclined to weary of him, it is because his character admits of no light or shade. He is a calculating machine, and anything you add to that simply weakens the effect. Thus the variety of the stories must depend upon the romance and compact handling of the plots. I would say a word for Watson also, who in the course of seven volumes never knows one gleam of humour or makes a single joke. To make a real character one must sacrifice everything to consistency and remember Goldsmith's criticism of Johnson that "he would make the little fishes talk like whales."

The Critic and the Snake

The impression that Holmes was a real person of flesh and blood may have been intensified by his frequent appearance upon the stage. After the withdrawal of my dramatization of "Rodney Stone" from a theatre upon which I held a six months' lease I determined to play a bold and energetic game and certainly I never played a bolder. When I saw the course that things were taking I shut myself up and devoted my whole mind to making a sensational Sherlock Holmes drama. I wrote it in a week and called it "The Speckled Band," after the short story of that name. I do not think that I exaggerate if I say that within a fortnight of the one play shutting down I had a company working upon the rehearsals of the other. It was a considerable success.

We had a fine boa to play the title rôle, a snake which was the pride of my heart, so one can imagine my disgust when I saw that the critic of the *Daily Telegraph* ended his disparaging review by the words: "The crisis of the play was produced by the appearance of a palpably artificial serpent." I was inclined to offer him a goodly sum if he would undertake to go to bed with it. We had several snakes at different times, but they were all inclined either to hang down from the hole in the wall like inanimate bell pulls, or else to turn back through the hole and get even with the stage carpenter, who pinched their tails in order to make them more lively. Finally we used artificial snakes, and everyone, including the stage carpenter, agreed that it was more satisfactory.

I have had many letters addressed to Holmes with requests that I forward them. Watson has also had a number of letters in which he has been asked for the address or for the autograph of his more brilliant confrère. A press-cutting agency wrote to Watson asking whether Holmes would not wish to subscribe. When Holmes retired, several elderly ladies were ready to keep house for him, and one sought to ingratiate herself by assuring me that she knew all about bee-keeping and could "segregate the queen." I had considerable offers also for Holmes if he would examine and solve various family mysteries.

I have often been asked whether I had myself the qualities which I depicted, or whether I was merely the Watson that I look. Of course I am well aware that it is one thing to grapple with a practical problem and quite another thing when you are allowed to solve it under your own conditions. At the same time a man cannot spin a character out of his own inner consciousness and make it really lifelike unless he has some possibilities of that character within him—which is a dangerous admission for one who has drawn so many villains as I.

I do not think that I ever realized what a living actual personality Holmes had become to the more guileless readers until I heard of the very pleasing story of the char-à-bancs* of French schoolboys who, when asked what they wanted to see first in London, replied unanimously that they wanted to see Mr Holmes's lodgings in Baker Street. Many have asked me which house it is, but that is a point which, for excellent reasons, I will not decide.

---

*Bus with rows of seating for sightseers.

SOME PERSONALIA ABOUT
SHERLOCK HOLMES

A t the request of the Editor I have spent some days in looking over an old letter-box in which from time to time I have placed letters referring directly or indirectly to the notorious Mr. Holmes. I wish now that I had been more careful in preserving the references to this gentleman and his little problems. A great many have been lost or mislaid. His biographer has been fortunate enough to find readers in many lands, and the reading has elicited the same sort of response, though in many cases that response has been in a tongue difficult to comprehend. Very often my distant correspondent could neither spell my own name nor that of my imaginary hero! Many such letters have been from Russians. Where the Russian letters have been in the vernacular I have been compelled, I am afraid, to take them as read, but when they have been in English they have been among the most curious in my collection. There was one young lady who began all her epistles with the words "Good Lord." Another had a large amount of guile underlying her simplicity. Writing from Warsaw she stated that she had been bedridden for two years, and that my novels had been her only, etc., etc. So touched was I by this flattering statement that I at once prepared an autographed parcel of them to complete the fair invalid's collection. By good luck, however, I met a brother author upon the same day to whom I recounted the touching incident. With a cynical smile he drew an identical letter out of his pocket. His novels also had been for two years her only, etc., etc. I do not know how many more the lady had written to, but if, as I imagine, her correspondence had extended to several countries, she must have amassed a rather interesting library.

The young Russian's habit of addressing me as "Good Lord" had an even stranger parallel at home, which links it up with the subject of this article. Shortly after I received a knighthood I had a bill from a tradesman which was quite correct and businesslike in every detail save that it was made out to Sir Sherlock Holmes. I hope that I can stand a joke as well as my neighbours, but this particular piece of humour seemed rather misapplied, and I wrote sharply upon the subject. In response to my letter there arrived at my hotel a very repentant clerk, who expressed his sorrow at the incident, but kept on repeating the phrase, "I assure you, sir, that it was *bonâ fide*." "What do you mean by *bonâ fide*?" I asked. "Well, sir, my mates in the shop told me that you had been knighted, and that when a man was knighted he changed his name, and that you had taken that one." I need not say that my annoyance vanished, and that I laughed as heartily as his pals were probably doing round the corner.

There are certain problems which are continually recurring in these Sherlock Holmes letters. One of them has exercised men's minds in the most out-of-the-way places, from Labrador to Tibet; indeed, if a matter needs thought it is just the men in these outlying stations who have the time and solitude for it. I dare say I have had twenty letters upon the one point alone. It arises in "The Adventure of the Priory School," where Holmes, glancing at the track of a bicycle, says, "It is evidently going from us, not towards us." He did not give his reasoning, which my correspondents resent, and all assert that the deduction is impossible. As a matter of fact it is simple enough upon soft undulating ground such as the moor in question. The weight of the rider falls most upon the hind wheel, and in soft soil it makes a perceptibly deeper track. Where the machine goes up a slope this hind mark would be very much deeper; where it goes down a slope rapidly it would be hardly deeper at all. Thus the depth of the mark of the hind wheel would show which way the bike was travelling.

One of the quaintest proofs of Holmes's reality to many people is that I have frequently received autograph books by post, asking me to procure his signature. When it was announced that he was retiring from practice and intended to keep bees on the South Downs I had several letters offering to help him in his project. Two of them lie before me as I write. One says: "Will Mr. Sherlock Holmes require a housekeeper for his country cottage at Christmas? I know someone who loves a quiet country life, and bees especially—an old-fashioned, quiet woman." The other, which is addressed to Holmes himself, says: "I see by some of the morning papers that you are about to retire and take up bee-keeping. If correct I shall be pleased to render you service by giving any advice you may require. I trust you will read this letter in the same spirit in which it is written, for I make this offer in return for many pleasant hours." Many other letters have reached me in which I have been implored to put my correspondents in touch with Mr Holmes, in order that he might elucidate some point in their private affairs.

Occasionally I have been so far confused with my own character that I have been asked to take up professional work upon these lines. I had, I remember, one offer, in the case of an aristocratic murder trial in Poland some years ago, to go across and look into the matter upon my own terms. I need not say that I would not do such a thing for money, since I am diffident as to how far my own services would be of any value; but I have several times as an amateur been happy to have been of some assistance to people in distress. I can say, though I touch wood as I say it, that I have never entirely failed in any attempt which I have made to reduce Holmes's methods to practical use, save in one instance to which I allude later. For the case of Mr. Edalji I can claim little credit, for it did not take any elaborate deduction to come to the conclusion that a man who is practically blind did not make a journey at night which involved crossing a main line of railway, and would have tested a trained athlete had he been called upon to do it in the time. The man was obviously innocent, and it is a disgrace to this country that he has never received a penny of compensation for the three years which he spent in jail. A more complex case is that of Oscar Slater, who is still working out his sentence as a convict. I have examined the evidence carefully, including the supplementary evidence given at the very limited and unsatisfactory commission appointed to inquire into the matter, and I have not the faintest doubt that the man is innocent. When the judge asked him at the trial whether he had anything to say why the sentence of death for the murder of Miss Gilchrist should not be pronounced upon him, he cried aloud, "My Lord, I did not know there was such a woman in the world." I am convinced that this was the literal truth. However, it is proverbially impossible to prove a negative, so there the matter must stand until the people of Scotland insist upon a real investigation into all the circumstances which surround this deplorable case.

A few of the problems which have come my way have been very similar to some which I had invented for the exhibition of the reasoning of Mr. Holmes. I might perhaps quote one in which that gentleman's method of thought was copied with complete success. The case was as follows. A gentleman had disappeared. He had drawn a bank balance of forty pounds, which was known to be on him. It was feared that he had been murdered for the sake of the money. He had last been heard of stopping at a large hotel in London, having come from the country that day. In the evening he went to a music-hall performance, came out of it about ten o'clock, returned to his hotel, changed his evening clothes, which were found in his room next day, and disappeared utterly. No one saw him leave the hotel, but a man occupying a neighbouring room declared that he had heard him moving during the night. A week had elapsed at the time that I was consulted, but the police had discovered nothing. Where was the man?

These were the whole of the facts as communicated to me by his relatives in the country. Endeavouring to see the matter through the eyes of Mr. Holmes, I answered by return of post that he was evidently either in Glasgow or in Edinburgh. I proved later that he had as a fact gone to Edinburgh, though in the week that had passed he had moved to another part of Scotland.

There I should leave the matter, for, as Dr. Watson has often shown, a solution explained is a mystery spoiled. However, at this stage the reader can lay down the magazine and show how simple it all is by working out the problem for himself. He has all the data which were ever given to me. For the sake of those, however, who have no turn for such conundrums I will try to indicate the links which make the chain. The one advantage which I possessed was that I was familiar with the routine of London hotels—though, I fancy, it differs little from that of hotels elsewhere.

The first thing was to look at the facts and separate what was certain from what was conjecture. It was *all* certain except the statement of the person who heard the missing man in the night. How could he tell such a sound from any other sound in a large hotel? That point could be disregarded if it traversed* the general conclusions. The first clear deduction

*Contradicted (from the Latin root meaning "to cross").

was that the man had meant to disappear. Why else should he draw all his money? He had got out of the hotel during the night. But there is a night-porter in all hotels, and it is impossible to get out without his knowledge when the door is once shut. The door is shut after the theatre-goers re-turn—say at twelve o'clock. Therefore the man left the hotel before twelve o'clock. He had come from the music-hall at ten, had changed his clothes, and had departed with his bag. No one had seen him do so. The inference is that he had done it at the moment when the hall was full of the returning guests, which is from eleven to eleven-thirty. After that hour, even if the door were still open, there are few people coming and going; so that he with his bag would certainly have been seen.

Having got so far upon firm ground we now ask ourselves why a man who desires to hide himself should go out at such an hour. If he intended to conceal himself in London he need never have gone to the hotel at all. Clearly, then, he was going to catch a train which would carry him away. But a man who is deposited by a train in any provincial station during the night is likely to be noticed, and he might be sure that when the alarm was raised and his description given some guard or porter would remember him. Therefore his destination would be some large town, which he would reach in daylight hours, as a terminus, where all his fellow-passengers would disembark and where he would lose himself in the crowd. When one turns up the time-table and sees that the great Scotch expresses bound for Edinburgh and Glasgow start about midnight, the goal is reached. As for his dress-suit, the fact that he abandoned it proved that he intended to adopt a line of life where there were no social amenities. This deduction also proved to be correct.

I quote such a case in order to show that the general lines of reasoning advocated by Holmes have a real practical application to life. In another case where a girl had become engaged to a young foreigner who suddenly disappeared I was able by a similar process of deduction to show her very clearly both whither he had gone and how unworthy he was of her affec-tions. On the other hand, these semi-scientific methods are occasionally laboured and slow as compared with the results of the rough-and-ready practical man. Lest I should seem to have been throwing bouquets either to myself or to Mr. Holmes, let me state that on the occasion of a burglary of the village inn, within a stone-throw of my house, the village constable, with no theories at all, had seized the culprit, while I had got no farther than that he was a left-handed man with nails in his boots.

The unusual or dramatic effects which lead to the invocation of Mr. Holmes in fiction are, of course, great aids to him in reaching a conclu-sion. It is the case where there is nothing to get hold of which is the deadly one. I heard of such a one in America which would certainly have pre-sented a formidable problem. A gentleman of blameless life, starting off for a Sunday evening walk with his family, suddenly observed that he had forgotten his stick. He went back into the house, the door of which was still open, and he left his people waiting for him outside. He never reap-peared, and from that day to this there has been no clue as to what befell him. This was certainly one of the strangest cases of which I have ever heard in real life.

Another very singular case came within my own observation. It was sent to me by an eminent London publisher. This gentleman had in his employment a head of department whose name we shall take as Musgrave. He was a hard-working person with no special feature in his character. Mr. Musgrave died, and several years after his death a letter was received addressed to him, care of his employers. It bore the postmark of a tourist resort in the West of Canada, and had the note "Conf films" upon the outside of the envelope, with the words "Report Sy" in one corner. The publishers naturally opened the envelope, as they had no note of the dead man's relatives. Inside were two blank sheets of paper. The letter, I may add, was registered. The publisher, being unable to make anything of this, sent it on to me, and I submitted the blank sheets to every possible chemical and heat test, with no result whatever. Beyond the fact that the writing appeared to be that of a woman, there is nothing to add to this account. The matter was, and remains, an insoluble mystery. How the correspondent could have something so secret to say to Mr. Musgrave and yet not be aware that this person had been dead for several years is very hard to understand—or why blank sheets should be so carefully registered through the post. I may add that I did not trust the sheets to my own chemical tests, but had the best expert advice, without getting any result. Considered as a case it was a failure—and a very tantalizing one.

Mr. Sherlock Holmes has always been a fair mark for practical jokers, and I have had numerous bogus cases of various degrees of ingenuity, marked cards, mysterious warnings, cipher messages, and other curious communications. Upon one occasion, as I was entering the hall to take part in an amateur billiard competition, I was handed a small packet which had been left for me. Upon opening it I found a piece of ordinary green chalk such as it used in billiards. I was amused by the incident, and I put the chalk into my waistcoat pocket and used it during the game. Afterwards I continued to use it until one day, some months later, as I rubbed the tip of my cue, the face of the chalk crumpled in, and I found it was hollow. From the recess thus exposed I drew out a small slip of paper with the words, "From Arsène Lupin* to Sherlock Holmes." Imagine the state of mind of the joker who took such trouble to accomplish such a result!

One of the mysteries submitted to Mr. Holmes was rather upon the psychic plane, and therefore beyond his powers. The facts as alleged are most remarkable, though I have no proof of their truth save that the lady wrote earnestly and gave both her name and address. The person, whom we will call Mrs. Seagrave, had been given a curious secondhand ring, snake-shaped, and of dull gold. This she took from her finger at night.

---

*A character, known as the "gentleman burglar," in novels by Maurice Leblanc (1864–1941).

One night she slept in it, and had a fearsome dream in which she seemed to be pushing off some furious creature which fastened its teeth into her arm. On awakening the pain in the arm continued, and next day the imprint of a double set of teeth appeared upon the arm, with one tooth of the lower jaw missing. The marks were in the shape of blue-black bruises which had not broken the skin. "I do not know," says my correspondent, "what made me think the ring had anything to do with the matter, but I took a dislike to the thing and did not wear it for some months, when, being on a visit, I took to wearing it again." To make a long story short, the same thing happened, and the lady settled the matter for ever by dropping her ring into the hottest corner of the kitchen-range. This curious story, which I believe to be genuine, may not be as supernatural as it seems. It is well known that in some subjects a strong mental impression does produce a physical effect. Thus a very vivid nightmare-dream with the impression of a bite might conceivably produce the mark of a bite. Such cases are well attested in medical annals. The second incident would, of course, arise by unconscious suggestion from the first. None the less, it is a very interesting little problem, whether psychic or material.

Buried treasures are naturally among the problems which have come to Mr Holmes. One genuine case was accompanied by the diagram here reproduced. It refers to an Indiaman who was wrecked upon the South African coast in the year 1782. If I were a younger man I should be seriously inclined to go personally and look into that matter. The ship contained a remarkable treasure, including, I believe, the gold crown regalia of Delhi. It is surmised that they buried these near the coast and that this chart is a note of the spot. Each Indiaman in those days had its own semaphore code, and it is conjectured that the three marks upon the left are signals from a three-armed semaphore. Some record of their meaning might perhaps even now be found in the old papers of the India Office. The circle upon the right gives the compass bearings. The larger semicircle may be the curved edge of a reef or of a rock. The figures above are the indications how to reach the X which marks the treasure. Possibly they may give the bearings as 186 feet from the 4 upon the semicircle. The scene of the wreck is a lonely part of the country, but I shall be surprised if sooner or later someone does not seriously set to work to solve the mystery.

One last word before I close these jottings about my imaginary character. It is not given to every man to see the child of his brain endowed with life through the genius of a great sympathetic artist, but that was my good fortune when Mr. Gillette* turned his mind and his great talents to putting Holmes upon the stage. I cannot end my remarks more fittingly than by my thanks to the man who changed a creature of thin air into an absolutely convincing human being.

---

*William Gillette (1855–1937), American actor who portrayed Holmes on stage and on film.

ENDNOTES

1. (p. 201) *Waterloo . . . Marengo:* Holmes uses battles from the career of Napoleon Bonaparte as metaphors suggesting his progress on the case. The Battle of Waterloo in 1815 marked the end of Napoleon. In the Battle of Marengo, fought in 1800, the French forces were first beaten, then rallied and eventually won.

2. (p. 233) *Porlock's:* One cannot help but think of the visitor from Porlock whose knock at the door awoke Samuel Taylor Coleridge during his intense opium dream about Kubla Khan.

3. (p. 234) *apocrypha of the agony column:* "Agony columns" were personal advertisements in the newspapers. Amid these anguished outpourings one could occasionally find coded messages. Holmes uses this ploy himself on several occasions.

4. (p. 236) *Machiavellian:* Niccolò Machiavelli (1469–1527) wrote *The Prince* (1513) to advise rulers of Italian city-states how to hold power. The first exponent of realpolitik, he was considered immoral if not wicked by the English. As no one is less like Machiavelli than Watson, Holmes comment is ironic, of course, as was his earlier referral to Watson's "innate cunning."

5. (p. 237) *He had spoken in jesting vein:* Holmes is indeed jesting because in the previous line he had irreverently quoted the Bible, *Isaiah* 6:5: "Then said I, Woe is me! for I am undone," and John 19:30: "When Jesus therefore had received the vinegar, he said, It is finished: and he bowed his head and gave up the ghost" (King James Version).

6. (p. 246) *the time of the first crusade . . . Red King:* The First Crusade lasted from 1095 to 1099. The identity of Hugo de Capus is not known. A fortalice is a small fort. The Red King refers to William Rufus, or William II (c.1056–1100), son of William the Conqueror.

7. (p. 272) *"Shocking, Watson, shocking!":* Holmes's clearly ironic retort reminds one of Claude Rains in *Casablanca*, who is "shocked, shocked" to find gambling going on in the gin joint where he seconds later receives his nightly take. It may even have been the inspiration for that scene.

8. (p. 280) *the concealment of Charles . . . a visit there by the second George:* During the English Civil War (1642–1651) between the Parliamentarians and the Royalists, King Charles I went into hiding in a futile attempt to escape being beheaded, which finally happened in 1649. The second George was King George II, who ruled from 1727 to 1760. Birlstone Manor has had a rich and eventful history.

9. (p. 333) *the repulsion and fear which the huge Danton may have felt for* *the puny but dangerous Robespierre:* Georges-Jacques Danton (1759–1794) was a leading voice in the French Revolution. His personal magnetism, a combination of his imposing physical presence and his grandiloquence as an orator, helped him become president of the Committee of Public Safety and the effective head of government in 1793, but his opposition to the Reign of Terror, largely run by Maximilien François Robespierre (1758–1794), cost him his head in 1794. Robespierre—slight of build and frail in health, but possessed of a steel will—lost his own head a few months after Danton.

10. (p. 340) *Pinkerton's:* The Pinkerton National Detective Agency, founded in 1850 by Allan Pinkerton (1819–1884), had many notable triumphs. One was foiling an assassination attempt against Abraham Lincoln in 1861. Another was the breakup of the Molly Maguires, the model for the Scowrers.

11. (p. 376) *the die was cast:* This is the English for a centuries-old Latin mistranslation (*Jacta alea est*) of the Greek phrase Julius Caesar uttered upon crossing the Rubicon with his army. Because by Roman law the Legions had to remain on the other side of that boundary, this crossing began a civil war. The Latin phrase indicates that a fateful step has been taken from which there is no turning back. Caesar actually quoted a half-line from the Greek playwright Menander. That line translates as, "The dice fly high," meaning "It's up to chance now—anything can happen."

12. (p. 382) *General Gordon:* It's difficult to follow Holmes's reasoning without knowing how the British public felt about General Charles ("Chinese") Gordon (1833–1885), so called because he helped put down the Taiping rebellion in 1863 and 1864. Years later, when a charismatic Sudanese leader claiming to be the Mahdi (the Muslim Messiah) raised a rebellion against British and Egyptian rule, Gordon was sent to suppress the uprising. He was besieged at Khartoum, called for reinforcements that never came, and was slaughtered when the city fell. Public outrage over lack of support for him forced the fall of the government. As an old soldier, Watson would naturally feel indignation at Gordon's betrayal.

13. (p. 382) *Henry Ward Beecher:* Beecher (1813–1887) was a Congregationalist minister and orator who became influential in the United States before the Civil War. His trip to England in 1863 to persuade the English of the moral right of the Union cause was initially met with hostility, but he won over many audiences with his eloquence. Watson, as a fair-minded man, a believer in progress, would have been sympathetic to Beecher's antislavery message.

14. (p. 389) *purchased his own Stradivarius . . . for fifty-five shillings:* Antonio Stradivari (c.1644–1737), a pupil of violin maker Nicolò Amati, made violins, violas, and cellos in Cremona, Italy. The two were preeminent in making Cremona synonymous with great stringed instruments. A Stradivarius violin at the time cost about 200 times more than Holmes paid for it at the expense of the unknowing pawnbroker.

15. (p. 416) *the most jealously guarded of all government secrets:* Dry humor obviously runs in the family. The most jealously guarded of all government secrets is something Mycroft assumes everyone has heard of. Exactly what sort of irony this implies is open to debate.

16. (p. 430) *Polyphonic Motets of Lassus:* Orlando Lassus (1532–1594; there are lots of versions of both his names, but this one is the most common) composed more than 500 motets, musical compositions for two to twelve voices based on sacred texts and sung without accompaniment. Holmes's achievement is the more impressive when one learns that these motets can't be meaningfully recreated by other instruments. To study them Holmes had to "hear" them, to paraphrase Hamlet, with his mind's ear.

17. (p. 483) *Duke of York's steps:* The first-born son of the English monarch inherits the title prince of Wales; the second-born son is the duke of York. The steps mentioned are a series carved in granite on the Island of Herm commemorating Frederick, the second son of George III.

18. (p. 533) *Negretto Sylvius:* An Italian word for "black" and the Latin for "woods" together make the name literally "Blackwoods," which was the name of a magazine that was a competitor of the *Strand*. *Blackwood's* once rejected one of Conan Doyle's early works. This, plus the too-cute-by-half address of "Moorside" for a black man, suggests to me that an editor at the *Strand* had a large hand in this story. Conan Doyle didn't need any revenge after forty years of prosperity. It is more likely a relative newcomer to the magazine, feeling a rivalry with *Blackwood's*, thought this in-joke would be oh so funny.

19. (p. 539) *the long-drawn, wailing notes of that most haunting of tunes:* No one who knows this piece could possibly characterize it this way; although it's a fine piece, it's neither wailing nor haunting, and if a musical piece had legal rights, it would sue for defamation for being labeled a "tune." It's another reason to suspect the authenticity of the story. Conan Doyle mentions many composers throughout the stories, but this is the only specific piece cited, and therefore the only one characterized.

20. (p. 553) *belle dame sans merci:* This French phrase means "beautiful woman without pity"; originally the title of a poem by French poet Alain Chartier (c.1385–1433), it is better known from a poem of the same name by John Keats (1795–1821).

21. (p. 567) *a queen in English history:* Eleanor of Castile (c.1245–1290), wife of King Edward I (1239–1307), was reputed to have sucked poison from her husband's arm; the story is most likely apocryphal.

22. (p. 617) *surds and conic sections:* Surds are sums of numbers at least one of which contains an irrational root of another number—for example, the sum of the square root of two and the square root of three. A conic section is the two-dimensional area obtained when a plane intersects a cone.

23. (p. 639) *in the days of the Regency:* The Regency was the period between 1811 and 1820, when the prince of Wales, later George IV, was appointed regent to rule England because of the insanity of his father, George III.

COMMENTS & QUESTIONS

In this section, we aim to provide the reader with an array of perspectives on the text, as well as questions that challenge those perspectives. The commentary has been culled from sources as diverse as reviews contemporaneous with the work, letters written by the author, literary criticism of later generations, and appreciations written throughout history. Following the commentary, a series of questions seeks to filter Sir Arthur Conan Doyle's Sherlock Holmes *stories through a variety of points of view and bring about a richer understanding of these enduring works.*

Comments

RONALD A. KNOX
Any studies in Sherlock Holmes must be, first and foremost, studies in Dr. Watson. . . .

If the sophists have been borrowed from the Platonic dialogue, one element at least has been borrowed from Greek drama. Gaboriau has no Watson. The confident Lacoq is an old soldier, preternaturally stupid, inconceivable inefficient. Watson provides what the Holmes drama needs— a Chorus. He represents the solid, orthodox, respectable view of the world in general; his drabness is accentuated by contrast with the limelight which beats upon the central figure. He remains stable amid the eddy and flux of circumstance.

—from *Blue Book* (1912)

A. A. MILNE
There used to be a song which affirmed (how truly, I do not know) that every nice girl loved a sailor. I am prepared to state, though I do not propose to make a song about it, that every nice man loves a detective story.

This week I have been reading the last adventures of Sherlock Holmes—I mean really the last adventures, ending with his triumph over the German spy in 1914. Having saved the Empire, Holmes returned to his farm on the Sussex downs, and there, for all I mind, he may stay. I have no great affection for the twentieth-century Holmes. But I will give the warmest welcome to as many adventures of the Baker Street Holmes as Watson likes to reconstruct for us. There is no reason why the supply of these should ever give out. . . .

The best of writing a detective story [must be] that you can always make the lucky shots come off. In no other form of fiction, I imagine, does the author feel so certainly that he is the captain of the ship. If he wants it so, he has it so. Is the solution going to be too easy? Then he puts in an unexpected footprint in the geranium bed, or a strange face at the window, and makes it more difficult. Is the reader being kept too much in the dark? Then a conversation overheard in the library will make it easier for him. The author's only trouble is that he can never be certain whether his plot is too obscure or too obvious. He knows himself that the governess is guilty, and, in consequence, she can hardly raise her eyebrows without seeming to him to give the whole thing away.

—from *If I May* (1920)

T. S. ELIOT
Sherlock Holmes reminds us always of the pleasant externals of nineteenth-century London.

—from *Criterion* (April 1929)

RAYMOND CHANDLER
The detective story for a variety of reasons can seldom be promoted. It is usually about murder and hence lacks the element of uplift. Murder, which is a frustration of the individual and hence a frustration of the race, may, and in fact has, a good deal of sociological implication. But it has been going on too long for it to be news. If the mystery novel is at all realistic (which it very seldom is) it is written in a certain spirit of detachment; otherwise nobody but a psychopath would want to write it or read it.

—from *The Art of the Mystery Story*, edited by Howard Haycraft (1946)

Questions

1. Do you agree with Kyle Freeman's argument in the Introduction that the Holmes stories in which Watson is not the narrator suffer for his absence?

2. Is there a sign in Holmes or Watson of what we would now call an "unconscious" at work?

3. Holmes's fits of melancholy or boredom, his resort to opium and strong tobacco, his lack of a need for female companionship, his skill as a boxer and fencer—are these just so many disparate traits, or do they add up to parts of a coherent personality? Is the absence of love or sex or romance in Holmes's life the flip side of his skill as a detective, as, for example, exceptional skill with computers is alleged to go along with a nerdy personality?

4. "From a drop of water a logician could infer the possibility of an Atlantic or a Niagra without having seen or heard of one or the other. So all

life is a great chain, the nature of which is known whenever we are shown a single link of it." So wrote Sherlock Holmes himself (in *A Study in Scarlet*). Do the stories bear this out? Is either the life observed or Holmes's method of solving crimes consistent with the idea that they are part of a great logical chain?

5. What does the reader get from detective fiction that he doesn't get from the other popular genres?

FOR FURTHER READING

Other Works by Arthur Conan Doyle

Fiction

The Exploits of Brigadier Gerard. London: George Newnes, 1896. Among the most popular books Doyle ever wrote, this is an account of an officer in Napoleon's army who could be a precursor to Inspector Clouseau, the bumbling Peter Sellers character.

The Land of Mist. London: Hutchinson, 1926. Those interested in Doyle's thoughts about spiritualism will want to read this novel.

The Lost World. London: Hodder and Stoughton, 1912. Still in print and the subject of more than one film, this novel featuring dinosaurs of all stripes is likely to remain Doyle's most popular work after the Holmes stories.

Micah Clarke. London: Longmans, Green, 1889. This non-Holmesian work was Doyle's first historical novel, and one for which Oscar Wilde expressed enthusiasm.

The Stark Munro Letters. London: Longmans, Green, 1895. This autobiographical novel is worth reading if only for the bizarre but fascinating account it gives of Doyle's friend and betrayer, George Budd, fictionalized as Cullingworth.

Nonfiction

The History of Spiritualism. London: Cassell, 1926. Reflecting Doyle's most passionate concern, this book is more revealing than his autobiography.

Memories and Adventures. London: Hodder and Stoughton, 1924; second edition, London: John Murray, 1930. This autobiography gives a surface account of the many colorful adventures Doyle lived but does not invite the reader into the workshop of his soul.

Through the Magic Door. London: Smith, Elder, 1907. This justification of the Western classics describes the books in Doyle's personal library and what they have meant to him; it contains some very fine writing.

Biography

Lellenberg, Jon L., ed. *The Quest for Sir Arthur Conan Doyle: Thirteen Biographers in Search of a Life.* Carbondale: Southern Illinois University Press, 1987. A good biography with an introduction by Doyle's daughter, Dame Jean Conan Doyle.

Nordon, Pierre. *Conan Doyle: A Biography.* Translated from the French by Frances Partridge. New York: Holt, Rinehart and Winston, 1966. A biography written at a time when access to private, unpublished material was not legally restricted.

Pearson, Hesketh. *Conan Doyle: His Life and Art.* New York: Taplinger, 1977. Brief, but highly entertaining.

Stashower, Daniel. *Teller of Tales: The Life of Arthur Conan Doyle.* New York: Henry Holt, 1999. A big, handsome volume that takes advantage of all the previously collected material.

Criticism

Baring-Gould, William S., ed. *The Annotated Sherlock Holmes: The Four Novels and the Fifty-six Short Stories Complete.* With an introduction, notes, and bibliography by Baring-Gould. New York: Clarkson N. Potter, 1968. If exact and minute detail is what you're after, you will find it to your heart's content in this massive two-volume edition. Baring-Gould and a host of subeditors combed every piece of published material about the stories and did some research of their own in compiling details about when and where every story was published, identifications of all the real people and places in the canon, speculations about the models for some of the fictional ones, historical information, opinions from doctors about Watson's medical pronouncements, comparisons of things like weather, phases of the moon, and train schedules in the stories to the historical ones—no, there was no 9:13 train that night, but there was one at 9:15—and attempts to establish the internal dates of all the stories.

Dakin, D. Martin. *A Sherlock Holmes Commentary.* Newton Abbot, UK: David and Charles, 1972. Packed full of rewarding material.

Green, Richard Lancelyn, ed. *The Uncollected Sherlock Holmes.* Harmondsworth, UK: Penguin, 1983. Contains all of Doyle's writings about Sherlock Holmes, as well as comments of others such as J. M. Barrie.

———. *The Sherlock Holmes Letters.* Iowa City: University of Iowa Press, 1986. Republishes a collection of letters from readers about the stories.

Hardwick, Michael. *The Complete Guide to Sherlock Holmes.* New York: St. Martin's Press, 1986. Solves many mysteries and satisfies many curiosities.

Shreffler, P. A. *The Baker Street Reader: Cornerstone Writings about Sherlock Holmes.* Westport, CT: Greenwood Press, 1984. A collection of essays.

Other Works Cited in the General Introduction

Doyle, Arthur Conan. *Arthur Conan Doyle: Letters to the Press.* Edited by John Michael Gibson and Richard Lancelyn Green. Iowa City: University of Iowa Press, 1986.

Hoving, Thomas. *Tutankhamun: The Untold Story.* New York: Simon and Schuster, 1978.

Other Works Cited in the Introduction to Volume II

Conan Doyle, Arthur. *Sherlock Holmes: The Complete Long Stories*. London: John Murray, 1929.

De Waal, Ronald Burt. *The World Bibliography of Sherlock Holmes and Dr. Watson: A Classified and Annotated List of Materials Relating to Their Lives and Adventures*. Boston: New York Graphic Society, 1974.

Hollyer, Cameron. "Author to Editor: Arthur Conan Doyle's Correspondence with H. Greenhough Smith." A.C.D.: The Journal of the Arthur Conan Doyle Society 3 (1992), pp. 11–34.

Howlett, Michael Anthony. "The Impersonators: Sherlock Holmes on Stage and Screen." In *Beyond Baker Street: A Sherlockian Anthology*, edited and annotated by Michael Harrison. New York: Bobbs-Merrill, 1976.

Adventures of Huckleberry Finn	Mark Twain	1-59308-112-X	$6.95
The Adventures of Tom Sawyer	Mark Twain	1-59308-139-1	$6.95
The Aeneid	Vergil	1-59308-237-1	$7.95
Aesop's Fables		1-59308-062-X	$5.95
The Age of Innocence	Edith Wharton	1-59308-143-X	$5.95
Alice's Adventures in Wonderland and Through the Looking-Glass	Lewis Carroll	1-59308-015-8	$5.95
Anna Karenina	Leo Tolstoy	1-59308-027-1	$8.95
The Arabian Nights	Anonymous	1-59308-281-9	$9.95
The Art of War	Sun Tzu	1-59308-017-4	$7.95
The Autobiography of an Ex-Colored Man and Other Writings	James Weldon Johnson	1-59308-289-4	$5.95
The Awakening and Selected Short Fiction	Kate Chopin	1-59308-113-8	$6.95
Billy Budd and The Piazza Tales	Herman Melville	1-59308-253-3	$5.95
The Brothers Karamazov	Fyodor Dostoevsky	1-59308-045-X	$9.95
The Call of the Wild and White Fang	Jack London	1-59308-200-2	$5.95
Candide	Voltaire	1-59308-028-X	$4.95
The Canterbury Tales	Geoffrey Chaucer	1-59308-080-8	$9.95
A Christmas Carol, The Chimes and The Cricket on the Hearth	Charles Dickens	1-59308-033-6	$5.95
The Collected Oscar Wilde		1-59308-310-6	$9.95
The Collected Poems of Emily Dickinson		1-59308-050-6	$5.95
The Complete Sherlock Holmes, Vol. I	Sir Arthur Conan Doyle	1-59308-034-4	$7.95
The Complete Sherlock Holmes, Vol. II	Sir Arthur Conan Doyle	1-59308-040-9	$7.95
Confessions	Saint Augustine	1-59308-259-2	$6.95
The Count of Monte Cristo	Alexandre Dumas	1-59308-151-0	$7.95
Don Quixote	Miguel de Cervantes	1-59308-046-8	$9.95
Dracula	Bram Stoker	1-59308-114-6	$6.95
Emma	Jane Austen	1-59308-152-9	$6.95
Essays and Poems by Ralph Waldo Emerson		1-59308-076-X	$6.95
The Essential Tales and Poems of Edgar Allan Poe		1-59308-064-6	$7.95
Ethan Frome and Selected Stories	Edith Wharton	1-59308-090-5	$5.95
Fairy Tales	Hans Christian Andersen	1-59308-260-6	$9.95
Founding America: Documents from the Revolution to the Bill of Rights	Jefferson, et al.	1-59308-230-4	$9.95
Frankenstein	Mary Shelley	1-59308-115-4	$4.95
Great American Short Stories: From Hawthorne to Hemingway	Various	1-59308-086-7	$7.95
The Great Escapes: Four Slave Narratives	Various	1-59308-294-0	$6.95
Great Expectations	Charles Dickens	1-59308-116-2	$6.95
Grimm's Fairy Tales	Jacob and Wilhelm Grimm	1-59308-056-5	$7.95
Gulliver's Travels	Jonathan Swift	1-59308-132-4	$5.95
Heart of Darkness and Selected Short Fiction	Joseph Conrad	1-59308-123-5	$5.95
The Idiot	Fyodor Dostoevsky	1-59308-058-1	$7.95
The Importance of Being Earnest and Four Other Plays	Oscar Wilde	1-59308-059-X	$6.95
The Inferno	Dante Alighieri	1-59308-051-4	$6.95
Jane Eyre	Charlotte Brontë	1-59308-117-0	$7.95

(continued)

Jude the Obscure	Thomas Hardy	1-59308-035-2	$6.95
The Jungle	Upton Sinclair	1-59308-118-9	$6.95
The Last of the Mohicans	James Fenimore Cooper	1-59308-137-5	$5.95
Les Liaisons Dangereuses	Pierre Choderlos de Laclos	1-59308-240-1	$7.95
Little Women	Louisa May Alcott	1-59308-108-1	$6.95
Lost Illusions	Honoré de Balzac	1-59308-315-7	$9.95
Main Street	Sinclair Lewis	1-59308-386-6	$7.95
Mansfield Park	Jane Austen	1-59308-154-5	$5.95
The Metamorphosis and Other Stories	Franz Kafka	1-59308-029-8	$6.95
Moby-Dick	Herman Melville	1-59308-018-2	$9.95
My Ántonia	Willa Cather	1-59308-202-9	$5.95
Narrative of Sojourner Truth		1-59308-293-2	$6.95
The Odyssey	Homer	1-59308-009-3	$5.95
Oliver Twist	Charles Dickens	1-59308-206-1	$6.95
The Origin of Species	Charles Darwin	1-59308-077-8	$7.95
Paradise Lost	John Milton	1-59308-095-6	$7.95
Persuasion	Jane Austen	1-59308-130-8	$5.95
The Picture of Dorian Gray	Oscar Wilde	1-59308-025-5	$4.95
A Portrait of the Artist as a Young Man and Dubliners	James Joyce	1-59308-031-X	$6.95
Pride and Prejudice	Jane Austen	1-59308-201-0	$5.95
The Prince and Other Writings	Niccolò Machiavelli	1-59308-060-3	$5.95
The Red Badge of Courage and Selected Short Fiction	Stephen Crane	1-59308-119-7	$4.95
Republic	Plato	1-59308-097-2	$6.95
Robinson Crusoe	Daniel Defoe	1-59308-360-2	$5.95
The Scarlet Letter	Nathaniel Hawthorne	1-59308-207-X	$5.95
The Secret Agent	Joseph Conrad	1-59308-305-X	$6.95
Selected Stories of O. Henry		1-59308-042-5	$5.95
Sense and Sensibility	Jane Austen	1-59308-125-1	$5.95
Siddhartha	Hermann Hesse	1-59308-379-3	$5.95
The Souls of Black Folk	W. E. B. Du Bois	1-59308-014-X	$5.95
The Strange Case of Dr. Jekyll and Mr. Hyde and Other Stories	Robert Louis Stevenson	1-59308-131-6	$4.95
A Tale of Two Cities	Charles Dickens	1-59308-138-3	$5.95
Three Theban Plays	Sophocles	1-59308-235-5	$6.95
Thus Spoke Zarathustra	Friedrich Nietzsche	1-59308-278-9	$7.95
The Time Machine and The Invisible Man	H. G. Wells	1-59308-388-2	$6.95
Treasure Island	Robert Louis Stevenson	1-59308-247-9	$4.95
The Turn of the Screw, The Aspern Papers and Two Stories	Henry James	1-59308-043-3	$5.95
Uncle Tom's Cabin	Harriet Beecher Stowe	1-59308-121-9	$7.95
Vanity Fair	William Makepeace Thackeray	1-59308-071-9	$7.95
Walden and Civil Disobedience	Henry David Thoreau	1-59308-208-8	$5.95
The War of the Worlds	H. G. Wells	1-59308-362-9	$5.95
Ward No. 6 and Other Stories	Anton Chekhov	1-59308-003-4	$7.95
Wuthering Heights	Emily Brontë	1-59308-128-6	$5.95

BARNES & NOBLE CLASSICS